THE TRAIL

A TRUE TALE OF THE CAMINO

ELIZABETH SHEEHAN

THOUGH NAMES AND IDENTIFYING DETAILS HAVE BEEN CHANGED TO PROTECT MY FELLOW PILGRIMS, ALL THE PEOPLE I MET ALONG THE WAY ARE REAL AND ALL EVENTS TRUE.

ISBN 978-1-4507-6362-2
PUBLISHED BY GREEN HOPE FARM PRESS
P.O. BOX 125, MERIDEN, NH 03770

COVER DESIGN AND PHOTOGRAPHS BY THE AUTHOR

FOR BABA & MEHERA

AND TO MY FAMILY WITH LOVE,
BUT MOST ESPECIALLY TO MUMMA.
I COULDN'T HAVE DONE THIS
WITHOUT YOU.

AND LAST BUT NOT LEAST, TO ALL ♥
MY FELLOW PILGRIMS PAST AND FUTURE
AND THE CAMINO HERSELF.
♥ THANK YOU FOR EVERYTHING.

PRELUDE

The dream was back. The one at the end of the world. Whenever I dreamt of this place, I knew I was at the starting gates again. Even its mere whisper was a preview of ominous ends tangled with the promise of unknown beginnings. It was more than a dream that visited me while I slept; it was a waking clue to a new life and a prelude to perilous journeys. With the return of the dream at the end of the world, I knew I was crossroads bound. The first time the dream had visited me, I'd been nineteen and unprepared for the forceful shove it had given me towards an unnerving new horizon.

Even after repeat visits, the dream was nothing I could hold in my hand as evidence or point to as proof that all would be well. It was as ephemeral as a memory of something yet to come. It was an almost pleasant nightmare that portended another quest into a world beyond the safe boundaries of what my life had been. The dream might have been formed of ether, but I knew it would push me to the end of my world and over the edge.

And once again, I was lost enough to accept a path that appeared to lead right off a cliff into thin air. Yet this time, the path was truly a path. It was a trail that crossed an entire country and moved six hundred miles from mountains to the sea in a far away and unknown land. This trail was even marked with the dream's name: Fisterra. Here was my course to follow when all other direction had been lost and all other forms of navigation had failed.

The map was clear, but this was small comfort. The trail's final stop was at a lighthouse atop the end of the world on the Costa de la Muerte, the coast of death. What would happen in a place known as the end on a shore marked as death? Where would this trail lead me? Who would I meet, and how would I find my way? I would trace the footsteps of the millions of people who had walked this road over the last thousand years. This was a well-worn path, but I still couldn't fathom what lay ahead.

Once before the dream had pushed me to boldly take a daunting road through unknown territory. That path had eventually brought me to something infinitely good and beautiful. Now all I could do was hope the dream would deliver once more.

ST. JEAN PIED-DE-PORT

STAGE ONE- 24.8K-15.4M

ST. JEAN PIED-DE-PORT TO RONCESVALLES

I woke before dawn and walked through the shadowy streets of Bayonne, aiming my feet in the direction of the train station. I'd arrived in Bayonne late at night and passed the hours until my early morning train in a nearby hotel with scratchy sheets and hollow corridors. It was my last night in the chaotic real world before the mystery of the trail began; these were the closing moments before the journey touched my every surface, reached down into my lungs and finally met my footfall.

The massive station was easy to spot with its thick tower soaring above every other structure. On its western face the hands and numbers of an ornate clock gleamed in the blue shades of first light. The station was empty, and the ticket booth was dark, but the warm glow of florescent lights shone deep in its belly. A café with small square tables was open, serving hot coffee. I knew I could choke down little else. It wasn't just the empty hour that turned my stomach but the place itself. Finally, I stood waiting on the edge of the beginning.

I thanked the woman behind the bar in rusty Spanish and held the warm cup with both hands. I'd taken Spanish for seven years but was far from field-tested. I had the basic tools to navigate a café, supermarket, train station or restaurant, yet I had a suspicion that Spain might ask more of me. This trail and its international community might demand more. Would my words fail me, forcing me to resort to pantomime, blushing and shrugging of shoulders? I hoped to prove myself wrong and make all my teachers proud, the patient souls who'd listened for years as I'd chased English thoughts around my head in a mighty effort to wrangle them to the ground and convert them to Spanish. Maybe this trail would lead me to the elusive goal of dreaming in Spanish and finally having words from the land of sleep and the subconscious cross the language divide.

This was the last leg. The last set of tickets, schedules and stations for the next month. A rusted behemoth of a train would deliver me to an even smaller village tucked in the foothills of the Pyrenees. Besides the option of a very pricey taxi, the slow mountain train was the only way to get where I was going. I bought my ticket from an automated machine and stepped out onto the platform. Several other pilgrims anxiously milled around the open space where gleaming tracks nestled between the station and a steep rock face. The tracks had been cut into the side of the hill, and it gave the space a comforting feeling even with wires dangling and a precipitous fall into the lanes of gravel and steel. Other pilgrims huddled together in the chilly morning air with packs by their feet and walking sticks in hand. We were all here for the same purpose. We'd all woken in the dark to catch this, the only Sunday morning train, and we would likely be its only passengers. I wondered if this train ran in the pilgrim off-season, or if the rail company knew that only determined pilgrims would wake at eight on a Sunday to ride the slow moving cars up the mountain to the border village of St. Jean Pied de Port.

As I waited, I distracted myself by talking with another pilgrim sitting on her own. The sixty year old Swede had traveled by a patchwork of transportation to this train station. Her inspiration was a Swedish television personality who'd walked the trail then written a book about her adventure. I was curious when the Swede pulled the worn book from the top of her pack, but my attention snapped into focus as soon as she explained how the woman had walked the trail in a mere eighteen days. All eight hundred kilometers in eighteen days. My mind whirled with numbers, but it didn't take me long to realize the woman must have walked nearly fifty kilometers each day. That was thirty miles. I suddenly felt daunted. How had she walked alone like me and still found the guts to walk so far and so fast? Taking the book in my hands, I realized to walk that fast and be that super human would perhaps not be my destiny, for the book was written in Swedish without a single secret diagram to ensure success. I would find no clues from a trail god here.

Handing the Swede back her book, we chatted about her plan for the day. I paced in a circle and listened to her valid argument for not hitting the trail until tomorrow. It made sense to wait. Rest, adjust and give myself the full allotment of daylight hours. She felt it was imperative to ease into this experience and get her bearings before moving forward. As she spoke I started to agree with her logic. It was wise and grounded. It held a cadence that suggested she was willing to pace herself to reach the end healthy and sound of mind. As the coffee charged through my bloodstream and rattled my nerves, I thought maybe I, too, should take a breath before beginning. It might be soothing. Or would it just give me more time to become agitated? I decided to wait until I landed in St. Jean Pied de Port to make my decision.

As I paced, a group of elderly Norwegians pulled out a map and laid it out on the platform. The map was large and colorful with names and information scrawled across every surface. One man made marks with a thick red pen as he leaned over the expanse of paper. Two of the women moved around the large square pointing, wildly gesticulating and talking in loud voices. This small dramatic production only added to the potent atmosphere on the platform. It felt like the start of a road race with all of us lined up at some imaginary starting line, looking around at the competition, trying to remember if we had everything we needed and becoming increasingly worried that we were under-trained or under-prepared. Nobody really wanted to talk or make eye contact beyond their group; instead they tended to their gear with an intense focus. At this point in the journey, when the Camino was almost in sight, it was every man for himself.

After so many days in the starting gate, planning and imagining the best and the worst, we all just wanted to get this thing started, feel the trail under our feet and go.

At five minutes to eight, the conductor arrived with his small son in tow. The duo hopped into the front cabin of the train, the father with one giant step followed by his son whose shorter limbs scrambled up with familiar determination. The only clue this man was the conductor was the confident manner in which he jumped up into the control room and began flicking switches. From the excited bounce of the little boy's limbs as he sat in the conductor's chair, I assumed he would be our driver as we climbed into the mountains. His father was simply the front man, getting everything set up for the real boss to take over. Since we were on a track and enclosed in a barrel chested metal car, I felt perfectly at ease with the qualifications of my driver. An eight year old behind the controls didn't bother me one bit. Actually, I enjoyed catching a glimpse of his obvious glee. Finally the conductor was done pushing buttons, and the engine roared to life. It echoed through the vast station like a starting gun. Suddenly everybody on the platform was up and moving. Some pilgrims had so much stuff with them, I wasn't sure how they planned to lift it on to the train let alone walk with it on their backs. I stepped up the wide metal treads behind the Swede, and we found a pair of worn seats near the middle of the car. It had been cold in the station, and the train was not much warmer. The seats were chilled to the touch, and I was glad I'd put on my only pair of long pants.

The train puffed to life beneath us as I took my seat. Nobody came to collect our tickets, and there was no warning as we pulled away from the station. The beast leapt into forward motion with a grunt and rattle of mighty wheels pulling and looping us up and away. This was our last rest, one last joy ride on the back of modern machine power before we became our one and only source of transportation. We were simply a bunch of pack mules in training, waiting for the big show.

The train wound its way up the mountain with purpose, slowing at the steeper inclines. From where I sat, I could see most of the passenger car and peer in through the door to the conductor's booth. There were roughly two dozen other pilgrims scattered about the car plus a few hearty locals in jeans carrying little more than a small purse or plastic shopping bag. Since it was Sunday, none of these early rising Frenchmen seemed in a hurry or affected by the jittery atmosphere clinging to the rest of us. They stood near the front of the train and chatted with the conductor or hung out the open door of the car waiting for the train to slow as it pulled into their stops. They seemed at ease and unencumbered compared to the rest of us. This was their home turf where they could travel with only a few euros in their pockets; they had no need to cling to their packs like life rafts. As we picked up speed, the Swede sat very still and looked out the window with an intense gaze. I let my eyes drift over the groups around us, wanting to absorb the scene but also a bit fearful it would amp up my nerves. I quickly noticed there wasn't a single young pilgrim in the whole of the car. Now that I was so close to the trailhead, I was on the lookout for traveling companions. Though ready and willing to befriend pilgrims of a wide range of ages, I was looking in particular for twenty and thirty somethings. These pilgrims would be my people. They were my compatriots in the chaos of early adulthood and the best age group for a romantic partner. I'd been unsuccessful in convincing any of my assorted friends to join me on this trek, but I'd always imagined that I wouldn't go it alone. Now I would have to make friends as I went, build a little moving community of my own from scratch. I wasn't attached to walking the length of Spain as some sort of proof of my independence. I didn't need or want solitude to be the main ingredient of this trip, and I wasn't running off to Spain to get some "me time". I was here to let go of a life that had included way too much time alone, a life that had been defined by loneliness even when in community and relationships. I was here to relish the chance to bunk with a bunch of other pilgrims, share meals and get close enough to know someone. Hopefully even know them well enough to love them.

I tended to see the world, particularly men, in a very specific way. I saw life as being about relationships. Past, present and most importantly, future. In the same way that men often wanted to understand how things worked, I wanted to understand how people would weave into my life. I couldn't deny that even though battered and bruised, I'd brought my relationship radar with me to the Camino, and there was absolutely no way it wouldn't get involved in the choices I made on the trail, for better or for worse.

Even as I looked around the dreary train car, I felt my current options were sorely lacking, yet I remained optimistic about what the next stretch of time might hold. It wasn't until I stood on the platform waiting for the train that I realized I'd never ventured out in the unknown so boldly. I'd never set my course to a place where anyone and anything could be right around the corner. Every experience, even leaving for college, had been safely tucked into a format and comfort zone that only pushed me just so far away from the familiar. This trail took no prisoners and held no guarantees. It was a mysterious and perhaps mythic creature that scared me on every level. I knew not a single soul, had never seen the towns and cities ahead and had never before subjected my body to a walking life. These elements were all unknowns on the practical level but worried me much less than how my emotional armor would weather the storm. Would I crumble under the pressure? I trusted my body to keep me moving down the trail, but I was utterly unsure of how my internal life would play out. Had it been reckless folly to set out on this journey right now, even though I was here under very clear and exacting guidance? Or was it just the answer to a moment defined by emptiness and my sudden release back into the world?

As we rode up the mountainside, the group from Norway sat in a huddle around their map. One of the men fumbled with the string on his beige sun hat, attempting to adjust it to fit snugly on his balding head. The woman next to him wrote notes in a small guidebook, only pausing to help her friend across the aisle apply sunscreen to the bridge of her nose. They all looked down into their laps, and so they missed the fields of sheep spray-painted florescent colors, the small houses with thin streams of smoke drifting from their chimneys and the mountains themselves. Their group was mirrored by another cluster of married couples in their mid sixties on the other side of the car who hardly noticed the rest of us as they chattered loudly in words that never came close to a language I recognized.

Across the car and down a few rows, a lone man with blonde hair and socks pulled up mid-calf sat on his own. His large red pack was propped up in the chair beside him, and he spent much of the ride packing and unpacking the outer compartments. I couldn't tell if he was taking inventory or trying to stow his things in the most efficient manner possible. It was evident from the way he sat apart from other pilgrims that he was traveling solo. He didn't look over as I watched him, and eventually I turned back to the window. Even though everyone in the car was acting out a different pre-race twitch, we were all thinking the same thing; those first steps were close. The air hung with unknowns and an energy of anticipation.

The train made a few stops where locals jumped on and off the old rusted cars. Most got off before the train stopped and gave a loud departing shout to the conductor. As I watched this easy flux of people, I knew I was finally on the local level, riding with natives who took this train every day. This mode of travel didn't involve any of the stress that had haunted me since I left home, and I felt soothed by the slow pace and relaxed management. As we crested the last rise in a set of steep climbs, the train slowed, let out a belch of steam and dragged to a stop. There was no announcement by the conductor, but somehow we all knew this was it. We had arrived in St. Jean Pied de Port, the French town where our trail began. This town was the Camino's last outpost in France. There were several popular Camino routes in France, but they all converged here before diving into Spain and turning west towards Santiago. St. Jean lay down in a valley, but on a clear day, pilgrims could look up to the mountains and see Spain. It was that close. The trail crossed the border and left France behind in its wake on the very first day's walk. France was merely a long landing strip of green propelling me onto Spanish soil.

And just like that, I leapt off the train and touched down on the dusty platform where the trail began. All the steps in the journey up until that point were suddenly washed clean and put behind me. The next leg of the trek would move me across an entire country on my own power. It felt calming to finally be able to rely on my own feet. No more plane flights, train schedules or fast moving sights. Now life would move only as quickly as I could.

Our carload of pilgrims filed out of the train and streamed through the small deserted station like an agitated swarm. We were funneled into the empty room only to be squeezed out the door into the street on the far side. The building was all business. It offered shelter from the elements but nothing more, and it perfectly suited this small village that was the most popular starting point on the Camino.

Virtually everyone coming into St. Jean came by train, a rite of passage I would share with almost all the people I later met along the trail. As we left the station behind, the group moved with quick and anxious steps towards the center of the village. I wondered if we were the blind leading the blind but didn't dare question the duo of middle aged women who directed our forward progress. Though I assumed most everyone was new to St. Jean, I doubted they were as understudied as I was. I hardly knew more than the name of this place. One thing was for certain, the unknown would loom over me like fearsome clouds until I finally stepped into it.

I had no idea how to find the trailhead. It also had not occurred to me that I had to register at St. Jean, but the Swede told me we needed to do this at the Pilgrim Office. Winding our way up narrow streets, I got my first taste of the type of town I would encounter on the trail. The buildings were arranged next to a delicate maze of cobbled streets. Everything was built on a slight incline with the Pilgrim Office at the top of an alley. I never would have found the place if I hadn't been caught in the group momentum and pulled there. On the way up the street, we passed half a dozen hostels with bright signs, rows of dirty boots lining the front stoop and bright flowers dripping off the window boxes.

The group splintered half a block before the office as a few pilgrims ducked into a small church while the rest of us pushed on. The better informed pilgrims among us knew they would have to check into one of the hostels before noon if they wanted to find a bed for the night. It was early June. The trail was starting to swell with the summer rush, and the Pilgrim Office was the place to set up accommodations and plan for the days ahead.

The office was a simple open room with a long table and a fountain in the corner. It filled the entire bottom floor of an old building with wide wooden doors open to the street. Even though the room was full of activity, there were only three people running the operation. They wore small nametags and moved around the backside of the table, arranging documents, speaking in several different tongues and handing out maps. Their job was to check everyone in, make sure each pilgrim had an essential document called a pilgrim passport and place the first of many stamps inside the fresh document. They were the pilgrims' personal assistants, helping with lodging, food and handing out warnings about weather and trail conditions.

The Swede went to the far end of the room to purchase a pilgrim passport while I hung by the main station to wait for her. I'd mailed away for my passport from an American fraternity of the Camino and already had this document that would guarantee me entrance into the hostel system along the trail. Pilgrim passports came in several different styles, but all began as a blank pamphlet. Mine was the size of a wallet and folded out in an accordion-like fashion. It contained my vital information and would eventually hold a stamp from each place I spent the night along the trail. Later, I would encounter other types of passports, ones that were larger, more elegant and book-like with designs scrawled across the cover. Mine was a simple affair, yet even in its plain state, it served me well. In the same way that a travel passport was absolutely vital for crossing international lines, the pilgrim passport was just as essential for entrance into the pilgrim hostels or "albergues." The rules were very strict and well enforced. If a pilgrim didn't have a passport, he or she was turned away from the albergues. I didn't doubt the sanctity of these rules, and in the days to come, I would hear tales of innocent pilgrims losing their pilgrim passports and having to face the cruel world outside of this pilgrim safety net. Not only was it upsetting to lose entrance into the pilgrim community but expensive to seek other accommodations. I would treat my pilgrim passport with the same reverence I held for my national passport and store the two in the most secure location in my pack.

Once the Swede and I reached the head of the line, we were divided into language groups. The office volunteers spoke several different languages but not a wide variety. The Swede and I clustered around the English speaking volunteer to be vetted and registered in the official pilgrim roster. The lone man from the train had stood back from the line for the past few minutes but joined our group once it was announced we were an English speaking lot. I was startled as he strode up next to me but even more shocked to hear him address us in nearly perfect English. I'd assumed from his stony silence on the train that he didn't speak English, but his was even more skilled than the Swede's. As he shook my hand and stood a bit too close, I learned he was Danish with an impossible name, one that I was too embarrassed to ask him to repeat lest I fail to understand it a second time. The Dane was several inches taller than me, stocky, with a nerdy haircut and in his mid to late thirties.

The three of us sat in a cluster as we were given maps and told about the first day's walk. It was over twenty-five kilometers with seven kilometers of ascent. This stage was known as one of the hardest days on the trail, earning this reputation due to the way it combined a massive climb with a long total distance. It also induced worry and awe because it was the first day for many untested legs and lungs. Such a day was hardly the easiest way to get the body accustomed to the trail, and many people gave up after this stage, beaten by the Pyrenees or its weather.

The volunteer handed us sheets that detailed the amenities in each town the trail passed through. He also gave us a sheet with the inclines for every stage. This would warn us of the tough mountain climbs and foretell the stages where we would walk on a flat plateau with no change in elevation. Though in French, the two pieces of flimsy white paper were vital, and I tucked them into my Camino guidebook knowing they would be safe and easily accessible in the days to come.

Even with the daunting sheets detailing kilometers and accrued ascent, I felt steady. I was confident about little else, but I was sure of my body. I was a good athlete with strong legs and a dancer's discipline. I tried not to let the mental aspect of the Camino spook me. Eight hundred kilometers was a number that could crush me if I thought hard enough on it. I would need to take it day by day.

As the older gentleman helping us pulled out a pen and circled the first day, I saw it was a climb unlike anything I'd ever done. On the elevation chart the trail out of St. Jean resembled an exponential curve going up and up. The Swede let out a startled noise, and the Dane looked grim. With the confidence of a man who had watched hundreds of people face the mountains and had learned to spot the ones that would make it from the ones that would take a taxi, the volunteer told us we'd better start tomorrow. Give ourselves a fighting chance. I could see his reasoning, for it was now nearly ten in the morning, and we were a motley crew, but the Dane had other plans. Shaking his blonde head at the man and speaking with firm resolve he replied, "No, I will be walking today!"

I could tell by the set of his shoulders and tone of his voice that he meant what he said, and nobody, especially not the man behind the table, was going to talk him out of it. After the Dane declared his intentions, I felt my mind start to swirl with pros and cons. I wasn't sure waiting until tomorrow would be the best plan, but I certainly wasn't sure that going was such a good idea either. I had tentatively agreed to walk with the Swede, but I imagined she and I would move at different paces. Walking together was a loose term. So in essence, walking with her might actually be more akin to walking alone. And if I stayed until tomorrow, what would I do for the next twenty hours with all my pent up physical energy? Empty time had the ability to unwind my emotions and might in fact bring on a serious meltdown even before I officially started the trail. Another concern was the weather. Would the skies turn nasty in the night and make me wish I'd gone today with its clear sunshine and mild temperatures? Unanswerable questions abounded.

Even though the fates controlled all the outside factors, I had a gut feeling I was being given a prod to get going. Maybe it was the forecast that called for rain tomorrow or the thought of others up ahead on the trail, but for whatever the reason, I felt a force pulling me onward. The choice to go felt hasty and unexpected but also sent a charge of energy through my system. Plus, I didn't like the feeling of being left behind, and I knew that is what I would feel if others from the train climbed the trail today, and I didn't. If they could start now so could I. I had the chops, and I could prove it.

My body flush with adrenaline, I made the snap decision. I would walk. I would start now and leave the wishy-washy state of in between behind. Turning with my most charming smile, I sought a companion in the Dane. From what I had ascertained in the last hour, I felt he was not only a safe choice but also a smart one. He looked ready to tackle the mountains with speed and endurance, and I had a suspicion he also was well equipped with extra maps and other survival gear. I hadn't a clue if I would need any such trappings, but there was no harm in walking with someone who had been willing to buy, pack and carry such things. He seemed unconcerned if I joined him but did remark, after looking me up and down, that he would leave me behind if I couldn't keep his pace. I could tell he was quantifying my potential strength and stamina with a cursory glance. I may have looked like a shell-shocked youngster, but I was no wilting flower. I held back any number of comments that rushed into my head because I needed the Dane's assistance, and I truly wasn't sure how I would stack up against the other pilgrims on the mountain trail. I'd never measured my athletic potential so evenly next to anyone else's. I'd always been involved in less easily quantifiable athletic endeavors such as dance.

I also wasn't sure if the trail would be well marked, and I had a fear of getting lost in the mountains, turned around and left to die alone of hypothermia. Well, maybe my fear wasn't that extreme, but I did worry about getting lost or running into serious problems. At least if I got lost with the Dane, we'd be in it together. Together with all his shiny and suddenly very useful new gear. My theory about company on an unfamiliar mountain trail was very similar to my theory about elevators. If something went wrong, the more people with me the better. At least from an emotional perspective. I was much calmer when faced with uncertainty and a suddenly scary situation if I was with another person. Plus, there was the added bonus of extra body warmth, though I felt sure that sharing body warmth with the Dane would only happen when and if things went very, very wrong. Only then might I consider a cuddle for survival's sake.

The Dane allowed a big smile to break across his face at his newfound popularity, while the volunteer squinted his eyes incredulously. After a few moments, the volunteer looked at his watch, shrugged his shoulders, turned and walked away. He was clearly done with us. I guessed if we stumbled off the mountain disoriented with frostbite, he would simply shrug his shoulders again and say I told you so.

Days later, I would hear of a group that ventured out of St. Jean on a misty morning that turned cold and dangerous. As the weather worsened, four of the eight people turned back to try their luck again the next day, while the other four pressed on. All four who continued to walk got lost and died of exposure. It was a deeply sobering tale and one I was grateful I didn't hear before I faced the climb myself. Our late departure time was working against us, but the weather was fair for crossing the mountains into Spain. There wasn't a moment to waste.

As the Swede and I followed the Dane out of the office, we admired the first stamps in our clean white pilgrim passports. They were the marks of our Camino's beginning, written in ink. After tucking away our documents, I sensed the Swede was rattled by my decision to leave immediately. She now had a choice to make, and neither I nor anyone else could tell her what to do.

It was nearly ten in the morning now, and though the sun was bright in the sky, there was nothing in the way of shelter between St. Jean and the next town over the mountains in Spain. We were headed up into the wilderness, and just like everyone else who climbed the mountain trail, we would have to keep going to the far side to find sanctuary. After a moment's thought, during which she fiddled with the straps of her pack and bounced on her legs as if to test their strength, the Swede decided to join us. Our group was now three.

We left the office in a rush but not before each of us picked out a white scallop shell the size of a fist to hang from our bags. The scallop shell was originally a symbol of St. James, the patron saint of the trail, but it had been co-opted as a broader symbol for all types of pilgrims who walked the Camino regardless of religious affiliation. As I juggled my pack and pilgrim passport, I took the first shell on the pile. Only later would I notice some people had dug through the stack and found ones with more aesthetic charm and fewer chips along the ridges. Nonetheless, my mutt of a shell, in all its imperfect glory, would mark me as a pilgrim on the long journey ahead.

The three of us moved down through town, passing groups of pilgrims and tourists with cameras and impractical shoes. We didn't speak; I felt shocked into a nervous silence. My whole body was humming. It was more than just adrenaline rushing through me. There was something else too. Scanning my thoughts and emotions, I stumbled onto the slightly absurd realization that I felt I was already behind. Behind what? Behind who? The extra pumping of energy was a genuine need to catch up, but this felt crazy. I had no idea what I was trying to catch. The rational section of my brain knew that during the summer the trail was like an ever-flowing stream. People entered, exited and moved along its path at every given moment. There was no single start time or arrival date. I could have come days before, weeks later or never at all. So why did I feel I needed to hurry? It certainly wasn't the threat of an imminent outbound ticket, job or relationship tugging at me. I didn't even own plants. So, if it wasn't a push from the world outside the Camino, maybe it was a push from inside the world of the Camino. Maybe it was the energy of people and places ahead that was drawing me forward. It had to be something other than the coffee, for I almost tasted the energy as my legs moved me out of town. It was a siren song yet of what I was still unsure.

The trail that would lead me across Spain was part of a greater web of converging trails. Here in the mountains at St. Jean, many of the branches merged. This was the spot a majority of pilgrims chose to enter the main stream. The stage out of St. Jean was legend, and its arduous climb led many pilgrims to start on the far side of the mountain in Roncesvalles, thus avoiding the whole experience altogether. I refused to take the skip card as the matter of principal. I was young, fit and I had all the time in the world. When else in my life would I be able to cross from one country to another on foot, not stopping until I'd walked the length of the second country stem to stern? Maybe never again.

I wanted this baptism by fire, and part of me sickly relished the chance to feel the burn. I wanted to prove I was tough enough to take on the mountains and whatever beating they handed out. In a strange way, I felt quite macho about this stage as if it were an entrance exam into Camino society. I wanted to claim my right to be on the pathway among the last trailing peaks of the Pyrenees. They were a grand stage with a weather system all their own, little if no inhabitants and a wild beauty that was somehow timeless.

The sky above us was a sheet of vivid blue as we wound our way out of town. I was immediately glad to have the Dane and the Swede by my side as we picked up the thread of the trail. Surprisingly there was no large sign or obvious marker in sight once we left the central streets of St. Jean. All that was given to us was a single yellow arrow spray-painted on the back of a road sign. This wasn't the most encouraging way to enter the trail's flow, but I soon found that a new arrow appeared along the trail every hundred meters or so. Like following a trail of crumbs, it turned into an exciting game. Watching for arrows, we followed the path as it switched back and forth up gentle slopes through small clusters of sleepy homes. At times, trees offered cover from the sun, and cars occasionally zipped by forcing us to step off the narrow road. As the signs of civilization dwindled, the slope increased, and all shade vanished. The path turned west, crested a small rise and revealed the mighty bulk of the mountains looming above us. My breath caught in my throat. This was what lay before us. This was what lay between us and Spain. We would walk up hill for five hours.

In the clear afternoon, we climbed through lush fields of green, surrounded by the clang of bells from roaming cattle. There were no gates or fences; the trail was the only break in the endless expanse of land. Small stone shelters were scattered along the way. Some were simple three sided windbreaks, but others had small roofs and thickets of brambles surrounding them. They all faced into the prevailing wind, and as it slammed the side of my body, I could see how important they would be if the weather picked up. At some point in the endless climb, we crossed from France into Spain. It was as stunning and strangely unremarkable an entrance as I could have imagined. I expected a sign, a marker or at least a fence, but there was nothing. Nothing but a horizon of distant blue peaks and inclines so steep I feared I'd lose my balance and tip over the edge into an open free fall. There were no manmade signs or fences to scramble over. Maybe it was fitting, for the mountains didn't distinguish their French bellies from their Spanish spines. It was simply all one body that was older and more settled than any nation state had ever been. In the place of a sign, there was simply a turn in a trail that revealed more wild green land rising up and up.

As the views fell away behind us, I spoke little with either of my companions. The Dane and I moved more quickly than the Swede, and within an hour, she fell out of sight behind us. Now it was the two of us lifting our feet again and again, calling on our quad muscles to keep propelling us forward. We came upon other pilgrims several times but overtook them with quick efficiency. Passing other walkers calmed my nerves and built a small foundation around my confidence in the strength of my own body. I reasoned we were all headed for the same place, and I couldn't be too behind the curve if I was now ahead of other walkers who had been wise enough to start at a decent hour.

Though I could feel my heart pumping faster than usual and a tender ache growing in my legs, I didn't let my pace slow as the inclines increased. I was singularly focused on the town that lay on the other side of the mountains. Within the first hour of walking, I knew my pack was too heavy, filled with things I'd meant to get rid of before starting out. I never guessed I would be swept up into the first stage with such speed, and I hadn't had a moment to change my outfit before we began to climb. Now with layers of sweaty clothing clinging to my body, I also contended with pant legs covered in mud. I daydreamed about being in shorts, but I sensed the Dane was all business and wasn't going to indulge in anything that stopped our momentum. Not on these inclines and especially not as the terrain changed. The ground was clear along the roadways for the first two hours, but as the trail turned to pathways, it became a mire of mud and slipping earth that threatened to suck my shoes right off my feet. Once I walked two paces beyond a sinkhole in my sock before I realized I'd lost a shoe. The Dane didn't share my plight for he wore tall hiking boots so expensive they looked as if they'd been specially engineered for his feet. The muddy sections of the trail became more frequent, and since the Dane and his wonder boots feared nothing of the sort, I spent much of the time scurrying behind him trying to catch up. As I slid, sidestepped and generally made a muddy mess of my lower half, he glided along with an unmistakably air of superiority.

The mountains kept winding upwards. As the afternoon fell closer to evening, I wondered, with wobbling weariness, if we would ever come down off these slopes. I craved the chance to be working with gravity. Downhill seemed almost too good to be true. The chance to let the cool air dry my clothes and sweaty limbs would be heavenly. Then, with only a few kilometers left, the land turned down, and the pain began. I'd expected the descent to be the relief of the day, a moment of pure triumph, but reversing the hard working muscles in my legs didn't feel as good as I'd hoped. After only a few minutes, the long tough muscles of my quads started to tremor from the stress of keeping myself from hurling down the side of the mountain. My whole body was so fatigued, it could do little to control my downward progress. Everything ached, and I prayed for flat land or even a bit of up hill again. As we descended, the trail moved back into thick wooded glades and grew very narrow as tree limbs closed in around us. I caught several branches in the face as watching my footing became a full time endeavor. I didn't trust my muscles or the slippery earth. Now all thoughts turned to the town of Roncevalles and the sanctuary it would provide once we finally stumbled into its outstretched arms.

When the land grew flat, and a river could be heard up ahead, the woods finally spit the Dane and me out into a cluster of buildings along a small road. It was like daylight after the dark. I rubbed my eyes, hardly understanding the shapes before me. We'd arrived at the end of the first day. The scattering of solid buildings, sounds of human life and the buzz of a car zooming somewhere nearby was proof of the fact. The Dane looked at his watch, grinned with manic delight and announced the hour with pride. It was only half past three. Most sane pilgrims would never start their day of walking as late as ten in the morning, but we still had managed to arrive before the pilgrim albergues even opened. I was relieved to reach the end of the first day but felt a wave of exhaustion-induced loneliness. I could see other pilgrims in the center of town sitting together, close and connected. I felt shy again. After the easy company of cows and mud, the wind and a grumpy Dane, I felt outside of the social life here and unsure of how to make a smooth entrance. I was painfully aware of my solo status and wondered again why the universe had called me here alone. Why had it drawn me into the mess of a relationship I'd known for the past year then spit me out the other side, sliced and diced into a thousand mangled pieces? I thought of the person I'd left not more than a week ago and how he probably hadn't noticed I was gone. In truth, he might not even have started to wonder where I'd disappeared to and why. At the same time, I was achingly aware of the breakup that had been so painful to inflict. I wanted to leave the past behind, put as much time and space between us as possible. Apparently putting space between us had been a quicker fix than time which worked on its own plodding schedule. I stood in the open square and waited for the unbidden and fresh memories to recede, waited to feel triumph that I'd crossed the mountains and survived the first day, but mostly I felt a haunting I couldn't shake. I needed to sit, rest, eat and sleep. Survival tools were all I had to get me through the first night of the first day of this new life.

RONCESVALLES

Roncesvalles was little more than a cluster of old monastery buildings and a set of rustic bars. Virtually everything in the small village was there to cater to the needs of all varieties of pilgrim. The three major categories of pilgrims were out in full force when the Dane and I entered town, and I watched in stunned silence as they moved in clusters and clogged the narrow main road. The walking pilgrims hung together outside one of the buildings, packs at their feet, water in hand, while the bike pilgrims milled around bike stands, checking tires, removing heavy panniers and unabashedly strutting around in full body spandex. The bus pilgrims were creating the most commotion and drawing the most irritated glances. A massive double-decker bus was pulled off to the side of the main square and swarms of camera toting men and women in ironed clothes and well heeled shoes were disembarking. They had come to see the church and the famous spot where the brave Roland, a decorated soldier under Charlemagne, had fought and died. Beside the small church building and the austere yet impressive monastery, there was little else to see in Roncesvalles. Visitors seemed to be the main attraction in town, and as I pushed through the groups, I realized there wasn't a local in sight. There was no store of any kind, just two restaurants with bars that served only late night meals and endless rounds of beer and wine. The lack of a food shop felt like a physical blow. Though I had some reserve supplies lovingly carried up and over the mountains, I didn't have much. For a trail that caters to so many pilgrims, I was startled to find basic necessities weren't available. Other than the cries of my stomach, it didn't bothered me that there was nothing more than the bare bones here. I preferred the closeness a small town could afford, and in Roncesvalles everybody was tucked together like hens in a small coop. All of us who weren't traveling by bus would sleep in the albergue and bind our trails closely together after just one night.

As the Dane and I made our way up the main road toward the albergue, I looked at the bus idling alongside the square. What would it be like to get on a bus and leave here? How would it feel to decide the trail wasn't the place for me to move forward with my fragmented existence? Secretly, it felt like sweet escape to imagine leaving the trail. I knew this transition would rough me up and toss me around as I found my footing, but I couldn't help daydreaming about stopping. If I toyed with the idea that I could stop, then I somehow didn't feel so trapped in this strange new life. Then I had freedom. Or at least the illusion of it.

Yes, I was free to get on a bus, call a cab, or even buy a motorcycle and ride off to the south of France, but I felt bound by deeper strings than those of practicality or pride. I was bound by the belief that there was some reason, some unknown but vital reason that had brought me here. I had to try and trust the instructions from the universe. I had to try a little longer than a day. I needed to show I had a bit more grit and spiritual determination than that. So for now my thoughts of fleeing were pushed aside in favor of the practical matters at hand.

Though the first day had been grueling, I'd found the physical element to be grounding. I'd taken refuge in the movement, the task of getting myself from one place to another and testing my body's limits. The physical part actually kept me tied to the trail instead of pushing me away from it. I could imagine for some, the walking and the toll it took on their bodies were the reasons to pack it in and call it a day, but not for me. They were my main source of sustenance, and even after a long day, I felt a bit helpless as we waited around town with nothing to do.

So I watched the world and kept scanning the groups of people, soaking in details. Were they English speakers? Were they in groups? Did they seem friendly and open to new trail acquaintances? I was searching for a posse. I couldn't believe that I would come to this popular trail and not eventually find a group of friends that accepted me into their clan. I couldn't believe I would remain on the outside like this for the length of an entire country. But as I surveyed the crowd sitting outside the albergue walls, I was no longer sure whom I would or wouldn't find along the trail. With the Dane at his leisure beside me, all I could see were couples and clusters of older pilgrims, all turned inward and deep in their own solar systems. When we checked in and were reshuffled, I hoped I might find openings to introduce myself to some of the thirty or so pilgrims lining the wall outside of the albergue. If the Dane was to be my only social interaction for the evening, it promised to be a long set of hours until dark.

As I threw down my bag along an open stretch of wall at the end of the line, I was happy to ignore the demands of my gear and slump down to earth. I knew I should take out my water and re-hydrate but decided it could wait. After just a day I was discovering that the whole water pack dynamic was a high maintenance one. I'd been lured into bringing it along because it was described as more user friendly, but I was regretting this decision already. The water pouch, which I would come to call by one of its goofier brand names of platypus, was a complicated contraption with a thick plastic pouch and a coil of tubing with a mouthpiece on the end. It required its own slot in my pack and had to be rigged into place just right so everything flowed when I wanted it to and didn't when it shouldn't. One of the more challenging elements was keeping track of how much water I had left when the bag was stored deep in the belly of my pack. The water device that was meant to help me stay hydrated inadvertently caused me to use the water sparingly, fearing I was always about to run out. I assumed in the days to come I would smooth out these issues, but I didn't expect the platypus to turn on me in the meantime.

Sitting a few paces down the wall from the Dane, I rested against my pack and completely lost track of the piping on my platypus. It took me a moment to feel the water seeping through the legs of my pants before I snapped out of my daze. I leapt up and found, to my horror, the whole seat of my pants was soaked through. It wasn't just a minor spot, but a total flood along the length of my upper thighs and across my butt. As I looked around for the culprit, a drain in the wall or a puddle, I realized I'd placed my bag on top of the mouthpiece. I was the culprit. The weight of my bag and my body leaning on top of it had pushed the valve open and leaked the water around me in a glistening puddle all of my own making. Suddenly I was that amateur pilgrim who wet her own pants on her very first day when she was trying so hard to be cool and make friends. I threw an invective or two under my breath while the napping Dane opened his eyes to laugh at me before closing them again. I scurried about, wrapping a shirt around my waist, unhooking the platypus's tube and moving all my stuff several meters farther down the wall. I didn't care if I lost my place in line now, and I certainly didn't mind putting more space between me and the Dane as he smirked in his sleep. Even though there were thirty or so people around me, no one offered to help and hardly a kind look was sent my way. What a welcome to pilgrim life off the trail.

After I sorted out my water explosion and repositioned myself against the wall, I felt very concerned. Was the lack of response and detachment from my fellow pilgrims typical? Should I be worried about finding a welcoming group? Was this trail, in fact, not as good place to meet people as I had imagined it would be? A set of Italian bikers rolled into the courtyard as my head buzzed with questions, and the Dane snored quietly down the row. I reached into the bowels of my pack and retrieved a chocolate bar, knowing it was the strongest drug I had on hand to ease my woes. Unwrapping the foil around the slightly melted bar, I tried to numb out everything but the rush of sugar. No matter what lay ahead, there was always chocolate. Little did I know this would be the first of many moments when sugar, mostly of the chocolate variety, was the only thing that would give me a bit of bliss. One euro and fifty cents, not a bad price for a moment's peace from my thoughts.

The albergue at Roncesvalles was one of the oldest along the trail system, and after St.Jean, this was the most popular starting point. Since so many peopled aimed to start their Camino here, the local bus systems accommodated this need. Well sort of. This was Spain after all, and schedules were loose enough to make arriving here a formidable challenge for any pilgrim. Later I would hear from pilgrims who had hired a taxi at the train station in Pamplona then were taken for a hair raising spin up and over the mountains to be dumped on the curb with rolling insides and a hefty bill. These fresh imports seemed worse off than the rest of us who had actually spent the day walking. I would also discover that people with tight schedules and most Spaniards picked this as their starting gate unconcerned about skipping the first hard day from France into Spain. It wasn't difficult to tell who had just arrived on the bus from Pamplona and who had spent the day climbing over the mountains. Beyond the cleanliness of their clothes, the carriage and tone of their bodies spoke the truth even from a distance. The energy behind each step and the ease of movement revealed those who had yet to walk. They still bounced while the rest of us hobbled around with sore muscles and new blisters. Yet even as their bodies were fresh, so too was their fear. We might have been less physically crisp, but there was a settled look in the eyes of those who had at least one day of walking under their belts. We had proved something and could sleep soundly, while the newbies would likely toss and turn, anticipating the next day's walk and their first test of pilgrimhood. Plus, they weren't tired, and I could only imagine that sleep in a bustling albergue would be much easier for those of us who had toiled.

At four, the doors opened, and the line of pilgrims flooded into a small office where the proprietors stamped our pilgrim passports as we each paid six euros for the night's stay. Behind me a group of Italian bikers with large bellies and deep baritone voices were waiting to check in and stow their bikes. Filling the small antechamber outside the office, they were passing the idle time by singing rousing ballads and laughing with one another. I smiled at their cheerful attitude and wished I knew a bit of Italian so I could eavesdrop on the subject of their songs.

Tucking my pilgrim passport away in my pack, I felt pleased about the cost of the night's lodgings. In the Camino guidebooks, I'd read much about the cost of albergues and found six euros to be a very reasonable price, even if I was only buying a bunk in a crowded room. Over the course of the journey, I knew I would encounter a varying range of prices, with cities, especially the destination city of Santiago, asking more of my wallet. Yet there would also be places along the way that were donation based or even free. No matter what happened in the weeks to come, I was certain that for me, this was the cheapest way to spend a month in Europe other than pitching a tent and subsisting on stale bread. Now curious to see what basic necessities my six euros had bought me, I crossed the street from the office and made for the door of the thick stone albergue. The wide wooden doorway, with a long flat flagstone out front, was narrow and dark. Once I stepped across the threshold, it widened into a single large room with a high vaulted ceiling, slightly narrower than a small gymnasium and stuffed to the gills with bunks. From the ceiling dangled a dozen chandeliers with small lights on their rough wooden surfaces, while a narrow set of stair in the far corner fell away into the basement. A beat up stereo played soft music, and three men sat at a table awaiting the arrival of the night's guests. Bunks clung to the walls all the way down each side of the room, and two sets filled the center aisle. There were over a hundred beds with no more than half a foot between every cluster. This was my bedroom for the night, just me and a hundred of my pilgrim compatriots.

As I looked around the most senior of the men running the albergue gruffly sorted the line, handed out pillows and sent people off to claim beds.

"Men to the left and women to the right," he mumbled to me as he gave me a slight shove to the right. Before I had made it very far, he jerked me back. "Are you alone?" he asked. "Are you in a couple, in a two?"

"No," I replied and he nodded his head to the right and turned away to manhandle the next person.

As I took a bunk on top, I looked around and suddenly understood the man's question. All the pilgrim couples were given bunks in the middle of the room and hadn't been forced to separate. If I had been a two then I also would have been in the warm center rows rather than flung to the outer edges of the room. Just the sight of the couples made my chest constrict. I wanted to be there. I wanted to be on the green grass of their world just feet away. But I wasn't. For tonight, I was still just a solo. I turned away from the middle of the room and began to unpack my bag.

As night fell, it grew cold in the stone room. Even though we had come down off the mountains, we were still in the foothills of the Pyrenees, and a cold wind seeped through the cracks in the walls above my head. I'd assumed the warmth of so many bodies in one space would keep us toasty, but the ceiling of room was very high, and our combined heat rose away from us. Though the presence of so many other people was strangely comforting, I felt utterly alone as soon as I crawled into my sleeping bag. There was too much space between me and everyone else. I was only a few feet away from dozens of people, but the short distance felt thick and impenetrable. In the first hours after the lights were turned down, the room reverberated with the sound of a hundred people settling into their bunks. Even though it was just the beginning of the peak season on the trail, almost every bed was filled. I'd never slept in a space with so many people, never fallen into the trust of sleep so unprotected.

That night I wore all my clothes in my sleeping bag. The air was icy and damp, causing my teeth to chatter as I tried to collect my own body heat in a pool around me. The invading cold kept my weary body awake and allowed me too much time to reflect. I wanted some help warming myself. I wanted a man with his radiant heat beside me. I wanted to know I could be held at a moment's notice, be cared for in the days to come. Night made everything worse.

I'd been carrying a letter from my mom as a talisman, waiting for the right moment to open the sealed pink envelope and read her words to me. As the volume in the room dropped to a murmur and the lights dimmed, I slid the letter out of my journal and broke the seal. The familiar handwriting brought forward the image of my dear mom in bed recovering from a terrible arm break that had befallen her just a month ago. It was all too far away now. My family's grounding support was thousands of miles away, unable to help me through this night or any of the days ahead. All I had was the letter. I cried at every word; the tears dripped down my face. No loud sobs or puffy eyes, just glistening tears rolling out of me in an endless stream. I tried to stay as still and quiet as possible. I felt too raw to involve anyone else in this, too fragile to share this private moment with any of the flock around me. The young woman preparing her bunk next to mine looked over at one point, pausing as if to seek my eyes and say something kind, but I couldn't look over and connect. I couldn't tell her that I was broken and far away from the only small cluster of people I was sure still loved me. The one cluster of people that had faith in the forward momentum of my life, the souls who stayed optimistic even when I was rife with doubt and fearful the life I craved might never arrive.

I awoke many hours later and realized the first night had passed. Though the room was as dark as night, it was just shy of five in the morning. I'd managed with surprising ease to fall into a deep sleep, thanks mostly to my body's thirst for recovery. I was also grateful I'd packed wax earplugs to close out the ambient noise of my sleeping companions.

On the trail, I quickly ascertained many things about snoring through extensive first hand experience. I discovered the hidden power of female snorers and learned that a room with five people in it and one snorer afforded the same quality of sleep as a room with a hundred people and a dozen snorers. Actually, the likelihood of being able to handle a snorer increased when there was a chorus of night noises. When snorers unknowingly accompanied each other, the results were often quite dynamic. That night in Roncesvalles, many nasal passages rose into song and somehow it made me feel less lonely, but this didn't stop me from attempting to avoid and evade snorers at all costs after that first night. I became somewhat of an expert at seeing a fellow pilgrim walking around in the evening and knowing he was destined to offer a marathon night concert. After years of nighttime dorm chaos, I could manage lots of random sounds, but the drone of a solo snorer left me awake and restless. Like the rhythmic ticking of a clock, the pattern eventually wore away my ability to ignore the sound. Only earplugs could counter the corrosive effect of such snoring. The wax had plugged my ears from the outside world and turned my hearing inwards that first night. My breathing had been the dominant sound, calming me with my own rhythm. Perhaps it was the strength of this tireless cycle of blood pumping and lungs inflating that had lulled me to sleep. Nonetheless, that night I slept a deep and dreamless sleep. Not an image or a noise, memory or thought visited my body as I slept curled on my side with my arms tight around my own frame.

ZUBIRI

STAGE TWO- 35.8K-22.2M
RONCESVALLES TO ARRE

The Dane woke me from a half sleep a few moments before six, shaking the end of my sleeping bag. I shot up as if zapped by an electrical current. My adrenaline was back, rushing out to my very fingertips and snapping my body awake. The rest mode I'd fallen into vanished. I was almost too awake and alert.

"I am ready when you are," he said with a maddeningly cheerful grin.

Part of me was thrilled to start the day, escape the inactivity of night and return to the trail. I needed the walking to give my existence purpose and structure. I wanted to be submerged in something concrete and measurable, rather than paused in my troubled thoughts. I craved to be in the flow of action where my mind could grow silent and passive as if subdued in a warm bath of endorphins. I hopped down off the wobbling set of bunks, trying my best to be graceful and not shake the other women still asleep below me. The leap was a little bit longer than I expected, and my knees buckled as I hit the ground. I could imagine that in the weeks to come, lofty bunks such as this one would be a challenge after a long day, especially if there were no ladders. And since there was no ladder for this tall frame, I didn't hold out hope for the other albergues down the trail.

I was busy groping around for my hiking shoes when suddenly the lights blazed on. It was six and officially time for the day to begin. The old men running the albergue had arrived with their morning coffee, pressed play on the stereo and flicked on the lights with unabashed brutality. They saw this every day. They were blind to the mild suffering, the shocked and startled groans. It was their job to get everyone out the door and on their way by any means possible. Within moments, the room was filled with the sound of shifting sleeping bags and creaking bed frames. There were people scurrying about with speedy determination, and others tossing and turning, trying to keep the light out for just five more minutes. With a swooshing rustle, women around me rose stiff and startled to face another day. The men on the far side were doing the same thing. Even the couples seemed to be stirring.

Once all my gear was inside my pack I double-checked that I had my three most vital belongings: my wallet, set of passports and sleeping bag. In the mountains, I'd realized there was little else I would turn back for. Everything else was truly expendable. It was striking how fast I'd realized what was really necessary. This viewpoint was refreshing and required a lot less of me in the early morning chaos. If I lost a shirt or sock, my watch or flashlight, it wouldn't be the end of the world. It was soothing not to care about the non-essentials I carried, to feel free to lose them and not be upset if I parted ways with these peripheral things. It was such an important practice for the part of me that grasped at things in an attempt to keep experiences, objects or people from leaving or disappearing. If I could take this small baby step of fluidity then maybe I could graduate to releasing my emotional grip on the bigger things like lost jobs and failed relationships.

As I secured my sleeping mat to the outside of my bag and prepared to hoist the whole thing onto my shoulders, two women hurried by. One turned to the other and in a gloomy half whisper said, "Have you looked outside?" Her face grew darker with each word. "It's raining."

As I overheard this weather report, I felt all the other ears around me swivel like antennas picking up a signal. Within moments, the news spread across the space like wildfire. This was bad, really bad. It was generally acknowledged there was almost nothing worse in pilgrim life than rain. Sun was to be expected and most, if not all, pilgrims were prepared for it. We brought sun hats and sunscreen, planned to wake early and keep hydrated. Wind was another manageable foe. It could tire us, slow our pace and batter our physical frames, but it was hardly ever an impossible obstacle. Rain was different. It was the most invasive of weather. It didn't just move around us it swallowed us, filled every fiber of cloth, adhered to our skin and settled into our bones. It got into everything in our possession and refused to let go. And it could go on for hours, even days. It could haunt a pilgrim through weeks of walking, falling on them by day and keeping the air damp and cold enough that nothing would dry in the night. Stepping into a wet pair of shoes to start the day or crawling into a damp sleeping bag at night could wear down even the heartiest pilgrim. Across the room, people were reopening bags and pulling out raincoats, hats and rain pants. Everyone had some sort of armor, some weapon against the weather, but it was generally understood that almost nothing could totally spare a pilgrim. Well, maybe a full body gortex suit coupled with a bag cover and waterproof boots, but that was a very pricy endeavor and would take up a sizable section of a pilgrim's tiny bag. I met very few people who had gone such a route. Most of us suffered to one degree or another. Some pilgrims had rain jackets with deep hoods; others carried bag covers to keep the expanse of their packs dry. Then there were the bold and statement making pilgrims who donned the infamous rain gear known as the poncho.

I could never have imagined how surprisingly popular a choice this goofy gear would be on the trail, and I watched in utter disbelief as several people around me took them out and started to crawl inside. The poncho was little more than a giant sheet of brightly colored plastic with a hole cut in the neck for the pilgrim's head, thus allowing the rest of the body and bag to live under the flowing waves of plastic. This type of rain protection made anyone look like a disfigured camel, assured that the pilgrim could be spotted from miles away and, unfortunately, said something about his or her fashion sense without the pilgrim uttering a word.

I didn't subscribe to the cult of the poncho. Instead, I sported a new rain jacket in light blue found at my favorite thrift store. It was a men's jacket with a large front pocket built for both hands. I loved it from the moment I picked it off the rack. Long and lean, it matched the color of my eyes. Though I understood that rain gear was meant to serve a function, I also wanted it to be pleasing to the eye. I might have been un-cool enough to suffer the embarrassing wet stains of a water hose malfunction, but I would never be caught dead in a poncho. I simply refused on aesthetic principal. Just because I'd signed on for this vagabond life didn't stop me from packing a few items that I felt were bright and beautiful in a utilitarian way.

While my body was swathed in blue, my bag got first class treatment and hid from the rain under a bright red bag cover that formed all my belongings into a neat, compact and rainproof bubble. This was the first time I'd used such a thing, and if it hadn't come with my bag when I purchased it, I fear I would have regrettably overlooked the need for such a cover. With all my rain gear in place, and my shoes tied with secure double knots, I strode to the door, dodging and weaving through the cramped aisle to finally emerge out into the open entranceway where the Dane had promised to wait for me. I pushed open the door, noticed a slightly mocking expression from the albergue volunteer in the entrance and stepped out into the new day. The smile made sense when I barely managed to dodge a wide puddle on the front step then looked up into a thick blanket of fog devouring everything around the building. Even the road which lay only a stone's throw from the albergue had vanished in the mist. The rain didn't seem to be cutting the fog but added to the feeling of isolation. The morning looked as if it would be one of no sight and no sound beyond the glow of opaque air and the rhythm of rain. The Dane was the only pilgrim outside, milling around under the eaves. When I emerged, he seemed to be absorbed in looking out into the water-saturated darkness of early morning. As I did some fancy footwork to quit the building, he swiveled in place so he could see me around the edges of his hood thus causing his long train of flowing plastic to swoosh around him like a cape. There was no mistaking it; the Dane was sporting the triple threat of a puke green poncho, knee high socks and an unusually smug grin. Day two had begun.

In the early morning, I walked behind the Dane through endless tracks of misty land. For the first hour, the pathway was narrow, cluttered with low hanging trees and speckled with overflowing puddles. As I trailed in the wake of the glorious poncho, I hopped around as if caught on a never ending hopscotch board. It was a vain attempt to keep my shoes dry, but I was soon convinced it made no real difference. Eventually, we moved through a small village, and the road widened into small farm lanes, allowing me to walk beside the Dane. The banks of fog clung to the ground and dripped from every green surface. All the houses were sealed tight and silent as we stole through neighborhoods and back into the open fields. There was something magical about being the only people awake, moving unseen at such an empty hour. The path felt soft like a sponge underfoot as it moved us around fields and farms. The only interruption in the trail came from narrow streams and farmyard gates that implored us to please close the latch behind us. We crossed the streams by way of crude but sturdy bridges made from large stones. There was an elegance about each crossing; it was clear the stone byways had been there for decades, maybe centuries. The gates were another matter all together; they were new, made of sturdy wood and hooked with metal rings. Even with the endless flow of pilgrims moving through these fields, farmers had to trust we would close the gates behind us and not allow the cows to escape. Since the trail had lived in its groove of land for over a thousand years, Basque farmers had to work around the flow of pilgrims walking to a city five hundred miles away. We didn't see a single person for the first hour and talked very little. The noise of the rain falling on the outside of my hood filled my eardrums and drowned out all other sound. There was something profound about the noise, and it filtered through me like silence. Everything in me was still, save the muscles and breath needed to move forward. At times, I lost sight of the Dane in my peripheral vision and felt I might slip through the edges of time. There were no markers of the present and no sense that the modern world still lay beyond this soft universe of trail, lush fields and sleepy eyed cows.

After several hours, the air started to break, and a film of white light leaked through with hints of the sun trying to rise behind it. Since the Dane had left me to my thoughts and I to his, we'd fallen into an easy dynamic. Even with all his oddity, I was secretly thankful I hadn't been forced to start out into the morning alone. Though I discovered the arrows were clear along this stretch of trail, the weather had made the day's stage a bit intimidating. Plus, it brought me a shred of comfort to know if I fell and broke a bone, someone would be there to drag me to civilization. The grouping that had taken place in the Pilgrim Office in St. Jean had been one of necessity and had given me the push up and over the mountain, but today the dynamic was different. The social outcast part of me was simply pleased that anyone, even the Dane, would want to walk with me, while another part of me was slightly concerned about creating a habit of clinging to any and all connections. In the mountains, I'd proved I wouldn't be a burden and slow him down. Near the end of the day, I even had to wait for the Dane to catch up to me. I knew I'd proved my speed and endurance, but why else had he chosen to wait in the eaves for me this morning? I had yet to reach out to many other pilgrims, but I knew this was due to a heavy dose of shyness coupled with extreme weariness. Hopefully, I would soon overcome both, but I noticed the Dane hadn't talked with anyone else either. And I could already tell that his reasons for such isolation were noticeably different than my own. From what I could gather, he spent most of the night in Roncesvalles sitting on his bunk making notes in his guidebook and ignoring the comings and goings around him. The other people hardly seemed to cross his radar. When I glanced over at the Dane, I realized that even though I felt gratitude towards him, I wasn't one hundred percent pleased we were walking together again. And as the morning wore on, the ratio of gratitude to annoyance shifted, making me less and less pleased that we were still moving as a unit. I couldn't help wondering what the trade off for this dependence and closeness with the Dane might be.

After many kilometers of field, the path ran into the woods. The downpour lightened and then turned to a fine mist. Little did I know, but luck had been on my side when the bulk of the rain had fallen in the night. The soft precipitation that now fell on us was the gods' helping hand, because I would have been a very miserable pilgrim if the rain had persisted. Though it matched my eyes, my rain jacket was no match for the rain. It was virtually useless, more of an example of what a rain jacket should look like rather than how a rain jacket should perform when faced with its one and only true foe. Waterproof was not a word that could be attributed to my blue fashion plate, and I had no one to blame but myself. It was a failure that allowed rain to seep through to my dry layers, drench the bare skin around my neck and cling to me with damp determination. I suppose it was karma for making fun of ponchos, and in a cruel ironic twist, I suspected the Dane was dry as a bone under his vomit colored tarp.

Besides the poncho, the Dane was decked out in some of the most high tech gear I'd ever seen. Everything gleamed with the fresh new sheen of plastic reconstituted into space age jackets and pants. All his sleek items were dark in color, cluttered with zippers and fit like a glove. He was prepared for every eventuality. I decided not to tell him that the most high tech items I had with me were a few pairs of bright colored quick drying underwear. His equipment made me feel a bit out of my league and wonder what the hell I'd been thinking when I packed for this journey. Had I totally lost track of what would be needed for this mighty trek and blacked out when stocking up on gear? I'd noticed a lot of other people with similarly intense paraphernalia and felt a bit silly in my drenched jacket. As a way of assuaging guilt that I hadn't arrived better prepared, I reminded myself of the medieval pilgrims, many of whom had walked these trails barefoot. They hadn't been decked out in expensive polypropylene clothing or gortex boots, yet their place of belonging on the trail had been just as legitimate. So my jacket and pack were a bit rough around the edges, not perfectly cut or brand new, but they would be able to get me to Santiago and the coast, and wasn't that the ultimate point? This trek wasn't about who looked the most skilled but who made it all the way to the end. There was a lot of talking going on with the gear, but I knew that the walking would sort us all out by the end. I wouldn't let my gear stop me, even if it made the journey a bit more uncomfortable. I could take it. As the Dane charged through puddles with high tech, high top, waterproof boots, I gingerly avoided the water holes, feeling my point was proven. Yes, I would have to be more dexterous and yes, my things might be damp when they could be dry, but I would improvise. Maybe the same could be said for the religious element of the trail. Okay, so I didn't fit into the easy category of straight forward Christian affiliation, but I was dexterous, and could navigate the elements of faith and spirituality that would come at me as easily as I could these puddles, with a lightness of foot and a nimbleness of spirit. Full of resolve, I ignored how my new sneakers welcomed water in to squish around my toes. At some point, it had to stop raining and when it did, I would dry out. Until then, I would keep walking, keep moving forward even in my less than perfect state.

As we wound our way down through the hills, the path moved from muddied ruts created by bikers to faux cobblestone roadways. I would have preferred an earthen trail on that wet morning, for I quickly discovered that the stones held a hidden slick. I feared for the bikers who passed us at high speed. Apparently they relished the sections of steep exhilarating descents, but I didn't long to be there if they were to meet with a stone or crack in the path. I'd seen the Tour de France and knew how a sudden bike dismount could end, even with a skilled rider taking the fall. The only time I'd ridden a bike at top speed on such surfaces ended with two black and blue palms and road rash that snaked up the side seam of my body.

Since the early days of the Camino well over a thousand years ago, the trail had been almost exclusively a walking pilgrimage, but during its modern reincarnation, the bike had emerged as another way to travel the road to Santiago. I always knew my Camino would be a walking journey, but every year more and more pilgrims decide to travel by bike. In the last five years, the number of bike pilgrims had grown exponentially and now roughly a fourth of the people who traveled the trail were on two wheels. Even after two days, I'd gathered most of the bikers were young men suddenly taking to the trail because of this emerging medium. For the walking pilgrims, it was hard not to curse the bikers and feel envious of them in the same instant. Moving at lightening fast speeds, they seemed weightless and free, broken loose from the grip of inertia and gravity. They were sleek and fast, light and agile. They were everything that walking pilgrims with large packs on their shoulders were not. And despite their speed, bikers carried much weightier packs than us walkers. They had more gear and weight, but a less direct experience of the load they carried. Because of their trusty wheeled vehicle, they had more stuff and still out paced us with deft skill. It was common to see the sides of the bikes cluttered with heavy bags full of gear, supported by the frame and the propulsion of the wheels. The panniers often held heavy tents, food supplies and extra clothes. The contradiction was clear to all of us moving on foot; as the bikers sped past loaded down, we were painfully aware of every ounce we carried. Leaving something behind and lightening our packs could create more speed, but the bikers didn't experience their gear the same way. They weren't thrown into a love/hate relationship, filled with angst about every single ounce in their possession. And they were still as fast and light as birds, zipping by with the ring of a bell or an infuriatingly cheerful shout. The only saving grace was that all pilgrims agreed who was on the most challenging road. Most bike pilgrims would concede that comparatively, they had the cushy life. Even they could admit to the deeper level of physical sacrifice required of us walking pilgrims.

As early morning drew closer to noon, we pushed on to Zubiri with the goal of arriving for lunch. The trail ran alongside the road for a while, and occasionally we could hear the hum of bikes rushing by us like a fleet of wings. My eyes barely had time to recognize their forms in the morning fog before they were lost again. And lost they would stay. Even though it was entirely logical, it took me a while to understand that I would never reconnect with the bikers I saw along the trail. Our paths would only intersect at the single point where my footsteps crossed their tracks. Then they would be vanish. All the herds of strapping young Spanish men with flowing hair and toned calves would be gone in the blink of an eye.

Fortunately the opposite was true of the other walkers I met along the way. Even within any given day, I might cross in front and behind a fellow pilgrim several times. I might meet a couple sitting along the trail in the morning, eating their bread in the new light, smiling as I passed. Then, as I was sitting under a tree at lunch, they would bound by, sticks clicking as they raised a hand in a wave of acknowledgement. It was comforting to feel, even after two days, that the trail could become a place of familiar faces. The only down side was that while the bike traffic was mostly young and male, the walking traffic I'd seen so far had been older folks and couples.

The existence of bikers on the trail was an unexpected wrinkle, but in that first day as they moved by us, I wasn't too concerned by the level of disconnection. Yet, I had to wonder, if in the days to come I would find it difficult to keep calm as packs of young men sped past giving me a parting view of their fit bodies and dreamy hair. If I was still surrounded by older coupled pilgrims, I might just have to bite my tongue so as not to yell out and call them back. What if all the handsome young men were no longer walking the Camino but biking it?

As the day warmed up and the rain lessened, I started to chat with the Dane. I was impressed with how well he spoke English, and I knew that speaking in my native language on such an international trail was a luxury. With English our stomping ground that early morning, I asked questions and learned more about my rather mysterious companion. The Dane's skill with English was due to several years of musical study in Florida, and he proudly shared his extensive knowledge of American slang to prove it. As we spoke, the cadence of my speech and my choice of words altered in response to my knowledge that English wasn't his native tongue. At first, the change was so subtle I didn't notice it, but then I realized I was pulling formal and antiquated words out of my brain. I was drifting into the language of Jane Austen and felt unable to stop this odd behavior. The Dane didn't seem to notice, but still, I wondered if I would do this with every non-native speaker I met in the weeks to come. It was disorienting. It made me wonder who I would become on the trail if I already felt myself shifting.

Even with the alterations in my speech, I still found myself in a half rabid state of delight to be talking with anyone. After the chilly social scene in Roncesvalles, I was feeling less confident in my ability to connect with people and have them actually want to walk with me for hours at a time. I knew being an American, on the eve of a crucial presidential election, wouldn't naturally endear me to many, and the fact that I looked so young might keep some away as well. I'd often been told that I would someday enjoy the fact that I looked so much younger than my years, but while it still had me appearing as if I was underage jailbait, I had a hard time finding the charm in it.

As we talked, we climbed a series of small mountains covered with scrubby pines, then finally felt the sun on our backs. Other people started to appear on the trail around us, and just shy of noon, we descended down a rocky trail into the town of Zubiri. For lunch, we crossed a bridge into town and located a place to buy food. A man on the bridge pointed us towards a small shop, tucked into a low beamed room on the bottom floor of an apartment building, As I stepped into the store, I was overwhelmed by how full the space was. It wasn't a large room but held at least a dozens haunches of meat dangling from the ceiling on lengths of twine. Legs and chops swayed slightly as I tried to navigate the maze of meat without bumping into anything. Eventually I found exactly what I was looking for in a bag on the counter. The fresh homemade cookies with thick white cream in the middle and dipped in chocolate had my name written all over them. I selected yogurt and some cheese to go along with the cookies, while the Dane bought sausage, bread and a large bar of chocolate. Just the sight of the cookies promised great things, and they didn't disappoint. Slurping down a yogurt, I plunged into the bag of cookies and dissolved into a momentary sugar blackout. Maybe my hunger and the many years I'd lived away from the lure of chocolate collided in those bites, but I knew I would never forget that batch of cookies. As I chomped into another sweet crunchy bite, I came to an epiphany. I could eat cookies for breakfast, chocolate for lunch, and pastries for dinner. There were no rules, no need to save treats for later, or cut back on the sugar. Forget savory and salty meats, olives and gooey cheeses. I could make sweet delights a regular part of this trek; I would certainly be working hard enough to earn them. Sitting on a bench in the shade beside the trail, drying my socks and feeding little pieces of meat to a stray cat, I could see glorious treats lining the path ahead of me. I was eight again, and the trail was like an extended version of Halloween but with much better offerings. When I was eight, chocolate and running around outside were enough to keep me happy for hours. Maybe the same would be true for the trail. Maybe if I willed it to be so, these two essential ingredients could be enough. Maybe I could forget I was twenty four rather than eight and needed more than just the freedom to run and munch on sweets to feel full at the end of the day.

After lunch, we moved out of Zubiri and headed into a sparsely populated stretch of trail. The clear sky was refreshing after a morning dominated by rain. It was energizing to feel the sun warm the surfaces of my clothes. The shift in weather necessitated I shed some of the clothing that had been indispensable when I began in the chill of the morning. The right balance of layers had been difficult to guesstimate when emerging from the cocoon of my sleeping bag. I'd piled on too many layers, but I was stubborn about stopping my forward progress to shed them when the weather shifted. There was something about pacing that kept me from taking the moment to remove the clothing overheating me. That sunny afternoon, I started to train myself in the skilled art of removing layers while walking, the tricky balance needed to pull one arm through and then the other and slide a sweatshirt out from my back. I had a feeling that by the end of the journey, I would be able to do practically anything while still walking and talking my way down the trail.

The land on the far side of Zubiri warmed both my body and my mood. As the narrow dirt path wound alongside roads, it was flanked by flowers in endless shades. The purples and pinks mingled with the sugar pumping through my veins, lightening my steps. Suddenly I felt my feet moving faster, each leg unfolding with more purpose and energy. I was out ahead of the Dane, and I could feel him dropping away behind me, unable to match my new burst of speed. I was moving ahead on my own, and I could feel every footfall recharging my legs for the next. For the first time ever, I felt I could fall in love with traversing far and wide all on my own power. I knew the Dane lurked somewhere behind me, but I didn't turn around to see how much space I'd put between us. After this morning and the initial rush of feeling lucky to have someone to look out for me, I was starting to feel another set of emotions creep in about my affiliation with the Dane.

ARRE

As I took my space from the Dane, my mind whirled with a growing realization. Even when I'd thought my connection with the Dane was little more than a pairing of convenience to last only a short while, I realized his presence was more than met the eye. He was a link in a pattern that scrolled all the way back to my early adulthood. He was a ghost of my past come to life.

The Dane reminded me that in the past I'd only attracted two types of men. As I considered the men who'd swerved, sprinted, circled and dodged into and out of my life, they all fell into these two categories. The first kind were forces of nature. They were boldly handsome, endowed with effortless magnetism and pursued success in their chosen field with ruthless abandon. They were wildly popular. They might have been nerdy once upon a time, but that era died long before I met them. As adults they sought approval yet operated as if above it. Their lives were littered with accomplishments in the arts, academics, athletics or all of the above. Extroverts in dogged pursuit of glory, they saw life as a fight and believed charm would win the battle. Narcissists to the max, they were the center of their own worlds, bound up in a desire to be famous, successful, beloved or all of the above. After such a description, it might be hard to understand what I saw in such men. It was simple; I didn't see any of this. I believed in the other side of them that they didn't show their adorning public. I felt I was behind the scenes in the drama of their lives, the one who saw their human need for love, acceptance and connection. I even believed I was the only one to fully understand the inner working of their hearts and their almost painful yearning for love. I didn't pay much attention to the show they put on for everyone else, because I was backstage and felt I knew the real truth of who they were. I wanted to believe in their best selves, but perhaps in the end, I should have paid more attention to the main show.

These were the lost boys who looked perfect in character and shone with blinding luminosity but were broken into shattered bits of loss and distress, fear and confusion. They were the boys who craved a rescuer to revive them each night after their daily theatrics drained them of all they had. Cue the quiet girl tucked behind stage with a willingness to pump blood, energy and life into someone with eyes drenched in sorrow and a delicately layered broken center.

Being in love with a lost boy meant action. Physical energy, emotional stimuli and mental adulation were needed at all times. Theirs were naturally caffeinated lives that hummed around a hidden center. With this activity came the manly pursuit of female attention, and they had great success with women, pulling them in by the net full. I was even told salacious details about one of the lost boy's rap sheet with the ladies a year before I met him. With this set of men, reputations preceded them. As to the matter of friends and close relationships, they had many acquaintances, but no one who was close enough to see below the facade. They preferred to be encircled by people who adored them for their worldly persona rather than understood them for their inner workings. They wanted an entourage not an emotional support system. Yet below all the layers of movement, there lay a shocking space of nothingness. A vast gaping hole where the center of faith and a grounding in love should have been. They were like towering houses built without foundations.

Fundamentally, they were absolutely clueless about who they were below all the action, theatrics and praise. And they weren't sure they could stand to find out, pause long enough to listen and be assured that they would like what they discovered. This running away from their own center caused a secret distress that ate away at them and sent each lost boy on the hunt, consciously or unconsciously, for a girl such as myself. A girl who might be able to go down into the cellar and shore up whatever was causing the house to slide and wobble. It was all about energetics. They could feel I wasn't scared of the hole or the emptiness, and that I even believed they could heal. And like a bell ringing across an open space, my vibration reverberated with them, so they sought me out even in a crowd of other more eager faces. And for the record, they came to me, not the other way around. Though I did make it a nasty habit of taking on these projects, they were the ones who stepped forward and asked me to do so. Maybe not in so many words but on every other level.

Once I entered their dramas, one thing always became very clear. These lost boys were ignoring the truth, turning away from it, shutting their eyes and evading it at each turn. Because they were waging such a campaign of avoidance, life and universal forces often gave them a mighty thrashing. It dropped the floor out from underneath them time and time again, attempting to wake them up and shake them back into their centers. In my family, we called this the two by four school of realization; if you don't get the message with a gentle nudge or a slight push, the intensity of the delivery method will increase until life is slamming you in the face with an energetic two by four. I watched each lost boy get his share of whacks and cringed every time. Yet in a strange way this also made them obsessed with the two by four. The school of spiritual hard knocks was a mortal foe in their own lives but an object of fascination and beauty they sought out in others. I could see they desired me almost more for my current of truthfulness than anything else. I felt sometimes they were mesmerized by the glossy surface of my energetic transparency, my ability and choice not to conceal anything. It wasn't that I spoke bluntly or displayed overtly candid outward behaviors, but I lived as if I had nothing to hide, nothing to run from and no fear of growing into the person I really was. No skeletons or emotional uncharted waters, just an earnest desire to unfold the layers of my life. It was a sort of innocence, but not of the naïve variety. It was an energetic tone of truth. And for that I was utterly fascinating, while perhaps also pleasing to look at and talk with too. And so we drew closer.

I hardly paid any attention to the lost boys upon first meeting. I was blissfully unaware of the role I would play in their lives and didn't feel I would ever be someone to garner their attention. I would notice their open demeanor and striking good looks but did so from a distance. The social world in which we moved was often rife with gossip. I was intrigued by the drama that swirled around them and discussed their comings and goings like those of movie stars. The lost boys, with their penchant for women, were often in relationships, considerably older than me and outside my close social circle. It was natural for our lives to hardly overlap, so they didn't. I made friends with different men, formed crushes on others and went about my life, for a while at least. But at some moment, often unbeknownst to me, I'd been spotted and marked. And then, it was only a matter of time until our lives did intersect, and everything burst into action.

When I collided with the first lost boy, I was living on my own at the time, in a small room in a quiet house up on a hill. It was late fall, and I was recovering from an illness that had kept me out of class and on the sidelines of dance rehearsals for over a month. It was cold outside, and all the studios were full. So I met with the Dancer Man in a small theater practice room with scratchy carpets and wood paneled walls. The lights were on, and the windows had turned into dark mirrors around us. I was new to the project but had been drafted to be a dancer in the piece. I expected to learn a few step then return to my bed for more recovery sleep. Instead, the Dancer Man turned to me and announced we were going to create a duet. The beautiful golden boy, with all the female adoration one man could hope for, drew me close and started to dance with me. Even in my haze of sickness, I could feel every surface of my skin where it touched his, and the air around us seemed to crackle. He was confident and bold as he lifted me, encircled my waist with his arms and touched me.

Dance is always a contact endeavor, but the one thing an audience or outsider might not understand is that touch in dance is all about tone. Nothing is romantic or sexual unless the dancer ordains it so; boundaries don't come from not touching, they come from clarity. The clarity of energy is the key. I'd been dancing for years, and it had always been clear, until that night. The lines were in shambles around me, and he knew it. It felt like an audition to be the object of his affection as if he was testing how much he really wanted to touch me, to hold me close, to pursue me. I was stunned and felt as if I was being pulled into a swift and all consuming current. He was no longer a handsome face or beautiful mover I watched from a distance. He was in my energy field as close to my grown up body as I felt anyone had ever been. It was almost more intimate than anything that could have followed. It was passion spoken in simple movements with no audience. Only the two of us and a silent space.

Until that moment, I'd never tasted such intensity of desire. I'd never felt it directed towards me or realized I too felt the same tidal pull. We certainly had requited attraction, but eventually, I conceded that we also had unrequited love. Yes, his attraction was strong and ever present from that moment on, but the Dancer Man was also a master tactician, so skilled in the ways of women that it took me years to realize how truly savvy he'd been. He'd honed a personality of open warmth and fake innocence that I and many others believed in. At the time, I felt the gravity of attraction pulling me into his life and believed his intentions were true. Little could my earnest nineteen year old self see that the deck had been stacked in his favor from the first moment he turned his gaze on me. I didn't know it then, but I hadn't had a prayer of holding my own ground.

After that night, everything I knew and felt about romance changed. In short, I was sunk. In retrospect, I could pin point that as the evening he hooked into my energy field, using all the skills in his arsenal to tie himself to me. And I let him. I was drugged by it all and had longed for such passion for years. During that ordinary night, I signed on for the project of trying to fix all that was broken in him, signed on to be backstage to ground his life. I naively thought I could help this lost boy if I surrendered everything to him. And in return, all I asked for was his love. The trade seemed fair.

My compassionate heart and its belief in the best in him was what hooked me on a deeper level. That night he discovered these elements and knew they could be used in his favor. It was as if we had known each other in another time and place. As if we had danced like this before. To dance with him was effortless, and it would be until the day we parted years later. It was like falling into something that fit perfectly and worked on a level deeper than thought or consciousness. I didn't need to think or plan. I simply moved, and he was there with me. He understood the mechanics and flow of my body upon first contact. We were even a perfect match in build and strength. We looked alike with wild torrents of fair hair and smooth flowing limbs that measured our heights to exactly the same number. Yet I would come to learn that lost boys, especially older ones, spend a great deal of time training themselves to attract people who would care for them energetically, so they could run through them and eventually discard the empty shell. More often than not, this was done through deceptive and calculated behavior. I was a prime candidate to take care of the Dancer Man's emotional strife, and he knew it.

Time moved around us both, but the center of the energy didn't waver. If anything, it took on a torturous ache. For as the months passed, his outer life moved not one inch. He was woefully stuck in deep ruts, digging his heels into an empty existence. He dragged me through periods where he wore black, spun stories of his victimhood and acted like a petulant child. There was no sense of a greater destiny or deeper balance. He didn't believe his life and the relationships that formed its fabric could be more than just bonds of convenience and advancement. He didn't believe it could be better, that he could feel grounded and safe, loved and in balance. In a way, he didn't believe in love at all. Not in its ability to manifest or create or its ultimate lasting value when all else fades. He simply discounted it as a sideline emotion that only deterred forward momentum. At times, I felt he feared my intensity when it came to love and hated me for how much I was willing to feel.

In my role as rescuer, I felt bound to fill in all the gaps, take on his imbalances and right the ship. His failure to create was my energetic project. And his failure to feel was mine to fix. I was always working to predict which way the wind was blowing, in hopes I could support him to someday create a piece of dance that spoke from the heart and make a course correction in his personal life that took him towards healing. I really believed he could get there. I suppose I believed this about all the lost boys. I knew they were projects, but I didn't think they were hopeless cases, just unusually dire. I could almost see the day, the moment, the words that would come when they got it, when the two by four school finally loosened enough teeth and drew enough blood that they saw me standing there offering a different way forward, a more soulful way forward, a way forward that included me.

Only years later would I start to understand the outer world drama was always going to win for these lost boys. Even when the Dancer Man's life was weeks of dark moods and depression, months of creating little more than reused and recycled shit from days gone by and years of parading around his hollow relationships, he remained invested in the illusion on the surface. For all I knew, this was still the case. It took me years to finally relinquish the role of fixing his life and standing by as he made his whole worth about the surface, devoting his creative flow, sublimely beautiful dancing and personal life to the shallow adoration of strangers and relationships of empty ambition. Being so young at the time, it had taken all the strength in my battered being to walk away and not look back. I had no help from anyone, least of all the lost boy himself. Lost boys only make messes and inflict wounds. They don't clean up or help things heal over. That job was left to my family. It was a lonely end and an end that took years to fully heal.

I would repeat this pattern again with another love where the particulars were very different, but the outcome was much the same. With the second lost boy, the Caveman, the secrets were deeper, and the evasion of the truth more profound. In some ways, the relationship was a darker version of my first brush with a lost boy. In an eerie twist of fate, both men had the same name. Right then, I should have known the end game would be similar. I ought to have seen the signs, been able to diagnose a lost boy when I saw one, but the tactics were different, and this one was avoiding the truth for vastly different reasons. These reasons poisoned us much faster than the slow killing toxins of life with the Dancer Man. And predictably, the conclusion was identical; it just took less time and left more dirty wounds filled with shame and fear that weren't even my own. Maybe there was no way to compare these two lost boys, for the Dancer Man was years in the past, and the chapter of the Caveman had ended no more than a week ago.

Even with their considerable dent on my youth, not all of my time was spent on lost boys. There was also a crop of different men who drifted in and out of my life. This was the second type. At first glance, this group seemed generally harmless, but something was always a bit off. They were glommers, connoisseurs who collected beauty, and more often than not, they were utterly clueless. They were older men who appraised me like a fine vintage of wine, and younger guys who felt they could charm me with their drug induced adventures. They were men who read me one hundred percent, totally and completely at face value. So I was often dodging and weaving these bogies in my spare time between gut wrenching sessions with broken men and the shallow lives they loved. The last decade had been.... well, something worth writing home about, but hardly anything I would recommend actually participating in.

As we left Zubiri, I had a feeling that my growing discomfort with the Dane and the way he hovered and spoke down to me all pointed to one thing. He was most certainly a classic version of a type two. He liked what he saw, felt I was suitably in adoration of him, even though I was so clearly NOT. His growing interest became apparent when he held my elbow as he spoke to me and sat too close for comfort. He had practically shouted the victory cry when I sat on his bunk to ask him a question in Roncesvalles. I realized I may have encouraged his thoughts in the wrong direction with my harmless inquiry about kilometers, but he was already lost. Lost in the dream of something of a scandalous nature unfolding between us. He had that gleam in his eye as I tried to assert my boundaries, placing bunks, packs and even other strangers between us as buffers. He felt he was very close to making me his own. I felt close to vomiting. He was asking himself which role I was to fill: booty call, easily claimed chattel or a doting indentured girlfriend, and I was starting to consider sleeping with a sharp object.

Unfortunately, this morning's banter had done little to quell my fears. During a lengthy and tediously dry dissection of Danish cinema, the Dane let his thoughts wander to the topic of women. His words were polite and perfectly proper in tone as he extolled the virtues of women in society and Danish cinema, but when the topic of his rambling veered toward sex, all his censor valves turned off, and he let his true thoughts fly. I must clarify that at this time I had known the Dane for little more than twenty four hours, twelve of which we had spent on opposite sides of a vast albergue. I wasn't ready for nor in need of his views on sex and relationships. Not now. Most likely not ever. He may have felt he was priming me for where we would go together in the days to come, but as my skin crawled, I simply wanted to take off at full speed and not look back. Or perhaps inform him that the last man who spoke to me in this tone, with this kind of false confidence and clear agenda had been a gay man with a girlfriend who refused to give up the charade. If I was meant to swoon and see the Dane as a big success with ladies, it wasn't working. And keeping in line with his breed of male, I was almost certain he hadn't even noticed that his pep talk had gone down in flames.

So the Dane was mutating before my eyes into a less than desirable Camino companion, but I hadn't met a single other young person or viable community of pilgrims pals. I had no idea if it would stay this way the whole journey; I wasn't sure the universe was willing to muster a gang for me. Was I meant to wallow in patterns of old or maybe break free and have to rough it on my own? When I was called to the trail, was there a clause that stated I was going to have to do it by myself in a sea of kind yet elderly pilgrims? I knew if I didn't start speeding up, I was going to be stuck with the same batch of people the entire way. Was my destiny cast when I arrived in St. Jean? Had I simply picked a lame starting day, or worse, were there just no young people on the trail this early in the summer? There were so many unknown factors and breaking all contact with the few pilgrims who were familiar felt too hard to manage in my tired and slightly freaked out state. Nonetheless, I mulled over this growing concern about how long I could stomach the Dane as I walked towards Arre, our final destination for the day.

Even after years of attempting to mend the broken lives of the men I'd loved and ultimately needing to release them back into the wild, I still had faith in love. Love had been the only element worth such taking on such trials for. Every time I began a new relationship, I still felt I was simply following the dream of love. Yes, I was often taken down dead end gullies and dry oxbows, but my thirst for realization of the dream hadn't diminished. If anything it had only grown. I came to see how damaging it had been to be with the men of the past, how to be with them had been to turn away from parts of my essential self. So now I was here on the trail. Awake and present. Strengthened through battle training and centered even deeper in my faith that the universe would eventually send the right man into my life. I knew it was only a matter of time. But I was impatient. After nearly ten years, two major failed love affairs, and half a dozen minor skirmishes to my credit, patience was simply not easy. Even as the trail neared Arre, it took a lot of soothing internal dialog to trust the timing. I wanted to believe that powers with a more lofty and clear view than my own guided the timing of my life. And because of my dream at the end of the world, I believed the trail might be the moment when enduring love would unfold.

But as I walked, I started to wonder if the universe had sent me on a wild goose chase. Was I here for something else, for another project perhaps or to more fully heal the past? That felt too cruel to entertain. Yes, I wanted to heal, but I certainly didn't want it to have to take so darn long. Couldn't I just wrap things up quickly, clean up all old business and get on with life? No more milling around. I wanted things to move as fast as I was. I wanted the scenery of my life to zip by. I wanted to go from the cold damp ends of something to the warm and delicious beginnings. This waiting game wasn't easy.

By now, I was only a few kilometers away from Arre, a small suburb of Pamplona. I estimated the Dane was at least twenty minutes behind me on the trail. As I looked across the valley toward the next cluster of civilization, I was no longer concerned about losing him, but I worried I might be lost. Catching a glimpse of him ambling along behind me signified I was on the right path, that I hadn't missed any way-markers or misinterpreted their directions. His presence was now solely about basic navigation.

I looked in the guidebook and calculated the distance of the day's journey to be just under forty kilometers. I hadn't seen another pilgrim in hours. My guidebook informed me that over 100,000 people walk the trail each year. Where was everybody? If I was moving so much faster than the crew who began in Roncesvalles, then shouldn't I be coming across groups that started ahead of us? Would it be better for me to keep going to Pamplona and stay in the big albergue there? I wavered about whether to stay in Arre and be forced to hold off the advances of the Dane or go on and be tired and very alone. With all the new elements coming at me each day, degrees of aloneness suddenly felt very real. To feel even that much less lonely after a long day made a difference. Plus, I might run into the Swede again if I stayed in Arre; she was a familiar bond that promised kind words and easy conversation. So for now, I would live in degrees of loneliness and stay in Arre.

THE TRINIDAD

The trail wound down into a narrow river valley. Pamplona lay just ahead but was hidden behind the valley walls, keeping the albergue at Arre tucked in a natural alcove off to the side of the busy city. As I descended down a long paved track into Arre, I imagined I would see Pamplona before me, but such a view would have to wait until tomorrow. Sometimes, a view forward was clear, and the destination could be seen from miles off, but often the land gave no clues which way the trail would turn. Buildings, villages, even cities that seemed to beckon would disappear out of view, never to be walked through.

The ancient albergue at Arre sat sidesaddle on the wide banks of the río Ulzama. The river was shallow, and rock outcroppings punctuated the swift moving water. The Ulzama flowed down a series of small waterfalls that kicked the water into the air and created an omnipresent rumble. An ancient bridge connected both sides of the river with a low arch made of massive stone. It was wide enough for a cart pulled by animal power but not big enough for a car; it was a narrow outlet for feet and slow moving wheels only. The albergue formed a wing of the church, and both church and albergue blended into the bridge. On holidays, the church community would parade through the streets and across the bridge with banners and musicians. I heard from a lucky pilgrim who witnessed the festivities that women made large vats of thick hot chocolate and homemade biscuits for all who joined in the celebration. Now the churchyard was empty. It was the peak of siesta, and everything was thick with sleepy silence. The Dane was nowhere in sight as I slumped down against the outer wall of the albergue to wait for it to open.

After twenty minutes, I decided to try the large metal knocker on the door of the building just in case someone was awake within. I hadn't finished my third knock when the heavy door swung open and a small old man wearing grey trousers and a wool sweater vest answered the door and beckoned me in. The building was dimly lit but cool. My body temperature dropped within moments of stepping into the narrow entranceway. My host spoke only Spanish, but his warm words were somehow easy to translate. He looked me in the eye as he spoke and let his hands help with the translation. He didn't seem concerned whether I understood him or not; remarkably this made me feel the same way. There was a subtle trust that information wasn't the most important part about sheltering pilgrims. He led me into the small anteroom that acted as his office, and with purposeful steps, he crossed the room and slid around the back of a large wooden desk. As I pulled out my documents, I heard the door swing open and large indelicate footsteps clomp up behind me. With impeccable timing, the Dane had arrived and taken his spot beside me. He was flush with sweat and panting slightly. I moved a half step away from him as he breathed down my neck. The peace of the moment was broken, but I wasn't about to let the Dane invade my personal space in the same way he'd invaded the calm of the room.

The man at the desk pulled out a fragile pair of glasses and drew forth a large discolored book. I could imagine that once it had been beautiful and unmarred brown leather, but time and human hands had worn its edges. As he opened the antique volume to the first half empty page near the back, I knew why it showed its years. Written in the tightest and most delicate hand were the names, nationalities and dates of arrival of every pilgrim who'd spent the night in this small albergue for the last number of decades. There could have been fifty years of pilgrim's names there, if not more. It was clear the man had spent much of his adult life doing this simple task, bearing witness to all the weary pilgrims who crossed this threshold. He gave them each a line, wrote their names with clear penmanship and kept the book safe. It was his mode of service, his way of being on the trail without walking its dusty pathway. He was in the flow of pilgrim life without having to be a pilgrim. There was a beauty to that, and I suddenly realized he and others like him were essential to our journey. They were the keepers of the trail. Across the years, they held the thread of the journey open so we could travel. They were stationary so we could move.

The recording of the information for each pilgrim wasn't unusual. In fact, almost every place I stayed along the way was meticulous about documenting all the details. At times, I wondered what all the records were really about, especially when they asked for my country passport number. But then I remembered that the elements of truthful passage were very important to those looking to prove they walked the whole trail. Each albergue was part of a system that honored all who walked the pilgrim journey with a certificate of completion called a Compostela. I'd begun to gather that for some, the certificate was a very important element of their journey. Here in this small office, the recording of names was also a way of acknowledging that each soul who walked the trail was a part of its lineage. Each name was given the same importance in one line of beautiful script. After recording the Dane and me in the book, the man brought out the stamp and ink from a small box on the desk. We watched as we each received our third stamp. The third circle of ink was proof once again that we'd reached a safe harbor.

With the formalities finished, the man beckoned us to follow him forward into the heart of the enchanting structure. Taking us under a small wooden door jam, he brought us into a lovely courtyard, hidden behind the rough stonewalls and cold exterior of the building front. The courtyard was a small rectangle filled with other pilgrims tipped back in white plastic chairs, taking in the last rays of sun or standing at the clotheslines with dripping garments. Multiple lines crisscrossed the yard and were already slung low with drying clothes as we ducked under them and made for the bunkroom. A narrow cobbled path curved through the lush yard, and on either side, rose bushes were in the first flush of bloom. The flowers, tangled in loops of thorns, were so bright and refined they almost felt out of place alongside the dirty utilitarian clothing and weary bodies. Even with their unmistakable contrast to the tone and color of pilgrim life, I felt drawn to them. With the soft light of late afternoon filtering into the courtyard, the flowers were a small gift of effortless beauty bestowed upon us all. They sat among us free of charge despite our slightly downtrodden state.

The gentleman led us onward and finally ushered us up the stairs and into the bunkroom. The cozy space was the size of a large bedroom but felt a bit tight with over thirty bunks filling the space. Some bunks were draped in unrolled sleeping bags while others had rough quilts thrown open across the narrow mattresses. Most pilgrims brought either a sleeping bag or a lightweight sleeping sack with them, but there were some pilgrims who opted to travel with neither. In an effort to lighten their load, this brave group stayed warm by using albergue blankets or sleeping fully dressed. In theory, using the albergue blankets seemed like a smart choice, but I was warned in Roncesvalles that bed bugs could and would become a presence in my life if I depended on such blankets. I assumed all who used the blankets knew the risk they took, and I wished them the best of luck.

I, on the other hand, had no need for blankets for I was besotted with my lovely rose-colored sleeping bag. It was my only place of comfort, my refuge from the storm of the new and unknown. It was my movable home that allowed me to escape and feel protected. There was something soothing and womb like about crawling into the small space and closing out the rest of the world. I called my bag the lady in rosy hues. I would carry her on my back for the next five weeks and share a bed with her each night. When I'd bought her I'd felt she was just itching to travel the world with me and be there each night when I needed a cuddle. She didn't disappoint.

We'd arrived at this riverside oasis late in the afternoon, but the promise of dinner was hours away. Since it was only my second day on the trail, I was still adjusting my body and mind to the rigors of the Spanish timetable. With food shops closed from two to five in the afternoon and restaurants not open until eight, I was suddenly on a new and jarring eating regime. My stomach wasn't always pleased with the shift, and apples or a handful of nuts did little more than take the edge off.

I wasn't the only one with a hunger to curb, and the Dane made heavy weather of his need for a proper meal. Not only did the Dane plan on dining out once siesta ended, but he was blindly confident I would be joining him. We had become an unspoken unit; even other pilgrims had started to treat us as a couple. When we picked bunks for the night, he'd chosen the open bed above me without hesitation. I slowly unfolded my sleeping bag and thanked my good luck that I was mere inches away from half a dozen other pilgrims. It made the Dane's company feel less intimate and his attitude less possessive. The mood around us grew almost unbearable when the Dane attempted to mark his territory and psychologically pee all over our narrow set of bunks. His movements and words declared me as claimed terrain; I scanned for the exits and felt my gag reflex sputter to life. Clearly, the Dane was going to be more of a handful than I could have imagined. I'd just made a covert escape from a relationship with this same tone of ownership built into its very foundation. I was horrified and more than a bit distraught to find its mirror image dangling his bare feet off the bunk above me. I'd literally taken flight and fled the country as part of my getaway plan from my toxic relationship, only to find myself with the Caveman's long lost twin. As bad as it was that the Dane had tried to mark me like cattle with familiar tactics, I also felt he was essentially disinterested in me as a person. Like the Caveman of my past, the Dane only wanted to claim me for the sake of claiming something worth having. I couldn't discern if he just wanted a girl to accompany him down the length of the trail or if it was something about me in particular, but the details didn't matter. He was another connoisseur, more interested in shelving me than knowing me. He didn't want to romance me; I wasn't even sure he wanted to sleep with me. He just wanted to feel he could. He just wanted me to be his girl, dutifully following behind him. We hardly spoke, and I could sense I bored him, yet he was rabid about keeping his eyes on me at all times. He saw our two days connection as proof positive that he was making all the right moves and reeling me in. I'd been marked maybe even from hour one, and foolishly I'd stepped right into the snare. Of all the people I could have hitched my wagon to in the early stages I'd "randomly" selected the Dane. Was my radar backfiring on me as it belched out the last putrid remains of my relationship with the Caveman, or was I simply feeling the sting of an unexpected trail truth?

The Dane's presence in my trail life was the first human sized red flag, revealing a curious trail phenomena. I came to the trail believing the ancient road would have many tricks up her sleeve, but one of its more magical, and at times tiresome, powers was its ability to conjure the past. Already on day two, the Camino had hurled people and situations into my path that represented old patterns in my life in a way that made them absolutely unavoidable. The strangers I met were not always strangers but simply new faces that reflected the past. These energetic doppelgangers were vivid and surprising. And frankly, ones like the Dane were making me severely uncomfortable but maybe that was the point. The glass on this trail could be either half empty, if I veered around trouble personalities, or it could be half full, if I was brave enough to resolve old conflicts once and for all. What this resolution looked like or how it would feel, I wasn't sure. The Dane was fashioned of a familiar fabric, and I knew something had to be done. And that something had to be done under my own steam. I had to stare this shockingly fresh pattern in the face and find out what I was made of. Like a wild west gunslinger, I had to call its bluff, show it I had no fear. Maybe going toe to toe with the Dane was part of true escape from my toxic relationship with the Caveman. If so, let the healing begin. I needed something, anything to help me move forward and away from the past. Maybe this move would release me from the energetic tangle. My actions with the Dane would have to be the proof, but with Pamplona awaiting us tomorrow, I was a bit gun shy. I had no idea what it would be like to cross a city, but I feared the passage more then I let on. Would it be wrong to let the connection with the Dane linger due to his usefulness? I couldn't say for sure.

My internal skirmish didn't keep me from putting one sore foot in front of the other to go out in search of food. The Dane went to find a bar to wait out the siesta hour, while I went on a delightfully solo hunt for a supermercado. As I wandered down the sleepy afternoon streets, my heels felt tight and my ankles slightly swollen. Though uncomfortable, I wasn't too worried; there was bound to be a bit of physical backlash after a thirty-nine kilometer day. When the body worked hard, it hurt in positive and less than positive ways. This sliding scale of pain was unavoidable in the pilgrim life; no matter age or fitness level a six hundred mile walk was going to hurt. I had more than a vague inkling of what I was signing up for with this trail, and much of my intuitive knowledge came from my years spent as a dancer. Those years of fresh adulthood had been defined by exhaustion saturated days filled with long hours of physical training and weary nights of recovery. It was a never ending cycle of building muscle and breaking it down only to build more, increasing lung strength only to find the limit once again. I came to understand the realm of full physical exertion and lived there for days, weeks and even months at a time. And like anything done to excess, it both wore me thin and fueled me to push harder. In many ways, it was easy to dive into such a life, for I loved dance with an insatiable hunger; the more I moved the more I craved the feeling and the energy I knew when in motion. Today on the trail out of Zubiri, I'd felt the twinges of that same hunger, that same self fulfilling desire to move. I could only expect that if the trail consumed me with as much gusto as dance had, then my body was in for a ride. My ankles would adjust, and in the meantime, I was more than familiar with moving through minor aches and pains. This moving life wasn't one without impact, but I was more than a little pleased to find such a worthy physical challenge after several years away from full time dancing. Bring on the soreness that hobbled and the weariness that caused one to pitch and sway; to me, it was all proof of a day well spent.

In my cloudy haze, I felt enormously proud to once again be involved in a life where my body was put to full use. I felt I'd been idle for too long. I'd spent too many months running to maintain, circling around myself with no direction or purpose. Now my body had purpose, and I loved it. Yet even as my understanding and familiarity with soreness kept me calm, the pain in my ankles was slightly unfamiliar. But, as I peered down each and every side street for a supermarket, I had too many other concerns to waste much time on physical pain that would, I assumed, sort itself out.

It was four thirty, and with little under half an hour until the shops sprang back to life, the Dane found me sitting on a bench waiting for the gleaming Día supermarket to open. He'd given up on the bar scene after tiring of Spanish TV that did little more than detail deviant crimes, bloody accidents and futbol. My stomach grumbled, and I tried to drift into a half sleep. Draping my arm over my eyes to shield my face from the dropping sun, I waited and tried to ignore the Dane.

An hour later, I returned victorious from the shopping trip and wobbled my way into the albergue. I was particularly enchanted by a large bar of chocolate that cost less than a euro and was roughly the size of my head. It would be sweet dense fuel for tomorrow if I could stow it some place where it wouldn't melt all over the inside of my bag. To my vast irritation, the Dane had abandoned his dinner plans to join me in shopping for supplies and now discussed at length his plans for a pasta feast. Distracted by his manly appetite and laden with a bag full of sauce, cheese, wine and dry pasta, the Dane made a beeline for the kitchen. As he disappeared into the communal room ready to muscle his way to the stove and claim a burner, I slipped outside and sought a moment of refuge. I was quickly learning that albergues were tight, offering little breathing space and few hiding spots for pilgrims like me who already had someone to hide from.

The light outside was soft yet remained remarkably bright. I was still coming to terms with my jet lag as well as the way the sun didn't set until ten. I'd abandoned my shoes with the rest of my belongings near my bunk, and the flagstones felt cool and smooth below my feet. Since most of the other forty pilgrims in the albergue were eating at this hour, there were only a few other people outside. I moved towards an empty set of chairs under a solitary cherry tree. The bright blooms of spring were long faded, but the fruit was not yet ripe. I'd met the tree on a night in between. We were crossing paths as it moved from one season of being to the next. Holding my journal in one hand, I arranged the two chairs to create an island to cradle my tired legs. The old walls around me held a visceral sense of safety as well as a secluded hush, as if this sanctuary was set out of time altogether.

I looked across the yard to a group of pilgrims. They were a quartet of women sitting in a tight circle and speaking Italian. Their familiarity with each other was clear, and conversation flowed without skipping a beat. They were also barefoot, and the woman facing me was absorbed in repairing her feet after the day's walk. With her foot in her lap, she hunched forward and went at the task with a determined focus. I'd been warned, assured even, that I would accrue dozens, if not hundreds, of blisters during my time on the trail. Though I knew there was some Camino exaggeration at work in the figures, I believed the basis of the intel; nobody here was above blisters. It was trail fact regardless of age, gender or fitness level; blisters were the great equalizer. Shoes never fit perfectly, and feet never seemed to cooperate as well as they should, so blisters became badges of honor we pilgrims gained through our daily footfalls. If one of us wasn't getting them, there was surely something suspicious, if not down right sinister, going on. I didn't dare contradict or question when a pilgrim in Roncesvalles told me that no TRUE pilgrim was immune to blisters. I didn't want to get kicked out of the pilgrim club on the first night, so I nodded, grimaced appropriately and made sure I had a cache of band aids handy at all times.

No two pilgrims agreed on how to deal with the common plight. Some strongly recommended a blister be cleaned and covered without puncturing the thin sack of fluid. This faction agreed one's body produced the fluid for a reason and to leave it was the wisest medicine. Those on the other side of the debate felt such passivity was foolhardy. They would puncture their blisters as soon as they formed, taping them up with anything on hand even duck tape. Often with little else to ponder after a long day of introspection, pilgrims became preoccupied with the prevention of blisters and deeply fixated on following the advice of every old wives' tale that crossed their path. One of the men I later befriended had heard it was best to never wash his socks. After great scientific questioning, he theorized this practice would build up a protective layer of molded material around the hot spots and keep blisters from forming. He beamed as he announced he hadn't had a blister for days. Even with his evident success, I choose not to partake in such behavior and from then on avoided the spot where he kept his boots.

As I placed my pair of sneakers in the racks of pilgrim shoes the last two days, I'd noticed that I was breaking with the crowd when it came to footwear. I'd chosen to bring a new pair of cross trainers for the journey in hopes that my feet would be soothed by their familiarity. Plus, I was a bit intimidated by boots. Having never been more than a day hiker, I had virtually no experience with clunky hard-soled boots, and I didn't want the Camino to be the testing ground. Scores of blisters certainly would have made a dramatic appearance if I'd been blinded by the bright laces and high ankles of a set of badass boots.

Looking across the courtyard, I could see that two of the women were clearly in a heated debate about blisters. One pointed to her friend's feet and spoke emphatically while the friend shook her head and proceeded onward with her chosen treatment. Pulling her foot towards her and angling her leg so the outside of the big toe was vulnerable, she picked up a needle and thread and with one swift move, lanced the blister. The needle and the lime green thread crossed through the center of the blister and out the far side. Though the move looked painful and slightly aggressive, she clearly didn't feel the area around the blister and treated her skin as if it were no more sensitive than a piece of cloth. Snipping off the needle, she left the thread dangling out both sides of her big toe. Fans of this technique had assured me that the string forced the fluid to drain and kept the skin from rubbing off completely and opening a wound that could, in the future, fester and cause larger more painful issues.

If a blister wasn't treated with respect it could turn nasty, open up and ripen with infection. But when given the attention it demanded, a blister was generally harmless though quite unrelenting. This was the beauty and the curse of such minor physical woes. They usually didn't cripple you or do long-term damage, but they certainly made life unpleasant. Walking through the pain of major injuries, such as pulled muscles, aching tendons, sprained ankles, shin splints or worse could cause serious consequences later in the trail and perhaps even later in life. To walk through a twisted knee could result in a hospital visit and maybe even surgery. Blisters were child's play in comparison. But like the scraped knees and bruised shins of childhood, they were annoyingly painful. So everybody talked about them, moaned and whimpered, shared their catalog of blisters and cursed anyone who claimed they were above such common trail maladies. Such braggarts were either showing off or lying and certainly failing to bonding with their fellow pilgrims. I was pleased I didn't have any large blisters yet, but I wasn't in the clear. My feet had only walked about sixty five kilometers; the true test lay ahead.

Though I didn't have any blisters on my feet, I sensed an emotional swelling in my chest that felt awfully akin to one. The spot was quickly filling with unpleasant memories that chaffed at my insides with every step. The images, conversations and moments that rose to the surface felt as nasty and unpleasant as pus. How was it possible that even here, in this strange place where I hardly felt I was myself, these memories could find me and hang around uninvited? I had believed in the decision to flee the physical markers of the past, to leave the places and people who had broken off with me, but now I wondered if such drastic steps were enough. I wanted the swelling to be anger and irritation that could be released by smashing something with a club or throwing a punch, but such hot fast emotions were a cover. I'd never broken something in anger and wouldn't even known how to throw a decent punch, but I felt a rush of physical energy careening through me that had to be released. The tidal wave was moving on the skids of my failed relationship with the Caveman but came from somewhere deeper in my history and was more than anger. It was what always lies behind, underneath and around anger. It was crushing sorrow. I could almost feel the pocket of liquid grief rising in between my ribs and bubbling up into my throat, closing it down tight as a clamp. I wanted to believe I could do something as simple as pass a thread and needle through this place in me. Pull the thread out, covered in the sour ruins of broken love affairs and heal afresh. But I wasn't sure how the universe intended to bring about such a healing in an environment like this and with me in such a state. I was a mess but just happened to be good at looking like I was holding it all together. I'd learned a few tricks about the art of the surface and knew I was using them so as not to induce looks of pity or panic in my fellow pilgrims. I needed to share my story with people, but I felt unsure if I could hold back the tears. Would I lose it if I broke the seal and began to tell someone why I was really here and what a disastrous relationship I'd just fled from like an escaped prisoner? Even in my loneliness, I knew it was a little too much for a kindhearted stranger to absorb. But the blister between my lungs was not a good sign. Holding in my story and not feeling at liberty to talk with anyone about it could cause serious problems. An emotional implosion or breakdown loomed on the horizon, but I knew neither would help me stay on the trail or keep going with my inner guidance. It was becoming clear that I needed to find the right someone or someones to be able to spill all my guts to. Yes, I'd met some kind people, but I hadn't yet stumbled across people who felt safe; people who might listen and not be afraid to hear the whole truth and nothing but the truth.

I picked up my journal intent on talking, even if only to myself, when I notice an older woman with tightly wound grey hair approaching cautiously. I looked up, and catching her eye, I smiled. She seemed to relax as I made friendly contact and continued towards me with more confidence. Once she reached the edge of the tree's shadow, she spoke,

"Do you speak English?" she asked in a soft hesitant voice. "You look as if you might."

I could tell she was in need of a bit of comforting conversation herself. From the click in her words she was charmingly Australian. I offered her the spare chair and as she sat down, she let out a small sigh, smiling wearily. I asked a polite opening question, and within moments I knew half her life history and everything she had done in the past three days. In a whirlwind of words, she told about her tortuously long flight from Australia and all the small travel legs that it took her to get to the trail. It was clear that every pilgrim, no matter where they hailed from, could agree that getting to the Camino was an astronomically complicated logistical nightmare. No one seemed to arrive here unscathed by the struggle of getting to a place that was close to nothing and easily accessible from nowhere. I could see the combined effect of time shifts and full days of walking colliding in this pilgrim's weary form. I was stunned by how many elderly pilgrims I'd already encountered who were willing to put up with the whole drama. I was young, able bodied and in no rush, yet even I found the transition from the outside world into the Camino universe to be jarring and absolutely exhausting. It wasn't until my new companion explained her devotion to this as a Catholic pilgrimage that I saw where the extra strength came from. She'd been planning this journey as a mark of religious devotion for decades, and now that she was here, there was no turning back or wimping out. When a pilgrim came from the other side of the world to complete an epic trek as a final act of faith at the age of seventy, there was no way she was going to treat it like a dress rehearsal.

Regardless of spiritual or religious momentum, I was in awe of the older pilgrims. It showed tremendous grit and a subtle form of bravery to take their bodies out into the world for a physical adventure when they were no longer full of the vim and vigor of youth. Yes, they might believe deeply in the greater meaning of such a pilgrimage, but they still had to survive it physically, and that proved quite a task for all of us, regardless of age. I especially relished the sight of older couples ambling along beside each other. As I slipped past them with a hello, I decided if the Camino were ever to call me back in my eighties, I was doing it that way. Two strong, side by side with the love of my life, taking it one step at a time and enjoying simply being on the journey with someone eternally dear to me. That would be a celebration of life and the soul. That would be worth everything.

Somewhere in the meandering progress of our conversation, I shared my plans for the next day. To get to Arre the Dane and I had walked nearly forty kilometers, and I felt it was entirely possible to keep up this tempo. I'd already mapped out a plan to walk at least an equivalent distance tomorrow. My declaration of intention wasn't seconds out of my mouth when the Australian's jaw dropped, and her brow furrowed in disbelief. In a blink of the eye, my docile seventy year old companion had gone from retired granny to pissed-off head mistress, and from the looks of her displeased scowled, I was in serious trouble.

"That is ABSOLUTELY too far!" she yelped at me. "Whatever could you be thinking to do such a foolhardy thing as walk nearly forty kilometers in a day?"

Her body had grown tense, and she'd even crossed her arms with an indigent flare. " Why are you doing this young lady? she demanded. Without leaving space for me to reply, she continued, " You MUST see that the trail is telling you to slow down. This is not the way a pilgrimage is meant to be. You are making a major mistake to push yourself in such a manner."

As I sat flabbergasted with little notion of how to respond, she rounded off her lecture with a hit where it would hurt the most, "Is it not utterly clear that going slow is THE LESSON that the trail is trying to teach you!"

I waited as she stared at me in fuming silence, willing me to concede and promise to change my plans then and there. I wasn't sure if she wanted me to sign an oath in blood that I wouldn't take a step over twenty kilometers the following day or if my word would be enough. Nonetheless, I was ready to do no such thing and felt my mouth clamp shut. There was no easy way to explain to this woman that as long as I stayed on pace with this group, I felt I WOULD be missing the purpose of my journey. As long as I kept even with this group that held no young people, kindred spirits or friends whom I could confide in, then I was lost. I was lost without people to care for and be cared by. From the surface, I looked a bit wild eyed and foolish as I pushed for the horizon, but I knew there were elements and forces at work in my journey that this woman couldn't see. She couldn't see what lay at the center of my trek, and she couldn't see who might be up ahead of us. Only the universe knew those particulars, and I felt I was being fueled with the energy and drive to keep pushing onward at top speed. I had to trust this energy had a purpose and a reason more divine than I could imagine. Just because she couldn't see the current sweeping me up and pulling me along didn't rule out its existence.

I decided to nod politely and bow out of our social visit. As I was getting up and gathering my things, another pilgrim wandered over, allowing me to gracefully slide out of the circle and away from the Australian. Even with my sore legs and dizzy weariness, I took the steps two at a time back into the albergue. As I peered into the kitchen, I found the Dane at home talking to two men who had walked from France. The duo of forty something friends had been on the trail so long, they were willing to cheerfully admit they'd forgotten the pace and constraints of every day life. Wives and children were like hazy half forgotten dreams; the tribe of the trail had claimed them mind, body and spirit. I would soon understand they were pitch perfect poster boys for the group of pilgrims, typically male, who used the trail as an extended escape holiday and cared little for anyone who had been in residence for fewer days than themselves. These characters were in it for number one and thought nothing of nonchalantly abandoning all things domestic for months at a time.

Recently, the two Frenchmen had met up with a woman who had ridden her vintage ten speed bike from Croatia to the French border. There she'd left her bike behind and had begun to walk. Now she sat silent and nameless in the corner, wearing a man's worn black tee shirt. She seemed to be sinking back into her nearly skeletal frame, and her large eyes were the only part of her that looked alive. It was distressing just to look at her, but I couldn't seem to stop. She was fascinating and frightening in equal parts.

Even upon first meeting, I was haunted by her strange clothing and detached presence. She was like a feral animal, eyes always scanning for the next attack as her body constantly sought the most protected spot in the room. She moved with quick smooth focus, didn't bump into anything and avoided all people. She was almost entirely removed from the social energy of the space and disconnected from the comings and goings around her. My reaction to her presence was immediate and visceral. I realized, as my body tensed automatically, that I feared becoming like her. I feared I would take on this haunted quality if I remained emotionally isolated on the trail. I was genuinely nervous about how to stay balanced without a support system as I knew I had a bit of feral blood in me too. I could survive with no other counsel but my own, yet such an existence would leave me withdrawn and entangled in my own thoughts. I'd been there before, in such places of isolation, and I was determined not to let this journey become another such place.

I slept soundly that night even with the Dane creaking above me. I couldn't be assured of much, but I did know I wouldn't have to face the trek into and across my first Camino city alone. The Dane might have been very low on the list of desirable companions, but he could keep up and was better than having no company at all.

Before I began the trail, one of my big fears was getting lost, especially in the wilds of Spain. I was seriously concerned about missing a marker and suddenly being in an unknown land, yelling at the top of my lungs with not a kind soul nearby to help me. It was an unnerving wilderness scenario and all the images Hollywood churned out did nothing to soothe my edgy nerves. I'd stopped watching scary movies years ago and didn't even allow myself to imagine the worst but indulging in the fear of getting lost was unavoidable. I'd grown up in a rural spot, spent much of my childhood in the woods near my family's farm and wasn't afraid of wild animals. Over the years I'd encountered moose, fisher cats, scores of deer, foxes, porcupines, coyotes, and even a few black bears. Being in the woods was familiar, it was places like Pamplona that felt like the wilderness.

It wasn't until Arre that I realized I would be crossing several large metropolises on my route across Spain. Only then had I learned that Pamplona was the first of five cities along the trail, and it was coming at me fast. I cannot claim I did a deep or thorough job of researching the Camino before signing on to walk it. In fact, I knew little more than it began in the mountains of France and ended at the Atlantic coast in Spain. I had shunned books, internet sites and stories of infamous spots along the way. I'd left myself out in the dark for a reason. I knew there would be elements, such as crossing vast cities, that would scare the pants off me, and I simply couldn't afford to jostle the thin thread of courage that kept me tied to this journey. I was actually terrified I would read something about the trail and, like a skittish horse, bolt from the undertaking at top speed. Since I felt I'd signed on the dotted line with the universe, I was unwilling to be tossed about on a sea of images, thoughts and conjectures beforehand. I didn't want to hear about blistering heat, pilgrim scoundrels, oozing foot wounds and bed bugs. I would have to face what came no matter what. I might as well not be filled with a vast array of potentially scary and unpleasant scenarios in advance. I knew the fear of something could be almost as bad as the thing itself, so I resisted my curiosity and kept my head in the clouds or maybe it was the sand. For this reason, I was woefully under informed, but I would quickly learn that other pilgrims weren't. Several pilgrims had already shared stories of uneasy moments, unreliable way markings and perilous crossings. They were thrilled at the chance to lounge around and share their knowledge with magnanimous grins of satisfaction. And as far as Pamplona went, while its swift arrival on my trail itinerary had been a bit startling, I'd view it as a quick test of my trail savvy and a preview of how I would fare in the urban lands to come.

In the fields and forests, the trail had proved to be very clearly marked and almost docilely bucolic. Often there was little need for clarification. A narrow strip of well trodden dirt was marker enough. I relished this clarity and noticed it allowed me to sink into my thoughts without having to actively seek reassurance about my course forward. In the city, however, I would discover that arrows were often more confusing than enlightening, and a wrong turn could take me far from the trail in a matter of minutes. As narrow streets forked, branched or just simply merged into the central arteries of the city, the directions for us hapless pilgrims were given less status. The spray-painted arrows that functioned so well in the small towns were seen as garish and unattractive graffiti by city dwellers. Businesses didn't want them on their outer walls, so the arrows were relegated to the backs of signs, and even the thin trunks of municipal trees. I'd never considered it before, but the arrow, in all its apparent clarity of purpose, could and often was, stunningly confusing. What did an arrow pointing up mean? If it was tilted to the side slightly did that indicate a turn up ahead or was it simply marked in a sloppy fashion? Sometimes it felt as bewildering to read the arrows as to read the weather for signs of rain.

In cities, there were times when the arrows disappeared altogether and were replaced by small artistic shells or tasteful signs referring to St. James, the patron saint of the Camino. Though beautiful and decorative, these weren't the most functional trail markers and were extremely difficult to follow through the maze of streets. In one of the cities, the markers were worked into the bricks of the street with shells and arrows underfoot pointing us on. At midday with swarms of people covering this map, the charm of such artistry was understandably lost on the average purpose driven pilgrim.

Arre was a mere four kilometers from central Pamplona. If I wanted to ensure company the Dane was my best bet. So with his overeager willingness to move at my side, I found myself indulging the most odious yet convenient choice. I hated that despite my growing annoyance with him, convenience and safety in the city could trump all else. As the Dane cheerfully set his alarm and wished me a lingering goodnight, he radiated a confidence that declared pure contentment with our continued partnership. I might have been his sweet little forgone conclusion, but in my eyes, this choice was a coldly calculating. I needed back up, and he was the most known person in a room full of paired off, coupled up and pre-grouped strangers.

At dawn, the streets of Arre lay in the thick shadows of towering apartment buildings. My bare legs were cold, and I tucked my hands deep into my pockets as we made our way out the back gate of the albergue. The door was an old stable gate with wide wooden planks and a large iron handle that clicked as I shut it behind us. We were both silent as we slipped away from the rest of the sleeping pilgrims. It had been another early wake up call courtesy of the Dane's watch alarm, and I had to admit, I got a sick pleasure from being one of the first pilgrims out the door and on my way.

As we walked down the deserted sidewalks, it felt like civilization had vanished and left behind the vacant and still remains of urban life. It was eerie and only reinforced the silence between us. Even though it was a bit unsettling to walk through a city at this hour, I was pretty sure the Dane's close physical presence and the way he seemed to veer into my personal space wasn't due to nerves. I almost stepped on his feet at one point, and he bumped into me with his pack and swinging arms several times. I knew his ability to manage spatial relations wasn't the issue, and no matter how much I tried to keep our individual walking lanes separate, he always managed to merge into mine.

Even the night before, as I'd organized my stuff on the floor around my bunk, he'd hovered as I packed then sat on my bed and reached out to touch my arm as he'd wished me goodnight. The hovering was little compared to when he'd sat back on my bunk, his body splayed across my sleeping bag. There was an understanding among pilgrims that almost everything was shared territory. Nobody had their own chair, clothesline or personal boudoir, but each pilgrim's bunk and sleeping spot was personal space. These few square feet were absolutely off limits to strangers, and in my case, creepy Danish men. Like other pilgrims, I reserved the right to keep my bunk to myself unless I invited company into said space. I hoped at some point I would share my sleeping nook with someone but the Dane would never be that guy. Just because he was entertaining delusional fantasies that he'd soon be curled up in my pink sleeping bag didn't make it a reality. In fact, I now felt his ick factor was surging from a low level buzz in my ears to a pounding alert. His moves, meant as the dance of courtship, made my insides squirm and my mind flood with thoughts of escape. Even as I'd tossed and turned, seeking sleep in the dark and noisy room, I could feel his energy seep down from the bunk above. My reaction was maybe a dormant strain of the fight or flight, but I trusted its wisdom and felt I would soon have to take advantage of its adrenaline side affects.

In addition the Dane was running interference with my connections to other pilgrims, even if only energetically. As he flounced around acting like we were a couple, people accordingly gave us space. This was what I did for other couples, waited to be welcomed into their circle and imagined their other half was their first social priority. I wanted to be open to all the people I would meet along the trail, and I knew if I stayed near the Dane for much longer, letting him act like my uber confident paramour, it was sure to throw off my socialization strategy. In fact, he might succeed in keeping me all to himself if I didn't nip this in the bud.

I'd needed his companionship that first manic morning in St. Jean, but now my trail savvy was growing. If I could learn to pick my way across not just country lanes but also city streets then I might have the tools to do this on my own. I was honing my brave streak and building up the muscles of self-trust, maybe even proving I could travel this Camino on my own resources and my own terms. The only question that remained was if I was emotionally ready to choose solitude and isolation over company if this company didn't offer support, comfort or exhibit healthy boundaries. Was I ready to face hours, maybe even days, adrift before new friends came into view?

To choose to be alone, when I'd already lived a string of rather lonely years, was hard to stomach. I could feel my own hesitation. I hoped I could shingle and overlap this unfortunate connection with a better one, hoped I could ditch the Dane and pick up the thread of new friends in the span of a single stride. But the flashbacks to the Caveman and the poisonous isolation I'd felt, even when in his company, was a searing reminder there was clean pain in the choice of solitude. Much more preferable than the dirty pain and tangled emotional struggles I'd faced when I'd sacrificed myself at the altar of my relationship with the Caveman. I'd hoped such soul mutilation would keep me from the loneliness I feared. But it hadn't, and I'd leapt for the single life again. Perhaps I'd needed a leap as wide as the Atlantic to make it stick. Now I had to put my money fully where my mouth was and risk being not only single but friendless for a while. But first, I had to master the art of city crossings on foot. The issue of the Dane would simply have to wait its turn.

PAMPLONA

STAGE THREE- 29.9K-18.6M
ARRE TO PUENTE LA REINA

The walled city of Pamplona was perhaps the most famous of the cities along the Camino, and enjoyed this fame because of one lusty, bloody week at the peak of summer heat. For the rest of the year, Pamplona lay in wait, crouched like an animal planning, plotting and salivating over its chance to perform. Pamplona wasn't a city to shy away from a dramatic show; it was well aware that it could capture the world's attention for a brief window each July. Maybe it excited little more than horror, jaw dropping confusion or impressed reverence, but it didn't matter. We all seemed unable to turn away from the show, the sport and the history. Eventually, most everyone caught a glimpse of the infamous running of the bulls and surely never forget Pamplona's name once they had.

Now I stood on the outskirts of the city, waiting for the streetlight to change and for me to get my chance to enter the old city and step where the bulls strode. I'd grown up with a crumbling poster of the matadors of Pamplona and I'd read the sweet and simple tale of Ferdinand the Bull many a time, yet I'd never seen the running of the bulls or a bullfight. The richly adorned and dashingly handsome bullfighters were mythical figures, young and handsome with tall lean bodies proudly puffed in a show of bravery, fully prepared to embody the theatrics and risk their safety to put on a show. I could see how a magic aura had grown around bullfights; there was something elegant about the aesthetic of the ritual. It was a ceremony that took all who watched it back in time to a land where heroes donned glittering jackets to prove that men were still men, fighting was still a graceful art and something tangible was still on the line. Later in the journey, I stumbled across a photo in the newspaper of a famous young matador, revered as a superstar, impaled on the horn of a bull. In the picture, the bull's horn was driven deep into the chest cavity of the matador right under his ribs. Lofted into the air, the matador's body was tipped back in an arch any dancer would strive for. The young man had been rushed to the hospital once they had detached his body from the horns of bull and he'd survived, how I cannot say. That said, there was much that was brutal and barbaric about the tradition, and I could see both sides of the argument over discontinuing the sport. Later, I would learn from a French pilgrim that in many cities in Spain they'd modified the bullfight to keep the spectacle and the glory but to remove the cruelty. In place of the long barbs of a picador and the killing sword of the matador, a ribbon was tied between the bull's horns. It was the job of the matador to use his skill and grace to pluck it from the horns of the fearsome creature. The bull wasn't harmed, and the human knew the risk when he entered the ring. It seemed like a balanced and clever way to shift the tradition rather than toss the whole art out as a pure blood sport.

Even with a growing shift in the bull fighting culture, Pamplona was solidly rooted in tradition. The festival of San Fermin, which encircled the running of the bulls, was a week long gala of red and white. It always began on the seventh of July and concluded seven manic days later. The bulls were run at eight in the morning without fail, and though this was an almost ungodly hour for the average Spaniard, the tradition had held its ground. A short poem of glory was read to the gathered throngs of runners, while many watched from apartment windows, street side balconies and the safe zone behind the blockades on the streets. The young and the old alike came out in force; no one was kept away from the scene. After the poem, a starting gun was fired, the doors pulled up and the bulls triggered the tide of runners into frenzied action. Two to four minutes later the bulls charged into the bullfighting arena across the city, and just like that, the show was over for the day. The speed of the run depended on the bulls themselves. Some days they were fast and caused the runners to scurry out of their way more quickly, and other days one or two of the bulls became turned around trying to return from whence they came or to engage with the herd of men clustered around them like flies. This was when men got seriously injured and when men died under foot or at the end of a horn. It was almost exclusively men who participated, but anyone could join the ranks of runners no matter their age, fitness level or nationality. In fact, it was often foreigners, especially foolhardy Americans, who died. I gathered that young Spaniards flocked to the event to prove their arrival in manhood, while the older participants wanted one more chance to flirt with danger, feel alive and prove they weren't going to be outdone by upstarts half their age. When all the bulls moved forward as planned, the runners shifted around them in a weaving pattern that was organized but subject to dangerous breakdowns. Dodging and crisscrossing in front of the on-coming animals, they took their turn then quickly ducked out of the way, leaving space for the next man to try his hand. It was a choreographed dance that often went very wrong. There were too many factors and too thin an edge of danger for everything to go well every time. If the spectacle wasn't inherently dangerous then, in the eyes of the Spaniards, it wasn't worth doing. There was a reason they picked an agitated bull in all its unpredictable glory; he possessed the ability to maim and kill. This was what made the show come to life and provide many an adrenaline pumping reality television segment for the nightly news. Later in the journey, even I would find it hard to turn away from clips of the madness.

All bull oriented activities aside, one of the other modern draws of the San Fermin festival was the parties. At all hours of the day and night, the endlessly energized mobs of drunken revelers took over the streets of Pamplona. There was music and excessive amounts of drinking and carousing, so much so that virtually everyone ended up covered in a sticky film of alcohol, drenched in sweat and dancing barefoot in the street with thousands of their favorite strangers. Since it was early June, I would walk into a dormant shell of Pamplona, but I wondered if I would hear echoes of the festival that would swallow the city whole in less than a month.

The streets of Arre merged into Pamplona as we crossed a series of quick moving four lane roads then picked our way down deserted lanes of chained gates and crumbling front walls. We couldn't see or hear the city and simply had to trust the few arrows we could find. The light was picking up in the east, and with an abrupt turn in the trail, we found ourselves at the feet of an ancient bridge. After crossing the bridge, we walked a path through a shady grove of trees that brought us to the edge of a wall of stone soaring upwards. We stood humbled below the walls of the old city for several moments. This was protection. This was defense. Standing there brought home the power of the fortress, the advantage of high walls and guarded gates. Once long ago this had been essential, yet now the city spilled over its walled edges and the gates hung open like gaping mouths. Did the people living inside even notice this wall, a presence that would have given shelter and safety if they'd been born to this land in another time? The past felt close around me as if I could slip through a hole in time and still be a pilgrim on the same journey.

Climbing up the steps under the stone arch, I reached out and drew my hands along the wall's thick body. As the cool stone met my palm and trailed along the length of my fingers, I snapped out of my daze and reconnected to the physical moment around me. There was pavement under my feet, small cars lined the streets and the Dane was busy zipping off the bottom half of his high tech pants. Nothing stirred in the row of towering apartment buildings ahead of us with their windows drawn like a hundred brightly colored eyelids. It was seven on a weekday morning, and the city was still asleep. Everything around the trail, including the cities, seemed to move on a slow morning tide, but the Camino itself was immune to this pace. The early morning hours were its active time. While the world around us slept, we moved with swift determination, taking advantage of empty thoroughfares and cool temperatures. The Spanish locals inhabited the hours we pilgrims avoided and vice versa. I felt it was a gracious way of giving each party the means to tolerate the other for the past thousand years. While we walked, they slept, then during siesta we were up and about, while they slept. Pilgrims ate dinner at the early hour of seven and retired to bed around ten, just the time when the average Spaniard was ready to go out and have a leisurely meal. Our clock filled the negative space in theirs, and like two puzzle pieces, it achieved a kind of harmony.

As we made our way up into the center of the city, I spotted another small group of walkers a few blocks ahead of us. The group appeared to be a trio of men. One was small and stocky with a balding head, but the other two looked like strapping twenty-somethings. It was incredibly energizing to catch a glimpse of this new trio. My thoughts had settled into a mellow tempo but instantaneously revved and flowered in a hundred directions at once. I tried to imagine where they were from, how they knew each other and what might have brought them to this alternate universe. I secretly hoped one might stop to tie his shoe or pause to take a drink of water, and I would have enough time to catch their swift moving band. As the group bobbed along just in sight, I felt things might be looking up, and with a bit of luck, I might find friends in the streets of Pamplona.

The arrows became sparse and ambiguous as we dove deeper into the center of the city. We navigated crosswalks and fast moving traffic circles before walking into a park. The space was large for a city park and contained old stone monuments and a network of paths. The grass was impossibly lush and still wet with morning dew. People on cell phones walked their teacup dogs, as couples jogged by us, asserting their dominance by forcing us to jump out of their way. The Dane fell a bit behind me, and per our agreement, I waited on the outer edge of the park for him. In all fairness, I also waited because I knew the group of men was just a bit too far out of reach, and the trail markings were proving troublesome. After several minutes, the Dane rounded the corner, hobbling slightly but trying to mask his difficulties. Despite his best efforts, it was clear there was a significant problem with his right knee. He often stopped to rub his kneecap as if he was trying to bring circulation back to the aching joint. The mountains and our rapid pace on the following day had caught up to him.

After leaving the park, we pushed on in silence. His progress was punctuated by a slight hiccup in his step and a faint grimace on his face; mine was marked by a growing irritation and a determined set to my shoulders. I'd lost sight of the trio while waiting for him, but I was still bent on catching them before the day was through, with or without the Dane. On the next block, I felt my stomach lurch with the displeasure of being empty too long, and I ducked into a crowded café, hoping to go in, fuel up and quickly get back on the trail. The shop was narrow and packed tightly with people but smelled like a heavenly mix of warm sugar and fresh ground coffee. Despite the morning rush, I managed to claim a small table near the door. I'd just sat down and turned to tackle the impossible task of picking just one kind of pastry to eat when the Dane entered the room. He made a beeline for me, pushing past people with his massive pack and leaving a wake of annoyed faces behind him. As he plunked down in the seat across from me, a waitress came over, and we both ordered. I suggested that we make the stop a quick one and began to explain about the group I'd seen ahead of us. As I gushed about the exciting possibility of new faces and more young energy, I suddenly realized the Dane had stopped listening and was glancing around the room as if bored.

After several moments of silence, he finally pried his eyes off something outside and looked over at me. I asked him if he'd heard me, and he nodded then said, "I don't care about meeting people on the trail. I prefer to keep myself removed from groups and such. There is something much purer about solitude or the company of one or two select others."

I couldn't even digest the absurdly haughty tone of his speech or the way he emphasized the word 'select.' At the tail end of his speech, he even tilted his head slightly as if to indicate I was one of those people he could tolerate to have around, that I was his right hand girl. I was bendable, moldable arm candy material, and that was all he wanted. The hovering axe finally dropped. He'd clarified his disdain for the social element of this trail, perhaps even for life itself; he didn't care to build connections or rely on others, and he surely wasn't interested in caring for his fellow traveler. He lived in a centrally focused universe where he was the center. And he was the antithesis of what I wanted to be, needed to find or cared to consort with. There was no delaying now; I was done.

I felt my flesh crawl. This rambling was further proof that he wasn't an innocuous or random companion on my journey; he was a slap in the face wake up call and the mirror image of the Caveman. Both men shared the same negative view of human community and sought physical and emotional seclusion even in magical places such as these. The Caveman had had a good life with me in a lively supportive community, but he'd entrenched himself in his apartment at all hours and given all his energy to work, computers and his own personal pursuits. He'd utterly failed to reach out to others with compassion or unconditional support. A narcissist to the maximum, he'd been so focused on himself he'd failed to see the swath of destruction he cut through other peoples' lives. And there'd been a coldness in the Caveman, a brash sense of righteousness about his behavior and his lifestyle that was now seeping through every word the Dane uttered. In some ways, it was the tone of his energy more than the words that made me snap. The vibration was like a trip wire, turning my body into a screeching fire alarm. I didn't even wait to process the words fully, my body knew what to do. I simply stood up without a word, dropped a few euros on the table and pushed through the crowd. As I broke out into the open street, I turned west and walked away.

The trail wound down below a train bridge and across a vast stretch of lawn surrounding beautiful old municipal buildings. Though there was no one by my side or even within spitting distance, I could see half a dozen new faces in view up ahead. I wondered if they were pilgrims who'd spent the night in Pamplona, beginning their walk here and blending in with those of us who came from farther a field.

As the city thinned out, the trail crossed a series of roads, railroad tracks and concrete bridges. This was the dregs of the city, the dirty, modern parts that clung to the edges of ancient Pamplona. A city is a big organism, and though I'd visited and even briefly lived in New York City, I'd never experienced one the way I did on the trail. To walk through a city on the Camino was to cross-section the whole being, move through its many rings, and for a brief moment, be in all its worlds at once. I wondered if the people living in the trail cities had seen as much of their home turf as pilgrims did, for we moved through the veins at street level only as fast as our feet could take us. No speeding glimpses from a car or train, blurred all the edges into something softer, more palatable. For us, an ugly bridge spanning a rumbling four lane highway or the jumble of train wires were experiences that lingered.

The presence of fresh pilgrim crowds emboldened me, and I felt my pace quicken like an excited pulse. Once the roads and railways were behind me and the land dipped down into a valley of fields streaming away from the city, I noticed a man up ahead walking with bare feet in the wet morning grass. He was moving so fast he almost skipped, and his bag looked weightless. I watched his apparent glee with unabashed fascination. Where did such buoyancy come from? Was it caffeine, sugar, recreational drugs or simply an ecstatic appreciation of the divine flowing through him at this early hour? One thing was for certain, what he had, I wanted. If I couldn't embody such lightness of foot, I certainly wanted to walk in its company for a while. Only as I drew within a few strides and he turned around, did I realize he was one half of the Italian duo who'd been with me in the bunk room last night. I'd met the younger half of the pair in the kitchen, but I hadn't met his accomplice. The caffeine and the scene in the café collided in me. As I watched the Italians fall into an effortless pace of long strides and speed, I felt my own legs stretching out, loosening their rusty hinges, tingling with the desire to push into a higher gear and leave everything behind. This was my window, and I had to jump. I knew nothing more than that. I didn't know if the duo spoke English or if they wanted company. I didn't know where I would land by nightfall, and I didn't know what awaited me in the days to come. I simply knew I was done with the Dane. And I didn't turn back.

Out of necessity, I couldn't be shy as I drew even with the Italians to introduce myself. Due to their tender hearted natures, they didn't turn away a stray in need. I could easily have been brushed aside since I didn't speak a word of Italian, and they had hardly a phrase of English between them. It would have been simple for them to fall into stony silence and radiate an aura of annoyance at my unwanted presence, but I'd stumbled upon a duo who were extraordinary. They would prove unperturbed to speak in a three way dialog that involved our own mangled form of Spanish, and unconcerned with the addition of a new member to their trail configuration. Alec, the younger of the two, was the only Spanish speaker in the pair and tirelessly patient with my rusty Spanish vocabulary. Within the first hour, we'd honed an odd but effective system of communication. I'd simplify the thoughts flowing through me into Spanish so Alec could translate them into Italian for Alberto. The current was reversed to send the response back to me, and so the circle of communication was complete. Even though it often made me feel left out of the conversation, wondering what might have gotten lost in all the linguistic contortion, I was happy to be involved at all. Alberto, the older of the two, tried to fill in the gaps with an expansive vocabulary of gestures and a never ending supply of cheery smiles. Nonetheless, it made me marvel at the subtlety of language, how a word carried a whole universe on its back, and how much could be lost in translation. During our conversations, half the meaning would settle back inside me, awaiting a moment when I might speak with all the fluidity and impact I desired. I knew I would have to wait for another English speaker, but in the meantime I had two new comrades in arms.

Alberto and Alec had met in Roncesvalles on the very first night and found something binding in their common disposition. Maybe it was the ability to be close but silent as they walked, or perhaps their roots in a shared country were key. I couldn't be sure, but the glue had held fast. On the Camino, nationality was a quick way to connect with others. It was a painless opener to ask fellow countrymen where they lived, how they got here and if they'd been to your neck of the woods. It was pleasantly disconcerting the way a stranger could feel like a long lost friend. No matter if a pilgrim was Canadian, German or Bulgarian, when he or she first meet a fellow countryman here, everyone had a special key to a shared place, and it felt down right wonderful. Well, for a moment at least, until the buzz wore off. Then we all felt that strange let down as we found we shared little if anything else. This very rollercoaster had besieged me in Roncesvalles when I'd met a young American girl from California. Our Americaness tied us to each other for a mere ten minutes, before the comforting feeling of instant bonding wore off. Our shallow shared well had run dry even with language, culture and age on our side. It was an astounding and slightly frightening discovery. I now had no guarantees about who I would be drawn to and who would simply slip out of view. As I traversed the land with all the time in the world, would I find I could push beyond the cultural edges, maybe even the language lines and fill my circle with a quirky but valued cast of friends?

I was encouraged that Alberto and Alec possessed the lucky combination of both a national bond and an easy friendship. They had age and professional choices working against them, but it didn't faze them that Alberto was in his fifties and earned his living as a yoga instructor in Milan, while Alec spent time as a twenty something working on computer software in a northern mountain village. The trail was an even playing field, a place they could both show up, walk and share a bit of conversation along the way. They were delightfully simple as well as typically male in their approach to friendship. And they opened the doors to their world for me with little fuss or concern. I was likable and could keep up with their highly athletic pace therefore I was welcome.

The visual appearance of the two countrymen was also strikingly dissimilar. Young Alec was tall and lanky but moved as if he had been a shy and awkward kid. A scraggly blonde ponytail dangled down his back, and his clothes hung off his frame. He wore round glasses, carried a tall old fashion umbrella instead of a rain jacket and a small daypack. There was something inherently nerdy about him that made him seem slightly out of place in the environs of the trail, as if he were a bit green to the whole backpacking experience. Despite the disadvantage, I was surprised at how well he was keeping up with his bionic companion Alberto.

As Alec and I trailed behind Alberto, I had a chance to study this mysterious Italian. Though he was in his fifties, Alberto's lined face and immaculately bald head were the only outward signs that betrayed his age. His body was fuller than Alec's but radiated strength through his long lean muscles and graceful carriage. He was neither muscle bound nor antsy when he was still. His every pause was full of purpose. For Alberto, there was no waste in stillness and nothing lost in a moment of rest. This ethos took on an almost mythical quality as I spent more and more time in his presence. I generally behaved like a caged animal when forced to wait or rest. I'd yet to learn how to be submissive to the stillness, roll over and expose my underbelly to it. Would Alberto be the teacher I needed for the practice of such arts?

One area where Alberto and I were kindred spirits was motion. He too moved at a higher frequency and every step or gesture brought energy down and out his body. Here before me was someone else who moved energy from above and out through the limbs of his body like a superconductor. We recognized this trait in one another but all we could do was stand on either side of our language gulf and smile in acknowledgement.

The real magic of Alberto's dynamic physical presence unfolded when he walked. His stride was unlike any I'd seen on the trail thus far, and I was shamelessly envious of such power. Each step was long and determined, yet clear and efficient like a dancer. There was no waste of energy and no apparent effort or struggle. It was a simple display of flow without fight. He didn't see gravity or physics as forces to be battled but as tools to be channeled. I'd come across fitness buffs and jocks before, but he rivaled even the dancer guys I'd known, because he wasn't trying to suppress the flow of emotions that came along with the flow of energy. He wasn't trying to disconnect from the greater source. Even without being able to speak to Alberto about this, I could see the mystical oneness of his progress down the trail, and I suspected he was aware of the link. Alec offered a more down to earth contrast to Alberto as he ambled along beside me, unfazed by tackling the trail with no experience and very little understanding of the energy moving beneath him.

Alberto carried a vintage red pack with no fancy straps or special attachments. He didn't even have a waist belt to help transfer some of the weight off his back onto his hips. Later, this feat seemed even more amazing when I picked up his bag and discovered it was much heavier than mine, filled as it was with homeopathic tinctures in dense glass bottles. Each bottle was a unique color and served a different ailment, but I was unable to understand the Italian labels. At one point, he pulled a bottle filled with bright orange liquid from his bag and rubbed a bit into the muscles of his lower leg. I had to admire his conviction, since I spent most of my time thinking about how to lighten my pack, while he happily charged ahead with a heavy pack.

From the albergue in Arre to Puente La Reina would be just over twenty-nine kilometers. Even though it was a shorter day than the previous one, I couldn't figure out why, as the afternoon wore on, I became so tired. I'd started the morning with so much coffee and adrenaline, then leaving the Dane behind had sent a surge of empowerment through my veins, but now the energy was fading fast.

Several hours outside of Pamplona, we started upward over a low ridge of mountains. Near the top, a small fountain clung to a hillside and gurgled water under the shadows of the white winged windmills dotted along the ridgeline. An older woman sat with her feet in the basin of the drinking fountain, chatting to her companion while smoking a hand rolled cigarette. She lazily rearranged the fraying scarf around her head while lamenting her new hiking boots with sharply enunciated curses. She appeared oblivious to the fact that her feet were hogging the spout meant for those of us thirsty from the short but steep climb. Instead, she waved hello and offered us well wishes on our journey as our trio continued single file up the narrow path. As we crested the ridge and stood beside a bronze pilgrim sculpture, we were able to look both east over Pamplona and west towards our destination for the night. After a brief pause on the windy spot, Alberto turned towards the village of Puente la Reina in the west and led our procession onward. I didn't dare ask Alec how many kilometers lay between us and our beds, nor did I try to calculate our estimated hour of arrival. I simply looked down at the bit of trail before me and dove back into motion.

I'd hoped to gain a bit of energy from the well deserved down hill off the ridge, but quickly remembered why the end of the day in Roncesvalles had been so unpleasant. At first the downhill was freeing, and I found myself buoyed by Alberto's joyful example. I was hopping, skipping even dancing with the delight of being just a bit weightless. But oh so quickly, the dense bulk of my pack pressed upon me, and the hill became less of a light hearted affair. When walking, my mind wanted to make the uphill stretches into the real villain. I'd look up ahead and see a gradient rising above me, and my mind would yell the battle cry, "Ok! Here we go! It's you and me, mountain, mano a mano." But all this bravado, though helpful in conquering the peak, was misguided, since the down hills were the true test of my body's will to withstand. The relentless way gravity sucked me down a slope at a rate faster than my legs wanted to go caused the real struggle. Resistance tired all parts, but if I let go, I became a rolling, tumbling and stumbling avalanche of limbs. With an extra twenty pounds strapped to my back, my muscles could do little else but shake with force while my joints and ligaments snapped from having to grip and take impact. In order to stay upright and ease the strain on my legs, I was forced to watch each and every foot placement along the rocky decent with diligent attention. It was a simple task but one that took a surprising amount of focus. I'd been awake and on the trail for five hours already. The task may have kept me from a smooth upright stride or an uninterrupted view of the valley before me, but it did keep me right where I was. Right there with the trail under my feet. Right in the now of the fight.

PUENTE LA REINA

Even with new company by my side, the trail to Puente La Reina felt leaden and never ending. Towns came and went, but we didn't stop. The stored adrenaline I'd built up during my mad dash out of Pamplona had now fully burned off. For the last two hours I'd had no stimulants of any kind, chemical or physical, to keep the engine going. It was sheer will and a small but powerful cluster of energy inside my chest that allowed me to stay with the Italians. Even as the sun appeared in bursts to beat down on us, and dust from the roadside trail filled my eyes and lungs, I still felt a powerful internal motor launching me forward. The fuel for this engine was little more than a tiny reservoir of liquid intuition. I felt I had a specific destiny to fulfill on this journey, and the destiny included other people. This hunch was no longer just a passing thought or daydream but omnipresent. It seemed to eat away at my insides, leaving me ever hungry for the next day when I would be closer to crossing paths with these unknown pilgrims. If this hunch was right, I was certain I was behind my flock, and it was my job to bring us together. I couldn't be certain these mysterious young pilgrims up ahead would be listening for signs to pause or slow their pace. I also didn't feel I could count on the universe to throw more than a few roadblocks or detours in their way to slow them down. All I could do was work from my side of the unknown and keep moving as fast and as far as I could each day. It was a daunting task but a concrete one that drove me to obsess over the fine art of balancing short-term stamina with long term endurance. I studied maps with intense focus, counted kilometers and monitored my physical limit. Today was my third thirty kilometer day in a row. I was heading into unknown territory as I faced another long day tomorrow. I would keep going as long as I could with this relentless pace, this hungry push, but I hoped I would fall into my place and my community on this trail sooner rather than later.

It was nearly three when the church spires of Puente la Reina came into view up ahead. Even the tireless Italians cheered at their appearance behind a thick bank of grey clouds. Since northern Spain was experiencing its rainiest June in recorded history, a soft cloud cover had been omnipresent for the last few weeks. One of the Spanish storekeepers I spoke with in Zubiri explained that such dismal days were keeping the Spanish pilgrim population down. Apparently a mild and rainy pilgrimage wasn't a draw for the average Spaniard, and since the trail was in their backyard, they could wait out the storms until fairer skies prevailed. With my current focus centering on speed and ever forward motion, the weather was a rare blessing. The partly cloudy afternoons sheltered me as I walked late into the day, sparing me dehydration or sun stroke. At first, I didn't see the weather as an ally in my master plan, but then, I'd never tried to walk in the true heat of a Spanish summer's day. That would come later, and only then would I feel the full magnitude of the cloudy blessings bestowed upon me in the Basque country.

An hour later, I sat at a long wooden table in the large municipal albergue staring down a carton of orange juice, willing myself to drink when all I wanted was to lay my head down on the wide smooth surface, feel the cool varnish on my flushed cheek and sink into drowsy release. Since the start of the trail, my body had needed more sustenance but had been willing to accommodate less. The space where hunger used to be was suddenly little more than a locked cage of ribs and muscle. Every bite or swallow was a small fight, and sleep was always a more appealing option. Alberto and Alec had chosen the latter and were next door in the dormitory, dozing in the dark cool room. When we'd agreed to stay together in an albergue in the center of town, I'd been immediately flooded with relief. These two familiar faces would be there with me, and no matter who else arrived, I would have some form of community

The albergue was a large solidly built rectangle seated directly across from the town church and only a few blocks from the center of the village. For a building that housed fifty pilgrims, it was marvelously space efficient. The dining room where I sat with my mid-day meal was filled with welcoming tables and benches, a guest book and a long row of windows facing the street. With the simple ingredients of windows and well-worn tables, the dining room was a space that connected strangers and generated new community each night. Once the light grew dim in the sky and the kitchen began to hum with dinner preparations, this room was the place to sit and talk, bask in the smells of the kitchen and meet fellow travelers. The large bunkrooms had just as many windows and were strewn along a hallway that opened out to a walled yard behind the building. Sets of muddy boots lined the wall outside the main entrance, tucked safely under the shelter of a wide portico.

The albergue was one of four in town, but being the municipal, it held the most beds and was always full by dusk. In most trailside towns there were usually a few accommodation options. The municipal was the public chain of albergues, often run by the local or provincial government. They were the least expensive, offering the basics of a bunk, a shower and a roof over our heads. When it came to municipals, the quality varied depending on who ran the albergue and how much funding the place received. Some felt so welcoming and warm that the five euro price tag felt like a steal, while others made me begrudge every cent I paid. Even with the risk involved, I always sought out the municipals first, for they housed scores more people than the other albergues in town and usually attracted all the thrifty youngsters who weren't afraid to rough it. The next level up in accommodations were private albergues. These were run by individuals and offered more amenities like personal bathrooms, a pool or a home cooked meal. This was a more plush pilgrim lifestyle and accordingly cost most. Last but not least, there were hostals, private rooms to rent in local apartment buildings and hotels. These were for the more financially endowed pilgrim or for those who wanted to remove themselves from the community of other pilgrims. If a pilgrim booked a room in a hostal, he or she had a hot shower and fluffy towels but didn't get to sit around in the evenings with other pilgrims, share meals and bond. Even if I'd been a bigger fan of such luxuries, the trade off of comfort for isolation would never have been worth it. The loneliness I already felt on the trail would have been crushing if I'd been forced to isolate myself in a hotel every night. Being with people, even if they were strangers, was comforting and made me feel connected to the human experience of this journey.

After packing up what remained of my lunch, I retreated to the dormitory and the comforting routine of unpacking. Once I arrived at an albergue, I typically spent a good part of the afternoon unpacking all of my belongings, unrolling dirty clothes and pulling out any food that remained from the day's supply. To unpack was to center myself and engage in a task that could be done with minimal brainpower while sitting down. It was also a chance to lay my things on the ground and see what I was hauling with me each and every step. All the small items, the extra pieces of clothing that meant nothing as I packed them back home, were now brought into question. In the last few days, I'd been cut loose from my moorings about the importance of the items I owned and carried with me. If the thing didn't serve my quest or support me in some vital way then suddenly it had no value. Belongings with no function could be shed like old skin and released without the slightest hesitation. I'd never felt this way before. I wanted my bag to be light and open, sleek and swift. I wanted to hollow out and not hold onto a single ounce that held me back or contained weighted memories of the past.

As I weeded through my dwindling supply of clothing, I unhooked my cumbersome and unused sleeping mat from my pack and placed it beside my bed. My pack had come to me in a round about way, but I'd never doubted its place among my trail gear. I'd known it was the right one as soon as I'd fit it to the arc of my shoulders and had felt it match me like a well tailored seam, yet I hadn't seen it at first. Disheartened after hours of trying on new high tech and pocket encrusted ill fitting packs, I'd made one more foray, digging through the racks low to the ground and unknowingly veering into the kids' section. There, among bags built for teens, I'd noticed a flash of blue like the wings of a bird. I'd pulled the narrow silver frame and blue body out from the pile and turned it over. A large white bird covered the expanse of the pack with its wings open in flight. The act of slinging the slender straps onto my shoulders had been simply a formality. I'd felt chills cross my forearms, and I'd known the wings of this Osprey pack would travel across Spain with me, give me flight and act as my snail shell. So maybe the bag was a bit small to crawl into each night, at least I would be assured it would have my back at all times.

My emotional relationship with my pink sleeping mat was a whole different story. The tight roll of inflatable plastic was still crusted with the dark mud it had picked up on the mountain passes. Out of pure neglect, I hadn't bothered to clean off the lingering traces of the early trail's wet grasp. My loathing for the Pepto-Bismol colored mat had begun almost immediately and had grown with every passing day. Only after arriving on the trail did I discover the mat wasn't necessary. I must have gotten the notion I needed it from an over anxious online packing list, one that probably insisted on such "essentials" as a SAT phone, a full medical kit and mace. Though I'd learned a wise lesson on whom to take packing advice from, I'd also shelled out a pretty penny for the mat and felt financially bound to keep it on board. Needless to say it was heavy, bulky, awkward and hadn't been of any practical use. I was more likely to trip over it and break something than unroll it and enjoy a soft night's sleep. Psychologically, it stopped me from feeling streamline and swift. And perceptions such as this could wear heavily on any pilgrim, for to be a pilgrim was to be part of a tribe that revered lightness of pack and foot. Though my mat was perfectly high tech, it wasn't necessary given the amazingly well organized albergue system. It was a dead weight, and it was dragging me down, literally. But the price tag still caused me to gulp. How long could I keep something on my back just because it was expensive? I hesitated each night, reasoning I could always jettison it tomorrow, but my economic resolve was fading fast.

After washing my newly sorted belongings, I went to find a place to hang them out in the last bit of daylight. Holding a dripping pile of clothes in my outstretched arms, I set foot into the secluded backyard surrounded by a high stonewall. A few small trees were scattered across the lush green lawn, and the well manicured space felt soft and warm underfoot. Many pilgrims had sought out parts flooded in sunlight to nap or read their guidebooks. To be warm and still was paradise to a pilgrim. The small clusters of people sat in beat up plastic chairs or sprawled out on the ground reading or talking in a low murmur. There was an air of relieved calm as if all was well for a few hours while we had shelter and the promise of sleep looming on the horizon. Each night I claimed a bunk and settled in was a victory. It was another chance to rest in a known destination before I set off tomorrow for somewhere new and foreign. This life demanded a rhythm of being in the moment, of cherishing the quirks and perks of my current home, for the now was all I could really know or contain. Everything else was too imaginary. The dry hot lands of the middle of Spain or the rugged coast of the Atlantic over seven hundred kilometers away might as well have been part of a distant solar system. For right now, this yard with its dozen or so pilgrims was my world, and to my delight and surprise, every face was a new one. I'd moved out of my initial group and leapt right into the group ahead.

As I uncurled the arms of a shirt and pinned them on to the clothesline, I noticed a young twosome sitting out on the edge of the yard. One was a German boy whom I'd seen from afar earlier and the other was a young woman with a stringy mop of mousey hair dripping all the way down to her legs folded underneath her. They were deep in conversation, but the banter appeared to be coming mostly from the girl. From the distance between their bodies and the slightly uneasy flow of conversation, I could tell they weren't a couple. I sensed they'd just met and were talking for the first time. Yet there was one element beyond speculation that made me immediately curious. Even at a distance, I could tell the solo girl was trying desperately to flirt with the guy. Since the German's back was to me, I couldn't fully make out his features, but he seemed to be fending off her enthusiastic attention with calm ease. As the girl continued to talk, I continued to shamelessly observe the German. As he replied to one of her questions, he turned slightly, revealing his profile. Then I got it. Suddenly I knew why the girl was working so hard for his attention. He was stunning. I pegged my last sock to the line and decided now was as good a time as any to make an introduction and throw my hat in the ring.

As I drew close, holding my empty laundry basket to my side, the girl didn't break eye contact with her prey, and I had a moment to make a full assessment of the German. And a quick look was all I needed to confirm what I'd suspected from a distance. Even after a day walking and little to no grooming, he was undeniably handsome with dark eyes and dark unruly hair. The long limbs of his tall frame were draped over the sides of the plastic chair underneath him. Here, not five paces in front of me, was the proof that cute young men still took to the trail by foot, and that perhaps I wasn't doomed to plod along behind crowds of middle aged groups and octogenarian couples. I had arrived in the promised land.

Since the German and his lady companion were sitting between the albergue and me, it was easy to stumble across them and introduce myself. After sticking out my hand to greet them both, the girl turned a chilly smile on me. Clearly, she would have preferred for things to remain an intimate party of two. As much as I'd made quick and bold conjectures about this girl's intentions, I couldn't blame her for trying. The German was a very promising prospect, and I hated to admit it, but I was also interested and willing to be bold. My normal level of shyness was withering under the pressures of the trail, and from those ashes was emerging a girl I hardly recognized, a brazen, daring girl who was willing to blindly jump into any social scene. The worst outcomes might entail a bruised ego, some fierce blushing and a few critical self-assessments after the fact, but that wasn't too strenuous a toll. I was willing to take a risk on the German's behalf.

As I settled next to the pair on the warm courtyard stones, I could feel the predominant force driving me was hope. Yes, I was a little behind the curve in wooing the German, but I would try and make up for that with a pinch of charm and a lot of effort. I'd come to Spain on instructions from my dream to walk the trail and fully submerge in the flow of this life. The land and the people were central to my mission. Finding love was in the bounds of my Camino contract. In fact, the promise at the end of the world seemed to imply love was part of the unfolding story. I could imagine falling for this attractive boy. I could see him as the one whose energy had drawn me forward for the past week, for the past month, for the past ten years. This trail was a series of meetings, during which my energy field expanded as if I was reaching out to take each new person's pulse, to see if the pilgrim held the cadence of the life I knew was coming. I knew if I could find the person who vibrated with my destiny that he would be the one. I'd come to Spain with an open heart about where this soul was coming from, and I was trying to trust the magnetism of the trail and the gravity of destiny. I just wanted to root around in the German's vibrational field for a while. Was that too much to ask? There was something sweet about him as if he was too shy, young and kind to play games and toy with me the way others had. He didn't feel like a no as the Dane before him had, but I needed time to sense if he could be a yes. I knew it sounded a bit crazy, but I'd always believed some part of me would recognize my person when I met him. And since the German was the first potential yes I'd met along the trail, his presence filled me with giddy excited energy.

My current competition was a young woman from French speaking Canada and a righteous vegan. With stories aimed to impress, she warbled on about finding the best tofu in Pamplona, saving animals from slaughter back home and surviving the rigors of medical school. She told stories of sneaking around the subway gates in London and sleeping in fields along the side of the trail. She even claimed she'd walked twenty kilometers in two hours. Later when I told the Italians of this boast, they laughed and suggested she had meant to say she rode the bus twenty kilometers in two hours. That was surely a more realistic notion. It wasn't hard to see where this cynicism came from, and frankly, I shared their hunch about her stories. The Vegan was a rather normal looking girl who claimed super human feats. On the surface, there were no clues she'd ever spent time engaged in any physical activity let alone walked for weeks at a time. I might have believed the tall tales had I been looking upon a sinewy marathoner with hard, weather beaten features, but buff she was not. I had to conclude exaggeration was at work but let the matter drop without interrogation. Time would sort out what was true. The kilometers ahead would be the test to see which of us girls could walk the walk.

Since the Vegan had clear romantic designs on the German, she dominated the conversation. He seemed unflappable and content to listen. He laughed kindly at her stories and in between the Vegan's soliloquies, he told us about his life as a teacher in Germany. His English was very proficient, but I wasn't sure how much content he gathered while listening to us girls. Talking with the German felt like looking at a puzzle that had most of its image showing but several key pieces missing. The lost parts made me wonder what was slipping through the cracks. I suppose I had no right to complain, since I spoke even less German than Italian.

As the German spoke, he nodded, flashed his charming smile and looked me straight in the eye. I learned he was two years older than me and the perfect age for all my romantic visions. His looks were absolutely suited to my tastes, and he would have caught my attention anywhere. I couldn't believe my luck to suddenly meet him after having encountered so few young people on the trail. I breathed a deep sigh of relief. Finally, things looked like they might be turning around.

After a while, our conversation veered to the future, and before the Vegan could take off on a tangent about dissecting cadavers, the German spoke up. He talked about his search for what came next, his desire to teach but also to see the world. The Vegan quickly interjected that the structure of med school was instrumental to her future. She'd already given away every minute of the next ten years but seemed unaware of the sacrifice. I spoke a bit about my own search and couldn't help drawing links between my ethos and the German's. We were both in a space of openness to whatever the universe presented, and somehow I didn't doubt that the Camino would show us the way forward. It did this every day on a small scale with its arrows. Might it also do this once this physical trail was done? I certainly hoped so.

I noticed the sky was starting to darken and rumble. I felt sorry for the pilgrims who would be caught out in the storm. As the rain clouds crept closer, the eastern sky became impossibly dark. We organized to move inside, and the German suggested we go out that evening to a bar to watch a futbol game. The European Cup had just started, and Spain was rumored to have an outstanding team. I could only assume that watching the national team in Spain, where soccer is practically a religion, would be vastly entertaining. I also wanted a chance to talk with the German alone for a few minutes, maybe even set a plan to walk together tomorrow. Since there wasn't a shred of privacy in the albergues, our excursion into the center of town would be a perfect chance to set plans for just the two of us.

When it was time to go to the bar, I noticed the German was attached at the hip with a tall Japanese guy to whom I hadn't been introduced. They'd met the night before, were already very tight and kept close to each other at all times. Apparently I'd met the German at a rare moment when his friend was otherwise occupied. The way they interacted could have fooled anyone into thinking they'd been friends for years. It was surprisingly hard to discern which pilgrims were pre-trail bonded and which had found each other here. Maybe it was the way the trail quickly thrust people into dependence and intimacy that caused the lines to blur. Or it might have been the sheer amount of time we all had on our hands to talk and the way pilgrims weren't shy when it came to sharing the deeper elements of their lives. No topic seemed to be "too intense" or "too personal" to share with a stranger here. If a pilgrim wanted to talk, there was usually someone who would listen, and both would be closer to each other as a result. So what was to become of us pilgrims who walked alone or with non-English speaking Italians? What was our fate? Strong bonds could form overnight or in the course of a morning. And once together, the bonds held fast. It made me nervous.

I couldn't stop from anxiously chewing my fingernails as I gazed around the scene of pilgrims milling under the eaves, waiting to head in to the center of town. Had I missed the boat by not finding a confidant or crew early on? In those first few days, I did the best I could, but what if the mere choice of my start date sealed my fate as an outsider in groups of young pilgrims? It was logical that groups of social twenty somethings would seek each other out, merge and solidify into bands. I was looking to do this myself, but would the walls of these clubs remain fluid and allow free rangers like me to enter? Living with others sped up the whole process of connection, and I loved this trail quirk, but I knew it was a double-edged sword. This quick bonding culture could work against me. I planned to be awake and open to a new face at any stage in the journey, but would others be so welcoming?

This whole issue made me think back to the massive effort I'd made to find someone to join me on the Camino. At first I'd been determined not to travel alone. I'd felt it was a deal breaker no matter what my guidance told me about heading off to Spain. I'd been unwilling to compromise on this point, so I'd put time and energy into the task of wrangling someone to join my wild scheme. Each of my previous trips had been filled with vast amounts of time alone, mostly in isolated coastal villages or unfamiliar city streets. During a summer working in Ireland, many long hours had been spent drinking tea with elderly cousins and walking for miles along deserted beaches. As a very young teenager on an exchange program to Barcelona, my host family had refused to speak to me in English. One all day boat trip, I'd spent a full twelve hours in the company of other people without speaking a word. The day had ended with my host brothers brutally killing an octopus for sport by beating it to death against the rocks. Clearly my track record with solo journeys wasn't good.

This time, I'd wanted company. Yes, it might be unfair to use a friend as a shield against loneliness, but I knew if a person agreed to go with me, then he or she was also meant to travel the trail. I'd called a handful of friends, floating the idea to them and trying to make the trail seem easy and glamorous even when I'd been relatively sure it wouldn't be. But I was dealt NOs again and again and again. From all directions, I was flooded with "sorry," "wish I could" and "I just can't."

Finally I'd gotten it. This trip wouldn't happen if I insisted on going with someone else, and I wouldn't be able to follow the directions I had from the universe and my internal guidance if I waited around for company. I had to make a choice between my insistence on a partner in crime or the trip itself. One morning I'd woken up and knew I couldn't wait around for someone else to shape the trip. I had to be brave enough to leap for it at all costs and blindly trust the plan. So I'd taken the bull by the horns, picked a date of departure and organized all the details. It was my dream and my prompting. I had to own it to do it.

In the moments when I felt safe and grounded, I could feel the purity of coming alone. If a friend had been beside me as I faced this wild unknown, our partnership might have locked us both into old patterns of the past. The balance of power and our view of each other might not have kept up with the internal changes this trail brought. I felt I was in a growth accelerator, and all the elements of my internal world were shifting and opening so fast that I could hardly keep up with the pace let alone expect someone else to.

Here on the rainy night in Puente la Reina, the connections I made were all about who I was today. There was no track record or history. There was only the present and the glimmer of who I was becoming. Nobody here knew I had an amazingly close family or that I'd once been a modern dancer on the rise. They didn't see the scars from my thwarted attempt to squeeze myself into the life of a boarding school teacher, and they couldn't make out the long line of failed romances that trailed behind me like a weighty and invisible train.

I was simply a fellow traveler. Other pilgrims and I could chat for hours or not at all. We could walk together from here on or purposely avoid each other at all costs. There were no rules of conduct, no laws stating we had to like one another, connect or care for each other. All relationships were voluntary, and there was a distinct beauty in that. For when people let others walk beside them or share a piece of their story, they did so because they genuinely wanted to. Time given to another was a gift here, especially in a world where we were all on our own internal quests. We each walked two roads at once, and I'd already crossed paths with pilgrims who did everything possible to stay on the solo road.

Only after escape from the Dane's company had I truly understood how important it was for me not to waste another single moment of this journey on company like his. This trail was too precious. I now knew there were others who felt the energy of the trail and listened. I was ready to search out fellow pilgrims with a matching view into this Camino life. For if we could meet on emotional and energetic common ground, then the outer details failed to matter. Age, nationality, gender, past or future would have no bearing on the tone of a connection. This trail was proving to be like the outer world but stripped of several layers. It was raw and often intimate in surprising ways, yet it was thrillingly real. I'd only caught a glimpse of this energy, but it had lodged itself in my chest and planted deep roots; I was hooked and on the look out for more. So the ever-present question hung over me like my own personal weather system. It was the simple question of who and when, with an elusive answer that only visited me in dreams and slipped away before first light.

As I mulled over the social world of the trail, the falling sheets of rain lulled me into a semi-hypnotic trance. With little energy left in my weary body, I found it easy and somehow perfectly natural to slip into an absent minded state. I'd come to see this glazed eye behavior as more of an exhaustion induced practice of meditation than a prelude to falling asleep standing up. But no matter the proper definition, I could easily be snapped out of it under the right circumstances. And the German bounding out the door and up to me was just the jumpstart I needed. My romantic adrenaline caused me to almost physically leap to attention. As he strode towards me, I couldn't help admiring what a beautifully constructed man he was, a quirky mix of all the attributes my most shallow self found enticing. Tall, but not freakishly so, he moved with shy grace causing his reckless dark hair to shift and bounce with each step. But it was his large soulful eyes as they met mine that encouraged me the most. His looks were undeniably top notch, but I knew myself too well to assume our bond could be formed on looks alone. I sometimes wished I could act on a whim of shallow indulgence, but it just wasn't in me, and I'd probably missed out on a whole lot of fun because of my intense view of romance. I only hoped one day I would see my position as more of a strength than an unusually boring weakness.

The rain had eased a bit as the rest of our party materialized, and we headed into the central hub of the village. With the Vegan and a fellow Canadian leading the charge, we set off for the far side of town in hopes of scouting out a bar and seeing a bit of Puente la Reina. I drifted towards the back of the group to walk next to the German. He smiled at my arrival, but continued to talk with the Japanese guy. Though they were in the trenches of a deep bromance conversation, I was willing to wait for an opening to talk with him. My shoulders gently bumped into his as we navigated the wet streets, and the physical contact reminded me just how much I craved closeness. As we crossed a busy road into the old center of town, I had to step around the puddles in the uneven roadway and leap from one dry cobble to the next. This activity took a bit of delicate footwork, but my feet were light and nimble in the vibrant blue ballet flats I'd packed as my spare shoes. Though the slippers did nothing to keep me lofted above the wet surface of the street, I loved feeling as if my feet were almost bare. Even feet needed to breath and rest in between bouts with tight-laced sneakers, heavy packs and the relentless tug of gravity. They were the source, the delicate bone and muscle that everything balanced on, and I needed to treat them as kindly as possible in the off hours.

After several minutes, the Japanese guy was pulled into another conversation, and I found my opening with the German. We chatted absently for a bit as I waited for a swell in courage, and then I looked him in the eyes and asked him if he would walk with me the next morning. What did I have to lose in asking? If all the rules of decorum and engagement were different on the trail, then a forthright question was a strong move, a fair move, a mature move.

After ducking his head and breaking eye contact, his face went expressionless. I was startled that my modest request had caused such a reaction. He fell silent for a moment as if his attention was drifting and he'd forgotten I was even there. Yet after an empty minute, he spoke casually, "If it works out then sure… no problem, but if not, that's okay."

His tone was extremely matter of fact, and his eyes were glassy and unreadable. The energy around us had shifted from a place of building intensity and eye contact to a disconnected and distracted vibe. He shrugged his shoulders slightly, patted me on the back and turned towards more entertaining company. Our little heart to heart was over, and I was even more confused than before I'd broached the subject.

Was he saying he couldn't be bothered to arrange plans? Was he simply implying he was a grump in the morning, or planning wasn't his trail style? Or was it an obtuse way of giving me the brush off? The BRUSH OFF? I'd hardly strung together more than a few sentences with this guy. Was he THAT uninterested in me? And if so, why all the lingering eye contact and flirtatious energy? I could still feel it humming off him as he walked beside me. Was I nuts or were there two conflicting sides to this German? I was finding it a bit dizzying to sort out which was the genuine energy. Was it the interest, noted via eye contact, or was it the disinterest, noted via shrugs and cryptic words? Suddenly the romantic buzz was less clear and seriously less fun.

Yes, I'd been bold in asking the German to walk with me, but I hadn't asked for his hand in marriage or if I could bear his children; I'd simply asked if we could walk together for a while. If he hated me or I him, I gave both of us the right to abandon the cause of being friends and take off at top speed. Our friendship was nothing, but it could be everything, and I was surprised he didn't see it the same way. In the last five years, and especially the last five days, I'd been on a course in random acts of boldness. Yes, the failure rate was disastrously high, and I'd had to develop a sophisticated system of fleeing first dates gone wrong, but I knew I wouldn't stop. I had yet to see long-term returns on my boldness, but I was convinced it would someday bear fruit. As they say, all the closed doors simply lead to finally opening the right one. But I sensed the German was missing the essence of risk; we can't only boldly risk once, we have to do it over and over and over. We have to try many doors, to eventually find the right one. I had such high hopes that the German would at least want to turn the handle.

We all had to walk. It was the unshakable core of a pilgrim's life. This was our task, our goal and our daily bread. But the silver lining was that it didn't have to be alone all the time. There was so much walking to be done that there was time to both revel in solitude and mingle in what good company we could find. And at this juncture in time, lively companionship felt scarce. I craved questions and answers, fresh stories and a view into worlds beyond our surroundings. I was restless when only part of me was engaged, and the blend of walking and talking was, to me, near to perfection. Only dance with its language of movement and energy was more vibrant.

As I looked over at the German, I felt the sickening pit opening in my stomach again. The German had gone from enthusiastic prospect to aloof conundrum in the span of an hour. I realized with horror that he might be another guy in a long line that I had to cajole into liking me. I'd gotten my hopes up all because of his good looks and lingering eye contact, but maybe that was all there was. Maybe he enjoyed the crackle of tension, but wasn't motivated enough to make a move or even respond to one. We weren't fresh-faced teens here; he was closer to thirty than to twenty. What was all this aloof social stuff really about? I guess it served me right to be thwarted in my attempts to woo someone I liked at first glance. I felt mistrustful of men who acted from such shallow impulses, so maybe the German had the right to be wary.

In truth, I distrusted it when a guy feigned romantic love after spending a few moments appreciating my outward appearance or thought we were a good match because I appreciated his. Yes, there was something visually alluring and aesthetic about beauty in another human being, but I'd found that beauty is not stationary and not always apparent upon first glance. A handsome man could fall into shadow when his character revealed a temper, arrogance or cruelty. And in the same amount of time, a less flashy man could grow in attractiveness as warmth and kindness radiated from his every action. Our vibrations and the energy we cycled through our bodies were the true marks of beauty, but I wondered how often we paid attention to anything beyond the image. I'd been fooled more than once by a handsome shell with an ugly core, and I imagined I wasn't alone in my mistake. Maybe love had nothing whatsoever to do with the immediate spark, maybe that was simply shallow personality business. I'd always fallen sideways into love, been swept up by a familiar character in the moment I least expected. I'd needed that comfort of friendship in order for anything romantic to flourish. So why was the German refusing to give me the trail equivalent of a mellow first date? I simply wanted to test the waters. Was it too much to ask?

I could imagine that a trail first date could be one of the more beautiful elements of Camino life, because it could have a flow and natural rhythm that such events often lacked. As we walked side by side, we could share the common goal of moving ever forward and be given the space to connect in as deep or as shallow a manner as we wished. He could share stories of his childhood, while I divulged the struggles of my recent past. I could flirt, and he could be vulnerable. It was all perfectly natural in the flow of the trail, for nothing was too intense or too shallow here. I could chat about the weather, not share my real name or personal history, lie about my age, profession and home town, then proceed to skip off into the sunset to never meet up again. From the very first moment I met someone, it had the potential to be everything or nothing. The only prerequisite was that we both showed up and jumped in.

My mind whirled on. Was his brush off a no? Or was it a coy yes? Or was it lazy maybe? I didn't know the German well enough to read his signals, but I could certainly try again. What did I have to lose by making the hard sell on a morning of walking together? He might be shy or not a morning person, or simply not sure his English worked before mid-day. I was determined to find out, for in truth he hadn't said no. Maybe wasn't a no. My old patterns crept to the surface, suggesting I needed to work just a bit harder to earn the first date.

As the clouds grew darker and hung like a low canopy over our heads, the group came to the unanimous decision to go to the famous bridge in Puente la Reina before finding a bar. The bridge was the oldest structure in Puente la Reina and lay on the very western edge of the village. It was the historical and architectural centerpiece of the village and gave the town its name, the Bridge of the Queen. Earlier in the morning as I trailed alongside Alec, he'd relayed the mythic story of the bridge and its infamous Reina. In loose hybridized Spanish, he told me a tale of a queen whose one true love, a young warrior not of noble blood, was killed in battle in the surrounding area. Though the death itself was tragic, it was the unique circumstances of the death that kept the tale alive. Legend told that the young hero was killed by the queen's brother whom she never forgave for doing her such a wrong. After her lover's death, she built this bridge to honor him and then died of a broken heart. I couldn't help wondering what traces of sorrow still resided in the old structure. What energy clung to something that had outlived generations of men? Could a bridge hold onto a window in time and simply refuse to let go, refuse to fully grieve and move on from its story?

The bridge was narrow and paved with large rocks, smoothed by hundreds of years of wear. Even in the falling light, it was a sight to behold composed of a series of sweeping arches that vaulted over the wide river. It was a sturdy form made more elegant by the effects of time. As our group crested the bridge, I was introduced to a few new pilgrims who'd joined our numbers. One was noticeably older than the rest of our young group. I guessed she was in her fifties, but she looked more at ease and rested than all the younger faces around her. As she shook my hand, I learned she'd come from South Africa to join the flow of the trail. Visually, she stood out from the rest of the group for she had a long mane of jet-black hair and a set of turbulent and steely eyes that moved as if she saw the world with ex-ray vision. At the same time, she lacked any of the typical

Camino nervousness and seemed very much at ease with the life of a pilgrim. Moments later, all the pieces came together when I discovered she had walked the trail once before.

Since I was standing next to this enigmatic trail veteran, I struck up a conversation. I was blatantly curious about the differences she felt here upon her second journey down the Camino. I asked her a slew of questions and was genuinely excited to hear her report. A mere six years ago, she'd spent virtually every night in the care of nuns or priests who'd washed and bandaged her feet each evening, and she'd met very few people who weren't on the trail for traditional religious reasons. Not only this, but the age of the average pilgrim had completely shifted. She'd hardly met a single person under thirty the last time, but now we were a growing demographic. She felt that with a younger more individually minded group of pilgrims, the reasons for taking the road were changing as well. Though I found this beautiful and thrilling, I wasn't sure if she felt the same way. I wondered what was drawing this new generation to the trail. Where was this thirst coming from?

As if to prove her point that youngsters were tainting the trail, she reported she'd spent the afternoon with a young Spaniard from Pamplona who walked his local stretch of trail a few times a week as a way to meet girls. The South African seemed horrified this young man was using the Camino as a dating service, but I found the image of him walking out to Puente La Reina over and over again in search of a girlfriend thoroughly endearing. I was amused and even charmed by his persistent optimism and dedication. He was willing to sweat and toil in the hot sun on a familiar road for the chance at love. In many ways, he wasn't too dissimilar from myself; he was following the path on the search for something more, something that would last beyond the dream of the trail. Even with my secret allegiance to the Spaniard, I didn't try and defend him. I wasn't sure the skeptical South African would understand there was value in all reasons for walking the trail. As much as we might try, we were all blind to each other's true purpose here. I still had no clue what mine would be; I just had to stay in my own guidance about the way forward and let that purpose take care of itself. I was starting to feel nothing was out of bounds as guidance. Though some would like to believe no one with a spiritual sense could be guided to seek romance on the trail out of Pamplona, I had to disagree. There were no rules, and even though the South African preferred the trail when the boundaries felt clearer and more tailored to her own beliefs, this new incarnation of the Camino was evolution in motion.

Eventually her stories veered away from the topic of her first Camino, and I asked her why she had returned to the trail. It was a typical Camino conversation starter and often revealed more than I could imagine. One thing was proving true; nobody came here for no reason at all. Everyone had a story and a mission.

The South African was no exception. Before she opened her mouth to speak, she turned to face me full on and took my eyes in a vice grip. Her words flowed thick with emotion as she held me captive. At first, I'd been enchanted by the slight click in her voice and warped British tones, but now her words merged together in a rushing blur. It wasn't the cadence of her words that held me now, but the substance and content. Suddenly, everybody else on the bridge was looking away into the town or deep into the waters below us, distancing themselves from what was being said. They'd even managed to shift away physically, leaving a widening moat of open space around the South African and me. It had started to rain and my hood was down, but I hardly noticed. I was lost somewhere else, transported into her story. She leaned against the side of the stone bridge as she spoke, her body was rigid yet strangely active. Though I was a few feet across from her, touching the cold stone to the flat of my back, she filled my field of vision. I'd suddenly lost all power of movement or speech. I was rooted in place as I was tossed into her past.

With sudden force, I was drawn into her dark story line, into sights from her world. She spoke of South Africa the only way she could, through her personal view of the land and her life there. Every word dripped with fear and chaos. Even in my absorbed state, I could tell the rest of the group was no longer listening. Maybe our group of fresh young pilgrims had finally betrayed our weakness as a Camino species. Each time the stories dove deeper into suffering, more drifted away. They evaporated from the drenched space until only the two of us remained in the darkening air around the bridge.

"I will never speak again of my country while I am on the trail." she uttered. From the finality in her tone, I believed her. Yet I wondered why she had chosen to share her open wounds with me.

"I have come to escape those thoughts." she said, thrusting each syllable into the night with force. I knew not what to say. Maybe there was nothing that could be said. The act of listening was all I had to offer.

I was shaken, thrown out of my own petty romantic dramas as we headed back into the center of the city in search of a bar. It was hard to find balance on the trail. Moments rushed at me in waves of intensity and then just as suddenly all was normal again. Would I learn how to soak it all in and not be too bogged down to miss the gift of each moment?

As we walked, the German fell even with me and introduced two French girls whom he'd met earlier in the day. The girls were students from Paris, both twenty years old and walking the trail from Pamplona to Burgos. They'd given themselves two weeks for this section. I felt it was a generous chunk of time considering the low number of kilometers, but they informed me this was their first time hiking, and they wanted to attack the trail at a leisurely pace. Neither of the girls had ever spent time outside of Paris, and I was amused to hear them talked about the trail as if it were a wilderness route, but then, I suppose compared to Paris, it was. Both were tall and lithe in an effortlessly chic way. The fair-haired one was slightly shorter but made up for the disadvantage with the graceful swing of her limbs. She was much more beautiful in motion like an unadorned fairy who was forced to keep both feet on the ground. Their clothes were understated layers of soft cotton in whites, and dusky grays with the outermost layers in protective black. Everything draped effortlessly and smelled of a sophisticated scent. If I hadn't seen their hiking boots, I would have been hard pressed to believe they'd traveled the same road as the rest of us. They still smelled of something other than sweat, and their clothes looked clean and dry. The only unattractive element to the duo was the matching set of cigarettes that dangled from their long boned fingers. The brunette's voice was deep and husky, while the other spoke softly, almost under her breath. I felt the fair-haired one was the more dynamic of the duo. Even though she wasn't traditionally beautiful and a bit shy, I could see the reaction she caused in others, especially men. Her delicate face and long limbs only added to the overall alluring damsel in distress quality. I was immediately intimidated and admiring at the same time. In all my imaginings, this was a breed of pilgrim I'd never seen coming. They were intoxicating and fascinating, yet slightly cold. They seemed to draw people to them and leave everybody else in the shadows.

Half way down the main street, the group at the front selected a bar and ushered us in. The space was small, with a long wide bar and many stools. Every soul in the place watched the TV in the corner with rapt attention. Even those being served drinks swiveled on their stools to keep an eye on the screen. The game had already begun, but we hadn't missed any goals or key offensive strikes. As soon as we corralled enough chairs and claimed our seats in the tight and smoky space, the French girls were ready for a second round of cigarettes. Hunting for a fresh pack and procuring a lighter, the girls were prepared to take full advantage of Spain's position as one of the last western nations to allow people to smoke in restaurants. I sat with my back to the TV for most of the game. Frankly, I was much more interested in the people around me than the match. The German sat directly across from me with the French girls squeezed together on his left. In between bouts of high volume yelling, I was able to gather a few key details about the girls' lives outside of the Camino bubble. Both were engineering students and lived in the center of Paris with their families. I was surprised to hear these most glamorous companions declare they still lived at home, for in the states the practice was considered the stuff of nerds, slackers and the anti-social. I'd spent time living on my parent's farm during and after college, but of all my friends, I was an exception to the norm. The girls explained they lived at home out of economic necessity and traded the ability to live in the city center with the downside of occupying their childhood bedrooms. They shrugged their shoulders with an air of resignation and explained they would most likely not be able to afford apartments in the city until they were married.

The German said little while flicking his attention back and forth between our ongoing conversation and the futbol match. He cheered at the right moments, took offense for any calls against Spain but also turned to our trio and smiled on a regular basis. He had one of those smiles that dominated his face and made him seem softer and sweeter as if he were more of a boy in a man's body than a pure adult. While he ate a Spanish omelet filled with gooey cheese, he returned to his charm mode, even more vibrant than at our first meeting.

I continued to ask more questions of the French girls, and our conversation veered towards their social life in Paris. I was almost rabid to gather details of their alluring life as young women in a beautiful city. Just because I preferred to live in the country didn't mean I wasn't voyeuristically curious about the life of an urban girl. They told tales of hip nightclubs, expensive restaurants and unpleasant French men. I was surprised to find both were outspoken in their distaste for French men and weren't afraid to explain exactly what caused offence. Perhaps to prove the point in a dramatic fashion, the fair-haired one shared the story of an evening when she'd gone to sleep in her family's apartment and awoken to find a friend of her parents climbing into her bed. The story was meant to demonstrate the arrogance and cavalier nature of French men, but her words fell into the pit of my stomach with a sickening thud. The story was clearly traumatic, yet she was willing to share this frank confession with virtual strangers in a crowded bar and wave her hand as if to dismiss the whole issue when my face fell into an expression of horror. I was taken aback and unsure how she really felt about the memory. Even as a stranger, I wanted to reverse the clock and defend her. For her sake, and maybe even for mine, I wished I could've time traveled to defend her as a nineteen year old. I wished I could've traveled to protected my nineteen year old self as well. And maybe my twenty three year old self too. I'd needed this current stronger, tougher version of myself to have shown up, and obviously so had she.

At this juncture in the conversation, I had to ask. I wanted proof that sweet girls like her could find a man that defied past experiences. I needed evidence of happy endings for girls who seemed to attract all the wrong kinds of men.

The brunette smiled and looked pointedly at the fair-haired one. She blushed slightly as she twirled an unlit cigarette in her fingers and let a bashful smile float across her face. From the look on the girls' faces and the way the fair-one seemed to disappear into some warm memory deep inside her, there was obviously a story to tell. The brunette gently nudged the fair-haired one with her elbow, as if prompting her to return to the present and tell me the tale. After a moment, the fair-haired one took a deep breath, looked me straight in the eye and told me she had fallen in love at first sight.

It was a story of an ordinary night at the end of an ordinary day, punctuated by an extraordinary moment. Several years ago, the fair-haired one had gone with her family to the opera, looked across her balcony to the far side of the theater and caught a man's eye. Even in a space filled with hundreds of other people, her eyes instantly locked with his. She confessed it had felt like being hit in the chest by a fast moving object shot from afar. Stunned, they had stayed locked together until the last note. When the show ended, the thread between them snapped, but the man had run through the theater looking for her before she was swallowed up by the crowds and evaporated into the night. And find her he did. They had been together since that moment over two years ago. She explained that people often misunderstood the story, believed it was a tale of outward attraction or desire, but for her it had been a moment of recognition, of something familiar and vital.

While the fair-haired one spoke, the German turned in his seat and relinquished his quest to give equal attention to both game and female company. The latter had finally won out as he listened to the story with rapt attention. As she spoke, I watched his eyes rest on her and remain there in an unwavering fashion. The rest of us had disappeared along with the game; only the fair-haired one held his focus. The eyes that had caught and held me several times over the course of the evening now glowed as she spoke. It was then I noticed how close he was sitting to her. They were just barely touching, and I sensed she wasn't even aware of the pressure of his shoulder resting against hers, but he was acutely conscious of every meeting cell. He leaned in towards her as if magnetized slightly by her presence. I'd been so distracted by my battles with the Vegan and struggles to decipher the German's mixed messages that I hadn't noticed he was sending a clear message, just not to me. I'd utterly failed to see he'd chosen this delicate French creature who already had love to be his romantic conquest. I was suddenly sure he would follow her tomorrow and all the days after that. As long as the trail allowed, he would follow unrequited affection in the form of this beautiful French girl. In this equation, there was no room for a rival. His affections were his to give freely, and he had given them to the fair-haired one.

At the very moment I slid the pieces into place, Spain scored, the crowd leapt to their feet and outside the skies opened with force. The rain fell fast and the streets flooded up to the threshold of the bar. I couldn't sit still anymore. I couldn't carry the conversation or hold the group together. I simply wanted to flee, go to sleep and disappear. I made for the door without even bothering to say goodnight and sprinted out into the rain. On my way back to the albergue, I came across a human traffic jam in the road. It was well past nine in the evening and darkness was falling behind the thick rain clouds. The narrow street was filled with groups of people in mourning. The women sobbed softly as their men huddle together and spoke in hushed tones, while children circled around in loops of innocent energy. The mourners were drenched in yards of black fabric now stained darker with rain. Clutching my arms around my ribs, I dashed by as silently as possible, skirting the churchyard while chills ripped through my body. I ran the rest of the way in the dark night. My shoes flooded with water, and my breath became ragged, but I only thought of escaping this day.

I woke the next morning at dawn. As I packed up my things in the dark room, I left my pink sleeping mat next to my bunk without a moment's hesitation. I was done carrying something I longed to leave behind, something that had no purpose. I was done with pulling people along energetically, willing them to share their time and their lives with me. I didn't go look for the German in the silent rooms of sleeping pilgrims. I saw none of the young pilgrims from the bar and didn't seek out the French girls. I put on my rain gear in the doorway, laced my shoes and secured my pack cover. Then I stepped out into the dark and wet city. The Italians followed me out the door, and without a word, we fell into our old configuration. I felt distant from their world as if we moved in parallel but disconnected tracks, yet they accepted me and wanted nothing in return. I couldn't tell them what disappointment and confusion had befallen me last night, but I garnered a shred of comfort from their sturdy presence. After the shifting sands of the night before, our slightly flawed trio was the support system being offered, and I accepted.

After leaving the center of Puente la Reina we crossed the Bridge of the Queen on the far side of the city and walked for an hour up the wrong road. The arrows vanished, and we found ourselves walking straight into the mouth of a four-lane highway. Each misstep of my stiff body and battered soul ached with a bitter sting. Retracing hard won steps dampened my spirits, but all I could do was right the ship and keep going forward.

ESTELLA

STAGE FOUR- 30.7K-19M
PUENTE LA REINA TO VILLAMAYOR

As Alberto, Alec and I climbed out of the valley of roaring vehicles, I checked my map for the number of kilometers to the village of Villamayor. I would now need to add three or four more kilometers to the day's total thanks to the forces of misdirection and confusion. The detour had been more than a psychological set back, it had been a physical one as well, and my legs were none too pleased with my navigation skills. The tiny town of Villamayor, thirty two kilometers from where we awoke, was Alberto's goal for the day, and neither Alec nor I put up a fight. I was simply relieved to be moving in his ambitious and quick flowing slipstream. To watch Alberto stride forward with an air of effortless determination was motivation enough to keep up my relentless pace. After a steep climb and a rough descent, the trail mercifully moved away from the highway and spread out into a network of vineyards that flooded right up to the edges of the large village of Cirauqui. The trail turned quickly from dry gravel path to dark and slippery mud. The ground was no longer brown and dusty but deep red and thick with water. Every pore of the land was suddenly full, and the trail became a slightly bowed groove that drew us into its wet center. After Cirauqui, the Italians conversed softly every once in a while, but mostly our trio moved in a silent formation up hills and across busy roads, through sleepy towns and into stretches of unending fields. The rain laden clouds shifted overhead and took turns unloading passing showers on our small band. Alec opened the wings of his umbrella, Alberto adjusted the bandana around his forehead to keep the rain out of his eyes, and I practiced the art of denial. I didn't want to admit the rain was minutes away from seeping through my every layer.

The small city of Estella, about twenty kilometers beyond Puente, promised a break from the weather and the blessing of open shops. As a small city, the place would have everything our group could hope for, but then, as pilgrims our needs were basic: food, water, shelter. And they were the basics for a reason. When fed and resting on a soft section of park grass, I would give in and float off in a daze of contentment. There was nothing to be done, no striving, just the happy practice of the pause.

About a kilometer outside of the city, we stumbled across a sign for a town called Lizzara. Both Alec and Alberto paused with furrowed brows, unaware we were scheduled to pass through any other towns before Estella. I quickly pulled my guidebook from my pack and hunted down the map. Low and behold, Lizzara and Estella were one and the same. This was Basque country, and here within its cultural walls, the Basque names for towns and cities took precedence.

The trail bisected several northern provinces in Spain, but Basque country was perhaps the most internationally known. Not only was it home to the infamous bull fights of Pamplona but also to a population hungry for independence. In the modern era, the province received lots of attention for its strong and often violent desire to be a separate nation. The Basques were more noteworthy than most other Spaniards with dreams of independence simply because they made their case with dramatic events such as car bombings and kidnappings. In the past, I'd been curious why the Spanish government didn't let the Basque country go if they desired independence so fervently. But the farther I traveled on the trail, the more I understood how much each culturally unique province wanted to break with the whole. The Basques and their separatist groups weren't unique; they were just putting on the biggest show and staging the noisiest fights. So letting the Basque region go might start an avalanche of departures. As we entered Lizzara, the space reverberated with the tension of being part of the whole while at the same time separate from it. There was even a push and pull of cultural identity in the simple lettering of a sign on the abandoned outskirts of town.

As we entered Estella, the trail curved along a river flowing straight through the center of town. From the path, we could see beautiful old homes perched on a hillside above the water and hear the roar of a dam. The streets of Estella wound into the old city like threads to the center of a web. We picked our way down a side street that opened up into a square with a large church. Across from the church, a bridge vaulted over the river with hundreds of tiny steps leading up its steep pitch. The church loomed above the water, its doors flung open to the street. The inside looked cool and hollow, while a large black horse stood peacefully next to the building in the tall grass of the churchyard. His glossy body shone in the bright sun as he bent to the work of cutting the grass, turning only briefly to look at us as we passed. The thin piece of twine mooring him to the side of the building dangled loose around his neck. He wasn't tied up against his will; the act of staying in the small yard was freely given. Even in relative stillness, there was a thrilling power rooted in the very muscles of the animal. The calm reflected in his sturdy frame did little to mask his physical purpose; this horse was built to move. Yet he waited for whomever he belonged to, lingered over a plot of sweet grass and chewed as the city buzzed around him. Evidently this stunning animal had mastered a few skills that still evaded me. It was the wait, the pause and the stopping that was the real exercise for me. I wondered if the people who had an intertwined destiny to my own on the trail were sauntering along behind me, and if so, how would I find enough strength to wait for them.

An hour after making our way into town, the three of us sat in a small park and ate cherries. I lay on the sidewalk and let my eyes close. The grass was still damp from the rain, but the hot black tarmac beneath me was blissfully warm. Alec found a spot in the park near the river, close enough to see the water moving and hear its quick progress. Just a stone's throw away, a small metal bridge crossed from the park to the land on the far side. A rambunctious group of young students huddled on the bridge engrossed in the task of repelling off the side of the structure. As each child began, the rest hung out over the edge hoping one of their classmates would be dropped a little too far and given a chilly dunking. They were loud and cheerful, chatting rapidly to one another, hooting and laughing even when encumbered by miles of rope. This gear reminded me we were, in fact, in a modern country. So much of the trail experience felt like going back in time to places untouched by modernity, but here were children working with high tech climbing devices. Here was a small piece of proof that the modern world was still out there even as we moved along the ancient trail.

The previous winter, I'd been the one learning how to rock climb, submerged into a whole new culture of movers. But it was a passing diversion that faded when my relationship with the rock climber ended. It had been yet another athletic pursuit tangled up in my search for love. I was most comfortable in motion and felt that was how people could know me at my most dynamic. Shy in almost every area of life, I found movement the one place I was a social butterfly, a confident player and a dynamic leader. Traditional athletics had been the warm up, but dance became the real universe of movement I belonged to. It was the language that flowed freely from me.

Now my physical language had become about steps and the moving life. It was my new athletic endeavor, and it didn't faze me to be thrown into the deep end. It suited my physical tailoring and easily wove into my strength at being solo with nothing but my thoughts for company. I hoped this daily meditation of footsteps might yield another romance, but it was in fate's hands. For now, the practice would have to be the gift.

The combination of a rest by the river and a belly full of ripe cherries was all the fuel I needed to face the remaining ten kilometers to Villamayor, but Alec and Alberto needed a bit more. The answer to their dragging energy came two kilometers outside of town at a fountain endowed with magical gifts for thirsty pilgrims. It was the most elaborate and lavish fountain I would encounter on the entire trip and the only one that caused grown men to cheer and leap around like jubilant children. Next to a much neglected font of clear fresh water was none other than an endless flow of rich pink wine. Camino history tells of many more of these 'fuetes de vino' during the middle ages, but this one on the outskirts of Estella was all that remained of a former pilgrim perk. The Italians were bent on sampling the local offering, so I took a break on the side of the trail. We didn't linger long, for they both knew that too much wine might seriously impair their ability to keep moving. A second round of naps wasn't in the cards if we wanted to make it to Villamayor before evening.

As I turned to go, I noticed a figure I recognized. The feral woman from Croatia sat on the bench beside the building, re-lacing her boots. I hadn't seen her since our meeting in Arre. We locked eyes for a moment, and I felt a chill rush across my flushed skin. She didn't speak, but stood up, shouldered her pack and took off down the trail. Her footfall hardly made a sound as she turned and retreated. She was wearing the same clothes from our first encounter: a black tee shirt and a pair of lightweight metallic overalls. Even in the sunlight, her skin was as translucent and white as rice paper. As in Arre, I was shaken by her strange presence. There was something ghostly about her. I couldn't pull my gaze away as I watched her dark form disappear up ahead. It was only after she'd melted into the horizon that I realized I'd never heard her speak. Though we all walked the same path, she felt separate as if she was on a different pilgrimage, on a darker more lonesome quest. I would never see her again and would always wonder if she wasn't a flesh and blood pilgrim like the rest of us but a ghost lost between the worlds, walking the trail again and again in endless loops until she could find her way to the other side.

After we left all traces of Estella behind, we entered a low valley full of vineyards. It took all afternoon to make our way through the mire of mud that swallowed every inch of the trail. It hadn't rained since early morning, and the sun was bright in a cloudless sky, but the ground refused to dry out. The pathway was dominated by mud, thick and red, the color of dried blood. It adhered to the soles of my shoes and weighted every step. My feet felt as if they'd gained a pound of mud, but every time I tried to kick off the clinging matter it returned with the next step. Advancing forward became a constant game of agility and balance as I aimed for the driest spots to place each step. As I tried to avoid swamping my low shoes with mud, I found I couldn't trust my footing. I was navigating impossible gullies where others had fought and lost. Alberto, on the other hand, left us in his wake as he moved with his usual speed and grace. The mud was no match for him; weather and water couldn't dampen his spirits. He walked in the middle of the trail with open sandals, unalarmed if his feet disappeared in the thick mire. Later, I would watch him wash his sandals clean with a cheerful smile on his face. Dry the next morning, his shoes and his feet would be none the worse for wear. It would take me two or three days to fully rid my sneakers of all the dirt and water they'd absorbed as I attempted to dance around the fields of mud.

The hours of mud wrestling dragged on. Most of the time I wasn't able to stay upright on the slippery ground; I often had to place my hand in the muck to catch myself. After several falls, my palms became caked in a thin layer of earth that turned dry and crusty. With every new fall came deeper irritation. I'd spent years practicing agility and balance, but I was no match for this new foe and found myself humbled by the wild sloppy pathway. The fight with the trail was more demanding than my weary body could contend with, and out of desperation, I picked up speed, hoping to get beyond this section. Adding speed to the mix didn't pay off, and I took an ungainly spill when my legs rushed up from under me in a moment of unexpected flight. I was at the mercy of gravity as my pack took me down, laying me out like a beetle caught on its back. The mud was warm and thick, but I didn't stay long it its grasp. I quickly scurried to my feet and looked around hoping no one had seen my fall. I still had a bit of pride left, even among strangers. Mud now coated both sides of my body and splattered every other exposed surface, but I was pretty sure no one witnessed my fall.

The pilgrims we passed didn't talk much, offering only polite "Hellos" or "Buen caminos." They, too, were absorbed with the battle at their feet. There was no escaping it, for we were boxed in on both sides by row of vines. Mid-afternoon as the three of us moved along a curved stretch of trail cut into the hillside, we noticed something a bit strange. A small section of the path was marked off with the bright yellow caution tape of the local police department, but there wasn't a soul about or any visible explanation. We slowed and drew to a halt at the edge of the roped off section. This very flat, very dry spot didn't look dangerous in the least. In fact, it looked downright pleasant. No mud, no incline. It was the definition of harmless. As Alec and I stood next to each other with perplexed looks, it dawned on us at the very same moment that if the land wasn't the issue, then perhaps it was something much worse than mud. Suddenly freaked out, I turned to Alec with a look of distress. What if something horrible had happened here? What if it had been the sight of injury or even worse, death? We gingerly stepped over the tape and walked through the spot but not without some trepidation.

Perplexed but with no answers at hand, we moved onward, and I assumed it would always remain a mystery. Little did I know that the very next day I would learn the full story of the yellow caution tape. The following morning, a man I walked with told me the story of discovering a woman trapped at that very spot, waist high in a mudslide. Apparently the banks beside the trail had collapsed and slid across the path during a heavy bout of rain. The woman, who was walking on her own, hadn't bothered to skirt the mudslide but had walked right into it and become horribly stuck. The man described in detail how he had worked for nearly an hour to try and get her out, but in the end, he'd needed another set of hands to pull her free.

As the man told me the story of the rogue slide and his valiant rescue, I couldn't help wondering what the universe was trying to tell this woman if she was caught in the land's grasp, and it wouldn't let her go? Maybe this was a not so veiled trail metaphor for the ways we can get stuck in negative situations. I'd been caught in such sloppy traps before, and it had taken all my strength to pull myself free of those places and relationships. If the trail was trying to speak to this woman through the medium of mud, I could guess what would happen if she continued to barrel through the sticky spots, rather than take another route. Though a cautionary tale, I felt there was a profound silver lining in the form of the rescuer. He was proof that even if we don't call for help or maybe even deserve it, help can arrive when we are most stuck and pull with all its might until we are free. I'd so often been the one up to my elbows in earth, tugging with all my strength that I forgot I didn't always have to be the rescuer. If I became stuck here on this winding trail, there just might be a person who would stick around and pull me out.

After the early part of the afternoon, the trail moved upwards through low hills, leading us alongside a large stretch of fields flush with the vibrant crimson blooms of thousands of flowers. Poppies had been sprinkled along the trailside since the first morning in the Pyrenees, but now they were in full riot.

The colors shone impossibly bright against fields of soft yellow and the blues of distant peaks. We passed derelict buildings covered in bright graffiti tags and the crumbling remains of Moorish well-houses that no longer supplied water. Walking along the gentle incline, I looked out across the valley. We were in a basin, a trough running forward with mountains rising up on either side. This channel had been worn through the earth eons ago and now allowed us to stay on gently sloping ground while the peaks off to either side leapt upward in mighty ridges. According to the guidebook, we wouldn't climb a mountain for another two weeks. It would be flat going for most of the trail, but the view of the land around the Camino was of a country of vast mountains and valleys often slipping by in my peripheral vision.

We passed through the last small village before reaching the day's destination. I noticed there was a small bar in the village but no food shop. This didn't bode well for what awaited us in Villamayor. We headed down and out of the village through an old farmyard with a sleeping dog tucked just inside the door of a large barn. He barely lifted his head as we passed; we were merely three more faces in an endless parade of pilgrims. Climbing a small incline, we paused to take our bearings. At the top of the rise, we could see ahead of us a lone peak with a structure perched on top. A cluster of buildings and a church spire clung to the base of the mountain. All logic indicated the cluster was Villamayor. We came to a collective stop as we looked across the valley at our night's destination. The majestic sight of the mountain against the sky and the building perched on its zenith caused us all to stare in wonder.

After a moment, Alberto turned to Alec and spoke. I continued looking forward, strangely absorbed by the sight. Suddenly Alec laughed and turned to me. In broken English, he struggled to find the words he need to explain that Alberto had a question for me. I waited with patient curiosity as Alec paused for a moment.

He pointed at me, " Very fast." then he said. "He ask, where you keep your wings." he continued. "He ask if at end of trail you show him your wings."

Alberto was smiling a large wide smile that shone out through his eyes. He was bursting with the joy of this life, and in the midst of his own journey, he saw power and beauty in my walking skills. I was suddenly blushing and more than a little bit flattered. I was moved by this sudden image. I would have liked nothing more than to prove his imagination right and be able to display a physical arsenal that included a pair of secret wings tucked in the fold of my shoulder blades. Maybe I would grow such wings over the course of this trail, maybe the image was a magical prophecy. Nonetheless, I'd proven myself to these men, these true walkers, and they had accepted me as one of their own. I dipped into a low bow in Alberto's direction and nodded my head. The end of the trail felt so far away, it was beyond comprehension. All I could do in that moment was keep up as Alberto took off down the trail at top speed.

As we drew closer to the shadow of the mountain, the steep slope filled the view, and the details of the building perched on its peak grew sharp. The walls had fallen into disrepair in several places, creating large puncture wounds in the fortress, but the majority of the building was sound. Yet when the clouds opened and light hit its stones, the building's rundown appearance was eclipsed by an aura of enchantment. In that moment, its former life was revealed. Its long faded identity as a place of power and splendor broke free of its current incarnation. I couldn't keep my eyes from the castle. I felt as if all the air was sucked from my lungs. I couldn't deny that I felt strongly for this place, that I'd maybe even known this place before. I knew its view out over the plains below. I knew its walls and their sturdy strength. I even knew where to find the old road that wound up the mountain to its door. For no logical reason, I was submerged in a deep sense of recognition. This had been my place and to pass under its shadow was to collect a piece of myself I'd left here long ago. The jolt of recognition held no answers, but caused a buzz of energy to flow through my system for hours afterwards. I'd been connected to this place once, and maybe here was my proof that not just this one isolated mountain, but this whole ancient trail had welcomed me before. I felt I was looking upon a familiar sight after a long absence and seeing again a place from my distant and buried memory. Images and emotions drifted through me like dreams just forgotten at the edge of sleep.

VILLAMAYOR

When we arrived in Villamayor, it was deathly still. I wasn't sure if the town was even inhabited, but as I rounded the corner, I noticed a man smoking outside the albergue. He was looking down in a contemplative fashion but turned his face towards us as he heard our advance. Alberto drew even with me, and Alec was only a pace behind us as the man snubbed out his cigarette and invited us in. From the outside, the albergue looked quaint and cozy, yet upon entering I was overcome with a completely different impression. The space was a single room broken into sections by cheap whitewashed cardboard walls and lit with a dangling row of florescent lights. I peered into the back to assess the sleeping quarters and found little more than several sagging bunk beds and mattresses flung on a dingy floor. As my eyes scanned the space, the man cheerfully took a seat at a small desk in the entrance and began checking us in. Across from the desk was a bit of open space cluttered with a clothes rack and a stack of washing tubs. Several sheets of newspaper were arranged by the side of the door, awaiting the muddy boots of incoming guests. There was no kitchen, and once I located the bathrooms, I found the stalls had no ceilings and virtually no privacy. Everything was worn thin, grimy and dark.

Though I stood in the doorway trying not to bolt into the road and take my chances sleeping in a field, the man welcomed us in as if we'd arrived at a five star hotel. As he listed off the "features" of the place, he explained that volunteers ran the albergue as a "donativo." This meant there was no set cost for the night's stay, but each pilgrim was encouraged to pay what he or she could. Most pilgrims treated a donativo as they would a normal albergue and paid the going rate, while others, usually cash strapped youngsters, would toss in a few coins and relish the chance to save a bit on lodging.

As the hospitalero stamped our passports, he explained more about the nature of the albergue. As he spoke, the state of the facilities began to make sense. Throughout peak season, the people who worked here changed on a weekly basis. Each caretaker did the best he or she could with what meager donations the place pulled in, but this was a space that belonged to no one. It lacked the energy and care of family run albergues or municipals with motivated teams of employees.

After retrieving my passport, I walked into the back room to claim a bunk. If possible, the beds were worse than they looked at first glance. But the quality of the bedding was really a secondary concern next to the quality and proximity of my roommates. Half of the mattresses were lined up in a row against the far wall and pushed together to form one long bed built for five. The only safe haven from the communal sleeping trough was a rickety set of bunks tucked behind the door. I quickly claimed the bottom bunk and reserved the other for either Alberto or Alec. I knew one of them would take the position as the front line of protection, and I felt thankful I could count on their guardianship.

As I placed my sneakers outside to dry, I noticed the afternoon was still hot, maybe even hot enough to dry some washing if I felt energized to procure a tub and slosh my things around. I wasn't sure what else I would do before the sun went down. I was painfully aware of the void in my life. With just the three of us in residence at the albergue, I had at least five or six hours to fill before I could crawl into my sleeping bag for the night. Having lively conversations with the Italians wasn't possible, studying my guidebook could only distract me for so long and the shower experience didn't look like one I would want to draw out. Yet I needed a good scrub all the same, for splatters of fresh mud mingled with sheets of dried earth to form a thin layer of dust across my entire body. My sleeping bag and fresh set of clothes wouldn't thank me if I punted and tossed personal hygiene to the wind.

Even though I'd showered the night before in Puente La Reina, I was amazed at how much dirt I'd accumulated. The multiple falls I'd taken as I crossed the mighty mud fields had increased the impression of dirtiness, but it was the grime accumulated from crossing roads and sitting on sidewalks that bothered me the most. Mud was used in beauty treatments; city dirt wasn't. As I stepped into the roofless stall not three feet from the bunkroom, I realized the shower, with its egregious lack of privacy, might actually offer me something other showers of late hadn't: a bright space in which to take stock of the damage walking had wreaked on my body.

Shedding all my layers, I was struck by several new sights. The skin over my hipbones was marked in deep blue crescents along the now boney ridge of my pelvis. Where the skin wasn't swimming in a sea of purple blue, small red cuts, like those collected after a run-in with a thorn bush, marked the edges where my pack met my skin. This blooming center of chaos and trauma was where my bag rested against my body, placed its weight against the arcs of my frame and chewed me up. I'd known I would be battered by the endless movement forward, but there was something upsetting about the pain inflicted on this sheltered part of my body. I was use to my legs getting cut, bruised and banged around, but this was different. This walk was now reaching every corner of me.

What else could I have expected? Even when in prime condition, dancing hours a day, the bruises, cuts and scars had a way of rising to the surface. During my dance training, I'd often felt weak but strong, bruised but fearless. Ironically the more beleaguered I was, the more resilient I felt. To push aside markers of weakness and still keep going meant nothing could truly fell me. And during my years of dance training, I found a strange comfort in being able to see the physical proof of what I already felt about the extremes of my life. The bruises were merely outward signals of internal pressure, signs that my rollercoaster relationship with the Dancer Man was real and intensely felt by all of me.

Now in the small shower cell, I could feel myself cataloging these fresh wounds the same way. They were physical markers of the energy and intensity with which I'd flung myself into this journey. No one could claim I wasn't pushing myself; all I would have to do is peel back my clothes and show them the proof. The bruises were evidence the land was taking a toll on my body, changing all my surfaces and maybe even bringing about a revolution that would sift all the way through me. Perhaps I really would be a different person, inside and out, when this was done: a fresh person, a less wounded person, a lighter person. Yet to all physical madness, there was an edge, and I worried I might be pushing my muscles and bones just a bit too hard. How would I know? Would something have to break, snap or rip before I knew my limits? As much as I sickly relished proof of physical endurance, I didn't want to seriously injure myself on a trail defined by ever-forward motion.

During my dancing years, it had taken me months of small agonies before I met my breaking point. By then all I'd needed was a slight bit of force from my dance partner, the emotional stress of a doomed love affair and no place for my ankle to come down but sideways. My body made only a small popping sound of distress, and I continued to dance on my ankle for another two hours, reasoning if I could endure the pain then all would be well. I believed I could push through the injury and reach a new level of toughness, but I was fooling myself. Later that night, I sat down to rest and was unable to walk when I stood up an hour later. It would be over a month before I was able to stand on my own again.

I feared an injury like that would come if I didn't pay closer attention to the signals. If I let my infatuation with being extreme take hold, I might have to face something I was unable to overcome. So as I scrubbed soap into the small cuts across the middle of my torso, I was thankful I had nothing more severe to be concerned about. I needed to watch the line, ride the edge with precision and hold real injuries at bay.

Once clean, I dozed in the sun outside of the albergue and listened absently to the Italians banter back and forth. An ice cream car rolled through town with loud music blaring from its speakers. Alberto bought a tall cone filled with dark chocolate ice cream. Too weary to be hungry, I tried not to look at my watch as I willed it to be night.

After several hours, the light started to fade, and the Italians organized to go to a restaurant. I decided to join them, to escape the dark confines of the albergue and find out if there were any other English speaking pilgrims in residence. We made our way towards the only bar in town which didn't usually serve food but made an exception for pilgrims. I assumed it would be a sit down family style meal better know as "the pilgrim dinner." I'd already heard many tales about the boondoggle that was the pilgrim dinner but had yet to partake in one.

The pilgrim dinner had long been a fixture on the trail, and in the past was recognized as a high point of Camino life, a way for a pilgrim to eat a hearty quantity of food inexpensively. The modern pilgrim had to be a bit more wary of this institution. I'd been told by countless pilgrims that the quality of the meal nowadays tended to be extremely variable. Each time a pilgrim chose to go for the pilgrim dinner, it was a roll of the dice. Only a few days in, I already felt the gamble wasn't worth it. I'd seen too many unappealing and steeply priced meals placed before a pilgrim after they'd waited for hours with shrunken bellies and aching hunger. I was inclined to cook for myself or compile a picnic in the late afternoon, fueling up before darkness fell and sleep called to me. Some nights, the thought of waiting three or four hours for food felt like torture, and it would only add insult to injury if the fare placed before me was worse than something I could have compiled myself. Despite my strong opinions on the matter, the pilgrim dinner remained popular among some who walked the trail; this group was mostly ravenous men who liked to sit down to a large glass of wine and a heaping portion of food regardless of taste or time of day.

As we approached the bar, I noticed most of the buildings along the main road were new and tightly built with a strange energy clinging to every surface. It was seven in the evening, yet there wasn't a soul about. A small park next to the bar held a set of swings glistening in the falling light with monkey bars driven deep into the earth. The space felt forlorn, and I realized I hadn't heard or seen evidence of a single child in this desolate town.

The door to the bar hung open, and as we drew closer, noise flowed out from the space into the street. Stepping over the threshold behind Alec and Alberto, we crossed from the bleak atmosphere in the streets into a startlingly different world. The room was dingy, cluttered and very narrow but hummed with the vibrant energy of a village sized family. We'd just stepped out of a haunted neighborhood into the belly of a family kitchen. A cluster of women sat at the bar with plump babies tucked in the wide crooks of their arms while a pair of old men sat by the window engrossed in a game of cards. But these commanding elders were no match for the central hub of the kitchen, and all eyes immediately gravitated towards the woman behind the bar. The small sturdy barmaid was the star of the show. Though her legs seemed as solid and rooted as tree trunks, she was amazingly animated and moved about with dexterous speed. Not only was she moving fast, but she was also running several conversations at once, tending to customers and family in the same breath. She served drinks while slinging babies over her shoulder, scolding the older men playing cards and directing the activities of a two year old who sat on the floor cradling a well loved doll. The door hadn't shut behind us before she was around the bar, seating us along a large family style table. It only took a moment to ascertain that the bar was actually her home, and most of its current patrons weren't paying customers. The women rocking the babies varied in age, but one was clearly the grandmother. Her arms were like a rotating door, holding one baby for a moment, then trading it off to let the two year old crawl up her knees, soon returning the toddler to the floor to place a third baby against her shoulder. I wasn't sure how the withered old men deep in their own pursuits were connected to the bevy of women, but neither group concerned themselves much with the other. Surprisingly there were no young or middle-aged men in the bar. The fathers of the many offspring were elsewhere, maybe beyond the town limits making a living to bring home to this warm circle hidden away in the cold town.

Despite the constant activity and plethora of babies, the women never let their conversation slow or break. They all seemed to speak at the same time in loud voices, waving their free hands in the air to prove their points. In the past few days, I'd noticed Spanish women had an intense persona they brought out into the world, especially the madres and abuelas. Just the day before, I'd stumbled across what I believed was a fight between two elderly women in the dooryard of a shop. As one woman gestured wildly and raised her voice, the other shot back with her own hand signals. I was sure I was about to see a couple of demure abuelas break into a cat fight and drawn blood, but just as I turned to go, I heard one woman laugh and bid the other farewell. As one went into the shop and the other passed me with a kind smile, I realized I hadn't stumbled across a fight, but rather a friendly gossip session. It was the high volume and aggressive tone that had thrown me, and later I would discover that if I didn't listen closely for the meaning of the words, most Spanish women sounded as if every conversation was a prelude to a fight.

With the chatter at top volume, I had no trouble hearing every word flowing between the women at the bar, but my brain was struggling to pick up any words I recognized. I wondered whom they were talking about. Was it absent talk or juicy gossip? Were they moaning about the good for nothing men by the door or recounting all the naughty things their older children were up to? The more I strained to listen, the more I failed to gather any clues. I could feel my memory hunting through lists of old vocabulary, and then it stopped as I realized this group wasn't speaking Spanish. Perhaps they were speaking Basque? This seemed logical, yet I couldn't say I had any idea what Basque sounded like. My confused look drew attention from the only other pilgrim sitting at the far end of the table. He was an older man with lean features and a pair of round spectacles that made him look rather scholarly. He was more than vaguely familiar. I had a suspicion I'd passed him walking in the last few days. As I caught his eye, he leaned forward with his elbows on the faded oilcloth. I asked him if he knew what dialect the crowd around the bar was speaking. He kindly told me they were an immigrant family speaking Portuguese. By entering the bar we had left Spain and the Basque country all together. We were now in a small tight-knit satellite, a family sized Portuguese refuge.

After only a few days in Spain, I'd learned new things about the way language worked in the tight confines of Europe. I'd seen first hand the beguiling way dialect could shift suddenly at all the many borders and shared communication could turn on imaginary lines. I'd crossed from France to Spain hardly aware I'd traversed from one distinct nation and language to another. For my body, it had been just one step in a long day through mountains, yet it altered the culture around me in profound ways. The farther I got down the trail, the more I found myself among people for whom language was more fluid than my narrow experience. As an English speaker, I had an unfair edge in most of the world, for English has been given a status unlike any other language in the global community. And this was true on the Camino as well. In this culturally diverse group, the default language was most often English, and this always worked to my benefit. Most of the Europeans I met spoke at least a bit of English, but I had no French, Dutch, Portuguese, German, or most notably Italian. Having grown up across the ocean from these intertwined nations, it had been permissible to learn just one extra language as a child. Yet the Europeans I met moved in a multi-lingual world and were more prepared for it. I could tell from his tight enunciation that the pilgrim at the far end of the table wasn't a native English speaker, even though he used an extensive vocabulary and spoke with little hesitation. My new acquaintance was German by birth, but had lived both in Scotland and Spain for many years of his life. The German Scottish Spaniard reached his hand across the table to shake mine and immediately dove into conversation. I felt my whole body release the tension it had been carrying all evening, and within moments I felt swept out of the boredom that now haunted my time with the Italians. This dull mood around our trio was even more frustrating because it wasn't of our choosing. If we could have found a common language, I would have delighted in talking with Alec and Alberto all day, but we could do little more than communicate the basics. And I had a deep seated belief that if I could have, I would have found Alberto a steady and wise counsel. But for now, I talked a bit with the German Scottish Spaniard and listened attentively to his stories of living in a Scottish new age community called Findhorn. As soon as he spoke the name of the place, it was as if a bell rung through my nervous system. I didn't know where I knew this place from or why it caused such a reaction, but I longed to know more. As I waited for an opening to ask further questions, another pilgrim entered and took one of the open seats between us. He lay a bulky black helmet down on the table as he pulled out his chair and settled into it with a sigh of relief. The new member of our party was a middle aged Spaniard with dark spiky hair still dressed in his skintight bike outfit. I had a feeling he was so eager for the pilgrim dinner he'd delayed showering or even changing his clothes. Those minor details were clearly secondary to refueling. My theory was confirmed when I looked down to the floor and noticed he still wore his bike shoes with their metal clips. As he pulled his chair into the table and tucked a napkin in the collar of his shirt, his shoes clicked on the linoleum, making him sound like a tap dancer warming up for a show.

Thankfully the meal came and went, devoured in the midst of endless talk. I'd eaten little so Alberto sliced the apple he was given for dessert into small pieces and placed them on my plate. He was trying to coax me to eat a bit more, and the kindness in the gesture was comforting. We may not have been able to speak, but we could connect, even if in a limited way. As we walked out the bar and its hidden bubble of human activity and warmth, I said my goodbyes to the biker. His trip would move at a speed double my own and for that reason our paths would never cross again. A young Italian I recognized from Puente la Reina arrived for food as we left the building. His eyes caught mine as he held the door open for us, and his sweet face broke into a smile. After the door swung closed behind him, I turned into the night feeling discouraged I didn't possess words he would understand. Even with such physical closeness on the trail, words or the lack of them, would keep us from knowing one another. He looked like a kind soul, but I'd never know for sure. All because his symbols of life, his letters and his words, were shuffled, reordered, spoken and constructed in a cosmos I didn't understand, we were mute ships passing in the night.

Once we arrived back at the deserted albergue, I unfurled my sleeping bag and formed a makeshift pillow from a shirt. The volunteer was gone for the night and though some of the other mattresses were occupied with gear, no one else was about. This gave me a head start. If I could plunge into a deep sleep before the chorus of snoring began, I might be able to stay in the deep blackness of sleep through the night.

At the early hour of six the albergue was abruptly brought back to life by the sounds of Handel's Messiah and clear directions to get out ASAP. And up I rose. Dragging my limbs back to life in the half-light, I tried to shake myself awake. The mornings were always disorienting, and the darkness never helped. My mind filled with grumpy questions like why exactly I was spending my vacation getting up so early and why was waking before first light so necessary. The questions only lasted so long for once up, I couldn't deny my desire to leave this town. Stuffing my sleeping bag back into its pack, I noticed Alberto was gone, his bed vacant and forlorn in the grey light. I quickly glanced across the room and was relieved to see Alec was still fumbling with his pack. Half a safety net was better than none.

LOS ARCOS

STAGE FIVE- 39.9K-24.8M
VILLAMAYOR TO LOGROÑO

With slight wincing steps, Alec joined me in the dark street and indicated with a delicate wave of his hand that it was time to go. Mud immediately reclaimed the surfaces of my sneakers as we stepped back onto the trail. It looked like another day of intimate encounters with Spanish soil lay ahead. The sight of the vineyards was breathtaking. There was a settled and wizened beauty to the rows of vines clinging to one another as if unwilling to survive without each other. But the edges of the immaculate fields had been worked, turned and unsettled by human tread and the sweeping hand of rain. This left the trail slipping one direction or another, tilting and flowing like a riverbed pushing us at its whim. It was like surfing on dry land and required muscles in my legs that had long been neglected. My gaze returned to my feet as I picked my way down the slope of the trail following Alec's lead.

This was day five. I had yet to wake to a clear sky, but this morning the east was breaking free of the last lingering clouds and rupturing warm yellow light over the land. I was so accustomed to grey and stormy skies that I stopped, turned back and marveled at the sun warming the surface of my face and arms. The land was no longer cloaked in a dull light that dimmed its brilliance. Everything alive now shone. It was barely eight in the morning. The day was both young and old at the same time.

After a couple of hours, the trail wound away from the swampy vineyards and into a long series of fields. As Alec walked beside me, I could tell something was seriously wrong with his foot. He dragged it slightly with each step and what weight he put on it was done gingerly. I didn't dare ask. He appeared to be in enough emotional turmoil without my useless prodding. Silence was our familiar medium and built on unspoken knowing. He knew it was bad, I knew it was bad and he knew I knew. Many of the injuries that befall the typical pilgrim are new and unfamiliar to them. Quirky tweaked nerves, mysterious strains or strange inflammations arrived like uninvited strangers. This walk was an unknown quantity. There was no real way to know how our bodies would hold up over the course of eight hundred kilometers. A test drive wasn't possible; everybody had to dive in headfirst and deal with the fall out. Being young and in good physical condition certainly helped, but here was Alec, twenty-five, fit and agile, tangled up in an injury he didn't understand and couldn't fix. Yet he didn't grumble or complain as his gait grew labored and his pace slowed. He was working so hard to stay on pace and not show any weakness that at first I hardly noticed, but soon a sizable distance had grown between us. He lost ground with each step, falling farther and farther behind. He didn't ask or expect me to wait for him, and there was nothing either of us could do about falling off rhythm and drifting apart.

After the trail veered away from the vineyards, it dove into a basin filled with fields of grain. The warm colored fields swept up the side of the valley floor and licked at the edges of the mountains. The vast space was defined by the change in color from one type of grain to another, while the mountains framed the edges of the wide space and ushered the trail forward down the valley.

I could see nothing but land ahead. There were no homes, sheds, plows, livestock, people, cars or bikes. The ground was clear of human imprint, untouched by movement or noise. I'd doubted a view could top the lookout above Pamplona, but this one did, and something about the sheer dimensions of what I could see before me was daunting. I'd walked through tracks of land as large but had never confronted their vastness so directly. The wide expanse of land and sky caused a physical reaction. As I stood on the precipice, a rush of wonder swept through me followed quickly by another gust of isolation that tightened my gut with one swift spasm. Both came quickly and coupled like the two halves of a breath. How could I feel such conflicting emotions so intensely? How could space make me feel connected and utterly alone all at once?

As I pushed forward, I discovered I wasn't entirely alone in this seemingly barren land. The open air was churning and alive with birds neither large nor brightly colored. Even in a dour shade of grey with delicately boned bodies no bigger than my palm, they were the entertainment, energy and pulsing life of the forlorn trail. In a constant buzz of activity, they twirled, leapt and balanced on the slender stalks of grain. Their small bodies rushed through the air in effortless arcs, twisting across my line of sight. I lost track of the world at my feet and even forgot about the easy swing of my legs and arms. I was a voyeur in the world of flight. When they changed direction, there were no signals given, no commands trumpeted and no leaders among their ranks. They flocked with effortless ease, assured of every move and every member. The birds were specks of movement in the massive canvas, but together their noise carried over the echoing space. As they swirled around me like a windstorm, I was encircled by a funnel of wings.

In that moment, I was jealous of the life of a bird. For even in this empty early morning field, they had a community. I was envious of their lightness, of their unspoken bonds. I longed to find the human equivalent of a flock, a community that would claim me, pull me into the pack with a dynamic swoop. The Spanish word for pilgrim is peregrino, a linguistic cousin to peregrine, the name for a falcon. As a pilgrim, I felt certain I was moving beyond the bounds of ordinary human life, but would I be able to form bonds like a bird and never need to move alone in the empty spaces of life again? Would my speed of foot be like flight, drawing me forward until I finally encountered my flock?

The birds and their comfortable ease with space reminded me of the thrill I'd felt in the moment before worry crashed in. There were always two sides to being tossed into the void. Even today, I was unhindered yet also unprotected. I was strong, but I was weary of my own company. As a way of taming the worry leaching into my system, I focused on arrows and way markers. I was now at least a kilometer ahead of Alec and didn't want to make a wrong turn down a side trail and find myself lost. I was again testing the limits of my independence. Could I go forward with trust that I wouldn't get lost? Would I be able to keep going if I never saw the Italians again? Alberto's disappearance and Alec's blossoming injury might leave me no other choice.

About an hour later, after a series of turns that took me towards another seemingly empty valley, I crested a rise and was saved. As I looked down on the outskirts of Los Arcos, I jumped in the air with a triumphant shout. This was the oasis that had eluded me all morning, the destination I'd walked towards blindly with little or no sign of encouragement. This was the town that hid until the last moment and was unable or unwilling to peek out from behind the topography to cheer pilgrims onward. Without a soul in sight, I did a small celebration dance and pumped my fists in the air for good measure. This was dry land after ocean, a clue I hadn't lost my way.

The fields ended with an abrupt halt, and the trail became hard concrete below my feet. I desperately hoped some kind of food shop would be open. My meager breakfast was now multiple hours and many kilometers behind me. The arrows grew sparse, and I forced my wandering attention to refocus. With only the occasional yellow arrow painted on door jams and street curbs, I picked my way into town.

Due to Los Arcos' tight collection of towering old buildings, the full light of day had yet to reach its cobbled streets. I'd been through other towns with constricted roads, but this place redefined the word narrow. The walls appeared to always be at a slant, creeping closer across alleyways as if funneling me down a long channel. They were made of imposing thick stone, weathered and rough. As I brushed up against a wall, I found it cold and damp. Wooden doors with faded paint punctuated the endless façade. They were sturdy and battened down with heavy locks. Even the smell of the chilled air clinging to the walls spoke of forgotten spaces and generations long gone. Very little broke the illusion that I was moving through another century. Ducking under dirty archways, I found myself in a den of thieves, immersed in an aura of shadow and mysterious peril. The town's charms had made this place the dominion of bandits, and the imprint of their activities remained here like a trapped echo. No car horns, electric lights or people marred the scene of the timeless alley. As the roadway took me down farther into the bowels of the city, a lone scrawny cat came out to mark my progress.

My eyes darted back and forth along the shadowed street as the alley began to grow very tight. It appeared the buildings might close ranks entirely, but at the last moment I found an opening just wide enough for my body. Squeezing through, my pack scraped both walls. Out I popped onto a wide street with modern stores, a cluster of men at work on a storefront and a set of motorbikes propped against an alley wall. Moving across the tight threshold with a single step, I was back in the modern world.

It only took a moment for my hunger to demand I refocus all my energy on locating some food. At this point, I would have eaten the strange salty meats dangling from the ceiling of a butcher shop. Anything to halt the grumbling of my insides. I picked up the thread of the arrows once again unconvinced I would find anything open so early, but near the end of the main road, there was a small shop with a sign dangling off the front window and a partially open door.

I could hear a woman moving about inside, singing to herself. Just the sound of her voice reignited my hope, and I pushed the door open. The shop was a long skinny rectangle with a tightly packed wall of goods and a doorway into a back room. Though seemingly unimportant, the door to the back was the key feature of the space, for it was the gateway into the kitchen where some diligent baker was making fresh bread and sweet pastries. The doorway was the reason for the shop's existence; everything else was secondary. I gave the shelves, dominated by dry cereals, biscuits, large tins of tomatoes, beans and slimy white asparagus little more than a glance. Even the crates of fresh fruit lining the wall were only slightly distracting. The real magic was born through the backdoor and lived in open trays behind the counter. The whole wall had been converted into a series of bins lined with parchment paper and each quadrant was home to a different pastry. Some were dipped in chocolate, others were dusted with powered sugar and stuffed to the gills with creamy filling. Several were compact biscuits of dense almond flour while others were high stacks of light and fluffy layers. They were all fresh, seeping smells of warm milk and sugar hot from the oven. The drab shop was no longer just another hole in the wall in a small town but a landmark of mouth-watering smells and stunningly sweet tastes. The sheer magnitude of choice left me dumbstruck, but I had no time to waste. My mouth was already salivating at just the sight of such trail fuel. How was I ever going to choose? I stood in front of the counter for several minutes as the woman behind it smiled patiently. I could weigh the pros and cons of chocolate versus vanilla crème all day, but a decision had to be made. In broken Spanish, I asked for a small assortment that attempted a range and depth of flavors, but in truth I was far from picky. I needed the sugar rush almost more than the taste. As a way of apologizing to my body in advance for the sugar hemorrhage soon to come, I also bought two apples. Later I wouldn't regret passing up the other fresh fruits and vegetables, but I would regret not buying a few more pastries. I'd selected only a modest amount, but what felt like a success in the shop would later feel like a rookie mistake.

The woman hummed as she rang up what I owed and placed the goods in a plastic bag. After paying, I tied the plastic bag to the outside of my pack, stuffed the apples into my side pockets and stepped back onto the street. Having the treats dangling off the side of my bag would assure that I could access them at any time. I found it strangely difficult to stop when I was on my own, even to eat or drink. Maybe it was linked to the internal motor that kept spinning me forward and whispered of people just over the horizon. If I could gain time by eating and walking simultaneously then I might find what lay ahead just that much sooner. Momentum was a powerful force, and it was near torture to sit down, rest and take a true break then get up and start my engine from zero all over again. The rest of Los Arcos moved by in a blur. It wasn't long before I was spit back out of civilization and into the endless kilometers of wide-open land. The rhythm of walking took over, and I let it pull me forward.

As the trail fell away behind me, the sun shifted overhead like the steady hands of a clock. I moved through more tracks of crop-laden fields and wound alongside a two-lane road. I walked for an hour with an older German gentleman from Madrid. As soon as I introduced myself, he proudly declared that his beloved mother shared my name, a happy coincidence that lit up his whole face and brought a little skip to his step. Though shared names were the full extent of our bond, we fell into easy conversation anyways. Before long, we were chuckling about all the little absurdities of trail life, discussing the manic ways some albergues shook pilgrims awake at the crack of dawn and how protective bike pilgrims were of their elaborate and copious piles of equipment.

The trail was now very dry and exposed as it ran alongside the busy road. The rusty dirt kicked up dust with each step we took. How dramatic it was to begin the day with slurping mud and end it with clouds of dust flooding my lungs. I pulled my hat on to keep the hot sun off my face while the German gentleman told me his story. He had walked the trail three times at different stages of his life and was utterly convinced that one could be a pilgrim and still remain civilized. He swore by the practice of eating a late breakfast, reading the local paper and waiting a half hour to digest before walking. I imagined strict adherence to these practices had been the key to his longstanding love affair with the trail. Yet without factoring in these habits, the three walks must have been shockingly different. The trail of a young man tasting the freedom of exploration for the first time was a far cry from the trail of a middle-aged bank manager who needed a moment for himself in the busy chaos of raising kids. And now here he was in his late sixties, in a new place altogether, returning to an old lover who had known all his many faces, one who had watched him grow. I wondered what she had in store for him this time. Had each trail held a different note, been defined by a different word, been painted in a distinct color? I could imagine there was little this trail couldn't do except remain the same, offer the same gifts, and deliver the same characters. Change was in her very blood.

An hour into our conversation, the trail traversed a busy road, and we were forced to make a mad dash across its wide lanes. As I sprinted to the other side, I noticed a wooden cross down off the edge of the road. The German gentleman arrived at my side panting a bit and drew a white handkerchief from his pocket. As he dabbed his forehead, I asked him if he knew what the cross was for. He glanced over, and his eyebrow drew together as if he was trying to remember something he'd once read. I was waiting for an old tale, a mythic Camino legend, but after he gained his breath again, he explained that it was for a pilgrim who had been struck by a car and died while crossing this intersection. Looking closer, I realized the cross was neither weathered nor worn by time. This was no history footnote; the woman had died just a few years before. This was no ancient battle, but fresh Camino history.

At the next small village, the German gentleman stopped to visit an octagonal church. I wished him luck on the rest of his journey and continued onward. The sky grew dark and molted with grey clouds. The light shifted, and the wind picked up. I could feel a storm creeping into the fabric of a day that had otherwise been pleasant and warm. I walked along the shoulder of a busy road, keeping my head down as the cars rushed past. The trail had been carved alongside the road, but due to recent rain, it was clogged with standing water. I was no longer sure what to expect from the land. Walking on the road with all its hazards was the best option, but after several hair-raising kilometers, I heaved a giant sigh of relief as the trail dipped away from the road. Once off the tarmac, the trail cut through scrubby land, cluttered with low lying trees and clusters of sharp rock.

I passed an older couple resting in a bit of shaded earth and a duo of young Irish women lying on rocks with their faces to the sun. I was delighted when I came across these girls and immediately stepped off the trail to introduce myself. They were from Dublin and in their mid twenties. After a brief hello, I told the friendly women I would look out for them in the next albergue. They smiled politely and waved as I took off down the trail. I promptly forgot their names, but it would matter little for I never laid eyes on them again. They wouldn't be in the albergue later that night, and I would soon forget we'd even met. It was strange how some fellow pilgrims, like the Italians, took root while the lovely Irish lassies simply vanished and were never seen again. Why was this? More to the point, how was this? The trail only had one direction, and feet only had so much speed to offer. It seemed there were a myriad of factors at work with the inflow and outflow of people on my journey. I couldn't begin to understand the delicate instrument of timing, and this scared me. How was I ever to find those I was meant to find if so much could go wrong or differently than planned? The margins of error felt painfully tight, and I wasn't sure I was ready to admit I was helpless to the flow of the trail. I still clung to the slightly manic idea that my speedy legs and crazy schedule could get me to the kind of life I wanted here. My pace was working for me as I strode towards the village of Vianna, but I wasn't convinced this would last.

I kept pushing onward. I assumed some of my extra energy was due to the sugar charging through me or maybe even the lightness of being on my own. I moved with unexpected speed and sureness. The city of Logroño was my goal for the night, but I didn't know if I could get there. I'd yet to really test my limits and truly see how far I could go in one day. I crested a hill and saw the village of Vianna in the distance. Arriving at the edge of the town marked my day's total at twenty-nine kilometers, and it was only noon.

Vianna rested about ten kilometers to the east of Logroño and was a final pit stop before the last push of the day. The village was built on a small hill perched up high enough to look out over Logroño in the distance. I planned to break for lunch in Vianna and assess my ability to keep going. It was only ten kilometers further, and I had all afternoon. Surely I could make it to Logroño. Yet my ankles had begun to ache in the last hour, and I had no way of knowing if walking would make the situation worse. I felt like a gambler hedging my bets, trying to figure out the fine line with my body; how much could I push it but still be able to walk as far the next day? There was no calculating where my body's breaking point might be or how long I could push before I found out. There was something mercenary about my attitude toward my body, and I knew my unraveling emotional state might only aggravate any physical issues. Part of me worried I was reading the tea leaves all wrong but wouldn't know until it was too late.

I referred to my guidebook and tallied the number of kilometers. To walk to Logroño would bring the day's total to just shy of forty kilometers. The albergue in the center of Logroño was built to house eighty pilgrims. If I could push on to the city, most of the pilgrims in Logroño would be new faces. The only way I was going to keep finding new walkers was to move outside of the major pilgrim traffic patterns. If I was to stay on pace with the guidebook, walking the allotted stages, then I would be with many of the same people the entire way. The only way to change the dynamics was to either speed up or slow down, and there was no way I was slowing down. Walking was the only element capable of lulling me into a state of semi-calm. The simple act was rocking me as if I were a fussy child.

Vianna sat delicately perched on the side of a small cluster of hills. From a distance, the city looked compact and contained, like a well constructed box with all the edges dovetailed together. I crossed through the decayed remains of buildings outside the village enclave and entered into the tightly curved city streets. Winding my way up through the slanted alleys, I moved deeper into the noontime city. Groups of children ran around the maze of streets alongside their abuelos and abuelas, while clusters of mothers stood in their dooryards and chatted with the many familiar faces that passed by. Small tables filled the sides of the central square, and several intense games of chess were in progress. I ducked into the first shop I came to, on the hunt for a large carton of pure liquid energy. As I walked into the shop with eyes only for orange juice, I nearly bumped into a tall, dark haired young man with a long walking stick. A fellow pilgrim, the young Spaniard graciously accepted my apology and introduced himself. He was also on this own and heading to Logroño after a short rest in Vianna. I paused for a moment, wanting to ask if I could join him for the last ten kilometers of his day but unsure of how my boldness might be received. He spoke first asking if I was on my own, looking me up and down with a discrete flicker of his eyes. He was clearly charmed by my answer, and I immediately asked him if I might join him on the trail to Logroño. He smiled a rakish grin and declared yes without a shred of hesitation.

After buying food for lunch, we walked down the street side by side and eventually stopped under the eaves of the church. At the far end of town, tucked in the cool shade, we sat along a narrow bench. Born in Colombia but raised in Spain, the young Spaniard was now a law student in Madrid. An adept multitasker, the Spaniard didn't hesitate to break out his food supplies and create a hearty lunch while we chatted. For the main course, he layered canned mussels dripping in oil and thinly sliced smoked meats onto a crusty piece of bread. In between conversation, he bent his head to the side, took large bites and made faces of pure enjoyment. I munched on a soggy granola bar and nursed my juice. I was more dehydrated than anything else and felt my body rebelling at the mere thought of solid food.

The Spaniard's English was strong, and he'd studied English for many years at a high level. Even with his depth of understanding, I found myself drifting into a distinct speech pattern. As in my conversations with other non-native speakers, I felt myself instinctively slowing down my speech and picking words that were simpler or more academic. On the trail, my accent may not have been British, but the cadence and tone were becoming more refined. I'd been told by the Dane and others that American English was very fast and littered with impossible slang. And to top it all off, the accent was much harder to understand than British English. This made sense but was slightly annoying. So our brand of English was rife with slang and a bit loose and fast around the edges. Did that mean it was a lesser breed? I couldn't deny that ours was the wild accent of rebels from the new world, and the more enunciated nature of British English was tight and clean in contrast. Maybe I was simply jealous and didn't have the heart to admit it. I'd wanted a British accent ever since I was twelve and swimming in a Regency sea of Jane Austen, but it was just now that I was beginning to face facts. There was no way I was going to suddenly awake with new sounds on my tongue and that distinctive click to my words. I was a new world girl, and I would simply have to come to grips with that.

LOGROÑO

An hour later the Spaniard packed up his lunch, I heaved my pack back into position, and we started off towards Logroño. After a morning of solo walking, I was eager to have some company in the last stretch of the day. Time moved at a more effortless clip when walking was coupled with human interaction. There was always something interesting to discover about a new acquaintance, a story to hear about the past or the present. Unless a fellow pilgrim had taken a vow of silence, there was usually some way for us to connect, at least for an hour or so. Shared anecdotes were the movies, newspapers and gossip magazines of the trail. We were each other's entertainment and the anthropologist in me was always on the hunt for a story. And now I was just as curious about the young guy walking beside me. I was starting to gather that those who took to the trail were invariably fascinating and bold in their choices. This journey wasn't for the faint of heart.

Yet walking with a new companion and falling into sync was always an adjustment, a balancing act of speed and stride. As we began to pick our way out of the village, I noticed the Spanish buck took long strides but with an air of lazy slowness. His was a low energy walk that accommodated his long legs but used as little oomph as possible. Even if I could have matched his stride step for step, it would have been impossible for me to move with such a molasses gait. I quickly realized he wasn't going to shift his style for my benefit, and I'd had been given the task of staying with him. Not until faced with this drastic mismatch in style did I realize how little shifting of pace I had to do with Alberto and Alec. If anything, I had to speed up a bit more than was natural. Somehow when I went slower, it tired my body as if I was working against the power of my own muscles. As I pulled back on my internal motor and concentrated on slowing my stride, I felt tiredness crash over me. This was harder than walking at top speed beside Alberto and more irritating, because the Spanish buck was completely oblivious. Yet, I needed to give him a chance and see who might lie below the slow stride and glossy hair.

As we walked away from Vianna, the trail wound us into a rather dismal section of land. Even though I'd been warned about this in my guidebook, I wasn't prepared for the sheer ugliness of the rundown industrial outskirts. My guidebook also mentioned the trail would cross a four lane highway with no light, crosswalk or footbridge to aid our safe passage. I'd become familiar with the typically ferocious rate of speed on Spanish motorways, and I wasn't sure how safe an unmonitored crossing would be. Our only choice would be to sprint to the other side with twenty-five pounds on our backs, hoping to evade the bumpers of oncoming traffic. The spot was evident when the trail made a sharp right turn and disappeared in the weeds along a set of gleaming guardrails. In the states, the sight of a walker on a highway, let alone crossing it, was rare and slightly disturbing. The danger level was just too high for any rational person to consider, but apparently here, pilgrims were expected to jump the rails and run for it.

At least I wasn't alone. Two bodies were easier to see and might induce cars to brake, if it came to that. As I turned to the Spanish buck to agree on a moment, he brushed by me, hopped into the road and sprinted across. His legs easily hurdled over the guardrail at the far side, and he was safely across before I even knew he was gone. Rooted in place, I was suddenly on my own, facing the crossing alone. It was several anxious minutes before I saw my opening behind the back of a small car in the closest lane and in front of the menacing grate of a semi truck in the far lane. Clutching the arms of my bag, I kicked my legs into motion and hoped nothing would fall off. When I reached the other side, the Spanish buck was kicking the guardrail absently as if he was deathly bored and had been waiting for hours. When we resumed our forward progress, I begrudgingly fell into his pace but felt a tide of rebellion rising in me. I wasn't sure why he waited if I was such a burden. Even though I no longer wanted to chat with him, he seemed delighted to take center stage.

He talked on and on, describing his childhood, life in Madrid and the ins and outs of political history. Breaking into the Spanish buck's conversation built for one wasn't going to be possible. It was shocking how fast I could swing from optimistic hope about a fellow pilgrim to a strong desire to flee his company at any cost. Now I would most likely have to endure him until Logroño.

Then against all odds, the tide shifted every so slightly, and he asked me about my Camino. I was startled by his sudden attention. I'd become resigned to the notion that I was little more than an audience. But as he turned and looked at me, I realized all wasn't lost. I might actually be a real person to this guy. He was asking me a question and leaving space for me to answer. I spoke with my guard slightly raised, unsure of how much to share about my real motivation for walking the Camino, but as he listened I warmed up. I divulged my strong focus on speed and distance at this point in the journey. Without going into the layers below my 'gut feelings' about the matter, I tried to explain my need to push ever onward. I knew it might have sounded illogical. I wasn't comfortable enough to tell him that I was following a dream or that I felt there were important meetings for me along this trail. Words often failed when explaining how my guidance got me places and he seemed to be only half listening to my ramblings anyways. The important thing was that I knew destiny was at play here, and for whatever reason, I needed to move fast to meet it.

After my vague answer, he laughed with a sneer and said, "You are disobeying the trail. You need to learn how to walk slowly and humble yourself before the wisdom of the trail."

At first I was startled. Yes, I couldn't totally explain what awaited me, for it was unknown, but I was following the dream and hoping that hindsight would prove me right. And yes, my guidance might look or feel totally wacky or wrong to another, but what made the Spanish buck think he could deem me in violation of the trail's code? My speed wasn't disobedience; it was the opposite. It was obedience to a plan that I couldn't see or understand. It was the marching orders I'd been given, and it wasn't up for discussion or dissection. I wasn't looking for advice and was unsure why the Spanish buck felt so free to give it with such a heavy hand.

My feelings of mellow annoyance toward the Spanish buck ignited into a wave of sheer irritation that flushed my cheeks and caused my blood to pump with a renewed vigor. I could have breathed fire on this stranger. In a flash of deja vu, I was reliving the exact same conversation I'd battled through with the Australian woman in Arre. Here was another person claiming he had his fingers on the pulse of the trail and was in contact with the true destiny of each pilgrim, believing this destiny was the same for all of us. How could this be remotely true? If anything, I sensed no two pilgrims traveled the same trail or sought the same end. I'd yet to meet a single fellow walker who shared the same energetic trail code as me. So how then could there be an overall trail agenda, an overarching to do list that we all had to complete and comply with? The mere thought of it was baffling. Yet I had now met several people who were willing to fight with me about it. Even the South African misunderstood the wisdom behind a young local's search for a girlfriend along the trail out of Pamplona. How could she know that God and the universe hadn't told him to walk that trail, told him to search every day for his destiny. Western religions had taught us rules, lists of do's and don't and finding a girlfriend on a holy trail wasn't within the "rules." But why would any of us presume we could understand the mysterious workings of another person's guidance? What was wrong with the search for a girlfriend or going faster than other pilgrims? Heartfelt guidance was astoundingly diverse, and if I was to compile hundreds of peoples' trail instructions, they would be awash with contradictions. Some would be told to walk slowly, while others would be prodded to pick up the pace. Some would be encouraged to stay only in small towns, while others would be guided to seek out the largest albergues along the trail. Nothing was right or wrong; everything was tailored to the life and destiny of each pilgrim. I knew this could act as a justification for doing as one pleased, but the experience of being with someone in alignment with his or her guidance was shockingly different than moving along beside someone who had chosen to do as his or her personality pleased. I would later meet a young guy who walked over sixty kilometers in a day, and to be around him was physically uncomfortable. The air around this man was charged with an energy of avoidance and fear. It reminded me again that it wasn't the choice that hinted at alignment, it was the energy around the choice. If the energy was centered and clear then even guidance to walk the trail in a tutu was a true way forward and beyond judgment or reproach. The inherent beauty of the trail was how it shaped its wisdom to fit each of us, knowing how to best push us to evolve.

Even though I had yet to know what I would get from walking so fast, I was grateful I hadn't faltered in my determination to keep following the thread of my guidance. If I'd listened to the advice the Australian woman had doled out so heavy-handedly, I might still be in the company of the Dane, and that was one break about which I felt no remorse. It had been a parting in perfect alignment, but only now, a few days later, could I see how right it had been. At the time, all I could do was follow the push and trust.

I couldn't deny the humming inside me. It was the intangible energy that had brought me here, so far from home. But I was the only one who could feel it. I clung to the hope that at some point I would have proof, real external, flesh and blood proof that this guidance was sound, that I was on the right track. It was human proof, in the form of friends and a man to love that dragged me out of my sleeping bag in the dark mornings and pushed me onward when I was weary to the bone. I hadn't just been waiting for the last week for such souls to arrive in my life; I'd been waiting for years. My trail to this spot was a long one and built on an invisible scaffolding of faith. These planks and beams had shaped my life. Even this run in with the Spanish buck was another chance to rebuff the naysayers and the doubters, the forces that would have me believe I was off course. Following this guidance was a marathon not a sprint, and as I pushed onward, I didn't need a heckler at my side.

At this moment, the Spanish buck's disdain for my current trail choices galvanized me, added a bit of heat to my energy system that had been lagging since mid-day. I used that jolt, funneled the energy down into the pistons of my lungs and legs. Even after a long day, I knew I had a few more gears left in me, so I pressed in the clutch and took off. I would deal with the physical repercussions later. My current aim was flight by any means possible.

When he fell silent for a moment, I picked up the pace. At first, he looked as if he would try and stay with me, but he quickly realized it would be more energy than he was willing to expend. The distance grew with each swing of my feet. Within ten minutes, I'd put a sizable gap between us, but he still felt uncomfortably close. When I rounded a bend in the trail and knew he'd lost sight of me, I broke into a full run, rocketing forward on sore muscles. My pack bounced around on my shoulders, but I didn't care. I'd already covered thirty five kilometers of trail, yet my desire to be rid of him trumped any tiredness. In no time at all, I was away from him and once again on my own.

A kilometer later, the trail descended into the outskirts of Logroño. The path ducked down near a broad river and turned onto a wide and elegant boulevard. Massive trees shaded the way, and the grass along the sidewalk was freshly mown. I lingered just behind a trio of middle aged pilgrims whom I vaguely recognized. I wanted to walk alone but knew tailing their movements through the city would steer me to the albergue.

The river was an impressive body of water, fast moving and as wide as any I'd crossed. It made the river in Puente la Reina look like a trickling stream. As I stepped out onto the bridge, I noticed one of the gregarious pilgrims in the group exuberantly attempting to climb a pillar on the bridge to get a better view while his companions cheered him on from below. The nearness of the end of the day had that effect. I knew it myself. The sheer relief of being allowed to slow the body and begin to recuperate could bring on spontaneous demonstrations of dramatic and slightly ridiculous behavior.

Logroño was a city in the aftermath of celebration. Broken banners hung from lampposts, and the streets were strewn with crushed petals, vibrant and bruised from a stampede of feet. Just the night before, the city had celebrated its Saint's day. Every inhabitant had come out in the evening hours to watch fireworks and enjoy live music in the vast central plaza. Even though the celebration had ended hours ago, the air of merriment still clung to every surface, and the people I passed still moved as if they had spent the previous day, if not the entire week, in a state of relaxed enjoyment.

Tucked discretely into the end of a street, the albergue lay just a stone's throw from the river. The large unmarked building was formidable like a solid fortress. The base of the building was windowless, but tall thin balconies dotted the upper floors. The front entrance was a large formal door, cold and unwelcoming. There was no indication at all as to how I was to gain entrance. I'd lingered at the river and lost the trail of the other pilgrims. I could only assume they were already inside. As I leaned into a locked door, a voice called to me from one of the windows above. My rescuer dangled half way out the window two or three stories up, his body bent over the railing and his arms full of pillows. With a warm but thick Spanish accent, the man told me to go around the side of the building, flashed me a wink and disappeared back into his tower. I turned the corner of the cold building and ducked through a wrought iron gate. After only a few steps, I moved from the austere front of the building to the bustling vibrant insides of a busy albergue. The open space hummed with pilgrim activity. The large courtyard was framed by wilting rows of plants and held a small rectangular pool with a gurgling fountain in its center. The pool, no bigger than a bath towel, was filled to the brim with icy water. Though a simple cure for the rigors of walking, it was the first line of pilgrim care and the main spot in which to sit and restore one's feet. As I entered, two pilgrims sat resting back on their elbows, chatting as their lower legs dangled in the water. Others sat at wrought iron tables with their feet propped up or lay sprawled out along a set of benches, catching the last bit of afternoon sun. There were at least twenty pilgrims in the small courtyard, and the interior room beside it was bustling with even more activity. Every foot I saw on my way inside was bare and gloriously free of our daily chains. Shoes and boots were both friend and foe. No words could explain the time we spent in them and the speed with which we tore them off at the end of the day. In the far corner, racks of clothing were splayed out to dry, and a group of girls was busy ferrying clothing from the sinks to the rickety metal frames.

I paid three euro and was given a bed number in return. After climbing three flights of stairs, I burst into my sleeping quarters and located my narrow bunk squeezed in amongst the beds of my thirty roommates. Though the night in Roncesvalles had broken me in, this space felt mighty intimate. Unlike Roncesvalles, the ceiling was very low and the aisles between the slender bunks were tight. This wouldn't have been such a problem if we all didn't have so much gear.

It was hard to know where to put my pack when I was given a top bunk, and the floor around my ladder was sticking out into a high traffic pathway to the door. Yet my intimate sleeping quarters weren't top on my list of concerns as I unpacked. The stairs had been a brutal test of my strangely weakened ankles and revealed things I'd been trying to avoid all day. Each step up the twisting stairwell was a painful stretch for my achilles tendons and sent a hot zing through my lower leg. This wasn't only an unfamiliar pain but a worsening one. I'd overheard another pilgrim describing the feeling of tendonitis earlier and had begrudgingly self diagnosed my injuries, but I was reluctant to embrace my conclusions. There was no mistaking the pain; I'd come down the pilgrim equivalent of the flu and staying off my feet and resting was typically the only way to get better. Not only were my tendons pulling on the muscles of my legs, but the tendons of my internal guidance were pulling on my ability to practice self care. If I decided to address my blossoming tendonitis, I would have no choice but to follow the conventional wisdom and rest. But if I took this path, then I would have to ignore the gnawing energy inside me that was still pushing me forward. If going slow wasn't an option, then stopping was throwing up the white flag and giving up on the core of this journey. In this no win situation, I knew my body would be the one to get the short end of the stick. I just I couldn't let go of the bigger dream. I hoped my body would thank me later when its pain and suffering had born me a new life. Bodies healed. Regret and lost chances didn't.

After unpacking, I hobbled down the stairs to the courtyard with my wash. As I made my way to the row of sinks, I passed three young women huddled around a beat up clothes dryer. It was one of the first I'd seen on the trail, and I could imagine how precious such a modern device could be during a particularly wet stretch of trail. Due to a gentle kindness from the weather gods, I'd been able to stay dry during the day and line dry my clothes at the night. Even my shoes were dry as a bone. I probably would have avoided the dryer no matter what. The glory of air-drying was free, and dryers have a nasty way of eating up small items such as socks and underwear. I needed all of those odds and ends to stay with me for the long haul. Many articles of clothing I could go without, but my meager cache of undergarments were rather essential; going commando had never been my style.

As I wrangled the water out of a shirt, one of the girls looked up at me and smiled. Though she didn't speak and wasn't wearing anything overtly American, I knew she was a fellow countrymen. It was often hard to pinpoint the specific trigger, but spotting an American was quite easily done. The clothing, the gear and even the body language were giveaways, and it always made me wonder if I was just as obvious as the rest. I spoke first, ready to be social after a long tough day, and thrust my dripping hand in her direction to introduce myself. With the day's work behind me and a bunk to my name, I was feeling cheerful and magnanimous, ready for a bit of company to ease the hours until sleep. After gaining the acquaintance of all three Americans, I was soon at the center of a boisterous four-way conversation. As the first group of American's I'd talked with on the trail, I was curious how they found this European mecca. While teaching together at a Catholic school in North Carolina, two of the three hatched the plan to come to Spain and walk to the Catholic shrine at Santiago. The slightly pieced together trio before me was comprised of an adult friendship, a childhood alliance and a brand new bond. Unfortunately the new bond wasn't taking shape as all had hoped. I got the distinct feeling the two girls who'd been strangers before this trip actually disliked each other but were trying to keep the flame low for the sake of the group. The third girl, the go between friend, looked haggard and a bit desperate for a new face. The lynchpin role was a stressful one, and I offered a bit of relief from their triangular dysfunction.

After half an hour of comparing notes about the day's walk, one of the girls looked around pointedly and asked me where my traveling companion was. I hadn't mentioned any companion, but I also hadn't shared the fact I was alone. As their eyes stared at me with genuine interest, I realized they were imagining a person, because they simply couldn't fathom I was adrift in the wilds of Spain all alone. I could see the image forming in their minds of a tall, rugged and adoring boyfriend who was just upstairs about to bound down and join us. It was almost painful to burst the beautiful bubble they had created around me, but that strapping lad wasn't coming any time soon, so I shook my head and told them I was solo. A single. A one. Just me.

The pause, as they slashed and burned their elaborate imaginings, only lasted a moment, but it was long enough for me to wish I had another truth to tell. Yet to my utter surprise, my solo status seemed to have elevated my cool factor, and their questions flowed quickly. They were simply fascinated, mesmerized by a peer much like themselves who was gutsy or perhaps foolish enough to come without back up. From the safety of their group, they wanted to hear every detail of my journey from St. Jean. I felt a bit heartened by how much they admired my journey. Listening to my tales, I noticed each of them lost in thought about their own Caminos, wondering if they would have taken this on without the others. To see through their eyes for a moment took the sting away from my feeling that this solo life was a second best. I'd come alone not as a righteous choice or declaration of my independence but as a fall back position. Regardless of how my story looked from the surface and no matter the downsides of messy group life, I was envious they had each other.

After my washing was done, the girls asked me if I wanted to venture into the city with them. One of them needed a new backpack because the straps of her old behemoth had given way. As we moved through the streets, I discovered Logroño was a city with many of the amenities uncommon in other sections of the trail. I understood why the American girls took this chance to get new gear but didn't need anything myself. I left them to shop while I wandered into the central square and settled down on a park wall to watch the city flow by. Abuelas sat on benches with their eyes on groups of young grandchildren while punky teens with florescent tee shirts and fashionable haircuts whizzed past on skateboards. Post siesta all the shops were open, and it felt as if every person in the city was out and about in the late afternoon light. The energy of the city absorbed me into its circle. Though Logroño wasn't a beautiful city, I hardly noticed. There was something restful yet deeply social about Spanish culture, and the plazas and parks were built to accommodate this. Crowds weren't feared or resented but embraced as the nature of life.

When the American girls reappeared, we went in search of food. It turned out to be more of a struggle to locate a supermercado in the center of the city than we expected. In the rows of fancy shops, cafes and open air restaurants there was little room for supermarkets, and we were told to search further afield in the working class neighborhoods on the outskirts of the city. On our path away from the center, we stumbled upon an underground market that looked promising. Only after descending into the bowels of the building did we realize we weren't in the average market. The large windowless basement was filled to the brim with every type and cut of meat imaginable. Racks of animal carcasses hung from metal hooks and tables spilled over with long links of sausage. The men behind the counters wore aprons stained with wide swaths of warm pink and deep red. Nothing in the dark cavern was immune from the seeping color, and the air was thick and pungent with the smell of iron. Local shoppers moved with swift determination and unbothered ease. This was the way they bought meat, and I had to admit they earned their carnivorous stripes, for this sight would induce even the most tough stomached person to consider vegetarianism. One of the American girls grew pale and plugged her nose to stave off her gag reflex. I ushered the wide-eyed crew up the stairs and back to street level as fast as possible, a bit concerned we might have to revive one or two of the girls if we lingered.

A supermercado appeared around the next corner, and we were returned to the no less creepy world of florescent lights and packages foods. This place was food with the blinders on. When shopping here, we knew as little as possible about where the food came from and how it ended up on the shelf before us. Even with the rough visit to the underground market still fresh in my mind, I preferred that reality to the disconnected world of the modern supermarket. But since I wasn't buying a slab of beef or a set of pig's ears for my dinner, I would have to wait in the checkout lines of a modern food machine just like the rest of the group.

When we finally arrived back at the albergue, I was greeted with an unfortunate reminder of my day's travel. As I walked into the courtyard, I noticed the Spanish buck sitting at one of the tables around the fountain. He had his back to the entrance and was deep in conversation with a fellow pilgrim. I hoped to avoid an interaction. I'd run away for a reason, and there was no need to re-engage. I was, however, a bit curious about the other pilgrim who was sitting with him. The young guy was an unusual looking pilgrim, if that was even possible. With a shaved head, he was squat, muscle bound and the proud owner of tattoo laden arms. I had a suspicion the rest of his body was also inked, but all I could see was the color snaking from wrist to neck on both sides of his body. He held a guitar in his much adorned arms, while the Spanish buck nursed a beer and smoothed back his freshly gelled hair. Even with a growing curiosity about Tattoo lad, I decided polite avoidance of the Spanish buck was the best tactic. I would just have to meet his new companion another time.

The kitchen was on the third floor above the courtyard. Large windows reached all the way to the floor, opening out to a balcony. The windows flooded the space with light and fresh air in the tidy well-organized room. Since almost all the surfaces were white, the whole kitchen felt like a clean slate, prepared to welcome a new group each night that would fill it with the smells of food and the hum of conversation. As we entered, there were already half a dozen people scattered about preparing food. I sat down with the American girls at one of the tables, and we began to unpack the supplies we had purchased.

Not long after we started to eat, Tattoo lad ambled through the door and made a beeline for our table. His guitar hung from his back, and I could tell that it traveled everywhere he did, maybe even into his bunk at night. He was already acquainted with the American girls, having met them a few days back, and he sat down with a manner of familiarity. It took him a moment to say hello and take a tally of who sat around the table, but when he stumbled across me, he introduced himself with a wide charming grin that was both flirtatious and childlike at the same time. It wasn't hard to imagine why the American girls were charmed by Tattoo lad. The thick Irish brogue gave away his nationality before three words had passed his lips, and he clearly relished the affect his accent had on the American girls. No matter the rubbish that he was spouting, they seemed to hang on his every word, enjoying the simple auditory thrill. I was fearful to think what would happen with the smitten trio if he sang to us or strummed his guitar. With his rock star's magnetism, there might be spontaneous shedding of clothes, swaying and pledges of undying love. I sensed it could get out of hand very quickly.

To divert Tattoo lad from reaching for his guitar, I asked how he ended up on the Camino. As he leaned back in his chair, he explained he'd been backpacking around Spain, enjoying the free life, when all his belonging were stolen. With only a guitar to his name and nothing pressing back in Ireland, he waited for a sign about what to do next. He didn't have to wait long. Later that day as he was sitting on a street curb smoking, he encountered a fellow traveler with a large backpack. When Tattoo lad offered a friendly hello, the two fell into conversation and the stranger told him that he was walking a trail called the Camino. Without hesitating, Tattoo lad stood up and joined the man in his westward progress. He'd been walking for a week at his new friend's side when he fell ill and had to rest in Logroño. The girls immediately began to cluck over him, asking about his symptoms and offering their help. He cheerfully refused assistance, insisting he was better. A recent trip to the pharmacy had done wonders. The inside of his mouth was no longer shedding layers of skin, and his temperature was back to normal after spiking over one hundred several times in the last few days. The graphic symptom rundown was a bit too detailed, but his fan club hardly noticed. As they fussed over him, I wondered what exactly was he sick with, but I decided it was better not to know.

As the girls finished their meal, I heated milk to accompany our desert of chocolate biscuits. The kitchen had filled. Only an hour before, everything had glimmered with newness, but now the ranges were cluttered with pots and pans full of boiling water, splattered with sauce and in constant use. One of the tables at the end of the room was dominated by a group of older men who were biking the trail. Even from across the room, I could tell they liked to indulge in a mighty feast after a long day in the metal saddle. Strewn across the table was a pot of steaming pasta, large rounds of cheese, two loaves of crusty bread, a couple kinds of olives and several bottles of wine. They were as dramatic as their food and became more and more boisterous as the meal wore on. They broke in song several times and offered food to every pilgrim who wandered by their table. Such generosity was the greatest strength of pilgrim groups; often I had to be quite forceful to convince them I was well fed and not in need of a pile of pasta, a glass of vino or a wedge of cheese. Later, I would meet a young guy who made hanging around kitchens into a fine art. All he had to do was lounge in the busy space during meal times and some family with a generous mama or group of older pilgrims with tender hearts would be unable to resist his puppy dog face. I watched one night as three separate groups took pity on my hulking friend. Needless to say, he never went hungry and rarely ever needed to buy food. His skill was a gift, and he used it with such sweetness, I swore the people who fed him always felt proud of their service and never noticed the remains of the four other meals he'd been gifted that night.

As one of the girls crumbled cookies into her hot milk, she mulled over my guidebook. Suddenly she looked up and asked me, "Do you know the Cowboy?"

The Cowboy? No, I didn't know any cowboys of any sort, but immediately wished I did. The girls started to giggle and told me that a few days earlier they'd met a man riding the trail on horseback. I was awestruck. How had I missed such a dynamic pilgrim, and how was I going to orchestrate a meeting? This rider was the stuff of myths and ancient lore, just the kind of thing I craved to encounter along the way. As I leaned over the table resting on my elbows and soaking up details like a sponge, the girls divulged all they knew, until suddenly they paused mid speech. Turning around slowly in my chair, I had a feeling I knew what I would see. There was only one thing or in this case one person who could cause the girls to fall silent and bloom into a trio of giddy smiles.

As he came towards the table, one of the girls informed me in a frantic whisper that the man crossing the room to our table was THE Cowboy, but she needn't have bothered. He required no introduction. In his early forties, he could have passed for a well worn thirty, especially when I caught sight of his thick crop of dark hair. Steely black eyes searched the room under a pair of dark commanding eyebrows while he radiated a self-possessed confidence that made him both attractive and a bit repulsive in the same instant. With cool ease, he spun the chair beside me around, plunked himself down and stuck out his hand to introduce himself. As his rough hand swallowed my own, his eyes never left mine. It was the look of the hunter assessing the skills of his prey. His voice was a hybrid of British and Irish, yet he gave off a distinctly well-educated air. His family roots were old and moneyed, but his current persona was one of a bohemian at home in the world. As soon as he settled down at the table, all attention turned on him like a spotlight, and he shamelessly sunbathed in the glow.

After the girls formally introduced us, they asked him about his travels since they'd last met. He spoke with an easy alluring style, one that lulled us into his tales and attached us to the unfolding drama. Just three days ago, he and his horse had been doing a bit of trail off-roading and got caught up in the mountains late in the day. Unable to make it down before nightfall, they sought shelter while a massive lighting storm collided above their heads. With his horse by his side, the Cowboy had walked in the dark down and out of the storm, navigating by the light of the cracking bolts overhead. It was slow halting progress, but by dawn they'd made it down the mountain and back to the outskirts of civilization. The Cowboy shrugged at the end of the story, as if the tale of tangling with the powerful hand of mother-nature was just another day on the trail. He claimed it wasn't an unusual story, for he was living this trail in what he considered its purest and most elemental form. He was conquering the land by horse and shunning the modern mode of pilgrimage. As the Cowboy digressed into talk about stabling his horse on the outskirts of the city, the conditions of the ride into Logroño and the nature of a "true" pilgrim, I had to ask what exactly he considered to be a genuine specimen.

The Cowboy explained he had little but contempt for all walking pilgrims and considered them a lower form of beings like invertebrates or insects. He was adamant about this, but did give the four of us around the table a stay of execution that excluded us from the category he so despised. His voice was sharp and intense as he talked about the "sickening way" walking pilgrims made a holiday out of their journey and relied on the trappings of modernity to aid their progress. Nothing, he claimed, could rival the struggle and suffering, the beauty and poetry of his travels by horseback. There was simply no comparison; he and his horse were true pilgrims in the purest sense of the word. Everybody else was just pretending. The American girls sat with their chins in their hands, enthralled by the Cowboy's charm offensive.

When the group disbanded, I settled out on the narrow balcony as the last light of the day leeched from the sky. The air was soft, and the view allowed me to see a great distance down into the center of the city. The moment was soothing and as near to private as anyone got in an albergue. I watched the activity in the courtyard three stories below with a detached interest; people moved about and chatted, but I couldn't hear their words or see their faces in the dusky light. Eventually the streetlights came on, and I felt a yawn rising in my chest. It was time to gather my things and head upstairs. I started to get up to go as the Cowboy rushed back through the door, scanned the room and strode over to me with a determined look in his dark eyes. Without hesitation, he stepped to within an inch of me, locked his liquid eyes on mine and said, "How about you come to dinner with me babe?"

I hesitated, caught in a moment of pure disbelief. Was he really making a move and attempting to advance with this offer? His bold tactics had certainly caught me off balance, and I was mustering some semblance of a response when he continued unbidden, "I am in search of a good meal, decent wine and a pretty face to look at," he said with a practiced smile meant to look innocent but coming off as smug. He paused again, perhaps wondering how best to convince me, then put the element of physical contact into play. As he reached out to stroke my arm, I backed up into the side of the table, and he stepped close, pleading, "I will pay and you don't even need to talk, you can just sit there."

We had come to the bottom line, the floorboards of the offer, and he was sure I couldn't possibly refuse. Resting perhaps on his charming looks and impressive stories, he'd failed to notice the way I'd put the table between us as he spoke. He'd also failed to notice the growing horror on my face now mingling with an almost unbearable desire to laugh. His was such an outrageous invitation that I didn't have the faintest idea how he'd ever succeeded with it before. But something told me that other women had lapped this up, and he'd rarely eaten alone. Sadly for the Cowboy, his dinner in Logroño would be a solo affair. As I made my way to the door, he made one last attempt, confiding with drawn brows and a slightly naughty tilt to his smile that he craved female company after a day alone with his gelding. Unfortunately for him, that wasn't enough to persuade me. So my first chance at a Camino date came and went in the blink of an eye. I'd never thought I would turn down a date with a cowboy for a date with my sleeping bag, but the Camino had a way of making us all a bit crazy.

NÁJERA

STAGE SIX- 35.2K-21.9M
LOGROÑO TO AZOFRA

The next morning took me out of the city under the glow of street lights. The path meandered in gentle curves through a long park system where groups of runners passed me at regular intervals. Even though we were both sweating, pushing, tearing muscle and pumping our lungs, I didn't feel much affinity with the runners. They moved apart in an alternate reality that had nothing to do with the trail. The hour they spent running was a brief hiatus from their busy days, just a strand in the fabric of their lives. It was a habit like brushing one's teeth or commuting to work. As they breezed past me, I felt alien. For walking was now a way of being that cut through my every thought, movement and emotion. It was the basic ingredient in every moment; it wasn't just something I did, but something I'd become. I wondered if the locals passing by with quick muscled strides could see the gulf between our worlds, if they could feel the contrast as viscerally and as deeply as I did. Their minds were elsewhere and would, I assumed, soon forget that they'd seen a girl with dirty shoes and a large pack alone in the park at dawn.

I could hardly remember a life where this movement wasn't rocking me awake in the morning, guiding me along in the afternoon and fueling my ravenous need for sleep every night. I had formed an attachment, and my whole world had changed. I wasn't sure I would ever be able to go back to the land of casual walking. Our relationship had gone to the next level, and there was no looking back.

I'd awoken in a low mood, and even the sight of Alberto and Alec waiting at dawn for me outside the albergue gate hadn't been enough to break me free of the gloom. The Italians and I walked together through the dirty suburbs of Logroño but drifted apart as soon as we hit the parkland. I had a feeling everybody craved a bit of space and relief from the grumpy moods we all seemed to be sporting. After leaving the park, the trail wound through a desolate area in the fringe of the city. The trees and shrubs were no longer meticulously cared for, and the trail grew rocky. The pathway had been open and uninhabited for the last hour, but suddenly I spotted another pack bouncing along ahead. Even from a distance, I recognized the form of a young woman I'd bunked beside last night. We'd traded genuinely exasperated smiles in the evening as a man traipsed by us in nothing but briefs then began to snore like a wheezy trumpet five minutes later. I quickened my pace. I wasn't sure if she spoke English, but I longed for a bit of company to launch me out of my slowly ossifying isolation. Just a few minutes of conversation would do wonders. It turned out the young woman was just as eager for some human interaction, and she spoke English. She was a museum curator from Prague, had studied English all the way through university and used it in her daily life. Though she appeared much more grown up than I felt, she was only a year my senior. Her appearance and way of moving was distinctly graceful and cosmopolitan. Her hair was long and dark, yet she wore it down as she walked, seemingly unperturbed by the way it gently swished around her. Her eyes were also dark and framed by the most astoundingly long eyelashes. The Curator's beauty was effortless, and I felt like a smelly, dirty, uncoordinated, fashion-challenged girl in comparison. The trail lifestyle had left not the slightest imprint on her appearance, and if she hadn't been carrying two sticks, shouldering a pack and garbed in tight synthetic workout gear, I wouldn't have been able to confidently identify her as a pilgrim.

As we moved along at a quick pace, her sticks clicking out our tempo, she explained that she had exactly thirty days to complete the trail without a single day to spare. The museum had given her only a month's leave, and she was devoted to the idea of making the whole journey. Before arriving, she'd planned out an extremely rigid schedule for the trek, and she knew she had to stick to it no matter what befell her. Illness and injury were unthinkable. There was no time budgeted for such misfortunes, no spare moments set aside for breakdowns of any kind. Her's was a steely mindset that left no room for error and made me a bit ashamed to admit to the general lack of organization in my pre-trip planning.

I wanted to believe there was a host of unknown factors along the trail, mostly in the form of new acquaintances, so there was no way I could predict my pace. I didn't have to plan a tight schedule, but the Curator did. Factors of time and space collided to shape her tour de force, and she seemed calm as she explained its general shape. Her voice was light and confident, but her body wasn't as good at putting up a strong front. There was tension in her frame and a slightly strained look on her face that she didn't have the energy to gloss over. The pace was clearly wearing, no matter what her itinerary said. I wondered if some deep part of her felt trapped by this journey, caged in by an impossible timeline. For me, there would have been two sides to such a challenge. One side would have relished the push and worked tirelessly; the other part would have lingered under the surface, strained and fragile, bursting forth in moments of pressure and flooding my eyes with tears. Was reaching the official end or refusing to catch a bus worth all this strife? I wasn't convinced, but knew if I were in her shoes, I would act just as stubbornly. There was a crazy but seductive purity to such determination. Nonetheless, I was relieved I wasn't on such a course myself.

Eventually, I drifted ahead as the trail came alongside a stretch of dismal highway. We nodded goodbye, but I knew we'd not seen the last of each other. We both were aiming for a long day and chances were our heads would hit the pillow in the same albergue tonight. The major traffic artery out of Logroño was loud, and the land was bleak around the throbbing four-lane highway. The only thing separating the trail and the tarmac was a high chain link fence, and there was no escaping it. Both trail and road were headed in the same direction and appeared to mimic each other move for move. Though the pathway was the senior of the two, with over a thousand years to its credit, the road had swallowed the valley and taken over like a disease. With nothing but chained link fences and industrialized land in sight, the only relief was the sky overhead. But even this view was not unmarred as a large bull shaped billboard dropped a wide shadow over the trail. Once I passed out from under the creature's thick silhouette, I noticed a section of the fence ahead cluttered with debris.

As I drew closer, fragments took shape and separated into individual forms. The holes in the fence had been swallowed up, and before me was a wall of crosses. I came to a full stop. The weight of my pack sunk into my hipbones, and my core felt hollow. I knew where I was. There was no mistaking this place. No two crosses were alike. Each varied in size and material. They were made from sticks, old plastic bags twisted into lines, shoelaces and colored pieces of wire. This was the work of many moments and a multitude of hands. Maybe this shape, and all the associations it carried, mattered little compared with the intentions of those who created these crosses. I could feel at the heart of hundreds of gestures was the desire by thousands of pilgrims to place a bit of their light in this field of darkness. Yet at the same time, the crosses were a demarcation, the signpost for a certain kind of spot on the trail, spots known as godforsaken places. I'd heard several rumors about these spots. They were universally acknowledged as cursed and understood to be locations that sucked the marrow from a pilgrim's will to continue and tapped the root of his or her faith in the journey ahead. These were the spiritual badlands. Beyond all logic, I could feel the energy sink through the layers of my skin and drop into my bloodstream like ice. This place was haunted but by something much more disturbing than a ghost. It was haunted by fear. And it seemed to mutate to fit the particular fear of those who walked through it. So there, surrounded by ugly industrial hum, a vacancy of humanity and submerged in the lonely stress of this walking life, I came face to face with doubt. Doubt in my every move, doubt in my choices and most especially doubt in my guidance and core belief this trail was taking me to a new life. Like many before me, fear had found me here.

I stood humbled by this realization. All I wanted to do was dive back into the refuge of movement as quickly as possible. Even this simple wavering moment seemed to crush my bones and tighten a winch around my lungs. I was in no shape to wait around here and confront my doubt. I had no answers, and the trail certainly wasn't helping me unearth any. Would the turn come? Would this journey shift and provide more or would I carry my forsaken place within me, like a leaden weight, until the end?

After dashing away from the wall of crosses, I walked alone with a pace verging on manic. As morning shifted towards mid-day, I realized I'd passed most of the other pilgrims who began with me in Logroño. I was at the head of the morning pack, on my own and striding into kilometers of empty trail. The small village of Navarrete came and went in a blur. Open tracks of fields and vineyards mingled together along the rolling stretch of land. Small towns appeared off to the side of the trail, bobbing into sight like corks, but the path never led to their clustered communites. I had only a bit of food with me and would have to wait until noon and my arrival in the small city of Nájera to restock.

Though I was weary of stalking every form of life ahead of me on the horizon, my thirst for company outweighed my fatigue. The hours had provided too much time for the Greek chorus of the Spanish buck and Australian woman to take over my thoughts. They proudly detailed their theory that not only was the trail telling me to go slow, but it was showing me how my journey was destined to be a solo one. They went on and on. Their points were so obviously defensible and their logic so sound, I was left with little but a stubborn hold on my guidance to keep me from sinking into despair. My divine instructions were all I had. I didn't have proof or fact to rebut the doubters. All I had was my iron grip and the dream so deeply soaked in light, it still felt true every time I picked it up and unfolded it in my memory.

Crossing a road and entering the dingy high-rises of Nájera's outer limits, I discovered a wide river cut through the city's core with a gracefully arched bridge spanning the river's widest point. Green parkland served as a buffer between the fast moving water and the old city blocks. The center of the city was churning with activity when I arrived just after twelve. I spotted several clusters of pilgrims among the crowds. Finding a spot along the banks of the river, I dismounted my bag from its perch on my shoulders. The grass was groomed and lush. It was soft under my arms and legs, and the noise of the moving river swallowed the sounds of the city. The sun was out and unhampered by clouds.

A man's voice yelled at me from the bridge down river. I held my hand up to shield the sun and saw a welcome sight. It was Alberto with Alec not far behind him. I was stunned but shouldn't have been. Every time I was sure they'd fallen back too far to reconnect, they would appear looking cheerful as ever. It was a comfort if only a small one. They were as dogged as I was, and their will to keep up brought an element of consistency to my fragile trail life. After a brief rest, they suggested we push on another five kilometers to a small town called Azofra. I was all in favor of the plan and started to pack my things at once.

After a short but steep climb through the backside of the old city, the trail dropped down into a beautiful valley of lush golden hues. The afternoon light was clear and warm. I walked ahead of the Italians, but took comfort in the low murmur of their conversation several yards behind me. The dip and fall of their words and its expressive flow had become music to accompany my wandering thoughts. After about a kilometer, I came across a lanky older man resting on a trailside rock, caught in deep ponderous thoughts that left a small smile on the edge of his lips. As I drew even with where he sat, he turned and offered me a warm but very gentlemanly greeting. Before the words had fully left his mouth, I already knew I was going to like this pilgrim. There was something slightly whimsical and timeless about his posture as he took a moment's pause. His face was old fashioned as if he could have fit anywhere in time. It was effortless to embrace the Philosopher's company, but a little bit more challenging to adjust to his stride. His long legs weren't just for show, and he used them with a youthful vigor I found thrilling. After several hours of monotonous solo walking, I was working to keep up while staying tuned to our unfolding conversation. As a retired Dutch schoolteacher who loved art and the classics, there was no lack of conversation, and I was ecstatic to get a chance to talk about dance with someone whose eyes didn't glaze over in boredom at the mere mention.

The Philosopher became particularly animated when explaining his basic theory on why the trail was such a powerful place. Detailing his extensive study of Greek philosophy and the nature of the walking, he concluded this was a life filled with a magical synergy of movement and discourse. I had to agree with his theory. In the past few days, my interactions with the land and others had taken on a greater depth because they were combined with the simple act of walking. Everything struck closer to my center and imprinted in profound ways, both positive and negative. Any and every genuine piece of community was treasured, absorbed fully and reflected on in hours of thought. No one came and went without reason. Every interaction was counted and recounted. Nothing was a guarantee on the trail, and no character was a known quantity. I was starting to get the feeling the only way to be prepared was to practice being unprepared, to live in the unrehearsed moment and to stay awake to the current of the trail.

The Philosopher agreed this life was extraordinary, and told me he never presumed to understand where it might take him and who might show up along the way. He was detached from outcomes. If I hadn't come along, and he'd walked into Azofra alone, nothing would have been lost. I wasn't sure I could claim the same detachment, for I was still tangled up in a desire to make all my divine appointments.

It was only a few kilometers to Azofra. Not surprisingly, they sped past. I was disappointed to have my conversation with the Philosopher draw to a close as we spied the village up ahead. I'd deeply appreciated the way he listened. It was a rare and much underrated skill that was effective only when one had truly mastered it. It was also a subtle talent that put me at ease and appeared to melt time. With an easy coming and going of words, talk flowed as swiftly as our feet, soon leading us into the village and down its sleepy main street.

Azofra sat upon an arid section of land, adrift in a sea of fields. The main road shot down through the center of town like an arrow and was tightly packed with low-slung stucco buildings. Nothing was higher than two stories, except, of course, the church. As we walked down the road, I noticed it was covered in a thin layer of yellow dust that shifted slightly in the breeze. A small band of kittens playfully rolled in the warm soot as we drew even with the central square. The main street came to a T in front of the church, and the right branch of the road swept down to the albergue. A large fountain gushing water punctuated the open courtyard as the sound of moving water filled the space. I'd seen many of these ancient fountains in the previous days, but none were in constant flow like this one. While the Philosopher and I stood and waited for the Italians to catch up, a local man lumbered by on an old tractor then jumped down to drink from the fountain. He didn't hesitate as he formed a cup with his grimy hands and scooped the cool liquid up to his mouth. He did this several times, drinking with clear relish. Apparently this fountain wasn't just for exclusive use by the never ending stream of pilgrims.

When the Italians arrived, we made our way to the large albergue. As soon as we entered the spacious courtyard, I was extremely pleased Alberto had suggested we spend the night here. The whole facility was brand new but still welcoming. A world of fresh paint, large windows and un-chipped tile greeted us at the gate. Despite my aesthetic preference for older albergues with years of wear and charm, I felt at ease here. A long series of international flags dangled off the side of the gate, and wrought iron tables with wide umbrellas dotted the space. A miniature pool was imbedded in the center of the patio, and a series of white clotheslines crisscrossed the far wall.

There were already a dozen other pilgrims roaming around in various states of activity as we made our way to the reception desk. A father and his young son sat with their feet dangling in the pool, playing cards. An older man reclined in the shade reading The Canterbury Tales with his legs delicately crossed. His wife moved efficiently around him, hanging dripping items of clothing and humming softly to herself. Another couple shared a chair under one of the umbrellas, their limbs intertwined as they chatted in animated tones with a woman across the table.

When entering an albergue, there were always two main attributes to inspect first: the bunkroom and then the kitchen. Was there a stove? Were there more than two forks and spoon? Was there a table and chair around which to eat? No two kitchens were the same, but this kitchen was a fine specimen with the added charm of a wonderfully roomy dining area with four large family sized tables. Our impromptu group took to the space right away, and Alberto deemed it the perfect spot for a pasta feast. The Philosopher joined Alberto in the kitchen to chop, stir and wait for the water to boil, while Alec and I set out glasses and plates. I even found napkins to tuck under the forks. It felt extremely civilized to be laying out our table and satisfying to return to such normalcy. Once the table was set, we took our seats as the open dining room flooded with pilgrims.

Across the room, a group of Korean pilgrims clustered around steaming dishes of food, speaking softly with each other. There was something peaceful and intimate about how they enjoyed their evening meal. I was drawn to watching them from afar. Eventually Alberto hauled the massive cauldron of pasta to our table, and we feasted on heaps of noodles. The Philosopher tried to recall what remained of his rusted Italian vocabulary and was jovial even when failing to make any sense. I half listened and let my eyes and thoughts wander. Silences were now a routine part of our travels together and no longer made me nervous. I filled the space with my eyes, watching the comings and goings of strangers at close range.

I continued to be mesmerized by the group of Koreans. Not only were they here with not a word of English, Spanish or French in their possession, but they seemed undaunted by such a gulf of communication. There was a settled calm to their group, and though they were clearly out of their element, never for a moment did they betray this. The group consisted mostly of tiny delicate women dressed in beautiful white linen kimonos. It was this touch, this element of dress, that really drew me in. I was utterly overwhelmed by their elegance. Here in this unlikely place, they dressed with a simple grace that defied the rules of dirt and sweat. I had no clue how they kept the smooth fabric clean and unwrinkled or why they even bothered. I had enough trouble keeping my own utilitarian clothes in a halfway decent state. As long as they were not overly muddy or smelly then I felt I'd won a small victory, but here was a whole new level of clothing care. I was in awe.

After dinner, I walked by their table and ventured to remark on how beautiful their clothes were. I wasn't sure they understood, but as I walked away, a young guy from their group stood up and came after me. This guy was the translator for the group, and he'd come to thank me and tell me he would pass on my message. As I turned to go back to my circle, he said, "They think that you are lovely looking and have especially pretty blue eyes." I looked back at the group and found them watching me with warm smiles. I was glad I'd ventured across the language divide and apparently so were they.

Another unexpected feature in this new albergue was my room itself. It was no large dormitory or group holding pen but a tiny stall like rooms built to accommodate just two beds. It was the first time in weeks I'd slept in a space with so few people. At first, I was relieved to think of the uninterrupted sleep this would offer, but then I became concerned about who my roommate would be. At least when I was sharing a room with a group, there were always a few people who made me feel safe and at ease. Somehow being one on one with a stranger in a small cell like room was more of a close encounter.

My fear was quickly put to rest when I shook hands with my roommate, a friendly middle-aged Canadian journalist who was traveling with her elderly father. She dove into her trail biography as she unpacked her things and asked a slew of questions without leaving space for them to be answered. After awhile, I wasn't sure if she was even drawing breath between her unending run-on sentences. She and her father were navigating the trail by a mixture of bus and foot travel. Her father was in his eighties, so this hybrid pilgrim existence was a smart one but left his able bodied daughter with energy to spare.

During the in depth description of her travels with her father, the Canadian mentioned an unfamiliar trail term that caught my attention. Apparently they were employing a pack carrier to ferry their bags from one albergue to the next. For a small fee, a taxi, bus or privately owned car would pick up their packs as they ate breakfast and deposit them at the albergue where they were to stop for the night. When she casually mentioned the luggage service, I was at a loss to understand why such a thing even existed. It had never occurred to me that my pack would cross the land any way other than on my back. My pack was mine to carry. Each ounce was in my control and there because I chose to shoulder it. Yet the Canadian and her father used this service to ferry their hefty belongings down the Camino. This modern service allowed them to walk free of a burdensome pack but still have their weighty baggage with them in the evening. I wondered how many pilgrims were taking advantage of this. I was startled to think it was utilized by more than just the injured or elderly.

After half an hour, I turned off my flashlight and curled up in my sleeping bag as a gentle segue from talk to sleep. I was surprised I didn't want to chat further with my roommate since I'd been isolated with the two Italians for the last stretch of trail. But after spending an hour in her frenetic presence, I was in shock and wanted nothing more than to escape. I'd grown accustomed to a slower pace of conversation with more space for stillness and deep breaths. Drifting off to sleep, I felt myself sinking deeper into trail life and moving farther away from my moorings in the culture I'd left behind in the states. This was a kingdom unto itself, and I was slowly becoming a native.

SANTO DOMINGO DE LA CALZADA

STAGE SEVEN- 39.1K-24.3M
AZOFRA TO BELORADO

The next morning Alberto left before dawn. He had a deeply quiet nature, and those moments traversing the land in the soft dark hours were the center of his pilgrimage. His daily departure before sunrise was his courteous way of declaring a desire to walk alone. Even though he'd become a trusted support, there was no understanding between us that our journeys would stay parallel. Each time he took off into the morning alone, I couldn't be sure I would ever see him again.

Alec and I stepped out onto the trail a few hours later, rejoining the main street and heading west out of town. We walked side by side for a few minutes, but I noticed Alec wince with every step he took. Both of his feet had been tight and swollen with tendonitis for the past few days, but now they seemed worse than ever. The cramping of the muscles had become so bad the previous night, he'd had to hobble to the pharmacy for help. There wasn't much they could do for his ankles. There was no magic pill or miracle ointment that could solve the problem. The cure was simple yet impossibly hard to swallow. The only way to heal was to rest, and this was the last thing he, or most any pilgrim, wanted to do.

At breakfast, Alec had declared that nothing would stop him from pressing onward, and he'd ordered me to keep moving at my own pace and not worry about sticking with him. I'd been torn, but he'd been adamant, so I'd moved ahead with renewed speed. Before I knew it, I'd lost sight of him behind me on the trail. It was that simple. Only a matter of minutes really, and I was once again on my own.

Outside of Azofra, the clusters of civilization I passed lay dormant in the morning light. As I came up a hill, I heard a strangely familiar sound that felt out of place. At first I couldn't identify the noise, then the trail turned sharply and I almost stumbled onto the gleaming surface of a manicured golf green. The tight florescent grass was wet, and a thick mist of water rained down on me. The noise I'd heard was the hissing of high-powered sprinklers. Backing up off the grass and continuing on the trail, I looked across the lush oasis. There was no logical reason for the golf course to be here in the middle of nowhere. The manmade landscape was garish, overly groomed and strangely uninhabited. As I skirted the course, a new development of houses came into view. Many were half built with construction materials strewn about.

As I moved away from the golf course, the arrows disappeared into the maze of the unfinished clone homes. Each lay in a different state of completion with walls open to the elements and naked beams rising from cement foundations. Nothing moved except sheets of thick plastic flapping in the light breeze. Near the edge of the housing development, I crossed paths with a lone construction worker. He was young, scrawny and moved with a weary lope. He wore a bright yellow construction hat and clutched a pair of work gloves in his hand. His boots were scuffed, covered in plaster and looked too big for him.

I was looking off into the distance as we passed, but still heard him say something. I failed to gather what he said and instinctively turned and asked him, "Que?"

He turned his face back to me as he continued to walk away and repeated, "Tu eres bonita."

I didn't ask him to repeat his words again. I'd gotten the message the second time, loud and clear and kept on walking purposefully away from the dejected slice of suburbia. He hadn't asked me a question, given me directions or even commented on the weather. He'd thrown me a flirtatious compliment as if it were as normal as saying hello. Over the past few days I'd come to learn that men in Spain were neither shy nor sparing when it came to complimenting a lady. It took some getting used to, even when it felt rather harmless. And this young kid throwing me a few flirtatious syllables was harmless; he lacked the dogged interest and physical intimidation other leering men possessed, and because of that, I found myself thanking him, at a loss for what else to say.

I crossed an empty road and entered a field of poppies stretching to the horizon. The endless trail was nothing but land and sky. I could have been the last person in the whole world, moving in place and never advancing anywhere. Each turn was into another string of fields; each crossroad promised four directions of the same. Even the sun had forsaken its early morning softness and turned harsh, whiting out my vision as it pummeled the ground with light. The land had taken on my qualities, and I had taken on hers. The both of us were full of longing for sustenance and marked with a crushing sense of endless isolation. The trail once again threw the nature of my journey back at me. This place was defined by aching beauty as far as the eye could see and a lone figure pressing onward.

Several hours later, I was relieved to arrive in the large village of Santa Domingo de Calzada. I welcomed the noise of cars and people bustling about in the morning hours. It snapped me out of the dreamlike state I'd drifted into. To return to civilization was to reconnect with the human world and have no time to slip into the hollow emptiness of waiting. That was the stuff of poetry, nature and the edge of sleep, all of which melted under the utilitarian glare of everyday life. I followed the trail through the center of the city. As I walked by the closed doors of the church, I noticed several pilgrims lounging on the steps, waiting for it to open. This church was a particularly popular landmark for it boasted a unique altarpiece of live white chickens. I was curious but had arrived hours before the doors would open. Even if the other pilgrims felt content to wait, I knew I couldn't muster the patience.

Leaving the city was as seamless as entering it. Santa Domingo came to an abrupt end when I crossed a small river and skirted a group of pilgrims clogging the trail. The stagnant group was a family too busy bickering with each other to glance up as I passed. Speaking rapidly in a tongue I didn't recognize, they threw volleys back and forth. The father's face was beet red as he hollered at the teenage children, skulking around him with sullen expressions.

The trail grew empty again. The tendons in my ankles felt raw and tight, and I tried to disregard the unnatural way they squeaked. I thought of Alec and then tried not to. Falling prey to tendonitis wasn't acceptable. How could I follow the guidance churning in my core, pushing me onward at top speed, if I was dragging gimpy inflamed legs along behind me? Was this the added endurance challenge? Could I keep following this nonsensical guidance even when injury and pain seemed like more reliable companions than any mythical pilgrim community up ahead? I needed a distraction to keep my mind from dwelling on such thoughts, hunting for answers I still didn't have. I needed some company, another pilgrim's story to fill my head. Squinting my eyes, I noticed a group ahead of me up the trail. One of the men appeared to be wearing a baseball cap. It was a small but not inconsequential clue about this mysterious group. I had a hunch they were English speakers, maybe even Americans, for I'd noticed that such headwear wasn't in vogue with European pilgrims.

Twenty minutes later, I was walking embedded in a group of three middle aged Irishmen and one of their wives. They were warm and inclusive, absorbing me like family and making genuine inquiries about my solo journey. Light on their feet, they carried small packs with water, explaining they had paid to have the rest of their things shipped ahead. Having just learned about pack carriers the night before, I was a bit startled to stumble across another group employing such modern means. They seemed at ease with their choice and weren't embarrassed in the least. Even as they praised the convenience and skipped along cheerfully unburdened, I knew I could never take advantage of such services. Carrying my pack and shouldering the burden of my things were core elements of my trek. In having to strap all my belongings to my back and carry them the whole way, I was acutely aware of what I choose to keep. I'd willingly pared down my life and set off on this voyage with just the necessities. In the past few days, I'd relished the chance to free myself from more items I no longer needed. It was as liberating as a hair cut: the snip, the locks falling to the ground and the immediate release of layers of the past.

One of my central aims on the Camino was to clear out the extra baggage in my life, and my penchant for unburdening my pack was a direct reflection of this ethos. Plus, I'd come to realize how little I actually needed. I wore the same clothes and shoes everyday, and it had no bearing on my life, caused no commotion in my inner world and changed no outcomes in my outer life. On the trail, what a pilgrim carried mattered only to him or her. Nobody commented on anyone's lack of things, and if a pilgrim chose to carry forty pounds versus ten, it was a choice that affected that pilgrim alone. Yet I felt my choice to be as light and streamlined as possible did have a reverberation out into the space around me, for it affected my mood, my pace and my general feeling of release. As my pack became lighter, I was becoming a more enjoyable person to be around, no longer weighted by ounces of the past.

That said, it was slightly bizarre to walk among a group who believed the opposite. They wanted their plethora of belongings, their heavy suitcases and overflowing packs so much, they paid to have this stuff dragged along behind them. I found a peacefulness in not being caught in the frenzy of needing things. In Logroño, I'd hardly looked in the shop windows. If I couldn't eat it or use it to tape up a blister then it just wasn't that important. This hard scrabble life as a pilgrim had already bestowed such gifts in its unburdening effect that it would forever outweigh being deprived of sheets, towels and fresh clothes. I wasn't convinced this pack of Irishmen could experience this while still tied to a mountain of luggage.

When priorities have a tangible physical impact, they seem to draw forward our real relationship and attachment to stuff. I wasn't willing to sweat and suffer over non-essential gear, and most gear was non-essential. There was very little pilgrims needed, especially in Spain in June with the guarantee of a soft place to sleep, running water and a roof over our heads each night. Camino life revealed the uselessness of most things. It undercut all need to collect, acquire and horde. On the Camino, contentment, security and happiness were all states of mind that had no allegiance to material things.

When the group paused in the next village in search of mid morning tea, I said my goodbyes and headed off alone. I crossed vast sun burnished fields and wound into another small village. As I followed the arrows down a paved lane on the backside of town, a bike horn rang out behind me. I turned to find Alec sitting proudly atop a shiny bike, wearing a very satisfied grin.

I couldn't believe my eyes. I'd left him behind me hours ago and didn't expect to see him until dusk. He'd made a habit of arriving just as doors to the albergue were closing for the night, snagging the last open bunk. I knew one of these days the doors might close without him, but I'd never dreamed he would abandon his feet and take to wheels. As my mouth hung open, and I sputtered, trying to figure out how to ask where, why and when he became a bike pilgrim, he jumped in and explained. He described how his ankles had given out in Santa Domingo, and a local had suggested he rent a bike. He would ride to Burgos, the next major city, turn the bike in at the rental shop and leave the Camino. The bike was little more than his end game. Our travels together and his solo journey along the trail were drawing to a close. I walked along beside him as he let the bike roll. He was planning to go to the coast to lie on the beach and take a proper holiday. It sounded both appealing and unimaginable at the same time. I couldn't stop now. The current was too strong in me. I couldn't allow myself to get where Alec found himself, a place where there was little choice but to jump ship and make for the mainland of everyday life.

After he explained his new plan, we stood for a moment in silence, neither of us sure what to say. Finally he stuck out his hand, and I shook it. Then he quickly hopped on this bike, shouting "Ciao!" over his shoulder. And he was gone. I watched him speed along for a few minutes and finally disappear. My trail life was changing. The few roots I'd managed to plant were being pulled up. I felt out of control knowing people came and went so quickly. They could be in my inner circle and then disappear in a flash. I was at the mercy of the trail, and no longer carried the illusion that I held any sway over its current or could predict its next move.

The day grew warm as the sun moved towards the center of the open sky. I had no clue where Alberto had gone, yet I was quite sure I hadn't overtaken him. The noon hour dragged, but my pace never slowed. To make matters worse, the trail left the quiet road and turned parallel to a four-lane highway. Only another flimsy chain link fence served as a barrier between the speeding cars and the dusty pathway. The air smelled of exhaust and was clogged with the constant drone of engines. With each footfall, I could feel the vibration of the highway rattling my limbs. My joints grew sore from the combined stress of my pack pushing down from above and the shuddering path rumbling from below. I looked down the expanse of open trail and could see the heat rising off the land. The terrain was flat with not a moment of shade. The only refuge I had left was my ipod and the world of music it held. At this point the voices and melodic sounds were more of a collection of dear friends than entertainment. My ipod was intended as emotional back up for moments when I needed comfort, but now it was an escape as the sights around me grew bleak. I'd only used it once or twice in the past week; but today it felt like an essential tool to get me beyond the juggernaut of desolate land and non-existent community.

With so many passing by me on the highway, I couldn't help wonder where they were coming from, who they were with and what awaited them when they arrived. They knew the route and destination; I couldn't say where I would be tonight, let alone the days to come. I was just as unsure of what awaited me when I returned from the Camino. What was the life that lay ahead? Would I find the thread here that would take my everyday life where it was meant to go? Just because I still clung to my ragged piece of guidance like a raft, didn't mean I felt safe or even saved from drowning. Even many days in, as I was hitting my stride physically, I still felt like throwing up. The proof of my guidance felt as illusive as ever. Where were the people? Where was the love?

Doubt had resumed its chokehold on my chest, and the desperation I felt with my Italian traveling companions only made things worse. With hours and hours of time together, the vacant silly cross language banter had run out. I longed for a deep substantive conversation. I wanted a chance to speak freely about the issues that filled my heart, to seek wise counsel and to be understood. I knew I could offer the same to a fellow pilgrim, but I kept shedding connections rather than building them. People kept disappearing, falling behind or taking off on bikes.

Even our trio which had managed to stick together was now finished. Now with Alec gone, I was in a more complicated situation with Alberto. We had a bit of dependence on each other but could never really be close. I felt a deep protective energy in our interactions, and I trusted his companionship, but I knew it couldn't last. Perhaps he did as well, and we were simply waiting for things to change, the cards to reshuffle and dynamics to shift. How much longer could we go with so little shared language? He could meet an Italian, or I could come across a group of English speakers, and we would drift. I secretly hoped a community was just a around the next bend, even if it would be the end of my friendship with Alberto, and I felt he wished this for me too. Neither of us felt this was the best way to travel this trail, but we were limping along until something better arose.

My goal for the day was to reach Belorado, a village that boasted several albergues and a bunch of shops. To arrive at this town, I needed to walk a normal stage plus an additional half stage. I'd been doing this for the past few days, and today it required me to walk roughly forty kilometers. Around two in the afternoon as I trudged onward, I found my body starting to weave with each step. The view up ahead gave no signs of a town anytime in the near future, causing my spirits to slowly sink lower and lower. Sometimes a town would appear over the crest of land with a surprising flourish. Like islands rising out of the fierce ocean, just the sight of these places brought relief, but Belorado was proving illusive. The trail seemed to continue endlessly to the horizon. Kilometers fell away under my feet, and the hours wore on. Time was a cunning creature, and in the bright sun of late afternoon, it dragged through me like a rusty hook. I'd been on my feet walking since before sunrise. My pace had dropped into a clear rhythm, but it didn't change the fact that today, like all the days before it, was a day dominated by endless motion.

As the late afternoon heat soaked my skin, and the noise of the highway drowned my ears, I felt myself slipping into a far away place. I might have been delirious with a mild case of sunstroke or wobbling dehydration, but I could feel the energy up ahead. I couldn't see their faces or be sure how close they lay, but my body seemed to buzz with the taste of something beyond this moment. Even though I was near exhaustion, I felt my pace quicken. The energy felt so vibrant, I couldn't stop myself. I wanted to reel it in, bring it to my arms and not just feel it from afar.

I remained upright by focusing on the twists and turns of the land, trying to interpret which fold hid Belorado. Crossing the road, I finally started to see buildings. Walking under a high rock, I reached the outskirts of civilization and found Alberto sitting under a tree. He sat very still as if sleeping or lost in deep meditation, but as soon as I drew close, his eyes flew open. He leapt to his feet and called out to me, "Elissabetta!!!" He ran over and grabbed my hand with a wide grin on his face. He was genuinely pleased to see me, and I felt the same way. To have finally arrived and to see a familiar face melted all anxiety, and for one precious moment, I felt light enough to hop around like a fool and laugh with Alberto. The dry rumbling land of speeding cars was behind us now, and my reward was a night of gloriously horizontal rest before I faced whatever the trail threw at me next.

BELORADO

Belorado was similar in layout to many of the other villages we had passed through. All the dwellings were clustered around an old city center with tight winding roads that led back to the central square. The village had just over two thousand inhabitants all of whom lived in a two kilometer radius from its center. My town at home had the same number of citizens but was one hundred square kilometers with people living scattered to the wind. The difference this brought to Belorado was immediately evident. In the late afternoon light, groups sat outside talking to each other as hordes of kids ran by. Women pushed strollers and chatted in their dooryards. Voices and movement were interwoven elements, producing abundant signs that this was a shared living space.

Alberto walked slightly ahead of me as we followed the arrows to the albergue. I was horrified to notice the ease of his steps. His pace was insanely vigorous, noticeably fresh and untouched by weariness, fatigue or soreness. He walked with the same sprightly air I remembered from our first meeting. This was simply not human. How could anyone be so untouched by a blazing forty kilometer day, especially when we had been moving at this clip for the past week? I was beyond envious; I was distraught. My strides were short and muscled compared to his, and every tight step sent sharp threads of pain down my ankles. I was young, but he was strong and impervious to injury. I couldn't believe I was the weaker of our duo now; I was the one dragging us down. Alec had fallen. Why did I think the same might not happen to me? Alberto didn't notice my weakened state or at least he didn't comment on it, so I kept my mouth shut. If he knew how bad the pain was, he might advise me to stop or insist I slow down. If he was in the dark, then I could make all the calls about my health, I could be the one to feel out the pain threshold, decide when my situation was about to go from nagging injury to permanent damage and stay just a hair's breath from that precipice.

As we followed the trail straight to the heart of the town, I knew we would stumble upon one of two things: an albergue or the church. If the past week had instilled any sense of pattern in a rather random existence, it was that the trail always went through the center of town aiming for the church like heat seeking missile. Tucked among edifices old and new, the arrows always pointed the way to prime real estate, the hub of community and the town's central show piece.

As promised, the trail delivered the two of us to the front steps of a solid deep-rooted church. The tall grey stones with three thick spires stretched upwards, looming above the river. I had to shield my eyes from the sun as I looked up at it. It was another sturdy church, and like others of its kind, it felt impressive, considering the size of the village. Who knew how I would feel when I came face to face with the mighty cathedrals of the cities ahead? I wasn't sure if they would endear me more to the small town churches or taint my eyes by forever casting shadows over these lesser buildings. I never desired more than an outward view of these structures. The insides held no draw, and I fully intended to keep our association one of curious detachment and surface appreciation. With my eyes on such buildings, I was an architect and an anthropologist but never a member of the club.

As I looked up, I caught sight of an arc of movement, a flash of white and a completely unexpected and rather enchanting sight. The spires of the church were covered with large bird nests dangling off the sides of the building. Regal long legged storks had fashioned nests out of straw and branches, perching them on the top of the stone surfaces. Small sets of beaks peered over the side of the nests, while adult birds cycled to and from the spires in endless loops. Apparently storks were notorious for creating their homes above the churchyards, but this was the first time I'd ever seen them there. I wondered if the storks knew they had taken up residence in the most coveted spot in each village, or if their choice of the church roof was simply for dramatic effect.

The albergue we sought was a small building tucked snugly under the side eaves of the church. Nothing marked its simple dooryard as a place of residence except a few scattered chairs and a clothes rack. Insulated by thick stone, the entryway was dark and cool but still managed to feel welcoming. There were several tables near the front of the room and a small kitchen at the back. The space had very few windows but felt well cared for. The albergue was a municipal run by a Dutch organization that cycled a host of volunteers through all summer. The married couple currently in residence had been stationed here for two weeks and would soon move elsewhere along the trail. Even with the language barrier, the duo were generous hosts. They welcomed in every person who came through the door with genuine warmth and used smiles and laughter as the glue when language failed. With not a word of Spanish between them, I was surprised they'd signed on for this assignment, but I discovered they'd figured out ways of getting around the language issue. Reading from cue cards and showing the pilgrims the lay of the land through a hands-on tour were two key elements; both techniques seemed to keep the albergue running just fine. Alberto stood behind me looking out the doorway into the street with an air of detachment, unfazed that he understood nothing that was being said. This wasn't a new phenomenon. He'd come to peace with isolation of this kind, and it showed. Pure acceptance such as his left no twitching anxiety in its wake; it hardly left a trace at all. Meanwhile, I still chaffed under the stress and strained to understand every word, determined not to lose connection.

Eventually the tour directed us up a very steep set of stairs. The stairs to the dormitory looked more like a wide ladder into a musty attic than a main route to the second floor. I summoned all my remaining balance and followed Alberto up the narrow treads, placing my sore feet sideways with care. On my way up, I was more than relieved to see a small shelf tucked next to the stairs with a first aid box sitting on it. I had a sinking suspicion I would be ransacking it for tape and gauze in hopes such simple tools would keep my deteriorating tendons limping along for another day.

The second floor opened into a wide landing that had been converted into space for sleeping. Two sets of bunks were tucked up against the far wall out of the flow of traffic heading to other rooms down the hall. A window overlooking the river filled the landing with soft light. The walls were a muddy red color that made the space feel cozy and safe. Alberto turned to me, and I nodded my head. This would do. I was too tired to go searching down the hall for something else. Alberto placed his bag down on a small table under the window as I claimed a set of the bunks then opened the window wider to let the fresh air in.

As the town lay in a soft siesta silence, I sought the showers in hopes that I could stay awake through the duration of the experience. Armed with only a bar of soap and my ratty washcloth, I limped downstairs and located the narrow set of stalls. Having under-packed in this arena and foolishly forsaken indulging in a super absorbent hiker's towel, I paid the price every time I got wet. I no longer felt so righteously proud of my space saving cloth. In retrospect, I could see it was one of the more idiotic packing choices I'd made, and that included the rain jacket with little tolerance for actual rain. No piece of slightly disintegrating cotton could be expected to take on the challenge of drying a full grown adult, so it often reached a breaking point around my face and arms then stupendously failed. I often spent long stretches of time covered in goose bumps, waiting for the wild curls of my hair to relinquish all the water they had thirstily drunk. I wasn't asking for the fluffy towels of materialist indulgence, just a bit more yardage or one of those marvelous squares of high absorbency material that looked amazingly spongy. A girl can dream, but until I could abandon my lazy good for nothing washcloth, showering would be a cold and lengthy affair.

Another one of my brilliant time and space saving items was my three in one magic bar of soap. Though a cousin of my disobliging washcloth, this soap had proven its mettle. Pilgrims needed to clean their clothes, wash their bodies and hair as well as scrub their cuts, bruises and blisters. With minimal space it didn't make sense to carry three separate cleaning products, so I had jumped on the chance to pack just one: a bar of old fashioned Castile soap. Other pilgrims had sought the same three in one solution and several had simply purchased a cheap shampoo to tackle the job. Though their clothes came out smelling like fruity perfumes, everything was clean and that was the bottom line. The only drawback to choosing a liquid was its nasty habit of shifting during the day and upending itself on the entire contents of one's bag. I'd only seen this once, but the emotional toll it enacted wasn't pretty.

If my goal on the trail was to be low maintenance, I was getting there, using the absence of a mirror in the last three days to help me along my way. I was driven by weariness to abandon my worries about what I looked like. In fact, I was starting to feel it had no bearing whatsoever on my journey. Besides the one or two licentious dinner invitations, I wasn't living in a shallow world, and nobody here was afraid of seeing each other looking rough around the edges. This was reality stripped of its smooth veneer, and it was delightfully liberating.

I was only twenty four, but I'd long ago grown tired of the never ending expectations to be primped, plucked and polished at all times. I thought back to my roommate at the London hostel on my way to the trailhead. She'd been horrified I couldn't take makeup with me on the trail. I'd decided not to tell her that I would also be using hand soap to wash my hair. She might have needed to sit down and maybe even put her head between her legs. The trail felt like one of the best places to rise above all the unbelievable things expected of women, offering a chance to let people know me just as I was, unfiltered and unadorned. Though I'd grown up away from the cultural mainstream, I'd had my moments of falling in and gulping some water. But the fight against the current of the culture could only be won by walking away. The appearance standards coupled with the cultural mandates that swore women would never be lovable without a whole lot of effort, dragged on my generation like self-induced shackles. We might have clipped ourselves in, but only because we'd been brainwashed to feel all the guise and artifice was needed. We lived in a two dimensional world of media and had given up our third dimension to stay with the times. But to set on out a journey like the Camino, we had to return to all three dimensions. The trail torched, clear-cut and leveled the omnipresent cultural ideas that we didn't need our bodies to be anything but attractive objects. This journey wasn't a tame endeavor for paper dolls. And all the while, I continued to stick my hand out, take a risk and introduce myself to anyone and everyone. I just hoped I could trust my three dimensional unadorned self even if romantic love did come along.

Above and beyond the small sufferings that accompanied a trip to the shower, I found it a moment to take stock of my new crop of cuts and bruises. That afternoon I discovered the cuts at my hips were healing over, and the bruises on my shoulders had receded to a light purple. After the first few days, the stress from my shoulder straps has lessened, and I'd grown accustomed to living with a waist belt cinched around my pelvis. I no longer winced every time I slid my pack onto the tender crests of my shoulders, and my hips no longer ached as I lay in bed at night. Maybe my body was finally coming to terms with the new conditions of life. I'd given it little other choice. I could only hope my lower limbs would take the cue from my upper body now that the trouble zones seemed to be shifting southward. Only when standing perfectly still did my ankles feel halfway normal. Any slight movement and the rubbery inflexible tendons shot a resounding jolt up my legs. Even lying down, I had to position my ankles just right so the tendons didn't ache. As I checked in with my body and assessed the damage, I came away feeling grateful I wasn't showing more signs of wear. Despite all my minor complaints, my body was carrying me along this trail with great fortitude. I owed much to my body's willingness to take a thrashing and keep charging forward. Even through my weariness, I knew I was more resilient than I'd been in a very long while. I felt a deep tenderness for all my physical frame was going through, and I felt sorry I'd been beating on it so relentlessly. The trail had driven me to it. My guidance, the dream, and all the signs in between had kept me going when my bones, muscles and internal working would rather have curled up in the fetal position and taken a long siesta. Even the emotional side of me would have heartily agreed, recognizing that all of this was too stressful after so much turmoil. But my body's pleas and the demands of my emotional self were team players, and somehow they were recognizing this push forward was good for the whole.

Eventually, I returned from the showers and glanced at my watch. I still had two hours before siesta ended. The middle of the day was always a hard time for my stomach. Having just finished a long day of walking, all I wanted to do was eat and promptly pass out into a deep, dream laden sleep, but the closed shops thwarted my plans for refueling.

I opened my book in an attempt to pass the time, but couldn't remember what was happening or where I'd left the story. I must have been so tired the last time I closed the book that I'd erased all mental notes on plot development. I lay on my bunk in the quiet room and wondered where Alberto had gone. I wasn't surprised we were spending more and more time apart; neither of us seemed to know why we were even connected anymore.

I hardly turned a single page of my book before the words grew blurry, and I let my eyes close for a moment. It felt deliciously easy to stay there with lids drawn and convince myself I was simply pausing in my reading progress. But within moments, I'd curled on my side and fallen asleep with the hum of the Dutch couple talking softly to each other on the floor below me. They would be there until late evening waiting for the day's pilgrims to stagger in through the doors. I had the feeling their energy wouldn't flag, and even the last person in the door would get a warm welcome. I was comforted by the noise of their voices, the distant comings and goings. It was like being home, safe in the soft center of a house filled with my people. And I suppose these pilgrim compatriots had now become my people: my large, wild, extended surrogate family.

When I awoke, it was clear Alberto had been through the room. While I slept he'd carefully placed a warm wool blanket on me, making sure to cover my bare legs. Its scratchy edges had even been tucked over my curled toes. I knew I'd been asleep for many hours for the light was low and the air much cooler. My body felt warm and displaced as if I was returning from some other realm. Dreams visited me each time I closed my eyes on the trail, and they were unlike anything I'd ever dreamt before. Each was like a long drawn out moment, one frame of a vibrant vignette. I sat up and decided to find Alberto to see if he wanted to go into the central square for food. As I stood, I felt my ankles were more disgruntled than ever. This didn't bode well for tomorrow. As I looked out the window, I could see there were crowds in the street. A large swarm of people clung to the stairs of the church like a colorful hive. Women in silk dresses with open backs and plunging necklines huddled around men in tuxes, while small children in floral dresses and pressed collared shirts weaved in and out, aware only of their own diversions.

Suddenly the bell in the tower of the church rang out, reverberating through the whole room and filling my ears. The crowd outside cheered and turned to face the doors of the church. As the gathering throng parted, I saw bunches of white flowers, a sleek black car and baskets full of rose petals. Hobbling as quickly as my sleep stiff legs could take me, I bounced down the narrow stairs and made for the front door. All I wanted was a glimpse, a fleeting splash of white, a set of newly intertwined arms, a look of pure joy. All I wanted was a taste of this celebration, a small still frame of this wedding on the edges of my solo trail. I rushed past the Dutch couple who leaned against the doorframe with soft whimsical expressions. Like a tight multicolored bloom, the crowd drew around the couple obscuring all view, until suddenly my line of sight opened as people fell away. The ground was coated with petals as the flower girls spun circles and waved their arms goodbye to the smooth dark surface of the car pulling away. The fleeting moment was gone, and I'd missed the bride and groom.

Settling myself in an empty chair outside the albergue, I watched as the last of the wedding party dispersed. The celebration had just begun, and spirits were high as they took off in various cars bound for a full night of merriment. Knowing the Spanish penchant for nightlife, I was certain even the children and grandparents would take part in the all night reception. Nobody was left out based on age or the hour; this wedding was an all community event. Once the revelers were gone, the courtyard felt hollow and empty. There were few pilgrims about, and no one to talk to. At times in the last week, I'd felt swept up into this strange caravan of international movers, but in these paused moments, I often felt the gaps. Living together and walking the same path gave wonderful fodder for shared experience, but community needed a bit more glue. In fact, I was starting to feel that grounded community could never just be. It needed to have an intentional strand, a sense of cohesion that required effort. There had to be people acting as stewards of the community and forces drawing the members together.

That night at dinner, I connected again with the Curator from Prague across a wide table in the dark albergue kitchen. As she sat rigid in her chair with her elbows spearing the wooden surface, her deep eyes reflected many of my fears back to me. Though she wore her tension like a weighted cloak, we were infected with the same ailment. The side effects were bone numbing weariness, a nostalgic longing for comfort and a twinge of sorrow at how the trail was unfolding. She was much more in control of her symptoms than me and noticeably more captivated by the fever of pace. There was something coldly unrelenting in her pressure on herself. I wondered what it would be like to reach across the vast space and touch her shoulder, pat her thin frame and call her back to the human world. I certainly felt in need of touch but had suppressed the hunger with physical exertion. In some ways, I walked to erase my feelings and replace them with aches and pains. I didn't know if the Curator was playing the same game, for her defenses were as thick and impenetrable as armor.

One revealing quality was her marked disinterest in company and community. She was unequivocally here for herself and herself alone. Once again, I was shocked to stumble across a fellow pilgrim who wanted to be alone. Did they not realize they'd chosen the most popular route of the trail during peak season? Or were statements like this a protection against arriving at the end with no friends to speak of? Meeting people was my central aim. Would I look even more the fool if I announced this along the length of the trail and then found myself alone at the end? Was it better to play it cool like the Curator? I wasn't sure, but I had the feeling people were more likely to embrace my warm friendly banter and desire to connect than her glamorous yet chilly sense of individualism. Only time would tell, but if she was speaking the truth about not wanting community she had an emotional leg up on me. She wouldn't be disappointed to reach the end and look out over Santiago alone, but I would be. She was cured of the want, but I still had it, bad. She said no more about what fueled her progress, and I didn't ask. Instead we ate in silence, talked of the weather and her plan for another forty kilometer day tomorrow. I was mildly relieved to see someone else struggling but was distressed to feel our inner turmoil only isolated us more. Alberto's effortless ease with trail life sometimes made me feel crazy as if I was the only one stumbling along through this experience making a total mess of things.

After the dinner dishes were done, Alberto and I set off into town to buy a few supplies and distract ourselves for a while. The albergue had become quiet as a tomb, full of long shadows. Walking side by side, we left the churchyard and made our way to the central plaza. Alberto slowed his steps to match mine as we wandered like a slow flowing current. The square was lined with outdoor cafes encircling a fountain with a slow trickle of water. Tables spilled out from the buildings to flood the cobblestones. One place was clearly the most popular spot in town; it was at least twice the size of the others and twice as busy. With red umbrellas sheltering its patrons from the last of the sun, waiters scurried about pouring drinks and serving plates of delicately constructed tapas. The groups were local as well as international, but one rowdy table caught my attention even from afar. There were no more than half a dozen people around the table, which by Spanish standards was a meager crowd, but they stuck out for another reason entirely.

The Spanish were notorious for meeting up with their extended family at cafes, so fifteen or twenty people around a table, laughing and talking as if they were in their living room, was a common occurrence. As I drew closer, interested in what had caught my attention, I came within earshot and realized the entire table was speaking English unabashedly with indifference to the mood of the café and with little regard for others around them. Yes, English was common, but it wasn't exactly popular and was especially likely to draw looks when traipsed around at loud decibels in public spaces. Even though the group was creating something of a scene, I couldn't resist the siren song of my mother tongue, and I veered toward the table. The ringleader was a woman with long grey hair leaning back in her chair and sipping a glass of wine in between spurts of uproarious laughter. Even from a distance, the clues to her background caught my eyes like florescent biker gear; the Native American talisman around her neck, her billowy layers, the pair of worn leather sandals and the wide turquoise bangles around her wrists were dead giveaways. I knew she hailed from either the liberal west coast or the liberal east coast and that she was involved in the alternative world to some degree or another. She was a known quantity and very familiar to a girl like me who had grown up playing in gardens where flower essences were made. Her familiarity was comforting as well as disorienting. This middle of nowhere Spanish town was worlds away from home, and the people I'd come to know, including Alberto the Italian yoga instructor, had no link to my life back in the states. But this woman did, and she didn't even know it. I was inclined to feel connected even before we met. Maybe I was just thirsty for anything familiar or for an easy distraction. No matter the reason, when Alberto wandered off to find a bank machine, I walked over to introduce myself.

As I stuck out my hand, the woman smiled a wide grin and pulled a chair out for me. She introduced herself with a flourish and went around the table familiarizing me with the rest of the group. Sitting across from me was the most reserved duo at the table, a Spanish couple with impeccable English and stern frowning faces. To my right sat a large man with long white hair whom the ringleader proudly introduced as her husband. Hailing from Connecticut, the couple was at large in the world and enamored by its every charm. When I asked about their home in the states, they laughed and shared the best joke of all. They'd sold their house several years ago, boxed up all their stuff and taken off. They hadn't lived stateside for five years and casually mentioned they didn't plan to ever go back. With no permanent address, they were homeless in the most glamorous sense of the word. They traveled around the world and lived wherever they landed, carving a home out of each new place and moving on when the time felt right. They lived as modern solvent gypsies.

The Gypsy wife took full charge of the conversation, letting her powerful voice fill the space around us, gesturing with bold sweeps of her hands and flicking the ends of her hair as she spoke. I found it easy, yet overwhelming to talk with them. The flood of information, the fast pace of banter and the strikingly familiar behaviors quickly filled my circuit board. I'd become acclimatized to the trail, and this was unlike anything I'd experienced since touch down in Spain.

In the rare moments when the Gypsy wife wasn't speaking, she stayed in motion, shifting and scanning the open plaza. When her husband spoke, his soft gravely voice was low, and he had a tendency to lean in as if confiding classified information. His presence was the calm at the center of his wife's storm of words and movement. I could see how she needed his sturdy presence to keep her feet on the ground and her life in balance. The Gypsy husband's face was worn from years in the sun, but when he smiled, he let the gesture travel to his eyes and displayed a large set of white teeth. Decades of laughter lines crinkled around his broad mouth and eyes and for that, I warmed to him. Even though he didn't speak much, I felt drawn to his words and curious how he managed life holding onto the skirts of a whirling dervish.

At home in India several years ago, they'd been told about this trail and felt a spine tingling sense of purpose. Even though they were a world away, they both agreed that someday they would make their home on the Camino. They pointed out that if they'd stayed in their rooted life back on the east coast, they would never have heard about this trail. It was true that very few people stateside knew anything about the Camino, but it didn't take much for those of us who were destined to be part of its flow. Our ears and internal radars were tuned to her frequency. All it took was a wisp of a mention of the Camino for me to sign on and take the plunge. Still, they had a point about Americans in general. I'd just started to understand how few Americans walked the trail. I could count on one hand the number of fellow countrymen I'd met here. We were a novelty along this famous European trail, and I had a feeling Europe wanted to keep it that way.

Still a bit sleep laden, I listened with interest to the conversation as it moved and shifted to different topics. It was effortless to sit back and soak it in. The Gypsy wife needed little back up as she hopped from one subject to the next like a well versed talk show host. It wasn't until she started talking about all the young people she and her husband had met on the trail that I was knocked out of my daze and brought to full attention.

"Have you met the American guys from New York?" she asked breezily. I, of course, hadn't met any other young people in the last few days, let alone Americans guys. With a feverish glow in my eyes, I quickly enquired when they'd last seen said guys and if they were here in town tonight.

"Oh they're so fast, they're probably way ahead now." she stated in a matter of fact tone, clearly unaware of the crushing blow her words delivered. "That's the thing about young boys, they move fast." she said with a laugh as she lifted her wine glass in the air and took a long sip. I hated the way so many of my fellow pilgrims assumed the fairer sex couldn't hold their own on the trail. She might have been impressed with the young turks from NYC, but she hadn't seen me out on the open trail in full health with an internal motor fueled by the scent of destiny. I was a pilgrim to be reckoned with, and this body could brave the trail with as much speed and stamina as any boy.

I would simply have to prove this doubting pilgrim wrong and catch up. It seemed to be a growing theme in my journey; always behind, always on the hunt. As the topic changed again, I stood up and said my goodbyes. I could feel my bunk calling to me now more than ever. Every day was a race, and sleep was an essential form of fuel. Besides it looked like tomorrow was shaping up to be another long one.

I returned before the sky started to get dark, pleased to re-enter the cool albergue and find it aglow with warm lights and several groups eating dinner. I was emboldened by the idea of trying to meet the mythical Americans. The view of the day had shifted, and now the course forward was transformed into something new and unexpected. As I hobbled back up the stairs and into our alcove, I found Alberto preparing his bunk. We nodded to each other, and I gestured for him to wake me when he was ready to leave in the morning. I wanted to get an early start on the day and could count on Alberto to roust me. I crawled into my sleeping bag, too weary to read. My limbs felt weighted. I tucked my head into the hood of my sleeping bag and plunged into a thick sea of sleep. It was good to turn off my anxieties, let the night flood around me and absorb all my bounding thoughts. Tomorrow would arrive soon enough.

Very soon, in fact. I was shaken awake in the dark. It was four in the morning and very cold. My skin shivered in the pitch dark room, and sleep lapped at me hungrily. This wasn't exactly what I imagined when I asked Alberto to wake me for an early start.

ST. JUAN DE ORTEGA

STAGE EIGHT- 51.4K-32M

BELORADO TO BURGOS

I gathered my things, stumbled down the stairs and plunged into the dark morning. Alberto stood in front of the church, tightening the straps of his pack and looking eager to be off. There was no clue to suggest he'd ever gone to sleep or was even in need of such pedestrian functions. Not only was he wide awake, but he was unbelievably cheerful. It was positively super human. I'd never met his equal. I, on the other hand, still felt half asleep. But with the open trail calling us and no reason to linger, I knew my moving body would bring me back to waking life in no time.

Without a word, Alberto flicked on his compact flashlight, and we moved away from the church. As we wound our way through the streets, Alberto swung the beam of light back and forth seeking arrows. It was absurdly easy to miss a way marker in the dark, and in order to avoid falling off the trail, we had to string the arrows together like a rope, always holding the edge of the last one in sight as we reached for the next. It was slower progress than normal, but our pace would change once we got out of town and on the earthen trail. Alberto walked swiftly between clues, and I hurried along behind him, trying to adjust my pack and ease my stiff muscles into a normal gait. My legs were well versed in autopilot, and they seemed to move unbidden.

Most of the town was dark and silent, but as we crossed the backside of the village, we heard a new rhythm breaking the stillness. As the trail drew us closer, I recognize the sound as muffled music. A set of nightclubs, with glowing neon signs and thick double doors, sat side by side waging a war of beats. Though the insides of the thumping clubs were the main attraction, the cobbled street filled with cool air was the second hottest destination. People came and went, leaking music with each swing of the doors. I drew closer to Alberto as we passed through clusters of staggering young people. Disheveled and covered in sweat, they looked like roughed up mannequins decked out in glossy fabrics and short dresses. The jewelry, the straightened hair and makeup were full on and a bit worse for wear. Groups of shoeless girls shared cigarettes as boys with slicked back hair and strong cologne leaned against the building with their arms slung around each other. Everybody moved at a slow, sloppy pace, in contrast to the crisp hyperbolic beats churning from the club. Their noise sensitivity was long gone and their eardrums shot, but their vision was still relatively sharp, and they didn't fail to notice the two of us. Our appearance was clearly the most bewildering experience in their long night. As a dozen or so faces turned to stare at us, I felt like an intruder caught in the act of sneaking away. Each face registered the same look of glassy eyed drunken disbelief. It was a draw who was more horrified: us or them. Neither pilgrim nor partier had expected to cross paths with the other. Even as their stares followed us down the length of the street, none of us crossed the line between the other's reality. I felt light years away from their drinking and dancing universe, and they watched us as if we were figments of their imagination, little more than ghosts. Our silence and the way we slipped by in the shadows only served to confirm their suspicions. We were made of ether, and like all things magical, could pass unheard, slip away into the rising dark and evaporate. But then again, I couldn't blame them for their disbelief; what kind of crazy people hike at four in the morning?

The trail wound us out of the shuttered suburbs of Belorado onto a narrow path. Alberto tucked away his flashlight, and we walked in the half-light. At first I couldn't see the puddles, but soon my eyes adjusted to the sight of the round glossy circles underfoot. An hour into our day, Alberto and I were still adrift in a silent world. Even on the Camino, darkness was a time of empty trails. Only the overzealous and irrational pilgrims walked before and after the light. I was reminded of the famous Swedish woman and her eighteen day Camino. She had seen the Camino in this half-light and known the land as it dipped into darkness at the end of the day. Her view of this trail was a different universe than those who rose at a reasonable hour.

With the sky blooming into warmer tones, the fields grew restless with birds, and several swung wide loops around us. One pair made games of orbiting above my head then bursting off ahead. Though there was always exhilaration in the first hour of walking, it didn't take long for the silence between Alberto and me to fill with questions. Even though I knew I was following my guidance and leaning heavily on my intuition, I still felt a tide of doubt rising around my feet. How had I come to be in the dark with an unreachable companion? Was this part of the plan? Could I trust this push, and if so, why did my ankles put up a fight with every step? Even with hours to think and plenty of time to wrestle an answer to the ground, these questions stumped me.

We passed through several tiny villages where the only light came from the church tower, and the narrow streets were empty and silent. There were no cafes to offer cups of coffee, no distractions and nothing to do but keep going. We didn't bother to look both ways as we crossed a freshly painted roadway to entered a small town. Like the towns before it, nothing stirred as we passed through. Then just as we skirted the very last building, a movement on the edge of my peripheral vision caught my eye. Turning, I noticed a scruffy ginger colored dog standing at attention in the dooryard of a solid little house. He sniffed the air as if questioning our smell as it floated towards him, then caught my eye and bolted towards us. He leapt off the porch with ease and came over to greet us as if this were his daily ritual. I'd already come across several dogs that lived along the side of the trail and filled their days with ambling out to meet the many new humans that passed by. These dogs eventually lost interest and returned back to their dusty porches or cool spots in the shade to await the next group to pass through their territory. Expecting a docile greeting, I wasn't prepared when the dog ran at full speed, leapt onto two legs and attempted to bathe my face in saliva. After I'd encouraged him back down to the ground, I patted the scruffy head, expecting the little guy to swoon under the attention, but he darted away from me as soon as I made contact. He twirled around me in joyful circles, coyly edging towards me then zooming away. The flirtation was with me alone; he barely noticed Alberto walking just a pace ahead.

As we lost sight of our new friend's porch, I stopped and called him to me. I wanted to give him a loving pat on the head and a gentle shove back home. Yet as he rushed towards me and I reached out, he ducked away and darted down the trail with obvious glee. Alberto turned back to me as the dog flew by him sprinting westward then shrugged his shoulders, sharing my confusion at the movements of this strange new creature. Unsure of what to do, we resumed walking, and I fell into place drafting behind Alberto. The ginger dog returned to rush past me, splashing through the trailside puddles, circling around and taking off forward again. I was hopeful that at any moment the little guy would lose interest in us and turn back, perhaps in search of something more exciting like his morning meal. But minutes passed, kilometers passed and the moment didn't come. As we walked farther and farther from the small village, I could feel a tension building in my chest, and each step became weighted. I was destined to go forward and keep on moving, but this dog wasn't. His life was back there, and the more we led him astray the more I felt responsible as if I were aiding and abetting his escape. I could no longer pretend that Alberto and I were in this together; the pup was highly focused on me and me alone. I was the center of his wild circles and the only one he attempted to knock over with his running leaps. So Alberto was off the hook and wandered ahead of us, unaware of the unfolding dynamics behind him. I was the one to notice my canine companion was spunky and sweet, but skittish and unkempt. His fur hadn't been washed or groomed in a long time, and his collar was frayed, all signs of a life of neglect. My heart ached for him, but I still felt he needed to return from whence he came; I couldn't care for him, especially if he hardly let me touch him. I was a traveler here, thousands of miles from home, and in no position to care for this dog, but I had the sinking feeling that he had chosen me.

I stopped and tried to shoo him back. I yelled and gently pushed his furry body backwards, but he slipped out from under my hands again, ran ahead then bounded back to my side. Standing just out of arm's length, he remained rooted next to me, tipping his head inquisitively as if he didn't understand why I was making such a fuss. He'd picked me, and that was that.

My temper rose as I felt a wave of powerlessness wash over me. I couldn't stop this dog from blithely going forward and in doing so, perhaps abandon his life and cast himself into a vagrant's existence. But worst of all, I couldn't stop myself from caring and feeling responsible for the naughty scamp. I couldn't bear to see any harm come to him, but I had no control or way to right this situation. I needed help, but there was nobody but Alberto, and he'd made it clear he wasn't getting involved. When we came through another small town, I tried to find someone, anyone, who could take the dog back to his home. It was only six a.m., and not a soul stirred. Everything was closed, and all the window shades were drawn. The only sign of life was a pack of village dogs that came out to spar with my ginger friend and eventually ran the three of us out of town.

As we left the village, we had to cross a river on a car bridge. A narrow path between the guardrail and the edge of the high bridge was the only space left for pilgrims. The drop to the river was nearly thirty feet, and the water was so low that the cement blocks of the bridge floor were visible. Unafraid of heights and assured of my balance, I charged ahead. I was exactly half way to the other side when the dog rushed through my legs, buckled my knees and tipped the top half my body out over the edge. I felt my center of gravity sway out over open space, the ballast of my weighty pack tugging my feet to the edge. The grisly cement blocks lay directly below me, and for a moment, I knew I was falling. I felt the empty space between weightless flight and gravity. With only a split second for any shred of agility to save me, I inhaled a sharp startled breath and grabbed the cool metal of the road railing with an iron grip. Every muscle fiber was focused on this one task. My feet were still planted as I hauled the tipped weight of my pack away from the drop. The knuckles on my left hand were white, gripping the sharp metal edges of the guardrail as I returned to a fully balanced state. Laying my chest on the guardrail and swinging my legs over, I dropped myself onto the hard tarmac on the other side of the guardrail. All my joints felt like liquid, and I was submerged in a rush of sweat. It didn't matter that I was lying in the road. It was safer than where I had stood as the kamikaze dog rushed at me. I had acted on pure reflex. My brain had nothing to do with my survival. Once again, I owed everything to my body. The instinctual animal part of me had saved me from the fall.

After a few moments, I walked to the end of the bridge and stepped back onto the trail. I remained deeply shaken, while the dog spun in circles, cheerfully chasing its own tail. My cheeks felt hot to the touch, and my nervous system was on fire, pumping heat and cold alternatively up and down the entire length of my body. Slowly my fear receded. I was young, I was agile and I was lucky. Yet I couldn't ignore the fact that the dog had almost taken me down in his idiotic flight from home and put me in peril with his wild uncontrolled ways. Just because he'd selected me as his person didn't mean everything was OK. I suddenly felt the same way for this dog as I had for the men of my past. I didn't want to see them hurt, uncared for or left to play chicken in high speed traffic, but I certainly didn't want them to knock me from a bridge with little concern if I fell.

The next few hours were spent crossing a small range of hills covered in dry scrubby brush as large glistening windmills whispered in great arcs above us. I passed a few groups of pilgrims, and the dog greeted them with overzealous attention. He jumped, licked, splashed in puddles at their feet and darted around frantically. I apologized for the naughty beast every time. Yet after his initial interest in new people, he always returned to my side. Despite my deep misgivings, we continued onward joined at the hip. We passed plenty of other pilgrims, but somehow I had become his alpha human, his one and only. He didn't seem concerned that he had nearly thrown his new love object off a bridge but trotted along with the light little steps of an oblivious innocent. I had no clue what I would do if I couldn't find some way to disentangle from his grasp without feeling guilty, neglectful or upset. Sure, there were cruel things I could do to cut the cord. I could tie him up to a signpost or a trailside tree, but then what? What would become of the little guy? It was infuriating yet impossible not to care. How do you walk away from a neglected lonesome creature even when you know you should? I was no longer sure I was seeing this dog clearly. He had become a furry canine representation off all those tragic lost boys, and I was finding it hard to unearth the energy to pull the trigger and make a break for it.

I didn't feel I had time to hunt for a local to help me with this inherited burden, and we'd gone a great distance from the dog's home. Would anyone here know where to return him to? Or even care? Could I be sure what was really best for the pup? The worst-case scenario would be if he followed me all the way to the city of Burgos. I feared his penchant for obliviously weaving through traffic would end his life right before my eyes, and that would be unbearably traumatic. All I wanted was for him to be safe and for me to be free. I went through all my options as I walked a terrain of dry ugly hilltops and the dog bounded around my feet, threatening to trip me if I lost my focus for a moment. This infatuation was a full time distraction and was bound to knock me down sooner than later.

The goal for the day was to reach a small village called St. Juan de Ortega. Though the guidebook went on at length about the beautiful church in St. Juan, it also intimated that there was little else in the town. There would be no shops, not a single cafe, and virtually no inhabitants. But it did have one advantage that drew the pilgrim hordes; it was the only albergue that lay exactly half way between Belorado and Burgos. Everywhere else was just a bit too close or a bit too far while St. Juan evenly split the fifty kilometers between the bustling town and the grand city. Just a kilometer out of St. Juan, the trail came down off the scrubby hillside and descended into a series of lush fields still trapped in morning dew. A group of men stood alongside a field, leaning against a small red car and talking to each other. One of the younger men held a handful of dirt, rubbing it between his fingers as if checking the earth for signs of health. The man next to him leaned on a shovel and watched closely as if he too were reading the lifeline in the soil. They wore tall rubber boots and well-worn work clothes. One of the older men held a cane and wore a tweed vest over his practical farming attire. As I drew closer he spun around and gave a startled look. Once again, I seemed to have snuck up on a group of unsuspecting locals. I said hello, and the rest turned to stare at me. They looked at me with puzzled expression, their eyes darting from the ginger dog at my heels to my long limbed form. Finally one of the men looked at his watch pointedly and spoke in slow Spanish as he asked me where I had come from. As soon as my answer was out of my mouth, his jaw dropped and the rest of the men laughed with startled disbelief. It was only nine thirty and I'd already walked over twenty-five kilometers. With a channel of communication now open, I tried to explain about the dog by my side, hoping one of the men would come to my rescue. But when I asked them what I should do about the dog, they shrugged their shoulders with little concern. Clearly, they believed in letting sleeping dogs lie and runaway dogs run. But as I walked on and said goodbye, the young farmer with dirt caking his hands told me the man at the bar in St. Juan might be able to help. I gave a smile of thanks, and he winked cheerfully before turning back to his crew.

With the dog following dutifully behind me, we trotted into town. I'd prepared myself for something small and remote, but I hadn't expected what I found. After walking by three houses, I stepped into a cold grey courtyard with a dark looming church and a tiny bar. I could look back along the path to see the beginning of town and could swing around to see the end of it just beyond the courtyard. I was surprised this village hadn't been abandoned long ago. Maybe it was the trail that kept it alive. I had to wonder what became of this place in winter when the pilgrim current ran dry. As I walked across the courtyard with the dog in tow, I looked around in vain for any sign of life. The church doors were firmly closed, and though there was light in the door of the bar, I wasn't optimistic about what lay inside. The sign was old and rusted, and all the outdoor tables leaned against the building up under the eaves. The weather wasn't helping to raise the charm factor; the sky was dark grey and the mist around me was changing into a light sprinkle. The farmers from the field pulled up in their small red car, piled out and made their way into the bar. The rain started to come down with a new intensity as I turned to look back for Alberto. I cursed the useless rain proofing my jacket afforded and made a dash for the bar. Alberto would know where to find me, and if the rain was here to stay, I needed to remain dry as long as possible. The longer I could delay shivers the better.

Alberto and I had made a plan to meet up in St. Juan with the shared belief we would end our day here. But as soon as I arrived in the rainy ghost town with a full two hours until noon, my attachment to the plan waned. We'd both underestimated the advantage of our brutally early start and the speed with which we'd traveled. Speed was one of our shared gifts, but until today we hadn't tested its limits. Though we hadn't walked together in the second half of the morning, I knew he was probably as fresh and energized as me. I also sensed I'd been granted this window of energy and endowed with temporarily resilient ankles, so I could keep jumping stages and stumbling across new faces. Not sure why and certainly not sure when this physical upswing would run out, I couldn't possibly sit around St. Juan de Ortega and let it drain away unused. When Alberto arrived and we sat down to determine the plan, my vote would be for flight and the onward march.

I walked toward the bar to wait, leaving the dog to sit under the eaves in a tight ball. The farmers sat at the bar and talked animatedly about the weather. I waved hello as I scooted past them and dropped my stuff beside a small table against the wall. The bar didn't bother to serve food, but specialized in all the popular beverages one could crave. At such an hour, the dozen or so people in the room were all sidled up to steaming cups of café con leche, and I was eager to join the club. There was nothing better to ward off the chill and drooping energy than piping hot caffeine loaded with sugar and a mound of froth. This hole in the wall may have lacked a bathroom with a lock on the door or a seat on the toilet, but it did have the basics and for that, I was supremely thankful.

The young farmer who had spoken with me in the fields stuck his head outside the door to check the weather. He motioned me over and pointed to the center of the square where my ginger friend was caught in a playful wrestling match with a duo of village dogs. As the three jockeyed for a stronghold on each other, they became a blur of orange and brown fur. I knew I had to leave the dog behind in this small town. Our romance had to end here. If I went on, the major city of Burgos would be in my sights, and its world of roads and busy human chaos was no place for this pup. I was leaning against the bar, in the process of ordering another coffee, when Alberto arrived soaked to the bone but with a remarkably cheerful grin on his face. Once again, I wondered if anything could faze him. There were so many pieces to this life that were pushing on me at any given moment, threatening to break me down; I had to wonder what got to Alberto? Was it being away from his wife and two young adult children or the isolation of spending his days among people who didn't speak his language? Or was it the way the journey had so far failed to be the spiritual quest he'd hoped for? I couldn't claim to understand what made Alberto tick, and he'd never shown me any cracks in his energized persona. But he must have felt some weaknesses, poked around in them in the afternoons and felt them ache in his sleep. We all had cracks, and the Camino was deft at finding them, no matter how hard we tried to keep ourselves locked up, tied down and fully armored. Maybe in Alberto's case, it was only a matter of time. He might be able to keep it together longer than the rest of us, but the Camino was lengthy for a reason, and eventually time was on its side.

After my second cup of coffee and a few chocolate biscuits from Alberto's pack, I pulled out my map. Side by side we bent over the charts, counted off the kilometers and looked longingly at street maps. He glanced around the bar, and I could see he shared my feeling of concern about staying in St. Juan for the night. He turned to me, tapped the next stage in my book, circled Burgos with his finger and nodded his head to the west. And just like that the vote was unanimous. We were off. The rain was still falling in persistent waves, and my outer layers were damp on the inside making my skin clammy. Besides being uncomfortable, nothing really bad could come from a few hours of soaked exercise, right? Was I really going to let the weather trap me into an afternoon, evening and night of incarceration in a ghost town with no food? OK, so I could develop pneumonia, bronchitis or a really nasty cold, but that was a pessimist's view, a procrastinator's excuse and a worrier's concern, all of which I had no time for. I'd always felt a Spartan vein in my character, so today was the chance to prove my chops. Plus, at this stage in the trail, I only had the energy to be an optimist and fill my imagination with the reappearance of the sun and a miraculously easy arrival at an albergue in Burgos filled with new faces and soft bunks.

I stood next to Alberto at the door for several moments, our bodies poised in perfect stillness and the door open only a few inches. I was suspended on the balls of my toes, ready for action, while his head was tilted as if listening for signs. After a moment filled with the sound of the rain and the view of a deserted courtyard, I tapped him on the shoulder and we sprang into motion, bounding out the door and out of town. My pack bounced around, the wet trail slipped below our feet and Alberto's sandals squeaked fiercely, but we didn't slow down. A few minutes later, I knew we'd made it; the coast was clear, and I was a solo again. I was no longer a leader with a follower or responsible for a male that delighted in running into traffic and endangering my safety.

After St. Juan de Ortega disappeared, we moved up through an area of tightly planted trees, evidence of major logging and fresh truck tracks. Then the trail descended into a lush wet valley with a main road cutting through its belly. Alberto strapped his sandals to his pack and walked with bare feet on the dark wet pavement. After my body had cooled down from the sprint out of town I'd begun to shiver. Now the only way to stop my whole body from shaking was to wrap my arms tight around my chest, holding in whatever heat I managed to produce. Soaked to the skin, it wouldn't be long before I was soaked to the bone as well. The rain had now seeped through my jacket, shorts and shirt. Even my underwear wasn't safe.

After the initial escape from St. Juan, our collective euphoria wore off, and we were faced with the reality of thirty more kilometers and very little hope of a quick passage into Burgos. It had been days since I'd carried on a substantive conversation with another human being, and my own internal dialog was growing tiresome. What was there to say to myself that would be of any comfort? I was following my guidance, pushing ever onward, but I still lacked any signs that it was taking me in the right direction. I moved on aching legs, wet from head to toe and aware there were many more hours of walking ahead. The empty trails out of St. Juan were a fertile ground for negative thoughts, doubt and unanswerable questions. With absolutely no sign of distraction in sight, I watched Alberto from under the edge of my hood, wondering again if his cheery nature filtered down through all the layers of his thoughts or if he was plagued with the same specters of doubt as me. I wanted to feel it didn't matter what shadows came across my path, what questions cluttered my brain and which thoughts made my insides squirm. I was still going, still moving forward on the steam of my guidance and the dream. In that way, Alberto and I were undeniably the same. No matter what was running on the internal ticker, it wasn't stopping my forward motion. I still fueled my Camino dream even in the face of this dreary reality.

As I chewed on the string of my raincoat and drifted kilometers away in thought, Alberto's voice broke through the sound of the rain and filled the space between us. As I turned to look at him and pulled my hood back to expose my ears, I knew for sure he wasn't just talking to himself. He was singing. His voice started low, but it picked up speed and volume like a rolling ball, and soon he was singing at the top of his lungs, swinging his arms around wildly and skipping around puddles. At first it was just jubilant sound, but then I began to hear words: words I recognized to songs I knew by heart. How it had taken us so long to find our true common ground was a bit of a mystery, but in the wet fields outside of Atapuerca, we finally shared a language: the Beatles. Swept out of my doom and gloom, I jumped with gusto into song after song, singing until my voice grew hoarse. The sound of the rain on our layers of gear and the squelching of our feet shifted from monotonous drone to exciting accompaniment. We were finally talking.

And so we sang as we crossed fields and wound our way up through a roadside village. As we faced a hill on the far side of town, our singing trailed off, but the buzz lingered, and I felt my muscles attacking the rise with renewed vigor. I sped ahead of Alberto and reached the apex to find two other pilgrims paused at the crest. The couple, dressed in full body florescent rain gear with sticks in hand, was outlined against the sky. When I drew close, I also could see the sight that had caused them to stop in their tracks. Ahead was a wide basin of land with a large cluster of civilization in the far corner. There was little else between where we stood and the city that looked like dollhouse furniture. No more illusions, no more sense the city was right around the corner. Here was the truth laid out before my eyes. There was something intoxicating about this view, and I could see why it made the woman in lime green beside me sway slightly, yet it only made me more determined. Now that I had Burgos in my crosshairs, there would be no stopping me. I would crawl into Burgos if I had to. The faint outline of buildings was a siren song rushing through me. I stood still on the very crest of the hill as the wind tugged me in various directions. This glimpse would keep me moving forward in the hours to come. It was nearly noon. I'd been on my feet walking for seven hours. I would need both the calming in-breath of this vantage point and the rushing exhale of a downhill slope to get me to the city. These elements would keep me on my feet and on the pathway. I just hoped nothing would snap, rip or break in the process. Maybe with the help of the universe, I would manage to keep from falling over or being run over. As I took off, I focused on these small, yet important goals.

Alberto was behind me, but I'd lost sight of him after the hill climb. I wasn't sure if he would make it to the city, but I was committed. If our paths diverged here I would trust it and try not to fear letting go of my only bond. I moved down the slope and wound my way through the empty fields and abandoned houses on the far outskirts of Burgos. The roads grew larger and louder. A hum could be heard and felt in every step. The busy roads rattled and my squeaky tendons throbbed, but the rain stopped and granted me one element of respite. The day stayed cloudy and soft, blowing sheets of air through my layers and drying my skin.

On the descent, I drew even with the young couple in florescent rain jackets. They were a trendy pair, taking a short break from their busy life in Madrid to stretch their legs in the north country. Even though they were walking on fresh legs, they weren't new to the trail. Last year they had come to Roncesvalles and walked to Atapuerca. When I passed them on the mountain, they had just begun the middle leg of their Camino and were trying to sink back into the experience amid less than gentle conditions. They planned to walk from here to León then return next year and walk on to Santiago. Their busy professional schedules allowed only a week of vacation each summer, and I appreciated their willingness to give it to this task for three years in a row. I sensed such a shared experience might bring the busy couple an intimacy they lacked in the larger world. It could give them a chance to need each other in a rough and tumble life, rely on the other when grumpy, tired, hungry and sore. I wondered if modern life had all but removed this element of coupledome, this human dependence and dramatic closeness. At home, there were other people to rely on, other places to be, other things to do, modern amenities and take out. Here there were only the two of you, a cast of zany strangers and the simple yet arduous task of walking across a country.

I walked beside the duo for half an hour, soaking in their story and basking in the human connection. The Madrilenian walked with me stride for stride, his tall lithe frame looming above me, while his wife took tiny steps and tried to follow our conversation. He was the English speaker of the two and though shy, he was friendly. His wife smiled often, working hard to stay beside us. I had the sense she was vivacious in her home life, but trapped in a bit of trail shock. They were strikingly opposites; she was blonde with a tiny compact frame, while he was tall and dark with an easy swing of limbs. Once again I was in wonder at how many overtly handsome men I'd met so far. This man was no exception, and I felt a slight physical pain to watch his dark hair bounce around his beautiful face and feel his warm contemplative eyes watch me. Thinking it best to take off and leave the maddeningly adorable married man and his wife to themselves, I waved goodbye and turned on the jets.

And the day wore on. The rain came to a full stop, and my clothes dried stiff against my skin. I no longer had permanent goose bumps, and my shoes stopped squeaking with each step. The trail leveled out, and I lost sight of the city. The yellow arrows kept pointing me forward, but time dragged.

Moments among fellow pilgrims offered me a change in pace and a refuge from my manic trends, but on my own, I found it hard not to drift into my bad habits. A creeping increase in pace added to a semi manic unwillingness to stop for any reason. The path turned to road then back to dirt, and all I could do was keep going forward faster and faster, leaving behind all sense of pace or distance. For lunch, I munched on half a soggy granola bar from the pocket of my rain jacket. I ate while walking, peed in the trailside woods without taking off my pack and didn't stop at a café, church or historic building for the next two hours. One moment I felt I was being hunted, fleeing on the run, and the next I was being pulled along by a rip tide, powerless to stop. The only solution for both was to keep moving. I didn't know how else to survive the pressure and make it to the end of the day.

As long as I could recall the sight of the city ahead, I would make it. I willed it to be so. My guidebook claimed the albergue in Burgos held over a hundred beds. A hundred new faces and a whole new cycle of pilgrims. A fresh batch with the potential for more young folks and a new line up of English speaking studs. The walk from Belorado to Burgos was a double stage, a distance that guidebooks recommended pilgrims take two days to complete. Most would never attempt the task Alberto and I had taken on this morning, for they were more rational, balanced and clearly less emotionally unhinged than yours truly. For better or for worse, there was no temptation to stop and stay the night along the trail between Atapuerca and Burgos as there was literally nowhere to stay. No doors were marked albergue, and I hardly caught a glimpse of human life. If my feet stopped and there was no hope of another step, then a roofless shed or roadside field populated by sullen cows would be my best lodging options. I'd thrust myself into a strip of barren trail tangled in the ugly weeds of city life and had to trust I would make it through.

As the towering buildings of Burgos stayed always at a distance, I started to feel genuine fatigue seep through my muscles. I'd run out of water, craved a cup of caffeine and had very little food left. The trail crossed a major highway, cut through a construction zone, petered out and vanished.

In the shuffle of the new construction, the arrows had been swallowed alive, ingested by progress in the dead zone of heavy machinery. I didn't know what to do. I'd always been able to rely on the aid of the arrows or a companion to make a choice, but I was alone and too tired to bear the thought of going in the wrong direction. In this dead stretch, there were no homes or helpful people.

I sat down in the hot afternoon sun on a new layer of pavement and breathed. It was really all I felt able to do. The arrows had been my unfailing guide these last two weeks. Now I had no arrows and no human backup. As I gnawed over the possibility that I'd missed a detour or a redirection arrow, the Madrilenian and his wife came up from behind. I turned to them, and with a slight waver in my voice and eyes brimming with tears, I asked if they knew the way forward. In response to a dignified nod of his head and a cheerful echoing okay from his wife, I stood up and attempted to keep going.

After twenty minutes of searching for traces of yellow flechas, the Madrilenian noticed a slim arcing stripe of yellow on a bridge a hundred yards away. We were back on the scent. If there had been any reserves of energy left in my body I would have danced a celebration jig, but all I could muster was a deep relieved sigh. Once we crossed the bridge, the city was under my feet. I'd officially arrived. So what if the albergue was another six kilometers across the city, tucked in a park on the western edge? I wasn't going to let such minor details ruin the moment.

I followed the Madrilenian and his wife off the far side of the bridge, but there we parted again as they dashed across the road for a cup off coffee, and I chose to push on. I was invited to join them but declined. The albergue was now so tantalizingly close, and besides, I wasn't sure I would be able to get up from a chair if I sat down in one. The lids of my eyes would be lulled into a false stop, and sleep might just swallow me whole. I had only a thin layer of momentum left to make it across the city. From the dark streets of Belorado to the albergue in Burgos was a distance of fifty-one kilometers. I had just six of those kilometers left to vanquish; there was no time to waste.

The couple dashed across the busy four-lane road and hollered goodbye over the traffic noise. I turned to my left and picked up the thread of yellow markers along the sidewalk. They were no longer hard to find. The road was unnaturally straight, man-made straight, parallel road straight. Every line cut a direct path to the center of the city and was crowded with giant warehouses. All the industrial buildings were gated off with security booths at the front entrance and pools of black parking lots leaking out in every direction.

This tunnel of ugly modern progress was utterly disheartening. The car traffic moved rapidly, leaving trails of exhaust in the air. I felt odd and out of place. There was no evidence I was on the Camino except for the yellow arrows along the sidewalk. I craved the comforting sight of another pilgrim, another walking soul battling this modern crush, but I saw no one else. I was the only person on foot in this vast suburb of concrete, metal and moving vehicles. In the most remote parts of the trail, I'd never felt this out of place. Those tracks of land were vast, but my legs, breath and movement belonged in the fabric of nature, no matter the scope or setting. The wild landscapes seamlessly incorporated pilgrims. We belonged there, but this industrial park was inhumane. It swallowed my view of the sky and sapped my strength as if some force was drawing blood from my veins. I crossed an intersecting highway at a quick sprint and wondered with desperation when the old city would begin.

The road bent slightly then continued on an endless track. My mind fell into empty space, and a profound weariness settled into my bones. My body propelled itself forward in an unconscious loop. Step and step and step. This level of fatigue wasn't one I'd felt in a very long while, not since my years as a dancer when days were filled with eight to ten hours of movement. I would wake at seven and be in class, rehearsal and the studio until I crumbled into bed late at night. And like all things physical, it became cumulative. As the months wore on, the weariness settled deeper and overcame me faster.

During those years, I lived in a small house off the top edge of campus. I had my own room and a view of a beautiful sloping field outside, but living there had its trade offs. One was the twenty-minute walk from campus to my front door. Most days I enjoyed the few minutes to be outside breathing fresh air. I liked having those walks built into my life, but on the nights when I returned home late from dance rehearsal, it wasn't as enjoyable. The biggest problem was the absence of streetlights in the middle section of the walk. I could always see the lights up ahead and move towards them, but would lose track of my feet in the darkness around my body. Sometimes, I craved sleep so much that I would break into a quick jog to get home faster. One night, I found myself speeding up, letting my head loll around. My eyelids drooped until I grew weary even of this action, and after a while they dropped and stayed there. Suddenly, I was in the ditch on the side of the road, well beyond the cluster of trees I'd passed with eyes open. I'd fallen asleep while running. I'd kept my forward momentum, and it was only the fact that I'd veered off the road that woke me. I later heard super marathoners often run during the night and have been known to fall asleep while running. Apparently my odd nighttime foibles were the stuff of great athletes.

If the afternoon light outside of Burgos were to drop into dusk, I worried I would be in danger of repeating my sleep running. The rushing cars would make such an event more dangerous, and I tried to stay focused. I'd lost feeling in the soles of my feet, and my mind lingered on the thoughts of food and horizontal surfaces. I tried to remember what had fueled my progress during the long day and recalled I'd eaten little more than yogurt for breakfast, biscuits and coffee at St. Juan and a granola bar for lunch.

So I'd failed at this aspect of my athletic endeavor. Somehow it hadn't kept me from the goal, and all I could do was be a bit more attentive to fueling in the future. Seeing the city off in the distance had consumed my focus, but now my thoughts swam with visions of sweet treats and cold drinks. Lost in apparitions of orange juice and croissants, I didn't notice right away when the buildings next to me began to change. They were growing older, richer in quality and more elegant. I was entering the first flush of the old city, and suddenly I could see other pilgrims up ahead. I picked up my feet just a bit faster and pushed off the ground with just a bit more force. With a jolt of speed, I could catch up, move out of the solo wasteland and into a whole new pilgrim circle. Now it was amazingly, tantalizingly and invigoratingly inevitable.

BURGOS

I glanced back as I crossed a busy roundabout, wondering if Alberto was in sight behind me. Could he have stuck with this endless grind, following like an echo just out of sight or had he sought refuge along the way? I hadn't seen him since Atapuerca, and the sidewalk was empty. The only fellow travelers were the strangers up ahead.

Dashing through yellow crosswalk signals and weaving around the growing pedestrian traffic, I kept my eyes on two blonde heads bobbing along with large rucksacks. They were unmistakably members of the perigrino tribe and looked like twenty somethings. After several blocks of huffing, puffing and squeezing through crowds, I drew even with the group and fell into step. As they turned to look at the strange new pilgrim at their side, I cheerfully introduced myself. The duo was a mismatched pair of Russian blondes who shared only three things in common: their nationality, hair color and this trail. One was very tall with a long braid dangling down her back and a rigid set to her shoulders. She wore an expertly tied bandana around her forehead and dressed it up with a stern expression that remained fixed in place at all times. Her companion was shorter, covered in extra gear: toggles, tassels, a hat, two walking sticks and clothing that zipped off at the elbows and knees. Her mood wasn't such a fixed attribute but a mercurial flow that shifted from block to block. The two girls had begun the trail together in Roncesvalles. They were strangers when they planned the trip, packed their bags and headed to the airport. Once past security and awaiting a boarding call at the Moscow airport, they'd recognized the telltale pilgrim regalia on one another and linked up. They hadn't even left their home turf before the trail provided them company. I was slightly sick with envy and wondered why my time in Boston and London had proved so fruitless. I knew it was a bit much to ask for instant manifestation, but I was now a third of the way into my journey and still on the look out. As I asked a plethora of questions and soaked in the quirks of these new faces, I noticed both girls were in a gloomy place. As they spoke, I realized they were more than downtrodden; they were downright pissed off. Apparently they'd spent the night in San Juan where they'd been served watery garlic soup for dinner, given a cold stone floor for a bed and provided with not a drop of hot water for washing up. Breakfast had been half a chocolate bar and a coke split between the two of them. And now it was Sunday. All supermercados were closed, and it was siesta, so most eateries were closed as well. I'd stumbled upon two cranky, hungry and aggravated pilgrim chicks, and part of me wanted to back away slowly before they tore my bag off my back and ripped through it in search of anything edible.

To distract them, I opened my guidebook and discussed how close we were to our target. Once in the belly of the beast, it was difficult to know how much more city lay before us. Had we crossed through the center? Was the park where the albergue sat just ahead or were we still a long way off? Several blocks later, we were visited by a small miracle when the gods took mercy on our group and led us right by the door of a bakery open at three in the afternoon on the day of rest. The small white room filled with cases of pastries was a heavenly manifestation of sorts, and I would take it. Ten minutes later, the three of us returned to the trail laden with bags of warm treats and fresh bread. I expected my Russian friends to cheer up but having to carry their food through the city seemed to perturb both to no end, and our trio quickly dropped back into a sullen silence. The shorter one resorted to dragging her sticks behind her dejectedly and cursing at passing cars. With fresh food in my pack and the realization I could navigate this city with or without my companions, I set all my energy on arrival and scanned for arrows at every turn.

Burgos was one of the most prosperous northern cities on the trail with a reputation for abundant glamour and moneyed elegance in both its structural façade and human inhabitants. The trail cut straight into the charming old city, then meandered down ancient alleys, traipsed beside glossy store fronts and eventually wound its way to a massive cathedral on the west side. Along the crowded route, we moved around cafes overflowing with people and passed large family groups dressed in their Sunday best. The spray painted arrows disappeared to be replaced by more decorative, discrete and artistic markers. Embedded in the cobbled roadway, golden scallop shells and tiles shaped into arrows pointed the way. Both markers were aesthetically pleasing and in line with the city's image, but they were difficult to follow, especially when faced with diminished brain power, gnawing hunger and wobbling limbs. I hardly noticed the road arrows as cars sped over them, and I struggled to find each of the scallop shells between the feet of the natives. I missed the crude yellow arrows on the back of signposts, tree trunks and along the curb. They were clear, supportive and functional even if they weren't glamorous enough for Burgos.

The streets curved on and on, withholding any view of cathedral spires. It had been several hours since my body began to tap deep reserves of primal energy. The body is a wondrous thing, and as my internal speedometer inched towards fifty kilometers, I was in awe of my own collection of cells. Though my body was resilient and sprightly, my spirit had hit the wall and was strongly in favor of lying down on the dirty sidewalk and surrendering. As the cathedral remained out of sight and the city showed no signs of ending anytime soon, my emotions took center stage and began to flail wildly. The three of us had given up on words, so I was cornered with my own thoughts. Even the people we passed, locals who barely acknowledged our presence and young travelers with packs but no Camino lineage, seemed to keep us out of their worlds.

Suddenly the moody sky broke into steely fissures of stone, and we all exhaled at once. Here was the cathedral and somewhere beyond it, were the most holy treasures of all: beds, showers and the knowledge that the day was done. Though the Russians had just spent the last half hour cursing the cathedral and glaring at the skyline where it should have been, they chose to stop, pay a fee, check their packs and venture into the great behemoth. Even though they invited me to join them, I was hesitant to step out of the flow. The sight from afar had filled my cathedral appetite for the day, so I kept moving.

I dropped a visor on my thoughts, ignored the commotion on the narrow streets and turned inwards. Deep in the quiet center filled with only the sound of breathing and pumping blood, city blocks fell away, roads were crossed and time passed. It may have been just a few minutes or perhaps closer to an hour, but suddenly I found myself in the middle of an ancient footbridge caught in the snare of another vanishing arrow moment. As I turned in circles, not sure where I'd lost the thread, an old man sitting in the shade of a tree on the far side of the river whistled to me. Shading my eyes from the sun, I looked over at him and found he was pointing to the right with a grin on this face. Even from a distance, I was a dead give away: disheveled, dirty and disoriented. I could have been the poster child for pilgrim-kind. At least I gave this man a good laugh in my role as vagabond in this notoriously chic city. I could pull it together if need be but maybe not when my entire wardrobe was crammed into a small damp pack, my skin was covered in sweat and dirt and I didn't have an ounce of spare energy to waste on vanity.

As soon as I stepped into the park, all struggle vanished as my body floated through a world of soft green shade and open circles of warm light. This place, this island of an albergue, was an oasis set aside for us alone, and I was ever so grateful to be in the club and welcome inside the gates. The parkland around the albergue was filled with ancient deep-rooted trees, and the vibrant green ground was covered with a film of fallen white flowers. Though the building itself was rather unattractive, the spot was drenched in an aura of rest. I moved towards the large rustic structure with renewed purpose. Groups of people sat outside on benches, and a man was asleep in the grass with his arm over his eyes. I had arrived. I looked down and took stock. All limbs were in place and functioning. Thirty one and a half miles, fifty one kilometers, sixty three thousand steps and I still had both shoes on my feet and my pack on my shoulders. I opened the wooden gate into the building complex, charged into the reception area and was assigned the very last bed in the place. I'd slipped in right under the wire, proved I had pilgrim street cred and been rewarded with a bunk alongside ninety of my favorite strangers.

When I returned from the bathhouse with clean hair, my grand plans of eating and socializing veered off course slightly as sleep threatened to pull me under. My sleeping bag was so soft and lying flat felt so deliciously easy. I awoke from my impromptu nap to find it had become evening while I slept. A tall blonde guy with a mop of curls sat on the bunk opposite me. He was reading from a small guidebook while his legs dangled over the end of his bunk. As I sat up, he flashed a toothy smile in my direction and introduced himself with a casual wave. We were too far apart on our floating top bunk islands to shake hands, but we did have a mighty good view of the rest of the room. Blondie was an American abroad like myself, but he considered himself a bit of a local too for he'd spent the last year teaching in southern Spain. He announced with an air of wistfulness that this was his parting embrace with España before he returned home. Extremely polite, he spoke with an open ease, telling me his rather academic view of trail life. When I asked him if he had been lucky enough to come across other young people, he looked slightly annoyed by my question. He explained the purpose of this journey was to be alone. Why would he seek out company to spoil his solitude? Why indeed? I could tell I might be fighting a losing battle to try and enlighten him about my differing views on the matter of trail community.

I nodded as Blondie spoke, rubbing my eyes to wake myself up. He explained the freedom of his year abroad, and the ways isolation had gifted him a more visceral experience of life. True, I couldn't argue that things felt alone were felt with more depth, but was that always good? At some point the world beyond our own thoughts, feelings and actions needed to take root. As westerners, we both had grown up in a culture so externally focused that coming to the Camino did provide a chance to reconnect with the internal, but could a life full of one and devoid of the other be healthy? I didn't feel human community was what cluttered western life and made it such a frantic external experience. It was everything else. It was our modern technology, the noise, the lights and the relentless pace. People and relationships weren't the reason we westerners were burnt out on the external world and in avoidance of our internal lives. Why then were so many pilgrims prepared to defend the fortress of their journey from any stray human that stumbled upon them and wanted to be friends? I'd felt the sting of a warning shot over the bow more than once and recognized Blondie's determined stance on solitude. Why did Blondie and the Curator want to be left alone? Alberto had spent much of his trail in my presence, and though conversation was not our forte, he hadn't pushed me away, and I knew he was living a rich internal trail. Why did one breed of pilgrim feel that a trail in service of knowing oneself was in direct conflict with a trail that honored human relationships? I was baffled and more than a bit surprised to find it so common in the younger people I'd met. Was it the wisdom of aging that allowed older pilgrims to arrive to this experience with a more open minded view? One thing was clear; Blondie was working very hard to stay isolated, to block out the hordes of people around him and to clip every conversation so it didn't become a lingering attachment. He was expending so much energy in fighting off the reality of this very close quartered trail that I felt exhausted just looking at him. How much easier it would be to let go, slip off the edge of his island built for one and join us. It would be no different than slipping into sleep after a day's walk.

As the lights flickered on in the large room and the sky outside grew dim, I fumbled to unzip my sleeping bag and extricate my legs from the silky cocoon. Blondie had lost interest in me and was absorbed in his guidebook again. Apparently our allotted moment of interaction was over. I left Blondie perched high on his throne to muse over his solitary course for the next day. I knew a lost cause when I saw one, or at least I did most of the time.

I managed to slide down off the high bunk safely if not very gracefully and collect my box of hard won pastries. I picked my way through the maze of bunks, stepping over packs, slipping by people sorting their things on the floor and made for the door. I wanted to go outside and sit in the grass for a little while before I returned to my sleeping nook. I had every intention of getting a full docket of sleep after spending eleven hours on the move, but I had landed in a whole new circle and wasn't going to fall back asleep before glancing around and checking out this group. The open lawn and fresh breeze were inviting after being in the stuffy confines of the bunkhouse, and I went in search of a bit of open grass with a prime view of the comings and goings.

The front yard was worn from all the foot traffic, but I managed to find a bit of grass near the entrance. I lay down on my back and let my body sink into the earth. I felt all my limbs giving in soundlessly to the ground's gravitational tug. Two massive trees filled the air above me, their branches forming a delicate lattice through which I could see the last of the color draining from the sky. Trees were often at their most beautiful from this vantage point. It was as if I was the roots looking up to where the very ends of my limbs met the sky.

My vision wandered from the trees, and I tilted my head to see the activity closer to ground level. It was comforting to see groups of people encircling me, talking, laughing and eyeing the scene with as much unabashed interest as me. It couldn't be denied: pilgrims were a nosy bunch, always thirsty for gossip, information and drama to fill the lazy hours of the day. But maybe I was being unjustly hard on my species and perhaps such keen focus on the comings and going of others was simply an essential human trait. By sharing the same spaces and walking the same narrow thread, we were part of a greater whole, and each individual's trek was out in plain sight to be watched, just as one might follow the movements of a celebrity. Granted, many of the pilgrims weren't as dynamic as the average movie star, but they were quirky and intriguing all the same. I'd found watching was a full time hobby here; I wondered who might be watching my progress and trying to solve the puzzle of my journey. After scanning the yard, I finally accepted what I'd suspected for the past few hours; Alberto wasn't here, and he might never reappear. The safety net that I'd had since Pamplona was now fully dismantled. I'd craved the change to a deeper community so badly, I'd forgotten it would be sad to leave this comrade behind to make room for others. Yet it felt right, painful but a bit like growing up and shedding outgrown clothes that had served me well. The hurt was necessary to mark the crossover.

I picked at the pastries and gulped down some water. My stomach seemed content with a diet of water and sleep, and I was finding it difficult to coax it into accepting a bit of sustenance. Stress had put a clamp around my throat the past few days, and it was as if the passage had grown narrower. For the sake of my brain and muscles, I tried to convince my body to accept more than it desired. It would be hard to go on if my muscles started to eat away at themselves and my brain slowed like molasses. Such breakdowns were not conducive to walking great distances or being able to carry on a conversation at the end of the day. I reluctantly gnawed on a protein bar, hoping the high density food would keep me going and steer me away from public melt downs.

I was lying on my back again, watching the trees move above me when a distinctly American voice wafted across the courtyard. Snapped out of my floating thoughts, I sat up so fast my head spun. As the freckles of light in my vision faded, I noticed two young guys walking side by side down the center of the yard. I could no longer hear their voices as they walked away from me towards the main building, but I could see they were laughing as a pretty dark haired girl led them into the office. Even from the back, it was clear they were in their early twenties. Sometimes I absolutely adored the exclusivity of the albergues system. In such a moment as this, it allowed me to be certain these guys were also making their way along the trail, and since they weren't wearing revealing bike shorts or carrying goofy helmets, I knew they were moving at my speed, tackling the trail by foot.

Though the two guys were a unit, they were distinctly different. One was tall and lanky with a long stride, while the other was more compact and walked with a limp. But who was the dark haired girl, and why was she wearing jeans and flip-flops? They'd moved down the path and disappeared into the albergue before I could meander over. I wondered what the reception desk would tell them. I'd gotten the last bed in the place and that was over three hours ago. What was a tired pilgrim to do when the largest municipal albergue on the outside of the city was full? Just the thought of backtracking into Burgos to hunt down a place to sleep was utterly exhausting and slightly frightening. Albergues were safe refuge, a constant that awaited me at the end of each day. After fifty one kilometers and a four a.m. start, I would have settled for a spot under the picnic tables rather than face the streets of Burgos again. I'd seen pilgrims dozing in the strangest of places at all hours of the day, so I was pretty certain hard ground and a bit of dirt was no real problem for weary travelers. But were these American guys as low maintenance as their European counterparts? I felt sorry for the guys, but at the same time, I felt a bit sorry for myself too. If they somehow managed to stay here, then I wouldn't miss out on the chance to make their acquaintance. If they were sent packing, it would be more difficult to meet them. I mulled this over as I kept my gaze fixed on the front entrance of the building. When the Americans reemerged five minutes later, my eyeball were dry from staring at the doorway, and my nerves were humming with a new energy. I was relieved to see the guys smiling as the dark haired girl kissed them goodbye and disappeared out the front gate. They both appeared to be in no hurry and were glancing around as I plucked up my courage and yelled across the yard to them to ask if they were American. They laughed cheerfully at my boldness and hollered back a resounding, "Yes!" Yes, oh yes!

When they ambled over to introduce themselves, we shook hands with enthusiasm. Jack, the tall one, smiled a wide grin, plunked himself down next to me and began to rummage through his pack for food. As we settled into a circle, I asked them what was happening with their accommodations for the night. The shorter and fairer of the two, Ivan, told me there were no beds left, and they were strongly discouraged from bunking under the picnic tables. Yet not all hope was lost, for the woman at the front desk informed them there was an overflow spot for just this situation. Located in a large community center across the road from the park, they would have to wait until after closing hours at nine, to go claim a spot. One of the albergue staff would take them over when it was time, but until then they were at loose ends and willing to pass the time in my company. I quickly thanked the albergue gods for getting me a bunk here in the park, but also keeping my new acquaintances around the place for a few precious hours.

The guys hadn't eaten dinner but had managed to put aside a few supplies at lunch, fully aware that dinner might be a dismal affair if they didn't plan ahead. They were learning the same pilgrim tactics I was; prepare for Sundays with the assumption that food would be impossible to find. As we chatted absently, Ivan settled across from me with his injured foot propped up on his pack, slicing cucumbers with a large woodsman's knife. Jack sat upright with his legs folded underneath him, spreading buttery cheese on a loaf of bread with absorbed focus. Even though both were working away at dinner preparations, Ivan wasn't afraid to multitask. He talked in an endless stream, moving his hands with an animated flare, slicing the knife through space as often as it sliced the green vegetable. When the task was completed and a pile of slices was all that remained, he leaned back on his elbows. The way he dropped into a fully reclined position and let his body collapse into the ground was effortless. He was active one moment, and then with little transition, drenched in an air of all encompassing ease. Yet even when released into gravity, his involvement in our conversation never flickered. Ivan was unmistakably the leader of this small posse and the central spoke of the conversation no matter the topic. His voice rose and fell in easy waves but was thick with laughter. To talk with Ivan was a fresh and delightful experience. He allowed no topic to be dull and spiritless, qualifying everything with boisterous opinions. He was an entertainer, and I was his happy audience. Jack seemed accustomed to the Ivan show and added his commentary when needed. He was the straight man, keeping a more deadpan tone in his voice, setting Ivan up for the laughs and following the thread of every tale.

I felt simultaneously hyper and drained. To be encircled by cheerful peers who spoke my language and exuded a genuine vibe of inclusiveness was something I'd sought from the very first step. I could have cheered with abandon or fallen into a deep sleep of release. I was a bit worried about betraying how much their arrival meant to me and thus scaring them back into the hills, so I tried to appear mellow. Even as I tried to act relaxed, I could sense they saw through me and were enjoying my puppy-like delight. I'd never been strong at hiding my emotions, and this trail had made me as transparent as tracing paper. Try as I might, every passing feeling was there to see. I still hoped it endeared me to my fellow travelers, for I was incapable of playing coy.

I relished the guys' curiosity. They had a refreshing sense of openness and held none of the dogma about this trail being a solo isolation driven event. I wanted to know all the juicy details about their Camino. I wanted to know where they'd slept last night, when they'd started, how they'd heard of this alternate universe and most of all if they had any blisters. My questions were endless, and they were generous as I soaked up their answers and asked for more. They said they were ready for whatever and whomever crossed their path, and they meant it. No mixed messages, no ulterior motives. They simply didn't have much guile. In fact, they seemed to thrive off of being vulnerable to the unknown. They were ready to be bowled over by the yet to be discovered. It was their central reason for hitting the trail. Ivan wasn't afraid to show off the dozen or more blisters he had earned for his troubles, for he was certain such humanness only endeared him to me more.

Comfort abounded in our small circle, both physically and socially. They sprawled out around their picnic as we left no stone unturned about our journeys. At first, I liked Jack's appearance more than Ivan's. I appreciated his tall frame and his clean-cut hair, but after an hour, my first impression shifted. I found myself drawn to Ivan's quirky charm and the way he told stories by punctuating them with jokes. Even as I was looking them over, I felt that neither would afford a romance. Ivan's charm could have easily morphed into flirting, and I couldn't deny I would have been drawn in, but he had a serious girlfriend at home. Her name came up half a dozen times in the first hour, and I got the message. He was taken and fully devoted to his girl. Amidst the background information, we discovered our lives mysteriously overlapped long before we jumped on this Spanish trail; we had friends and beloved places in common back in the states.

Above and beyond the outer world links, I realized I'd been trying to find them before I knew who they were. Ivan and Jack were the infamous American boys that had filled the Gypsy couple with such admiration. I'd walked this longest of long days because of them. I felt sane enough not to share this slightly nutty link with the boys, but I had fun merging the picture the Gypsy couple had painted with what sat before me now. How often I accepted the words of fellow pilgrims as truths when they were, like all things, totally subjective. It had never occurred to me to doubt the description of an albergue or the praise of an upcoming city. Why would a person bother to distort or embellish such information? But pilgrims did, and I was finding a gap between what had been confided to me, whispered in the albergue halls, shouted down the trail or told with stern caution in roadside cafes from the things themselves. What had the Gypsy couple meant when they called the American guys lightening fast? Had they even seen them walk? Waxing poetic was a Camino hobby and the Gypsy wife was no slacker; she could turn a phrase with the best of them, and with her words make gods out of mere mortals.

Yet everything I'd seen so far made it abundantly clear why the Gypsy couple had grown attached to the American boys so quickly. The guys harnessed a seemingly effortless flow of charm and warm accessibility that surely endeared them to people of all ages. It was easy to see that Ivan and Jack in top form could charm both granny and kid brother with equal ease and in record time. They were that good, or goofy, or funny or endearingly warm depending on which was needed most.

They'd also been on the trail for nearly two weeks, connected every second of every day. They'd been sleeping, eating and breathing alongside one another in endless loops of daylight and dark. Often they ran into amiable pilgrims such as myself, but most of the time it was just the two of them. Just like the Madrilenian and his pretty wife, theirs was a close and intimate trail, and it would rest squarely on the shoulders of their friendship. Best friends since childhood, they had a long lasting and sturdy base that had already weathered a prolonged separation when they attended different colleges. Thus the coming together here was a bit of a throw back, a renaissance to their days of closeness in childhood and a way marker before they graduated college next year and ushered in bigger changes. The trail was more than a manly physical challenge; it was a moment of bonding, a moment they could always share. I sensed they were already collecting stories, constructing myths around this moving life and building lore for the tales they would take home.

Jack spread more gooey squares of white cheese on a long baguette, while Ivan sliced an under-ripe tomato into chunks with the wide blade of his knife. When Ivan kicked off his shoes, I noticed the boys were wearing matching blue hiking sandals. Munching on the heel of a baguette, Jack pulled out a wine bottle from his bag, uncorked it with his teeth then took a big swig to wash the bread down. As he put the bottle down, I raised my brow slightly at Ivan who laughed heartily and explained how the wine bottle was now a water bottle. Jack hadn't even drunk the original contents of the bottle but swiped it off a café table in Belorado when his original water bottle failed him. In a dramatic turn of events, both Jack and Ivan had purchased traditional Spanish bodas in which to carry water. Both bodas had torn open, split and hemorrhaged liquid after only a few days of use. The charming culturally authentic water pouches were meant to be bad ass additions to their trail life but turned out to be a boondoggle instead. Even though they sorely missed slinging the animal skin bladders over their shoulders each morning, the wine bottle still added to their coolness factor and set them apart from all of us with modern bottles of gaudy plastic.

When Ivan finished his last sandwich and began to dive into the pastries I'd offered up, he explained why the two of them had arrived so late in Burgos. Jack looked a bit bashful as he admitted they'd expected to find an albergue beyond Atapuerca but before Burgos. When the mythical hostel for pilgrims didn't appear in the outskirts of the city, they became disoriented and lost the trail altogether. They had no idea where any albergues were, because, staying true to their thirst for adventure, they were proudly walking sans guidebook. They felt this made them part of the long lineage of great explorers before them who'd traveled without such pedestrian means of navigation. They scampered over the fact that a guidebook might have been a source of wisdom today and went on to their favorite part of the story: the rescue. It was nearly four when they wandered back to a yellow arrow. They sensed they were many kilometers short of an albergue, but they didn't wallow long in defeat. For out of the soft afternoon light a bright red compact containing two Spanish women with a fondness for cute foreign men screeched to a halt and offered them a ride and personal tour of the city.

The cavalry had arrived. The dark haired beauty who'd lead them into the albergue was the younger and fairer of the two. She was also the only one who spoke a lick of English and unlike her aunt, she was able to say goodbye to the boys without a bit of friendly groping.

I was slightly in awe of the relaxed way Jack and Ivan shared this story. Among the cult of walking pilgrims, getting a ride or taking a bus was a major faux pas. The belief was that once you missed even a single meter of trail, your journey was flawed, chipped and tarnished irrevocably. If I'd done such a thing, broken the code so blatantly, I certainly would have kept it to myself upon first meeting. But they were just happy to have an entertaining tale to share. Apparently the notion that their experience this afternoon was a blemish on their record was of no consequence. They could no longer claim they'd walked the whole trail stem to stern, and it didn't faze them one bit. I wouldn't have taken such a wrinkle in stride, I was still a bit too attached to proving I could do this by walking every single kilometer to the end. Even though this dogma had taken hold in me, I was excited to be around others who weren't so bent on perfection. I needed to move more into Ivan's way of thinking, one that embraced the quirks, the mistakes and unorthodox help.

As the sun went down, the grass where we sat fell into shade, and I slipped on my sweatshirt. The guys seemed oblivious to the cold and happy to sit around until darkness fell. They told jokes about the wacky people they'd met along the way and detailed the weird Spanish foods they'd already come to love. I was lost in their world, thoroughly entertained and hardly noticed the comings and going of other pilgrims. A flush of relief filled my body as I looked upon the two of them; Ivan was sprawled like a dog stretched out before a warm fire, and Jack lounged against his pack, sipping lazily from his wine bottle like a sleepy drunk. They were my people, new, vibrant, dynamic and inclusive. They had been strangers just three hours ago and now they were the closest people I had in the whole of Spain. I couldn't claim I was a hundred percent certain about what tomorrow would bring or who else might be around the next bend, but they were the building blocks of a new trail. After eleven hours of walking, I'd stepped out of a solo trail and into a communal one. My muscles and nerves vibrated with this new energy. I was finally here among the beginnings of my Camino community, and there was no worry about going back to what had been, for the trail only moved one way. Forward.

As I gathered my things to retire for the night, two unfamiliar female pilgrims walked over and introduced themselves. They were a pair of college aged Americans who had joined the trail here in Burgos and had yet to take their first step. Ivan welcomed them into our circle with his usual warmth. I made a snap decision to delay my move towards the albergue for a bit longer; I suddenly felt I had to stay connected to the guys so I wouldn't lose them to other charming pilgrimesses. Jack asked the girls how they found the trail and why they had picked to start here. The more animated of the two explained they'd spent the last few months living in Barcelona with anarchists but finally decided it was time to move on. A look of intrigued puzzlement spread over our three faces, and I knew we were all thinking the same thing; what did living among anarchists entail, and what was the breaking point that forced them to leave? For these two rather normal mid western American girls, it entailed squatting in buildings with no running water and jury-rigged electricity that could electrocute them at any moment. Their days were spent dumpster diving and evading the police who were always hot on the trail of their group. They had to flee from derelict houses several times with police in pursuit, yet spoke about all this with a disturbing air of nonchalance. One of the girls was nursing a large wound on her leg received from falling on broken glass in the last squat house. Apparently this was the final straw that had ushered them here. I was both fascinated and horrified in equal parts. Ivan was the most hungry for details but also seemed distressed by the tales. I'd never heard stories from the life of an anarchist but was pretty certain there was a high level of danger that these girls still seemed unable to fully appreciate. Their affect was dull and off hand. It was hard to tell what emotions lay under their tales.

As they recounted their life in Barcelona, they spoke slowly as if disembodied. Perhaps they'd been on drugs during their stay with the anarchists; perhaps they still were. As I looked them over, my biggest concern was that they had little idea what they'd gotten themselves into by joining the Camino. This trail wasn't the best of places for a radical detox. It was hard enough without that twist. It made sense that if they'd underestimated the scope of their life in Barcelona, then they would also fail to accurately assess what the trail would demand of them now. The trail was no cakewalk. It had a great spiritual energy that drew people to it, but it was a very physical experience. I wondered how often this weeded out the people who loved the vibes but couldn't handle the sweat and toil.

I stayed silent as the guys flirted with the girls. Jack pulled out a piece of paper with daily stages scribbled on it and showed the prettier girl where the trail went from here, while Ivan asked the other girl about the cut on her leg, peeking below the layers of bloodstained bandage. I was willing to guess that we would outpace these girls, and this might be our last encounter. The guys seemed willing to make the most of it nonetheless.

The call of sleep was now tugging on me with greater force, so I quickly set a plan to meet Jack and Ivan tomorrow in a town called Hontanas. After agreeing on this rendezvous point, I took myself off to bed and left the co-eds to bond. As I crossed the lawn and headed towards the main building, a voice called out my name. I turned to find Alberto standing at the entrance to the bathhouse. We smiled at each other across the open space, and he walked with weary steps towards me. He drew me close and placed a hand on my shoulder. I hadn't expected to see him again and yet his miraculous appearance changed nothing. He knew it just as well as I did. Change was rushing around us, and the past way of being was disappearing with the falling light. His touch honored what we both knew as true. We had shared some good moments, but with the entrance of the American boys, everything was changing, perhaps faster than we could know.

HORNILLOS DEL CAMINO

STAGE NINE-29.6K-18.4M
BURGOS TO HONTANAS

At dawn, I paid the price for my late afternoon arrival and learned why my bunk was the last to be claimed. Tucked on the outer edge of the room, it sat right next to the busiest traffic route: the path to the bathrooms. It took only a few pilgrims waking at four, hobbling to the stalls, banging around and flicking on the row of florescent lights to fully rouse me from my coma like slumber. This unusual alarm clock wasn't only grating to my sleep drugged nerves but woke me at an unacceptably early hour. With sleep no longer a possibility, there was little choice but to rise and join the ranks I'd spent the past hour cursing under my breath. To abandon my warm sleeping bag was sometimes the most painful moment of the day. I preferred to get that inevitable event behind me as quickly as possible and usually flung myself off the bunk and scrambled into motion. Once banished from the cocoon, I hurried to get out onto the trail and generate warmth through my layers of clothes. Even though Spain offered hot days and lots of sun, the mornings were a dark chilly affair, and albergues were far from cozy at this hour. After attempting to exit the packed bunkhouse as silently as possible, I sat on a bench outside in the half-light, threw on an extra layer and tied my shoes. I had a piece of bread left in my pack from the night before and chewed absently on it as I gathered my things.

There might not be a rule about when pilgrims could rise in the morning and begin to fumble around, but there was a code of silence. No one spoke a word in the open yard, even though there were nearly a dozen pilgrims milling around. We all recognized we were just outside the cardboard thin walls where people still attempted to sleep. To speak felt like blasphemy. Even whispering could garner a glare or two from older pilgrims. I could imagine this atmosphere might come off as tense and controlling, but it felt far from it. I treasured the holding of the peace, the silence of the first steps and the understanding there were times to be silent and times to talk. This quiet usually lasted until the first café stop a couple hours down the trail; by then most everybody was ready to open out into the social world of the Camino. As I chewed the last of my bread, a duo of older men sitting on a bench down the row from me heaved their packs up and started off down the trail. Unsure how many more kilometers of city were before me, I quickly followed, hoping they wouldn't mind my company on the first part of the walk. I still felt nervous navigating a city alone. I drew even with the men, and in a hushed tone, asked if I could walk with them for a while. Both were typical forty or fifty something European pilgrims, already deep into their journey. Their legs were too toned and their limbs too wiry to explain it any other way. I wouldn't have been surprised if they had come from deeper in France or maybe even farther a field. Their clothes and packs were worn, but everything was in good condition and well cared for. All my musings were shattered as soon as I made my simple request. One of the men didn't even acknowledge my presence. His companion looked me up and down with a critical eye then told me he would prefer I didn't join them. It was evident they thought I was little more than an inexperienced kid who would slow them down. The fact that I was a girl also seemed to work against me. Nonetheless, I was genuinely startled by the blunt rejection and slowed my pace to drop behind. As evidence from their none too subtle physical assessment of me, I was being judged by my cover and dismissed without a second thought.

All I really needed the pair for was navigation anyways, so I lurked a few blocks behind and made sure I didn't lose sight of them. As soon as we moved out of the urban area and the trail became a clear dirt track, I picked up speed. My muscles were warming and the chill was leaving my layers. It only took me a few minutes to draw even with the duo, but I didn't pause as I cruised by them and kept on going. I could feel both men look over, slightly startled as I passed, but I didn't dignify them with a single glance. They may have been pilgrim pros, but their error in judgment and blatant unkindness had been a rookie mistake. Having to eat my dust was the price they had to pay.

The land to the west of Burgos was desolate in a peculiar way. There were few signs of human life, only tangled highways lofted on concrete pillars and large road signs that glowed with reflective letters. It was an in between place, one visited only by people on their way from one cluster of civilization to another. I hadn't expected to see any other pilgrims, but several kilometers outside the first village, I came upon Alberto walking with a young woman whom I recognized from the albergue the night before.

Last evening, as I'd flopped on my bed in a sugar and exhaustion induced daze, I'd watched the comings and goings of the other eighty people who shared my sleeping quarters. It was always an endless form of entertainment, but never overly gripping. If I fell into a dozing sleep and awoke an hour later, the scene would be relatively unchanged. Yet, as I'd reclined on my sleeping bag in Burgos, I'd seen this young woman across the room in a top bunk passionately embracing a fellow pilgrim. Blithely unaware of their audience, the guy had stood up against the bunk with his limbs dangled over the woman, drawing her to the edge of the mattress. She'd been tucked up against him, curling her knees in tight, with arms folded around his torso as she'd kissed him slowly with her eyes closed. There'd been something searing and intimate about the moment as if they were somewhere else, adrift in a world all by themselves. They'd been drenched in a circle of energy where everything melted under the heat of touch and the now was vibrantly alive. I'd assumed they were a couple and couldn't help staring in envy at their blatant enjoyment of each other.

Though being a pilgrim involved living day-to-day life in the company of strangers, what I'd witnessed so far had been quite innocuous. Yes, I'd seen old men in sagging underpants and had stood in a crowded bathroom with other women as we flossed and brushed out teeth, but such moments felt like being part of a large family. The moments of stripping down to one's underwear or sharing tight sleeping quarters were rather innocent. The energy had never been like this, never full of heat or desire. The vibrations that had rolled off the couple a stone's throw from me had felt different and to be so close, had somehow felt invasive. It was as if some line had been crossed, by them or by those of us in the pilgrim gallery I wasn't sure. To be fair, they'd only been kissing, but somehow it had been the sexiest thing I'd seen in weeks and by far the most sensual moment I'd stumbled across on the Camino. Others had told me stories of frisky pilgrims making noises in the night and abusing the rules of the public living spaces, but I'd been unable to believe the risqué tales until now. This raw intimate moment should have been the couple's to unfold in private, but we'd all been there, all eighty of us, and humans will be humans. We were too curious and gossipy for our own good. I'd met couples on the trail and seen them cuddling, but it had always felt very PG, very in line with the family atmosphere. This unfolding moment had been more akin to an R rated feature. Yet the scene had been enticing, and I'd found my predominant feeling was one of wistful envy. I'd assumed couples on the trail struggled with the lack of privacy and usually chose to err on the side of too much restraint rather than too little. This couple clearly didn't subscribe to that school of thought, but who could blame them? They were young and knee deep in love. I'd read it all over their faces as they came up for air, and I hadn't had the heart to deny them enjoying the perks. My bunk had suddenly felt too big for just my solo sleeping bag, and I'd wondered if it had been a kindness of the universe to keep the sights and sounds of adoring couples from me for the past few weeks. Looking around the room, I'd noticed others were entranced too. An older couple, three rows down from me, had paused while unpacking their stuff, their jaws dangling wide open. Another woman had walked by on her way to the bathroom, noticed the couple and then caught my eye. We'd exchanged grins, and she'd rolled her eyes with a humorous flare. Apparently I wasn't alone in feeling there was no stopping love.

And now, here I was being introduced by Alberto to one of the lovers. I was more than curious to meet this young woman and gladly fell into step beside her. The female half of the couple was a Hungarian actress. She was tall with flowing clothes, beautiful tan features and a low velvety voice. Her hair was thick, dark and matched her very round eyes. Her beauty wasn't of the obvious kind, but there was an air about her that was intriguing, especially when she spoke. It made perfect sense that she was a performer. I'd been entranced by one of her performances just last night. It was nearly impossible not to watch her, and I wondered how much of this gravity was training and how much was purely innate. We spoke only for a brief time before the path curved upward and delivered us into a small village. I enjoyed walking with her and listening to her speak Italian with Alberto, following the trail of smooth sounds that looped between them and for the first time not caring that I couldn't understand a word. When we reached a small village, she went onward and left us as we stopped to get a cup of coffee from the first open café. We crossed a road and made a beeline for a dingy cafe as the Actress disappeared down the trail. The door of the place hung open, and several packs rested against the outside wall. I could hear people talking and smell fresh coffee as I placed my bag with the others. The promise of caffeine buzzed through my muscles, and I felt the morning brighten.

When we got back on the trail after our brief pit stop, it took only a few minutes to cross through the sleepy neighborhood. Near the edge of town, we turned a sharp corner and came upon the Actress sitting on a bench with the boy she'd been kissing the night before. She sat in his lap, and he played with a piece of her hair. They spoke softly to each other in Hungarian while the young man looked up at her. The guy was clearly besotted, and frankly I couldn't blame him; she was absolutely mesmerizing. He hardly turned his eyes to us as we passed, but the Actress waved hello. Later, I would learn he was also Hungarian and had only met the Actress the day before. Now that I understood this love was fresh, in the first throws of desire, all the dramatics of the night before came into focus. There had been no beds left when the Hungarian Lover boy had arrived last night, and he'd been forced to walk another ten kilometers to the next town to find a place to sleep. Everybody in the bunkhouse had been witness to their goodnight farewell. As we passed the bench, I could tell their good morning hello was going to be just as gripping, but perhaps not as well attended as the previous night's show in the packed house of the albergue.

Once the village was behind us, the land and sky opened up into unobstructed spheres. Both Alberto and I stopped to put on our rain gear as we spied dark clouds ahead. Rain came in alternating intervals, according the whim of the clouds, and kept us in a constant tussle of too many layers or not enough. I pulled the red bubble around my pack and slipped on my useless rain jacket. As the air was already warming, I knew I would be wet most of the day. Even when the rain held off, the thin layer of my jacket over my warm body left me sticky and damp with sweat. There was really no way to avoid such a problem on a restless day like this.

I walked for an hour or two a few paces ahead of Alberto, and he seemed content to have his own space. Somehow the two of us had an understanding that we would walk together, but by this point, we both seemed at a loss as to why. We were familiar, known quantities with a working short hand, so our connection lingered. I preferred company even when silent, for there was something soothing about companionship.

Though we walked along in our usual formation, I no longer felt a shred of dependency on Alberto. His role as protector was now finished. The paternal energy he'd kindly bestowed on me was no longer vital to my ability to keep putting one foot in front of the other. I wasn't so scared of what lay ahead or what might befall me if I didn't have trusted allies. I'd survived the day from Belorado to Burgos and had managed to meet two wonderful English speaking guys at the end of the long day. No matter what the trail threw at me, I felt grounded, ready to move and improvise, make choices and trust my gut. The guidance that had brought me to this place outside of Burgos, the border lands of the mighty Meseta, still hummed in every nerve. With or without the characters of the past few weeks, I would keep going. Yes the land was changing, and the appearance of the American duo was a wonderful moment, but I was changing faster than my feet could keep pace. My body was growing lighter in everyway, yet it was stronger as well. But the more profound changes to my life were under the skin. I was shifting, settling into a rhythm and moving faster and farther away from the past. The clutter of thoughts, the tangles of memories and sting of brokenness were being shed with every step. I was revolving and resolving in every moment of silent thought and simple interaction. This trail had become a mirror and I was caught in the reflection, caught in the hopes that it would guide me forward after this journey.

As I strode out onto the wide-open plains, the shifting dynamics with Alberto didn't occupy my thoughts for long. My stomach and ankles were suddenly demanding the majority of my attention with visceral bulletins. Even with my growing endurance and strength, I couldn't ignore the physical breakdowns that were opening chinks in my armor. I wanted to wish them away, be as strong as I could, rebuild my fraying tendons and rise above the humbling affects of injury. Since I couldn't arrange a miraculous mid-stride healing, I settled for some ibuprofen. If I didn't ignore the growing pain of my tendonitis and refuse to give into its fear mongering, then I wasn't sure I'd make it to Hontanas today. And I just had to make it to my rendezvous with the American boys. Now that I'd found them, I wasn't going to lose them in such an ironic way. I'd been able to tough it out this far, it was no time to crumple in an injured heap on the side of the trail and let these guys move on without me.

As the day neared noon, the fist sized loaf of bread I'd eaten before leaving the albergue was no longer holding down the gurgling rumble in my stomach. Even the quick shot of caffeine from my mid-morning pit stop had burned off. I would need to find supplies soon and restock my pack with almonds and cheese, apples and bread. These had become my staple foods. Even if I'd craved a bit of meat, there was nowhere to purchase the white loops of cured sausage that most of my fellow pilgrims gnawed on with gusto. The Spanish had a flare when it came to making a grand feast out of simple fare. Sliced meat, cheese and a loaf of bread with an accompanying bottle of wine was all it took to create a moment of pure culinary delight.

In regards to food, the issue of supply and demand was continuing to be complex. In normal life, I rarely let my energy dwindle so low or let my hunger rise to such a pitch of discontent, but here it seemed to happen almost every day. The only comparable experience was during my dance training years when waves of weary hunger would hit me near the end of a long class or after a performance. But these moments were easy enough to resolve, and there were always snacks at hand to bring my blood sugar back into balance. But here, hunger snuck up on me with speed and force. One moment I was fine, and then the next I was ravenous and woozy. Walking was deceptively draining. I'd been a runner since my early teens and with running I'd always understood the extent to which I was working my body. I felt the muscles burn, my heart race, lungs churn and the sweat drip into my eyes. The effort was short and intensely felt. Here my body was working at a more moderate level but doing so for hours on end. Since my heart wasn't pounding out of my chest, and my breathing hardly changed cadence, I was lulled into believing I wasn't working very hard. But I was, and my stomach was the first to alert me of this fact. There was a certain irony in the need for food on a trail where it was so challenging to get supplies. In desolate sections of the trail such as this one, everything had to be planned like a science, and carrying more supplies than normal had to be factored against the extra effort needed to lugged said food down the trail. I liked to err on the side of carrying a heavier food laden pack, but arriving in Burgos on a Sunday had thrown me, and I was still trying to recover my base of emergency snacks. As I scanned the horizon, I didn't see the next town, but felt it had to be close. My guidebook hadn't led me astray yet and indicated there was a little shop just ahead in Hornillos.

Several minutes later, I crested a small hill and saw a tiny village down on the valley floor. The rain had started to come down in earnest. My face was wet as I pushed into the oncoming weather. The wind snapped the plastic of my jacket with fierce shakes as the layers under my raincoat grew damp and sticky. The trail had been vacant for the past few hours, but as soon as I crested the rise, half a dozen new shapes dotted the pathway ahead of me. The nasty gusts of rain grew bolder as I strode onward pinned against the prevailing wind. I was moving a bit faster than the groups ahead and was sure I would catch some of them before they made it into town. With such open views, I often felt like a tracker following unsuspecting prey. On a wild day such as this, I knew they wouldn't hear my approaching footfall until I was even with them. As I drew closer, I enjoyed the chance to watch and gather clues about the new pilgrims. One group of pilgrims moved in a small cluster, huddling close to each other to help cut through the sheets of cold rain. The group stopped a few paces ahead of me to put on rain jackets as fast as they could. They were hollering to each other in French as I passed, fully preoccupied with donning their gear and attempting to keep themselves dry.

Further ahead, I noticed two pilgrims walking side by side. I was quite certain they were a man and a woman, but with their heads tucked down as they pushed against the wind, I couldn't see their faces. Both were tall and looked swift of foot. The duo seemed to be battling the wind with determined grit but also fully absorbed in the flow of conversation between them. Even from a far, their clothing and lithe movements betrayed their relative youth. They were most certainly peers. I charged forward, feeling my ankles protest at the change in tempo. I felt torn, literally, but knew my cranky tendons would have to adjust. Making new acquaintances was worth a little bit of suffering since there was inherent suffering of the emotional kind if I let such a glimpse of community disappear over the horizon.

The trail leveled out as it hit the bottom of the valley, and in no time I'd drawn within a few steps of the lanky young man with a large worn backpack and the girl in a neon jacket, leggings and a clear plastic poncho. As I came closer, fragments of sentences and familiar words flew back at me through the driving wind. I was almost positive they were speaking English even though I had no clue what was being said. The weather had created a bubble around their conversation, and I was still just outside their circle.

After meeting Jack and Ivan the night before, I felt things were changing, and this only confirmed my theory. The long slog to Burgos hadn't been in vain, for somewhere in those many kilometers I'd crossed a threshold, stepped away from the dynamics of the past weeks and entered a new phase of my journey. Maybe it was even bigger than that; maybe I'd left not just my old patterns since day one in Roncesvalles but my old patterns from the years leading up to this trail. Maybe this shift resonated more profoundly through my whole life, drawing a line in the sand marking the past and the future. One thing was certain; this new trail made me bold in a way I'd never been before. Jack and Ivan had been the first to meet with my social daring, and I couldn't have asked for a warmer reception.

With less than a kilometer before we reached town, I strode up beside the twosome to introduce myself. After offering my name, I asked if they spoke English. It was perhaps a silly question since I was pretty certain I knew the answer, but it was an easy opener and a quick way to glide into conversation. The girl answered my question with a curt yes. The tall guy said nothing. She was from Australia and her friend was from Belgium. I smiled as I spoke and sought to catch their eyes during my warm greeting. The girl was directly to my left and seemed to lean away from me as I spoke. Even before the words were fully out of my mouth, I felt their chilly reception. When I'd finished, she let her mouth hang open as if I'd cut her off in mid speech then curved her brows inward while drawing her lips into a thin line. The combined affect was one of the most beautiful scowls I'd ever encountered, but as she turned to look at the guy next to her, all her features rearranged themselves into a more neutral palate of disdain. The guy by her side was pensive as he finally spoke up and returned my greeting. I could see the tension in his frame and his sense of being on uncertain social ground. Worried as he was about the wishes of the girl beside him, he wasn't sure how nice to be to me. They didn't strike me as a married couple; I wouldn't even have assumed they were dating, but the girl was certainly in control. Turning my gaze back to her, I felt intense waves of hostile energy flow off her every surface. She wasn't in a daze over my sudden appearance like her companion; she was pissed off. Seconds ago, I'd been flush with excitement and now all I felt was awkward and intrusive. The confident open energy I'd felt soaring out to meet this duo curled up as if blasted with arctic winds and rolled back into my core. Suddenly, I wanted nothing but to be away from this tense encounter and back in my own easy company. I battled on in vain for a few minutes, doing whatever I could to bring a pulse to the interaction but to no avail.

As I scrambled to figure out how I'd taken such a social misstep, and why I'd fallen immediately out of favor with this duo, the Australian girl gave up her mild charade of subtlety and turned her back on me to re-engage in her one on one conversation with the Belgian. She lowered her voice and drifted further away from me, using the wind as a buffer. It was as if they were talking about highly confidential secrets, and I didn't have clearance. Giving the two of them the benefit of the doubt, I drifted ahead, wondering if I'd interrupted a deeply private conversation.

It now felt rude to stay, so when the young man stopped to pull on his rain pants, I said farewell. Maybe they had engineered the break, or maybe I'd taken the opportunity on myself. Either way, it was a relief to stride away from the dark looks of the girl and the silent uncertainty of the guy. As I walked on, I heaved a sigh of relief. I'd wanted so much to connect with other young people, but that encounter had been brutal, nothing like the easy moments with Jack and Ivan. The Belgian guy said they were part of a larger group that included two British girls and two German guys. This sounded promising at first, sending a jolt of excitement through me, but now I wasn't certain. How much could I expect from a group that traveled with that duo? I'd been brimming with confidence just minutes before, and now I was a collection of jangling nerves and doubting thoughts. Maybe things weren't changing as I'd hoped. It was a sobering thought and one I wasn't sure I wanted to entertain.

The one positive outcome of the interaction was my increased thankfulness for Jack and Ivan. I hadn't fully appreciated how generously they'd welcomed me into their trail life. It had all felt so effortless. As I watched the town up ahead drawn closer, I set my internal sights on Hontanas and reconnecting with the American guys. I would hold on to the good stuff now and let the threads of that messy trail run-in fall away behind me. After the evening in Burgos, I'd collected real evidence this trail might not be a solitary endeavor. To sit in the falling night with two young guys who had opened their circle willingly was a scrap of proof I could touch, recall and ground to. They hadn't run away, ignored me or frozen me out. Their body language and swirling current of enthusiasm for our growing connection was real, and it was a talisman against every group who moved with locked doors and closed ranks.

Once I stocked up and made my way out of town, all traces of civilization fell away, and a rise in the land led me upwards into an endless sky. I'd reconnected with Alberto on the far side of town and now walked a few paces ahead of him in our usual pattern of silence. All that could be heard was our double set of echoing footsteps. After a kilometer or so, we passed two bulky forms in ponchos, a son and father from Madrid who were on their third year of walking the Camino together. They planned on completing the trail in four parts and had just begun stage three in Burgos. There was a freshness to their clothes and a slight hiccup in their step, all evidence their bodies were still getting use to being back in the pulsing rhythm of the walking life. The father had a tightly trimmed white beard and spoke some English with a thick accent. The son had tied a tee shirt around the crown of his head and smiled as I came even with them. Taller than me, the son was fashioned of solid muscles and boasted the dark shadow of a day old beard.

As the father asked us questions about where we had come from, I thought about the multitude of factors that got in the way of a potential friendship or romance on the Camino. Just kilometers ago I'd run across two English speaking peers who wanted nothing to do with me, and now I'd met a handsome Spanish lad who flirted with determination but could never become part of my journey. It wasn't just his lack of English and my lack of Spanish, but his devotion to making this journey about the father-son experience. It was all a bit maddening.

As I walked stride for stride with the Spaniards, I knew I would move on and perhaps never see them again. Such was the rhythm of the trail and I was starting to surrender to it patterns. What could I do but trust? Trust that if I was meant to spend more time in the company of this pair, then they would reappear in my life further down the trail. The flow of people in and out was now moving unimpeded. I no longer felt I was grasping at bonds or pushing them away. The illusion I was in control of who came along and how was fading. Some might say Jack and Ivan had been a turn of luck, but maybe it only appeared as luck, and instead was all part of a plan that my dreaming and scheming had no control over. I liked the energy of this father and son pair but would hold them loosely and trust a journey itinerary I was clearly not privy to.

As the plains topped out onto an open grassland, I picked up speed and waved goodbye to the duo, while Alberto hung back to walk by himself. It didn't take long for me to lose sight of them altogether. Suddenly, the dirt track was empty except for my feet. I was alone, afloat on the sea of land. As I moved forward, the weather rushed from all corners of the sky. The sun cracked the ceiling of white and heated the thin layer of my raincoat. Then just as quickly, the dark clouds rushed in and black wisps of rain fell. No clothing configuration was exactly right. The weather was in a state restless indecision. On the track leading up to Hornillos, the weather gods had been in favor of a wet, dark and blustery state of affairs, but now the sky was a kaleidoscope of elements in constant motion, moody and delighting in its own range.

Unlike the weather, I was settled in an unfamiliar sense of calm. It was startling to find this place after so many days of stormy waters. Yet the mood felt ephemeral as if it could vanish on a passing gust and leave me ghosted and cold. I couldn't have asked for kinder conditions; a belly full of food fueled my system, and the path was wide and flat. My mind was blessedly vacant, and I felt my body ease into a rhythmic pace. With little on my mind, my senses took over. The surface of my skin grew light and thin, water and air moving through it as the swing of my arms measured the time. The land was absorbing me, and I was one of its elements rather than an outsider walking against its conditions. I longed to be rolled into the clouds, tumbled into the endless fields of green, plowed over like a curling wave to disappear altogether in this wild place. My feet met the land sole to sole, and the kilometers fell away behind me. I was caught in the temperaments of the churning skies but found exhilaration in her restless disposition. This was the weather to be outside in with no polite distance or courteous sense of space. The elements were drawing close and smelling my every surface, breathing deep into my lungs and hugging my very limbs. This was the weather to feel alive in.

There was no human imprint for miles. Just two equal spheres of sky and land meeting along a delicate seam at the horizon. No buildings, roads or other people. The only sound was the even cycle of my breath and the churning gusts of the wind. We were alone together, the land and I. This was the duet of a solitary figure traversing the open space between grass and sky. Even with weary legs and mangled ankles, I almost wished our moment alone would never end, that we could stay so close, tucked away from the messy human world forever. But after an hour of walking straight towards the skyline, the path dropped down a gentle slope, and I returned. My tendons were the first to welcome me back.

It was only reasonable that I would have to endure some consequences for my fifty-one kilometer jaunt the day before. I couldn't, in my right mind, expect that a toll wouldn't be exacted for pushing my body to walk the longest distance it had ever walked in a day. But somehow I'd hoped I would be able to ride out the backlash. Even during my days of extreme training, I'd very rarely met a physical challenge I couldn't grit my way through. I could recall dance performances where I would get out on stage and feel my muscles eating away at themselves. They would burn in protest at yet another vigorous workout but never hinder my ability to breathe through it with an appearance of dynamic ease. I had very little experience with being humbled physically, but now my ankles were crumbling underneath me, and this localized injury was derailing my whole trail.

I'd agreed to meet Jack and Ivan in the small town of Hontanas, tucked in the folds of the Meseta. The next few days would be spent on the Meseta where most of the towns were very small, often without even a food shop. I would come to refer to many of these towns on the horse scale. A small but well provisioned town was a one horse town. These spots were nothing too exciting but met a pilgrim's basic needs. A two horse town was pure decadence. My guidebook informed me, though charming with a wild west aura, Hontanas was most certainly a half horse town.

On the edge of the plains where the land fell away into a swooping valley, a tiny glimpse of Hontanas came into view. The tip of the church spire broke the surface of the land and looked as if it were a few feet off the ground. The clouds reached right to the edges of the earth. As I got closer, the houses and old streets appeared down in the scooped out land. Hontanas was a protected spot, one that had been given the best advantages the land could offer to defend itself from weather and attack. A full circle turn confirmed the village sat tucked in the only hollow for miles. Even though I'd come through plenty of rain during the day, as I entered the edge of town, the earth was dry and crumbled into dust under my feet. It was a quick descent down a steep slope into the main network of streets. As soon as I dropped down, the wind died away, and I could hear the sound of birds rushing from roof to roof. This sweet and mellow town was unaffected by the constant change in weather that brought blazing sun one minute and torrential rain the next. It was sheltered from the passing moods of the mighty Meseta and protected it's half horse well. I only hoped it could offer an equally safe harbor for my reunion with Jack and Ivan.

HONTANAS

As I ambled down the worn streets of Hontanas, it was good to know Jack and Ivan were back there somewhere on the trail coming towards this place. I wondered when they'd rolled out of bed and how much longer their journey across the plains would take. I spun the numbers and tried to guess at their arrival time. No matter how I counted, I knew I would have a handful of hours on my own before they arrived. I already felt a bit edgy at the thought of waiting for them. They'd been slightly concerned about their ability to do a full thirty kilometers with Ivan's foot injury, and I wasn't confident that my sparkling personality had won them over enough to encourage acts of heroic walking. If Ivan's foot acted up, they would stop in Hornillos ten kilometers back, and I would have no way of knowing until darkness fell and the last few stragglers stumbled into town. Unsure if they could keep their promise, I felt shaky about keeping mine.

As I stepped into the tiny central square, the church bell declared the noon hour. Hontanas held a peaceful atmosphere tight around itself. Everything seemed to pause and breathe here. To call the space in which I sat a central square was somewhat of an exaggeration; it was little more than a hexagonal opening between several alleys. Three roads in the village descended on this point and filtered all life into the center of activity. The town's two cafes and two albergues were located on either side of the block, and the church sat beside it all. Filled with a few red plastic tables, wooden benches and a sprinkling of pilgrims, the space was the village's central hive of activity.

The church was an unassuming structure possessing a simple beauty. The walls were large smooth stones covered with tangled vines that clung to the seams of its facade. The front entrance was a set of tall rust colored doors with thick arms of black wrought iron trim. A small fountain with a rounded stone bowl hung beside the doors. There was something sturdy and grounded about the building as if it had planted roots in the side of this basin and become a part of the dusty earth. It was drenched in its own history yet calm and confident in its identity. It fit the town flawlessly, mirroring back the tone and carriage of the place. It didn't try to be gaudy or pretentious; it was a perfect match.

Ready once again to dive into my food supply, I sat down on the bench outside one of the albergues. I cringed as my tendons squeaked and behaved like unyielding rubber bands. Both lower legs felt as if they were strung too tightly, bunching and cramping at the same time. I tried to flex my toes and massage feeling back into the gathering of tendons around the back of my ankles. I'd heard pilgrims recommending heavy doses of ice, elevation and rest, lamenting that such practical solutions were the only remedies for this plight. With no ice available until the albergues opened, I resorted to an embarrassing elevation tactic. I was more than willing to stick my legs up in the air like a fool for a while but was still firmly against any prolonged periods of rest. My body would have until dawn, and then its allotted rest period was up. I had to be firm and not give an inch to my finicky ankles. I just couldn't afford the emotional, social and even spiritual ramifications of taking a longer layover. It wasn't in the game plan.

I propped my legs up in the air against the wall of the albergue and let my head dangle off the edge of the bench, while the sun reappeared and covered me in warm light. I garnered a few curious glances but was too invested in ankle health to care. Yes, I was acting weird, but if I'd gathered anything from the past two weeks, it was that pilgrims were a strange breed, and we were all a bit nutty in our own ways. People who stayed inside the boundaries of normality just didn't seem to end up on a six hundred mile pilgrimage in the wilds of Spain. And when normal folks strayed onto the trail, they became as zany as the rest of us by the end. Everyone had a freak flag, but in normal life some just didn't fly it. On the Camino, people strapped them to their packs and let their flags flow with pride.

Despite how it might have appeared, I was hoping that seeing everything upside down would make the sight of uninjured pilgrims moving through town easier to bear. I watched from my inverted vantage point as those who had arrived for lunch began to pack up and leave. I couldn't look away as they disappeared one by one from my upside down line of sight. Everything was reversed, thrown on its head, and I was powerless to right the ship. I was the one who was always strong enough to keep going, able to go to the edge of endurance with ease. I was the one who led the pack not the one left behind.

Even when tipped upside down and nursing a set of throbbing legs, I couldn't let go of the pace that had brought me here. I couldn't give up the sense of purpose that came from always pushing onward. What was I suppose to fill my time with now? I was aimless, set adrift without the focus and structure of walking. I didn't know what to do without this task of walking to consume my fidgeting limbs and aching chest. The push was easy. It was about grit. It was about energy. This void was something else all together. I could feel my bone tighten at the joints, a sense of panic grip the outer edges of my rib cage and an overwhelming need to rock back and forth tug on my body. I wanted to hold my knees to my chest, crawl into a small dark space and feel contained. I wanted to be brought back into stillness by human hands, by something outside of myself. But I was alone on the bench, and my back-up boys were hours behind me.

The only Camino life I'd known up until this point was one of battle. Every day I'd waged battle with the terrain, my body and the clock. I'd pushed, proving my strength kilometer after kilometer, over and over again. I'd used my Spartan skills to keep myself going, to draw closer to love and community. To wake at six, eat while walking, arrive at the albergue at four, buy food, eat, sleep and repeat, was nothing. It was nothing if it garnered the two elements that had eluded me for so long. But once I'd crossed the threshold of Burgos, community had arrived, and I felt unprepared for the shift in dynamics.

My face was now beet red as all the blood in my body collected in my upper half. It was time to return to a sitting position. I swung my legs down gingerly and felt a rush of darkness cloud my eyes. A whoosh of sound filled my ears like rumbling surf, and I quickly stuck my head between my legs. I wasn't sure I could handle a public fainting spell at this juncture in time.

Eventually the black shapes in my vision receded, and I could hear the noises of the outside world again. How could I even consider walking more today when it might jeopardize my ability to walk in the days to come? If I stayed in Hontanas, I would be able to walk another full day tomorrow, but if I continued on to the next town I might cause serious damage and have to come to a full stop. Oh, the dreaded full stop. Just the thought made me shudder. It would be agony to wait out an injury in an albergue for a WHOLE day and see people blithely funnel through each hour. If I was forced to stop, I might as well lie down in the trail and let people stomp on my internal organs and wipe their shoes on my face.

No sooner had I returned to a fully upright position then a large group of walkers came down the lane and into the courtyard. I heard them making their way towards me long before I could see them, but as soon as they came into view, the courtyard filled with bodies, voices and buoyant movement. Two blonde girls with tan limbs led the way, their chatty British voices rising above the rest of the noise, echoing down the stone alley. They sauntered over to the fountain, oblivious of the commotion they were causing and began to refill their water bottles. Trailing behind were another girl and four guys. It was unnerving to see such a large group of young people arrive out of nowhere. Were they a hallucination, a conjured hope from somewhere in my addled brain? I would have believed it if not for the vast amount of noise they made as they flooded into the space like a herd of cattle. Even though I was caught off guard by the sight of them, their vivacious energy was intoxicating. I watched as they bumped into each other, fought for a spot at the fountain and laughed with open glee at their own escapades. They were so alive, extroverted and completely unaware of the stares they were collecting. No internal strife. No sign of injury. Not a care in the world. It was such a contrast to what life in the courtyard had been a moment ago and a world apart from my own Camino. I was stunned into a shy silence.

One part of me instantly wanted to be one of them, to be drawn into the fold of their solar system. I felt ready to be an outlying planet, if it meant I could be so light and move so unencumbered by worries, desires and a sense of mission. I wanted to be light as clouds and fall as easily into laughter. I could feel my body itching to leap up, introduce myself and do whatever it took to be adopted into their ranks. For not only were they having fun, but they were unmistakably and undeniably cool. The outcast in me felt a chance to belong and was not pleased that my shy limbs were having trouble standing up and throwing me into the fray.

I was almost on my feet when I noticed something that caused me to pause and stop myself. The third girl in the group was the Australian who had been so cold to me earlier in the day. She hadn't noticed me on the wall, and I suddenly hoped she wouldn't. If her reception outside of Hornillos was any indicator of what the group sentiment would be should I seek introductions, I had reason to stay silent. I'd already failed once today with this girl and was still recovering from our run in.

Just as quickly as they arrived, the group finished refilling their water bottles and whirled out of town in a flash of movement and sound. I let them go without uttering a peep. The fears of being snubbed, turned away and coldly rejected had won out. I'd never been so tense and anxious about approaching other people on the trail, so why was I worried now? Was it something about the sheer size and energy of the group, or the fact that they were peers, or maybe that they were a posse flush with females? I'd spent most of the past two weeks in the company of men. Only upon touching the edges of this group did I recall how different a trail life among girls could be. As they disappeared out of town, I slumped against the albergue. I already missed the energy of the group and wondered if I'd just let something good slip away in the span of a water pit stop.

At two o'clock, I had a choice to make. I expected a town as small as Hontanas to have only one albergue, but there were two. Normally this wasn't an issue, but the guys and I hadn't agreed on a specific albergue. I had to pick and hope for the best. I chose the older municipal albergue with beautiful ancient beams and stone floors. Once I checked in, I found an empty bunk and curled up in my sleeping bag. As I squirmed around, I dropped my flashlight on the floor with a loud bang, sat up to retrieve it and managed to knock my head on the bed frame with a resounding thud. Rubbing the crown of my head, I noticed a woman across the room smiling at me sympathetically. I said hello, and she said hello back in a soft flat American accent.

Sitting across from each other in our respective beds, I struck up a conversation with my new roommate. Our dialog flowed easily as she leaned against the wall with her glasses pushed up into her wild burgundy hair, and a journal rested in her open hands. Before the trail it would have been a bizarre moment indeed to meet a stranger and strike up a conversation all from the comfort of my own bed, but on the Camino it was often the best place to chat. In the wide room protected from the sun by cool stone, the middle aged woman and I traded background information. She'd danced since childhood, but when her life as a professional dancer had ended, she'd become a cook and eventually had found herself working on fishing boats in Alaska. I listened closely as she unfolded stories of dancing and slinging food for sailors. One world intrigued me, and the other felt just like home.

As soon as she began to talk about dance, I settled back in a state of pure delight. Not only did I see her life as a young dancer with sparkling clarity, but I felt it. When she spoke of partnering and talked about injuries, I knew exactly what she'd gone through. We'd both grown up in the circle of dance, lived and breathed a life of movement. She knew what I meant as I warbled on about the crossroads of pure athleticism and artistic content. We were the athletes with a deeper message, the artists with a physical grounding. She didn't tip her head and draw her face into a doubtful scowl when I announced my love of dance.

She got it. I was preaching to the choir. After more tales of life in the studio and at sea, she asked me about my journey and why I'd come all alone. Before my pre-rehearsed and rather guarded answer could escape my lips, I felt my throat closing down and my eyes tingling. I didn't have the heart to fake it, spin some self-reliant answer or show no weakness. So instead I spoke the truth in a wobbling voice and spilled my emotional guts onto the floor for the first time in many weeks. Because the Cook had lived so many years inside the dance bubble, I felt free to talk about the ways dance both completed me and ate away at me, the way I craved a dance community, yet found the existing ones to be toxic and imbalanced, bereft of nature and a deeper mission. I didn't feel at home in the New York circles of ambition and scarcity, and I soaked up the Cook's stories of dancing in a different era. My censor valve was off, and my audience didn't even flinch. Amazingly she hung with me through it all.

Eventually our conversation turned away from dance, and we spoke about the group of young pilgrims who'd blown through town. I expressed how torn I was by my conflicting feelings at their sudden appearance. One part of me longed to join their lively group full of boisterous fun, and the other part felt the Camino was meant to be more than a joy ride across Spain. I was captivated by the festive energy swirling around them but wondered if maybe they were missing the whole point of the journey. Was I the only one who believed there might be something with more gravitas here for each of us? Fun was fun, but could this trail offer a gift more profound than pleasure? I couldn't claim to have a full understanding of their journey; I'd only crossed their path for a few minutes, but I wasn't sure I would ever see them again. The Cook countered that perhaps I hadn't seen the depth of their experience through the circus of activity. Maybe her benefit of the doubt was fair. Maybe I'd judged them too harshly and let a good thing slip through my fingers. Was there a balance between the punishing road I'd walked so far, devoid of community yet rich in a sense of inner strength, and their road of omnipresent community and bacchanalian fun? Like myself, did they have a face they showed to the world; a blasé attitude shown to outsiders that concealed their connection to a deeper journey? I was suddenly sorry I might never know and that I hadn't leapt up from the bench to find out.

Only as the light started to grow dim outside the open windows did the conversation veer towards a place that made my words come thick and slow. My eyes filled with tears and threatened to spill over when I told her about my dream of having a family, how much I wanted to be in the throws of good love and have babies of my own. The Cook laughed in a gentle sweet sort of way that meant she understood but wasn't as worried as I was. Her face softened, and her eyes grew deep as she told me not to worry.

"Don't be concerned about getting all the things you want." she soothed. "You have time, and if these dreams are your heart's desire, they will be so."

She murmured in a low lilting tone as if singing a lullaby to me, comforting me with her grounded sense that it would all turn out well in the end. I felt blessed to have her there. It dulled the regret I felt about letting the group of young people walk on.

The shifting weather continued to change the light outside the window, yet nothing slowed the encroaching night. The Cook fell asleep sitting up with her book splayed across her chest. Two older Spanish men arrived wearing bike shoes, dragging heavy bike gear behind them. As I sat on my bunk with my legs hugged close to my chest, I opened my guidebook and looked ahead to the next few stages. I'd become addicted to my guidebook, fanatical about scanning it each night and thrilled to turn a new page. Sometimes I allowed myself to read a few stages ahead as if by doing so I was privy to the future. The unfamiliar names and charts pulled the promise of the land ahead towards me. It was escapism of sorts but practical too. I had to set a strategy for the next day, and this meant tasting the promise of something yet to be found. Almost every pilgrim I'd met was besotted with his or her guidebook. It was always on their person or tucked securely in their packs, ready to be held at a moment's notice. It was filled with markings, ticked pages and bent corners. The guide was their most cherished companion and trusted ally.

When I'd walked with Alberto and Alec, we'd spent a lot of time trading books and looking through the pictures and unknown words of each other's tomes. It hadn't been hard to understand the Italian guides. The kilometers, photographs and place names had all been the same. After all these weeks, my guidebook was no longer a stranger to me with weird maps that had no logic and cultural advice that made no sense. It was a worn and wise companion about all things Camino, explaining the ins and outs of this alternate universe. The book's outer appearance had shifted too. It had been caught in the rain several times and thumbed through by dozens of people. It even boasted a cracked spine. Now loose and aged, it had character. I silently thanked my mom each day for selecting this book before I'd left the states. She'd done a bit of sleuthing and discovered it was considered one of the best. She'd loved it so much, she'd bought a second copy for herself so she could follow my journey from home.

The book was a wonderfully quirky manuscript. There was something deeply satisfying in how the guide gave equal attention to practical matters as well as the bigger spiritual and emotional challenges that could and often did, arise. Need to know where to find the next water fuente? No problem! Need words of motivation and support? Look no further. It was an all in one, inclusive experience that wasn't bashful about linking the physical experience to the spiritual one. There was no attempt to be cold and solely informative. There was a personality behind the guide, and the author's advice was honest and sensible. As I read and reread each section in the evening hours, I felt I had a quirky and astute trail mentor helping me along, but I'd begun to meet others who had a different bond with this particular tome. A trio of Irish girls I'd stumbled upon several days back noticed my book and showed me they too were carrying the brightly colored guide. They giggled as I confided how supportive I found it, for apparently they'd been reading the slightly effusive passages out loud to each other for entertainment. So I'd taken the author's meanderings to heart a bit more than some. Did it matter since we were all still relying on his stewardship to keep moving forward on the path? Even the sarcastic trio of Irish girls felt a sort of affection for the author, a sense that he was a real character in their journey.

One element of the book I found both complex and upsetting was the lengthy discussion of the religious history of the trail. Since men had been walking the Camino for over a thousand years, the path had been a coveted entity worth fighting for. The trail's history was chronicled in ruined churches, battlefields and markers at the spots where men had fought and died. Some of these men had been famous, some had been religious and others had been fighting in service of the powerful and the papal. As the guidebook detailed each stage, it explained the historical underpinnings of the land along the day's route and shared stories of men long dead.

I struggled to keep all the information straight in my head and felt overwhelmed by the magnitude of the fighting. But even the chronological descriptions of bloodshed couldn't explain how all that was done was done in the name of faith. Away from this trail, one might wonder about the history of such a place, but here with my feet rooted to the land, I could feel the energy that had drawn such human chaos to its shores. This pathway hummed with an unmistakable vibration. And it was only thinly veiled by the layer of human energy, tension and conflict placed upon the land. I'd felt moments when the ground beneath my feet literally shuddered with the memory of violence, and at the same time known the eternal vibration of the path was still strong, serenely separate from its human past.

It reminded me of a story my dad told about a friend who grew up on Lookout Mountain in Chattanooga, Tennessee, the spot of an infamous and bloody Civil War battle. As a young boy, he would go into his backyard with a shovel and dig a few inches down to uncover ammunition and rifle fragments. The history of the land was that close to the surface even though the battle had taken place more than a hundred year before. The trail felt this way too, as if I could scrape a thin layer away and find the remnants of conflict and struggle lodged like physical remains in the earth. Yet like the backyard in Tennessee, it was only the skin, the top most layer of dirt that had been wounded by human history. The beating center and its current of energy was still strong, still drawing people here from all over the world like a silent pulse magnetized to something timeless in us.

At the same time, the human history of this trail affected every person who walked it. I could see the way it intensified every exchange, brought forth core conflicts and drew out the energy of battle within each of our small lives. It charged the air and seeped into the community dynamics. For if we were in a place that held a timeless energy, then how could we avoid feeling the affects of all the Camino had known? Could anyone doubt the shadows of the past lay thick around our shoulders, and we were in the energetic fray as much as those before us?

Now that I was on the trail, I knew the fight for religious control of the Camino was due to the undeniable intensity of this pathway. There was an internal motor below the path, a golden hum linked to the ley lines of the earth and the track of the stars. This trail was no creation of accident or folly, no random trajectory. It had been carved by the earth itself. We humans simply followed the current. This was a mythical land, hidden by the cloak of modernity. Abandoned in the early part of this century and returned to the wild after astounding popularity in previous times, it was an Avalon of sorts, set apart from time and rooted to a source of eternal wisdom. And now it was experiencing a renaissance, and I was part of the rebirth and human reconnection to this trail. Even the South African woman in Puente la Reina had remarked that the trail was twice as full and teaming with more young people than ever before. This new generation, my fellow twenty and thirty somethings, were thirsty for the Camino and willing to dig below its wounded surface. Whether these pilgrims had gravitated here consciously or unconsciously mattered little. We were all part of this new chapter in the history of the Camino, and I wondered what my guidebook would say decades from now. How would it understand this new paradigm? Would we be better stewards of the trail than the men before us?

This journey was a symbiotic encounter. We mere mortals depended on the Camino as much as it depended on us. We were all locked in a tussle with her, yielding at one turn and fighting back at another, adding to the light in one moment and lurking in the shadows the next. This wasn't a static relationship and certainly not a generic one. The bond with this ancient space was surprisingly personal and refreshingly alive. The Camino was at times coy and ever unpredictable; I was surprised by the heady combination of sheer irritation and deep affection I felt for the thread of land on which I attempted to balance like all the rest.

Even though I'd heard murmurings of the trail's gravitational pull before I arrived in Spain, I hadn't considered the depth of the relationship between the trail and the pilgrims who walked it. Not only did we benefit from the gifts of the Camino and the intensity of the energy here, but we were participants in her flow and helped to cleanse her energetic field. I'd felt this dual purpose running through the length of my conversation with the Cook. We both felt the internal unfolding prompted by the trail ley lines, at the same time I felt the Cook was serving the light of the trail with her support of my journey. She aided me to untangle my own internal logjams and in the same instant helped clear the energy of the trail around us. This service could be done alone as well. During the afternoon on the plains, it had felt as if my movement forward was opening a wider current of light, raising the vibration just a bit by moving across the space with such purpose. I'd been like a street sweeper, wheels whirling and pushing any detritus off to the sides, breaking up what was stuck with the sheer force of my movement. In that moment, I had no doubt in the power of our delicate and dynamic electrical systems. And I was just one among many. Others were striding along with whirling dusters, caring for the trail without even knowing it.

On a pathway defined by movement, nothing could really get stuck. Nothing got stuck in the rushing streams of the first snowmelt in spring, and the Camino seemed to be in perpetual spring: flooding and flushing, sweeping and swooshing. It had taken all my will power not to be swept up off the bench in the central square today and lofted down the trail. Everything here wanted to keep going forward, and even the people caught the sensation like a highly contagious fever. It was stunning to see how it affected each and everyone of us, to look around and see the revolutions unfolding and wonder what "normal" human life would be like if we were always riding these waves, always shifting and changing at this extraordinary cadence.

The energy wanted to keep evolving, absorbing more light faster and faster. I'd never before felt such momentous and speedy change rip through my life as in the past weeks, and the Camino didn't even seem winded from keeping up. Evolving was her game, and she'd seen her fair share of change. As a child, I'd grown up in a world where energy was as important and vibrant as the physical world around us. So in my early adulthood, as I spent more time out and about in the world, I began to practice clearing my energetic field with the same regularity and nonchalance as if I was taking a shower. For in a way I was showering, brushing off the layers of energy collected like dust and grime from my interactions with other people and places. It had so long been part of my life I hardly noticed the practice, but here on the trail, I'd fallen out of the habit. I'd lost touch with my regular routine, for the act of walking was cleaning my field for me. Along with the obvious occupation of walking, I was also unknowingly engaged in deeper work: pumping, inhaling, contracting and sweating the toxins from all the layers of my energetic system not just my physical frame. The tone and texture of my vibration was shifting. The most visceral proof of this stealth work was a shift in tone, not only in my interactions with others, but in my feelings about myself. The Camino was no stranger to mess, and I'd already released my fair share on her pathways. Yet she was a stickler for openness. I wondered if some pilgrims would flourish in such circumstances and others would writhe and squirm. It was hard to tell so far who was blooming out and who was crumbling inward in search of an escape. In any case, we were of the trail as well as on the trail, and perhaps its history was now ours by rite of passage. Ours to hold, carry, settle or perpetuate. Or maybe lay to rest.

Around dinnertime, the American guys still hadn't shown up. I wondered if they were staying at the other albergue just up the street. Since it was close to seven, I assumed they'd covered the thirty kilometers by now even with Ivan's bum foot. I slipped on my blue ballet flats and eased my way down the stairs. I couldn't bend my ankles or stretch my achilles at all and getting downstairs was a slow maneuver. I tried not to bend or point my toes. I had no flexion. It was like trying to walk in ice skates that were laced too tightly.

The rain had resumed so I hobbled as fast as I could up the road to the private albergue. Slipping into the doorway, I did my best to avoid the water gushing off the eaves. I entered into a small room with a low ceiling and dim lighting. The space appeared to be filled with every person in the village, both of the pilgrim and local variety, all taking refuge from the weather. Groups sat clustered around tables covered with half empty glasses of wine and snubbed cigarettes. With several people smoking in the small hot space, there was no way to avoid the clouds that lingered in the air.

Through the crush of people, I spied Jack and Ivan in the far corner waiting in line for the internet computer. When I joined them, we managed to find a few bar stools. It was lovely to see the guys again. They were in high spirits with many stories to relay about their night in Burgos. They'd slept in a large echoing gymnasium with a crowd of drunken Spanish school kids. The group of rowdy boys had stumbled in at three in the morning then proceeded to sing loudly and pee in the corner of the room. I felt a bit sorry for them as they recounted their night on the cold hard floor of an impromptu Spanish fraternity. I'd dodged a bullet with the sleeping arrangements in Burgos, but the guys took it in stride. They felt the experience was part of toughening them up, making them a more evolved breed of super pilgrim, and they were quite proud of their fortitude.

When I arrived at the bar, they were debating the pros and cons of waiting another hour for the pilgrim dinner versus eating dodgy bar food and calling it a night. Their empty stomachs were in favor of the first option, but their sleepy trail battered bodies favored the second. Jack and Ivan's debate about dinner plans raged on for nearly half an hour. Much of the time was spent with each attempting to persuade the other to be honest without being honest in return. The elaborate dance was a bit too muddled for me to follow. There appeared to be a general fear of pushing an agenda and a whole lot of effort spent trying to uncover what the other one really wanted.

We decided the following day we would meet in a town called Frómista. With a medium sized albergue and a host of supermercados and pastry shops, it sounded like a perfect choice. A guarantee of a bed and the promise of fresh food before siesta hours was all I needed to be sold on a place. It was especially easy now that Ivan and Jack had pulled me into their posse. Though they wanted to walk later in the day, I now knew both parties could be counted on to keep our plans, even if I rose in the early morning and walked ahead as the advanced guard.

I sipped a cup of tea and laughed while Jack raved about the way the dry meat sandwich in the case on the bar grew more appealing by the minute. Ivan confided in me that the last food he'd eaten was bread with slightly rancid cheese. This wouldn't have been so bad except that this cheese had been part of every meal for the past three days. No pilgrim could claim variety was a central fixture in his or her trail diet. Life on the Camino meant any piece of meat, no matter how dubious the quality, could be an object worth craving. Ivan kept flicking his eyes up to the clock above the bar, counting down the minutes until eight when they could go into the dining room and feast on the pilgrim dinner. At eight on the dot, the guys jumped from their stools and dashed off. I yelled goodbye, certain I would see them again tomorrow, hoping the meal that awaited them in the back room would live up to the wait.

It was fully dark as I left the bar, but the rain had stopped. I skirted around the puddles in the wet cobbled street and ducked into the thick walls of my albergue. The air was cool, but I could hear the steady hum of snoring above me. I climbed the steps slowly and slipped into the room, tiptoeing between the low slung bunks of two large Spanish men with equally large bellies that rose in rhythm with their loud exhales. I had the forethought earlier in the afternoon to pack my bag for the next day, so I crawled into my bed without further ado. Tomorrow morning would be one of the first times I would wake and have no one to walk into the morning with. It comforted me to realize I felt at home on these wide plains. They didn't carry the lonely energy of the trail in earlier days. In a mysterious way, I was enamored by what I'd seen of the Meseta. The land and the hum of the path would to be my companions for the morning, and I suddenly felt unafraid to rely solely on them. The arrows wouldn't lead me astray and Jack and Ivan would follow behind me. I had let go of my training wheels, lost sight of Alberto and those early days. I was trail savvy, equip with all the pluck I'd cultivated over the past one hundred and eighty miles and ready to walk out of this albergue unaccompanied. I wasn't sure what lay along the track to Frómista, but I wasn't worried about stepping into the unknown. In many ways I'd been on an endless loop of crazy adrenaline laden steps for weeks now. Tomorrow would be just another step into the rosy morning light with a set of cranky ankles and a curiosity about what lay ahead. As I drifted to sleep lulled by baritone snores, I couldn't help but wonder if community or even love was in the cards for the days ahead.

CASTROJERIZ
STAGE TEN- 35.9K-22.3M
HONTANAS TO FRÓMISTA

The windows of the room had been drawn together to keep out the rain, but when I awoke the slight gap in the old wooden slats revealed a sliver of grey dawn. I eased my bag on to my shoulders, trying to make as little noise as possible as I tiptoed out of the crowded room. The flagstones in the hall were cold, sending shivers down my arms but soothing my swollen feet. The kitchen and entryway were dark and the air soft. A light wind blew down the alley as I pulled the albergue's heavy wooden door closed behind me. It would be a matter of minutes before the sun rose above the edge of the basin, spilling golden light into the valley to awaken the hushed town. There was only one road west out of town, but I hunted for a faded yellow arrow all the same. Finding the first arrow scrawled on the side of a building down the road, I headed toward it, preparing to thread the distance between these markers all day, playing leap frog along the many kilometers ahead. I didn't glance back at the albergue as I left town. There was no one following, no trusted companion or Italian escort just a few paces back. There was only an empty street and the faint sound of snores drifting out of the albergue walls.

Testing my feet against the hard pavement, I was dismayed to discover rest hadn't been a cure-all, and my ankles were far from a hundred percent. But they still moved, and I would try to walk all the way to Frómista. What my ankles were asking of me was to exercise patience and restraint. In other words, I would have to walk slow, very slow. If I'd confirmed anything in the last few weeks it was that my body had only two natural speeds: fast and extra fast. I'd spent vast amounts of time during my training as a dancer practicing how to move slower, stay in the stillness and not revert back to top speed. Fast power driven dynamic movement was my wheelhouse. While others ran out of steam or never revved up, I zipped across the studio. It was going to take all my will power to keep the pace my body was calling for today, to feel the roaring flow of the trail move by me and not get swept up. I hoped not too many people would come along and pass me. I didn't know how much of that I could stomach. Thankfully the morning hours leant themselves to centered quiet, slowness of step and the illusion that nobody else populated the trail.

Waiting had never been one my fortes and patience wasn't one of my strengths. In the past five years I'd summoned patience by necessity, endured its desire to hang around with little more than a grimace and worn it around my neck for vast lengths of time out of a sense of obligation. In truth, I hated the virtue and would have preferred a young adulthood where we hadn't had to become such close companions. Even now, patience irked me. I could see the trail unfolding before me, but I had to wait, hold back and draw myself forward with less than I could give. Such behavior just wasn't my style. If I could see my path, I wanted to be on it, giving every ounce of energy to going forward. The same could be said for the larger scheme of my life. I'd come here on the shoulders of guidance. My dreams had weight and substance; they were rooted to my every action. I'd come here chasing the scent of the dream, of love and a family of my own. So why, if I could sense these parts of my destiny up ahead, must I wait so much? Why must I plod along here and hold back, unable to sprint ahead until my lungs seized, muscles cramped and I puked from the effort? I would rip my ankles to shreds to draw love to me, and if love was just up ahead of me, why was I being asked to go so darn slow? The endless questions, fears and worry circling through my head were maddening, and the day had just begun. I had to put them away, go back to basics and focus on the mechanics of the walking. What other choice did I have? I was following my guidance from above to the best of my ability, and I hadn't been given any smoke signals in the sky saying I was on the wrong track. I couldn't be, for today there was really only one track and one speed.

I navigated away from town with deliberate slowness, making every step take just a bit longer than I wanted. Scanning the village outskirts, I noticed a municipal swimming pool clinging to the side of the town. The aqua blue water was unruffled, clear all the way to the bottom like an unbroken plane of luminescent earth. The lifeguard tower leaned out over the water, forming a long shadow. I wondered what it would feel like to crawl over the fence, slip into its watery void and float weightless in the still hours, released from gravity and washed clean. It was hard to return to the trail every morning showered and rested only to find that I hadn't been able to scrub off the nagging uncertainty, throbbing injuries and troubling sorrows. Cleanliness was a moot point, because most of the time we perigrinos had bigger fish to fry and deeper forms of dirt and muck to wrestle with. And such things waited on the trail for us no matter what hour we rose and began to walk.

I turned off the main road and picked up a winding dirt track cutting along a sloping basin. The tall grass brushed my bare legs, licking my shins and leaving trails of morning dew on my skin. The path turned slightly, and a young woman appeared up ahead. She was standing very still with her hand above her eyes as if she were looking for something down in the valley. As I drew closer, I recognized the dramatic colors of her clothes and the beautiful contrast of olive skin and dark hair. When she heard my plodding footsteps, the Actress turned and gifted me with a wide smile. She wore a bright green scarf wrapped around her head and looked utterly peaceful. There was nothing stiff or sleepy about her demeanor. She was fully awake in the early morning light. As I drew even with her I glanced out over the valley to see what held her attention, yet I saw nothing but fields. Only then did I wonder if she'd been looking across the expanse of her memory, seeing images of the past across the backs of her eyes. I felt sad for a moment as if I was never going to see what had caught her in such deep stillness on the ridge. Nonetheless, she motioned for me to walk beside her, and we took off down the slope.

The Actress was also moving slowly. She had severe shin splints in her left leg and felt the ripping of muscles off bone with every footfall. Her orthopedic issue was a one legged affair and caused her to hobble in a more dramatic fashion than me. After walking with her for a few minutes, I felt it was a kindness to have pain in both my legs. At least I was a balanced gimp.

I was thirsty for company and intrigued by this mysterious creature, for she was both vulnerable and illusive. Her energy moved like quicksilver, dancing before me and shifting as soon as I saw any deeper layers. It was impossible to stop watching her, and I stumbled several times as I lost track of my footing. Even with her injured leg, she moved with an articulate awareness of her body. This was her instrument and even in the flow of everyday life, she understood how to use it to her advantage. Yet with all her magnetism, there was a refreshing naturalness to her. Nothing felt forced or gilded. She wasn't play-acting, but then again she didn't have to. I wondered if acting and the craft of being watched had chosen her rather than the other way around. She was the most naturally glamorous pilgrim I'd ever met. Most of us were goofy looking with strange dusty clothes, massive packs and unwashed hair. She made us all look a bit more alluring by association.

As we walked down into the valley beyond Hontanas, I was drawn into her energy field and immersed in stories of her life in Hungary. Even though we'd hardly spoken before, the trail allowed us to dive right into the juicy arenas of life, and I didn't feel a speck of hesitancy in asking about her blooming romance with her Hungarian Lover boy. She was open with her answers and spoke in a slow even cadence that drew me into a world so unlike my own. Since the Actress was more of an urban bohemian than a nature loving hiker, I had a hard time figuring out the rational behind her trek. Eventually I asked her why she'd come, knowing this question often proved the most fertile ground for understanding the core of a fellow pilgrim. The forces that drew each of us here often revealed much about our mission on the trail and beyond. In true dramatic fashion, she had a twisting tale about how she found her way to the Camino when her life had fallen to pieces. I hung on her every word, traveling back in time with her, following like a ghost in the halls of her memory, and seeing a story that resonated to my very core. She told of finding, suffering and eventually losing something she believed was love. It had felt like love, looked like love and spoke all the right words of love, but wasn't. I knew this story. I knew the feeling, and I knew how it would end. The cast, setting and timeline were distinctly hers, but everything else could have been direct scenes from my own story.

As the Actress's deep voice floated out into the still morning, she held me captive with her narrative of the long trail from Hungary to Spain. A year before her arrival on the Camino, she'd met a fellow actor while auditioning for a play then tumbled head first into an intense love affair with him. By the spring of the following year, the relationship had died but the memory was still fresh. She blamed herself. There'd been a brief flirtation with another man that had led to bouts of insurmountable jealousy. In the dark of sleepless nights, she'd seen the trail, felt her feet settling into a rhythm below her and known she must come here. The space of darkness and loss had been too great to banish in the real world. She'd needed this place of intensity where the bridges to the past could be burned to the ground and the ashes left behind. There'd been little fear in her choice to come to the Camino, instead there'd been the understanding that the past and the memory of this love affair were still holding sway over her life, and she'd have to take drastic measures to break free. Along the trail she'd collected rocks in her pockets, letting each soak up the memories of the past. When she had as many as she could carry, she'd taken them out one by one and hurled them into the trailside fields. She'd shed every filament of memory and every strand of emotion, one stone at a time. The cleansing had culminated when she'd walked until dark then flung large rocks into a growing rain storm and finally hurled her guidebook into the night with a single heave and no remorse. It had been a ritual sacrifice, a final gift to the memory of the past. She was done with collecting rocks and didn't miss her guide one bit. In one dramatic string of days, she'd wiped the past away and shown that she was done. She was done carrying a love that was dead weight. Even with a clean edge to her voice and the easy tone of her story, I knew what it had taken to banish the ghosts, for I was still in the fight. We both had the same scar. Hers was just a bit more healed over than mine, not fresh to the touch, not so open and raw. She'd turned to face the wound and had a healthy scab to show for it; I'd been avoiding mine, letting it gape and fester.

Even though I knew I was the walking wounded and could do with a bit of first aid, I'd spent the past weeks bent on avoiding the gash in my energetic and emotional field. Open wounds made me queasy and left me craving a return to the moment before things had broken, and my escape to the trail had also been my escape from the latest chapter in my broken attempts at love.

Upon hearing the Actress's story, thoughts flew back in time and pulled up the fresh memories of the Caveman, the man I'd just left. I couldn't claim I understood who this man was; the memories revealed nothing but a stranger. I couldn't fathom why he'd rolled out the red carpet and invited me into his life, wooed me with dogged intensity and made all efforts to convince me of his affection when he'd never wanted me. I couldn't say I understood how a man so many years my senior could be so absurdly young, so blind to the needs of the heart and so willing to play manipulative games with the affections of others.

I hadn't sought the relationship that had begun in the cool days of autumn in a blueberry field. I'd never expected to be chased with such competitive fervor. I'd just rounded the corner of empty numbness from the first broken love affair of my life, just recovered from a sleepwalking life of sorrow when I'd arrived at the blueberry field. I'd finally given up the ghost of the Dancer man and relinquished the faint hope that this first love would show up at my door and fold me back into his life. On the edge of my first real adult job after college, I'd felt ready to abandon my childish hopes of fairy tale love, of inexplicable love between artists who spoke in the same medium. I'd finally drawn back into the realistic side of my nature and decided to be more practical about love. I would be open and accept someone, anyone who showed a bit of interest in me. The Caveman had just happened to be the first to knock on my door.

I couldn't have known in those crisp days of fall what awaited me in the cage of winter. I couldn't have known I was being played, drawn into the life of someone who'd been telling secrets since his youth, who'd been selling a version of himself that was nothing short of a lie. By the beginning of winter, the threads had begun to unravel, and I'd become lost in a sea of uncertainty and shame. Unbeknownst to me, our relationship had been based around many deep lies and some of the things that had been presented as truths were proving hollow and empty. He'd said he cared, wanted me, maybe even loved me, but these tales had been nothing more than polished words executed to keep an illusion alive. In a world where he was beloved and touted as a hero, I'd found he only wanted me to act as a display, something he could show off like a coveted prize so others could admire him. I'd been the eye candy for his public image as an ardent suitor with the purest of intentions, a role he'd immediately dropped in private.

I suppose I could have done better to disconnect myself when the ground had begun to shift below me, once I'd realized the world he'd promised was hollow, but I'd become emotionally entangled and confused, and he'd been skilled at pulling every thread. He'd been a Bluebeard hiding behind the mask of popular acclaim in our small community. And like the fable, I couldn't see the darkness lurking until I'd opened the room of secrets. I cannot say there was one moment when I'd suddenly realized I was being energetically poisoned and emotionally abused all to protect his secret, but the nights had reverberated with dark dreams and had revealed cracks in his highly sophisticated masquerade. The space between us had become charged with a thick cloud of his shame and self-loathing that for many months I'd taken on as my own. He'd projected and I'd tried to absorb at the same time as he'd shunned and shamed me in every way possible. He'd rarely touched me and he'd blamed the distance on my behavior, my looks, my neediness. He'd made me the villain in our story while ignoring his role in fostering isolation and emotional trauma in our relationship.

Any self-respecting girl would have run for the hills, seen the signs and hightailed it out of there. Yet he'd worked round the clock to convince me that I was the problem in our relationship. I'd felt that if this was true then I could be better and summon the power to heal us. I could be more attractive, more desirable, more lovable and then all our problems would vanish. But the harder I'd tried, the more our bond had failed. He'd used words like weapons and had starved the physical side of our relationship until there was nothing left. I'd struggled to see beyond the moment, struggled to understand how I could make things right, and then I'd known what I'd been unable or unwilling to feel all along: there was a secret at the center of our relationship, something powerful that was hidden but guiding every move and every emotion. The secret was all around us, unspoken, un-actualized and greatly feared. This secret was not mine; it was his. I could never be the person he wanted, and I wasn't the true target of his anger, blame and disgust. I was simply the closest punching bag. So I'd fled from his life.

Leaving that small community and boarding a plane to the Camino had been a leap in the direction of accepting my truth and realizing that fear of the truth can be a mightier foe than the truth itself. Here beside the Actress, I had to lay to rest my self doubt, my sorrow and anger at myself that I'd been drawn into such a toxic and ill fated affair and let myself be used and abused. I wasn't here to lay a broken love affair to rest, but rather to lay to rest my sense of guilt about wasting energy and love on a mirage and allowing myself to be wounded by a man who was running from the truth. I needed to hurl rocks into the night until I could forgive myself for being human, for falling into a bad relationship on the heels of a broken heart and for not valuing myself enough to walk away long before I did. I knew I wouldn't be able to explain the intricacies of this release to the Actress, so I told her I was here to make amends with someone I'd hurt, someone whom I could have loved better, someone from my past that deserved more than she'd been given and that someone was me. The uncertain, fractured and love starved girl who was worthy of better than what the past year had given. The Actress turned to me, then looking across the valley, she remarked that the only way to let go of the past and make amends with those who had been hurt was to move forward less burdened, less wounded and more centered. She could only make amends with her former lover now by being more loving with her next love.

"The trail is ever forward, and it is our duty to evolve with it, our duty to heal the past with the movements of the present," she said with a soft assurance. And as if knowing this was the key line in the whole play, I leaned in and gathered every word like stones to fill my pockets.

Even with all the talk of the past, I was most intrigued by the details she shared about her current Camino love affair. The unfolding drama between the two Hungarian pilgrims was more diverting than my own trail interactions, and I craved the escapism their story offered. My ankles had begun to warm up under the touch of the rising sun and the fresh blood pumping through my body. The empathetic exchange and intrigue of the Actress's words also added a spring to my step. I was charmed by the trajectory of her story and the way she had begun the trail still caught in the snarl of broken love but had moved on and begun a new chapter with such speed and gusto. She hadn't gotten lost, had an emotional breakdown, fled the trail or wandered off into the forest to be eaten by wild dogs. No, she had boldly shed the past and found romance and the promise of new love. She was the poster child of all I hoped for. She'd rounded the corner, fulfilled the dream and was blissfully immersed in the new reality of fresh love. If her tale wasn't a fabulously successful advertisement for what might come if I really let the past go, then I didn't know what was. She was the living, breathing, kissing proof that it was possible to make it out the other side of traumatic love affairs here on the Camino and begin again.

She paused at the bottom of the valley to rest her feet, and I felt the pull to keep on moving. Surprisingly my ankles obliged. Perhaps they got the memo it would be better for all involved if they didn't impede my forward progress. I thanked the Actress for the pleasure of her company, and she nodded with a faint smile of contentment. Even her blooming injury wouldn't spoil the day. The trail skirted a field of unfurling poppies then spit me out onto a narrow paved road as a rabbit with a tuft of white and silver dashed across the path in front of me. I'd followed the magical clues and white rabbits many times before into territories unknown. The white rabbits of my life had brought me here to this trail, to face the gauntlet of the past head on and keep moving. Now I had to keep walking until I crossed to the far side and found the dream of love and community I'd always felt waiting for me up ahead. Somehow I felt the rabbit was a soft reminder that sometimes life took a path that led us through grief and uncertainty, but it was the kindest way to evolve forward as souls. It might curve and loop, take mysterious and infuriating detours, and even hit roadblocks before it helped us arrive at the life we craved, but like it or not, the route was our best way forward.

The last stretch before Castrojeriz was a long road lined with beautiful old trees, filtering the light and framing the pathway into town. The center of the village sat sidesaddle on the mountain with the church tucked below. Like all other small villages on the trail, Castrojeriz was compact. Buildings huddled together as if to protect themselves from any threat the open plains of the Meseta might conjure up. It was only human nature to plan villages in such a way, to crave a defensive formation and the comforting intimacy of small spaces in such a vast land. The trees offered sweet tempered shade as I passed under their arched wings. I could hear each branch moving ever so slightly in the growing wind. The trees lulled me back into the soft edges of childhood summers and the almost physical memories that drenched me in wonder. It was staggering how nature could still unexpectedly crush me with its beauty, long after I had lost my childhood to the turmoil of growing up.

The trail entered the town at the base of the mountain and wound up through narrow neighborhood streets to a sleepy center. The first sign of life arrived when I came across a small café with a tiny front yard tucked back from the road. Empty tables were clustered on either side of the door, and a sandwich board announced the specials for the day. Even though my ankles were warming up, I felt there was no harm in spiking my energy system with a bit of caffeine. I ducked under the small arbor and walked through the yard into the long dark café. As I sipped a foamy café con leche at the bar, the Hungarian Lover boy came in and scanned the space anxiously. I smiled at him and told him the Actress was not far behind. He looked relieved as I paid for my drink and headed to the door. He even ran outside after me and yelled a cheerful thanks as I crossed the lawn and made my way back to the trail.

As I ducked under the arbor and stepped back onto the trail, a young man was passing. He shouldered a large pack on his lean frame as if it weighed nothing, and he held a sophisticated walking pole in his left hand. By the time I found my voice and hollered up the road to him, he had his back to me and was slipping away on the tide of long determined strides. I wondered if he was an English speaker for he looked like a northern European, but there was a chance he was from somewhere like Switzerland, Austria or even eastern Europe. There was no sure way to know until I heard him speak. Since I knew the Actress would be occupied with her Hungarian Lover boy for the rest of the day, I hoped he would be willing to walk with me for a little while. I was still hungry for a bit of company, and he was noticeably on his own. I dashed into the dusty road as my voice rebounded off the low stone buildings.

"Hey, do you speak English?"

He turned, a bit startled as if my words had knocked him out of some deep internal place, then lifted his hand to shield his eyes from the sun.

"Yes I do," he declared softly in crystal clear English. There was no mistaking it. I'd finally stumbled across my first British pilgrim.

After hesitating yesterday afternoon to connect with the boisterous posse of pilgrims, I was back to my guerrilla style introductions, no matter how foolish it made me appear. I couldn't bear the weight of regret and vowed to myself I wouldn't miss a single opportunity to connect with fellow pilgrims, no matter the size of the group, nor the age or nationality; I would befriend them all. Carried on the confidence boost of my growing bond with Ivan and Jack, I dashed up the street to draw even with the stranger and introduce myself. As we shook hands and exchanged names, I hardly noticed how such moments had become commonplace, such social risks easily taken. Francis dropped his hand from his eyes as we turned west side by side, and I finally had my first proper look at his face. Even from paces away, I'd appreciated the tall lanky build of his frame and the grace of his stride, but his true handsomeness was in the details that I noticed only after falling into step beside him. The delicate articulation of his hands, the high bones of his cheeks and soft rich tones of his voice seemed to change him. I felt the heat flush to my face as I realized I was already slightly attracted to this new acquaintance and suddenly looking forward to the hours of walking that lay ahead.

Thus with little more than a dose of boldness and desire for a bit of company, Francis and the British boys came into my life. Later Francis explained he'd seen me long before I'd accosted him in the street. Apparently he'd also spent the night in Hontanas and had been trailing behind me most of the morning, but only in the straightaway of the tree lined road into Castrojeriz had he caught sight of my brightly colored pack. He'd grown curious as to why the pilgrim up ahead looked unfamiliar and seemed to get farther and farther ahead no matter how much he tried to catch up. He claimed the final straw of annoyance had come when he figured out that the quicksilver pilgrim who challenged the speed of his long legs was, shock or all shocks, a girl.

The trail sliced through the center of town, but I hardly noticed the buildings until we were past them, and the open sky was before us again. In the heart of Castrojeriz, I lost track of the world outside our conversation. Though we began with shy pauses on Francis's side and rambling questions on mine, soon our strides fell in sync and the current of the conversation found a life of its own. It was like I'd been fumbling with the radio frequency for the past few weeks, waiting to find someone on the same station and suddenly here he was, coming in with startling clarity. Francis moved with swift determination next to me, yet his speech was tight and contemplative. It was as if all the edges of his energy field were dovetailed inward, bound into a beautiful shell that was difficult to penetrate. At first, I wasn't sure if he was just being polite, exercising his good British manners and indulging me out of curiosity. But after a while I saw his shoulders loosen and the formality fall away. I was becoming less frightening, and our common ground was growing. He was learning that I enjoyed the task of plundering for information with questions, and I was discovering that he was different than the typical male and gave more than monosyllabic answers. Francis appreciated details and paused before each response. I was giddy with the discovery of such company.

We passed other pilgrims as we headed out of town, but I hardly registered them. I'd become the kind of pilgrim I'd so loathed, the kind that became so lost in her own circle she failed to see anything beyond it. But I couldn't help it. I was drawn to the energy of familiarity, the pervasive feeling of connection that had appeared out of nowhere. I was mystified and fascinated by this bond, intrigued and curious about Francis. I'd followed the current thus far along the trail, gravitated to places and people with whom my energy resonated, and this was no different. Maybe the novelty was that he was new or of the male variety, but I couldn't be sure. There was really only one way to know. I wanted to walk with Francis, even if just for these brief morning hours, and talk in the open air on a trail where nothing was out of bounds.

It couldn't have been more than twenty seconds between when I'd looked up from the dooryard of the café to when I yelled over to Francis, but apparently it was plenty of time for my mind to leap to several false conclusions that would soon be unwound from my over imaginative brain. As a female, it was perhaps my birthright to assume and imagine a mirage of things upon first glance, but the Camino had proved many days ago that it was a place where little was as it appeared. Best just to ask heaps of questions and soak up the truth straight from the source walking beside you. I'd assumed Francis was traveling alone like myself since he'd stood solo in the street when I fist clamped eyes on him, yet he wasn't. Instead he was one of three; a small nucleus from home comprised of three male friends from childhood. Francis confided that the trio had been on a punishing schedule for far too long, and his other mates had taken this morning off from a pre-dawn start to bask in the decadent thrill of a sleep in. Even the thought of doing such a thing made me grind my teeth with anxiety. I would never be able to indulge in such a luxury, and I had a sense Francis was the same way. Like myself, I could see he took pleasure from walking the trail in the early hours when few were around and everything shone with fresh light. Just the fact we'd met in the middle of the road at seven in the morning bright eyed and energized was proof enough we were kindred spirits. Francis even confided that he secretly relished the chance to walk on his own after weeks of moving as a small herd. And the mention of weeks was no exaggeration for Francis and his posse had been on the Camino for more than five. Whereas I'd jumped head first in the flow of the Camino on the outer rim of France, they'd taken the first steps of their quest from deep in her heart.

As Francis moved beside me with a settled emotional tone I'd rarely felt in other pilgrims, I surmised that the long weeks of walking had drawn him into this place of easy calm. His stride was rhythmic and flowed smoothly from the line of his leg to the bend in his elbow. The whole mechanical cycle was so effortless I sometimes forgot we were in motion as we spoke. I'd met several other pilgrims who had come from deep inside of France, but all had been wizened middle age men with thirty day beards and a strong disregard for the family life they'd abandoned in favor of a solo trek. I tended to avoid this grumpy, laconic sub-sect of pilgrims and for this reason had heard very little of the trail before St. Jean. Francis was a breath of fresh air compared to his long distance counterparts. He cheerfully took all of my questions, but I still sensed a core of intensity in his silent pauses. These moments were the only things to betray that he and the grumps shared something in common, some essential quality that lent itself to the harshly beautiful and isolated trails of France. Above and beyond the energetics, there was no denying Francis was another breed of pilgrim. He was a marathon pilgrim where I was merely a long distance runner. Francis explained that they'd entered the trail in Le Puy, France making St. Jean Pied de Port the halfway marker in their journey to Santiago. My beginning was his middle, and from my first step I was about five hundred miles behind.

The distinction made me feel a bit lame after so many days of pride in my St. Jean start, but Francis put me at ease and refused to make a fuss over the difference in our trail credentials. Beyond the obvious strength and sinew, there was little to mark Francis apart from us mere trail mortals except perhaps his hair. Before I could ask, he volunteered the tale, rubbing his closely shorn hair back and forth in a bashful gesture. He confided that both he and one of his trail compatriots, Elliot, had shaved their heads before starting the Camino. As he absently mussed his hair, I felt a shy side emerge. I was suddenly aware he was aware I was unmistakably female. It must have been some time since he'd been in the company of anybody but his two male friends, and now after many weeks, he was a bit concerned with how the radical hair cut might look to the outside world. I laughed softly at his story, and I could feel his body release its sudden bout of self consciousness. Still I wondered what his features would look like framed by longer locks. The initial buzz must have been quite a sight to see, and perhaps the desolate trails of France were just the place to let it grow back. The Camino roughed up the edges of everyone who traveled her length. New beards, unkempt hair and burnt features were the marks of a pilgrim and often added an unintentional allure. Now that my hair had begun to soak up the yellow light, and my limbs had crossed over from red to more golden hues, I was willing to admit that time on the trail, whether we buzzed our hair or not, improved our looks without even a shred of Hollywood magic.

We were so engrossed in our conversation, we hardly noticed the groups of elderly pilgrims as we moved by them. There was something magical and dance-like about the unspoken way I moved to the left of the groups in our path, and Francis moved to the right. Our words paused in mid-air and then reclaimed themselves as we met on the other side, falling back into rhythm without missing a beat. After all the talk of morning solitude and days of uninterrupted group dynamics, I felt a surge of guilt as I realized I'd taken his solitude from him. I'd crashed his solo morning, snatched it up and thrown it into a trailside field with a mighty heave and the smile of a naughty child. But as he talked, I didn't detect he was bothered by my company, and the fresh energy in the space around us was as vibrant as a dose of restorative solitude. As I walked beside him, I felt the unfamiliar pulse of a momentum that was distinctly outside myself. It was unnerving, yet I'd never walked so swiftly and with such little effort.

Once beyond town, the trail crossed a small valley and led up a short but steep incline. As the trail snaked its way upward, our conversation continued but I could feel my lungs burn from the effort of speaking while climbing. As we reached the top, we fell into a sudden mutual silence. Looking back, Castrojeriz seemed to float on the surface of the land while the thread of the trail was easy to spot as it dove into the circle of buildings then wound up towards us. Rarely did the land bequeath us pilgrims such views of where we had come from, such panoramas of the many kilometers. An old ruin clung to the peak of the square mountain and the church on the outer rim of town stood in relief. The land was losing all traces of green, and as we swung around to view the next sweeping valley everything shone with golden light. We were entering the dry burnished kingdom of the Meseta. Pilgrims often waxed poetic about the Meseta and its uncanny ability to push the average pilgrim towards either meditation or madness. The trail ahead would be flat, but it would also be hot and unrelentingly straight. We would have to face down kilometers and kilometers of unchanging terrain. The challenges of old, the rain and muck, the damp and hills were behind us.

As we made our way down the valley, Francis explained the particulars of his journey. Teaming up as a trio, the British guys had come to the Camino as a traditional pilgrimage. Though one of the lads had no real connection to the religious thread, Francis and his companion Elliot had been raised on the bread and butter of the Anglican church and saw the experience of pilgrimage as an important one. Francis explained that his father was the rector of a rather large urban population in southern England, and he'd literally grown up in a religious house. They'd moved from parish house to parish house throughout his childhood but never left the city where he'd been born. His lineage was also one of religiously minded men. His parents had met when his father had moved to the country to work as a curate in a rural parish and had fallen in love with the rector's daughter. Within a month, he'd made her his wife. Despite his religious credentials, Francis insisted it was just in the past year that he'd come to the decision to walk the trail. First he'd taken time off from school and arranged to live with a group of Franciscan monks. Working for them as a gardener, he earned meager wages but was able to live in community with the brothers. Only then did he finalize plans with Elliot and their third member John, to give several months to the Camino quest. I was curious about what would motivate such an articulate and engaging man to spend nearly a year of his time apart from the world, tucked away in such a lonesome place. He seemed to be forever caught in the cross hairs of deep thought, even when speaking with me, as if part of him was always tucked away in a fortress of contemplation. It was a wonder he reemerged and came back to the world as he did, for I could imagine his nature might just let him slip below the surface of solitude and settle to the bottom.

Yet even with his meditative silences and the way he gathered his thoughts carefully before speaking, he was funny and deeply thirsty to understand the world around him. He wanted to know about my Camino thus far and broke into soft chuckles as I recounted my goofy missteps and minor disasters. The outer edges of him felt light and innocent, but in no way naive. I was shamelessly intrigued by someone born of such a different spiritual upbringing, and he seemed open to my unabashed curiosity. The more he explained his roots in the church and the religious underpinnings to his journey, the more I felt we were polar opposites, disparate constellations on the sky of belief. And despite it all, I liked him. I liked him very much, almost more than I was willing to admit. Maybe there were different coverings to our faith, but I sensed we shared some core spiritual values. In some surface ways, he was part of the group of pilgrims who didn't interest me, but at same time he was a person I felt strongly drawn to. Ours was the most instant connection and chemistry I'd felt since the beginning of the trail. He was the most unlikely friend and the one I somehow wanted the most. I wanted to tell him every reason I was here, spill all the messy tales and wait for his words in reply. I wanted to understand our stunning familiarity and follow this new current of energy across the plains that lay ahead.

It wasn't until deep in the morning that I stumbled across my last and maybe largest assumption about Francis. I'd begun to talk about my studies at college then asked Francis what he'd chosen to study at school. As I waited for a response, he paused. He rubbed his shorn hair as if he'd suddenly become vulnerable, shy almost, and he replied that he'd yet to begin university. The time he'd taken off to work for the monks and this summer journey was all part of his gap year before university began. All of his posse were on the verge of adulthood rather than deep in the weeds as I'd blithely imagined. Upon meeting, I'd looked this tall, put together and articulate man up and down and imagined he was in his mid twenties just like me, out in the world trying to find his place. I was startled to realize I was in the presence of a rare male who was more poised, emotive and adjusted than his age would suggest. It is an accepted truth that females are often wise beyond their years, but men? Before this moment, I believed I would more likely have a run in with a yeti than the mythical mature young man, but here he was, bashfully announcing he was a fresh nineteen years of age and not afraid to talk to a girl like me. I was pretty sure I frightened grown men, so how was it that Francis was hanging with me? Was it the uncanny and rather unexpected familiarity, or was it simply an openness that resulted from trails of solitude? I wasn't sure I knew the answer, but it would take me a little while to accommodate the idea that Francis was nineteen. I could feel my brain whirling, sorting all the information and trying to figure out how to absorb the shift in the lay of the land between us. Since I was still on the quest for love and a partner to share my life with, I couldn't lie and say I hadn't thought Francis was a potential contender, but his age had brought the damper down rather quickly on such daydreams. I felt a bit sorry such a dynamic person, one to whom I felt so drawn, was suddenly off the table. But as we matched each other's pace, I felt a wave of comfort roll over my body; I felt less lonely than I had in weeks, maybe longer. Even if I couldn't open the avenue of romance with Francis, I could be close and find solace in his company. I needed friends here just as much as love, and though it wasn't the most exciting of the two choices, it was a necessity I had long lacked. And it was a necessity he was willing to offer me without question even on a morning when he had hoped for a few hours alone.

Traversing the long open plains, we talked at the speed of light, passing groups of walkers, puddles and roadways without dropping the thread of conversation. The cadence and direction of our words took on a life of their own. Perhaps my conversation with the Cook had served to loosen the doorframe, but suddenly I was taking about my love of dance again. I told the vivid tales of a time in my life when the dream of who I wanted to be and reality were so close to finding each other, when every moment was a swift moving current of bliss with only a thin edge of emptiness I couldn't banish. I let my voice drop low and found my vision sliding into memory, even my body moved as if it remembered how it felt to be so in love, so consumed and endlessly hungry for more. I explained how the very core of my desire hadn't faltered since the first dance step. It had only grown, but the expression of this love had lost its stage, its avenue, its place to belong in my solo journey. Francis waited until I paused to let the outside rush into my lungs, then he asked me a question that encircled me with its swift sight and filled the space around my suddenly paper thin walls.

"If you still love and long and seek, how can you doubt this true love of dance will come back to you? It has never left you, it just placed its roots in deeper soil and steadied itself to wait until it is time to bloom."

He had heard it all. The way I'd fled from the fame hungry circle of NYC modern dancers then pined for dance when I'd allowed myself to fall into a job where dance was only a peripheral perk I had to earn. I'd craved the feeling of being a dancer and tried to re-embody who I'd been during my years of training, but it had been hard to capture the thread as I moved alone in cold studios or met for late night clandestine rendezvous with movement in any space I could find. The love I'd once lived and breathed now felt unavoidably lonely and a bit unrequited. Francis saw the luck of having uncovered such a passion, but he wouldn't let me rest back on my assertion that I was also unlucky to be separated from the community that had nurtured my dancing. I tried to explain the way a social art felt when lived alone, and how sometimes I longed to be a painter, sculptor or welder, anything I could practice without the company of others. But I quickly withdrew my statement and confessed that in truth, much of my love for dance was because of its communal energy. The energy of bodies moving was the poetry I longed to live over and over again like a beloved sonnet.

Francis confessed he was a stranger to the world of dance but listened as I explained the dynamics that both attracted and repelled me from the world. I was an improviser. Near the end of my training I'd abandoned the traditional format of choreography to give the flow of my creativity to the art of improvisation. I'd always been drawn to dance that was crackling with energy, so alive it felt intimate and vulnerable. I wanted to see people move from impulse, be in the now and share the present experience. Pre-rehearsed choreography so often veered into a dulled series of executed moves, but a dance that was improvised and alive in the moment could go anywhere; it was true to the present and a gift of energy that was felt by all who watched. I would rather have seen Baryshnikov stumble and recover than execute a perfect series of pirouettes. For in the slip up, his humanness would arrive on stage, and we would be part of a moment when he was making choices and reacting to the unpredictable nature of life. He would be alive to the next move just as much as we were. The greatest art I knew felt raw as if created in a space of vulnerability to the now, a willingness to share the questioning rather than churn out an end product full of answers.

Small children were the best at embracing improvisation as a way of performing; it was the practice of play. They followed the current of interest or wonder where it took them. Play wasn't pre-rehearsed or confined; it took on a flow of its own. To my eyes, dance was simply the grown up version of play. Yes, the movement tools were sharper and the topics deeper in tone, but we all craved the chance to live through art, to feel through movement and emote essential truths. Dance was my voice. More specifically, for skilled dancers with physical grit and emotional depth, I believed improvisation and the art of performance were the tools that brought a revitalized gravitas to dance. They could plug our art form back into a deep eternal source and make our artistic voices viable again. If forced, I couldn't separate the energy of love from the experience of dance. The feeling of oneness or pure fullness was the same, and an audience felt that as we performed. Why else had we been enraptured by romance in plays, fables, books and movies for most of human history? It was because we got a taste of the feeling we craved from the tales of others. Dance was no different. We simply told human tales with the body: the most essential of all human elements.

Francis told me a bit about his schooling, and I saw the traditional academic wheels spinning in his brain. He'd always used writing and the precision of finely crafted words to express his creative voice, and he'd clearly never imagined stumbling across a wild heathen of a modern dancer such as myself. I could feel him follow the current of my enthusiasm with a steady ear but pull back slightly at my zealous tales of an art form that was so physical, so bound to others and so uncontrollable. But we kept walking, and he continued to listen with a genuine desire to help as I questioned what was next for me and dance. At first I worried my emotional dialogue would produce a chilly reception, but he remained steady, holding out an arm of support as I ventured to share the building blocks of my voice. Movement was my first language and maybe the clearest vocabulary I could offer others. To see me dance was to know me. In the past few years I'd become adept at social interaction and the art of chatter, but I knew when I danced for people they saw into me, and all was revealed. All the wounds of the past and strengths of the present were there to see. I was a bad liar with words but utterly incapable of mistruths with my movements.

And I knew there was a beauty in that. Because of this it was profound for me to dance for others, especially those I cared for. To dance for someone I loved was the ultimate act of vulnerability. No more walls, no more hiding how I really felt for them, all would be revealed. It had been too long since I had danced for another, but I was drawing closer to the beauty and the risk again. I could feel it. As soon as I touched down on the trail, the shift had begun. Now it was only a matter of time and universal scheduling. I was at the Camino's mercy but had to admit with the arrival of new life in the form of Jack, Ivan and now Francis, I was happier with the leap that had brought me here.

As I stepped gingerly around the muddy trail, my body suddenly hummed with a new combination of comfort and exhilaration. I felt cared for as if the hours by Francis's side had curbed a ravenous hunger that had been eating through me for days. He actually listened as I told tales of dance and art, dreams and the unknown. From the way he nodded optimistically at my boisterous rants, I felt a momentum build inside my chest. Suddenly I felt I might actually be able to read the tea leaves scattered around the edges of my cup and discern the divine code that promised a life of love and kids, dance and community. It was out there just up ahead, waiting for me to grow up and arrive. This young man who hardly knew me believed it could be so with such a lack of guile or doubt that I felt immediately bonded to him. Not only did I want to stay by his side to keep hold of the threads that were now strung between us, but I wanted to hear his story too. I wanted to be his friend, for I sensed it had been too long since he had unburdened his own heart.

In the meantime I'd completely forgotten about my ankles. I wondered if it was the talk of dance or the promise of such good company for the rest of the day; I concluded it was both. If there was something deeply reflective about Francis, this quality only grew when the tables turned and the story was his own. I wondered what gears were shifting and moving down below his composed façade. I was curious as I sought to uncover the things I couldn't see by just glancing at him. An attuned listener, I'd felt Francis might be shy about becoming the topic of conversation, but I made him squirm in the spotlight for a bit until he gave up the fight and began to tell me about his early life as a writer. Even though he was only nineteen, he'd already explored many parts of this calling. When he was sixteen he'd spent every waking, breathing, living hour sitting at his desk writing a novel. After months of hiding away in his own words, of seeking intimacy through a bond with the characters of his own imagination, he'd shared his story with two people. The first had been a literature professor at Cambridge University and the other had been his father. The professor had enjoyed the novel and felt there was real potential in the creation. His father had been politely baffled and felt the book had no foreseeable future. Thus with two such reviews to its credit, Francis had tucked the manuscript back into his desk and abandoned it. He wouldn't even tell me what it was about or why his father's words had eclipsed all else. With that chapter shut, he'd turned back to his search through the veil of religion, sought solace in spaces of stone and gathered congregations. His life at the monastery had soon followed and then this moment, this trail of reflection: a thousand miles of space to talk with voices deeper than his own. I was astounded by his ease with stillness. He was one of the first people I'd ever met who seemed to be still even as he moved. I lived in a state of perpetual motion and had even awoken at times to find myself dancing across the surface of my bed. I could make silence move and stillness vibrate. I wondered if we were polar opposites, facing off with wide-eyed curiosity about the internal workings of the other. I certainly admired his skill yet found it maddening at the very same time. I could imagine him sitting still for hours a day, crafting letters into words and words into lines strung together in an endless chain. I wondered if writing was his dance, stillness his movement. At the center, I felt the vibration of two very different notes, each somehow ringing true.

I asked questions, but mostly I listened. I heard his writer's voice flowing beneath every tangent; it was as if we were making a fair trade. I spoke of dance and he of his novel. For each reveal there was an equal disclosure of something vulnerable. I'd felt this effortless current in the trail many times since St. Jean, the way it almost pushed us to tell what lay at the root of our search, but Francis was the first person who seemed to match my intensity and absorb my tales fully. Besides my moment on the bridge with the South African, I couldn't recall a conversation as honest. Yet Francis's confidences were of a different breed than those shared by the South African. His weren't about the intensity of the world outside of himself but rather about the intensity of his internal life. In telling the story of his novel, he wasn't explaining an outer world disappointment, but divulging the nature of his internal world, the movement of his creative voice and the things that he held most dear. Such tales involved a risk, subtle and profound. Until Francis, I hadn't met a fellow pilgrim who had seen the difference between sharing his view of the world and sharing his feeling for life.

I couldn't figure out how we had sized each other up and determined the other was worthy of such confidences, but we had. I enjoyed watching my questions settle before Francis spoke. It was as if they had to sink with gravity through him before he could respond. The trail had provided us with dusty flat lands and created a space where soul searching hours in the company of a stranger was possible. I felt once again this land, the solar system of the Camino, was a rather dramatic and magical place where tides shifted at the whims of some unknown force. Nothing was out of bounds, not even a surprising friendship with a most unlikely confidant. I couldn't curb my flow of words, my flat vowels betraying my American identity at each turn, but Francis with his reserved penchant for contemplation, seemed willing to hang with me.

Even so, I wondered what it felt like for him to walk with me. On the way out of Castrojeriz, he'd admitted he hadn't talked to any young females while he worked for the monks. In those months, he'd had little contact with the outside world and even less with the fairer sex. I could tell I was a shock to his system, but I wasn't entirely convinced it was a bad thing. After explaining about his life with the monks and the quick transition into a journey of all male companionship, he admitted I was the first girl he'd talked with on the trail. After his self-contained month in France, maybe he felt it was time for the alchemy of his journey to shift. He must have felt the draw to stay by my side, for I'd learned that on the Camino moving off and away was a way of life. Nobody owed time or space to another pilgrim. Bonds here were of a voluntary nature. It was very easy to push off and disappear, and he had done neither. So we marched onward, and I briefly wondered what would come of my changing trail. Would I be able to stick in the life of all these young turks who now flooded around me? Would I meet again with the group of other young pilgrims? Maybe love awaited me in that group or still another group ahead. I couldn't know, but I felt relieved from the constant burden of worry as I basked in Francis's company on an otherwise empty road.

As we talked, the world around us changed. The landscape wasn't nearly as beautiful as the day into Hontanas, yet the land had somehow become secondary. Yesterday there was a fierce connection of weather and skin, but today the land was more of a backdrop for the air between me and this new pilgrim. The ripe fields of grain had given way to yellows and oranges, and everything living was in an arid form of hibernation. The trail no longer meandered in wide loops but choose the straightest line forward. No more twists and turns to accommodate hills and trees, no more thick swatches of wet earth. I wondered if this dramatic and increasingly dry world was more typical of the Meseta. Maybe the trail into Hontanas was an anomaly of beauty all its own. The directness about the trail was startling, and there was a dizzying sense that we were crossing a barren land along the fastest road. I felt my water bag every few hours, trying to keep tabs on the amount of liquid I still had, for there were no fountains out here. Yet with Francis as company, I felt at ease in the open land and wasn't concerned when the kilometers ahead showed no signs of a village or town.

After climbing up and out of the basin where Hontanas and Castrojeriz nested in the earth, the trail would spin us out for over a week on a plateau. The charts in my book confided we wouldn't change elevation for nearly eight days. This was flat desert land. After walking on our first true taste of Meseta lands for several hours, we came to a cluster of lush trees, an old monastery and a bridge spanning a glassy river. As we headed to the bridge, I noticed a large bus was pulled up alongside the trail with groups of elderly people milling about. As we crested the bridge, a woman asked if she could take our picture. We exchanged a bemused look and shrugged our shoulders in compliance. As we posed and the flash clicked, I felt like a zoo animal. Here we were: the rare walking pilgrim captured in our natural habitat. I am sure my dusty limbs and wild hair only added to the authenticity of her shot.

It was odd, considering all the walking and rough living quarters we faced, to feel sorry for the pilgrims who rode buses from town to town, but I did. They didn't have the same intimacy with the trail. I touched this pathway every day all day. I spoke with it, fought with it and praised it. I was in a serious committed monogamous relationship with el Camino. I loved my new mate more than I could have ever imagined, and yet to bus pilgrims, the trail was a virtual stranger with whom they connected briefly before moving on to something new. I was in the trust tree, and the trail was beginning to show me its secrets, virtues and vices. They, on the other hand, watched it from a distance as if it were a movie, a flat image from a guidebook. How could it affect them the same way? It could entertain them with churches and historical sights, old stone bridges and scallop shells galore, but never lodge itself in their bones and muscles with the same truth and intensity. The trail's essential self was as a trail. To know it fully, it had to be walked.

Near noon, the endless ribbon of hot exposed trail ducked into a shaded glen of trees and a small park on the outer rim of a town. Stone picnic tables dotted the space, and the grass grew tall and soft, lapping around the edges of the smooth benches. The glade looked cool and inviting, but we didn't stop. All our senses were attuned to the hunt for water and fresh supplies.

The cluster of muted stucco buildings in Bodilla could hardly be categorized as a town, and the streets were vacant. We ducked our heads into the municipal albergue but found a hollow building with the lights turned off. My guidebook had promised a food shop, but we found only a small store with an odd collection of items in the front window. It looked more like some crazy nana's house than a food shop. Once the wizened old woman opened the door to let us into the tiny space, the feeling only grew stronger. The place was weathered with age, dust clung to every surface and the air smelled musty. The small woman ambled around to the backside of the counter, and her equally tiny husband came out from the back to help us.

Francis and I picked out a few items, and in a gentlemanly fashion, he offered to pay for them. It reminded me of the small kindnesses of Alberto. I wasn't used to men being so courteous. The shopkeeper tallied our purchases on a piece of scrap paper with a pencil retrieved from behind his ear. We gathered the small pile of food into our arms and thanked the couple before stepping back into the sunshine.

Settling on the stoop of the store, Francis cracked open a can of peas, while I unwrapped triangles of cheese and broke off pieces of bread for the both of us. Other than my infatuation with sweets, I continued to wallow in an appetiteless malaise. As Francis spread cheese on a piece of bread, I noticed with envy that he had a brightly colored set of utensils. A knife, a fork and a spoon, the whole civilized gang was there. We spoke on and off between bites but mostly sat in companionable silence, letting the sun warm us. The road was oddly still for noontime; a few passing pilgrims were the only activity.

The Cook came by and sat with us for a while. It was nice to see her again. We'd crossed paths a few hours before, but it felt as if a lifetime had transpired since then. Time had bent and stopped, opened up and pulled us into some past that might not even have been this lifetime. Everything about the trail had begun to shift the moment I met Francis. I didn't see this at the time. It was just another day, and he could very easily have been just another passing acquaintance, but even as I sat on the stoop in the sun, I felt something had occurred. It felt similar to what happened the evening in Burgos when I met Jack and Ivan, yet deeper in tone, more sustaining somehow. Time on this trail was divided into before and after. Before Burgos and after. Before Francis's arrival and after.

As we sat on the stoop, Francis pulled out his cell phone to call Elliot and John, the other members of his Camino posse. They had yet to make a plan about where to spend the night, and Francis now seemed keen on ending up in Frómista with the American guys and me. Earlier in the morning, I'd been pleasantly surprised to hear that Francis's group was already acquainted with Jack and Ivan. The five of them had shared the pilgrims' dinner with each other last night in Hontanas. It was strange to realize that when I bid Jack and Ivan goodnight, they walked into the next room and met Francis and his crew. We could have missed each other by a matter of seconds this morning. We'd already passed by one another last night unbeknownst to the both of us. It made me wonder who else I might have missed by fractions of time or space.

Francis was excited about a rendezvous in Frómista but wasn't sure how the other two in his group felt about opening their circle. I could see the trail thus far had been about devotion to his two friends and to the religious roots of his journey. This fall they would scatter to the wind when they attended different universities in different corners of England. They all knew they might never live parallel lives again, certainly not as young men, open and unattached. This was their last shared trail before their paths in the outside world diverged. It was odd to know how much their lives would change in the next few months. I was only five years older than Francis, but those years had been dense with experience, crushing and expansive in the same breath. They had shaped my bones and my view of the world. As I listened to Francis talk, I felt any lingering feelings that age determined wisdom begin to evaporate. If I'd learned anything in the past ten years, it was that we all did our growing at different moments. I seemed to have set a trail through adolescence and young adulthood that was all about steep climbs and endless marching. Just from being allowed into the edges of Francis's story, I felt he too might have had more than his fair share of trying times swimming against the current of the culture and his peers. Maybe that was why I felt so at ease with him. All of us had a different timetable for emotional and spiritual growth spurts. This was extremely evident on the trail. I'd met older pilgrims called here to navigate great change and face the last chapters of their lives with heartfelt openness. I'd also met pilgrims my age that didn't seem interested in change or growth at all. I'd found solace and community in the conversations with the older group but craved just a few younger pilgrims who might also be rooted in the search for balance. This very tone was what I'd found so lacking in the German and his group of beautiful Parisians. They'd been here for the surface. I wanted to go deep. Francis, on the other hand, had a gravitas beyond his years, a centered and calm energy lacking in pilgrims decades his senior. And if we hadn't had this morning's trail, I might have overlooked a kindred spirit and simply kept walking.

I was curious to meet the other two British boys, but I would have to wait until Frómista. Jack and Ivan would be there later in the afternoon as well, hobbling into town with broad grins and merry hoots. Regardless of their inability to get up in the morning, I had a feeling they were unflaggingly cheerful as they walked. The trail might take them most of the day and leave them with another layer of burnt skin, but they would be in high spirits come dusk. And I would be effortlessly part of a group, suddenly not such a sore thumb of a soloist. The pieces were snapping together like magnets suddenly flipped over to their charged sides. Perhaps this was what it felt like to have a bit of calm in my trail life; it was something akin to chocolate, coffee and warm sun all at once.

I left Francis to finish his lunch, feeling I should give him the space he had sought this morning. It was only about six kilometers to Frómista, not too far to walk on my own before being reunited. I didn't explain my decision to push on. As I gathered my things together, I knew I was making a prudent choice if I didn't want to burn Francis out with my intensity. Plus, I needed to get back on the trail and feel the balancing calm of walking. I needed space to digest more than my meager lunch. Things were changing, but I couldn't be certain Francis or any of my new trail acquaintances would stick. I had to stay contained, stay prepared for anything to happen. These boys, though kind and inclusive, had no formal ties to me; they were free to take off or fall behind as they wished. I felt a surge of uncertainly about whether they would want to keep me around. So many people had already come and gone from my life, both on and off the trail. I would push my muscles harder and force my legs to take longer strides. I would prove I'd be fine if all these new friends vanished. I'd done it before: pushed onward when things fell apart and fell away.

After only an hour, my pack dragged on my shoulders, and the skin on my arms stung from the touch of late afternoon sun. The trail wound along the banks of a canal system, and flocks of rotund sheep milled in the fields on the far side of the water. Trees planted along the edges of the trail in straight lines formed perfect grids, but none were old enough to provide much shade. There was something desolate about them, something too symmetrical and tidy. Even with a slight wind, they didn't move or make a sound. They lacked the soothing randomness of nature. I wondered if in the next hundred years these grid forests would find some form of chaos and reclaim something from the perfection of their plantings.

FRÓMISTA

Frómista was built beside an old lock system now almost empty and no longer carrying boats through its veins. I crossed into town on a narrow gangplank, watching my shadow chase me along the rusty red surface of the metal canal. The drop down into the belly of the old locks was quite far, but I stood on the rickety overpass anyway, enjoying the view. It was like looking down a metal bound stream, mysteriously forlorn and strangely aesthetic. The town center was a paved intersection around which the village shops clustered. Though there were plenty of distinctively Spanish stores and restaurants, the town felt oddly American. Maybe it was the proximity to the infamous N120 highway or the unwelcoming block of storefronts, but whatever the reason, it felt uncomfortable. The roads were too wide, not cozy and intimate like other villages, and the town felt like a quick weed beside the flow of modern traffic. The only redeeming features were a large plot of green grass with a fountain in the middle and a beautifully designed church just out of view behind the new developments.

Everything was closed as I entered town, and it took some time to find the albergue. Eventually, I got directions from a cheerful tattoo laden woman running a bar with playboy style pictorials covering the walls. As I stepped through the gated archway into courtyard of the albergue, other pilgrims were already settling in. The space was rather ugly and utilitarian but offered a large section of clotheslines with exposure to the sun and a shaded arbor filled with tables.

As I stood in line to check in, I wondered how long the sun would stay warm and bright. My clothes were begging for a wash, and the task would distract me as I waited for the American guys and Francis's crew to roll in. I claimed a bunk, showered and changed into clean clothes. Everything felt easier without layers of dirt and sweaty fabric clinging to me. I hardly noticed the state of my clothes while walking, but once my sleeping bag began to beckon, I wanted to be dry and clean. As I moved about the bunkroom organizing my things, a man lay in the bunk below mine reading a book while he absently chewed on his toothbrush. I kept my shoes off as I gathered my washing. My ankles were still in rough shape, and it was easier to move around on high-strung tendons in bare feet. The only way to make it downstairs was on tippy toes as both of my achilles ached and refused to stretch. The tendons were still bunched tight and continued to squeak unnaturally. It was unnerving to hear my body make a sound it normally didn't. A click, pop, snap or even a squeak wasn't good news. I resolved to hunt down an ice pack and keep my ankles elevated as much as possible. I knew I had tendonitis but didn't feel it was any worse than before. Maybe it was actually getting better. Or maybe I was simply willing it to be better, improvising moment to moment, just hoping I could keep going as I had for the last two weeks.

The wash station in Frómista was a set of large outdoor sinks and a stack of plastic bins. Though rough and basic, it was in the sunshine and stocked with bars of milky white soap. I scrubbed my shirts, shorts and underwear against the washboard in a basin of soapy water while the cold water stung my wrists and sent chills up my arms. As I pinned my clothing on the lines, Francis arrived with Jack and Ivan by his side. My chest released in a deep sigh of relief, and I realized I'd been holding my muscles tightly since my arrival. Though my mind had wandered off into other thoughts, my body had remained alert like a high-strung watchdog seeking any hint of the guys on the horizon. It was silly to feel this way but part of me had been on guard since I left home. Now it felt as if that tension might not be an omnipresent energy I would have to carry with me the length of the trail.

They noticed me in the tangle of washing and hollered hello before going inside. Word came via cell phone that Elliot and John, the other British boys, were still a few hours out. For the last bit of the afternoon, the four of us sat around a table in the courtyard soaking up the sun. Jack and Ivan were in full entertainment mode and proved they were nothing if not skilled at instantaneously lifting the mood.

As I leaned back in my chair and closed my eyes, I listened absently to the boys chat with each other. I started to wonder about the group that passed me in Hontanas. I wasn't sure how many of them there were. I could only remember a few guys scattered in among the girls. Would they come to Frómista for the night? I had no idea what their pace was, but with fewer places to stop during the Meseta stages, we were bound to run into them again. I felt mixed about the potential arrival of this group, wary almost, yet at the same time inexplicably curious. I was intimidated by the Australian girl and her two confident blonde sidekicks. I remembered the chill flowing off the Australian and the way I'd become just another piece of the bench when the British girls whirled through town. Maybe I felt more at ease with boys or maybe it was just these boys. How could I not feel at ease with Ivan as he proudly showed off his camouflage colored compass- thermometer-watch wristband made especially for this journey? According to Ivan, a true journeyman needed essential survival tools on an epic trek such as this. He'd sewn the band himself so it could contain his perfect customized blend of gear. When the thermometer failed to read anything other than his body temperature, he was sorely disappointed, but I tried to comfort him with the notion that no matter what, he would always know if he was coming down with a fever.

A large commotion at the door of the albergue caused me to open my eyes and glance over at the entryway. Looking to the open gates, I watched as the group of young pilgrims I'd been thinking about made a dramatic arrival, captivating every eye in the place as they flooded into the courtyard. They moved like a synchronized flock with one of the blonde girls leading the way. Though abuzz with conversation, their words were for each other's ears only. As they swarmed past and disappeared into the building, they appeared not to even notice our small party or the half dozen other pilgrims hanging their wash. Once again, I didn't get the feeling they were overtly unfriendly, but a wave of exclusivity settled in the small courtyard after they'd gone inside. I could sense the drop in energy as if some great novelty had just gone out sight, and now we all felt a bit left out. Francis was the only one who seemed immune to their energy; he sat beside me leaning against the building, hardly bothering to look up from my guidebook as they passed. The albergue was small. At some point in the evening, we would bump into each other, and I intended to introduce myself. I'd been exercising this small bravery muscle with every other pilgrim I'd met. These newcomers would be no different. Until I knew this group of alpha females and their dutiful guys, I couldn't be sure about their circle. I couldn't be sure there wasn't room for more among their ranks.

Jay, a bulky college student from Florida, was the first of the group to reemerge. After chatting for a few minutes, I realized our residency in the states was perhaps the only thing we had in common. Jay had family in Spain with a gaggle of relatives in Madrid but spoke hardly a word of Spanish. He'd started on the Via de la Plata with his mother but had to stop after she injured her leg. The Via de la Plata was a Camino route that wound its way up from southern Spain to join our route, the Camino Frances, in the middle of the Meseta. When Jay's mother went back to the Madrid to recover with relatives, Jay had caught a train to Pamplona to walk the main route on his own. As Jay lumbered over to talk with Ivan and Jack, I noticed he was wearing a pair of beat up Nike high tops and using a piece of rope as a belt. He settled himself on the edge of the albergue steps and continued the tale of his Camino, but I couldn't shake a feeling of disconnection. I had a hard time picturing this frat brother from the land of beaches being interested in the rigors of the trail, but I'd been shocked before by those who stuck with it. Jay was perfectly friendly but talking to him felt remarkably arduous after a day of easy banter with Francis. From the looks on Jack and Ivan's faces, I could tell they were bored as well but trying to hide it. After a few minutes, I became distracted by Francis's questions as he thumbed through the charts in my guidebook. Gratefully, I shifted my body back towards our small group.

Not long after, Jay drifted away to sit with another boy from his group, a tall and skinny German with hair the color of orange marmalade. Luc spoke not a word of English, but I got the distinct feeling he was the silent and rebel type anyway. Luc felt a bit like the French girls I'd met in Puente la Reina, too urban for the trail and cool in a grungy effortless sort of way. I could easily imagine he was a bit of a troublemaker, a candidate for drinking in excess and clubbing all night. I would learn that he hardly ever did anything, including walking, washing his clothes or napping, without a cigarette dangling from his lips. Our first glimpse of him was no exception. As he placed himself down beside Jay, they disappeared into their familiarity with each other, and I started to wonder just how long this group had been together. Clearly the smooth German with no

English and the beefy Floridian had met on the trail, but their shoulders touched as they sat side by side. I wondered how far they'd come together, and how they'd managed to build this manly bond with no shared language. Maybe typical male friendships, even here on the trail, didn't need many words or passage of time to grow strong. As I glanced over at Jay and Luc, I gathered that for these two the simple of activity of smoking a cigarette in shared silence was the stuff of intimacy.

Moments later, the blonde English girls came bounding out of the building. Their arms were full of clothing, and their bodies bumped into each other as they darted towards the washing tubs. Their laughing voices filled the courtyard, and I knew they must have been friends from before the trail. Even though the Camino could bring people together in a hasty and intimate fashion, their closeness was layered and comfortable. They spoke in a shorthand that was distinctly their own, and made fun of each other and playfully jostled one another with revealing ease. It was as if they felt the other was simply an extension of self. The duo's banter was thoroughly enjoyable but made me feel very far away from the world they lived in. We were on the same physical pilgrimage, but my reality was so different from their world. It made me wonder if I had the skills or resources to change the ambience of my own lonely trail, shift away from what it had been thus far and reinvent myself. They looked so light and so present to the joys of the moment that I felt it was worth a try.

After scrubbing and pummeling their laundry, they hung it on the last bit of open clothesline and came over to introduce themselves. Ava was the unofficial head of the pair, and she strode over to us first, sticking her soapy hand out to shake mine. She was neither tall nor noticeably petite but commanded the air around her nonetheless. Her deep brown eyes, cheeky smile and curvy figure drew all attention to her. She had one of those unbelievable bodies that was both thin and voluptuous, shaped like a perfect hourglass. Her platinum blonde hair slipped out all over the place from under a loosely tied scarf and fell over the curve of her cheekbone as she shook my hand. Her nose was punctuated with a glittering stud, and the upper crest of her ears were dotted with earrings. Even with all the hardware, there was still something soft and inviting about her as if she were a fifties pinup on vacation.

Her second in command, Iris, was also a blonde but a bit more understated. Upon meeting both girls, all eyes seemed to gravitate to Ava first but linger on Iris longer. There was more to be figured out with Iris, her looks were tucked behind a veil of reserve which beckoned only the most intrepid to leap up and try to know her fully. Her face was delicate and refined under her sweeping bangs, and her blue eyes matched the blue paleness of her skin. Even in this climate and on this trail, she appeared to be made of porcelain. Her long hair dangled down her back in a silky ribbon of pure blonde. She'd never lost the golden feathers of babyhood like most of us had. Though I rarely saw her fuss with it, Iris's hair always looked effortlessly beautiful. It appeared as if there wasn't a wild and rebellious strand on her entire head. She was taller than Ava and built like a string bean. Her voice was softer and something about her felt distant, more cautious and private than her partner in crime. She was the fixed center around which Ava swirled, collecting people and energy to the both of them through the laws of attraction.

The Brit girls had been friends since childhood. Like Francis, they were living out the last few months of their gap year before university began in the fall. While Francis had lived with monks, Ava and Iris had spent six months traveling around India. They'd gone without a plan to jungles and white sand beaches. They'd ridden crowded trains, docile elephants and rickety bikes. Ava had relished the chance to get lost, and I wondered if because of India, the trail now felt like a very safe sort of adventure. After all, it was a planned out and well marked route in a more westernized country. Was that why they moved with such ease? Or was it the safety net of their duo and the fact they never had to be alone? They acted excited to meet all of us despite the vibe I'd felt in Hontanas, and I began to relax in their company. Ava seemed genuinely curious about my solo trek and the adventures of the American guys, but I wasn't convinced her hungry questions were more than curious banter. She was bold and entertaining, absorbing the stories of others, but I couldn't tell if she was opening her circle to bring us in or simply filling the empty hours before dinner.

On the trail, there was lots of talk that went nowhere, and albergues were entertaining places to collect conversations that evaporated as soon as they finished, but like most of my peers, I was looking for friendships, romantic relationships and everything in between. Even Luc and others with language barrier issues understood it was important to connect and fill the social element to the brim. I'd come here with a sense that the social thread of my trail might be the most important strand. The dream portended this, and the guidance I kept following with dogged determination wasn't about keeping myself open to historical sights or Spanish cuisine but to the people who crossed my path. Yes, the girls had an inner circle and maybe it was locked into place, but Ava had the unmistakable air of a welcoming host, and I had to trust that. She was an infectious whirlwind of activity, and Iris had spunk as well as a hint of depth. I was drawn in.

My guidebook was on the table in front of me, and at one point, Ava glanced down at it. A smile bloomed on her face, "Do you like your book?"

"Yes, it's been a trusted companion for the past few weeks." I replied. "It's been my only consistent ally on the trail, and I've become attached to its quirky charm." I'd come across other English speaking pilgrims with the book and expected Ava to have a strong opinion of its narrative voice and content.

Ava laughed and said rather cryptically, "I am glad to hear that." I felt my forehead wrinkle questioningly. I was about to ask her if she too carried the book, when Iris filled me in with a shout from across the courtyard, "Ava's dad is the author!"

I felt a sweat break then cool on skin. I quickly scrolled back through every word I'd uttered and was relieved I'd passed the first undercover test of coolness and likeability. I sensed a critical book review wouldn't have been a harmonizing moment for me and the Brit girls. There had been a Camino rumor that the daughter of this author was on the trail, but I figured it was just a piece of gossip, traded around to fill the hours. When a fellow pilgrim in Villamayor had told me about the author's daughter, Ava wasn't exactly who I'd imagined. I'd conjured up a vision of a tough super athlete, the type who climbed Himalayan peaks, an outdoorsy person that bushwhacked through the woods, slept on pine boughs and started fires without matches. Ava, on the other hand, was an urban girl. Though a determined walker who clocked long hours, she wasn't exactly a wilderness buff. And this didn't faze her one bit. She seemed to have embraced her trail persona with panache. Later she told me her brother was a professional mountaineering guide who traveled around the world leading treks. As Ava moved about in a light gray pair of harem pants, I noticed she was washing a bright fuchsia bra. The girl was certainly her own person even on a trail where she couldn't avoid people who considered her father the ultimate Camino guru. She seemed undaunted by making something of her own out of a trail her father had walked every year for longer than she'd been alive. It was refreshing somehow to find her so normal and so human even if she did descend from a blue blooded Camino family.

Not far behind Ava and Iris were Zara and Tomas, the two young people I'd met the day before in the rainstorm outside of Hornillos. I still felt a bit stung by the chilly interaction, and Zara continued to have an unapproachable air about her. She was about the same height as Iris, but her hair was jet black and held no light. Her thick locks were cut at a severe angle under her chin, and her skin was a warm olive color. She was the visual opposite of the British girls but drew just as much attention as the blondes.

Tomas carried his lanky frame with shy weariness. He was built like a full-grown man, but his energy betrayed his youth. He was just a year out of university and a fresh faced twenty-two year old. It was hard to fully grasp why the Cook had gushed about Tomas during our conversation in Hontanas, but I was willing to try to figure it out. It was difficult to uncover much of anything about the new guys, because they all seemed so deeply focused on their group, talking in an insider shorthand, rife with shared trail experiences. Again I felt lucky that the boys sitting around the table had let me be part of their world. They could easily have kept me on the outside or made me jump hoops to gain entrance, but they hadn't. I looked over at Ivan as he fiddled with his survival wrist belt, and my heart melted just a bit.

Another German boy came out last. Gruff and determined to deter friendly conversation, he sat with Jay and Luc and didn't engage with us. He was slightly shorter than Tomas, built of a leaner muscle and further distinguished from the group by a scruffy blond beard and a wild tousled crop of sandy blond locks. I wasn't sure the three baby faced lads by my side could even grow beards. He further set himself apart from the boys by sporting a large tattoo of a compass on his forearm. Later I would learn he was a boat builder's apprentice, hoping to craft sea vessels for a living.

Ava announced their group wanted to go to one of the cafes for drinks. To my surprise, they invited us to join them. We left our laundry drying stiff on the cluttered lines and flocked back into the center of town in a mass of young pilgrims. In the central square beside the row of cafes was an open park with lush grass, prime real estate for pilgrim gatherings. My aching body approved of the decision to sprawl out on the grass rather than squeeze around tables at one of the cafes. The men in Ava's group went in search of beer and wine to share. Ava, Zara and the blonde German had made it a priority to hunt for the cheapest wine in each town and reveled in purchasing many a bottle of wine for under a euro.

We lay on the grass in a clumped configuration of small circles. The groups unconsciously sat across from each other as if both still felt the need to remain buffered and self-contained. I sat close to Francis and Ivan as if I'd known them for months, and they leaned towards me with the same unspoken familiarity. They were my safe harbor in the large group arena, and all my animal instincts pointed to these boys as the ones to trust. Even so, my social self wasn't going to be satisfied with playing it safe and hunkering in. I didn't want to limit the number of connections I formed; closeness could come from unexpected places. I wasn't ready to let go of any future friendships with the nine people around me. Even though Zara had already given me a taste of her chilly demeanor, I was ready for the challenge. I could thaw out her cold ways; I just needed to get my foot in the door. This gathering was the first step. As a free agent in Camino society and an unattached immigrant to the shores of this trail, I had no original tribe or cause to bind me, and I belonged nowhere by default. There were strengths in being free, but often those benefits weighed on me. I craved nothing more than to trade in my credentials as a solo pilgrim for a new set as someone who was connected, linked and involved. I no longer desired the so-called gifts of the hours alone. I wanted to trade them all for just a bit of time among the company of kindred spirits, maybe even alongside the company of love. It would take work to form friendships that didn't evaporate in the current of the trail, but after so many days of this walking life, a little bit of sweat and honest grunt work was nothing new. I just wanted to form something more than easy banter. I wanted to be needed, to have a shared reliance and to be missed if I suddenly stepped off the trail and disappeared.

While the wine flowed and the guidebooks circulated, Ivan and I fell into an easy banter about pirates. He was obsessed with the topic, and it was amusing to hear his treatise on how to become a modern day equivalent. Ivan was impressed by my knowledge of the first female pirate Granuail, an Irish clanswoman who lived in the sixteenth century, and he wanted to hear more about this feisty female. I shared the tales of my summer on her lands, traipsing among the ruins of her stronghold and exploring the ragged coast of her domain. I'd known Ireland with an aching homesickness even before I'd stepped on to her shores. Even as I recognized the land, I felt confused by how much I disliked modern Irish culture. I loved Ireland as she'd been. On the hill tops, in the rain, on the bow of a ferry boat on its way to an island stuck in a time, I found her again and wept with joy at holding someone I loved close to me even if only for a moment. Though I didn't share my candid past life recollections with Ivan, I did feel a swell of connection as we spoke of ships and the lore of the sea. I'd found our common bloodline, and I knew if I traced the energy back far enough, I would find a life where we'd known each other on the current of the sea rather than the current of the trail.

As I lay on my side listening to Jack and Ivan talk with Francis, I noticed a pilgrim enter the far end of the square striding with purpose towards the albergue. I noted his bright red pack and then something else caught my eye. A flash of orange and streak of unmistakable ginger trailed behind him with an eager bounce. The dog that had been my trail companion into St. Juan de Ortega trotted beside the pilgrim. I turned my head away in horror. The dog had found another pilgrim to follow. Three days after I'd seen him leap from his porch, he was still on the trail and now over a hundred kilometers from home. The sight caused my stomach to twist with associated guilt, but once again I felt powerless to stop his onward progress. Maybe all that was left was to feel grateful he'd found another alpha human to follow, another steward to protect him along the way.

Even after an hour in each other's company not everyone had been introduced. We went around the circle and said our names as if it were the first day of some alternative and very international school. I listened carefully when the quiet blonde German spoke his name. He lay on his side with a straw hat tipped forward on his head, keeping his face shaded; he hadn't spoken to anyone but Iris and Ava who sat close beside him. There was something mysterious about him, a quality of reluctance or wary disinterest. It was obvious he thought we shouldn't have been included in the gathering, and he was going to keep his distance until he'd figured us out. I learned his name was Konrad but didn't find the moment to bridge the circle and speak with him. If he needed proof of my willingness to put in the time and effort to really connect, then he would get it. I was fully prepared to prove I was more than a fair weather pilgrim friend. And in the meantime, I'd give him space and trust he would come around. From his body language, it was clear Tomas and Iris had garnered entrance into his world. He seemed particularly focused on Iris as she leaned against his shoulder with her legs tucked underneath her and played with the frayed edges of her dress. Every so often, he would look up from under the brim of his hat, and she would tilt her head down to talk with him. Ava was on his other side reclining as she took long swigs of wine. Beyond the girls and the gruff Konrad, I hoped to get a chance to speak more with Tomas, the Belgian, but Zara sat next to him guarding access with her long tan limbs. No matter. The hours on the trail were long, and I would get my moment to know them all. Tonight was just the beginning. If I was unable to circumvent all the barricades now, then hopefully tomorrow the magic of the trail would assist me in having time with Tomas, Iris, Ava and maybe even Konrad. I'd been given such a moment with Francis, and it had drawn us together. I could only smile at the promise of these fresh links.

As the sun went down, thoughts turned to dinner, and Ava's group wandered off on their own. I was happy to avoid a big scene that involved the whole group invading a restaurant, but I also felt there were some hidden agendas a foot. Ava's group seemed keen on enjoying dinner by themselves and dodged off before we knew what was happening. Turning to Francis, I shrugged my shoulders and fell in step beside Ivan and Jack who were already following their noses to the closest source of food. Our disbanding had been uncomfortable, but it passed so quickly I wasn't prepared to let it upset me. With glazed eyes and woozy footsteps, Ivan and Jack ducked into a small restaurant along the central square. Francis and I bowed out of the all you can eat pilgrim feast and headed home. We crossed the empty lawn and walked in silence up the narrow side street towards the albergue. I could feel Francis digesting all the swirling dynamics, but I wasn't sure he was ready to share his conclusions with me just yet. As we were about to step through the gates to the albergue, a sharp whistle resounded up the alley, and we spun around to find the source.

Francis' companions were just as I imagined, a pair of gawky young guys with a set of sheepishly cheerful grins. Francis threw his arms up in the air with a mixture of relief and excitement as the tall duo strode towards us. I had to admit that even I was beginning to wonder what had happened to the guys. It was nearly six, and though there were many hours before the sun began to set, the albergue was close to capacity. As soon as the boys drew even with us, breathless and a bit dusty, introductions were made all around. John was all limbs and floppy hair. A bit shy, he seemed to hang just a half step behind Elliot. He appeared frazzled to meet new people and especially jittery because I was a girl. Yet he had an endearing quality that made me want to put him at ease. John was still growing into his tall body. He seemed at a loss about how to control his limbs and organize his grown up form. The shyest of the bunch, he made a habit of ducking his head bashfully while he spoke, yet his eyes were a bold, crystal blue with long blonde eyelashes. In a few years when he filled out and gained in confidence, he would be a dreamboat.

Elliot was very different looking, but it was his energy that really set him apart from the gangly John and the slightly ethereal Francis. Elliot was rooted, grounded and sturdy from head to toe. He was the bulkiest of the three Brits, but that wasn't saying much, for they were all tall and slim. He was remarkably present in his body, and though he was trim, there was a feeling of solidness in his very muscles. He wore a scruffy beard and had wide set shoulders that made him feel approachable and comfortable upon first meeting. He was settled in his own skin, enjoying all the physical elements of pilgrim life. Elliot had none of John's shyness around females and seemed utterly charmed to make my acquaintance. There wasn't a moment's hesitation and no cautious assessment of my desirability as a trail companion. I felt Francis had given me the seal of approval, and apparently that was enough. Even though they seemed curious about why I wanted to befriend them, I sensed I was a bit of a novelty to each of them in different ways.

We didn't linger long in the entrance of the albergue. As we entered the building, Elliot asked where Ivan and Jake had gone. The Brit boys had met the American guys the night before and were already big fans. It was fascinating to meet the other two parts of Francis's triangle, watch the shifting energy between them and feel the dynamic of three such different guys. They didn't rest back on a point of balance, but shifted constantly as if the movement inside the group helped keep everything flowing. If they had claimed roles and become entrenched, things would have crumbled quickly. This was a living breathing group organism, and I was a new element in the mix as were Jack and Ivan. We would force the boys to figure out a new balance, but I got the feeling the weeks in France and the isolation of those days made the risk worth it. I was very aware of my strong energy system and the difference I presented by just being a female among a tribe of men, but they didn't draw back and neither did I. I soaked it up and delighted in the two new faces that somehow already felt like close friends. In two days I'd gone from zero to five with hopes for more. Against all odds, the Meseta had proved fertile ground. It would take me a few days to settle into my view of Francis as part of a trio, and because of the intensity of our morning together, I would always see him as separate from the other two. Closer somehow, more vivid and more alive to the current of my energy.

After a quick trip to a food shop, the Brit boys created a feast of canned vegetables and readymade omelets as if such thrown together meals were now routine. I didn't join the boys in their feast for my stomach had begun to roll and turn in queasy circles as soon as we arrived back at the albergue. As I sat next to Francis with my back up against the cool stonewall, I drew my legs up to my chest while my internal organs twisted and turned. Maybe something I'd eaten had disagreed with me, but more likely I was in the midst of a spine deep, energetically triggered stomachache. My stomach was a delicate barometer. When it began to toss and turn, I knew something bigger was a foot. I'd gotten stomachaches since I was a child trying to digest the energetics of my life at school. As I grew older, I saw a link between physical digestion and my desire to digest the energy of the people and circumstances around me. Yet even with this information in my back pocket, I often had a hard time pinpointing what had flicked the physical switch. Tonight I was baffled why I suddenly needed to crawl into the fetal position and rock back and forth.

I was among a new group of kind friends. The Brit boys had been on the trail for over forty days, but today they let me start again with them. I was finally comfortable with the demands of trail life. Even my ankles were proving to be a bit more cooperative. What was this thick energy I was trying to digest? I couldn't share my nutty thoughts on energy digestion with the gang, but I did tell Francis my stomach was bothering me. I tried to breathe and let Elliot's cheerful banter distract me. I didn't want to leave the warmth and comfort of our circle especially when I felt ill. Every so often, Francis glanced over at me with a look of soft concern on his face. At one point, I felt he wanted to reach out and touch me, lay a hand on my knee, rub my back or simply make some physical gesture of comfort, but he didn't. Even after the intimacy of the morning's walk, we still hadn't grown close enough to use touch as a medium of connection. Though we lived very close to one another, there was no need for pilgrims to touch beyond the shake of a hand or the accidental bump of the shoulders. We seemed to live in small bubbles orbiting around each other but rarely making contact. And now, as I felt this growing pain, all I wanted was that reassurance of physical connection.

As the boys finished their dinner, I excused myself and went to crawl into my bunk, re-center myself and elevate my ankles. I lay on the top bunk listening as people moved about, whispering to each other, rummaging through their bags and shuffling back and forth to the bathroom. I noticed Alberto's stuff on the bunk across the room. I hadn't seen him in at least a day, but I would have recognized his red bag anywhere. Just the sight of his things threw me back into the trail before Hontanas. Suddenly all the twisted energy inside my core made sense. I was no longer feeling the push. The drive that had eaten away at my every thought and pushed me beyond my physical limits was suddenly quiet. It could only mean one thing. This was my place. I'd finally found the groups I'd longed for. I'd caught up, and now my job was to be here with Francis, John, Elliot and the American guys and forge a deeper bond with Ava, Iris, Zara and the guys in their group. It was all swirling around me, and I was suddenly deeply grateful and achingly scared of what awaited me now. Who would these new faces be to me, and who would I become to them? I felt an image sink into my very bones. After so many days in the quiet tributaries with no sight of what lay ahead, I'd finally sailed out into the open sea, swirling and churning with waves of energy, vast and alive. No wonder I felt so awake and so seasick all at the same time.

The light started to fade around ten, and just before I decided to click off my flashlight, Francis came into the room and hopped up on his bunk. The large room was split into two parts by a partition that only reached a few feet above the top of the bunks. By chance, my bunk was on one side of the partition, and Francis's was the other side. After he'd climbed onto his bunk, he leaned over, and dangling his arms along the wall, asked me if I needed anything. The tone in his voice was heartbreakingly kind. There was a transparent earnestness to everything he said and did. Since he chose his words and connections with such sensitivity, I knew he wasn't making a flippant remark. If I'd asked for something he would have crawled out of his sleep nook, hobbled about on his tired limbs and gotten it for me. I was startled by how close I already felt to him and how much solace it afforded me to know he was just over the partition if I needed him. I shook my head, curled my limbs tighter around my core then whispered goodnight. He wished me goodnight, told me he would wake me when his alarm went off and disappeared out of view. Eventually the room fell into the hush of sleep with a lone snorer keeping time in the far corner. In the middle of the night, I drifted into a shallow pocket of sleep and heard the drunken arrival of the other group back from their adventures in town. Even as my stomachache eased, and I found relief in the comfort of gravity, I knew the change I'd craved with such passion was upon me, and I would have to take all she brought in her wake. When I awoke the red bag was gone, and that was the last I would ever see it.

CARRIÓN

STAGE ELEVEN- 20.1K-12.5M
FRÓMISTA TO CARRIÓN

The next morning just after sunrise, I walked out of town with Jack, Ivan and the three British boys. At breakfast, Francis had poured me a bowl of cereal and lent me his spoon. I'd neglected to include eating utensils in my pack and was delighted to rediscover the luxury of a civilized meal. It had been gratifying to share the large tupperware bowl of granola with John and Elliot. I knew I was a member of the posse and part of the man clan when they'd let me eat from the same container as if I were family. While the Brits and I'd huddled in the corner crunching away, Jack and Ivan had sat at the dining room table with napkins in their laps, sipping on glasses of fresh orange juice. They'd paid extra for breakfast and relished every bite. The American guys didn't mess around when it came to meals. Food was a serious concern, and voluntary hunger wasn't an option. They wanted to be full and enjoy the experience regardless of time or cost. If they could get a hot fresh meal served to them, they wouldn't worry if it put them behind schedule. I cared more about beating the heat of the day and enjoying the sunrise than tucking a napkin into my collar, and the Brit boys felt the same. Yet we'd waited for the Americans, if only because they were so darn charming and much funnier with full stomachs. They were a bit like toddlers in that regard. We would need to be focused on keeping them well fed if we wanted to avoid midmorning meltdowns. After Jack had polished off his fourth pastry, licking the frosting from his fingers, and Ivan had consumed enough cheese to induce a serious nap, we organized to leave.

The streets of Frómista were empty when we slipped out the albergue gate. The sun was rising warm and golden behind the dome of the church. I walked next to Jack and Ivan as we strode down the wide street. Ivan continued to limp due to his foot injuries. Even though his body was rested and he had a full tank of fuel in his stomach, he moved as if his injured leg was wooden. He obviously relished every swing of his peg leg, knowing it lent his gait a dramatic swagger and made him more pirate-like. Jack, on the other hand, was perfectly healthy but walked so slowly it was unnatural. Each leg unfurled at a calm gentlemanly pace, and his whole body reclined as if he were resting back into himself. I was at a loss to understand how these guys had made it this far with such strange habits. Sandwiched between them, I could hardly stop twitching. I tried to distract myself with chatter and the early morning topic quickly fell into a groove of all things seafaring. A conversation Ivan had with the Cook the night before about her life on a king crab fishing vessel was currently fueling the boy's giddy banter. Talk of this dream job was endless. Their eyes glazed over as if they were reciting fairytales, drawing themselves into a mythic world far away from our dusty tracks. In their mind's eyes, they were already swaying on the deck of a mighty fishing trawler, battling the salty swells and living the life of modern day adventurers. For now, I'd lost them to another realm. I scanned forward on the trail and saw John and Francis moving out ahead at a livelier pace. It was time to jump ship.

Jack and Ivan stopped to fix something on Jack's shoe, and I made a graceful break. I strode up beside John and Francis, skipping the last step as I caught them. They were moving fast, and my legs rejoiced at the speed. I felt a momentary stab of guilt. I probably should have practiced slowing my tempo with Jack and Ivan but decided I would stick with their seafaring strut another day. Francis and John looked up in surprise at my arrival, but Francis's face quickly shifted from a startled tilt of the head to a warm grin. That was all I needed. If he was OK with me crashing his walking hours again then I couldn't help myself. Even John, in his bashful way, seemed excited about the new grouping. Nonetheless, the majority of my attention was attuned to Francis; John's reaction was an afterthought.

For much of the stage, the trail paralleled a straight road. Its black pavement was the only dark color in sight. The rest of the world was golden brown, coated in layers of sun-drenched dust. The section of trail was a thankless one with the same endless view and not a spot of shade. The one upside was the width of the trail. Due to the flatness of the land, the path was wide enough to accommodate the breadth of our trio. I was curious to observe Francis and John together and begin to understand their friendship. I knew full well it would take some time for John to loosen up in my presence. In time, he would realize that despite his view of me as an intimidating female, I wasn't going to bite.

Each of the Brit boys had an obvious sweetness about them. At first it made them seem young, almost naïve, but soon I realized it wasn't inexperience that made them sweet but an overall kindness of spirit. They weren't concerned with machismo and knew the importance of being exceedingly polite, sometimes to a fault. They had a genuine desire to be ever more sensitive to the world around them. In other words, they weren't afraid to feel life. They hadn't embraced the cultural stereotype that defined men as gruff, unemotional and disconnected. The Camino called all her pilgrims to balance action with intuition if they wanted to make it through in one piece. The Brit boys seemed to lean more towards their intuitive side, and I already knew my strengths lay with my action based side, so I had a feeling our easy configuration was no accident.

Francis seemed to be engaged in a balancing act that sometimes took all his effort. John was a bit more unconscious about the Camino challenges, but who knew if that would change in the days to come. Though he wasn't the youngest, he was the baby of the group and apparently resigned to occupying that role. At times the shadow of this position upset him, but his tantrums blew over quickly. He spoke with a soft voice as our conversation turned from one topic to another, and though he was full of opinions, they felt untested. A three-way conversation is never easy, but we found a flow. After several hours, my ankles began to ache, and without hesitation Francis lent me his pole, handing it across to me silently as John talked on. He'd noticed my tender steps. My worry about my injury had now grown to mythic proportions, but his simple gesture vanquished my fears of being permanently broken. I thanked Francis several times which caused him to blush slightly and brush off my words with thoughtful nonchalance.

The morning's trail was a new incarnation of the Camino. The route had been named a UNESCO World Heritage Site. This meant the EU supplied the Spanish government funds to invest in trail up-keep. One of the more soulless uses of the money was to make this section of the trail into a road accessible path. This increased bus pilgrims' ability to access the trail but took away from the authenticity and beauty of the original Camino. Newly placed stone pillars resembling gravestones were set at frequent intervals along the roadside trail.

Before leaving the albergue at Frómista, we'd agreed to rendezvous for the night in Carrión de los Condes. Francis and Elliot insisted we stay in Carrión because a nunnery there held great importance to both of them. The albergue de Santa Maria was a thirteenth century nunnery that now doubled as a pilgrim hostel. Trail history claimed that while on pilgrimage to Santiago, St. Francis of Assisi communed with the nuns here and slept within the nunnery walls.

Francis felt a deep connection to his namesake, St. Francis, and cultivated a living devotion to the saint. The monastery where he and Elliot had lived for six months prior to the trail was Franciscan. Even the saint's connection to plants and animals struck a chord in Francis. After several months in the monastery gardens, Francis felt irrevocably linked to nature and the saint himself. I had a feeling those months and gardens had given Francis shelter in the aftermath of something that still reverberated in him, an event I could only sense the edges of but hadn't yet been shown. We all had such vulnerable places in the past we kept to ourselves. I hadn't shared mine with him, so for now it was only fair his remained a mystery as well. The energy of St. Francis and the feeling of refuge were now fused in his heart and his thoughts. I knew he would stay with the nuns even if he had to sleep in the courtyard all by himself. Hopefully it wouldn't come to that; we were all happy to go along with the plan. I certainly didn't care where we stayed as long as we were together.

We arrived in Carrión around eleven. We'd made excellent time, getting off the trail right before the sun became unbearably hot and our water ran out. The shift to the blazing Meseta lands was still a shock to my system. Part of me missed the cool rainy mornings and cloudy skies of my early Camino days. Yes, my things were dry, and I was able to stow my rain jacket at the bottom of my pack, but the sun sapped my energy faster than ever, and the land felt vast and unforgiving. No nooks of fog, no groves of shade, just air and heat, light and horizon.

The three of us sat on the curb outside the nunnery in easy silence, leaning against the building to soak up the shade while waiting for the albergue to open. My body always felt light and unburdened in the moments after I took off my pack as if I had been released from gravity and my limbs might begin to float weightlessly upward. Carrión was a large village and despite the heat, it felt alive. Kids hollered at each other from the park down the block, and a pair of older ladies with aprons cinched around their waists swept their front stoops while trading bits of gossip. A couple appeared in the doorway of the apartment building directly across from where we sat. The man scooped the woman into his arms, kissed her goodbye, then darted out to a small yellow car and pulled away in one decisive motion.

Minutes later the clock on the church tolled the hour, and the tall wrought iron gates of the nunnery opened. I ducked my head down through the archway, following Francis and John inside. The nunnery was small and built like a perfect fortress with the insides scooped out. The center was a beautiful courtyard with a rough wooden cross rising like a lone tree in the middle. Birds filled the eaves, casting shadows on the smooth flagstones. The space held a blended tone of protection and isolation; this was a world unto itself, insulated from everything beyond its walls. There was safety in this space untouched by the messy energy of the outside world. This was a beautiful refuge but divided from the flow of human life, a separate realm in which people had sought God but also fled the complicated jumble of faith amidst human community. It struck me this was an easier life of devotion to God than some. This was a clean, black and white, all or nothing, no distractions world of faith and a less demanding way to live close to the center of oneself and God. Though I was curious about Francis's life with the monks, I didn't feel that life was the best for me or for my connection to the divine. I liked the mess and the chaos, the beauty and the flow of the drama beyond the walls. But as we spoke, I began to wonder where Francis felt he belonged. What did he feel in this space? Did it call to him more than the light, the children and the passion outside the door?

I wasn't sure how many beds this small nunnery held for pilgrims and wondered if the other group would join us here later in the day. I'd tiptoed past Ava, Konrad, Iris, Zara and the rest of their gang dead asleep in their bunks in Frómista. Ava's arm had dangled off the side of her bed; there had been piles of clothes and other belongs wildly strewn about, and two of the guys had been snoring loudly. I'd no idea when they would wake and begin their day's walk, but I had a sneaking suspicion they would rematerialize in Carrión eventually. There weren't many options in this desolate stage of the trail, and this was a desirable place to make camp for the night.

After we checked in, Francis, John and I went to explore the village. The albergue was on a side street that wound into the center of town. Like Frómista, Carrión was loosely bundled around an intersection of two busy roads. Unlike Frómista, Carrión had charm and a settled softness. I took a shining to the town and was delighted to have hours to explore it. The inner ring of the city was built at the feet of a large and sturdy stone church with graceful doors and thick towers. The streets were flooded with people, many of whom were camera toting tourists. Beyond a quick glance, we paid no attention to the rows of shops that catered to these crowds. We meandered deeper into the stone paved streets and soaked up the activity around us.

There were several empty hours before siesta ended, so we walked down to a shady riverside park. The spot by the river was an aberration after our day walking through dry heat and tracks of arid land. The densely forested park wound its way along the banks of a wide but shallow river. Trees sheltered the ground in dappled light; benches lay strewn about in a random fashion, afloat in circles of grass. A bridge loomed upriver, and a group of young kids were fly-fishing from it. Francis wanted to swim and pleaded with us to join him. John agreed to watch our stuff, and I joined Francis at the edge of the river. He waded in with fierce determination, but I could tell from his startled face and clenched muscles that the water was very cold. I stepped gingerly into the icy river, moving out only far enough to draw the water up to my knees. Francis was determined to dunk himself, but his body was fighting the notion with rounds of teeth chattering chills. I wasn't a natural wader. I was a jumper, and if I couldn't fling myself into the cold water then I wasn't going under. As I stood on the edge of the river, the chill of the water seeped through my system, causing my arms to rise in goose bumps and my feet to grow numb. Despite the cold temperatures, Francis seemed delighted with the river, entranced by the chance to swim. As I watched him from afar, I could tell he was one of those people who adored water and loved rivers, oceans, baths and running under the sprinkler. While we stood in the water, he tried to coax me in and told me about a river at the end of the trail where medieval pilgrims bathed before entering Santiago. Apparently their trio planned on skinny-dipping there. I could safely assume if Jack and Ivan were still around, they would gladly join the Brits in a bit of streaking, but I wasn't sure how I would fit into the nude arrival celebration. Being the only girl did, at times, have its disadvantages.

The children on the bridge yelled and laughed as Francis attempt to swim. A pilgrim came by to deliver a message from the children. They wanted us to know swimming in the river was illegal, but not to worry about them ratting us out, because fishing was also against the rules. If anybody came by to enforce the regulation, we wouldn't be the only ones getting in trouble. Or maybe we would. The gang of ten year old fishermen probably had a better escape route planned than our troupe of clueless perigrinos.

Finally, I abandoned the cause of full immersion and returned to dry shores. John lay absently under a tree pulling fresh stalks of grass from the ground as I settled myself beside a neighboring tree. We both watched Francis without speaking, each wondering if he would without warning drop out of sight like a stone. Even though I'd spent the morning with John, I felt the age gap between us swell without Francis nearby. John seemed young even when caught in pensive silence. Francis had warned me John was a realist and always game for a verbal sparing match to defend his position. Francis admitted the two often clashed over their differing views. John digested events with a right and wrong, cause and effect logic. For him, facts always trumped feelings. He was the most soft spoken and romantic in his looks but the most analytical member of the well educated trio. With his innocent good looks, I imagined girls would start to notice John very soon, if they hadn't already. What then would become of his purely rational way of being? I had a sneaking suspicion that falling in love would change his opinions about the importance of feelings. His heart would demand his attention whether he liked it or not. John wasn't immune, none of us were.

As I considered the contained worldview still flowing through John, part of me envied its clear simplicity. The other part of me knew it couldn't last. The emotional threads of life would find him eventually, and they would shape who he would become. The ripping apart, the building back together and the endless cycle. Like muscles, our hearts had to be torn to create the capacity to hold more light and love. Even during this lazy afternoon, I sensed he was on the edge of change. This was the last journey of his boyhood; I could see it in his eyes.

Francis stayed in the river until his lips turned a light shade of blue, but he never managed to let himself go all the way under. As he trudged out of the riverbed and towards our spot in the shade, I told him I would swim with him in the next river we came to. He looked triumphant as we shook on the deal. I felt intent on keeping my side of the bargain; it was a promise. We gathered our shoes and walked back through the cobbled streets in bare feet, leaving wet footprints behind us.

Back in the albergue, I fell asleep sprawled on my stomach, half in and half out of my sleeping bag in an awkward tangle of limbs that normally never would have engendered comfort let alone sleep. While I dozed, Jack and Ivan arrived with Elliot trailing close behind. I awakened from my nap to a room full of packs. The boys promised they would be ready to go back into town to buy food once they showered. As I waited in the sunny courtyard, feeling disoriented and slightly nauseous from hunger, Ivan joined me on the bench against the wall. As he cleaned the toe wound he'd had since the Pyrenees and taped up the cut, he proudly showed off his foot tan. His new sandals had gifted him not only a gaping pus filled wound and a limp but comic tan lines a la Spiderman. According to Ivan, the sun had tattooed his feet, branding them with the mark of greatness. He couldn't have been more pleased with the effect.

As the siesta hour ended, our boisterous group walked up through the center of town. I couldn't get over how wonderfully different it felt to be imbedded in this clan of boys. Every activity, no matter how small, took on a new life. The mundane business of going to buy food was now an adventure with Ivan and Jack leading the charge and the rest of us bouncing cheerfully behind. Off the main square, we found a modest shop run by a mother and daughter duo who displayed wide smiles on two versions of the same face. The pair hung with us when we spoke in broken Spanish and were endlessly patient as the boys hemmed and hawed over what to buy. They were particularly charmed by Ivan and Jack's inventive Spanglish and laughed with delight at every language misstep.

With bags of food in tow, we made for a small park across from the church. The group settled in a loose circle under the shade of a large tree and unpacked our meal. The bit of green space in the center of town offered great people watching. After a few minutes, a large albino husky wandered over, spying the chance to be fed. Like the other stray dogs we'd met on the Camino, he was gentle, timid even, and a little the worse for wear. His coat was rough, and he cowered under Ivan's touch. We resisted the temptation to feed him, despite the heartbreaking vagabond look in his eyes. We all worried he would adhere to our group if we bestowed a meal on him, and I for one couldn't handle having to ditch another dog. Ivan tried to distract the dog by talking with him in a playful lilt of rhetorical questions and making coy eye contact. I hoped the worn red bandana around the dog's neck was proof that someone was caring for the creature. I couldn't help but wonder where the ginger dog was tonight. Maybe his new pilgrim had been the right alpha human for him, and they would travel the length of the trail together in a balance he and I couldn't find that morning outside Burgos. Maybe his new alpha would give him the home I couldn't offer.

As this new dog milled around, Ivan gleefully unwrapped a chocolate yogurt, slurping it straight from the container while Elliot arranged the components of his sandwich with precision, stacking layers of bright green peppers on top of watery tomatoes and thin slices of cheese. The boys viewed meals as feasts and the highlight of their days; I still experienced food as basic fuel to move me forward.

For my dinner, I'd selected a boring medley of yogurt, nuts and cheese. I was never one to shy away from adding strange ingredients together, and apparently I'd found a crowd that could embrace my talents. On the Camino, yogurt was in and milk was out. Spanish shops didn't sell cold milk. For reasons unknown, Spaniards subsisted on milk packaged in ultra pasteurized boxes and stored at room temperature. Called "UTH" or "long life milk," this product supposedly lasted for months, even years. I had some serious concerns about the product. Wasn't the essence of milk its freshness? Wasn't it only natural that milk would and should, at some point, go off? The cartons barely contained any life force energy, and I had a hard time convincing myself I could be sustained on such food. The product wasn't milk; it was milk's scary cousin, vacuum sealed in slim containers with splashy names. When planning my journey, I'd been under the impression I would be eating local foods along the trail, sampling the early summer produce as I traversed farmland. I'd assumed each day would provide fresh gooey cheeses and regionally grown foods like almonds and cherries, but alas, this was not to be. Most of the time I was forced to stock my pack with mass produced western food, all too similar to the dismal foods that littered supermarkets in the states. I lamented the fact that another country had fallen under the trance of westernization and embraced all the crappy American brands. It shocked me that as I traveled the ancient Camino, I was forced, out of necessity, to buy too much from the modern world.

Another problem I faced was the difficulty of shopping for one person with nowhere to store extra food. There was only a tiny space in my pack, no bigger than a few square inches, designated for supplies. The British boys had a much easier time with food storage. They could buy a whole carton of milk and a box of cereal in the afternoon and polish it off as a group at breakfast with no fuss about leftovers. On the other hand, I had to carry my food supplies like a pack mule. Each purchase literally weighed on me, for I knew I would have to eat the product for several meals in a row and drag it with me for dozens of kilometers. Dairy and fruit spoiled quickly and were off limits unless I could eat them right away. Eventually, I began to buy four packs of yogurt and bestow the extras on the boys as gifts. I could always count on them to be grateful and hungry no matter the hour of day or the amount of food they had already ingested. Plus, I liked exercising my mothering muscles in this small way. Food was a sneakily complicated element for all of us. We had to eat, we had to move and we had to maneuver around the Spanish schedule, all of which seemed to work against us. I had a feeling the tussle with food would continue; maybe I just needed to embrace the complication and stop trying to perfect an imperfect dynamic. The guys had embraced it, and I needed to take a page out of their book.

The amount of food we needed also upped the ante. We all required three to four times more food than normal. The physical energy required to walk all day was much more intense than what I'd expected coming off the heels of a life as a dancer. Yes, I was moving for six to eight hours like my dance days, but the tone of the energy was different. With dance there was a subtly to the exertion and a deep internal motor that didn't demand fuel with the same intensity. Dance unfolded in a set space and circled around a fixed point in the center of myself; this trail forced me to keep that center on the move, constantly recalibrating, adjusting to new pathways and new environments. The primal part of my body was working harder, swimming around in the energy of flight or fight more than it did in the safety of the studio. This was an exercise in endurance and survival. It cut deeper and was draining in a whole different way. Here we were crossing the land, cutting through space and interacting with vast surroundings. This required us to be more dynamically expansive. And having begun the Camino on my own, it had immediately asked even more of me energetically. I'd been called to push physically and also to push outside of my shy circle. Being with the boys was the first taste of consistency I'd known in Spain.

There was also the challenge of carrying twenty pounds of weight on my back and becoming accustomed to a new relationship to gravity. There was no easy way to feel light, fast and sleek. Our packs weren't like layers of clothing we could shed. They were necessary evils that extolled a price on our bodies. Even through the seemingly endless cloud of nausea, my body ached for sustenance, calling for proteins to rebuild and carbs to burn. We were engaged in an intense cycle of energy, pulling in greater quantities and moving it out just as quickly. I felt the flow of my body becoming faster with stuck energy breaking up and releasing like never before. This physical life certainly got everything moving on all levels. The physical was just the most obvious, but I could feel my energy system shifting, growing deeper and increasing its current and flow.

Of the American duo, Ivan made the boldest choices in all arenas of trail life, be it food or fashion. His pants had originally been a rugged brown but had faded in the sun to a slimy green. He often wore them with one leg rolled up to the knee hip-hop style with a dark green army surplus belt strapped around the middle of his thigh and a pirate flag draped over his pack. Each detail sought to invoke the essence of pilgrim cool and make Ivan look scruffy yet tough, but they had the opposite effect and only added to his approachable charm. There was something too boyish and jolly about his demeanor to allow any of us to believe he was the rebel he pretended to be. He lacked the intensity of a real rebel and the hard edge of a true bad boy. The main feature of Ivan's leg belt was a pocket designed for his prize knife. The blade in question was a five inch hunting knife that would have been frightening to discover on almost anyone except Ivan. As he showed me the long blade and smiled with pride, I was sure there were great tales about why this knife had been chosen and why it would ultimately mean the difference between victory and defeat. Like actors who couldn't get over how cool their props were, both Ivan and Jack loved to talk endlessly about their knives On the trail, the knives were used mostly for cutting cheese and bandages, but one knife was set apart from all the rest and wasn't sullied by such common uses. Big Blue, as she was called, was the official third member of their group. Jack and Ivan doted on her so much they never let her out of their sight. Because of Big Blue's revered status, there was a need for lesser knives to fulfill other lowly functions that often included gooey jam and greasy slices of meat. The only knife that didn't live in the pockets of Ivan's worn pants was a blade shaped like a whale that was attached to the buckle of his belt. Disguised as a fashionable beluga shaped buckle, Ivan was confident he would always have a back-up knife if the rigors of pilgrim life demanded action. In contrast, my first and only line of defense was a bright orange whistle and my speedy feet.

With the knives having served their domestic purpose for the day, we rested in the spotty grass as late afternoon rolled into evening. Francis and Elliot left us to go to the church to say their night prayers before the sun dipped below the horizon. I shouldn't have been surprised to stumble across young pilgrims who were here for religious reasons, but I was curious why such pilgrims would want to consort with the likes of me. I was on my own trek of faith, but I was well aware this element of my trail life wasn't evident on the surface. I hadn't really shared my full story with anyone. Yes, bits and pieces to strangers along the way, but I hadn't worn it like a public badge as some pilgrims did. Francis was fast becoming a valued confidant, and I knew it was only a matter of time before I told him the whole story of why I was here. As he walked away beside Elliot with his head ducked and his long legs making soft footfall, I wondered how the journey was playing out inside him. How did we mere mortals fit into his trek? Would he ever be able to believe that maybe he and I had trusted the same source of guidance to arrive here? Perhaps the center our Caminos were more alike than anyone would guess.

As we lazed around in the park, Elliot and Francis took refuge in ritual, and I marveled at how public and formal it felt. Even though I'd walked two full days with Francis, this part of him, this surface framework of belief, still felt mysterious. Although Francis was British, I'd felt few major cultural gaps, but his life embedded in traditional religion was utterly foreign to me. I didn't know the rituals, hadn't learned the rules and certainly didn't crave the structure. I wondered if his contained nature felt more comfortable in the boundaries, history and security of a widely traveled path.

But below the pomp and circumstance of his religion, I felt akin to his energy. One reason I felt drawn to Francis was of because his deep affection for God. It was just the man-made framework of organized religion built around this love that baffled me. I'd grown up with a freedom of belief that was elemental, hand made and internally cultivated. I felt no desire to leave my freedom for a cage, no matter how gilded. It made me wonder what Francis felt. Was this journey testing his attachment to religion or strengthening his connection? Even from our first conversation, he struck me as a questioner; so was he questioning this part of his life? What was our boisterious group doing to his internal workings? Since the Middle Ages, the trail had held deep Christian roots, but in the last few decades the spectrum of belief on the trail had blossomed into a melting pot of faith. The Camino was no longer dominated by one spiritual tone, and the proof was all around me. Jack, who had studied in India, loved to discuss his interest in Buddhism. Ivan, on the other hand, felt nothing but distain for organized systems. Instead, he was still unfolding the mystery, still trying to understand how to connect his inner and outer life. He was a musician's child with a carefree view of life that didn't buy into what others were selling. For the American guys, this journey was more about mythical gods and epic adventures than deep introspection. And then there was John. The odd man out in the Brit trio, his analytical plumage unruffled by that fact he had no connection to the religion his friends followed with such devotion.

There was too much space and time on the trail for any of us to entirely avoid the spiritual undercurrent in our journey. Just because Francis and Elliot were coloring inside the lines of traditional faith didn't mean the rest of us weren't using the crayons in our own way. Maybe our connection to spirit and God was more illusive, individual and private. Maybe it wasn't always available at first glance or in an easily recognizable package, but it was just as vibrant. As I pondered Francis and Elliot's religious excursion, I wondered if growing close to them might allow me to see their faith in action. Might it help me be a less jaded observer of their traditional ways? Maybe in the days to come Francis's faith, in combination with our growing friendship, would remind us both that it wasn't the outer shell that mattered but the truth at the center of our beliefs. For I sensed behind his guarded stance, his essential truths weren't so different than my own. Beyond words and practices, there was a root and source we both shared.

Perhaps coming to the Camino was the first time I'd seen my faith actualized in my outer life in such a dramatic turn, but if spirituality had been a minor part of my life, then I certainly wouldn't have followed its pull to Spain. The trail was undeniable evidence than I cared. I was raised in a family where a connection to God was like a romance; we could talk about it, share hopes, dreams and questions, but ultimately it was a one on one love affair. I'd never had a public structure like Francis and Elliot and didn't particularly want one.

Both the Dancer Man and the Caveman had been atheists with a hatred of anything related to spirituality. I'd tried to keep my faith to myself because they'd both thought my beliefs were crazy. As for their lack of faith, I'd tried to view one's elusive nature and the other's overtly romantic connection to the arts as proof they had spiritual depth. In my naiveté, I'd believed I could be the safe harbor they'd needed to reconnect with God. Ultimately I came up against the issue of free will. Their fight with faith would never be more than a silent stalemate unless they wanted more and reached for it themselves. I'd failed to see where their free will lay or how they'd felt love and faith were one in the same. And eventually, I'd learned they believed in neither enough to be with me.

It had been wrenching to be emotionally and physically linked to men with no faith; their deep disconnection from their spirituality had eaten away at me. I'd felt empty around these men as if I was always pushing them to go deeper and connect to the core of their lives. It had felt like playing tug of war with a boulder and had left me shredded with exhaustion. Even though I'd propped up their energetic fields with my own in an attempt to get the boulder rolling, it had never budged.

But both relationships had shown me that my faith was woven into my every moment, the way I saw the world and how I connected to others. It was my roots, alive just under the surface and ingrained in every cell. It was in each movement, flowing through me as I danced. It was only with the trials of these relationships that I began to learn how valuable this piece of me was. It was more than valuable; it was an intrinsic part of me as indivisible as blood and bones, muscles and memory.

Not long after Francis and Elliot disappeared into the church, the crew from Frómista rounded the corner. It was déjà vu as they moved in a herd, drawing all attention to their cluster. Their group threw off an air of easy fun and exclusive coolness without saying a word. Even from a far, everything about the ensemble was designed to intimidate and impress. Yet Ivan waved to them with brazen confidence, and Ava led her posse over to join us on the lawn. I wondered how long it had taken them to get to Carrión. If the morning had been any preview, the afternoon on the Meseta must have been scorching. They looked a bit tanner but no worse for wear.

As we opened the circle to them, I felt my shy side emerge out of nowhere. I'd been perfectly at ease with the boys all day, but the energy of our conversations altered as soon as the larger group sat down. The structure dramatically shifted, new hierarchies and alliances were suddenly at play. I sat next to Ivan and felt relieved to have such easy company by my side. Despite my immediate misgivings, I was mostly pleased to see this crew again and connect with them in small ways. They were undeniably exciting, glamorous and entertaining. Ava sat at the top of the circle with Konrad's straw hat propped jauntily on her head, drinking from her brightly colored water bottle and laughing at each passing joke. She was ringleader to the circus of activity and read from her father's guidebook in a silly voice that we all supposed was an exaggerated impersonation of her dad. Zara showed off her less than fashionable leggings tan that ended mid-shin and chatted almost exclusively with Tomas at her side. Iris leaned over the spread of food, opening cans of corn, chickpeas and olives. She then mixed other raw vegetables in a plastic bag to form an impromptu salad while Konrad sipped a beer with contented ease beside her. And I watched, soaking in every detail.

Being part of this large group felt easy in some ways. I didn't have to be the social director. There was no pressure to entertain or keep the flow of conversation rolling. In fact, the boisterous chatter from the outgoing newcomers left little room for the shy members to join in. John and I were quickly relegated to the sidelines and became merely audience members. He sat very still with limbs crossed and his face tipped down at the grass as if he were digesting each word. I knew John was engaged, following each story and joke, but not feeling bold enough to jump into the fray. Ava was the center of all conversation and as the hub, she was unaware of what was happening on the fringe. Suddenly the trade offs for frivolous company seemed too much, and my mood shifted. A wave of exhaustion washed across my chest, and I felt tired, distant and a bit lost.

As the group munched on their dinner, I excused myself to go hunt down a pay phone and call home. I crossed the intersection, walked up to the doors of the church and looked deep into the cool interior. Inside two figures were alone and apart in the large space. They sat bolt upright and completely still as if they were hardly breathing. Even though I was drawn to the dooryard by curiosity, I had no desire to go in. There was something cold and vacant about the shadowy space. Yet as I looked in, I longed for Francis to come out and come back to life beside me. He was already a source of comfort and grounding, but the person I saw deep in the church felt like a shadow of the Francis I'd come to know. We shared energy on the trail, but we didn't share this. As I stood on the threshold, my body was out in the open air with my gaze fixed on Francis's back. I desperately wanted him to turn around, to unconsciously know I was there and come be by my side so we could, like runaway children, escape such confinement. I wanted him to leave this stuck energy and come away. But he didn't turn around. After a while, I felt the temperature dropping around me and noticed the shadows had grown around the edges of the building. Without a sound, I stopped waiting for Francis, turned away from the vault of stone and moved back into the warm air of the living city.

I called home then made my way back to the albergue and the room I shared with the Brit boys. When I arrived back, Francis was asleep in his bed on the far side of the room. Making as little noise as possible, I lay in my sleeping bag, writing in my journal by the beam of my flashlight. I dozed off for an hour then awoke to the sounds of my roommates jumping on each other's beds. Elliot sat on top of Francis's body crushing him playfully while he spoke in silly voices and tried to bait Francis into joining their revelry. I knew they were trying to cheer Francis up, and it made me smile under my covers. These boys were, in many wonderful ways, still boys.

Nineteen. I tried to remember who I'd been at their age. I'd been on the brink of major change and not seen it coming. I'd known so little about myself. But if I could go back in time and leave a small note for nineteen year old Elizabeth under her pillow, I'm not sure she would believe anything I could tell her about what lay ahead. There would be too much change to understand or absorb. Perhaps in this instance, it was better not to have known what awaited me, to have lived those moments one at a time, ever hopeful and never seeing how far the tumult stretched ahead. I wondered if these boys knew they stood on the edge of great change. Were they aware of what was to come? The answer was most likely no, but this blindness wouldn't be a disadvantage; their growth would be just as painful and beautiful without a view of what lay ahead.

I felt a bit old and out of place as they bounced around the room. I didn't know if the boys could really understand what had transpired in the five years that separated us. Those years had gutted who I was, given me gifts I couldn't have imagined and drawn sorrow out of me to depths I couldn't quantify. Growing up in the purest sense of the word wasn't a free ride. All that hard earned knowledge hung in the space now and made me feel lonely. I wanted to feel less damaged and understood, but I wasn't sure the Camino could give this to me. I wasn't sure the Brit boys or American guys could grant me this either. That evening, the other group could be heard talking down the hall late into the night, past curfew and quiet hours. They too were in a different cosmos, distant and unreachable. I turned my flashlight off, and the light around me went out.

TERRADILLOS DE TEMPLARIOS

STAGE TWELVE- 39.9K-24.8M

CARRIÓN TO SAHAGÚN

Francis and I woke before the rest of the group and set off into the morning together. It was seven and already hot as the sun rose around us. The trail led straight into the horizon with not a turn or tree in sight. We walked on a deserted one-lane road, lost track of time and eventually slipped out of it all together. The brown earth, dry and freshly turned, receded as we both fell back into the past. As I spoke, I found my vision clouded with images from other times and places where I saw younger versions of myself attempting to navigate the mire of falling in and out of love. It felt like gravity to divulge some of the aching tales of my broken love affairs, especially to Francis. I hadn't trusted many others with these tales, and none of my confidants had been men. With Francis it was different. His compassion was tangible, and I felt we'd been broken in many of the same places.

Just to speak, to drop the words out along the trail, released some of the power the memories still held over me. To say names so familiar and so lost helped to snapped the ties that still bound me to unchangeable moments of the past. It was effortless and at the same time poignant to speak into the open silences Francis created. His deep listening was not a skill many possessed; it was a lost art especially among our generation. But it was an art the Camino pushed us to hone; the trail gave us a few jobs and one was to listen. Any way a pilgrim sliced it, there was listening to be done both when alone and when in the company of others. The definition of listening widened here; it crossed from the outer world to the inner universe and back again every day. There was something delicate and sophisticated about the art of listening to the outer world, acknowledging every energetic cadence and holding a clear space for another being, but to listen to the inner flow required even more. It required practice, nose to the grind stone diligence and constant centering. When things were good on the surface, it was harder work and easier to lose track of. Yet I couldn't deny the practice had a revolutionary effect on me. And it was the one skill that held fast when everything else was in chaos. It was the one skill I attributed to getting me to the Camino. If I hadn't listened, I wouldn't have heard the guidance that called me to leave all I'd known and leap.

That said, I still felt I was better at the external part of listening and certainly enjoyed practicing it more. I longed to soak in all the details of Francis's life, to fall deeper into his world with every confidence and memory shared. Here on the trail, just the two of us, I didn't feel the distance of age as I had last night. Instead I felt we were back in a configuration and bond we had know many times before.

And once Francis began to talk, I was swiftly drawn into the winding tale he told of his life before this moment. I saw the characters, learned their names, imagined the places and pictured Francis there amongst them. I felt people told their stories better when their words were contained by an attentive listener, so I tried to be a good container, and Francis's story spilled out with clarity even though it was undeniably raw. As we talked, there was no rush, no fear of being interrupted or dismissed. We mirrored each other's stride with each word and held the space even in the relative freshness of our friendship. The trail served to create a bubble untouched by other voices, a place where bikers rushing past were the only signs of the outer world. We were alone, yet I felt not a hint of loneliness. I actually felt free of the ghost of emptiness that had followed me since I'd left home: a ghost I'd known intimately during my relationships with other men.

Eventually, we turned away from the smooth road into a barren sea of grain. Only the wide and cloudless sky marked our progress. The land shone bright golden below our feet, and dust shimmered on our arms and legs. The tempo of our conversation slowed, and every click of Francis's stick and crunch of our feet in the gravel became sharp and voluminous. Into the easy silence, he spoke his morning prayer as I walked next to him. Usually this was a private moment away from the company of others, but today his morning included me, so he folded me into his solitude and began. He sang, spoke words of thanks and sent blessings to the people in his life. Among the list of names was an old love of his whose vowels still felt fresh as they left his lips, and to my surprise, he spoke the name of my ex's as well. I must have flinched visibly at the name that had haunted me through two ghastly love affairs, for I felt as if I'd been struck by someone I trusted. It was a name I desperately wanted to forget and felt unwilling to forgive. Its vowels and consonants were ugly and thick with dark memories. It was hard to feel Francis drop it like a weighted rock onto me. I felt guilty when I instinctively wished the blessing could be taken back and the name unsaid. For the first time, I felt Francis had broken my confidence and overstepped his bounds. To say the name and offer compassion was my choice. I had my reasons for not blessing that name.

Morning prayer was all about compassion, but I knew I couldn't extend that branch to my former loves. Compassion had been the doorway those toxic men had used to control me. Indulging in my compassionate heart had drawn me back into believing it was my job to save them from drowning in their lives. I'd had to leave. In doing so, I'd embodied the part of me that was unflinchingly self-protective. For when I'd made it my job to keep those men afloat, I'd always found myself slipping below the water, sinking slowly away from the true course of my life and towards the bottom. Part of me wanted to extend compassion and fill the situation with light and love like Francis desired, but I knew certain battles called for certain weapons. To be free from those men, I'd had to be stronger than ever before, cut all ties with one swing of a sword and trust it was the kindest and cleanest way forward. How could I explain to Francis this was the true prayer, the true act of kindness no matter how it looked on the surface?

It was the tone in Francis's voice that unnerved me the most. He truly felt prayer, forgiveness and a softening of the heart were the only way forward, but such things only caused me to slip backwards. I'd worked so hard in the past few weeks to defend myself and construct an emotional fortress around my heart when it came to the end of my relationships. Francis's unexpected move rattled me greatly. I was trying to un-connect the dots between having love, feeling compassion and thinking it was my duty to put up with anything because of those emotions. I didn't know how to articulate to Francis what it had taken to step forward and prove that love wasn't always about seeking to be more vulnerable and more forgiving. That in times like the ones I'd just come through, love had to be ruthless. That the most loving thing to do with those men had been to turn away, break all contact and feel no remorse. How could I tell him I was practicing being a warrior about this chamber of my heart, sharpening my sword so I could know what to defend and what to cut loose? I was wielding the swift blade of self-protection with more assurance than ever before.

Being fiercely loyal and steadfast meant once my heart was given it wouldn't waver. I felt these qualities would serve me in the long run, but in the past, they'd worked against me with the lost boys. In those relationships, my positive tendencies had brought on a hefty dose of negative consequences. Holding fast only worked if I was holding onto the right people. Clinging to the fraying edges of tortured love affairs had worn me thin, turned my strengths against me and pushed me to try and make the impossible work.

Just because I could love an unkind man, a man who didn't care about me, a man who was vain and shallow, or simply the wrong man, didn't mean I should. In my eagerness to love, I'd lacked discernment. In the past, I hadn't understood that love should be a meeting of equals. Now I needed to exercise my volition and strength. I needed to wield both to find a bond that nourished me. I'd been too willing to merge my energy system with the other person, too willing to forgo essential parts of myself to be loved. I'd believed love was about energetic sharing, so I'd attracted men who were thirsty for energy and seeking the life force they were unable or unwilling to generate for themselves. On a more basic level, I should have chosen a man who was kind to me. Not just in public or around my friends and family but in the hidden moments between just the two of us. I had needed less of an actor, more of a true friend. I should have known I deserved more than a major fixer upper. I deserved someone who was grown up, but not afraid to keep growing. Someone who was aware of the way he moved through his life and his destiny as a soul, someone who viewed me as an equal and central part of his life. I should have ignored the ones who lay around whimpering in a pool of their emotional lifeblood just waiting for me to run over with bandages to stop the hemorrhage. Yet above all these things, I wish I could have turned back the clock and sought wiser, gentler and truer souls to have given my young heart to. But clocks only move forward, and though I felt far from nineteen as I walked beside Francis on the plains of the Meseta, I knew I could only remedy the past by imprinting the future with something better and a little bit wiser.

These epiphanies were swirling around in me fresh and untested as Francis brought up my past by name. Though it felt like he was poking around in a deep wound that sliced right down my middle, I said nothing. I had yet to truly heal the past by picking a better man and didn't know how to explain any of this. So Francis, unaware of what my silence meant, kept right on listing off names without missing a beat. As morning prayer came to an end, I realized there were things I couldn't explain to Francis. Instead, I had to let his words drift into the space between us and fall to the ground as we walked over them and away.

On we went, straight towards the end of the land, feeling as if at some point we would bisect the soft blue sky and stand on the very seam of air and earth. It wasn't until late morning that we came upon any sign of food, shelter or the basic structures of a town. The cluster of buildings was no more than a few houses tucked under each other's eaves, all encircling a fancy hotel. Several groups of pilgrims sat outside eating a late breakfast. After so many hours with just the two of us, I was startled to remember we weren't alone on this journey. Among the diners, I recognized the Madrilenian and his blonde wife. We exchanged cheerful hellos as they sipped steaming cups coffee, and I noticed both had more color in their cheeks and a relaxed tone to their bodies. Even after a couple of days, the trail had sunk into their very structure, and they radiated a revitalized energy.

Francis and I agreed to keep moving. I was too jittery to sit in a café and wait for food, and neither of us needed the formality of tables, cups and chairs to take a midmorning break. Outside of town, the trail clung to the road again with trees planted in the grass on the far side of the pathway. They were young and thin but managed to convey a sense of purpose in their planting, and like Francis, their lithe bodies felt bound for more growth and substance with age. As I looked at my watch, I suggested we stop for a break under the trees.

A thick bed of tall green grass was a deliciously enticing safe harbor on the endless plain of heat. Francis reclined against his pack, and I lay on my back using my bag as a pillow. We were close enough that my feet rested against his legs and one of his arms arced above my head while the other draped over his ribs. We sat in the center of the tree's shadow with the long stalks of grass splayed out around us in a circle. The grass fell away from the center, but our limbs formed their own loose circle and seemed to draw our still bodies inward with a gentle centrifugal pull.

For weeks I'd been moving through the land, but the solid ground had rarely touched the surface of my skin. The earthen path was shaping the muscles of my body, the sun was burnishing the outer shell, but I was still thirsty for touch. My eyes felt weary. My sense of sight had been overloaded. Often the land and the people I met were felt only by my eyes, and I sorely missed the texture of touch.

I relished the way the Camino plunged me into a physical life again; it was like waking up after years of sleep. This life was the heartiest substitute I'd found to fill the void where dance had been. Yet there were marked differences, and touch was one of them. My dance life had been centered on motion but defined by contact. It had been filled with the smooth surface of the floor, an arm draped over another's shoulder or the breathless moment of hands encircling my rib cage preparing to lift and toss me into open space. That life of movement had been an endless loop of skin, air, limbs, floor, weight and balance. A silent dialog had existed between the surfaces of the ground, gravity and the movers. It had been a language that had become ingrained in my cells. And it was entangled with love: my love of movement and my belief that good love would feel as heavenly as dance. Even the endorphins in my brain told me so. I couldn't separate my longing for dance from my longing for touch and love. They were irreversibly intertwined.

I chewed on a stalk of grass and felt torn. I was rooted in the moment, present with Francis but still my pulse quickened with anxiety. Maybe it was because I'd traveled here to heal old wounds and find fresh love, and I had nothing to show for it. Because of this, my body felt strangely tense. It made me wonder if all my jitters might actually be a signal I needed to keep searching. Was I wrong to rest on my laurels with the Brit and American boys? I wasn't sure I could handle playing it safe, and I was starting to feel that perhaps staying with this posse of boys was blatantly safe. Since day one, I'd flung myself into situations headlong time and time again. What was the harm in continuing to be bold and taking big risks? I might always regret not knowing.

As Francis lay peacefully with his eyes closed and his breathing deep and even, I stopped chewing on the grass and started chewing my fingernails down to the quick. Part of me wondered what it would be like to inch closer, ask to be held and find out if he wanted to hold me too. Would it cure the hunger gnawing at me? If this group had love and touch to offer would I feel content to stay? I shook my head as if to banish a question hardly worth asking. The group had shown me many things, but I pretty was sure romance wasn't one of them. I felt an idea brewing, and I knew Francis wouldn't be pleased. Last night as I was studying my guidebook, I'd discovered that a mere ten kilometers beyond our deserted destination albergue was a large albergue with over a hundred beds and a bustling central square at its feet. I wondered if perhaps my destiny lay just ten kilometers beyond our designated stopping point. The odds were certainly in my favor with a larger number of potential pilgrims. My mind grasped hold of this idea with sharp teeth that refused to let go.

I'd come to Spain weighed down by a hefty dose of doubt in this hair-brained plan. I wondered why I had to walk across a country alone in order not to end up alone. How would this bring me what I wanted most: love and a family of my own? It felt unimaginable, non-linear and mysterious, but my guidance had been clear; this was the way forward even if I couldn't understand why. Now I had to make a move, decide if I should keep pushing, keep seeking and part ways with this group.

I finally broke the easy silence that had fallen over us as we lolled in the shade and shared my brewing plan to go ten kilometers past our predetermined rendezvous point. Francis's eyes snapped open as if he had woken himself suddenly from a dream he longed to escape and turned to look at me with an intense gaze. I met his stare and instead of finding the irritation or anger I expected, I found concern and maybe even traces of something else. He understood why I thought it was wise to go, so he didn't try and talk me out of it as I'd expected. He simply started to pack his food away in the top of his bag and insist no decision had to be made right now. It was true. We were still five or six kilometers from the meeting point, and I had time to make my choice once we arrived. But his mood had switched like the weather, and I couldn't be sure what had brought on this new chill. Was it my rash decision making style or simply the way I'd entered his journey like a whirling dervish and now might leave just as dramatically? I felt a bit crazy to keep following my dream so doggedly as if I was always unsettled, always looking around the next corner for something more, waiting to meet the future. Francis didn't have this energy humming off of him, this restless impatience, this deep ache for more, and I knew he felt slightly wary of its hold over me. I felt torn as he packed up and said nothing. I couldn't see past his detached manner to sense if he was genuinely upset at the prospect of my departure. The shades had fallen over his internal world, and I was on the outside again.

After we had slung our packs back into place, we stepped on to the trail and fell back into our comfortable side by side formation. We hadn't gotten more than a few feet when Francis stopped. Turning towards me with a slight grimace, he asked me if he could have some space to walk the next few kilometers on his own. I could tell he was attempting to give this message with polite kindness, but I immediately felt chastened as if I'd been crowding him or causing him to feel uncomfortable. I agreed, plastered a smile on and assured him it was fine. Maybe it was selfish to ask Francis to keep me company, to stay with me when he wanted me to be alone. So I quickened my pace as he slowed his, and before long a wide gulf of dusty trail had opened between us. After several minutes the trail rose slightly then dipped downward, and he was gone. I hardly dared to look back as I walked out ahead, feeling that even glancing back at him might be misconstrued as invading his space.

The land grew more desolate, and the temperature rose higher after I lost sight of Francis. With no other people on the trail into Terradillos and the unchanging sweep of land before me, I began to imagine what thoughts tumbled through Francis's head, but I realized I couldn't even begin to guess. Even though we'd drawn close, and I felt connected to his past emotional trials, his thoughts and feelings about our group and especially about me, were a complete mystery. There was something deeply contained about his energy as if he was in control of every action, aware of how much he was revealing with each word or movement. Others like Ava were the antithesis of such restraint, falling on the far side of the spectrum from Francis. I knew I could be like Ava at times; an open books of wild flowing emotion. Even though I didn't know her well, I identified with her way of being and understood her better somehow. We were people whose insides were transparent for all to see; each swing of emotion and motivation were declared without an energetic censor. I had a terrible poker face, but I found it even harder to play coy with my emotions. I wished Francis was easier to read, for in the absence of understanding his thoughts and feeling, all I could do was guess, speculate and gnaw at my conclusions along kilometers of empty track.

It took me only an hour to arrive on the outskirts of Terradillos, but it was enough time to slide back into the sea of loneliness. Francis had left me. Maybe it had only been for an hour, but it had been at a tipping point. He'd put space between us and made me feel the distance acutely. When Francis fell away behind me, the tether anchoring me to the group lengthened and grew thin. His physical presence with its tug of warmth and connection was the main element keeping me from going ahead. Our friendship was the talisman that prevented me from falling back into a current of deep restlessness. Ironically, I felt he'd withdrawn it at the moment I had a choice to make about whether to go forward. So as I walked alone surrounded by vacant land with only my own thoughts as wise counsel, I decided I would go on. I must go on and seek what awaited me ahead.

No longer being caught between divergent courses of action, I was filled with energy. No more limbo. I'd made my choice. When I arrived in Terradillos, my lower legs felt tight but strong. I was disappointed but not surprised to see the town didn't have a central square or store. It didn't even boast a church or water fountain. The albergue was the only building that looked inhabited.

As I walked by the gates of the albergue, the Actress lay sprawled in the shady grass alongside the building. She was scribbling madly in her notebook with a half smile on her lips. Her Hungarian Lover boy was nowhere to be seen. I stared at her relaxed body, loose hair and bare feet in disbelief. I couldn't fathom how she'd arrived here before me. Just last night I'd seen her in the park along the river, cuddling with her Lover boy in the late afternoon shade, his hands full of her hair and her eyes closed with that same half smile upon her lips. Francis and I had begun our day very early, and I knew the Actress walked at a slow methodic pace. I could out march her any day. None of the pieces matched up. I called over, she looked up and waved then immediately dropped back into the pages of her notebook. I set my bag beside hers and scrounged around in it for the carton of orange juice I'd thankfully deemed worthy freight to carry all the way from Frómista.

After several minutes filled with only the sound of her pencil wildly scribbling across the rough pages of her journal, she turned to say hello. I couldn't resist asking her how she'd gotten here so fast as disbelief and a bit of envy coursed through my system. She rolled onto her side, the wide neck of her shirt revealing elegant collar bones and a deep tan then proudly explained she'd walked in the hours before dawn. Packing up her things silently around midnight, she'd headed down the trail without a flashlight or guidebook. Luck had been on her side, for the moon had been nearly full and had acted as a soft nightlight guiding her along the path. Her face glowed as she recounted the beauty of the air, and the way even the dirt shone like phosphorescence. She rolled around in the grass as if just the memory of the night gave her physical pleasure. I sat perfectly still, feeling every muscle gripping my bones. We'd crossed the same land, taken the same steps and lived such different realities. Where I'd found little more than bleak endless heat she'd found magic and harmony.

A little while after I sat down, the Actress suddenly closed her journal, looked around and asked me where we were. I was startled, then I remembered she had no guidebook and absolutely no clue where she was. Though she'd asked the question, she seemed unconcerned with the answer, and I suddenly felt in awe of her ability to let go. Here was a woman who was truly throwing her life to the gods without giving an ounce of energy to worry. She made my bids to relinquish control look rather pathetic. Once I told her the name of the town and explained where it lay in relation to Frómista, I discovered she also didn't know where her Lover boy was or if he knew where she'd gone. She had slipped out without waking him in the early hours. For all he knew, she'd vanished completely and evaporated from between his arms in the night. Though I admired her ability to let go of the details, I couldn't admire the way she had left Lover boy in her wake. I was distressed to read little if any concern on her face as she told me about leaving him, and I felt sorry for him. At this very moment, he was surely speeding along towards us, wondering if he would ever catch her again. I couldn't imagine what I would've felt to awake in the middle of the night and find my new love gone with no idea where he was. And even worse, wonder if he'd broken away on purpose and moved ahead with the aim of putting space between us.

I couldn't be certain of the motives behind the Actress's night walk but felt too distracted to do the detective work to find out. Instead, I picked up my things and went through the gates of the albergue in search of water. I knew Francis and the rest of the guys would be there soon, and I wasn't sure I had the strength to say goodbye. I knew Francis would be able to talk me down from my decision, and the warmth and laughter of the rest of the guys would be irresistible. I felt a bit woozy but determined to head off across the open land. I ducked into the albergue to use the bathroom and collect myself. The interior of the place was cool and inviting, but I didn't pause to soak in the details. I couldn't. It might crumble my reserve. When I came out a few minutes later, I planned to dart through the main room and escape back onto the trail as quickly as possible. Upon entering the room, I was brought to a full stop. Francis sat at the small desk checking in. As I came in, he stood up in one fluid motion. Even in that moment, his head tilting as his eyes caught mine, I sensed he knew. He knew I'd made a choice to break away, knew I was going on and this was where our journey together would end. Maybe the conflicting emotions I felt were written all over me, but he too had many things written across his face, and the only one I could read clearly was disappointment. Whatever else I wanted to see, I couldn't trust as truths. I might be imagining worry or sadness because I wanted to believe my departure mattered. Maybe he really felt relief to see me and our growing intensity go.

As I stood with the full room between us, I told him I was leaving, almost whispering the words in the hushed air. He crossed the space swiftly to hug me and held me there for a silent moment. As his arms wrapped around me with delicate tenderness, I realized it was the first time anyone had touched me, let alone embraced me, since I left home. It was the taste of rain after a drought. I stood stunned for a moment then turned and ran. I darted out into the bright day, through the gates and away. My legs took over, and my eyes looked ahead to the horizon. I didn't even stop to say goodbye to the Actress.

Terradillos ended abruptly. Stretched out before me was a savanna with a distant cluster of buildings glistening in the midday sun. I turned my music up and plunged into the sea of heat. It didn't take long before the beat of my music was no longer driving me. Instead it was panic and a sense of alarm that rushed through my whole body. I'd thrown myself out into the intense heat of the day, and there wasn't a shred of shaded safety in sight.

For the first time, I felt the land was dangerous and could hurt me. Almost immediately, the backs of my calves turned bright red and began to throb. Walking west every morning meant the sun always hit my body in the same way. The backs of my lower legs were particularly vulnerable and took the brunt of sun's attention.

After about an hour, I looked down to see my legs had started to drip with blood. The sun was cutting into my flesh. I didn't know what to do. I was too far out to go back but to go forward meant keeping the sun behind me. I'd cut my only pair of pants into shorts so I dug through my bag in a panic, squatting over my clothes in the middle of the vast plains. There was no one ahead or behind me. It was the first time since the early days of the trail that I couldn't see a single other pilgrim for miles around. Apparently everybody else had been smart enough to stay out of the sun at this hour. As I dragged a set of black leggings out of my bag, I had no time to beat myself up. I was very much on my own. I stripped off my shorts in the middle of the trail. The barren stretch of land was as private as any dressing room. The leggings were hot, but they kept the sun at bay. I set off quickly for the next oasis of buildings three or four kilometers away. The only way to fight my rising panic was to keep walking.

My body moved forward, and I kept my eyes on the trail ahead. I was too freaked out to think about the repercussions of the choice I'd made. The physical backlash was quickly becoming the least painful aspect. Somehow I hadn't understood that leaving to seek new acquaintances would mean completely losing others. The less than rational part of me thought I could keep both. I'd had a failure of imagination, a blackout of sorts where I hadn't understood what it would mean to leave the guys. I'd just let go of my safety net, because I told myself it would keep me from risking but was that really it?

What was so scary about safety, especially after weeks of feeling very little in my life was safe? I'd given myself only two nights of comfort before I'd thrown myself into the void again. I'd voluntarily given up a precious thread of community. I'd given up Francis and the gaggle of Brit and American guys. Why? Maybe I was afraid I would miss the chance at love and let a romantic interest slip through my fingers because I was content to hang with the boys. I wasn't sure how I belonged in the guys' world. I was the odd woman out, and they could at anytime do just what I had done, push on, push off or push me aside. Then the comfort and intimacy, dependence and ease would be stripped from me, and I would have to face the trail alone again. Maybe I abandoned them before they could abandon me.

The land was drenched in blinding heat. A far off highway buzzed, and cars shimmered as they rolled by. For the first time, I was pleased to see a highway running parallel to my course. It was a sign that somewhere up ahead was my destination, the city of Sahagún. I pushed through the only cluster of buildings I'd come across since leaving Terradillos. A small group of older gentlemen in long slacks and wide brim hats stood in the shade of building. They looked at me with critical eyes. They knew the sun was at its zenith. They knew better than to go out into their fields at this hour. Hardly a breeze stirred in the narrow dirt lane. I avoided looking into their eyes as they turned their heads to watch me scurry out of town. I knew I looked like a wild creature on the run. I was just glad my ravaged legs were well hidden from their sight.

Beyond town, the trail sidled up to the highway and ran alongside the monstrosity until I entered the outskirts of Sahagún. The approach to the city was downhill but seemed to stretch forever. I crossed through a crumbling set of apartment buildings, traversed rusty train tracks and squinted my eyes against the sun, trying not to miss the arrows.

The edge of the city was defined by wide streets, towering apartments, deserted shops and vacant lots. I didn't see a single person until I reached the old city, embedded deep in the sprawling mass of modern Sahagún. The albergue was a large building a few blocks from the city's central square. It was so immense it took up a whole block. Once a church, its old stone structure spoke of its history as a consecrated spot. Church officials had deconsecrated its holy walls so pilgrims could spend their nights under its roof. It struck me as odd to suggest a small group of people had the power to take back the spirituality from a space. And why did it need to be whitewashed with such intent for pilgrims to be allowed to stay within its walls? I imagined during the Middle Ages pilgrims often found the only dry and sheltered place to sleep was the floor of a church.

The large side door to the building hung open, and as I entered, my feet echoed in the vast space. There was no welcome desk or hint of human habitation. I climbed the smooth and wide stairs to a large vaulted room. Broken into cubicles of four, there were at least one hundred beds in the room. By this point in my journey, this configuration was nothing new. It actually made me feel safer to see lots of bunks. Sweat had started to dry and form chills on my skin. I peeked my head into the room and found there was only one person in the whole space, a girl asleep fully dressed, face down on her mattress.

I was alone. Again. I'd given up the chance to spend the evening in the company of people I knew and liked to arrive here. I felt the weight of my choices crush me. I'd rushed away from the first group on this trail that had truly cared about me. I'd chased a figment of my anxious imagination away from a good reality.

By necessity, I was distracted from my emotional chaos. I needed to buy supplies to deal with my blistering and bleeding legs. I peeled back my leggings and found the red flush had crept up to my knees. Fortunately, it stopped there. The leggings had saved me, but I still needed to tend to my wounds. And unfortunately, my emotional wounds were hemorrhaging in a much more distressing manner.

Since there was nobody to check me in, I lay down on the wooden bench by the door and stuffed my pack under my head. I had to keep the raw skin of my legs from touching anything. Specks of blood from my legs clung to my hands. I wanted to fall asleep to distract myself until siesta ended. Then I would then be able to buy sugar to help with my nerves and band-aids for my ruptured legs. But then what? My mind kept rolling over and over. I started to let my panic rise. Why had I done this? Could I even find my friends again if I tried?

My timing couldn't have been worse. This was a moment when I might actually lose track of the boys for good. Virtually the entire length of the Camino Frances was a single track, but the next day's stage had two options. One route went through a small Meseta town, and the other followed an old Roman road. I couldn't be sure which way my friends would go. Even if I chose right, I worried I would miss them, go too far or not far enough. I'd picked the worse moment to fall apart and do something rash. I'd believed this albergue would hold new friends and potential loves, but it was a ghost town. Was the universe trying to tell me something?

As I sat in a daze in the cavernous albergue, I realized that somewhere in the long hot kilometers of this afternoon, I'd crossed the half way mark between St. Jean and Santiago. Without even knowing it, I'd left the first half of my Camino behind me, tripped and fallen face first into the next part of my trek.

SAHAGÚN

I fell into a light doze, my body dangling off the sides of the narrow bench. I was close to dropping into some deeper form of sleep when I woke with a start. In one quick motion I sat up, tipped my hat off my face and swiveled around to pull my guidebook out of my pack. I flipped through the pages, madly searching for my own scrawled handwriting in the margins. And there it was, a long fourteen-digit number written across the top of page one hundred and eighty six. I clutched the book to my chest. I could have shouted for joy. The series of numbers was more than a random list of digits; it was the key to finding my way back to my group after my irrational blunder. It was Elliot's cell phone number. I hadn't lost all contact. I could make things right again. I was no longer sleepy as I pulled on my blue shoes and eased myself down the long flight of stairs. I could check in and claim one of the dozens of empty bunks later. Now I needed to find a phone.

The walk into the center of town was downhill, and I clung to the shade on the right side of the street. The main square had several phones scattered around the edges. I was better with the phone system now and managed to get it to ring through on the first try. Elliot picked up on the third ring, his cheerful voice a bit confused to hear mine. In a flurry of words I told him where I was and how I needed to reunite with the group as soon as possible. His voice was friendly, but he seemed slightly flummoxed by my level of intensity; his tone suggested he felt I was being rather melodramatic. It was hard to explain to someone who'd never been alone on the trail what it felt like to be in my shoes. It was hard to describe how arduous it had been in the early days and why the scars of those kilometers had caused me to act as I did. I asked Elliot about the group's plan for the next day. Which road had they chosen? Elliot was the Brit boy I knew the least, but he was rebounding and now seemed comfortable that he'd picked up his phone to find me on the other end. He laughed in a kind way and told me he would love to see me again, then explained their plans for the next day would take them to a town called Bercianos. They would travel the main route to this small village rather than take the Roman road. I told him I would meet them there. When we said goodbye, I felt my body exhale for the first time in hours.

I would have liked to talk with Francis, to hear his voice and be reassured he was OK with my return. I knew he was probably in the room as Elliot talked to me, but I hadn't asked to speak with him. I would just have to wait to reconnect with Francis tomorrow. It would give me time to recover, organize my feelings and dissect my choices. I knew Francis would give me that look, see to the core of my every move and find the truth of why I'd scampered off without saying a word. I needed to uncover my motivation before he looked through me and found it first.

As I let the blue public phone click back on the hook, I allowed my shoulders to fall. I was safe again. I was back in the loop and knew the plan of action for the next day. Every nerve in my body suddenly felt soft and loose. I let myself look up and around the square, see the buildings and notice the falling light. I could be here now, breathe again and know tomorrow I would mend what I'd torn today. It was nearly six. The streets were filling with people as shops reopened. I walked slowly through the town searching for the bare necessities of food and medical supplies.

I bought band-aids in the local pharmacy with a neon green cross hanging above the door. Most of the larger towns we passed through had a pharmacy. In Spain, this was the first stop when a pilgrim fell ill. If the illness or injury necessitated a visit to the hospital, the pharmacy would refer the pilgrim to the nearest one. It was a different system than in the states, but I imagined it kept down the volume of traffic in Spanish emergency rooms.

I went into a strange clothing shop and picked out a pair of cheap knee socks. I needed to cover my legs for the next few days, no matter how silly it made me look. When I returned to the albergue, there were half a dozen people milling about. The slumbering girl was now eating a bowl of cereal, and four French men sat around a spread of crusty bread and sliced meats. A woman came through to collect money and give people tickets for their beds. It was strange and informal, unlike anything I'd experienced in an albergue before. The bed tickets made me feel like I was buying a seat in a movie theater rather than a place to sleep. After a cursory glance around the facilities, I was relieved the night's stay didn't cost more than three euros. It would have been almost criminal to charge more.

The kitchen was a large hallway with a broken microwave, a random assortment of plastic dishes and one dull butter knife. There was a small refrigerator, but it wasn't cold. The bathrooms and showers were worse. The stalls were made of cheap plasterboard. Half of the showers didn't have a hot water nozzle, while most of the toilet stalls had no lights. Everything flowed into drains in the floor at the center of the space, and the sinks were dark with layers of rust. The beds were small, and the mattresses had no covers. It was obvious they'd never been aired out. Their ends were sagging and dingy. I tried to find a clean mattress and opted for one on the top bunk, hoping these were used less often than bottom ones. No wonder they were slightly cleaner. There were no ladders. How did anybody manage to reach the upper beds? I stayed exclusively on my sleeping bag, trying not to make contact with the surface of the mattress. Despite the size of the room, it was a hot and airless attic. I wasn't sure I would want to get into my warm sleeping bag that night, but I didn't want to roll off it's safe clean surface either. Was this penance for my choice to take off alone? Was I paying the price by being forced to stay the night in this creepy and derelict albergue?

As I pulled my sleeping bag from its tight compression sack, two young people came in and settled on the bunks across from me. The young man from Colombia was very tan and had a long mane of unruly dark hair matted in a way that suggested he'd been lying on it for most of the day. The woman was a blonde German with glossy hair that hung in a curtain around her face. She wore a long brightly printed skirt with a rosy colored tank top over her tanned body. They held hands and spoke in Spanish to each other as they settled into their bunks. The man moved slowly as if groggy and the girl fussed around him, arranging his sleeping bag and offering him sips of water. Once they were settled, I introduced myself and chatted with the German girl. I sat cross-legged on my top bunk, and she sat beside the boy on the bottom bunk across from me. He lay on his back as if he was listening but unable to sit up.

The cross-cultural couple was traveling the trail together, but they'd begun their journey a year earlier when they met at a university in Madrid. They'd shared a class and fallen in love, but knew after their year of study, he would have to return home to Colombia. This walk was their last joint adventure before his departure. I could sense the tension of opposites in everything they did, the feeling of pulling each other closer at the same time as they imagined how to be apart. Their trek had begun in Pamplona, but they'd been forced to ride the bus a few times because of illness. Today they'd taken the bus from Burgos to Sahagún because the Colombian was too sick to stand up, let alone walk. It was rare to see someone on the Camino who was sick with a normal run of the mill illness. I'd seen plenty of people laid up from injuries, but things like the flu were unusual. Pilgrims were either healthy or really sick, but rarely in the nebulous in-between of normal life. The Colombian boy had a glazed look about him as if he was trying to stay awake and alert but deep down ached to be asleep in a familiar place. This albergue was one of the last places I would want to be sick. Everything about it was cold and grimy. Even the bunks were too narrow for the two of them to sleep in the same bed. I wondered if the sickness was a physical reaction to the rapidly approaching separation. When I asked the girl what lay ahead for them as a couple she confided she had no idea how it would fall together with such distance between them or if it would just fall apart.

They were friendly but preoccupied with their own concerns. Nonetheless, it was comforting to have other English speaking young people sleeping in the room. Later in the evening, I watched them whisper to each other in Spanish and hold hands as he lay on the bottom bunk and she draped herself over the edge of the top bunk. Their intertwined hands hung in space as if floating, fingers laced together in an unbreakable grip. I envied that closeness. Envied the way the German girl lay totally relaxed across her bunk, confident all would be well, even when she had no solutions to sickness, grimy bunks or the approaching separation. In this now they had each other. Everything else was less important.

Other people wandered in to find a bunk, but still there were only about twenty people occupying a room with over a hundred bunks. This place was meant to present me with new community not a deeper reflection of loneliness. I cursed myself for my fumbling choices. I looked around the dark space and knew this was what had come of my attempt to control the fate of this trip. And I knew I would taste this bitter pill again if I insisted on letting my personality, anxiety and overactive brain take charge. I'd been shown the universe was much too delicate and wise a creature to need my abundant controlling energy. I hadn't waited to listen to my gut in Terradillos; I'd just run. My divergence from the flow and doubt of my guidance had given me little more than a few new bloody scars, a creepy old church and a bunk across from a young couple in love. The last hardship was the most challenging to endure. It was hard not to be melancholy when given a sideline view of the sweet romance I wanted but didn't have. Slowly but surely, I was starting to get the message. The current of my guidance was the kindest way forward even if my personality wished for something more.

The albergue was on the second floor of the building but filled only half the upstairs. On the other side of a thin wall, the top floor fell away into a two-storied concert hall. As I read, I suddenly heard the rush of voices in the space beside our sleeping quarters. Soon the noise hushed, and out of the silence bloomed the soft and unsteady sound of piano keys being played by hesitant fingers.

That night, as I tucked into my bag, I was treated to a concert of Chopsticks, Happy Birthday, Mary Had a Little Lamb and a bit of Beethoven by a group of very young musicians. We couldn't see the supportive crowd or the young performers, but their brave little solos filled the space around our bunks. The clapping from their adoring fans rose up to us at the end of each short piece. I felt like I was up in the catwalk, off stage in the still blue lights, while an orchestral performance went on below. We pilgrims were the silent observers, part of the experience, yet unseen. As the notes from the piano rang through the hollow space around me, I could feel every tentative touch of the keys and reverberated with every proud volley of applause.

I didn't remember the end of the music. It faded into my sleep along with the German girl's attempts to stifle her throaty laugh. We had to be a good back stage audience, and I did my part by drifting away, seeking tomorrow and reunion.

BERCIANOS REAL CAMINO

STAGE THIRTEEN- 10K- 6M
SAHAGÚN TO BERCIANOS

I woke early. I had only ten kilometers to walk to my rendezvous point, but I wanted to escape the shadows of yesterday as quickly as possible. I needed to cleanse myself of the fear that had pushed me into the unpleasant night in Sahagún. Leaving the city was the first step. No one was awake when I launched myself off my bunk and began to gather my things. The German girl had crawled into her boyfriend's bed in the night, and though it was tight and her limbs spilled out over the edge, they looked peaceful and didn't stir as I moved past them. I quickly laced up my shoes and slipped out the door. The streets were empty except for the arrows that led me down through the center of the city and out across a footbridge. It wasn't unusual to cross over a bridge at the end of a town or city and then suddenly be out in the countryside. Today I was more grateful than usual for the swift exit from the urban sprawl. The pale moon lingered in the sky but was no match for the blooming sun. The trail was open and dry with no promise of hills or turns in the near future. Storks waded on nimble legs in trailside marshes. Once I left the city, I felt strangely isolated and lonely in a way I hadn't felt since before Burgos. Even though I was bound for a reunion, an echo of last night lingered. It would be the shortest day of walking I'd done since day one. Ten kilometers was a distance I usually covered before breakfast, not a real work out. I hardly considered it a walk; it was more like a well deserved rest day. My ankles were still raw and ached with the last twinges of tendonitis. They were long overdue for this rest.

My most rational self knew a short day would be good for my body, but another Spartan part of me felt I was wimping out. My sense of perspective was officially warped. I'd survived a day of over fifty kilometers, and now I only was walking ten? That seemed like a weak effort. Spartina Elizabeth made it extremely hard for me to take days off. She focused on pushing physical limits and loaded on the guilt with memories of dancing eight hours a day. I'd had too many first hand experiences of how far the body could be pushed. I was no longer in possession of rational or normal expectations about physical exertion. Spartina ruled.

There was only one factor that could silence my concerns about taking a short day and divert Spartina: human community. I would swallow my discomfort with this ten kilometer day, because it would bring me back to my people, to the guys I already missed. It would allow me to rest but not fall behind. I worried how Spartina would fill the idle hours waiting for the group, but I shuddered at the thought of another Sahagún. I wouldn't make that mistake twice. The solo pursuit was over; the push and the chase simmering down inside me.

I tried to walk slowly but within three hours I'd entered the tiny village of Bercianos and arrived at our rendezvous point. The town was flat and dusty with simple houses in a spectrum of cream, brown and rusty reds. It was only eleven when I arrived. Not even a curious dog came out to greet me. I set my pack down on a bit of lawn off the main street and made camp in the shade offered by a few scrawny trees. It was a good spot to rest and provided me with a clear view of the trail and each and every pilgrim who came into town.

And so I waited. I tried to become engrossed in my book, but it was hard to still my body. I felt jittery as if I had too much caffeine in me or perhaps not enough. Even though I tried to be calm, I felt revved up. I nervously checked my watch a dozen times an hour, struggling to convince my squirming limbs it was OK to stop. I'd only brought two books on the trip and since they were two parts of the same series, I had little choice in my reading material. Pulling the crushed paperbacks out of my bag, I tried to disappear into The Fellowship of the Rings. I'd never read the book, but as I'd tucked it into my pack at home, I'd known it was about an impossible and perhaps foolhardy journey taken on foot. I'd felt we were a perfect match, but I could never have guessed just how apt the parallel would be.

Beyond the obvious, there was another strange connection with the books. The first night around the dinner table with the Brit lads and the American guys, The Fellowship of the Rings had come up. Within seconds, each and every guy had professed their undying love for the trilogy and had begun to discuss its characters, battle scenes and underlying conflicts. There was an eerie kind of luck I'd brought the now rather ratty copies with me. The boys had spent a great deal of time hemming and hawing over details as they'd assigned matching characters to each member of our group. It had been a task Elliot and Ivan took very seriously. Each character had been allocated only after great debate and general blessing from the rest of the group. Ivan had been the first to stake his claim as Boromir. After his well thought out pitch, the role had been bequeathed to him without a fuss. He'd explained he liked the dramatic flare of a character that possessed both immense goodness and a powerful shadow side. I'd wondered why Ivan had never been an actor. I could see him relishing the chance to play warriors and kings, heroes and villains. In this dramatic vein, he loved Boromir's epic death, the great honor mingled with the stain of disgrace. It was in line with his dream of a warrior's life and an honorable end.

Jack had been a bit disgruntled that none of the group had been willing to cede the title of Aragon to him. Aragon was too distant and stern for Jack. There was much more of the naughty hobbits in Jack's easy banter with Ivan. As we'd clustered around the table, Ivan and his lively monologues had been the center. He was the storyteller at meals and into the night. I often preferred his tales to the meandering narrative of my book.

The British guys had claimed their trio was Frodo, Sam and Gollum. I wasn't sold. In my eyes, none of them deserved the title of Gollum. Out of principal, I'd wanted to be a female character, but had felt there were few strong women in the story. Ivan and Elliot had hopped around in their seats with glee when they realized I would make a perfect Gandalf. Well fine except for the white beard. It had taken me a while to give up the dream of being dubbed Aragon myself. We all secretly wanted to be the ranger who would be king, but perhaps I would warm to Gandalf in time.

With my book in my lap, I drifted off into a light sleep around noon, then woke a while later still protected by the freckled shade of the small trees. The air hung heavy, and not a person or car passed. The grass was rough and spotty underneath my limbs. The sky was opalescent blue and unmarred by a single cloud. I took slow breaths, inflating my lungs and watching as the air made my chest rise and fall in a steady looping rhythm. This action was like the gentle swing of my legs, the lift and fall of my feet to the ground. Yet my breath was not forced or muscled. This action had been at work since the moment I was born. I was in awe of its ability to keep on going through every moment of chaos. This action was my most devoted ally, my ever constant support; it was my fuel even when I lost track of its steady circle. I could forget about this most basic action during fear and excitement, pain and pleasure and yet my lungs would still kept rhythm. Their only rival for steadiness was the heart, but the workings of that organ were a greater mystery to me than the perseverance of my lungs.

The building across the square was a solid stucco house with sagging eaves and a roof alive with motion. Dozens of swallows were in constant flight, circling out into the sky then back to their nests, flowing in endless loops of perfect choreography. Occasionally smaller birds would appear from the nests, waiting for the return of food to fuel their growing bodies. I wondered what it would be like to live in that house. Did the inhabitants feel the vibration of hundreds of birds living within their walls? My eyes wandered from the eaves to the far side of the building where the wall turned the corner and disappeared. There a lone swallow dangled from a piece of twine. The bird had hung itself and now remained there, twirling in the wind. The other birds moved about the corpse as if it was simply part of the building.

The hours slunk by. Two women came out of the small church and swept the porch with straw brooms. They chatted softly to each other without noticing my still form tucked in the shade. I must have drifted into sleep again for suddenly I awoke to find myself in a sea of backpacks with the sun blotted out by three tall figures. After so many hours adrift in the empty town, it was thrilling to be surrounded by a hive of voices and movement. I leapt to my feet, and as swiftly as that the boys came back to me, and I came back to life. The current swirled around me again, and all feelings of being lost evaporated.

Francis stepped towards me, and I drew him into a hug. My arms folded over the tops of his shoulders as his bare arms encircled my rib cage. I embraced his tall lean frame with unabashed happiness but felt there was a reserve in his body as if he didn't want to get too close or hold on too long. He held his center away from mine like he was fighting a gravity he couldn't understand. His body felt rail thin in my arms but deeply familiar as if we'd known this place before, this looped embrace. A second spun out into reels of time, and I felt my lungs push against his, breathing through both our bodies. Without missing a beat we dropped the hug, and I received quick bashful hugs from John and Elliot before they crashed to the ground ready for lunch. My arms still tingled slightly, caught in the echo of Francis's embrace, but I shook it off and turned to the cheery crowd around me. As he pulled food supplies from his bag, Elliot commented on how nice it had been to receive my call. Francis looked over and smiled but said nothing. He sat farthest away from me and seemed to be holding his energy tight around his limbs. The rest of the boys ignored Francis's grumpy mood and delighted in sharing all their news with me. It was soothing to be re-embedded in their posse. I sat back and soaked in the tales. It felt like I'd been away from them and the rest of the group for ages.

Elliot reported that the British girls, Zara, and the German guys had gone the way of the old Roman road, but Tomas, the Belgian, was due to join us in Bercianos that night. I was curious why the groups had chosen divergent trails. Elliot smiled mischievously as I asked him about Jack and Ivan. He explained the American guys had settled upon the crazy idea of walking through the night. They'd broken company with the Brits in Terridillos that morning and would walk all day, take a small nap and then walk until dawn. Their aim was to accomplish two days of walking in one marathon of a day. Since they didn't plan on sleeping, time wasn't an issue, and they could keep a slow pace. I was disappointed I wouldn't see them in Bercianos, but apparently they'd agreed to rendezvous with us in León in two days. This was comforting news. There would be more reunions to come.

I felt a warm glow when I imagined us all back together in León. It was characteristic of Jack and Ivan to have gone for a bold and perhaps foolhardy plan. They were obsessed with doing the Camino in an epic fashion. Though plagued by injury and inadequate conditioning, they wanted to be great. Ivan was a scholar of the classics with dreams of being a writer as well as a pirate when he grew up. It was a vague plan currently still in the works, but this didn't stop the riveting talk about a future in constant danger or the plot of his yet to be written Odyssey inspired novel. Ivan's medium build and tawny hair made him look rather ordinary, but once he opened his mouth that presumption vanished. He was an entertainer, a weaver of tales and a dreamer hungry for experience. His enthusiasm knew no bounds.

When I'd met Ivan and Jack in Burgos, I'd introduced them to Alberto. Though they didn't speak Italian, they were taken with Alberto. He became a mythical figure as soon as they looked down and realized he was wearing the same shoes they were. While Ivan could hardly walk because of the damage his sandals had done, Alberto had nary a blister. From that moment, Alberto was dubbed the "Guru" and became the guys' unofficial idol. They wanted to learn his shoe secrets and more, convinced there was great wisdom underneath Alberto's polite façade. The guys even tried to follow him for a day to watch their champion in action. With time, their theories grew wilder and wilder. When Alberto vanished from our lives in Frómista, they claimed he'd never been human but was a god who materialized at will, down from Olympus to mingle with us mere mortals for a while.

Even though Ivan appreciated the Italian's Camino skills, his own trail choices were unorthodox and made forward progress difficult. Reality always seemed to get in the way of his imagination, and his dreams were often more delightful in conversation than in action. He shouldered a large pack that contained a thick book about how to tie complex seafaring knots as well as set of heavy metal hand strengtheners to improve his grip. These looked like small nunchucks and were used infrequently. Ivan either drew people to him or drove them away. Men had especially strong reactions to him. The British boys loved him unequivocally. John was deeply smitten by Ivan and had developed a serious bromance crush. Ivan called himself "the captain" and Jack was his official first mate. Their lively company would be missed tonight, but I was still euphoric to be back among the Brits.

As the boys opened their bags and pulled out bread, cheese and an assortment of withered vegetables, Tomas rounded the corner. I was delighted to see him strolling toward our impromptu picnic. He smiled his wide smile as he spotted our gathering. I was encouraged he was here in Bercianos on his own, connecting with us. The absence of Zara and the rest of his group might actually allow us to get to know him.

The sun shifted overhead as the picnic feast continued. I felt the joy of being in no rush. Time was easy and full. Francis had even warmed up during the length of the meal; he was now stretched out like a lanky cat in the shade next to me. Tomas was busy eating seconds and thirds, while the other guys chatted. Though all within a year of each other in age, Tomas was the manliest in build, and I could tell his tall body longed for food all the time. An hour later, the mood was still light as we gathered up our packs and headed across the village to the albergue.

Our home away from home for the night sat at the far side of the village adrift between town and field. The pilgrim hostel in Bercianos was a large building made of the same straw and mud as the rest of the village, but somehow the structure had a jaunty elegance to it, a quirky sense of individuality. It was part of the town, but not of it. It radiated a lived in quality even from a far. The outside was painted a warm earthy red with two small windows and a large door like a yawning mouth. A row of benches hugged the front, and an overgrown garden clung to the side of the building. The double doors hung open as we arrived, and a pilgrim sat on one of the benches reading his guidebook. The entrance hall was narrow but cool. The space felt clean and orderly. A French couple welcomed us warmly as we put our packs down. They were in residence as volunteers for two weeks, spending all hours of their day devoted to our migratory flow. When their time ran out here, they would be placed in another albergue along the route. The couple cheerfully explained they would be moving about on this cycle for the rest of the summer.

Though the entrance hall of the albergue was lovely in many ways, it was the floor that caught my attention. A mosaic of colored tiles and polished stones formed the shapes of the sky and trees swaying in the wind. Someone had spent a great deal of time to create this moment of beauty beneath our feet, and I longed to take my shoes off to feel the lustrous stones. I wondered how the piece of art had come to be here. Was it as old as the building itself or a recent project taken on by one of the many hostel volunteers? Like everything in the space, it looked as if it had always been part of the building and folded into its aura. After the French couple offered us slices of juicy watermelon and stamped out passports, the woman showed us where to stow our boots. The long rack at the back of the entrance hall was already half full with muddy shoes and dangling laces. On the trip up to our room, we dodged a small white mess caused by a family of birds who had taken up residence in the ceiling of the stairwell. The boys and I were led into the smaller of two bunkrooms. It was wonderful to check in at the same time as everyone else, for it insured that we could claim bunks close to each other. This made me feel safe as if surrounded by a layer of familiar warmth. There were only about a dozen bunks in the room, and our group clustered to one side, spreading out our things in a whirlwind of activity.

Ever the group of gentlemen, the boys gave me first choice of bunks, and I choose a bottom slot near the window. Tomas took the bed above mine, and the rest of the boys splayed out around us. The floor was soft caramel colored wood and as I slumped down beside the bed, it felt cool to the touch. Just being on the floor drew me back to the many floors I'd known and the hours I had spent in their arms. All those dance floors had moved gravity through me and caught me in their lines of soft beauty. It was a strange existence to be moving so much but not dancing. There was rarely ever the space to move in the bunkrooms let alone dance. Other times in my life I'd lived and danced in small rooms, pushing back furniture, pulling up rugs and braving the consequences of slamming my head on the floor or flinging an arm into the side of a door jam. But here I had to play nice, behave and share, so I daydreamed instead.

In college, I often danced alone in large empty studios. I sometimes missed the close spaces of smaller rooms, but the floor in these studios made up for this feeling of dislocation, enchanting me like nothing before. Its soft endless plane drew me in, sliding me like a smooth current from movement to movement. It made my joints feel liquid and my limbs light and amazingly long. The floor's color changed across the length of the surface, but it was always cool. It breathed with every action, and the springs below its surface gave life to the moments when muscle and energy met. I'd start my warm ups on the floor, staring up into the space above the lights into the place where the room fell away into nothingness. My bones would settle and sink deeper as the floor rose to meet all my surfaces. It seemed to yield, reach up and dip me down below its surface without a fight. Once I'd begun to move, all the force and strength, balance and stillness rose up through the floor to meet me. It was the roots. It was the element of dance that touched us all.

The boys were busy unpacking and getting in line for the shower. I could feel both of my achilles acutely. They still worried me, but I distracted myself by warming up other muscles that needed attention. As I stretched, it was lovely to once again be close to others while I moved. I could pretend they were dancers, and we were all warming up together for class or rehearsal. John, banging around on his bunk and dropping his pack off the side in a noisy heap, shook me out of my nostalgic daze. I got up off the floor and went in search of ice for my legs.

With an ice pack in hand, I sat on a sagging orange sofa in the cool entryway nursing my achilles. I'd been overjoyed to discover the gooey blue packet tucked behind freezer-burned vegetables. This was a rare albergue with a family style kitchen. The small space was cluttered with dangling pots and pans, cups of silverware and a drying rack filled with ceramic bowls. It was home to both the French couple and the passing hordes. With delicate lace curtains over the windows, the small space felt chaotic in a comforting way as if the remains of lunch dishes sat unwashed because someone would get to them when they had a spare moment.

Sitting prone on the sofa, I didn't want to draw too much attention to my current physical plight, so I wrapped the blue packet in a shirt and tucked my feet between the worn cushions. I was irrationally convinced that to acknowledge the problem, to give it a name and talk about it would give it power. It would make it real and give other pilgrims free reign to pour on advice and send me into a downward spiral of panic. The pain forced me to listen to my own body, but I wasn't willing to receive further input. It was less likely that someone would point out the obvious need for slower speed and more rest if I kept my mouth shut.

Tomas came and sat with me at the far end of the sofa, folding one of his legs over the other and watching the steady hum of activity. He asked about my ankles, and I brushed off the question with a joke then turned the questions back on him. I'd been curious about this mysterious young man for sometime but always felt he was just out of reach behind the fortress walls of his tight group. With nothing else to do and no human barriers in sight, we began to talk. There in the peace of the albergue, his demeanor shifted before my eyes. The person beside me was so different from the guy I'd first encountered walking alongside Zara outside of Hornillos. Here on the sofa, he talked with warmth about anything and everything. I realized I'd let my snap judgment about Tomas take on too much weight. I'd bound my view of him to Zara's icy chill and dismissive attitude, but he was kind and solicitous.

As he spoke, I watched him fold and unfold his limbs, swing his arms in slow looping gestures and play with the tattered edges of the armrest. His solid body was so adult compared to the lithe Brit boys, yet he was still settling into this evolution. Tomas wasn't particularly handsome but made up for it with a cheerfulness that radiated through his cherubic face. It was impossible not to be drawn into his sweetness, and this shifted his attractiveness before my eyes.

We continued to talk as new pilgrims buzzed in and out of the entrance hall. It was a blessing to have conversations built into our duties on the trail, and today it was a blessing to talk to Tomas. He sank back into the dusty old sofa while he told me about the night several years ago when he'd stayed at this very albergue. Tomas was the only person in the group of twelve who'd walked the trail before. When he was eighteen he'd come with his mother, stepfather and stepsiblings to bond as a new family. It was a 'two birds with one stone' experience: a pilgrimage that also attempted to build intimacy into their newly formed family. Tomas explained that here in Bercianos, he'd made a connection with some of the nuns running the albergue. He'd promised himself if he ever returned to the Camino, he would stay here again. As Tomas shared this story, everything made more sense, both his relaxed style on the trail as well as his decision to come here rather than stick with his group on the Roman road. Tomas hoped to give the nuns a letter he'd written them, but they were no longer in Bercianos. I was touched he'd broken from his tight group to seek out strangers who'd been kind to him one night long ago.

That evening, our French host opened the chapel in the back of the building, and everybody piled into the small whitewashed space. I stood on the outer edge against the wall as the collection of pilgrims sang prayer songs and held hands. It was the first religious ceremony I'd taken part in during the trip. A combination of curiosity, courtesy and prodding from the Brit boys lured me into a scene I'd avoided thus far. I was well aware that every town we passed through conducted a pilgrim's mass at the church in the evenings. Many of the pilgrims I befriended attended these services without fail. In the early days, I'd been very determined to stay far away from the rituals that held no sway for me. The conventional world of the church and its customs had never been a part of my life and held no allure. I wanted to spend the soft hours around dusk outside under a beautiful tree, soaking in the last golden glimpses of the sun or tucked deep into my rosey cocoon talking to a fellow pilgrim. I'd grown up in a different church: a church of vegetable gardens with towering sunflowers, lawns of thyme, arbors of twisting grapevines and spires of sweet pea topped with flags of cloth and feathers. Church had never been a room cluttered with icons and benches, heavy with stuck energy and buried in gloomy light. These churches felt as if they'd rarely been scoured of the dense energy people shed in their halls. I felt the only place up to the challenge of absorbing all our chaotic human energy was nature: the wind, water and the land below our feet. This was the ultimate restorative gift nature gave us, the gift of taking our burdens from us, of accepting our run off and refilling us with light and the memory of oneness.

In my eyes, buildings of stone, confinement and enclosure never stood a chance against nature. They were no match for her wild beauty. If the root of church going and prayer was to nestle closer to the divine and to fall into the silent arms of the heavens then I wanted to be out in the open where we could kiss unimpeded with nothing but air and light between us.

With the three British lads front and center the group sang Ultreya, an old French song about the courage it took to walk the trail. The French couple asked the Brit boys to lead the group through the song since they knew all the words and had lovely singing voices. As I stood beside the singing trio I felt a rush of warmth, a desire to move closer to their energy. They had become so familiar, I felt as if I was home. This new family was permanently changing the nature of my journey, and I finally felt ready to embrace it, even if it meant abandoning my quest for romance. The night in Sahagún had been a brutal harvest, allowing me to feel my trail life without them. To be with Francis again was especially important. I glanced over, watching as he sang with deep concentration and feeling. I wondered if he would forgive me for fleeing so gracelessly from Terradillos, for not explaining and for wanting more than I'd been given. It was hard to know on the surface what might have shifted in the thread between us. I had a feeling it would take me a while to unravel what Francis felt in the wake of my sojourn. I hadn't had a moment alone with him since my return. I both dreaded and craved the trail ahead where we might find a time to talk, just the two of us. I was already racked with guilt about taking off. I didn't know if I could handle Francis's stern face and cold reception. I wanted everything to be as it was before. I wanted him to see I could be still and calm, centered and grounded. I wanted him to see that I wasn't flighty or indecisive and that I was no longer caught in the worry that this wasn't the group for me. I knew my destiny was with them now, and I wanted him to know it too.

The singing drew to a close and the service ended. I dashed out of the chapel as soon as we were done. I was glad to have joined in with the rest of the pilgrims, but I'd gotten my fill of church and suddenly felt queasy. Francis, on the other hand, was beaming as he trotted off to say his night prayers with Elliot bounding behind him.

The moment in the chapel was yet another reminder we were all guest stars in each other's distinctive Caminos and would never see the trek the same way. Our pasts were here with us, packed alongside the rest of our gear, and this changed the nature of our individual treks. I was beginning to understand that other peoples' choices and behaviors on the trail had nothing to do with me or anybody else. The experience in the church was neither purely nauseating nor completely inspiring; it was both at the very same time, carrying different truths for each of us. This light bulb realization was liberating. The physical pathway itself was the only common denominator; the land, the albergues and the towns bound us together. The rest was colored by a unique assembly of beliefs and memories, choices and desires that often had been built into our bones since birth. These elements made the journey our own as did the unique twists and turns that befell us on the trail. This intimate relationship with the environment, people and interactions created a distinctive Camino that mattered to each soul. Each of us was dealt just what we needed, and I knew now that they were never the same cards. The journey was as distinct as a fingerprint; even twins would navigate a different course along this path. The only thing we all shared was intensity. This was no stroll in the park, and no one could sleepwalk in the shallows of the current. We were all moving and being thrown about in our own ways; it was impossible not to get roughed up in the flow because sometimes we all wanted to resist where the universe was taking us.

I grew up on a farm that grew flowers, embraced the spirituality of the earth and was the hub for a flower essence company. I saw fairies when I was a small wild child. I dressed myself in bright leggings and tutus and had a whole universe to embrace. I was ever in motion and the lush terrain of my home was the setting for endless adventures. Even in the early days of my childhood, there was a current of belief and a love of the God in all things coursing through my family's farm and my soul.

As I grew into a young adult, I liked my eclectic beliefs. They were a hybrid that suited me. When I planned this trip, I knew the historical and religious underpinnings of the trail were very deep, but I was more interested in the astounding volume of earth energy held by the trail. I felt this energy couldn't be claimed by one group or organization no matter how hard they tried to own it. In the last few decades, people of all kinds had begun to fill the trail, and I felt at home among their diverse ranks.

Outside of Terradillos, Francis had asked me about my beliefs and listened to me with a contemplative ear. I tried to find the language to truly describe my faith, but the words felt elusive. A better description came through my actions and my life in motion. My connection to the universe felt like a deep internal ocean of golden light that filled every action and spilled out onto each person I loved. I imagined the description of the ebb and flow of this golden sea didn't make much sense to Francis, but I felt galvanized to explain it to him or at least give him the chance to see the waves in action.

That night, like the nights before, Elliot and Francis disappeared for evening prayer. Both had confided in me that they'd considered becoming monks. Elliot spoke about his decision not to become one with a grounded clarity, and I genuinely agreed with his assessment that his place was in the outer world. Just his relish of food, laughter and human community was proof enough he might feel caged behind monastery walls no matter the magnitude of his love for God. Francis wasn't as forthcoming with his reasons for forgoing the monastery, and he seemed to hold the memory of his time with the monks in a romantic hue as if it was a place he wished he could always belong. His nature was more suited to it, but I felt such potential in his heart. Choosing the monastic life felt like closing down a valve I wished he would open further. I hoped to see him come to life in a fuller way, not recede further into the corners of human community.

Later, as I got ready for bed, a group of pilgrims sat outside watching the moon rise. I could hear their murmuring voices down below as I took off my extra layers of clothes and crawled with bare limbs into my bunk. The light from the moon fell into the room through a small window and illuminated the boys as they moved about quietly readying themselves for sleep. John lay sprawled on top of his bunk. Elliot had borrowed my book and was lost in its pages. Tomas hopped onto the bunk above me, drew his long legs out of view and then all was still. Finally when all was quiet, Francis came back into the room, slipped into his bunk soundlessly and receded into the shadows.

EL BURGO RANERO

STAGE FOURTEEN- 28.3K- 17.6M

BERCIANOS TO MANSILLA

Leaving Bercianos, I walked alone as the moon dropped in the sky. I'd agreed to reconnect with the Brit boys and Tomas in a large village called Mansilla de las Mulas. The other group following the Roman route would be there as well. I'd left Bercianos with Elliot by my side, but he now sat somewhere behind me, leaning against a church wall and waiting for Francis and John to catch up. The dusty track clung to the side of a deserted road with frail trees lining the way. Their wiry limbs offered no shade. In a few years they might have more to give, but that morning, they looked naked and ineffectual, forming an endless single file line to the horizon. As the sun chased the fading moon from the sky, the light warmed the crown of my head. I pulled on my hat from where I stowed it on the back of my bag and slid my bandana down around my neck.

Nothing moved on the dusty open plains. I could see mountains off in the distance, but they looked days away from where I stood. All at once, I heard a bell behind me and turned just in time to see a cluster of bikers rush by. It was a group of young men, one of whom whistled as his spinning wheels flew past. He turned to look at me for a brief moment, revealing a fox like smile and a flirtatious wink. Then, as swiftly as they'd arrived, the bold stud and his fleet were gone. Their tight spandex covered butts evaporating like a mirage I'd conjured up out of a different kind of hunger.

Time on the trail was only alive within the radius of my fingertips. If the future of this journey was anything like the past few weeks, it was ripe with unknowns. I had no way of predicting, let alone imagining, the sights, places and people that would enter the scope of my trek, but all these future experiences would have to wait. Even as I waded through the endless heat of the Meseta, I could only meet with the future as quickly as my feet could get me there. And right now, that was slowly. Just as the future stayed out of sight, the past also remained locked away behind me; the present belonged to neither land. My eyes were always looking west to the horizon. I didn't reminisce about where I'd slept last night or who'd constituted my trail before this moment. People like the Dane and Alberto had become characters in an old story, and I wasn't the only one who felt this way.

Everything on the Camino looked forward, both the internal current and the mundane external world. There was a deep trail taboo about turning around and going back for any reason. I knew people who'd left gear behind because they didn't want to retrace their steps and walk into the past to retrieve it. Others went in loops when they got lost, so as not to tread on the same path twice. To walk backwards was to move against a strong current. There was almost a physical aversion to the act, a link between the emotions and the body that kept everyone on a forward trail.

If I could easily let go of the bunk I'd slept in the night before or the park I'd napped in during the afternoon, why couldn't I forget other things? If the Camino encouraged each of us to keep our view forward, why was it so hard to do this in normal everyday life? I was still haunted by locations in the history of my life, the feeling of a particular space, the texture of a piece of clothing, the smell of someone loved and lost, the thrill of contact. They were all physical landmarks in my life, and I had a nasty habit of revisiting them as if something could be changed by reviewing all the still frames. At times I even used them as a mild form of self induced torture. Yet these stories and characters were calcified in time. Going back to them didn't change the information or the feelings. It couldn't even change the outcome. I was powerless in the past, a specter of no consequence who could only watch and formulate more questions that might never be answered.

I wondered if the trail could teach me how to let these visions go, sweat out the grime of the past and literally walk away from the characters who still haunted me. I felt a dawning hope the Camino might be up for this challenge. I'd been drawn to its shores long before I understood this ancient trail only traveled forward. The Camino brought us all into the only moment that had a pulse; I hoped it would help me lay down for good everything beyond the bounds of the now.

I could feel the heat of midday approaching, and there was no tree cover for kilometers. The trail from Terradillos to Sahagún was still fresh in my mind and body, making me skittish and desperate for shade and any hint of civilization. My legs were still covered with the socks I'd bought in Sahagún. I'd cut the toes off and made them into a very odd pair of leg warmers, choosing the health of my legs over fashion. I knew Ava, Zara and Iris had already shared a giggle about the lumpy waist pack I wore slung around my hips. I'd sacrificed fashion for function with that choice and even I was a bit embarrassed about the trade off. Now I was glad they weren't around to see me in my sock monstrosities. It was already a struggle to prove my worth to these girls, and I didn't want to fall any deeper into the outcast role.

I'd come from a college where fashion was half the fun of waking up in the morning. In the counter culture world nobody cared what you wore and everybody appreciated the theatrical nature of clothing. My friends would go to class wearing combat boots and vintage couture with a fresh blue hue in their hair. It was a fishbowl of freedom, a dynamic place where clothes were dramatic and risks were exuberantly embraced. On the trail, I wasn't sure what I wanted to be or how my clothes could tell my story. They had been selected a million years ago. I'd been a different person in those hectic days before departure. The clothes I'd brought were simple and functional: two pairs of shorts, several tops that were very light with long sleeves, a few pairs of socks, and bold colored underwear. That was it. Perhaps for this chapter I'd have to settle for saying a little less than normal through my wardrobe, and for the sake of my battered legs, I'd have to run the risk of looking totally weird in an unstylish way.

I passed through the last town before Mansilla then plunged back into the white heat. I only had a few more hours before I would be forced to stop and take cover; I wanted to be in Mansilla by then. I was now living in extreme caution when it came to the sun, but I was still addicted to meeting my distance goals.

A physicist once told me the natural state of the universe is to be in motion. The real struggle arises when things are forced to stop. Energy wants to be in motion. Stillness is in many ways the less natural state, for even when we think we are 'still' we are swaying, pumping blood and breathing. I seemed to crave movement with an unquenchable thirst. I longed to stay in flight, in the flow and in the rhythm as long as possible. On the trail to Mansilla, forward momentum was easy. I had the stamina and a deepening comfort with this life. Maybe now that we were in the second half of the trail, the gravity of the land was funneling us down to the sea, drawing us all towards the end. It made me jumpy when others wanted to take breaks. I didn't always know how to moderate. I felt like a racehorse who was let out of the gates each morning and only knew one way to make it across the finish line at the end of the day. I'd come to see how unusual this was and recognized its central side affects was isolation. This was a pattern I was trying to change, but my body had a mind of its own.

The British boys loved to take breaks. They had no agenda about momentum or pull towards arrival. I'd left all of them behind on numerous occasions when I couldn't keep myself still long enough to sit with them and rest. I'd left Elliot under the eaves of the church in Burgo Ranero just this morning, and he'd seemed effortlessly relaxed. My internal engine was set in a gear that kept me moving forward, always seeking the next rise, the next cluster of buildings and the next place to stop for the night.

MANSILLA DE LAS MULAS

The trail wound itself up and over a small bridge into the outskirts of town. Mansilla was another Spanish village that had managed to hold onto its old frame of buildings, small lanes and ancient storefronts. I found my way toward the central square to try and get my bearings.

I came to a halt, struck dumb by a modern pilgrim statue at the entrance of the old town. The white stone monstrosity depicted a male pilgrim standing wearily beside the crumpled figure of a female pilgrim. Not only did it do an injustice to all pilgrim kind, but it seemed to be picking on us ladies. As a self-proclaimed badass female pilgrim, I found the obvious sexism both unoriginal and chauvinistic. I'd gathered from many Spanish perigrinos that Spanish women weren't as interested in the trail as their men-folk. Was this a cultural choice? Yes, Spanish women were bold, fiery and dynamic, but they weren't encouraged to be athletic. Was the trail considered a place of male superiority even in our modern times? The physical trials and tribulations of the trail were an equal playing field, and many of the women I'd met proved there was no weaker sex here. Or was it history creeping into view, the lingering truth that for hundreds of years this trail was populated solely by men? As a lass among lads I was the best walker in my group, and I wasn't about to let an absurd artistic rendition of the trail tell me otherwise.

As in other towns, I wasn't sure where the albergue might be, but I had time to hunt around. Most of the albergues opened between eleven and two but each had slightly different hours. To show up at the entrance before then meant a pilgrim could claim a spot in line but would have to sit against a wall outside until the doors opened. I'd been told that during the busy months on the trail, it became more important to know the albergue's hours. In the high season of July and August, pilgrims needed to be there before the doors opened to ensure a bed for the night. In the French part of the trail, pilgrims could reserve a spot in an albergue, and the places often filled up days in advance. I was thankful Spain had different rules and all the albergues lived by a first come first serve policy. This allowed for improvisation. Pilgrim knew they could change their plans at any time and still find a place to sleep.

The central square in Mansilla was a small tiled space with a circle of benches punctuating its center. People were scattered around the edges of the courtyard moving up and down the connecting roadways and drifting in and out of shops. It was Saturday, and a large crowd had gathered around a favorite local shop directly off the square. Old women with large baskets, couples linking arms and small children with sweets in hand were stuffed into the tiny shop. The two women behind the counter dodged and weaved as they pulled hot loaves of bread off the shelves and weighed bundles of fresh fruit. I didn't want to risk knocking over a fellow shopper, so I decided to wait to go into the shop until I could put my bag down.

I headed toward the cluster of park benches, fully expecting to be the first one to arrive at Mansilla. It took a moment to recognize the three familiar faces sitting there. I thought the crew walking the old Roman road would wake late and wander into town in the afternoon hours. As a group, they were notorious for sleeping in. They claimed it was a good day when they were out the door by eight, but now to my astonishment, three of them sat sprawled in park as if they had been there for hours.

Iris sat in the sun with her long legs tucked up around her chest, deep in conversation with Zara who lay on her back. Konrad lounged against Iris with his limbs splayed and his hat shielding his face from the sun. I'd often seen him like this for he only had two speeds. I marveled at the way he effortlessly shifted from action and purpose to a state of total relaxation. There was something lean and primal about the way he moved, and his pervasive silence only added to the allure. Even though his body was in rest mode, I could tell he was attuned to every inflection and energetic nuance of the words flowing from Iris. Zara had kicked off her shoes but was still decked out in her monochromatic walking ensemble and matching visor. Though I was sure they were made from expensive and high tech fibers, there was something inherently safe and boring about her clothing choices. I might be labeled quirky and strange for my fashion sense, but at least I stepped away from the mainstream. Iris also made her own fashion choices and looked positively elfin dressed in a light cotton dress that fell below her knees. Patterned in sweet garlands of pink roses on a white background, the garment made her look ethereal as if she didn't sweat or simply wasn't human. She seemed cool and comfortable as the thin strap of her dress dangled on the edge of her shoulder and the bottom hem waded up around her hips revealing a dark pair of spandex shorts. Konrad also wore his usual attire, a tight faded white shirt tucked into the waistband of light blue shorts. His socks were pulled half way up his downy legs, bleached golden from the sun. Even though I'd encountered other northern European men with such taste in socks, Konrad succeeded in conjuring effortless cool where the Dane had fallen short. He and Iris seemed to match with their soft colors and fair hair.

As I walked towards the group, I noticed Ava arrive and leap into Iris's outstretched arms. After they'd hopped around holding each other for a moment, they broke apart, and she said hello to Zara and Konrad. The British girls must have walked apart for the morning, and I wondered if it was the first time they'd spent away from each other on the trail. How rare and strange it must have felt for the intricately bound pair to be parted, even if only for a few hours. Ava dropped her pack and began to wave her hands wildly as she described her morning's walk. I hadn't seen any of them since Carrión, and I felt jittery with social energy. It was still a novelty to reconvene with familiar people along this pathway. They were like newly minted friends, and I longed to dive deeper into their circle. As I put my stuff down beside Ava's, she and Iris turned towards me and offered a set of cheerful hellos. Zara glanced over but quickly turned back to the vastly more important conversation she'd dropped to acknowledge my presence. Konrad said nothing, but I could feel his body bristle at my arrival. Zara's eyes flashed towards his, flush with words unspoken, but I couldn't see his return message. I appreciated Ava and Iris's mild enthusiasm and as I sat on the ground beside them, I asked more about their walk on the desolate Roman road. After a few minutes and several awkward pauses, Zara and Konrad's silence grew louder, pushing me to the fringes of their chatter. I'd realized back in Frómista that it would take time to infiltrate this group, and I was willing to pace myself, hoping Zara and Konrad would warm up eventually. A fellow pilgrim walked by with an ice cream cone, and I got up to go in search of one of my own, asking the group to keep an eye on my pack until I returned from the shop.

I crossed the square into a small sweets shop and came out a few minutes later with a giddy grin and a cone of bright green mint chip ice cream. The cone began to drip as soon as I stepped into the sun, but as I re-crossed the square, I realized this was the least of my worries. The courtyard was deserted, and my pack abandoned on the ground with none of its protectors in sight. I looked at my watch; it was now past eleven. They'd taken off down the street to check into the albergue and left my belongings without a second thought.

Slinging my pack over my shoulder, I was shaking with adrenaline, my mind racing as I imagined what I would have done if all my things had been stolen and my moving home had vanished. Even though I was just across the square, nobody in the group had come to give me my pack or tell me they were leaving. I felt rattled. I wished I hadn't entrusted them with my bag in the first place.

As I walked towards the albergue I read up about the place and learned it was highly recommended. Though it had no lawn, it did have a charming interior courtyard and a fresh clean feeling. After I checked in, I wandered into the sun drenched patio and found myself surrounded by walls of vivid color. In contrast to the harsh Meseta lands, the sides of the courtyard overflowed with hundreds of blooming geraniums; their bright pinks and glowing oranges transformed the walls into a breathing garden. Tables and drying racks filled the area below while a narrow stairway made of old planks rose into the sleeping rooms on the second floor. Everything was light and airy with open windows and freshly painted walls. All the surfaces felt lived in but meticulously cared for, welcoming us like guests in a friend's home. After our walk tomorrow, the Meseta would be a thing of the past. This comfortable place felt like a fitting transition into the next stage of the journey and the lush lands that led to the sea.

The British boys had arrived but were still out in the street buying lunch, so I was on my own when picking a bunk. I peered into the first room on the right and found Zara sitting on one of the bottom bunks. The three girls, Konrad and Tomas had claimed beds in the room, but there was one empty bed left. As I stood in the doorway, I felt my pulse skip a beat. Part of me wanted to move on to the next room, but I knew this was my window. I needed to show no fear or hesitation. If I wanted to be close to this group it was now or never. I had to prove I deserved the open spot in their lair. I could ignore Zara's chilly looks and in doing so perhaps cultivate friendships with Ava, Iris, Tomas and maybe even the gruff and laconic Konrad. Even though Ava and Iris came together as best friends, they'd made space in their friendship for Zara. There had to be room for one more. I longed to be included in the girls' boisterous fun. My track record with all female posses wasn't very promising, but I'd changed. Maybe this dynamic could too. Female peers of the past had misunderstood my reserve as chilly unfriendliness and had strong reactions to the way I didn't play by the cultural rules. Yet this situation was a fresh slate. New faces in a new place. What was the worst that could happen? I decided to find out, and threw my bag on the last empty bunk, welcoming myself into the lion's den. Perhaps I was in for another dose of schoolyard bullying, but I had to take that risk.

In the past few days, afternoons had taken on a peaceful quality that didn't exist in my early Camino life. Today, I sat in the bright courtyard with Elliot and Francis munching on slices of cheese and crusty bread. I tipped back in my chair and luxuriated in the company of the boys. Our wash hung on the metal racks sprawled across the patches of sun as I arched my back, stretched my arms in the air and sipped peach juice from a carton. The sun was high and bright, but we were draped in the shade of the building. Around us we could hear the activity of other pilgrims unpacking, showering and washing their clothes in the outdoor sinks. A gaggle of Italian men walked by in nothing but their underwear while a couple of French women sang a duet in the kitchen. I felt right at home. I was no longer walking in the afternoons but resting and napping in the company of others. Mellow afternoons were as they should be, and I was ever so grateful. As the guys ate their lunch with gusto I relished having found my place.

The trail was helping me make peace with the sorrows of the last few years. It was showing me that nothing had been destroyed by my struggles. I hadn't lost irreplaceable pieces of myself or been broken irrevocably. It was hard to think back to relationships of the past and not cringe, feel bereft and stupid or all of the above. It was hard to release my self from a sense of shame or guilt over whom I'd loved and how much I'd given them in the process. Yet in the last few weeks, I'd felt a revolution brewing inside me; I was beginning to feel differently about the past. I could suddenly feel all the muscles I'd built up in these battles. I could see my own courage and fortitude. But above and beyond it all, I realized how well my young adulthood had trained me to listen and follow the universe's guidance. Every trial and tribulation had worked on a different muscle group, helped me dial into a deeper frequency and often left me with little else to turn to but myself. I'd jumped hoops and chased the thread of my life because I somehow knew it was the only way to survive. For many years I'd resented the struggle, but that view was changing, shifting and blooming before my eyes. I was leaving the past with each step, shedding what had been but marveling in how much of the good remained with me, how much of the growth I got to keep. There were areas of my life I still wanted to tie down, shore up and lock in, but the trail had become the playground on which I could breathe and let some of that pressure dissolve. I couldn't control the details, but I didn't need to, for I had something better than control. I had trust.

When Elliot and Francis disappeared upstairs for a nap, I joined Ava, Iris, Konrad and Zara on a scouting mission to a shallow but fast moving river on the west side of town. The girls flopped down on the grass and opened the chocolate treats they'd bought before siesta hours. Busy licking their fingers and lolling in the shady grass, they temporarily forgot about swimming. Konrad roused a small group to go in the water, and the rest of us fell into a sleepy silence. Feeling restless and slightly out of place, I slipped away to wander back through the town's twisting maze of streets. I didn't know what I was searching for but eventually decided to seek the sanctuary of a nap.

I peeked into the Brit boys' room when I returned. Elliot was asleep with my book covering his face, and Francis dozed peacefully on his back. Their room was cool and dark, an inviting space not my own. I closed the door silently, a bit disappointed Francis wasn't awake. Group life was stuffed to the gills with other people, and since our reunion in Bercianos, Francis and I had had little more than stolen fragments of conversations. I craved time to talk with him about everything that had happened since Terradillos. I longed to be back in his inner circle and close the way we'd been. Instead of breaking into his siesta dreams, I returned to my empty room. The space was unbearably hot and thick. My sleeping bag roasted under me and clung to my clammy skin as I tossed and turned.

When I awoke, my face was stuck to my bag's silky shell. I noticed some of my roommates had come and gone, dropping things, dumping out their packs and changing clothes. When I found my way downstairs, John told me Zara and Tomas were making a group dinner for us. The two of them were already in the kitchen opening slim packets of pasta and drinking wine from plastic cups.

The rest of the group sat around a table in the shaded courtyard. Konrad had found a guitar and was bent over it, concentrating on the delicate strings and the movement of his fingers. Ava and Iris sat at the head of the table breaking into laughter while swigging wine straight from the bottle. Iris played with her blonde hair and rolled her eyes at Ava's jokes. Both managed to make their bold drinking habits seem sexy and alluring. Francis had kept a seat open for me next to him on the far side of the table, and I caught his eyes as I moved towards him. As I sat down, half asleep, I pulled my unruly curls into some semblance of a ponytail; I was sure I looked as if I'd just awoken from a wrestling match with my sleeping bag. My vision was blurred, and my limbs felt loose. It had become automatic to gravitate to Francis's side and to be near him as much as possible. I'd taken the seat next to him almost unconsciously and felt more comfortable because he was there.

Even a celebratory style meal such as this was a social audition that caused my stomach to churn. It was as if the Brit boys and I had finally arrived on the other group's radar and been admitted provisionally into the outer ring of their journey. I sensed Elliot, John and most especially Francis had very little interest in venturing past this easy ring. They didn't need to; they had each other. Their social card was full, and none of them struck me as friend collectors in search of total peer acceptance. Elliot enjoyed the laughs. John liked the entertainment. Francis, on the other hand, seemed a bit wary of Ava's posse but was willing to play along to keep harmony among his group. As I sat beside him I could feel his thoughts wandering, his body sinking back from the center of the action. He really was the rare guy who craved solitude and intimacy over this kind of event, and the trait endeared him to me even more. I loved his clear preference for open spaces, easy silence and the deep connection with just one other person. There was a side of me that felt the very same way.

As Elliot and John took seats opposite me, Ava continued to ramble on while the rest of us listened with amusement. Elliot was the most outgoing of the Brit guys. He had a whimsical sense of humor and interjected into the main conversation often, but the rest of us sat back like spectators. Zara and Tomas made a grand entrance with a massive pot slung between them, and it was just in time, for the girls were in need of some food to fill their wine soaked stomachs. The large vessel held several pounds of steaming red pasta flecked with gooey white cheese and threads of spinach. The muscles in Zara's arms strained as she stirred the massive coil of noodles and heaved large clumps onto outstretched plates. There were nine of us crammed around two rectangular tables, elbows bumping and feet knocking into each other below deck. I laughed as the boys twirled and shoveled pasta into their mouths, while Ava made a toast to our feast.

It never ceased to amaze me how much men could eat. As the piles of pasta disappeared into thin air, I began to feel the boys had some sort of hidden second stomach I didn't possess. Elliot and Tomas took seconds, thirds and then helped me finish my plateful. Elliot smiled and rubbed his belly as he finished my portion. There was something very cheery about his enjoyment at being over-stuffed. Ava sat at the head of the table giving them a run for their money. She grinned at me as I handed her a large second helping, telling me she never felt there was any reason to decline the offer of more.

Ava had a voracious appetite for all things. She wasn't satisfied with just a taste or a few hours of fun. She wanted more. She wanted it all. She wanted it forever. She consumed the pleasures of life, each relationship and every moment to the fullest. For Ava it was all or nothing. There was something free and appealing about such a lust for life, the way each experience was lived to its height, the way it seemed to open her up and let everything flow. But as I felt into the energy of her appetite for living, it left a funny aftertaste. It felt as if she had so much riding on sensation that she'd lost all feeling of roots. There was too much happening in her energy field, too many strands from the outer world spinning in and out. What was all the hyper stimulation about? What was Ava in search of or avoiding? For her, was this journey only about the realm of tactile experience?

As the meal wound down, Iris asked the group a series of questions. She wanted to know would we rather be a little too full or a little too hungry? Ava shouted her answer across the space, and it was, of course, a confident vote for fullness. When my turn came I chose the opposite side. I choose hunger. The past five years could have answered the question for me. They were marked by deep lines of hunger in all areas of my life. I still felt my life was leaning in a direction that always kept me on edge, hungry for something just beyond my reach. I could see the way this had shaped who I was, shaped my fear of being alone on the trail and my sense I would have to fight for everything I wanted. My hunger kept me focused on the life fuel I lacked, but it also made me frail and withdrawn. I'd lived all my adult life with some level of hunger for romantic love. Hunger had fueled my dance, my need to express myself and be seen, but now I felt it was a weary choice, a choice that kept me off balance and disconnected from myself. Ava had clearly made a different choice. She'd opted for a life that was overstuffed with activity, people, places, sights, sounds and tastes. Yet I sensed deep down, she had many of the same feelings about her choices as I did about mine. To be overfilled was still uncomfortable, exhausting and disconnected in its own way. All the activity weakened her bond to herself and the genuine flow of her life just as much as hunger did. We'd chosen two sides of the spectrum, yet neither was optimal; neither was balanced.

When we finished dinner, a woman with a large head of blonde dreads began to play the guitar and sing. As our table lolled in a food coma, she came over to ask if anybody knew how to play. Zara offered to give it a try, and we began to sing. The random songs were chosen whenever a few of us knew the words and Zara knew the chords. There were twenty or thirty people sitting at other tables in the courtyard finishing their meals. They fell into a hush as voices rose from our table. As we put on a rough impromptu concert, the singing drew us closer, sealing something into the framework of the group that hadn't been there before. The Brit boys had such wonderful voices that we all sounded better in harmony with them. There was something timeless about the moment as if we had been here before, joined in song along this trail once long ago in a time none of us could recall.

The growing stillness in the albergue encouraged us to draw the singing to an end and make our way to bed. It felt like summer camp in our room as people rummaged through their stuff, went to brush their teeth and crawled into their bunks. I lay inside my sleeping bag with my legs and arms out as far as possible.

Ava and Iris complained about the oppressive heat, while Tomas rubbed his knees, dangling them off his high bunk across from mine. I could see worried thoughts darting around inside him. He had been struggling with his knees for the past few days, and his anxiety about injury was shifting before my eyes into worry about being left behind.

Tomas had been walking for more than three months. He'd stepped out his front door in Belgium and begun to walk towards Santiago. After all his time walking alone, I could see Tomas feared the pain of losing community more than he feared the physical pain in his knees. I felt the same way only to a much smaller degree. My achilles were still causing me problems, but they were healing. Tomorrow the walk was only eighteen kilometers into the city of León. It would be a shorter day and kinder on all of us slightly injured pilgrims. While Tomas continued to tend to his knees, the girls still moved about in high activity. Konrad lay sprawled on his mattress with his hands behind his head, allowing his eyes to drift shut for moments at a time. Other than Tomas, I knew so little about each of these people in the room. I was now socially part of their circle but couldn't say my foot was in the door yet. There was something impenetrable about them, something guarded and elusive. The lights went out, and I threw my sleeping bag off. My legs were hot and sticky, and the air rested thickly on my chest. I wondered if Francis and the Brit boys had already drifted off to sleep in their cool room. As people started to go silent, nothing remained but the tossing and turning of restless sleepers.

PLAZA DE SANTA ANA

STAGE FIFTEEN- 18.6K-11.6M
MANSILLA TO LEÓN

Over breakfast I plucked up the courage to ask Zara if she would walk with me during the morning trek to León. I knew she was my toughest critic, and if I managed to sway her into camp Elizabeth, then the rest of the group would likely follow. She was the gatekeeper of what I had come to call the Iron Six. This group, forged in the fires of early Camino tribulations, consisted of Ava, Iris, Konrad, Tomas, Jay and Zara. There were ranks within the group, and I knew it would matter little to warm up someone like Jay who was low on the totem pole. Getting to know Zara was the most vital step if I hoped to get anywhere with their tribe. Above and beyond that, we were the oldest members of our Camino community, living more adult lives than the rest of the school bound gang. We were also the only two girls who'd come to the Camino on our own. I was encouraged by all this overlap and genuinely curious about her life down under.

I acted more confident than I felt and boldly plunged into the situation, because I had an ace up my sleeve no matter how my chat with Zara went. My honorary membership in the Brit boys and American guys man-camp was growing each day, and I felt proud to be among their ranks. The trail was the first time in my life I'd been consistently outnumbered by men. My college was seventy percent women, and half of the meager male population was openly and happily gay. The school had been all female for most of its history, and the vibe still lingered. Though I loved my gay guy friends very much, I graduated feeling I was still a bit clueless about the culture of men. Being a dancer didn't help as the field was notorious for its lack of straight men. I topped my college years by working at a small and isolated boarding school where I taught artsy teenagers with a tiny group of graying faculty. Now I found myself, at twenty-four years of age, without having spent much time with young men.

It was thrilling to discover how much I enjoyed the company of men on this trail. They could match me stride for stride and wanted to talk about the inner workings of life as well. I liked that they were rarely catty and enjoyed companionable silences as much as I did. There was something effortlessly fun about these men. They didn't leer or creep around me like many men before them had but moved beyond the surface of my appearance. I was proud my solo strength and open friendliness endeared me to them instead of igniting feelings of irritation or rivalry. It was a delightful surprise to be suddenly submerged in a sea of men, but there were things that existed in close female friendships that I missed, and I couldn't help wanting to win over a few female pilgrims.

As we left the albergue, Ava, Iris, Zara and I moved as a group. Crossing a bridge, the four of us found the trail tucked between a straight flat road and fields filled with young crops. Zara and I walked side by side while Ava and Iris followed behind us lost in their own conversation. Zara currently lived in London but was from Melbourne. After the trail, she planned to go back to London to reestablish life with her businessman boyfriend then return to Australia to start business school. She was only a year older than me but in an entirely different place in her life, and as the morning wore on, I felt we had almost no overlap except our year of birth.

She had a long-term boyfriend, lived in a city and was enrolled in graduate school. Her life was pinned down and mapped out years in advance. I, on the other hand, felt as if all the pieces of my life had just been thrown up into the air and burst apart by some sort of explosive device. I'd just ended a relationship, been let go from my job along with other young faculty and exiled from a community; I had absolutely no idea what came next. My view into the future was terrifyingly open and unknown. For Zara this was a holiday, a stopgap between the bigger events of her life; for me, this was a life raft and a launching pad all in one. It was shelter from the emptiness of endings and a sprung coil ready to fling me into the unknown. Zara knew how her days would look for the next five years; I wasn't even sure how I would be getting back to the states after the trail.

As we talked, I struggled to sink beneath the surface and learn something more than the details of her outer life. I longed for an emotional foothold, a place to build a real connection, but it never came. While she did not bare her teeth or hiss at my questions, she was clearly unwilling to engage in anything more than surface chitchat. Her energy field was rock solid and her affect slightly bored. We swiftly came to a place where we ran out of things to say.

As Zara and I reached the modern and industrial outskirts of León, Ava and Iris came forward to join our conversation. It was diverting to walk with Ava and nice to have girls there to watch out when I needed to duck into the trailside brush to pee. If I'd been male, I might not have needed such protection and foliage coverage. I'd already stood by a dozen times while the men in our group had turned their backs and peed off the side of the trail not more than a few feet from me. Even Francis, with his code of modesty, had done so on our first day walking the Meseta together. Apparently guys were nonplussed about sharing the moment; I was both envious and slightly annoyed they didn't have to go wading off into the scrub.

We hadn't been on the dusty path very long before a large billboard welcomed us into the city suburbs. Its gleaming surface loomed over the sidewalk with a picture of a woman in a tiny set of matching lingerie. Her long silky hair dripped down her shoulders, and her deep red mouth was parted seductively.

Our group came to a collective stop and looked upon the cultural cancer we all knew so well.

"Bloody fuck." Ava retorted. All of us nodded in silent agreement with her apt assessment of the situation. This was one reason it was so tough to be a woman in our modern world. This open-mouthed come hither, rail thin, mostly naked woman was impossible to contend with and just one of millions of similar images that filled our lives. I realized I hadn't seen such familiar media shit in weeks and had found the dearth thoroughly relaxing. These pervasive images created a culture that pulled female friendships into competition and caused delusional beliefs that women could and should be plucked, waxed, coifed, tanned, toned and sexually available twenty-four seven. It was the imaginary charade that this was womanhood. I found it a degrading lie we were forced to live with.

The stream of curses coming from the very real woman next to me only confirmed I wasn't alone in chafing against the rules placed on women of our generation. Here we were, four women brave enough, strong enough and bold enough to travel across a whole country by foot, and yet we were still under the shadow of this cultural pressure. Literally! We were still shamed about who we were and how we stacked up to impossible standards. It made me feel sick. Why weren't there pictures of girls like us up there, badass pilgrim chicas who were doing something rather than simply being something? When did it become OK for women to just be; to embrace passivity and values based purely on looks? When did we become little more than two dimensional images? Why was every media outlet churning out stories about girls who just looked cool rather than girls who went out and did awesome things proving their three dimensional coolness? What would the life of young girls be like if they were encouraged to be more than an image, to seek action and motion, activity and bold choices? What if we became a culture that praised attractive deeds and beautiful works of action rather than attractive bodies and beautiful features? Would us Camino girls be sudden cover girls? Would youth be a more rewarding experience and aging less of a loaded one? Would life feel fuller and more vibrant for the millions who watched the few, rather than the opposite way around? Would girls need bodies with muscles and strength that could do more than pose?

Not only did it teach men what to expect from female kind, but the current media expectations had the power to conquer and divide us from each other. The propaganda set us at odds and kept us from finding solace or supportive community in which to make choices that defied the norm. It also presented a toxic and shallow ideal for young men. I was deeply irritated to have so little recourse against the powerful gleaming image, to know that the people who produced the picture and added to a corrosive culture wouldn't hear our invectives and simply didn't care. Though I did enjoy Ava's enthusiasm in trying. I swear she would have thrown her shoes at the billboard if she hadn't needed them to walk with. It was a constant battle, and the more of us engaged in it the better.

As the trail dove into the city, it clung to a noisy highway and widened its berth. I walked at the front of the group as we dashed across the road and hugged the guardrail on the long descent down into the city. Our talk shifted as the four of us entered León. Zara described a wedding she'd attended the week before she'd left for Spain. I felt us all rush into a state of frenzied excitement; no topic could bring forward more emotions, interest and discussion among a group of women than weddings.

The group shifted to a place of total focus. Ava's voice became low and strong, while Iris smiled non-stop. Each of us took turns gushing. It felt as if we were talking about an unimaginably delicious dish we'd been told about in mouthwatering details, shown the recipe to and smelled the ingredients for but had yet to taste. We could savor the idea of it rolling around inside our palates, yet there was a deep element of the unknown.

Despite our differing sensibilities, marriage seemed to matter greatly to all of us. Zara seemed slightly smug during the conversation, and when she made a comment, it was in a matter of fact, nonchalant tone. I wondered if there was no longer as much mystery or uncertainty for her. Maybe the place of the faceless groom was filled in her mind's eye with her current boyfriend, giving her a clear edge over the rest of us. Somehow, I wasn't convinced the boyfriend in London was "the one," though I guessed she might marry him anyways. I sensed she liked being at the top of the heap, first to the finish line no matter what.

When her turn came, Iris spoke about her wedding day in a soft voice as if lost in the theatrics of the day. I knew she was picturing the vintage clothing, detailing each voluminous curve of her dress. Everything down to the fabric's vibrancy and texture leapt forward in her imagination. It was as if she could see the image, but had little understanding of the energy or emotion of the moment. There was something very guarded about that area of her life. She hadn't once spoken about love, romance or men around me and seemed deeply contained when it came to matters of the heart.

In my case, the event and the details of the day were never important, the moment in time was just a threshold to a new life. Though I was independent, I was made for such a partnership. I longed to build a life with a good man by my side and creating a home for the children I'd always dreamed of. It was the ultimate sense of belonging and the dream by which I navigated. It was a north star I'd been following for many years.

Yes, I enjoyed the visions of wedding dresses and romantic ceremonies, but they were dust compared to the life that came after, the hours, days, months and years that would follow. I'd spent so many years thinking about this while knowing I was still too young, biding my time and being patient. I'd been given a choice of birthday cake decorations when I was eight years old, and from the large store filled with a million baubles, I selected a bride and groom. Little had changed since that day.

Except now I'd arrived into adult life, and I could live the dream in the present. This knowledge hung heavy around my chest. The feeling it was now time and yet love hadn't arrived was the weightiest item I carried in my pack. I'd imagined marrying both of the men I'd loved and though I saw the supreme gifts in parting from them, I still felt as much at the starting gate as ever. Blank slate. Begin again. Wait for a stranger up ahead in the unknown.

The city of León came into view as we followed the busy highway down a steep pitch. A flock of bikers advanced towards us, wearing official looking outfits with numbers strapped to their chests. There were over a hundred of them. Some were off their seats pushing hard and passing their fellow riders with intensity. Others sat back and chatted with the bikers around them. Most were young, but some were middle aged and had the telltale belly hanging down near the handlebars. A few glanced over at us. One even yelled a cheerful hello. I wasn't surprised. We were a collection of young, mostly blonde girls, and Spanish men enjoyed the harmless flirt even when peddling up an impossible incline.

The city looked much bigger than any I'd encountered on the trail with the spires of its famous cathedral gleaming a radiant white in the distance. I knew it wasn't the most populated along the Camino, but the valley was filled to the brim with a sprawling metropolis. Besides Pamplona, it was the only city we walked through that I was familiar with before leaving Spain. The arrows would lead us down into the old part of the city near the cathedral to an albergue run by Benedictine nuns.

Jack and Ivan had arranged to meet us there, but I wasn't sure if they would pull it off. Walking through the night to enrich their trail experience might have been too much. Hiking by the light of the moon on an old Roman road certainly sounded epic and fit with the duo that dreamed big, but I wasn't certain they would enjoy the night trek as much as they imagined. I hoped they hadn't overestimated their prowess, but even if they had, they would make it into a great story, and we would live vicariously through their travails.

In the past few days, I'd heard much of Jack and Ivan's pre-trail training regimens including dragging rocks across a field for endurance and throwing knives at tree stumps. Ivan had met his girlfriend during one attempt at warrior training. He and a buddy had been improving their endurance by running up and down a flight of dormitory stairs wearing a thirty-pound set of chain mail. His friend had passed out on the second floor landing and Ivan's future girlfriend had rushed to their aid. From there love was born, or so the story went.

When Ivan wasn't discussing the need to build strength in his sword arm, he was explaining the ways pirate tales taught valuable lessons in strategy. I'd spent many years training as a dancer and during the long days of endless movement, I'd known the life of a warrior. I could see this journey was Jack and Ivan's first true experience of such a physical challenge. Theory was becoming practice, and the metamorphosis was unfolding before our eyes. We all wondered if they would meet the challenge and get to León.

And of course it was a Sunday. I had a particular skill for arriving in cities on the one day of the week when all the supermercados were closed. It was ironic to be in places that offered the best choice of food and yet find myself unable to buy anything I could take with me. The shops in the outskirts of town were shuttered and dark as we passed through the outer ring of the city. The arrows threaded us deeper and deeper into the swarming metropolis. Our conversations drifted to a halt as we took in new sights and sounds. Contrasts on the trail were often overwhelming. The way we moved from the open isolation of ancient villages to the fast moving cogs of modern cities was jarring. The lights signaled for us to cross a four lane intersection, and the arrows led into a small park filled with benches, tightly manicured grass and tall palm trees. Busy city dwellers traversed the web of sidewalks, slicing through the park with determined speed, but one figure remained stationary like a fixed point.

Konrad sat on a lone bench with his arms crossed behind him, cradling his head. Beside the bench sat his abandoned boots, stuffed with a pair of dusty socks. It was his routine to take off his shoes at the end of each day's walk. He stood as we came along and picked his boots up by the laces to walk with us towards the albergue. Once he was standing, I couldn't help noticing the length of his torso. It was if he was stretched in one smooth line from clavicle to pelvis. I'd observed his lean body before, but with one sudden movement, I saw how attractive he was and wondered what it would feel like to touch him. He'd been so grumpy since our first meeting I'd always overlooked his physical attributes.

We moved in a clump, but Konrad hung near the back with Iris. Crossing roads, sidewalks and bits of city green, his bare feet collected a layer of black dirt. Even though he was away from the open land, he wouldn't let the mire of the city stop him from going barefoot. I'd also lived a life of bare feet, unbound by shoes. Each toe took its own stretch as the many bones of my feet absorbed the shock when limbs and ground met. One of my professors had told me the physics of feet meeting the ground was a sly trick of the universe. The ground was encouraged by the forces of the earth to rise and push our bodies away as gravity anchored us down. Each step was a dance of forces beyond our control.

THE OLD CITY

The albergue was closed when we turned up the lane at eleven o'clock, but there were already thirty bags lined up along the wall next to the entrance. Clearly, we were in the second wave of pilgrims entering the city that day, and all we could do was claim a spot in line. The albergue held ninety beds, but the number was a moot point. Some pilgrims were always worried about claiming a bunk no matter the size or season. The number of pilgrims afflicted with this nervous territorialism and scarcity model only grew worse as the summer wore on. As we walked toward the line of bags, I wondered where all these people dispersed to when not in the city albergues. Most of the people milling about were unfamiliar faces and hadn't stayed with us in Mansilla. Cities acted as collecting pools, depots where many pilgrims began their journey and others departed.

We placed our bags at the end of the line and made camp against the wall on the other side of the street. It would only be a short wait for the doors to open, but Ava and Iris pulled out their remaining food, constructing bread and cheese sandwiches on the tail end of a baguette. Zara read her guidebook hoping to locate the closest post office, and Konrad talked softly with Iris, flexing his feet every so often to reveal his blackened soles.

When the doors opened, the throng of pilgrims broke into a flurry of activity, darting to the door like moths to a flame. We collected our things and took our spot while I nodded to a few familiar faces ahead of us. Knowing people this way made the trail feel like a hometown. One of the familiar faces was a Spanish woman and her husband whom I'd seen several times in the past two weeks. Even though we'd only spoken once in broken Spanish, I felt she was looking out for me, and I would never be without help if she and her mild-mannered husband were around. I wondered if they had a daughter my age; they seemed so accustomed to their role as parents that they couldn't help but care for young strays like me. Maybe there was something in the way I moved or spoke that helped them connect the tenderness they felt for their own children to my weary frame. Whatever the reason, I was grateful for the extra buffer of warmth.

After several minutes, Francis and Elliot arrived at the back of the line. We waved them forward. The front was moving lethargically, but our group buzzed with chatter. As we drew close to the check in point, I listened to the pilgrims stating their home nation, age and starting point. The pilgrim records were no laughing matter on the trail, especially when staying with nuns.

Suddenly there were hands on my shoulders. I jumped slightly, spun around and saw Ivan beaming from ear to ear. His tan was more red than brown, but his body looked rested and bubbled with energy. My face broke into a matching grin. I'd doubted, but the American guys had prevailed. I was happy to have been wrong and pleased they'd survived to keep their promise. It was especially generous of them to reconnect since it brought them back into the sphere of the Iron Six. The guys had never been resistant to meeting new people, but Ivan was clearly put off by the vibes of Ava's group, and I could sense Zara and Konrad's barely concealed disdain for him. But for the moment, I didn't care about the brewing drama and hugged both boys with genuine excitement.

With Ivan and Jack back in our midst, a missing puzzle piece had returned to our fellowship. From the joy on John's face, it was obvious the Brit boys felt the same way. Ivan and Jack had spent the night before last on the trail, walking under a full moon. They'd arrived in León yesterday then dropped into a day and night of recovery sleep. Today their energy was restored. In fact, they could have used a walk to take the edge off their buzz.

After checking in at the front desk, we girls were led into the bowels of the building to the women's quarters. It was the first time since the beginning of the trail that I would be in a room filled only with women. The men's quarters were on the top floor. The guys climbed a short set of stairs on the side of the courtyard and then disappeared into the all male realm. There was something mysterious about being separated by gender. It felt like summer camp with boys' and girls' bunkhouse and created a level of curiosity that was rather unfounded.

I followed Zara down into a dingy cellar filled with thirty bunks. The room was empty at this early hour, and since we were in the basement, it was deliciously dark and cool. Ava and Zara were especially thrilled to be able to change without the need for covert stealth. Even though we were now practiced in the art of changing clothes without revealing too much to a room full of strangers, it was relaxing not to have to go to such measures. On top of that, we could all appreciate a night without strange old men wandering about in their saggy tighty whities. As we unpacked, Ava swaggered around the bunks, imitating the offending characters and dropping us all into gasping laughter.

The room was broken up into groups of four beds. Two bunks on the top and two on the bottom. Ava and Iris claimed the top, and Zara and I took the bottom. The math made it obvious I would be part of the equation, but I still felt a thrill of delight to be included in the group. Zara had been perfectly cordial as I set up my sleeping bag, and I felt a sense of calm growing. OK, so we didn't have the easiest of bonding sessions today, but that wouldn't stop me up from sinking deeper into the Iron Six fabric. The bunk arrangements felt like proof that change was happening.

Even though it was noon, the basement was dim. The only windows in the space were small squares that looked out to the street at foot level. As sets of feet walked by, I wondered if people sometimes stopped to look in. I was glad my bunk was on the far side away from the windows. I didn't put it past Spanish men to peer into a room of female pilgrims in hopes of a lucky glimpse.

The central courtyard of the albergue was enormous and cold with a few parking spots for the apartments next to the nunnery. Only a small alcove near the door was slightly inviting with a cluster of tables and chairs grouped together. Despite its lack of charm, this area was the gathering spot. Split by men and women's quarters, this place became our Switzerland and the central hub for our group during the afternoon and evening.

When I emerged from the all female dungeon, Jack and Ivan were regaling the Brit boys with their night adventures. The boys smiled as I pulled a chair out and sat down. As my attempts to crack the circle of girls amped up, I felt physical relief at being among my guy posse again. I needed a soft place to land, and these five boys had my allegiance first. Jack and Ivan were a tight duo, but I knew they felt close to me since our meeting in Burgos. Perhaps it was the fact we were all Americans, or all from the same area in the states, or that Jack went to the same college as my sister, or that Ivan had spent a summer studying at my college in Vermont. Or maybe they just loved how I laughed at all their jokes and was willing to be bold and zany right along with them. But I chalked much of it up to how far we three had come.

In my early days on the trail, I'd met many Spaniards walking the Camino in sections. They'd walk a part one year, saving the next stage for the following year or years depending on how many pieces they broke the journey into. Europeans typically asked me how much of the trail I was planning on walking. They seemed to have a failure of imagination about the geographical and cultural distance it took for me to arrive on the Camino, and why for a handful of major reasons, this journey had to be a stem to stern trek. I always laughed a bit after the question then told them I was going all the way to the coast. This journey was no holiday; this was my odyssey. Just getting to the first step had been a major undertaking. Now so far from home, I wouldn't allow myself to stop short of the finish. I wouldn't be done until I stood at the sea.

The friendly pilgrims who asked such questions had often hopped a train or bus to arrive at the trail. They had taken a week off from work to walk on familiar terrain. Home with all its comforts and complications was relatively close by. The pathway was a known quantity, involving a culturally accepted activity. Most people in America had never heard of the Camino, let alone understood the tradition of pilgrimage.

Jack and Ivan knew what it had taken to get here. They knew it in a way that none of the Europeans could. Each of the other members of our group had the ability, at any moment, to get on train and be home within a day. There was a safety net in being able to step back into their old life at any moment. Perhaps that was why the trail held different challenges for them. The ease with which they could get on and off the trail could also be a temptation. It might make it hard to stick it out when the escape route was so accessible. Yet the American guys moved forward with a marked difference from me; they had each other and I was flying solo. Nonetheless I hoped we would stay connected for the duration of the trail, linked like family members: odd, theatrical cousins who regularly drove each other to laughter and the brink of insanity.

After an hour of tall tales from Jack and Ivan, Ava and Iris came running over to me with a bounce in their step. The very distinct sparkle in their eyes could mean only one thing. They were on the hunt for chocolate and knew I would want to be included. As Ava and Iris chatted with the boys, I collected my wallet, and we organized a hunting party. The Brits and the Americans decided to stay at the albergue, but Konrad, Zara and Tomas joined our group. Jay and Luc had disappeared along the Roman road a few days ago, and none of us were sure where they had gone. Neither Tomas nor Konrad seemed worried, so I assumed all was well.

I said goodbye to the guys and joined the search for sugary delights. Tomas walked at the front with me, while Ava, Zara, Iris and Konrad trailed behind. Since the night in Bercianos, I found it easy to be with Tomas. He was always willing to include me both in action and attitude without the slightest hesitation. There was an open kindness in his manner and no hidden agendas. He seemed incapable of lying and blushed often. I found the reflex endearing and felt myself gravitate to his side.

Closed off from car traffic, the main street in León was a wide cobbled boulevard that rose uphill to the open courtyard around the cathedral. The large promenade was thick with people out in the bright afternoon. The edges of the road were lined with overflowing cafes. Families and clusters of hip young adults moved past in swarms, crossing paths with the occasional clump of American tourists. As I moved around an English speaking family, I felt like a tourist in the land of tourists. My life on Spanish soil felt a million miles away from their reality. I was grateful for my experience of Spain: its heat and dust, desolate villages and vast skies. I'd earned an intimate friendship with the trail and every place along its route. I no longer felt like an observer to this culture, making a brief moon landing. The trail had given me the gift of residency. Because we pilgrims were willing to follow an invisible thread, we could see this world differently and feel at home here even though we had no permanent address. I suddenly longed to get back on the trail, to flee León with my band of fellows and return to the flow.

I'd only been within the city limits for a couple of hours. How could I already want to leave so desperately? I tried to match Tomas's steps, fill my eyes with activity and saturate my senses. The shops were mostly fancy clothing boutiques and cafes which hummed with conversation while people crammed around dainty tables cluttered with half eaten meals. Groups of friends smoked, drank coffee and nibbled on desserts. Tomas announced he was looking for ice cream and asked me if I would join him for a scoop. As I stood in the hot glare, the thought of ice cream sent my taste buds into a frenzy. I nodded enthusiastically, and Tomas turned to ask the rest of the group if they wanted some as well. Swiveling around beside Tomas, I was hardly able to see more than a few feet back down the roadway. The space swarmed and vibrated with the movement of hundreds of people, and I didn't recognize a single familiar face. No set of blonde heads or guy in bare feet. The group had vanished. Tomas and I had been set adrift.

Tomas turned to me, shrugged his shoulders and nodded towards a café with a large ice cream bar in the front window. I chose coffee and he picked lemon. The cathedral was closed so all we could do was stand beneath it and look up, licking our cones before they melted. The cathedral weighted the whole space at the center of the city. It was so tall I had to let my head fall back to view the vast, ornate and inhuman structure. I thought back to the small village churches we'd passed in the days before and knew I preferred their rough but sturdy walls to soaring spikes.

We wandered back towards the albergue down unfamiliar side streets, moving against the churning current of people. Unperturbed by the turn of events, Tomas didn't say much, and I let the silence be. Not only was I confused by the swift exit of our companions in the central square, but it seemed that all of León was blooming and ripe with life. Everywhere I turned pregnant women walked by, long dresses hanging off their large bellies and a warm flush to their skin. I saw at least half a dozen men holding small infants to their chests, cradling heads and slinging the squirming toddlers onto one hip. With each sighting my chest contracted tighter, and my quiet state grew deeper. I didn't want to be chasing groups of youngsters trying to pin them down until they declared friendship. I wanted this life of young couples and babies that was swirling around me. I didn't want to be a kid backpacking across a foreign land alone anymore; the glamour of the solo adventure was gone. I was tired of jumping hoops for the girls and the rest of the Iron Six. I was sorry Tomas had been a casualty of the social maneuvering, a sacrificial lamb to the slaughter. He could see my spirits were nose-diving and tried to cheer me up with stories of his earlier trail days. I tried to stay focused on his voice, avoid lingering views of baby prams with graceful umbrellas and wobbling kids in hip little sneakers.

I was thankful for Tomas's cheerfulness. It was such a gift. I'd often felt the general perception about cheerfulness was all backwards. Cheerful people were often criticized as being naïve or unbothered by the cares of the world, silly or just plain crazy, but this was rarely the case. To be cheerful was a much harder and more beautiful gesture to give the world than to be cynical, dark and moody. Those were easy slopes to slide down and lazy dark spaces for people to dwell. I knew this moment with its tense group dynamics wasn't easy for Tomas, and he had faced many other rough spots along the trail as well, but he was still trying to be cheerful and add to the light around him. I felt better, and it calmed me to be close to his sturdy frame as we pushed our way back to our temporary home.

When we arrived back I was less than surprised to find Ava and Iris asleep in the women's quarters. The remnants of a giant chocolate pastry lay abandoned next to Ava's head as she slept. The croissant must have been the size of her head but was now almost completely decimated. They'd found what they were looking for after all. The rest of the errant group was asleep or reading in their respective areas. I decided to ignore the slight, take Tomas's lead and let it slide off my back. It wouldn't do any good to bring it up now with the moment past. Tomorrow was a new day. Hopefully things would improve.

Later in the evening, I went back into the city center with Jack and Ivan. This time, the hunt was for pizza. They had been daydreaming about Mexican food and pizza for the past week. Hours were spent talking about quesadillas and tortillas, melted cheese and pepperoni. The more time they devoted to culinary dreamscapes, the more powerful their hunger grew. Jack was now willing to scour the city to satiate his appetite. He and Ivan were prepared to devote the whole night to the quest. After an hour of wandering down shady alleys, we returned victorious to the albergue to eat our Spanish style pizza. Despite strangely doughy crust, Jake was happy. The rest of the group joined us as we ate. Ava, Tomas, Iris, Zara and Konrad also had pizza, but the Brit guys had already eaten a meal made from leftover supplies. Though it didn't seem to bother Francis and Elliot to watch us eat, I could see John looking longingly at our takeout feast.

Though it wasn't glamorous and sometimes involved slimy white asparagus from a jar, I had to admire the Brit guys' approach to food on the Camino. Their mode of operation was more my style, and tonight I felt a bit like a turncoat with my fancy takeout. Jack and Ivan, on the other hand, were massive fans of meals out. If their budget had allowed it, they would have eaten out every meal.

As more of the group arrived, the circle became wide and loose. I sat on the ground submerged in a sea of conversation. The mood was light as Ivan bantered with Ava and Elliot and John beat-boxed an original and truly epic rap about The Lord of the Rings. The well-crafted song sent Ava into an uncontrollable spasm of laughter that caused her to double over and slide off her chair while a flattered John turned a deep shade of red. Though I'd learned days ago that the Brit boys were witty, the rest of the group hadn't seen this side of them until now. Ava's humor was apparent on contact, whereas Elliot and Francis's humor built slowly and appeared when you least expected it. Tonight both engines were running side by side, and I ached with laughter. It was terribly hard to retain a grudge when Ava and Iris were so engaging and unconcerned with the events of the afternoon. And I was a sucker for harmony.

After the meal was done, I was buzzing with energy. The shifting terrain of group life was filling my limbs with a restless ache. I was often overwhelmed by the need to move when I was in emotional overload, but as I sat on the edge of the group, it was more than that. I had to move to digest not only what I was feeling but to process all of the energy around me. The complex dynamics with Ava's group, the return of Jack and Ivan and my deepening connection to Francis were coursing through my system. We'd hardly spoken in days, but I now felt linked to something deeper in his journey. I could read his slightest movement and decode his most ardent effort at remaining neutral. I knew we were kindred spirits, reading the dynamics swirling around us through a similar lens. I felt what he felt. And yet I knew he was baffled by my blatant attempts to woo Ava's group. I could sense his concern for me as well as his irritation. He'd avoided me today and though I'd found others to while away the hours with, I was rattled by his behavior. I felt as if I had too many balls to keep in the air, too much grunt work to stay afloat in the social network around me, and the problem was that I cared. I cared about becoming closer to the girls, and I cared about my bond with Francis.

I just had to move. Walking generally took the edge off this need, but our eighteen kilometer trek now felt like a million hours ago. I crawled through the center of the group as several lively conversations continued on and slipped out of the circle into open space. I began to walk around a bit and stretch my limbs.

My feet were bare, and I felt whole and healed for the first time since my arrival on Spanish soil. My ankles had let go of their vice grip, and I could articulate my feet once again. The tendonitis in my ankles had kept me from dancing, but now for the first time in weeks, I was free to move again. Suddenly I missed dance with a fierce ache. I longed to move the energy churning in my chest and stand in a large space with a bare floor. This was an imperfect stage with cement below my feet, and there were thirty or so pilgrims lounging about, but I didn't pause to think, worry or care.

Slow and subtle at first, building into smooth lines and quicker tones, my arms swung in long arcs, my knees cracked as I sunk into a plié and circled around my center. I let the momentum build, and everything around me fell away into a liquid blur of light and color. I didn't care if it was strange or inappropriate to be dancing. I would gladly face the teasing, a squadron of criticism and jokes if I could just have that moment to move. I ceased to worry who was there or if they were watching. The feeling of moving again, of tracing lines and shifting energy pulled me under: limbs strong, spine rolling on each curve and my mind peacefully drifting into stillness. It was like diving into a clear lake, falling blissfully into bed, running down hill and embracing someone you loved fiercely all at once. It was simply bliss.

From the corner of my eye, I could tell no one from our group was paying much attention, but other pilgrims who had been sitting out in the late evening were watching. They sat silently on the outer fringe of the space, caught in the shadows of the falling light. I didn't dance for them or for my group, but if they wanted to watch then I was happy to entertain. As the movement warmed up my body, I was flooded with adrenaline as if I had reconnected with love again after a long absence. I felt every surface of my body and let the air encircle me with force. All the moments before and after fell away.

When I finally stopped, I let the momentum uncoil within me and drifted towards stillness. I didn't look over at the group but walked toward the door. Nobody seemed to notice. I wasn't even sure they had seen me begin. I darted out into the empty road by the albergue and stood on my own. The rapid filling and draining of my lungs made my chest rise in rhythm. Now that the moment and the rush were gone, I felt lost again. I hadn't danced with any aim or motive, but it was strange to feel unseen by my group; to be invisible even when on show. The lights were coming on in the empty streets, but the only sound that filled my ears was my own breath. No one mentioned my dance when I returned, and I would never hear anybody except Francis refer to that moment. It simply evaporated as time and the journey rushed on.

MAZARIFE

STAGE SIXTEEN- 23.1K-14.3M
LEÓN TO MAZARIFE

It was still dark as our large group wound through the empty network of central streets. The cathedral loomed overhead with its dusky spires filling the sky. Bisecting its center, we moved away from the glossy nucleus and into the ragged edges of the city. The suburbs of León were the one area of the trail I'd been warned about. Less that a week before, I'd spoken with a female veteran of the Camino who felt this path was one of the last trail systems in Europe, or perhaps the world, safe for women to walk on their own. She added that her only moment of discomfort and worry took place in the vast rundown suburbs of León.

Always a bit more on guard in the cities, I was glad she'd shared this story with me, and I'd made it clear to some of the guys in my group that I needed to leave the city by their sides. They'd kindly patted me on the back and told me not to worry. But since they were sweet boys, they indulged my concern nonetheless. After I made a verbal pact with Francis and Tomas to be my companions and/or bodyguards, I was less concerned over the whereabouts of the rest of the group. Yet in a stunning stroke of synchronicity, all eleven of us were up and out of the albergue at the same early hour. Given the various factors, this was nothing short of miraculous. Now, it was comforting to be on the trail out of the city with all of us strung out along the path and within sight of each other.

Though I'd contracted Tomas to be one of my henchmen, I almost immediately found his slow pace hard to keep. I quickly jumped ship and strode off in search of my other protector. I found Francis engaged in a conversation with Iris about their approaching life at university. It was unusual to see Iris without Ava; I'd rarely witnessed her fend for herself socially. She was shy and clearly preferred the familiar. As I drew closer, I sensed the two of them were having an interesting and easy conversation. I noticed Francis was even smiling. It was startling to trail behind the two of them and recall they were contemporaries. They could have been friends or gone to school together or even dated. They had the instant connection Jack and Ivan had with me. This unnerved me somehow and caused me to dwell a bit too long about what they thought about one another and what our group would be like if we all had come solo. What would have become of Iris if there had been no primary bond to Ava? And what might have happened if Francis, Elliot and John were all here but didn't know each other? Would different friendships have occurred between us or more importantly, would romance have been given more space to flourish? The thought both intrigued me and made me slightly jittery. Iris was so lovely and fragile, sweet and softly aloof. Everything about her was like the delicate roses on her dress, not flashy, sexy or aggressive but striking all the same. I found her intriguing and distant, whimsical and slightly reminiscent of a young child with loosely bound locks of hair. I felt all my hard edges around her, all my lanky height and long limbs. But most of all I felt battered and bruised by forces that had so far left her untouched. I was damaged, and I felt it showed. I knew men felt drawn to her. I could see it in the way they looked at her and the way they moved around the edges of her thin frame. I saw Francis falling too. This group was a growing web of relationships, and I'd wanted that, invited it even, but now I felt caught off guard by what might unfold and who might move closer to others and farther from me.

The trail leaving the old city followed one of the main roads westward. We spent over an hour walking past dozens of large factory buildings and gaudy storefronts. The cafes were dimly lit and sparsely populated by clusters of old men bent over their morning coffee. The sounds of the city waking up grew louder as the sun rose and more cars filled the roadway.

León was a metropolitan city, and the excess at the center of the city was opulent and chic, sparkling and high priced. The clothing stores sold fine goods, and the cafes boasted beautifully paneled walls and ornate furniture. It was materialism at its most elegant, and yet it was only a small taste of the city. Here on the fringes were stores as far as the eye could see selling unglamorous products in unglamorous ways. Both types of stores existed for the same reasons, but the ones we passed in the morning didn't mask their objective with perfumed air and thumping music. This was where most of the city indulged their material needs.

It disturbed me to wade through all this consumerism. I'd been on the trail so long I couldn't fathom anything but a streamlined life where all I needed was on my back. I looked into store windows at rows of furniture and racks of clothes and couldn't imagine ever wanting any of it. Was I being brainwashed by the trail or was the trail rubbing off my strange western attitudes about the need for material goods? I thought back to my stuff at home. All I owned lived in a series of five or six cardboard boxes in the barn at my parent's farm. The stuff consisted of books, artwork, blankets and clothes. I'd spent the past few years moving around, leaving places behind and packing up so often that those things were all I had left.

As I looked down at my faded shirt and worn blue shorts, I had a hard time remembering what clothes were even in those boxes. My day-to-day reality was this ensemble and the few other things in my pack. I was living to satisfy my basic survival needs and much of the time I felt full and happy in ways that had eluded me since childhood. Any collection of things couldn't equal the land and the humans, the light and thrill of this life. My whole body was alive to the now: lean and strong, valuable and vital. It had a purpose and once again, so did I. Even the company of the people around me, no matter how challenging and imperfect, soothed my soul and made me feel full. Forget hunger for food, I had been hungry for life, for movement and relationships, and finally I was tasting these longed for things. Francis and Ivan, Elliot and John, Jack and Ava, Iris and Tomas, these people whom I'd just met had taken root in me. They helped the hollow places in me feel less voluminous. I was more than willing to carry a bit of them inside me, to care and be present to the shifting tides of the group. I would carry their stories and be the richer for it. No matter how it had come about, by luck or destiny, these were my people now. I was content to leave the materialistic rules of the culture in the dirty outskirts of León. Life in this vagabond group brought me closer and closer to the energetic tone of the life I'd dreamed of, a life where happiness flooded over me, sometimes for no reason at all.

Yet with the sight of Francis and Iris walking side by side, I couldn't deny my ongoing craving for the one supreme element I didn't have. That's the trouble with being a romantic. I liked romance and was deeply infatuated with love, sometimes beyond reason and rational behavior. I was willing to go to crazy lengths for love, and my romantic side was always there to back me up, shove me out of the skydiving plane, nudge me off the bungee jump station or dare me to leap flippers first into shark infested waters. My romantic side cared about me keeping my limbs and sanity intact, but let's face it, it fancied the experience of love just a bit more. It would keep me risking regardless of the consequences.

I wanted to be grateful, satisfied and at peace with the terms of this journey. I wanted to be like the guys, at ease with solo adventure and at home in the pack, but I wasn't. Many years before I'd been shown a view into a life of family and community all my own. It had been a glimmer of who I would become, a dream more real than waking life. Since that time I'd never doubted it would be so, but I wondered when. My eyes were always on the horizon, always waiting to catch a glimpse of the dream, to turn a corner and step into the energy of that man and those children. I believed in destiny, understood that some elements of our journey through life were rooted way markers we simply would not miss, but timing was an element I couldn't begin to grasp. So I had to let destiny move me, pull me forward to a spot in time when the dream would arrive. Despite my early desires to rush through the trail, I now felt it was rushing through me. The trail was drawing closer and closer to its final days. I wasn't sure how much time I had left in this pilgrim life and if that time would provide love. I certainly couldn't predict what foolish messes I might get myself into before this trail was done.

Jay and Luc had gone ahead in the days before we entered León. It was surreal how people came and went, often with little rhyme or reason. One night I was sleeping beside someone and the next he was gone, vanishing without a trace. As for Jay and Luc, we had no idea where they were and though they were close to the Iron Six, they had taken off on their own. The trail was shaping up to be a miniature diagram of life, a small stage on which we enacted some of the major flows of the human experience.

The trail was like a train with all of us as passengers on its rails. Sometimes we switched cars, losing touch for the day but reconnecting at night. Other times, one or another of us would get off at a stop, change lines and perhaps disappear for days or all together. This path was a flowing container we had willingly gotten on, yet there was endless activity, infinite chances to appear and disappear, to link up or break apart. I hadn't fully understood the nature of the train until the morning on the far side of Hontanas, the moment when I moved a few cars forward and suddenly discovered a new community filling my boxcar. Then I'd slipped off the moving creature that bright afternoon in Sahagún and felt the coldness of a hollow car.

After my return to the group, I felt there was something profound about the ever forward motion of this train. It was a shared journey with a complex web of comings and goings, but such was life. Moments in time were defined by the blessed arrival of a dear friend or the loss of a lover. The cars would be full one moment and vacant the next. We all had our times of getting off and our times of letting go and moving away.

In the dusty fields on the far side of León, my Camino train felt full and in no danger of changing anytime soon. Even though it was unclear where some of the group had gone, there were many still aboard. That morning I was in a small car near the front with Francis and Elliot. After the suburbs of León fell away and we moved into the rural countryside, the group reshuffled its configuration. Iris hung back to reconnect with Ava and Elliot moved forward to walk beside Francis. For a moment, it felt like the mornings couplings were a bit of an aberration, and we'd all secretly longed to shift back into more familiar grooves.

The trail was a wide dusty track of red dirt that allowed us to walk three wide. The boy's spirits were high, and I was swept up in their infectious exuberance. Since Bercianos, I'd known the three Brit boys were wonderful singers and León proved they could also claim to be songwriters, maybe even aspiring rappers. As we crested one small rise after another, I asked the boys to sing for me. I also taught them one of my favorite sea shanties, aptly named Spanish Ladies, and a three part African vocal round. As an encore, Elliot lifted his voice up with the chorus of Lean on Me as Francis beat-boxed with mock seriousness.

I liked life on this train in cars filled with these friends, but I couldn't predict who would stay onboard until the end or what the last legs of the journey might bring. I wondered who would slip off in the night or drop behind in the late of the day? Who would draw closer and who would fall out? I was scared to realize it was all out of my hands but relieved to feel those moments of change were far away from today.

I was familiar with the momentum of another train. I'd grown up in a family on a farm that moved forward with light and pure momentum. When I was eight, my mom worried about my siblings' winter colds and my childhood stomachaches so she began to make flower essences from the plants in her gardens. It started with the delicate blue borage flower and grew from there. At first the bottles of flower essences filled a few shelves in our pantry, then a whole wall of shelving and soon there was no room to store anything else.

The next summer my mom and three of her friends expanded the gardens on our property. The designs were circular and dynamic. The main vegetable garden had a large tent of living green vines growing in its center. It was spacious enough to allow people to stand under its leafy walls. My mom and her friends put up twenty posters in our local area and opened the gardens to the public. That summer we had hundreds of visitors each week. They came from all over the country, even from abroad. We weren't exactly sure how word spread, but visitors flooded in at an astounding rate.

One afternoon we arrived home to find an unfamiliar person in the shower at the same time a group was pitching tents in the back yard, and strangers were eating food from our refrigerator. It was bedlam all summer long, yet through it all, one thread shone bright and strong: the flower essences.

On a whim, my mom put a few out for sale at the farm stand, and they sold as fast as she could make them. When fall rolled around, my parents were comatose from the stress of such a summer, and the gates to the farm closed to the public for good. Yet the essences kept going out into the world.

Over the next decades, the business grew from a kitchen operation into one with several buildings for bottling, shipping and inventory. And through it all, the flower essences kept speaking to the world. By word of mouth, the company grew. Healing filled the lives of people who used the essences and the collection of flowers expanded too. We made and sent into the world collections of flowers essences from Bermuda, St. John USVI, Ireland, the Adirondacks and the deserts of the west.

Even here on the Camino, I was creating a collection from the flowers along the trail to bring back to the farm. The Spanish flowers were with me every step of the way, from the very first bloom that called to me on the outside of St. Jean weeks ago. I would carry these flowers the length of the trail, they would move with me and carry me as I carried them on my shoulders. My journey was shaping their gifts, and at the very same time, their gifts were shaping my journey. Soothing and purging, coaxing and strengthening, their vibration hummed through the walls of my pack and into every cell of my body. Each delicate bloom and trailside cluster of color continued the thread of my destiny. I'd grown up among the flowers of our farm, and it was only right their Spanish cousins were here with me. On my return to the states, they would move out into the world to reach others.

The trail had been carrying the tide of pilgrims along this lay line for over a thousand years. The flowers that lived on its tidal edges knew exactly where they had planted their roots. They were part of the energy grid as much as the land. They were interwoven with the healing energy of the trail. A poppy along the Camino was unlike any poppy that grew farther a field in Spain or France. These were trail flowers, and it was ingrained in their energetic gifts. I was simply the porter from Spain to the states, and it was a service I was honored to render.

Life on our flower essence farm was very much a fast moving train with purpose and direction. The universe had laid a track for the healing and light that moved through the business. Characters were given a chance to board the train, to come and go. I was born to the land, to my mom and to the life in and amongst the flowers. This meant I was a permanent resident on the train as was the rest of my family, but at times, I had to get off and painfully go out into the world. I needed to go to school and create other connections, but part of me was always on the train, always part of the forward momentum of the vehicle of light.

My mom was the center of the train, she was the driver, the stationmaster, the chief engineer and the coal stoker. Yet she wasn't the architect and she didn't lay the tracks. That was the work of the universe, the work of the light, the work of God. My dad was the roots. He was the dedicated craftsman who built every structure on the farm. He was the steady strength that threaded our lives together. The farm demonstrated my parent's faith in each other and their combined effort to bring a dream into reality.

Even though my family members were regulars on the train, many people came and went at different stations. My mom's three friends who boarded the train that first summer left the next year, getting off at a station to never re-board. New staff got on, and more often than not, got off at a station down the line. This flow was ever present, yet the destiny of the train, the destiny of the business and the mission of the flowers was always an absolute.

This was true of the Camino as well. We were on this very ancient road of travelers, and the course was clear; the stars defined the way forward. It was written where we would go, and I wanted to believe it was written where I would go beyond the last step in Spain. There was momentum building in all of us. There was a great destiny laid along the tracks ahead. I just couldn't figure out what that destiny was, couldn't figure out who would stay together on the train, and where we would go at the trail's end. It was too early to tell, yet the tracks were laid. Perhaps all I could do on this dusty stretch was to have faith that as long as I kept moving and kept listening, the rest was destined. The contracts were clear and would unfold in their own time.

I glanced back to discover we were now the lead group for the morning. I secretly relished being at the head of the pack. The land had flattened out into gentle hills that pulled the trail down like a wave and then flung it up and over a wide crest. The singing died down and talk veered toward home and family. Elliot and Francis talked about their sisters and I wondered how my life would have been different if I hadn't grown up among a gaggle of siblings. Suddenly I was telling the boys about the complex and upsetting dynamics surrounding my extended family. In a flood of words, I told them about the death threats directed towards my siblings and parents from my mother's brother, and my grandparent's refusal to protect us. It was difficult to explain the extent of the destruction my grandparent's alcoholism had wreaked on my mom's side of the family and how it had caused such pain in our small family circle. I talked about this piece of my history in an even tone until I started to talk about my parents. They'd spent the last decade actively fighting to protect us at all cost, cutting off all contact with my mom's family and letting the local police know about the threats. Once I started to talk about all the ways they'd gone against the cultural norms, turned away from an inheritance and given up relationships and places they loved simply to protect us, I was overwhelmed. How much sorrow and isolation they had endured. How brave they'd been in the face of so many lies and so much criticism, I burst into tears. I hadn't expected to cry, and I could tell both Elliot and Francis were startled by the intensity of the tale .

I wiped the tears from my eyelids as the boys slung their arms around my shoulders to comfort me. Before they could say anything, a whoop of joy resounded from behind us, and we turned back to see Luc and Jay coming up the trail with Konrad. The two missing members had returned, flowed back into the group just as easily as they had departed. Our train was full again. Within minutes the trail wound out of the dusty open plains into the edge of a small town of tightly clustered buildings. This was to be the last bit of civilization before we reached Mazarife.

We rested in the shade of a tall garden wall, and I asked Francis if he wanted to walk with me. He nodded yes, and we gathered our things as Ava and Iris settled in for a leisurely feast of chocolate doughnuts and coffee. I figured they might be a while. After we left the small town, the trail followed a flat straight road all the way to Mazarife. As we strode along, Francis and I talked about various things and moved effortlessly at the same pace. My lungs delighted in deep breaths, and I felt light and unbound by the stress of social maneuvering. I was alone with my confidant, and all was safe. Everything about Francis drew me in. Our matching cadence was something I'd taken for granted until I'd tried to walk with Tomas and the American guys. I had so many observations to share with Francis, so many things to discuss about the group. I also wanted to know what he felt about all the new characters in our drama. It had been too long since we'd been on our own like this, and I relished our honesty with each other. Time slipped away, the kilometers rushed by and I was startled to see Mazarife appear on the horizon.

Before departing from León, the group agreed to stay at an albergue called El Refugio de Jesus, a place recommended by Ava's dad. After our four hour walk from León, Mazarife was an oasis of color and activity in the dry and barren remnants of the Meseta. And Jesus was the brightest, most welcoming spot in the whole village. As soon as we stepped onto the front lawn, we were swept into its embrace. Francis and I walked through the front yard, past a giant pirate ship and paddock with several horses into an inner courtyard where a large tree grew. The walls were bright tropical colors, both inside and out. Hundreds of drawings were scribbled on every open surface. A table full of crayons, colored pencils and markers sat next to the pilgrim ledger, encouraging us to add to the artwork. The walls looked as if pilgrims had been drawing on them for years. There were beautiful depictions of ships and mountains, names, words of wisdom and notes of hope. Everything about the albergue felt cherished. The place brought on a wave of relief, the very same kind I felt when returning home after a long absence.

While I worried about what I would do when I returned to the states, on the trail, my body had finally found a rhythm all its own. I'd discovered the beauty of rising early, working hard for five or six hours and then resting and simply practicing the challenging art of being. All the restless energy and physical intensity had dissipated, leaching into the trail and leaving me deliciously empty. This town held that sweet mellow emptiness in its very bones, and somehow it felt warm and welcoming. The young woman running the albergue had walked the Camino several years ago and loved this town so much she'd come back to fix up the albergue and shelter other pilgrims. Once a pilgrim, always a pilgrim. Her connection to the pathway never vanished. It moved through her even now that she was rooted to this place. I wondered if I too would always be a pilgrim, always feel the pulse in my core. I wanted to be changed, altered, cut to a new form and cast away from the familiar shores of who I'd been before this trail. I wanted to believe change wasn't fleeting and a vibrant, freshness could rush over me. I wanted to believe this brief piece of time mattered.

By the time we were done checking in and exploring the downstairs, most of the group had joined us and together we climbed the stairs. We were given two sleeping choices: shady bunkrooms or mattresses on an open-air porch. I nearly flung myself over the edge and into the courtyard below as I bounced around in glee. The rooms looked fine, but I'd spent too many nights inside and couldn't wait to sleep out in the soft night. Soon Tomas, Ava, Iris, Zara and I were lined up like ducks in a row on beds under the protection of the eaves. Tomas offered to go deep into the far corner, and I took the spot beside him; I had a feeling the other girls would prefer to sleep in a cluster. Along the other side of the porch Luc, Elliot and Konrad had also claimed mattresses, but our side of the outdoor abode was the happening place to spend the afternoon. Francis picked a spot in one of the rooms off the porch and later John, Jack and Ivan would join him in the small bunkroom. I felt badly that in the scramble, Francis hadn't gotten a spot outside, but he seemed unperturbed even visibly relieved to have a bit of space. Or maybe I didn't notice how he felt because I was caught up in Ava and Iris's swirling excitement as they pushed mattresses together and jumped around with delighted grins. I wondered, for a brief moment, if mild mannered Tomas was up to the challenge of sharing this space with a bunch of rowdy girls.

With the mattresses pushed together, it was a continuous soft space of cushioned fabric, scattered clothes and bags. As I sat cross-legged and unpacked my bag, Tomas reclined next to me and we chatted about the day. I was flush with the delightful feeling that there was nothing else to do but enjoy each other's company without fear the outside world would whisk anyone away to something more exciting.

In the afternoon, the girls lay sunbathing with rolled up tops and exposed stomachs. They chatted warmly with me, and I could tell their spirits were high. Even Zara laughed at our silly antics as I attempted to teach Ivan, Francis and Tomas a bit of yoga. I'd started to notice the girl's warmth and inclusiveness was directly linked to their contentment with themselves. When they were happy, it rubbed off on everyone in the group. We were all bathed in the glory of the day. The moment of inclusion felt like gift maybe even a sense of promise about how the tides would soon turn.

The Hungarian Lover boy sat forlornly in the hammock, removed from our silly fun. The Actress hadn't shown up, and none of us had seen her in several days. He was rife with anxiety over her disappearance. He knew she was safe. That was never the issue, but he worried he'd lost her into the cracks again. It was clearly exhausting to keep falling in and out of company with her. To be drawn closer and then spun farther out with each moment of connection fading just as it grew ripe.

The lowering sun brought sleepy yawns and card games on our porch beds. The boys gathered into a circle as I looked at pictures with Ava and Iris, only pausing to take new shots to add to our camera libraries. In those moments, I felt as if the divide that had kept our group slightly fractured was mending. I had Tomas to thank for much of that. I even felt a bit more tolerated by Jay and Konrad but just a bit. I couldn't seem to get past Konrad's gruff exterior. He made it abundantly clear he had no interest in talking to me, but I was positive his grounds for rebuffing me were totally unsubstantiated. He had me all wrong and seemed uninterested in shifting his view. He didn't speak to me and never made eye contact. Nonetheless, my joy in this afternoon couldn't be dimmed by grumpiness. I'd known he would be the hardest nut to crack, so I had to give it more time, fight that fight another day. Eventually he would tire of his resistant stance and relent. He was wasting more energy than he knew in trying to keep me out of his circle; his defended energy asked more of him that my open energy asked of me. I had the easier position, and time was working in my favor. Maybe the battle with Konrad was simply one of attrition.

A letting go had started back in Puente La Reina where I'd left my sleeping mat. Since then I'd become less fearful of not having. I worried less about when I might shower next or where I would sleep or what I would wear. I was given the chance to see even when all those elements were not a part of my day-to-day life, I was happier than I'd been in months. I was sleeping on dingy mattresses, eating weird foods out of cans and unsure of how I would get home at the end, but I was awake to the world around me. These friends and the trail had given me hope. Even as it took some not so graceful juggling to keep up with all my growing relationships, I was delighted by the new challenge.

Despite my sun dazed optimism, there were small signs that day in Mazarife that perhaps portended the future. I tried not to let the way the Iron Six ate separately or the Brit boys removed themselves from the group keep me from relishing Mazarife. I didn't think about what this might mean later in the trail. The next day and its challenges would come soon enough.

I awoke with some unease before dawn. Rain had rolled through while we slept and the flagstones in the courtyard were damp, the air full of release. In the night, I felt the weight of phantom limbs upon me and dreamed of the past, of warmth so close and familiar it stayed with me even as I crawled out from the trenches of sleep. I wanted to know when all the memories of men past would be far enough away to be forgotten, to know when the memories I traversed like a rutted road would hold no more power.

I once read that memories aren't static in our brains; they shift and change. They lose detail as we loop through them again and again. These details start to turn fuzzy and their visceral world melts under repeated touch. We forget smells, noises and tactile moments the more we revisit them. A memory frequently recalled becomes two dimensional and removed from the current of emotion. It no longer leaves a zing in your abdomen or dashes across the nerves under your skin.

After scrolling through memories repeatedly, we stop being able to recall how someone's skin felt or the sound of their voice. Then one day we arrive at the hollow moment when our brains scratch around for some clip, some sound bite, some taste of the past and can find nothing to hold on to. This is when it has passed and died soundlessly within us.

I remembered the ache when all the details vanished from my first love, when I hardly recalled anything at all. It made me know it was truly over, that I could no longer fool myself into thinking I was still connected to him. Now I wasn't just letting the memories erase themselves, I was hoping to speed up the process. I was working to dissolve and erase fresh and traumatic memories so I could clean the slate and move on.

I especially wanted to forget everything about my last relationship. I wanted the night, these new friends and their sleeping sounds to replace all the spots in my brain that held the memories of the past year. I wanted to be free of the endless cycle of questioning, the hashing and rehashing. Released from the burden of guilt and shame he'd laid upon me. Tangling with memories of the past year wore me down and only ever brought me to the same conclusion. It was over. It had always been destined to be over. I'd escaped but not without wounds. Even though I knew the trail was ever forward, I suddenly felt sorry to leave Mazarife and a bit weary to carry on. This small village had cradled me, if just for a moment, and I didn't want to lose this memory, turn one day and find it was gone.

HOSPITAL DE ORBIGO

STAGE SEVENTEEN- 30.1K- 18.7M
MAZARIFE TO ASTORGA

The next morning as we walked out of Mazarife, I fell into step with Iris, Jay and a very sullen Konrad. It was an unlikely combination, but two out of three didn't seem too bothered by my presence. The sun began to rise into the dusty pink sky as we headed west along the flattest and straightest road we'd traveled to date. The roadside fields were filled with a riot of green leafy vegetables as far as the eye could see. Sprinkler systems snaked across the fields, fed from old water troughs that lay half full along edges of the road. There were clusters of walkers ahead, and the rest of our group was only a little way behind, but the four of us were as adrift and self-contained as an island.

I was a bit nervous with this group, but I wanted to connect with Iris in a moment where it could be just the two of us. Ava had already displayed a certain level of possessiveness towards Iris, but somehow Zara had managed to get close to them both. I, on the other hand, still felt like the younger sister and tagalong. At one point, Iris needed help with the straps of her pack. We stopped, and Konrad went to her aid, adjusting the belts to fit her back. His muscles worked in his forearms as Iris braced herself against the tugging. His free hand held the curve of her hip as he poured all his concentration into the task. It was all done without question or hesitation. The way he helped to put her load at ease was tender, and I paused to watch as they stood intertwined with the rising light behind them. Even in the brief seconds of touch, I saw a small current of energy run in a full circuit through the loop of their bodies. Finally the glare of the sun caused me to drop my eyes, and when I looked up, they were apart and striding towards Jay and me as if nothing had happened.

We crossed roundabouts, train tracks and backyards then entered the large town of Hospital de Orbigo around ten. As our small group wandered into the village, empty streets hung with festive banners, a long ancient bridge and a medieval jousting field welcomed us in. The river in the center of town only ran through a small section of the bridge and the flat lowland below the other arches was now home to the jousting grounds. The dirt was still freshly stirred from a recent set of battles. This town's celebration had been in honor of its most famous knight. This young knight had been deemed unworthy of marrying his lady love, so to prove his valor, he proclaimed he would joust one hundred men to win her hand. As with all good tales of gallantry, he succeeded, became a legend and won his fair lady.

After the morning with the group, I felt adrift. The American guys and Brit boys had declared they wanted to walk with their respective groups or on their own. Francis, in particular, had made his sentiments clear and announced he desired a full solo day. Though I understood the need for space, I was forlorn without his company. I felt a shift between us and wondered if it was him pulling away or just fall out from the blooming social configuration. Maybe my growing connection to Tomas and the rest of Ava's group was breaking apart the familiarity and intensity of our connection. Maybe now that there were twelve of us, everything was becoming diluted, more surface fun and less subtle links. I couldn't be sure, and I had an ache in my stomach as I wondered if it had less to do with the social whirlwind and more to do with what lay between us. He was the only person in the whole group with whom I had an unwavering connection. I knew instinctively he felt the same way, but his energy had been distant, withdrawn and distracted of late, and I had seen very little of him. We'd grown close so quickly. Why was he now stepping aside and lowering the intensity level of our friendship?

Jay and Konrad wanted to stop for bocadillos at a small café overlooking the jousting fields, so Iris and I tagged along. Bocadillos were sandwiches made of omelet, potato and melted cheese. They were a common staple in Spain and particularly favored by the guys. Twenty minutes later, Ava arrived to rest and refuel. I knew she and Iris would want to finish the day on their own, so I left the café and bumped into Konrad and Jay heading out of town. I wasn't sure if they would tolerate my presence without the rest of the group around, but it was worth a try. I walked with them for five minutes before their pace slacked, and they drifted away behind me. By the time we reached the edge of town, I was alone again. I'd seen these guys sprint after walking twenty kilometers. My pace wasn't the problem; I was. They'd made their feelings known in a subtle but effective brush off, and I took the hint. It was a discouraging litmus test, but all I could do was keep walking. The cure for everything on the Camino was to just keep walking.

Navigating dusty fields, I kept my hat on and occupied my mind with finding the next arrow. Whenever I was alone I worried I would get lost and head down the wrong trail. It seemed to represent all the things I feared about my life. Being physically lost would just add to the trauma of being lost in general, unsure of my direction or purpose beyond this moment.

I moved through a sun-drenched town where children played in rough grass then passed through a barnyard with tractors on the move. A large St. Bernard sat in a puddle inside the farmyard gates. He looked up slowly as I passed but only shifted to his feet to stretch before thumping to the ground again. His size was impressive, but he was about as interested in me as Konrad. It was hard to know the intentions of dogs on the trail. More than once, I'd been surprised by the fury coming from pocket sized dogs and the sweetness of larger canines. There was no hard fast rule, but I always tried to be cautious, prepared to take off at a moment's notice.

The city of Astorga lay down in a valley and hinted of the coming changes in the topography of the trail. At the scenic vista above Astorga was a small cross. An older Spanish couple I'd seen before sat at the base of the cross admiring the view. We acknowledged each other with a smile. Some relationships on the trail were just that simple. We could see in each other the strength it took to keep moving forward and take a moment's pleasure in the sight of something familiar.

A view of a city up ahead could be a deceptive thing. To see the destination made it feel close, yet I'd noticed the outskirts of such places tended to drag on much longer than I expected. I could see the towers in the center of Astorga but knew I needed to wade through all of the buildings and road systems spread out from the heart of the city. I stopped to buy a carton of juice and hoped the liquid sugar would propel me forward. All of the group was behind me except for Zara who'd dashed ahead to mail a letter before the post office closed.

Even though I'd been relegated to solo status for the past three hours, I no longer regretted coming to Spain on my own. In fact, I didn't believe I'd come on my own. I felt there was some universal mapping that had brought me to the trail and made sure I came upon the American guys, Brit boys and even the Iron Six. Calm pervaded my whole body as I wound my way across empty streets in the bright sun of the cloudless day. I knew the initial lack of companions had been a gift I couldn't fully appreciate until now. It had opened me completely to these new acquaintances and made me hungry to connect beyond my comfort zone.

As I thought again about my new friends who'd come in groups of twos and threes, I considered the challenges they faced. It took more work to change the dynamics, to make uncharacteristic choices or seek new social circles with a familiar person by one's side. And it was dangerously easy to become insular and rely only on each other for companionship. Plus, when a pilgrim brought a friend along there was a hierarchy of allegiance. The pair was bonded to each other first and everybody else second. I could tell my connection to Francis was causing a small rift between the Brit boys. My closeness to him threatened their group dynamic and caused an imbalance in the trio.

The American guys solved this added complexity with a blend of easy connection to outsiders and unquestioned allegiance to each other. Jack and Ivan had polished social personas and were delightfully entertaining, but they left hardly any space in their close friendship for others. Because of this, they were the most distant in the group and perhaps the least known. I suppose I was lucky Francis had let me close to him. Even though I was drawn to Ivan and found him endearing, he wasn't interested in building a lasting bond with me.

As my mind drifted, I knew I was only counting my blessings about being free, because I didn't want to admit I would have put up with almost anything to have the right someone by my side. The day before I'd walked past a middle-aged couple along the trail. From a distance, they'd caught my attention because they were holding hands as they walked. When I came upon them, we chatted, and I asked them their story. I wanted to gather some of the love dust off the edges of this couple and collect more proof of Camino love. When I asked why they were walking the trail, the husband told me his wife wanted to do the

Camino and since he loved his wife, he was doing it for her. It was that simple. His words stopped every darting thought in my head and flooded my heart with tenderness. Here was someone who said, "Yes I will walk this trail with you, just because I love you." That was what I wanted.

ASTORGA

Elliot caught up with me as I charged up the streets of Astorga. As he walked, his stick clicked in rhythm on the black asphalt. I knew Elliot was a fast walker when he wanted to be, but since I'd met him, his only walking style had been a leisurely stroll. Apparently the Brit boys had held themselves to a punishing schedule across France, walking all day and never stopping short of the day's projected goals. This had been easier to accomplish since very few people walked the French section of the trail, and there had been no social distractions. They'd often gone days without seeing other pilgrims. Our group, and the communal buzz that came with it, now sidetracked them from such a pace, but Elliot told me their group ethos had shifted even before we met them.

As I walked next to Elliot, he told the story of injuring himself in France. A few weeks into their journey, a series of blisters on his foot had broken open and had become dangerously infected. He could hardly walk, but he'd been determined to keep going, stay on schedule and walk all one thousand miles of their journey.

I knew this wasn't machismo at work but a pilgrim's sense of honor. We all wanted to be able to declare we'd walked the whole distance. I was unwilling to accept that I could get injured, not be able to finish the whole trail or have to take a bus. Elliot had felt the same way. There was pride involved. We loathed the bus pilgrims so much, partly because we all secretly, or not so secretly, feared becoming one of them out of necessity.

That was exactly what Elliot had faced in France. He'd become delirious after a day of walking on his infected foot, and a doctor had told him he couldn't walk for at least a week. It had been tough to face the limitations of his body, especially as a young man, and challenging to make choices that broke with his plan for the trail. Elliot had caught buses and rode with bag carrying services in order to stay up with the other boys. I could tell he'd been very angry at himself and his body during those days. After ten days of riding in cars and experiencing the kindness and generosity of strangers willing to help him keep going forward, his anger had eased. He'd accepted he was going to walk the trail imperfectly. After that, he'd walked at whatever pace felt right for that given day. He wasn't afraid to be the last one to arrive at the albergue or to take detours off the beaten track to see churches. He'd already broken one of the walking pilgrim's cardinal rules. Nothing else he could do would trouble him as much.

Francis and John had jumped on board with this new attitude when a couple of weeks after Elliot returned to the trail, they'd both fallen ill with the flu. In order to fully recover, they'd been forced to stay in a nice hotel. In doing so, they too had broken another unspoken pilgrim rule of conduct. I could see the way it informed all the things they did as a group. I marveled at how events such as injury or illness that were often considered bad luck could sprout things that were so good. I was sure the boys would have been more reluctant to stay with our group or bond with me if they'd still been committed to their tight schedule. And if they hadn't been waylaid for three days cooped up in a hotel, we might never have met.

The albergue in Astorga was newly constructed and rose above the roadway like a gothic monstrosity. Buzzing with activity, the building had a small chapel and four stories of bunkrooms with beds for more than one hundred pilgrims. Each of the rooms held six people and was named after a place along the trail. Since we wanted to stick together, the hosts allowed us to reserve rooms for all the people in our group. I'd become spoiled by having friends in my room at night and hardly recalled what it had been like in the early days. Jack, Tomas and I sat out front, eating lunch and enjoying the chance to rest in the shade. A small public rose garden was situated next to the building, and local people were coming and going through the gates draped in fresh blooms. Later in the afternoon, Iris came back to the building with a dark pink rose tucked in her fair hair and Ava by her side. Both had a naughty and somewhat guilty look in their eyes.

My room looked east, back the way we had come and was directly above the small yard. Housed by order of arrival, I shared a small room with Tomas, John, Konrad, Zara and Elliot. I claimed a high bunk but was pleased to find it easy to climb onto. Zara disappeared to explore the town, while John fell asleep with no shirt on, arm dangling off the bunk and mouth open. I peeled off my sweaty layers and leaned against the cool wall of the building with my book in my lap. The window hung open, allowing the sound of traffic and a slight breeze to enter the still space.

Late in the afternoon I went down three sets of stairs into the basement and found a tiny kitchen with a large dining room, opening onto the lawn. The space was no more than a small patio with a bit of green grass and walls that rose up twenty feet on either side with crushed glass bottles sprinkled along the top. Ava lay on the grass with Iris. Tomas and Konrad sprawled around a table.

The group was planning a large dinner of American pancakes. As soon as siesta ended, Jack enlisted me to shop for ingredients. On the way to the supermercado, I noticed shiny blue public phones. I suddenly craved the chance to call home and hear my parents' voices. I decided to call when my shopping duties were complete.

Ava and Iris met up with us in the aisles of the brightly lit grocery store, while Konrad and Tomas sat outside drinking German beer from large silvery cans. Jack and Ava were the official cooks, so I let the group go back without me. As I lingered on the edge of the central courtyard waiting for a phone to be free, I noticed a very tall man leave the albergue and disappear into the center of the city. I was curious, drawn in by a glimpse of an unfamiliar pilgrim but became distracted when my turn came at the phone.

It took over twenty numbers punched in through the stiff metal keys to connect with home. Just hearing my parents' voices brought tears to my eyes and caused my throat to tighten. They were used to this. I had a long history of calling them on the verge of tears and then spending most of the phone conversation letting the tears out. Normally I hardly went a day with talking to my mom; she was my grounding, my most precious counsel and the one that relayed all the drama of my life to my dad. They each had their different roles, but both were invaluable. The duo had been there for me through two broken love affairs and everything in between. This evening, I needed to talk to my mom more than ever. I felt a strange unsettled force inside me. I knew there was no pressing reason to feel so sad. Behind all the joy that came from finding my place in the group, albeit an imperfect one, I still felt a nagging emptiness. Until I spoke the words to my mom, I couldn't say them to myself, but I was worried.

I worried that having a group of friends wasn't enough. I still craved a relationship. Friends had a way of coming and going from my life like the tide. But a love would stay. He would be ready to root himself in my life and embrace the role of being a friend who wouldn't leave. This craving drenched me in loneliness and made me question my destiny on the trail. The images of the dream at the end of the world were slipping away, and I felt out of touch with my underlying guidance. There was no longer a pressing need to hurry forward. Instead, I felt the days were slipping by too fast, leaving less and less time to connect. Half an hour passed, and my phone card ran out with an abrupt click. It had soothed me to speak with my family, but I felt woozy and disoriented.

As I walked back to the albergue, I met Tomas sprinting past on his way to buy Zara some juice. Apparently she'd almost fainted in the middle of the kitchen floor. As Tomas disappeared into town, I felt a growing warmth for him. In Mazarife, he'd told me he'd come to a deep realization while on the trail. Early in his journey on a day in northern France, he'd gotten lost, and as night fell he had nowhere to take shelter. He'd knocked on a stranger's door in hope of getting directions to an inn, but instead he'd been offered a hot meal and place to sleep. The woman refused to be paid or even thanked, and he knew she'd taken care of him for no other reason than to be kind. The giving had been reward enough. After this, Tomas had a revolution of thought and realized taking care of people and bringing happiness into their lives was to be his goal from that moment forward. He told me if the chocolate bar he'd bought would make me smile, he would give it to me. Or if any of us were in his hometown, he would offer his own bed to make us comfortable. For Tomas, the trail was a course in selflessness, and here he was doing the course work, dashing across the city to help another.

He was a visceral reminder of the importance of staying present to my fellow pilgrims. I needed to stop worrying about if and when love might arrive. I simply needed to embrace those around me, go forward with faith and an open heart. I rushed back towards the kitchen full of my friends. Though the thought of pancakes made my stomach heave, I craved the sustenance of company and connection.

When I arrived in the kitchen, there were at least twenty people crammed into the tiny space, all trying to cook, chop, clean or plate their dinners. This was the downside of staying in such a vast albergue; everyone converged on the kitchen facilities at the same time. Jack was holding his ground at the stove as Ava kept the pancake batter flowing. The rest of the group sat around a large table.

The dining room was one of the stranger spaces in the building with walls paneled in wood the very same color as the table. Everything blended into a sea of dark brown, making seven o'clock feel like midnight. When I entered, Francis was busy with salad preparations. The special salad of the night involved kiwis, chickpeas and fresh tomatoes. I went over to him to help, pulling up a chair and offering my services. He smiled and let me cut up the tomatoes. I realized it was the first time I'd see him all day. He was still in his trail clothes, his skin dusty, but he'd at least taken a moment to abandon his hiking boots before pitching in. Francis had filled my thoughts as I walked alone, but I hadn't seen him since the previous evening. In trail time, this felt like weeks. He seemed weary and a bit coy about his day but perked up as we worked side by side. I felt my own mood shift in the same direction. It was uncanny to realize he had this affect on me. I'd only known Francis for a handful of days but time just didn't seem to play by the same rules on the Camino.

Zara sat at the end of the table with her head in her hands, looking like she might drip off the table into a puddle on the ground. Her skin was white to the tips of her fingers, and I couldn't see her face. Iris was trying to tempt her with some jam from a sticky jar while glancing towards the door, anxiously awaiting Tomas's return.

Other pilgrims sat outside on the patio, but our group claimed a prime spot at the table. I wasn't hungry but enjoyed being given a concrete task and being useful. With such a large group, the cooking duties had become a touchy subject. I was starting to gather that some people, primarily Zara, felt they had already done their fair share of cooking and were disgruntled about what they considered an uneven distribution of labor. I didn't let it faze me. I was willing to help but, like Francis, I hadn't been given a window in which to do so. Slicing and dicing was all we could do to contribute, at least tonight. The thought of being head chef for a group of twelve under these conditions was daunting, especially when right now, I had so little interest in food. And besides, a meal put on by a girl that is satisfied with chickpeas from a jar wasn't always appreciated by those with more refined palates.

Finally Tomas returned with a large carton of juice. As he caught his breath, he filled a tall glass for Zara. His face was creased with worry, and he didn't take his eyes from her face. Even though she was sick, her hair fell in a lustrous wave from her face, and her hands delicately cupped the vessel of juice. There was a magnetism about her even in the throes of illness. I imagined all of the boys in our group had noticed her striking looks, but she was a taken woman, and they all knew it. This permitted her to be close with the boys, let them dote and adore, but made it clear she was never expected to return the affection. Tomas hovered near her as she slowly stood up. She wanted to sit outside in the air. Tomas offered his arm, and she leaned her weight into him. His willingness to support her was gallant and genuine. As they moved out towards the small lawn, her body rested against his, and his knuckles grew white where they gripped her side. I didn't need to wonder if he had a crush on her. It was encoded in every gesture. And even through her haze of sickness, she knew it too.

The pancakes were slow to come, but it gave us time to set the table like proper adults. I darted through the traffic jam of people in the kitchen to search for forks and plates. It was always nice to have real silverware. Not all of the albergues had such amenities, and I seemed to have been the only member of the group who hadn't thought to bring my own. We set twelve places at the table, because Luc had shown up out of nowhere. Nobody was particularly surprised by his arrival. He was always disappearing and reappearing like some sort of magical creature. Maybe some of this had to do with his lack of English. It was the common language in our group, and only Konrad could speak German. Despite his chain smoking and lack of shared vocabulary, Luc was very charming. His long red hair shone bright against his pale skin, and it would have been considered stunning had he been female. It was clear he and Konrad had a bond that couldn't be replicated, but it was anybody's guess how long he would stick with the group before vanishing again.

Later that evening, the remains of the meal lay scattered about the table. Its large surface was littered with half empty jars of jam, the remnants of our well intentioned but very strange salad, dirty knives covered with chocolate goo and empty bottles of wine. The pancakes had been a success, but I guessed that was because the group was rather ignorant about what a good pancake tasted like, and after a day of walking, they were delighted with anything that was edible. The steady flow of pilgrims moving in and out of the kitchen had slowed, and our group fell into clusters of contented conversation.

I was listening to Ivan regale the group with a tale about roasting a whole pig when a man stepped out of the kitchen and glanced down the long table at our group. As I looked up, I recognized the new arrival as the tall pilgrim I'd seen leaving the albergue earlier in the afternoon. While he stood searching the dining room for a place to sit, I got my first good look at him. His face was long and lean with a small beard that matched the rail thin quality of his very tall frame. He must have been over six foot five and looked as if he'd been hungry a lot in the last few weeks. In each of his large hands he held a bowl of noodle soup. He looked our table up and down then turned to Ivan to ask if he could sit. Ivan welcomed him by making more room at the head of the table. The new addition to our party sat down with careful attention to the full bowls in his hands.

Since I was sitting in the middle of the vast table, I watched him from a distance. At the moment he was too ragged to be considered classically handsome, but a pleasant change flooded over his face as he answered Ivan's eager questions. Ivan asked him if he was expecting company or if both bowls of soup were his. It was a fair question, but the answer opened a floodgate. No, he wasn't expecting a guest, but he'd walked over fifty kilometers that day and was very, very hungry. Jack nodded and casually asked him when and where he'd started the trail. The man lifted his spoon up towards his mouth, paused and with an absence of feeling said, "Two years ago in Brazil."

The rest of the group around the table were involved in their own conversations about parties back home or the quality of one beer over another. They were transparently uninterested in our new guest, but Ivan's face told a different story as it bloomed with childlike delight. He turned and yelled to me. I stood up and moved to join him at the end of the table. Our new guest had returned his concentrated focus to his dinner. He ate with the dedication of one who'd gone a very long time since his last meal. I pulled my chair up next to Ivan as Jack scrunched his chair closer. Our minds were cluttered with eager questions. Why had he started on a different continent? How had he gotten here? What had he seen? And why? Why? Why?

We wanted to give him a chance to eat, but the questions spilled out of us. At first, he addressed his remarks to Ivan, lifting his gaze up from his dinner and speaking in a low voice. Born and raised in Tasmania, he spoke with a strong accent. Ivan was giddy as the details of this pilgrim's epic story unfolded. Over the past two years he'd walked from Brazil up though Central America, the United States and into Canada. From northwestern Canada he'd taken a plane to Vladivostok in Russia then he'd walked west to Santiago with a detour to Rome. Here, right in front of us, was a real life adventurer in the flesh and blood. I waited my turn to ask a question and finally found the nerve to push my way into the conversation. He turned to me as if noticing me for the first time, looked into my eyes and smiled. In an instant I knew. I knew what had happened to Ivan to make him so infatuated, for it had just happened to me. Our new guest had the power to make anyone he turned his gaze on feel he or she was the only person in the whole world. He romanced with his deep eyes and soothing voice; he was a born charmer. The rest of the room melted. All the chatter turned to distant murmurs.

Hours later, I tumbled out of an alternative reality to realize it was half past eleven. Only Ivan and I remained with our new acquaintance. Ivan was still so overcome with awe that he asked if he could hug the Tasmanian. It was as if he wanted to make contact, to prove this real life hero was made of flesh and blood. There was a slight awkward pause before the Tasmanian acquiesced. Ivan grinned from ear to ear, and all of us rose to depart to our respective sleeping quarters. Suddenly I realized I didn't even know his name. As he stood and stretched his long limbs, I turned, stuck my hand out and said my name. His large hand swallowed mine. His fingers brushed the tender underside of my wrist, and we were formally introduced. I took the three flights of stairs two by two and wondered if this new acquaintance, this epic Tasmanian, would cross my path again. I certainly hoped so.

That night as I brushed my teeth, Elliot and Francis joined me in the co-ed bathroom. As my mouth foamed with toothpaste, they rushed upon me and began to sing. They serenaded me like a barbershop duo through the mirror. Fellow pilgrims gave us odd glances, but the boys sang louder in response. They were so sweet, and it was soothing to feel Francis cheerfully by my side once more, but my vision was clouded. In a matter of hours, everything had changed again, and I couldn't begin to predict what lay ahead.

RABANAL DEL CAMINO

STAGE EIGHTEEN- 31.4K-19.5M
ASTORGA TO MANJARIN

The next morning I decided to walk alongside Tomas. Once again Francis had fallen behind the main pack in search of space, and genuine allies were thin on the ground in Iron Six territory. As we left the outskirts of Astorga, Tomas seemed glad to have me by his side, and if not for a niggling worry about my original pack of boys, I would have felt the same. I worried I was losing touch with the American guys and Brit boys. Now on the trail out of Astorga, it was me and the Iron Six. Konrad strode at the front with Jay on his heels, while Ava and Iris walked side by side. The city was dark and still, but soon we were out beyond the last scattering of buildings. The urban world vanished, and we were back in the wilds. Flocks of small birds darted from islands of trees, afloat in a sea of fields. The birds were poised and still, then without a hint or gesture, they rose and darted through the air in total unison, forming a voluminous cloud. Their direction changed, yet every set of wings knew when to turn and how to follow the group plan.

There were times when our group felt like a flock moving across the land, but we weren't like the birds in the air above us. Our movements, words and emotional connections weren't as seamless, and we often failed to move as one. Instead, we moved as individuals careening and slamming into each other, often unaware of boundaries and flow. Emotionally, we couldn't find that wordless state of oneness or move in a way so we didn't crash and inflict damage on others. Nothing felt harmonious and synchronized about my position in the group that morning. I felt out of place and distant from my posse of boys. Among the Iron Six, I was an outsider, and they made me feel my place. I still was trying to crack the code and find my way into their illusive inner sanctum. As the days progressed, the casual and snide gestures of the Iron Six had begun to build up like layers of dust I couldn't scrub clean. As the configurations stayed the same, I began to wonder if they would ever make any reciprocal effort. Part of me wanted to confront Konrad and Zara, sling curses and bring the tension to a boil, but the rest of me knew too much was on the line. I'd grown very fond of Tomas and even Ava and Iris were warming to me, and I didn't want to lose their friendships as a casualty of war. For now, I would stay on the fringes of our uneasy flock.

I first learned about flocking as a dancer in college, and since then I'd found its echo in my life reached far beyond the studio or the stage. Flocking is the term used for a wordless understanding of movement, space and other dancers. It is a sixth sense that is in us all but must be coaxed forward through the practice of listening with our whole selves. It is the awakening of every cell and every sense to the practice of awareness. Flocking allows us to feel the energy of the room, the movers around us and the flow of where the dance is going. It is a way of communicating without a leader, a skill beautifully expressed by birds. It is a physical skill but depends greatly on our ability to the read energy and make informed choices. There is no planning, and nothing exists ahead of the now. The skill is about feeling and responding in an instant. It is taking charge and just as quickly relinquishing control, all with effortless ease. Many species flock. Fish move in spatial perfection and turn simultaneously on a dime. This is possible because they have sensory lines down their sides that are tuned to feel pressure and change in direction. We, unfortunately, don't have such high tech equipment built into our bodies, so we have to work harder.

When humans flock, we have to pay attention. We have to focus on the health and well being of the group and read the energetics below the surface. We can't just see the situation and take it at face value. We have to feel into the moment and stay aware of all parts of the whole, acknowledging the interconnectedness of the distant members of the group as well as those closest to us. And most importantly, we have to be ready to play every role in the group. In a flock there is no permanent leader and no resident followers. The reins of control are always on the move, shifting through the whole organism. This clearly wasn't happening in our tribe, especially with the Iron Sixers. Roles were set, power was concentrated, and so we moved in a destructive flock without balance or flow. I could feel our energy slipping and sliding all over the place but felt helpless to stop it. I was only one, and Konrad and Zara needed to get on board with inclusion and connection if our group was going to make it to the end. I could feel the seams beginning to rip in all directions. The American guys begin to drift away. Slice. The Brit boys hang back. Rip. The Iron Six leave me in the dust. Crunch. I was holding this tenuous frame together as best I could, but it was becoming too much. Nobody else seemed to notice all the physical cues or read the many markers of discord.

To study dance is to be immersed in the language of the body. Everything we do is a form of speaking. When attending a performance, we feel the sorrow or joy shown through crumpled bodies or effortless leaps. We read the expression of emotion, because it is a space where we're asked to look deeper. We see a message in movement because a choreographer placed it there and trained dancers to reveal it on cue. Why then do we so often fail to see that even when the language of the body isn't intentionally set, it is still very present?

The stage isn't the only place where the body talks, and professional movers aren't the only people who speak with their bodies. We all spout prose with our limbs and features. Time, space, focus and energy are the raw materials of human movement. They are the alphabet of our vernacular. The way we move comprises a whole language. Movements are jumbled, reassembled, shortened, lengthened and enunciated differently but speak as eloquently as the words that escape our mouths. Perhaps they speak with even more fluency and truth, for it takes much more training to control and manipulate the signals of the body than it does to tell a lie or deceive with words. The mind can be crafty; the body can't help but speak the truth.

If the Iron Six were asked about the nature of our group, the story could be told many ways. Konrad might disassociate with the rest of us and keep his alliances clear. Iris would be polite and insist we were all one big happy bunch. Ava might speak with a jovial tone about how marvelously we got along. Tomas would kindly applaud the way were all equals and valued as such. The messages from their lips via their brains would have a different flavor and slant, but all it would take was one morning in our company to read the body language and know the truth.

When my dance training began, I was almost completely ignorant of the language of the body, but the practice of connecting through movement alone opened a new view. The dance form called contact improvisation is built completely on our ability to read the language of the body. When dancing this way, a dancer's safety depends on this type of literacy. Contact improv is a fast paced practice of basic partnering defined by duets, lifts and physical contact. The difference between the partnering in Swan Lake and contact improvisation is that contact improv is unplanned, un-choreographed and unrehearsed. It is raw and alive. The performers are as new to the dance as the audience. They are bonded in the exhilaration of the unknown. Everything is created on the spot, and the dancers can't pause and set a plan. The essence of the form is that it is spontaneous and alive to the present, so the audience is drawn into the now along with the dancers. The dancers have to risk, trust, be ready to move, change and adapt depending on the sensory information they read off their partners and the group. They have to listen and know what they are looking for. Listening and being able to read the body is the key to success.

Giving off signals is easy, and dancers train themselves to be subtle and smooth with their cues, but while everyone speaks, few can read. We all have plenty to say with our bodies, but few of us bother to read each other. Reading is a general as well as specific skill. Dancers learn the basic shifts in weight centers of another body or the arc of gravity from the floor to the air. Yet at the same time, each mover is different. As dancers become familiar with one another, we learn each other's specific tones.

I was reading the group almost out of habit as we moved away from Astorga, yet I had the distinct feeling I was the only one paying attention to this telling undercurrent. Contact improvisation isn't just based on an individual dancer's ability to read movement clues, but the whole group's capacity to do so. Everybody has to be paying attention to the flow of the group or things can quickly disintegrate into chaos. I knew as long as things didn't change, our group of twelve had a shelf life. We wouldn't be able to navigate what lay ahead if the rest of the group didn't pick up their heads and look around. Every member of the group was an equal part of the flock, but I sensed the Iron Six didn't understanding this. They weren't able to see beyond their tight circle and sometimes, as with

Ava and Iris, beyond their pre-existing bonds.

The group of twelve was certainly talking volumes with their bodies, but some I could read with more depth than others. Francis's body language was the easiest to discern for I knew him the best, yet I could tell he was working extremely hard to control the impulses beneath the outer layer. There was a slight tension in his frame almost all the time, and of late, he seemed caught in two conflicting currents of energy. He was working to organize the way his movement spoke, and it showed. I'd begun to wonder if this was the reason he was avoiding me. We'd both opened up to a point of near transparency to the other, and now he knew I was reading his every gesture, and he was feeling my every emotion. He was aware more than anyone else that I was listening to movement and paying attention to the flow of energy.

Others were more unaware of their movements. Ava's relaxed pleasure with the world was clear in the easy tone of her limbs, the set of her shoulders and loose swing of her head. At the same time, there were bigger clues floating around the group. Zara's defensive positioning in group situations and Konrad's swift and determined actions to physically break the group apart often created a groove in our moving flotilla. The two of them divided us as clearly as if they were drawing a line in the sand. Konrad rarely turned to face me and never initiated contact of any sort. Even in the early morning hours, the movements of our group were telling truths no one was willing to speak.

Within the hour, Ava and Iris stopped to shed layers, encouraging us to keep going. It was a thinly veiled way to be by themselves, but we played along and gave them space. Tomas and I were near the front, and after a few minutes, we pulled away from Jay and Konrad. I was relieved to stay by Tomas's side as we moved ahead on the winding dirt paths.

The tainted memory of my first meeting with Tomas outside of Hornillos was all but erased. I'd long felt there was something earnest and curious about Tomas. He wanted to grow from this journey. At first, his goodness appeared goofy and simple, but now I could see it was a real practice and sprang from a life touched by pain and suffering. Tomas was honest not just in word but in action. His story of arriving at the Camino was an epic filled with integrity and humility. His father had died when he was ten and since that moment, he'd felt an emptiness in his life. In the last year, he'd begun to look at that space inside his emotional life and had started the slow process of healing it. He'd trained for a year to be able to cover great distances and eventually had decided to walk for a total of seven months.

In March, he'd strode out his front door in Belgium and begun his journey. His family had accompanied him to the end of town, waved goodbye and turned back home. Until he'd reached the Camino in southern France, he'd met few young people and had been very lonely. When he'd met the other five Iron Sixers, they'd become his group. It was hard to hear him talk about his closeness to them. But in this moment, he didn't exclude me from knowing him and didn't make me feel the lesser for not being one of the six. For this I was grateful. I could use as many easy and uncomplicated bonds as I could get.

Not surprisingly, we lost sight of everyone ahead or behind. The trail was relatively flat, but as we moved closer to the tiny village of Rabanal, I could see clusters of unfamiliar people on the trail. We'd started a bit late that morning and the proof was in the amount of people clogging the path. Among the groups was the trio of American girls I'd met in Logroño, the ones who'd introduced me to the Cowboy. They smiled and said hello as we passed.

We came upon John at the entrance to the small village of El Gonzo. He was absorbed in picking a hat from a group hanging on an old stonewall. A small white haired man was also selling sticks and calabash gourds. His collection of walking sticks was small but tenderly crafted. This wasn't the first time I'd come across someone selling the famous pilgrim sticks. When Francis had lent me his pole for the afternoon outside of Carrión, I'd become a convert to the joys of walking with a stick. Now that I knew the support they offered, I looked upon them with fresh eyes.

Many in our group had walking sticks. Some only used a single pole, but most people had two poles that could be collapsed inward and strapped on their bags when not in use. On the road out of Mazarife, Jay had lent me a titanium pole he didn't need. I thought it might help my ankles. Within hours, I was grateful for the small and unexpected kindness.

Last night, the Tasmanian had confessed he too was a fan of walking sticks. Since his original sticks had been broken during a brutal fight in the dead of winter with two drunk Russians, he now walked with a brand new set. He admitted he'd been sad to abandon his beloved poles in a trash can, but they'd become too associated with the fifteen kilometer mad dash away from the fight. Running down a deserted road with ten foot high snow-banks and no place to hide had been a rather searing experience. It was good to know poles could serve as weapons when needed, but I hoped I would never have to test them that way.

Poles were the modern equivalent of the medieval wooden stick though some modern pilgrims still carried a wooden stick. A medieval pilgrim often found his stick along the trail, but with the growth of the tourist industry, it was now much more common to buy one from a local like this old man. He would do the legwork of finding the wood and peeling off the bark until the smooth tender insides were exposed. These sticks felt soft and buttery. Even when carved for sale, there was a sense of magic about them. Since day one in Le Puy, Elliot had walked with a stick he'd made at home. He'd spent hours carving it, shaping the handle and varnishing it with endless coats of gloss. He'd taken on the pilgrim's tradition with gusto, and it showed in his careful attention to his stick. He'd never left it behind at an albergue or trailside café, and that was a feat in itself. Even with all the benefits of a stick or pole, some braved the trail with neither. Tomas had walked twice as far as Elliot without a stick to his name. His arms swung with an easy rhythm, and his fingers were calm.

The trail wound into Rabanal through dense clusters of blossoming shrubs. The air was full of the pungent smell of the cloying yellow flowers. I walked behind Tomas and noticed the way he'd tied down all the odds and ends of his journey to his pack. There was a sun hat, compass, rolled sleeping mat and long baguette stuck through two vertical straps. That was the magic of a Camino meal; sometimes pilgrims could just strap it to their bags and go. Tomas walked in pants that zipped off at the knee. On top he wore a long sleeved black turtleneck. Its arms were faded from the sun, and it looked hot as well as worn, but he'd become fond of its energy and kept it as a good luck token. Though the ensemble was far from cool, he managed to pull it off and seemed thoroughly unconcerned with his appearance. The trail made us all a little less vain, and I found that refreshing.

Rabanal was a small cluster of buildings along a cobbled main street with a single shop and church. When we reached the top of the main street, Tomas and I sat on the narrow benches outside the shop. I bought a bar of chocolate for us, and we lazed about in comfortable silence. It didn't last long. Within moments the three British boys came striding up the hill looking like rock stars entering a venue. Ava, Iris, Jay and Konrad followed not far behind with a flood of sound and energy. The group put their bags down and went inside to buy supplies. The tight roadway was full of people milling around. When I looked up, I noticed a man on horseback making his way down the street.

The white horse held a single rider wearing a cowboy hat above a familiar face. There was no mistaking it, here, more than two hundred kilometers and many days later, the Cowboy was sauntering towards me on the back of his dashing gelding. For a moment I couldn't believe my eyes. I'd never expected to see him again.

I hadn't seen the Cowboy since I politely demurred his flirty dinner offer in Logroño. Now he was dismounting right next to me. As he came down off the horse, his eyes traveled around the group and quickly spotted me. In a moment, he had found me out and with a shocked but obviously delighted look he kissed me on the cheek.

"You look like you've been on a tropical holiday!" he remarked with a lascivious look in his eyes. It was stunning how quickly I felt like prey again and how close he lingered after I broke from his greeting. I darted towards his horse to get a bit of space between us. I figured it was best to act oblivious to such blunt advances; it had gotten me out of a jam with him before. The beautiful but nervous young horse was named Fernan, and he was a stunner. Pure white, he contrasted against the brown buildings and was remarkably calm. As I stroked his neck, he hardly moved his feet. I too worked hard to ignore the antics of the Cowboy, but I hadn't escaped as easily as I hoped, and suddenly the Cowboy was by my side slinging his arm around me.

"Come over here gorgeous," he said. Then turning to Tomas he asked, "Will you take a picture of me and my girlfriend?"

It was more statement than question. I blushed and worked my way out of his embrace as soon as the camera clicked. Our little reunion was creating something of a commotion, and everybody seemed to be watching the show. Into the fray came the Tasmanian who immediately engaged the Cowboy in discussion. I felt a thrill course through my body at the Tasmanian's sudden appearance and noticed him look over at me. I wasn't sure he remembered my name, but I knew he remembered the jolt of attraction that had passed between us when we shook hands last night. I could still feel it along the insides of my wrist. The two men discussed the trail as the horse began to move in an agitated fashion. Fernan pulled at his reins and flicked his head up into the sky. Standing close to his powerfully strung body, I lay my palms on the sides of his face in an attempt to sooth him.

The Cowboy retrieved an apple from his pack and smashed it on the cobbles. The flesh of the fruit broke with a soft crunch under his heel. In a split second Fernan's teeth were on it. Suddenly a small man appeared out of the front of the shop and ran over to the Cowboy.

"Move your fucking horse!" he shouted.

The way the curse came forward, tinged with contempt and a deep Spanish accent, made the insult seem even stronger. The Cowboy turned on the man, ready for a fight.

The shopkeeper continued his rant. He didn't want the horse blocking the entrance to his shop, and the Cowboy was required by law to leave. The Spaniard's machismo demanded he show his strength in front of the group. And the Cowboy wanted to have his horse in front of the store where there were fellow pilgrims to impress. I felt a bit guilty knowing he might not have stopped if he hadn't recognized me.

The two combatants stood facing each other as angry words flew across the gap. Balding and elderly, the Spanish shopkeeper only came up to the Cowboy's shoulder. The Cowboy with his dark features and dramatic eyebrows towered over him. I worried he might turn and slice the spurs of his boots into the man if things really started to get out of control. Their voices rose louder and louder. The shopkeeper's wife came to the doorway of the building and started yelling as well. This only increased Fernan's agitation. Many in our group were stifling laughter. The scene was as entertaining as a circus event with nothing more than a pair of egos on the line.

The Tasmanian took out a video camera and chuckled to himself from behind the eye of the lens. Suddenly the Cowboy leapt onto the horse, and with a final curse towards his opponent, rode out of town. It was the classic scene from a western, an exit with flare.

CRUZ DE FERRO

We moved as a large free flowing group out of Rabanal. I fell into step with Ava and Iris who wanted to sing. As we moved towards the Cruz Ferro, I began to teach them a few songs I knew. The Cruz was the highest point on the whole Camino. The incline of the trail increased, and I was acutely aware of the Tasmanian just steps behind me.

I laughed and pushed a good pace as I taught the girls the African round I knew. My lungs scratched for air as we climbed higher into the folds of the mountain. I repeated the parts of the song again and again. It was lovely to feel close to the girls, to be sharing something fun and easy. The Tasmanian was a bit behind our trio and deep in conversation with Francis and Elliot. The others dotted the mountainside like a processional.

As had become routine, we would reconvene as a large group in the evening. Tonight the destination was a mountain refuge on the far side of the Cruz in a place called Manjarin. It was no longer a town but a series of abandoned buildings with a solitary albergue. There would be no store to buy food or fountain for water. My pack was light on supplies, and I would have to rely on the albergue's supper for sustenance. Zara had started the day alone, moving ahead of the rest of us. We assumed she was already at the mountain albergue in Manjarin, awaiting our arrival.

Zara remained an elusive person, dodging and weaving away from me. The first and last time we'd spoken anything of substance was before León, and I'd gotten the sense she wasn't interested in forging any kind of bond with me. We had virtually nothing in common, and she clearly saw me as a peripheral character of no value in her Camino community. She generally avoided me, making it hard to exist in the same circle while feeling her resistance.

By the time I met her, she was close to Ava and Iris. Something had bonded them before I joined their trail. I sensed I would never know what it was and would always feel I'd missed the moment when all their relationships were open and nothing was locked down. I'd slept in the same set of bunks with Zara countless times, and yet it didn't engender closeness. It only felt like an attempt to keep your friends close and your enemies closer. She continued to strategically place herself between me and the rest of the Iron Six. Maybe that was her unofficial duty. There was a clear line drawn between their six and the rest of us.

Our group appeared as if it should split down the keel: six on one side and six on the other, but the American guys, Brit boys and I didn't set up an exclusive dynamic. The composition of the group didn't seem to matter much to Francis, Elliot and John, for they seemed a bit ambivalent about the Iron Six. Jack and Ivan were lone rangers who took off when they felt like it and never really tried to lock anything down.

This left me as a solitary figure, close to lots of circles but never fully allowed into any. I thought time would change this, that all we needed was the opportunity to get to know each other individually and something would shift. All I could do was hope every day would bring another chance to know each person I walked with a little better.

All group drama aside, I could feel my interest in the Tasmanian growing like a slowly rising temperature. It fluttered in the back of my mind as we crested the hill and came upon the long slender cross known as the Cruz Ferro. The sky had cleared off, and bright shafts of light filled the open ground around the Cruz. After winding our way up through a narrow path of high mountain scrub, the trail now opened into a large clearing. Ava and Iris had gone quiet behind me. We'd all stopped singing as if on cue.

In the last few days, I'd spoken to several different pilgrims about this place. As the highest point on the trail, it was considered a turning point for all pilgrims passing over its crest. My mind knew this was the peak elevation, but it didn't feel that way. The mountains that dropped off beside us were wide and green. We were certainly up high, but these peaks didn't have the breath stopping grandeur of the Pyrenees. When crossing them on the first day, there had been mountains as far as the eye could see. I'd felt as if I was being swallowed by the earth itself and thrown into the goliaths of the land. There had been a sliver of danger in every view, but this range was different.

The land around the Cruz was docile in comparison, yet people had found reason to mark the spot. At the Cruz Ferro, pilgrims felt the need to leave something they could carry no further, and so the tradition began.

Set on a large mound of rocks, the cross was a tall thin rail that ran straight into the air. This place had become a repository for sorrows from lives and worlds far away. Jay was the first person to tell me about the tradition of the Cruz. He explained that for the last thousand years people had left home for their pilgrimage with a small stone or object in tow. They carried these objects with them as tokens representing pieces of their lives they wanted to leave behind on the trail. Jay had brought a stone from Florida. Tomas had a stone from earlier in his journey.

As I walked closer to the large base of the Cruz, I fingered a small smooth stone in my pocket. I'd only picked it up a few days ago. Almost a perfect oval, it was the size of a euro and metallic grey with a milky white line running through its core. I'd found it among the thousands of other stones that fell beneath my feet each day, but somehow it had caught my eye. The way the line cut through the two spheres felt exactly right. It represented the current state of my life, this place in time between the old travails of young adulthood and the beginning of a new existence: the past and the future. It was the promise of a new skin, a new way of being. I wanted so much to leave this stone full of all my past failings. I wanted the pile to accept the pieces of my past I couldn't carry anymore.

Jay sat on a fence leading up to the cross. Tomas sat next to him with his pack at his feet. They nodded hello to me, but in a show of respect for the sanctity of this place, they didn't speak. I looked up at the cross and knew instinctively the climb up was an individual experience. Konrad was at the top of the mound. His back was to us, and the sun shone through his bent legs and elbows as he squatted down deep in thought. I couldn't see his face. It was tilted down and away. His hand reached up towards the cross where the small tokens of strangers dangled and swayed in the breeze. The curl of his fingers as he touched the other objects was instantly strong and vulnerable. I didn't see him leave what he'd carried the length of his trail but felt him brush by me on his way down.

As I moved up toward the base of the cross, I found myself wading through piles of stones: stones that had no link to the land around us, stones that were sharp and clear, bright and worn by the ocean. These were stones that had come in the packs and pockets of thousands of pilgrims. The base of the cross was covered in a collage of loss, sorrow and release. An old pair of boots worn through to the soles. A handwritten note of love. A frayed cowboy hat and a pair of sunglasses with no lenses. A small picture of a baby, its body covered in the tubes of modern medicine, its delicate face turned to the side with eyes closed.

The weight of brokenness hung off my limbs, yet the immense capacity of human love to carry on through suffering and sadness, grief and loss was profound. The Cruz spoke of our need to love no matter the risks and against all odds. Here was the proof. To my own disbelief I felt my eyes fill with tears. The drops hung on my eyelids. This was a place exploited by bus pilgrims and tourists, but somehow it still held wisps of its ancient integrity. I was surprised to feel its energy as I stood at the apex. Here among the discarded sorrows was the stream of wisdom and faith the trail gave each that walked her path.

I came down the heap of memories with a clean emptiness. I'd left my stone among the others and could feel the weight slipping from me, evaporating into the land. I'd held the rock for only a few days, but in that time I'd given it all my sorrows. I'd given the rock failed loves and lost communities. In return, the rock and this moment had given me the gifts of letting go. What exactly I'd left with the small stone I didn't know. Only the rest of the trail could answer that question. I'd crossed the milky white divide to what lay ahead and moved away from the past of what was.

Weightlessness coursed through me as I walked down the other side of the Cruz Ferro. Tomas, Konrad and I set off from the top, ahead of the rest. I wanted to leave the girls to have their own moment at the Cruz. I'd felt earlier that day there was something fragile about Ava that she hadn't shared with me. The way Iris had held her with the utmost tenderness as they stood beside the cross spoke of things I hadn't been shown: internal worlds to which I wasn't privy but could sense the edges of.

The combination of downhill gravity and the rush from the experience at the Cruz allowed us to practically skip down the mountain. My legs bounced with each step. Even though none of us spoke, it was clear we were deeply excited to see what this night would bring. It was the tangible feeling of reaching the summit and knowing after so many days on the trail that we had finally climbed the highest peak.

Konrad was leading the charge down the mountain. This was fitting since he was the person who'd encouraged our group to stay in the small and isolated mountain refuge of Manjarin. The evening before in Astorga, he'd described the refuge. It would have no running water, no electricity and nothing more than mattresses on a barn floor. It was located in a mountain town deserted for over fifty years. In my life before the trail, this kind of accommodation would have been tolerable but not something I would have sought out. Now after all these days of living on the road, I felt a blooming excitement about what might await us in such a refuge. I relished the idea of being on a mountaintop, pared down to the essentials with my trail comrades.

The Camino lived and breathed the life of shared experiences. That was how it stayed alive and what kept people going forward. I knew I would have abandoned the trail if I hadn't been living in some vague form of community every stop along the way.

Most of us had grown up in a culture that considered it a necessity to have our own rooms when we traveled, but this meant living in isolation from each other. I loved the shared spaces of the albergues, the way we all congregated in the evenings and how in the night we heard each other sleeping, breathing, shifting and snoring. Despite all the downsides, we were in and around each other all the time, and I relished this interwoven life. In my eyes, it was worth more than any five star accommodations. When Konrad told us about the albergue in the mountains, I knew I wanted to stay there. It would be an adventure. It might be uncomfortable, but I was willing to take the risk. Even from a far, it had the scent of magic.

MANJARIN

For most of the descent into Manjarin, I walked a few paces behind the swift movements of Tomas and Konrad. There was a determined set to Konrad's face, and he hadn't spoken since we left the Cruz. As we moved down into the village, we arrived in a world long dormant. All that remained were the decaying ruins of houses so crumbled that only a few feet of stone remained. The insides of the foundations were overgrown in a riot of weeds. The buildings had become a part of the land itself, slowly melting back into the wild hills. I now understood how settlements vanished. The land was swift to reclaim, and human memories quick to fade. Beside the handful of men running the albergue, no one had lived in this village for over fifty years. Yet there was life in every place along the trail, even here, and each pilgrim traveling through this forgotten town energized it, if only for a few moments.

Outside the albergue a large sign made up of individual planks of wood marked the distance to Santiago, New York, Rome, London and other places around the globe. Many of the distances were a bit rough considering they included thousands of kilometers of ocean, but the sign suggested this small albergue deep in the mountains was connected to the rest of the world, a spot on the map just as relevant as other more illustrious places. The sign seemed to mark our progress and honor the determination of the pilgrims who came to the albergue's doors from far off lands.

The bell in the dooryard of the albergue rang loud and clear as we arrived. After several rings, an old man with a crisp white beard stilled the bell above his head. It was his duty to ring the bell as each new pilgrim crossed the threshold. This had been his task for nearly twenty years.

There were so many tiny gestures and small greetings given to pilgrims along the length of the trail. Each gave a feeling of welcome and recognition. The cheerful honk from a passing car or a nod of acknowledgement from locals in the streets were proof this was no easy task, and people respected us for sticking with the trail. Most greetings were energizing or made us laugh. Others, like the soft, "Buen Camino" from a grandmother pulling weeds in her garden, filled me with calm. The phrase "Buen Camino" literally meant good trail and was a term honoring those of us on the Camino. This trail culture reminded me how even a small gesture can encourage people to keep going. We never know how a smile or a moment of connection can shift people's feelings about their world and the rough journey they are on.

The group of building that comprised the albergue were mainly old sheds converted into usable space. Most were narrow and dark on the inside but quirky and eclectic from the outside. The dining room table sat vulnerable to the elements in the center of the front courtyard. Its top was little more than a few thick planks worn with weather and age, nailed onto a rough base, but it was sturdy and could welcome at least twelve people on the stone benches built around the edges. A canopy of scrap wood hung over the table, keeping most of the elements at bay. As we checked in and had our pilgrim passports stamped, a family of kittens emerged from under the table. Konrad and I chased their tiny bodies around and scooped them into our hands. The litter was a rainbow of warm colors, deep oranges and creamy yellows. I managed to gather a handsome grey and white fellow into my arms and let him delight in chewing on my fingers with his sharp incisors.

It was lovely to be holding a living thing again even if only the skinny limbs of a squirming kitten. I realized how much I missed physical contact and the warmth of bestowing unfiltered affection on a living being. The kittens made me miss my connection to babies and children. The Camino was an adult's world, and it had been weeks since I'd done more than smile at a passing child. Though there were benefits to adult company, I longed for a bit of uncomplicated human contact. I missed the chance to just be playful and see the wonder in the moment as only kids can.

As I held the furry wriggling body, I was less upset about the dearth of kids on the Camino than I was about their absence from my life beyond the trail. My friends in college had often joked that I was drawn to any little kid who crossed my path, and if they didn't stop me, I would adopt every one and put them in a pouch like a mother kangaroo. My bond with children and my desire to be a mother were essential parts of me. When asked in college what I dreamed of being when I grew up, I'd told an assembled group of liberal feminist hipster artists that I wanted to be a mom. The incredulous silence that had followed was intense, but ultimately the opinions of other women or the current culture meant less to me than pursuing the life I craved. The desire to have children of my own was engrained in my every cell. It might have been blasphemous and perhaps a bit foolish to admit this truth to my classmates at the time, but nothing could shake me from this desire. And even as time drew me deeper into adulthood and offered very few clues as to when I would be able to live the dream, I didn't let go.

Konrad managed to capture one of the bigger kittens to stroke its soft cheeks as our host led us to the sleeping quarters. Across a rutted lane was a small barn with thick stonewalls and a roughly fashioned wooden door. This was the main sleeping room with six beds downstairs and five up in the loft. I was a bit concerned whether there would be enough space for all of us. There were already two young guys occupying a pair of beds. A large flat wooden frame that held four beds all in a row dominated the downstairs sleeping area. I quickly threw my stuff down and claimed the beds for the girls and me. Even though the young guys seemed harmless, we girls needed to stick together. Tomas and Konrad climbed up into the loft where mattresses lay on the floor under a sagging roof. The room had no lights, but a small candle sat in the only window. Once again, I was glad I'd brought a flashlight.

Zara appeared, looking thoroughly relieved to see us. She'd been there by herself, nervous we might not show. The tension in her body dropped as soon as Tomas came down the stairs to greet her. I recognized Zara's fear since I'd felt it myself earlier in the trail. It was strange how quickly we became attached to each other as basic survival supports. We all seemed to feel safer because we were a group of many. Zara was pleased I'd claimed the large sleeping area but took charge and assigned spots. I was given the far left side of the bed, and she placed herself to my right. Ava and Iris would be next to each other on the other side. In the night, I knew I would be pushed to the very edge of the bed, but I was too tired to fight her instructions.

Not long after, Iris and Ava arrived to claim their beds. Jay and Konrad had settled into relaxation mode at the outdoor table, talking, chewing on sunflower seeds and cracking open their ritual "arrival beers." They'd bought the beers in the morning, anticipating this abandoned town wouldn't have much to offer in the way of refreshments. The beer added a few extra pounds to their packs, but they were dedicated to the nightly ritual and went to great lengths to keep the tradition alive.

I wondered where Francis, Elliot and John were, but I wasn't expecting Ivan and Jack. The American guys were going to stay on the other side of the Cruz Ferro. They wanted to wake early to see the Cruz at sunrise. They planned to sleep in a small village we'd passed through earlier in the afternoon called Foncebadón, a village known in Camino lore for its wild dogs and haunted buildings. I wondered if the boys would be treated to either of these experiences during their night's stay. As we'd passed through the rundown village, I only saw one ragged ancient dog, and he'd been sleeping so soundly that until I'd drawn close, I'd worried he was dead.

Ava and Iris flopped down on the bed, unlaced their boots and complained of their general dirtiness. There was no running water, but the head of the albergue told us we could use the abandoned village well to wash up. The girls convinced me to come with them, so we took off in a noisy cluster towards the well on the other side of the village. We figured we could protect each other from prying eyes and general male intrusion if we stuck together. As we headed to the west side of the village, I glanced back to see Francis and Elliot arriving at the albergue gates. I waved to them before turning down the road towards the well. Walking barefoot, we spotted the well house down in a grassy valley. The tiny hut was the size of a large doghouse with a spout protruding from its side. The water pooled at the edge of the building into a small indent in the land. Even though the flow from the pipe was constant, the water couldn't have been more than a foot deep. Nonetheless, it was fresh and held the icy tang of mountain streams.

One of us kept watch on the road as we took turns bathing. I tossed my layers off into the grass and stepped into the shallow pool. Chills ran up my bare skin as I stood in the open breeze. My fingers turned a light shade of blue as I scooped the water into my hands and doused my body. That afternoon in the lowering rays of sun, we were nymphs, hopping around under the touch of cold water, part of an enchanted moment.

Iris kept several men on the trail from peering over the side of the bank and down into our private world. One man went up to the hill above and turned back in hopes of catching a glimpse. Iris swore he even pulled out a camera, but we had thrown our clothes on before he could seek us out with his telephoto lens. Ava laughed as the peeping tom gave up and disappeared over the backside of the hill. The moment was ours alone, weary and wild and something just the four of us shared. No matter the dynamics past or future, we would always have our moment at the mountain well.

As I sat in the tall thick grass and let the sun dry my skin, I felt a hum fill my body. I knew this moment was just as it should be. That somehow the combination of this place and these people was destined. It had always been part of me, part of the promise of the trail. I suddenly felt each of us had arranged to meet here, to be here together for this time. We just hadn't known it until now. I'd been unable to identify why I'd needed to walk so fast in the first weeks, but some part of me had known I had an appointment with these souls. I'd understood the universe was pulling all of us together like individual threads to a larger weave. It was a mighty feat to bring us to the trail and feed us into the flow so we could meet here. Tomas had already been walking for weeks before I'd bought my ticket to Spain. The Brit boys had battled illness and injury, while Jack and Ivan had hitched a ride outside of Burgos to bump them ahead. Now I knew this was my divine appointment. The soft contentment pulsing through me was proof that even with zero information to control my entrance and movement along the trail, I'd found those whom I was meant to find. Alberto had been a gift to me in service of this appointment. He'd helped me move faster and farther than I might have on my own. He'd aided me in connecting with this group of twelve and then had disappeared ahead into the current of the trail when his duty was done. After he'd evaporated in Frómista, he'd moved away from my life and onward with his own quest, knowing he'd delivered me to my destiny. He'd delivered me here to this perfect, imperfect flock.

When we returned, Konrad, Tomas and Jay were bare-chested at the table, still eating salt encrusted sunflower seeds. When Zara shared the story of our peeping tom pilgrims, the guys thought it was entertaining. They laughed a bit at our expense and carried on with their card game. Their blasé reaction was a blunt reminder that we females faced different challenges on the trail, and in the world, than our male counterparts. They would never be worried about an overly aggressive member of the opposite sex groping them, leering with determined intensity or violating their privacy with a telephoto lens. Even though I'd accepted this gender gap, I was a bit irritated at how unsympathetic and aloof the guys were. It was an immature moment and quickly reminded me no matter how grown up they acted, this bunch of dudes were rather clueless when it can to women. I wondered what the Brit boys and American guys would have done, if they would have fallen in with the general sentiment or displayed something more genuine. My guess was the latter.

It should have slid right off my back, been another conversation that drifted away forgotten, but as I unfurled my sleeping bag in the late afternoon, I found myself thinking about their reaction. I sometimes wondered if people really understood the damage they inflicted when they stood by and watched others get hurt. I'd wanted one of the boys to jump up from the table and pledge to protect us from such scourge or at least feel something, any pulse of emotion. So many people had sat on the sidelines doing nothing as men of the past had violated me. These witnesses, both men and women had been complicit in the acts unfolding around them. They'd chosen not to stand up and defend me. I'd seen this same thing happen with my extended family as swaths of relatives had stood by and done nothing to protect me, my siblings and parents when my uncle had repeatedly threatened to kill us. And most pointedly for me, I'd seen it in my relationships, where communities of mature adults, mentors, teachers and close friends had stood by and let me go to the wolves. Older people, with more perspective and a deeper understanding of the man in question than my young self, had not come to me in the trenches to stand beside me, didn't follow their hunch that something was amiss. I understood ultimately I was responsible for the relationships I choose to embark on, but I also knew I would defend the ones I loved tooth and nail. People either worked for the truth or they didn't. There were no innocent bystanders. If I had been in the guys' shoes this afternoon, I would have defended my tribe, defended the girls of my group without question or scorn. As I fell into a warm afternoon doze on top of my sleeping bag in Manjarin, I realized we were drawn into challenges almost every day here, moments that laid bare what we were willing to risk and how much we cared about protecting each other. When it came to this group, I was all in.

Night fell swiftly in the mountains. When I awoke, the light had shifted and shadows cluttered the room. I didn't know how long I'd been asleep. When I emerged into the falling light, I was greeted by most of the group sitting around the table, still playing cards and finishing the last of the beer and wine. With dinner an hour away, I could feel my stomach grumbling. I was surprised to find John at the table, but no Francis and Elliot. To blend in with the other macho males around him, John sat at the far side with his shirt off and a pair of dark sunglasses covering his eyes. Ava shuffled the cards and asked John if he wanted to be dealt in. He declined reluctantly and said he needed to find Elliot and Francis. I told the group I'd seen them arrive a couple of hours ago. This sent everyone into a burst of confused chatter. If they were here, where were they?

The albergue wasn't that big. They might have gone to the well, but they wouldn't have stayed there for hours. John was noticeably agitated and went off to look for them. Once John was out of earshot, Ava turned to me with a look of sheer irritation and told me she was pissed at Elliot and Francis. John had a bit of a lost puppy attitude about him, and by this point, we were all sure he'd been ditched for the afternoon. I understood Francis and Elliot's need for space, but I was surprised they would do such a thing to John after all these weeks together.

The assembled crew at the table wasn't pleased with the afternoon's events. I was particularly startled by how indignant Ava and Iris were about John's temporary abandonment. They clearly thought it was rather mean spirited. This was a bit of the pot calling the kettle black. These girls, especially Zara, had made more obvious moves of exclusion than this small slight, but now they were feeling righteous and convinced me to go in search of the head of the albergue to see where the boys were. I was a little worried myself about where Elliot and Francis had gone. If I hadn't seen them arriving earlier, I would have been just as anxious as John.

I needed to check if there was anywhere else pilgrims were housed on the property, and if so, had two stray Brits been placed there. Walking into the small courtyard around the main building, I couldn't find the older man, but a young guy in his twenties came rushing out of the house as I approached. He was wearing a mechanic's suit and was the spitting image of the head of the albergue. After navigating a rough Spanish dialog with the scruffy but handsome young man, I learned he was the son of the owner and there was, in fact, another building for pilgrims down the far side of the hill. He pointed up and over the side of the hill away from the road and winked at me as he dashed back into the building.

I thanked him, and he returned to the kitchen to prepare dinner. I tried not to think about what an auto mechanic might put before us. The trail had offered up some very strange and rather disgusting meals, but at this point, I was committed to the dinner no matter what. The group at this albergue clearly cared about pilgrims. It was imbedded in their every action, and even though it wasn't evident in the state of the facilities, this place held an energy of pilgrimage unlike any place I'd stayed. I had to trust the meal would follow suit.

Walking to the backside of the property, I spotted a small wooden house tucked down out of sight from the road. This was a prime place to disappear, a quiet hollow away from the rest of the buildings. I knew Francis and Elliot would be inside. After following the narrow grassy trail to the house, I entered through the low door as Francis came down from the loft through a hole in the ceiling. He stepped gingerly off the ladder and landed with a soft thud on the floor, offering a smile of welcome. I wished I felt so cheery. He was obviously pleased to see me but skilled enough at reading my energy and furrowed brow to know I was the emissary from a disgruntled faction. He stood back from me as I unfolded a description of the scene up at base camp. As I spoke, he seemed to withdraw slightly, pull back and dig in his heels. I suddenly felt I'd placed myself at the center of a mess that had nothing to do with me, and now it was causing Francis to pull away. I admitted as much to him, and we lapsed into silence. He felt he was right to seek a bit of time and space apart from John, and yet understood how callous the gesture appeared. I sighed deeply and suggested we go up and join everybody for dinner. His shoulders seemed to drop their defensive stance and accept my imperfect truce. Elliot joined us on the walk back up to the albergue. They both promised they would go see John right away and make amends before the dinner bell rang. I hated to fight with Francis especially about something like this. As we crested the rise in the land and the albergue came into view, I felt Francis look over at me, and returning his glance, I knew he was attempting to make peace. I gave him a half smile as he dashed off to find John. I'd missed his company in the last few days and realized I'd gotten in the middle of the fight just so I could reconnect with him again. Anything not to feel like ships passing in the night.

Later after dinner, Francis would take me back down the winding path to the house and show me the peaceful spot where he'd spent his afternoon. Lying on his low tidy bed, I would drink in the building's smell of fresh pine and feel insulated from the world. We would talk with our usual flow, relishing the feeling of being adrift all by ourselves. I would wonder what he was thinking and realize for one of the first times that I didn't know. Closing my eyes, I wouldn't be able to read his body or feel if he was watching me. The attic space would be small and close, warm and intimate like sleep. I would lie with my legs dangling off the edge of his bed, my eyes tracing the boards on the ceiling. His voice would be low and melodic as the edges of his energy field spread over me, and I would suddenly be aware of every breath. We wouldn't touch, but the air would be thick with the question of the open space between us. I would feel Francis silently wrestling with the moment, caught in a soundless struggle with what would come next, both of us sharing an unsettling feeling that the vibration between us was slipping from our control, becoming something different than before. And I would be glad when Tomas arrived unexpectedly to say hello, yet strangely disappointed as if all the energy had drained from the room as soon as another person arrived and cut the air between us. I would be curious what Francis was feeling as I bid him goodnight and traipsed back up the hillside with Tomas but find myself at a loss, unsure where it was all going.

The table was being set for the meal when we returned. I helped place the tin plates around the edge and folded napkins as Elliot and Francis went off to talk with John. Tomas reappeared from his afternoon nap, and the group waited in anticipation for supper. After we found our places around the table, I crawled out from my spot to help serve the first course. A large pot of creamy soup sat just inside the albergue. The head chef, a pirate in both looks and demeanor, scooped the liquid into the shallow bowls and gave me a wink in return for playing waitress.

Our hosts were Knights Templar, an ancient fraternity of men who'd protected pilgrims since the middle ages. In medieval times, they'd protected pilgrims' money from theft as they walked the trail. The Knights Templar had been in essence a moving safety deposit box for those on the Camino. Here in this deserted town hundreds of years later, this small band of men running the albergue were a part of what remained of that order.

As I passed out the fragrant soup, the elder statesman of the albergue sat down at the head of the table. For a place with no electricity or running water, the soup was an astounding miracle. Large bowls of crusty bread were scattered around the table. The bread was warm and homemade. I hadn't known what to expect in this isolated land among the mountains, but now I was caught in a wave of grateful awe. I took my place next to Elliot on the far side of the table. I was close to the top of the table where the head of the albergue sat quietly until the food was plated. He waited until the noise settled into silence and then in soft deep tones thanked the universe for the bounty of the meal. I was rather sure I was the only person who caught any of the meaning of his words, but we all felt the tone. When the prayer ended, the Knight motioned for us to begin eating. As we slurped from large spoons and broke pieces of the bread into the silky soup, he told us the history of this town.

During the meal, I translated the Knight's words to the rest of the group. The light was nearly gone as we finished, and the air carried a new chill that cut across my skin even though I was sandwiched between Elliot and Francis. Looking around the table, I felt all the battle lines had come down. We had paused for a time, stalled the engine of complicated group dynamics and accepted this night, accepted the beauty of the meal and the gift of kindness coming from the wizened Knight and his son. We had embraced the adventure that many a pilgrim passed up for more plush accommodations, and this was our reward.

I had no trouble slipping into sleep. My body was warm with food, and our room was filled with the magic of childlike delight. Just for this night, we had found a dream-like kingdom of old, of mountain air, knights and feasts. We had drawn together despite all odds and shared something precious, something fleeting and irreplaceable.

MOLINASECA

STAGE NINETEEN- 23.5K-14.6M
MANJARIN TO PONFERRADA

At dinner, the Knights had told us we couldn't leave the albergue before seven the next morning. This was an unusual request on a trail where hospitaleros made sport of kicking people out of bed at dawn and sometimes even shook pilgrims awake with obvious delight. The Knights relished their chance to restore and care for us weary travelers and believed a grueling morning schedule wasn't a healthy one. They despised the new trail ethos of waking at four, racing to finish the day and competing for bunks. It wasn't how traditional pilgrims traveled the trail and threatened to erode the real importance of the journey.

Nonetheless, I was accustomed to waking at five or six, loved the quiet morning hours on the trail and subsequently felt a bit put out by the request. Tomas woke me at seven as he promised he would, and we navigated our way into the Knights' dark and cluttered kitchen for breakfast. Every surface in the room was covered in tilting stacks of books, yellowing papers, large cast iron pots and faded china. A blackened stove belched heat in the middle of the room while a window the size of a picture frame offered the only natural light. Swinging vines of garlic and salami dangled from the walls, and jars of pickled vegetables lined the shelves next to plastic bottles of orange soda. Apparently, even Knights Templar had their modern vices. One of the younger Knights was boiling water for coffee, and the table was cluttered with biscuits, cups, saucers and jars of butter and jam. I ate cereal with warm milk as Tomas drank coffee from a chipped mug. I was startled when Konrad came striding into the room, his hair sticking in every direction, rubbing his eyes awake. He looked down the table at us and paused as if he was debating his next move: to sit and join our small posse or to return to sleep and wait for back up. As he dropped down into the seat at the end of the table, he seemed to have made up his mind that food and Tomas's presence outweighed the slightly irritating company of a certain American girl. The morning was shaping up to be quite eventful.

After I thanked the Knights for the warm breakfast and slipped more money into the donativo box, I slung my backpack onto my shoulders. It was a true delight to know the trail was downhill today; psychologically, it made everything feel much simpler. All I had to do was let my body ride the current of the trail down into the next valley and watch where I placed my feet. Gravity was a changeable creature that worked against you one moment and then tilting her face just so, was suddenly your dearest friend. She was the definition of a frienemy; always keeping you on guard for a change of heart.

As I departed the three girls were still deep in sleep, curled around each other on the large bed. They looked sweet and docile in the dusky light of the barn, and I did my best to slip out without a sound. Poor Iris had the far side of the bed near an old Spanish man who snored deeply all night. Later she would lament there hadn't been more than an inch of open floor between the edge of her bed and the beginning of his.

At half past seven, the day wasn't warm yet and the air felt crisp, smelling of all things fresh and green. We rejoined the only road that ran through town, passed the well house and looped down into the valley. Konrad disappeared ahead, so I stayed just a bit in front of Tomas. We both took out ipods and disappeared into our own realms. It was such a still morning each of us needed time to wake up before we broke into conversation. The line of rising sunlight could be seen ahead, tracing across the valley and inching toward us. As I walked in the shade, I could see Konrad up ahead entering the new light.

Tomas hummed beside me, but as the trail took a serious turn downward, all our attention focused on putting each foot in front of the other. It was the first time since the Pyrenees I'd experienced a steady downhill. My knees started to ache. I had to concentrate harder and harder to place my feet in a way that kept my balance but didn't stop my momentum on the slippery trail of fragmented rock. Ivan and Jack had assured me several days ago that the best way to tackle the back side of a mountain was to run down the slope, to never put the cartilage brakes on to begin with and go with the flow. I'd seen them demonstrate the technique shortly after and felt they looked slightly nutty as their limbs flailed wildly by their sides and their packs jostled them to and fro. It was a bit too dramatic for the slopes outside of Manjarin so I plodded away with aching care. Both Tomas and I were relieved to reach the first small town on the descending mountain trail. Our path cut through the main street of the sleepy village, and we stopped for a short break. After a second coffee Tomas and I were ready to continue onward, but Konrad lingered at the bar bent on giving us the slip. Tomas shrugged his shoulders to me, and we headed out of town. Apparently the magic of Manjarin hadn't provided the full healing moment I'd craved between Konrad and me.

After several more hours of walking, lunchtime came. I bought a fresh loaf of artisan bread with walnuts and raisins while Tomas purchased savory pastries for each of us, He ended up eating both as my stomach had been agitated all morning. Only later in the evening would I learn that Zara, Francis and Ava all had felt the same way. Eventually we traced it back to the drinking water from the well in Manjarin. The Knights had assured us it was safe, but they'd been drinking it for decades, and their stomachs were clearly more tolerant of the water's microbial life. Still, the experience in the mountains had been worth the sacrifice of a touch of intestinal discomfort.

Tomas and I found a bench along the trail and dropped our packs with grunts of freedom. I'd bought a carton of fruit juice and forced some on Tomas as part of our midday picnic. I was laughing and trying to keep the juice from dripping down my face when around the corner the Tasmanian appeared.

As his long legs strode into view, I was caught off guard, surprised to see him walking in behind us. I could feel my cheeks flush and a delightful glow build in my core as he caught sight of our duo and came over to say hello. I'd hardly thought about him the night before, but back in his presence, I recalled how good it felt to be around an eligible bachelor.

He leaned on his poles and talked with us for a bit, arching his back into long curved lines and pausing only to receive the next question. Not only was I fascinated by his Camino story, but I was curious about his life beyond the trail. I wondered if there was a lady in his life, and what he felt about trail romance. It was hard to imagine he still had vibrant connections at home if he'd been walking for almost two years. He couldn't possibly have a girlfriend waiting back in Tasmania even if he'd left one behind when he set out.

His body and way of speaking were rangy and rough, but he wore a faded shirt with delicately worn holes at the collarbone. He wasn't overtly handsome, but his charismatic persona eclipsed everything else. A two dimensional photo would never capture his magnetism and the aura of charm that hovered around him. He was alive and rakishly good looking when encountered in the flesh. I especially relished his height and the never ending length of his limbs. Even his hands were long and wiry as if they understood both hard labor and refined movements. I felt small and feminine next to the lean manliness of the Tasmanian and savored the feeling. I could imagine the way I would be able to feel his bones beneath his skin if I touched him. I looked at his face and wondered what it would be like to kiss him. How far he would have to bend down to scoop me up and how high I would have to stretch on my toes to meet him. Something about the attraction was immediate and blushingly visceral. And I sensed it had the potential to be reciprocal.

Even amidst my daydreaming, I could tell the downhill was starting to take its toll on my legs. My front tendons were aching with the familiar sharpness of tendonitis. We could see the city of Ponferrada ahead but would have to cross through several small villages before reaching it. I tried to ignore my legs but was worried my body was sending me a signal.

The Tasmanian walked with us towards Ponferrada, chatting with Tomas and Luc who'd appeared out of nowhere. We watched in amazement as the Tasmanian used his long wingspan to pluck cherries off roadside trees and toss them to us. Eventually Luc and the Tasmanian dropped back out of sight as Tomas and I charged forward, the tireless advanced guard. I wanted to reach the albergue so I could sit and rest my legs. I was beginning to wonder if my legs were acting as a universal telegraph line, tapping out a signal I needed to decipher but was attempting to ignore. It had seemed like universal organization when the Tasmanian had come upon us this morning; I couldn't be too far off course. His return had brought on a flood of energy, and wasn't that what I was following?

The outskirts of Ponferrada were deceptively vast. I could see the city off to the right as we crested the top of the valley, but it took over an hour to wind our way into town. Konrad reappeared ahead, and I wondered how he had overtaken us. Now he waited on a hot barren strip of road between two outlying towns. He walked around in tight circles and glanced up occasionally as we got closer. I knew he wanted to be with Tomas as they entered Ponferrada so they could share an "arrival beer." Since the epic portage of beer to Manjarin, I was now aware of this revered Iron Six tradition.

The three of us stopped to wait for others at the first café within the city line. It was a prime location right along the trail, so it would be easy to add other pilgrims to the arrival party. I felt awkward as I sat in the middle of a tradition that was Iron Six territory. The fact I wasn't a drinker didn't ease matters. As we sat down, the Tasmanian came around the corner. His long strides quickly dissolved the distance between him and our table. He stopped for a short hello to Konrad but said he wanted to get to the albergue before all the supermercados closed for the day. I had the same desire and asked if I could walk with him to the albergue.

It was a bit of a calculated move, but I wanted to go, and he seemed genuinely delighted to have me join him. Just the tilt of his head as he accepted my company and the way he soaked me in fully, perhaps for the first time, confirmed my theories. There was a bit of a spark, and it wasn't all coming from my side of the court. With his sudden interest, I knew I had to dive into the chance to be with him one on one. I had to follow the pulse. Potential loves interests often made me retreat back into my shyest self, but as I leapt up from the table, I felt a rush of bravery. This trail had drawn me away from comfort and towards the new. I had to keep trusting her flow and the seemingly random coincidences.

PONFERRADA

The albergue was a large squat building on the edge of town. It housed one hundred and eighty pilgrims in vast low slung rooms. The front of the building had an inviting but utilitarian patio with shaded tables and a swath of lush lawn. If the sun hadn't been so bright, I would have sprawled out on the green, but I had things to do before siesta. I'd eaten the last of my supplies in Molinesca, and food shopping beckoned.

The Tasmanian and I dropped our bags inside the gate. A friendly older pilgrim said he would keep an eye on our stuff while we dashed into town. He and a crew of others were waiting in line to get into the albergue, even though it didn't open for another two hours. Most of the determined pilgrims were older, and I could sense they were highly focused on securing a place to sleep and being first to the showers and washing machines. Lines and worry over accommoda-tions were becoming more prevalent as we drew closer to the more popular pil-grimage month of July. I imagined everything would become even more chaotic as we neared Santiago.

I didn't fret too much about the scarcity model when it came to beds. Sleeping on the floor or outside if necessary wasn't a problem; I was certainly tired enough at the end of the day and knew some of the bunks offered little more padding than a patch of grass. As long as I had a group encircling me I could adjust to anything. I could see the way anxiety laid waste to pilgrims even more than walking did and the way fear ate away at their enjoyment of the day. I had my own things I wanted to churn over in endless worry, but all I could do was practice the fine art of distraction. If I filled my moments with people and movement, I could banish the worry. I'd wasted too much of the early trail gnaw-ing at those bones of doubt and fear. I wanted the second half of the trail to be defined by blithe hope and trust in the swiftly approaching end of the world. The nervous pilgrims in line were a helpful reminder of how not to waste my energy in the days ahead.

As we went in search of a supermercado, time was of the essence, for si-esta hour was fast approaching. I tried my best to keep pace with the Tasmanian's strides, but even with my long legs, I had to take extra little hops to keep up. I could feel my limbs were jumpy and my movements slightly twitchy. I was more than a bit nervous to be alone with the Tasmanian, and I found it nearly impos-sible not to overcompensate with endless chatter at a million miles per hour. For a shy person, I was amazed my nerves caused me to get stuck in this strange gear filled with verbal overflow and run on sentences. Perhaps I feared open air and what an empty pause might reveal. My general strategy was to ask questions and keep them coming at a fast clip. Luckily for me, the Tasmanian was a genuinely fascinating pilgrim and loved to talk about himself. So I used both elements of his character to my advantage. It felt like a fact-finding expedition, digging below the surface and feeling into his energy as the topic swung from his homeland to being stalked by a hungry puma in the jungles of South America. I didn't expect him to ask any questions in return, and he didn't. My journey was dull as paste in comparison to his, and I didn't think life in New England had the same mystique as a childhood in Tasmania. Nonetheless, I wondered where the vibration humming between us came from if he knew little more than my name and what I looked like after a day on the trail. It was a high-strung conversation, but I tried to make it seem effortless. If we could get beyond this moment, there would be time and space to settle into a more equal dialog.

A group of women standing in the entrance of an office building directed us to the supermercado. I was surprised to notice my Spanish was better than the Tasmanian's. I wondered how he had managed to get through Central America on so little. The supermarket was a large white space filled with rough metal shelves and rows upon rows of florescent lighting. It made American supermarkets feel cozy, a feat I thought impossible until now. I was reminded once again that not all food shopping in Spain took place in quaint markets. Some local markets lived on, but the modern Spaniard was a fully westernized breed of shopper, and it showed.

The shelves were filled with American brands and packaged in an excessive western fashion. I'd already eaten more Special K and Dannon yogurt on this trip than I had in all my previous years. The Tasmanian led the way through the wide aisles, moving like a man on a mission. He threw items into his cart, exclaiming how thrilled he was to be able to count on food at the end of the day. One day in Central America, he'd walked seventy kilometers on an empty stomach and finished the hike by feasting on the only food available; a raw onion and an under ripe mango. He'd eaten the onion first in hopes of masking the taste, but confided it had been hardly worth the scant calories as its pungent flavor had filled his taste buds all night long.

As we paid, he tossed a few bars of chocolate onto his pile, explaining he'd lived on chocolate and canned tuna for much of his trip. They were easy to transport and densely packed with protein and fat. He was only twenty-eight, making him just over three years my senior, yet he seemed much more worldly than his years. A fellow Aquarian, he was born on his family's large cattle station when his mother went into labor while working in the yards. Apparently, she'd needed to race back to the house to get to a bed before he came charging into the world.

The age gap between the Tasmanian and me was narrower than it had been with my previous relationships, but I still felt the gulf. Four years was much more digestible than ten or thirteen, but the Tasmanian had lived a bolder existence, risked more and seen more of human life. He'd pushed the boundaries of his twenty eight years, and I found this energy of adventure captivating. Unlike the men of my past, he'd tested himself against the places and people he'd encountered, and I assumed he'd uncovered more about his essential self in the process. Even with all its allure, the distance between us made me feel younger than my years in an unsettling way. It was as if I'd been strangely scrubbed clean off all the independent strength and wisdom I'd grown into on this trip, and I was hardly good enough to make a blip on his romantic radar. Or maybe I just felt this way because my confidence was now eclipsed by my sudden desire to be close to him.

It seemed as if the Tasmanian had lived many lifetimes before he arrived at this moment with me. He'd broken his nose three times, most of his ribs, both the bones in his forearm, his right tibia, dislocated his shoulder which frequently had to be popped back in place and received countless stitches in various spots across his body. His spleen had been sliced in half during an Aussie rules football game, and he'd pulled his middle finger fully from its joint. He was a Frankenstein of repaired parts, and as he towered above me, I had to wonder how the other guys fared.

Even though I'd never broken a bone, I'd been an athlete and dancer all my life. I too had stories to tell of epic physical moments and years filled with sweat and toil. I was a warrior in my own way but knew it couldn't match the drama of his tales. Some of my un-brokenness was no doubt luck, but I also felt injuries were external markers of something unfolding on a deeper energetic or emotional level. Everything I'd learned about the mind/body connection suggested even the location of an injury was telling. That said, I didn't even know how to begin to unravel the deeper roots of the Tasmanian's countless injuries, so I let it be.

The supermercado locked it doors behind us and pulled down the heavy metal window grates like weary eyelids. All the other shops had also closed for siesta. The heavy plastic bag twirled from my hand, spinning as it bumped my leg and twisted its thin plastic loops around my wrist. We crossed the empty street and made our way back to the albergue. The trees lining the sidewalk afforded shade to our pathways. Beyond this shade, the world was ablaze with light and harsh reflective surfaces.

Arriving back at the albergue, we found the check-in line had grown even though there was still an hour until opening. We sat under the shade of a grape arbor in the patio and watched the swirling activity flow around us. The Tasmanian stretched his long muscled limbs out under the surface of the table, and I tucked my legs up to my chest.

He told me about his family back in Tasmania. His eyes shone with great pride as he described how his sister had punched a man in the face for groping her in a bar and the way his brothers wrestled to resolve every dispute. I got the feeling he wasn't exaggerating about the toughness of his siblings. They'd all grown up on the cattle station and had spent their childhood roaming the land around the farm. I could see how that kind of wild youth would grow into the desire for a life as an adventurer. I talked about my own family and how I missed the comfort of their presence. I wondered again if they would be different when I returned. I felt so changed. Would they appear different through my transformed eyes?

I'd always been torn between being home and feeling life was calling me out into the world. My parents and siblings were treasured friends, precious beyond all measure, yet the world was out there beyond the edges of our small farm. It had been pulling at me with a fierce tug when I left for Spain, and I was helpless to its siren song.

As I looked across the table at the Tasmanian, I hoped I was ready to trust where love took me. If I gave up control, there was no telling where I would land. I'd leapt for love with this mysterious journey and knew I would give everything to the dream at the end of the world. I just wasn't sure this man from down under was leap worthy or if he was part of my destiny. Only time would tell, but I craved to know now. I wanted to be closer to the answer and the dream, wanted to stop questioning at every turn.

The doors opened as we finished our late afternoon meal. The line rose to its feet, and the giant processional funneled itself by the graying hospiteliero stamping passports and allowing entrance. The Tasmanian tilted his head towards the organized chaos and suggested we wait until the line diminished. I agreed with a sleepy nod. I was happy to sit here with him, to recline in the sweet shade and listen to his thick accent spill into the space between us. I wanted the words and this moment alone to pull us closer and bind my trail to his.

The older man who'd watched our bags arrived at the front of the line. I could see his weary triumph as he ducked into the building and made a beeline for the showers. Finally we joined the queue. Within moments the rest of my group materialized through the gates of the courtyard. The Iron Six stumbled in, now drowsy and a bit drunk from their early afternoon beers. The British boys weren't far behind them, their faces flush with the effort of coming down off the mountain in the heat of the day.

They dropped their bags at my feet and enfolded me with their voices. Ava and Iris were laughing and telling a funny story about leaving Manjarin, while Tomas and the Tasmanian talked to a seventeen year old American from Wyoming. The Tasmanian had walked through this young man's town earlier on his trip. Of all the places he had been over the past two years, one was a town nobody had ever heard of in Wyoming that just happened to be the hometown of this goofy kid. While this overlap brought the boy and the Tasmanian into shared territory, I noticed we'd all drawn closer to each other. Hailing from such different places mattered little at this point, because in this here and now, the Camino was our address on the planet, and this moving location had become our home.

I grew up in an area of the states that had long winters, and I wasn't accustomed to the way warm air and closely entwined lives could produce such community. Winter raged for too many months in northern New England. It broke into the morning air in October, crushed the delicate geometry of flowers in bloom and froze all the liquid life in the grass. The world crunched beneath our feet and bruised the tender canals of our ears. And that was just the beginning. With all autumn's tangible beauty I couldn't love the season. I couldn't love the messenger who came to tell me winter was coming. I couldn't fully befriend the herald that foretold with elegantly drawn proof that everything would grow cold, hibernate or die. With this brutal cycle, we forgot how interwoven human communities could be. We chose space and distance over connection and interaction. Or perhaps the climate chose it for us. Other cultures found a different balance. They lived, slept and worked in a close circle of vibrant interaction.

Here in the albergue, filled with pilgrims on this night in June, closeness was given to us. Thrust upon us by necessity, economy and tradition, we were given no choice but to embrace it. As our group hung together in the advancing line, I smiled at the way we'd drawn tighter as a pack since last night. After sleeping in the mountains under the cover of a rundown barn, we'd settled into an interwoven life. The community around me now was unlike anything I'd known.

With my large close family, I knew how to exist in the energetically chaotic realm of shared space, but it had never been this diverse or vibrant. It was in no way perfect, but perfection was neither the aim nor destination. There was beauty in the wide age range, the varied backgrounds, multiple faiths and strange groupings. Here I was part of a group that accepted me, at least in general terms. Last night proved that. I felt I would only be drawn deeper into this Camino life. I didn't have to earn a merit badge, prove something or be of the same blood, nationality or gender to be in the pilgrim community. There was no entrance exam and no golden key. I just had to show up and walk.

The man at the desk stamped our documents with a resounding bang. I got the feeling he wasn't as thrilled by the endless stream of pilgrims as I was. It was such a contrast from the outpouring of welcome we'd received in Mazarife and Manjarin. The one thing the trail promised was a new experience around each bend. I held out hope tomorrow night we might stay again in the warmth of a place that cared for the pilgrims crossing its threshold. And in the meantime, I'd give the benefit of the doubt to the men running this albergue, for it was large and obviously required a vast amount of energy and patience from its staff.

Our group checked in together, and we were led downstairs into a large basement room. Our feet on the concrete resounded in the hollow stairwell as we descended into the bowels of the building. The room was sizeable but full of rows and rows of bunks standing tight against each other. Each of the beds was covered in a bright blue plastic cover, and the walls were stark white against the florescent light. It felt like a jailhouse, and I unconsciously looked for bars on the windows. I found none because there were no windows at all.

The way we picked bunks was often very random, and the results depended on who was there when we first checked in. I claimed a top bunk as usual, for I didn't mind being up off the ground and sometimes felt better without a rickety structure above me.

As I put my things down, I noticed Konrad had claimed the bunk below me. I realized we'd never slept so close. When we'd been in the same room, he'd always claimed the bunk farthest from mine. I was now well aware of his preference for distance but felt less and less concerned with his clear dislike of me. As I drew closer to the others, I found a sense of fullness that didn't have to include the gruff German. I didn't dwell long on the bunk assignments of my group but instead looked around to see where the Tasmanian had settled himself. My radar was on high alert.

The Tasmanian was on the top as well, two bunks over in clear view of my bunk. I felt a small smile creep across my face then ducked my head down and rummaged through my pack to conceal it. We would be able to see each other from our respective perches, and I felt a thrill of energy just knowing this was so. Ivan claimed the top bunk in the row across from me, and Francis was in the top bunk in the row across from the Tasmanian. The rest of the group was sprawled out around us. I hadn't talked to the Brit guys, Jack or Ivan yet but knew they would be around later to chat with. The Tasmanian was drawing all my focus, pulling my glances into him and making it hard for me to pay attention to anything else. I felt a familiar woozy, slightly hypnotic sensation pumping through me. I was sinking fast. Apparently the speed and intensity of the trail reached into all areas of connection not just that of friendship.

The albergue flooded with pilgrims wandering to the showers or dashing through the halls in search of the washing sinks. I could feel a fine layer of dirt across my shins and a stiff mass of hair on top of my head. Since I'd swapped soap for shampoo, my naturally curly hair took only a day to turn unruly in what I hoped was an effortlessly bohemian sort of way but probably wasn't. Today the sweat on the back of my neck had crept up into my hairline, and I needed a shower badly.

The bathrooms in the albergue were on the main floor. I took the steps two by two as I climbed out of our basement cellblock and found the door marked with a stick figure sign. Unfortunately, the sign held both a skirted woman and a stick man. The bathrooms were co-ed. I crossed my fingers the showers had doors, preferably with locks.

As far as my personal safety went, I'd always favored the better safe than sorry route and looked out for moments when something struck me as strange or uncomfortable. So far on the trail, I'd only felt this way once. It was weeks back in the city of Nájera. Easily identifiable as a pilgrim with my pack, I'd been standing along the edge of the main road, waiting for Alec and Alberto to catch up with me when suddenly a large man had crossed the intersection and had made a beeline for me. Bulky with every exposed surface of his body covered in dark hair, he'd worn a pack on his shoulders and held a wooden walking stick in his large meaty hand. I'd decided to turn and ignore him. Aloofness was my first way to avoid interaction with men who made me edgy. As soon as I'd turned, he'd jumped up on the curb and stepped in front of me, drawing close and asking if I was a pilgrim. His voice had been thickly accented, and he'd stood between me and my escape route out of town. It had been noon, and we'd been standing in the middle of the bustling lunch hour activity. Wearing a straw hat too small for his large head, the Corsican pilgrim had leaned in way too close to me as he'd introduced himself.

He'd asked me if I was sleeping Nájera that night while drawing his words out and looking straight at me. I had a sudden disturbing vision of him trying to crawl into my bunk. I knew there was another town just five kilometers beyond Nájera, so I'd lied to him and told him I was staying in town. He'd smiled a wide grin, winked as he told me he would see me later and went off in search of food. He'd kept his eyes on me as he walked away, running them up and down the length of my body with unabashed interest. As soon as the Corsican had disappeared across the road, I'd made for the bridge and got back to where the trail wound out of the city. I'd felt it was vital to put kilometers between me and him as soon as possible.

Even as I stood at the door of the co-ed bathrooms and remembered my interaction with the Corsican, I still felt the albergue system was safe. Maybe it was the sheer number of people in one space or the way many of the pilgrims took on the duty of being protectors. Regardless, these hostels were my homes, and I felt safe in them. At this point in the trail, I was also insulated by a bubble of protective young men. They knew me and would defend my honor if need be. As I entered the bathroom, Ava and Iris were at the sinks, brushing their teeth, toothpaste foaming out the corners of their mouths. They promised to keep an eye out as I dashed into the shower before any men arrived to share the facilities. We had each other's backs, and it made all the difference.

I returned to the basement room with wet hair and a sopping washcloth in tow. It felt good to be chilled and clean. I swooped my hair up on to the crown of my head, but the wet locks dripped down my neck and splattered across my stuff as I sorted my clothes. The Tasmanian sat on his bunk holding a small journal. I could tell he was looking at me, but I didn't dare look up to meet his glance. I was wearing a dark blue top that had grown too big for me over the course of the trip. I now had to tie its thin straps together with string to keep it from exposing my chest. As I pulled the innards out of my bag, I could feel his eyes returning to me with a dogged frequency, tracing my every movement through space as if he was unable to look away. I wondered what kept drawing him in, and at the same time, didn't want him to figure it out and stop the pursuit. Zara rummaged around in her pack a few bunks away, and Francis lay asleep on his bed across the narrow lane. As Zara grunted and tussled with the straps of her pack, Francis didn't shift in his sleep but lay still on his back with his arms draped delicately over his chest. Sometimes he almost looked dead when he slept, laid out with precision in long straight lines. His rising and falling chest was often the only sign that he hadn't departed his body all together.

People were still being assigned bunks in the large room, and the noise level grew as the albergue filled to capacity. There were at least two more rooms just like this one. As I scrambled up on to the top bunk, I wondered if they were as ugly as this space.

The Tasmanian turned his body towards me and began to talk. He was closing in on the end of his journey. I could feel his disorientation at being so near to the end of this life. Just a few days before he'd met our group, he'd been walking through the town of Santo Domingo early in the morning. The streets had been filled with mist as he'd strode along, lost in thought until he'd noticed a duo ahead. It had been early for other pilgrims to be on the road, but he'd thought nothing of it until he'd come closer, and the forms had become clearer. There had been something familiar about the figures. As he'd drawn near, his pulse had quickened, and then he'd known. The people coming towards him had been his parents. After a two-year separation, they'd surprised him and come from the other side of the world to be with him at the end of his journey.

As the Tasmanian talked, he leaned against the wall and gestured with his long hands, I could see joy spread over his face. He'd been able to hold his parents close to him, hear their voices and be surrounded by their love after a very long absence. I could only imagine how thirsty he'd been for that. I myself was parched with the desire to be close to my dear ones again, and I'd only been gone for three weeks. The feeling came over me in waves, and I wondered if similar waves had followed the Tasmanian across the surface of the earth.

He munched on some of the food we'd bought and as he ate, I talked about my own departure from home. For the first time in our conversations, the topic veered towards romance. Turning his head to look me straight in the eyes, he asked me if I'd left a boyfriend at home. His eyes held mine as they waited for an answer, a small curious smile hovering on his lips. I told him I'd left no one but ex-boyfriends in my wake, and I was a solo perigrino here as well as back home. For both of us, the trip was the end of the end and the beginning of the beginning.

He nodded in agreement and asked the question that fuels all pilgrim talk at one point or another; he asked me why I'd come. I looked down at the shirts I was folding, suddenly tongue tied and then answered as best as I could. I was here because everything had ended in my life, my relationship, my job and my clarity about what came next. I'd come because I'd been given a dream. I'd come because I'd been guided to. I'd come because every other trail forward had closed, and this rough road was all that remained. I felt my pulse flutter at such a wave of honesty, and I worried my words betrayed the intensity of my feelings about this journey. I didn't want to scare him off, but I believed in following the energy, and there was major energy between us. I wanted to swan dive into it, but I felt myself holding back, waiting and watching the tides.

The Tasmanian was looking up at the ceiling as I finished explaining how I arrived here, and I let a small silence grow after my words trailed off. Then he turned to me, caught my eyes again and said, "I hope you find what you're looking for on this journey." The room melted away, and I was unsure of my balance, even as I sat firmly planted on the stiff plastic covered bunk.

A moment later, Ava and Iris broke the silence as they clattered down the stairs, filling the low space with cheerful banter. I noticed Francis was still lying on his bed in the same configuration as before, but his eyes were open looking absently up at the ceiling. This afternoon he'd been withdrawn, bothered by something I couldn't identify and had chosen to avoid my company. I suddenly wondered if he'd been awake all the time I believed him to be asleep. Maybe he'd heard what passed between the Tasmanian and me when I'd thought no one else existed but the two of us.

The afternoon processional of events rolled on. By the time my washing was clean and hung, I desperately wanted some chocolate. I knew Ava would be a reliable accomplice on the mission, but I couldn't find her; something intangible suggested a small bit of drama was suddenly floating in the air. The courtyard of the albergue abutted a wide field of scrub grass with a large tree anchoring the open space. Stepping into the field, I noticed two figures off at a distance.

One was sitting on the ground, and the other stood against the wall. Iris looked like a small child at Ava's feet. For the first time since I'd known them, I felt they were in deep conflict with each other. The struggle seemed to pit them against one another so dramatically I could almost see the fissure of disagreement in the air between them. They had fled into the field for a bit of space in which to resolve their disagreement. It was only right to retreat and give them the space they craved. It was often hard to find places in an albergue to speak alone with anyone. We all lived so intertwined; privacy was virtually non-existent.

I returned without chocolate to the inside of our basement room now fully lit with a harsh florescent glow. The Tasmanian and Francis were gone, but Ivan lay on his top bunk, a packet of chocolate malt balls clutched tightly in his hand and a glazed look upon his face. I climbed up the riggings of my bed and turned towards him. He'd been drinking and wasn't pleased with the state of himself.

The British boys, Jack, and Ivan rarely drank and the Iron Six didn't make an issue of it or at least never to our faces. They enjoyed their beer and wine but could still engage in social pleasantries with us sober folk. Our daily activity surely helped create this dynamic. Hangovers and long hours of walking didn't blend very well. Yet today at lunch Ivan had indulged in several glasses of wine, and now his face was bright red. Touching the palms of his hands to his face, he tried to soothe his flushed skin. He rolled from side to side and told me he hated how drinking made him hot and bothered. After a few drinks, he always felt as if he was coming down with the flu. I tried to hold back my laughter, for he was a quite a sight to behold. He lay with his body splayed across the bunk like a strung out rag doll, occasionally reaching into the bag of malt balls to pull one out and pop it in his mouth. This favorite candy was apparently his way of distracting himself from his self-induced plight. Malt balls were the only silver lining to his groaning state of affairs

As dusk was falling, I left Ivan to go out to the field again. A warm golden light was settling across the rough grass, and the girls were nowhere to be seen. I wondered if their conflict had resolved itself. No matter what drama was still floating in the air, it felt good to be alone with my back against the wall.

I sat with my knees drawn up to my chest and felt wonderfully compact and contained. I spent so much of each day sending energy out into the world, crossing vast tracks of land and connecting with new faces. My life was expansive, and this felt good after the past year of being so contracted and closed off in the woods of Vermont. But tonight in Ponferrada, I needed time alone in stillness to the digest everything that was rushing by. As I sat breathing deeply, a boy jumped the wall on the far side of the field. Since he wasn't seeking refuge in the albergue, I guessed he wasn't a pilgrim but more likely just a young traveler hitching across Spain. My eyes were drawn to him, and I watched with curiosity as he unpacked his bag, blanket and mat under a tree. The thought of sleeping in the open air tonight felt slightly delicious compared to the hot and noisy box that awaited me back at the albergue. I could tell the boy had a thick crop of dark hair and glasses, but I was too far away to see more. I felt like I was watching a young animal prepare its den for the night, unaware he was being observed.

After some time, darkness crept into the field around me. Suddenly I felt lucky to be able to stand up, stretch my stiff muscles and return to the building full of other people, some of whom now meant a great deal to me. Though the night air would be cool, it would be a lonely night for the mysterious traveler on the outskirts of the field. On the walk back to the albergue an explosion of sound startled me. Car horns, cheers and firecrackers ricocheted through the city streets. The ground shook. Spain had won their futbol match. It was the same rumbling we'd felt as we slept underground in León, another night of victory for Spain at the Euro Cup.

The lights were low in the dormitory now, and the bunk below me was empty. There was suddenly something forlorn about the space. Then I realized all traces of Konrad were gone. I looked around, trying to find some answers. Had he moved bunks? Down the row Ava lay on her bed. I went to her and asked what had happened. As soon as Ava began speaking, the pieces clicked into place. I knew even before the actual confirmation came out of her mouth. Konrad's departure was about Iris.

Konrad had fallen for Iris. I must have been the only one who didn't see what was right in front of me each and every day. Ava spoke in a low voice as she explained that this afternoon Iris told Konrad she didn't want a romance on the trail. He'd disappeared not long after they'd spoken. No one knew where he'd gone. I could feel a small space open in my chest for him. The pain of love unrequited was so sharp and ached like nothing else. He must have leapt, ventured towards her, taken a risk and now it was over. He'd lost his place in the group in the gamble and was out in the night alone, set adrift. Though I held no great regard or warmth for Konrad, and he clearly disliked me, I knew how distressing such a shift in tides could be, and how escape and solitude were sometimes the only tourniquets in the aftermath. I slept restlessly above the empty bunk and wasn't sure what caused me to spend the night hours in endless tossing circles.

VILLAFRANCA DEL BIERZO

STAGE TWENTY- 35.8K- 22.3M
PONFERRADA TO TRABADELO

The next morning, I left the albergue with Francis by my side. We'd agreed to spend the morning together after he'd left a small note on my bed requesting the honor of walking with me the next day. I'd found the note on top of my sleeping bag late in the evening. I'd wondered if he'd felt the distance that had fallen on us in the past few days as acutely as I had. The letter was on a piece of paper torn from his small journal, folded in half with my name scrawled in his handwriting. He'd signed his name at the bottom of the penciled request. It was all very Jane Austen and made me recall exactly why we'd gravitated towards each other many days and several hundred kilometers ago.

The city was dark except for the spaces illuminated by street lamps. I'd forgotten how much easier it was to walk with Francis not only from a physical standpoint but an emotional one as well. I was simply bursting with thoughts, feelings and reflections, and he was a safe harbor for it all. Matching each other's tempo, we dove into the swirling group drama, free to discuss everything. It was no mystery we both preferred to digest the social whirl by talking about it and breaking it down to what lay at the core. Even so, there was one topic I was hesitant to dive into with him: my growing connection to the Tasmanian. In equal parts, I didn't want to jinx what might be evolving by uttering it out loud, and I wasn't exactly sure if Francis would approve of my crush. He'd seemed interested in the Tasmanian but wary of the hype around the adventurer.

I chose to skirt the issue of my blossoming connection to the Tasmanian, but I certainly hadn't given up thinking about our dynamic. I wasn't sure what was happening with the Tasmanian but had plenty of time to chew over all the clues. When I'd seen him at breakfast, he'd sat at the head of the table, pouring milk over his cereal, smiling charmingly to all around him but hardly breaking eye contact with me. The room had buzzed with oblivious early morning activity, yet the space between us had crackled with a familiar intensity. I'd finished my meal and prepared to go while he'd remained at the table. When Francis had opened the door, letting us both out into the dawn, I'd turned away hoping to see the Tasmanian later.

As we walked, Francis shared more of the story about his last relationship. Once again, I felt myself moving deeper into Francis's world as he made me his confidant. It wasn't an easy task to share the messy endings of a relationship with another person, and I admired his willingness to be open. I'd heard parts of the story several days ago on the Meseta, but like all heartbreak, there were many layers to reveal before one reached the root. I knew it helped to go over the story, and I couldn't deny him that solace. He needed to feel understood especially about the pieces of his past that still haunted him.

I'd felt the same insatiable need following the end of my first relationship. In the months after the end, I'd needed to keep talking, saying his name and living in the memories until the day came when I no longer craved the past. Until I woke up one morning and it was done. I saw that Francis was on that road, even though he still thought of her often. One morning he would wake up, and she would be in the past. And all these conversations where someone listened and contained the story would have helped him get there. As his words flowed into the dawn on the far side of Ponferrada, I wondered when he would wake up drained of the past and what he would choose to be on the other side. Part of me longed to be there when the ghost vanished; part of me wondered who he would seek to love next.

As we pushed onward through a cluster of homes and old vaulted arches of vine covered stone, I confided in Francis. I told him how, in my most assured moments, I knew a great love was out there for me. He grew silent for a minute, turned slowly and told me he was in awe of my certainty. Francis cupped his chilled hands and blew warm breath into them as I spoke softly about this unknown man who was so real to me I would cross hundreds of miles to find him.

Even though I had no proof this person or the life we would share actually existed, the dream and my guidance kept hope alive. It was still hard to explain the powerful symbology of the end of the world and how it galvanized me to walk the walk for love. With the romantic adrenaline of my flirtations with the Tasmanian coursing through my blood, I felt giddy and wanted to fill Francis with my hopeful excitement. It had been weeks since I'd held a scrap of tangible proof that this trail could yield romantic love. And now, in the wake of all that was unfolding for me, I felt good things were coming for Francis as well. He was too lovable, too precious a soul to go through life alone. My one worry was if he would be open to it when love arrived. Some part of him seemed willing to drift back into himself and pull away from human life. His fragile silences sometimes made him seem distant and cold. Often in these moments, I felt the shadow of his time at the monastery drift through him. I knew there was a part of him that still wondered if his life belonged to that path, but he never spoke of his feelings on the matter. I felt such life in our interactions, a pulse of energy that was so human and so vibrant. I knew he had the stuff to be in the world, to cultivate love and be a father one day. But I felt for now, I might have to hold that faith for him. Maybe my role as his friend was to anchor this hope until he recovered enough from heartbreak to reconcile his past life pull to the world of monks and believe again in the beauty of messy human community. I was resolved to hold my ground as I walked beside him in the crisp morning. I would watch over the dream for him as long as he needed. I would be there until he was ready to claim the love that awaited him up ahead.

We grew silent for a moment as we thought about the dreams of great love, but it was an easy silence that neither of us felt the need to fill. Several minutes later, we came to a crest in the paved trail, and Francis abruptly drew to a halt. Looking down to the ground, the air grew full, but neither of us spoke. On the earth below our feet we read the words freshly carved on the trail's surface. Written in Konrad's hand and scrawled across the pavement in white chalk was a message to Iris, " Iris, It is / was good." After the words he'd signed his name.

I stopped short and caught my breath. Here was the grand gesture and the blunt complexity of holding tight and letting go. The words reverberated with a tone of refreshing simplicity. The message was short, but the energy lingered and was hard to ignore. Konrad was obviously trying to make it right, to mend the break, to connect one last time with a shred of dignity. I found him suddenly a hundred times more real. This was a human note and a private gesture laid public. So this was how he treated those he liked and maybe even loved. The hostile German's willingness to make a gesture touched me.

And I suddenly felt a bit sorry for Konrad. I knew Iris might not read the sincerity of the note as I did, and she still might be unwilling to give him a chance. I guessed Konrad had been steady in his affection for Iris all along, and just the thought made me wistfully envious. There was a beauty to consistency and sturdy devotion. I longed for someone to make such a gesture on my behalf, to feel them step out with such clarity of intention. There was nothing tentative about this note, and I knew Konrad wouldn't have entered into a play for Iris lightly. Everything he did held weight and seriousness, even his campaign of disdain towards me. As I went to sleep the night before, I'd thought Konrad was somewhat conceited and had fled out of shame, but now I knew he was simply human and vulnerable to the ache of dashed affection just like the rest of us. I somehow liked him more, and all it took were four words to shift my view.

As Francis stood close to me above the markings, I swayed a bit and found myself leaning into his side. There was something stable about Francis and despite his rail thin frame, he was comforting in his own particular way. We must have paused for a minute or two, and in that time, the Tasmanian came up beside us. He looked over the words, laughed a soft chuckle and stepped over the inscription. Evidently not much of a romantic, he was less than impressed by the note and moved on without missing a beat.

And so the trail rolled onward, and we gathered steam and followed after the Tasmanian. As we drew up beside him, I could sense I wasn't the only one who was happy we'd linked up. Francis was suddenly very cheery and ready to chat about anything other than notes in the road and quests for true love. I was back in the boy's club again and somehow OK with my place. I couldn't think of two other people I would rather have to myself for a day of walking. The trail gods had smiled on me once again.

As we moved along the twisting road, it was hard to walk three across without having to continuously step to the side of the road as cars roared by. Francis and the Tasmanian were so deep in conversation they hardly noticed how I had to drop back or risk becoming roadkill. Their conversation was very focused, and each was deeply drawn into what the other was saying; I was simply trying to keep up, dodging and weaving. I expected after a while they would tire of each other, and the Tasmanian would be interested in a bit of a flirt, but the hours drew on and he hardly turned in my direction the whole morning. I drifted into daydreams, watched the lanky movements of their astoundingly graceful limbs and felt the hours drag.

The day turned bright and extremely hot as we crossed towns and open fields. The land was arid and afforded little cover in the way of trees. After a short trailside pause for water, I noticed Francis become more agitated with the exclusive banter. He started to ask me questions and break the locked walking configuration so I wasn't always on the outer ring. If Francis was aware of the dynamic, how had the Tasmanian failed to notice? He seemed to be able to turn on and off the flirt valve at whim and had decided this morning wasn't about that. I could tell from the tense set of Francis's jaw that he was becoming concerned with the way the Tasmanian continued to ignore me. But I didn't want to ruffle feathers. I longed to feel light and happy, still caught up in the swell of yesterday's romantic energy. I certainly didn't want to shift my feelings about the Tasmanian any great distance; I enjoyed the pull of our connection too much. So this morning wasn't ideal. I assured myself it was nothing to be overly worried about.

As I walked a bit ahead of them, I tried to pick up snippets of their conversation. The central aim of the Tasmanian's journey was to unify all Catholics, and he'd arrived in Spain via Rome where he' been given an audience with a group of high-ranking cardinals at the Vatican. In his worn backpack, he carried a thick stack of documents from several Australian archbishops endorsing his journey. The documents were another kind of pilgrim passport, giving proof of his mission and credentials, and they seemed vitally important to his sense of purpose. Francis was an Anglican but deeply interested in the Catholic Church. The Tasmanian loved to pontificate on the ins and outs of Catholicism and hardly seemed conscious of his surroundings as he spoke of rules, doctrines and the court of the church. They discussed the pope, papal changes in the last few years and the reasoning behind many of the church doctrines. It was strange to hear Francis carrying on conversations so strikingly different than the kind we shared. Having no link or affection for organized religion, I felt their talk was nothing more than rhetoric about boring dogma, but I respected them enough to leave my opinions out of it. If these talks were engaging and pertinent to their search on this trail then so be it. At times, I was tempted to throw in a thought or two but I held my tongue. This was one fight I was never going to win. In any case I cared very little about fighting for converts to my school of thought. I felt deeply rooted to my own core beliefs and the divine love and guidance I found within. I didn't need to wage a war of words, especially not with dear Francis and the swashbuckling Tasmanian. Plus, I guessed that to tangle with the Tasmanian about religion might be as dangerous as taking him on in Aussie Rules Futbol. I liked my unbroken bones and vibrant spirituality too much to rise to the bait.

The path stayed on a small road for most of the morning. One perk was the abundance of cherry trees lining the route. Trees dripping with the bright fruit tumbled out over the gates and walls of orchards along the side of the road. The Tasmanian told us it was acceptable to pick the cherries that dangled out into public property but illegal to reach into someone's front yard for a handful. We used the sharp ends on our walking sticks to knock the bundles of fresh fruit into our hands. It was a challenging task involving both sharp aim and quick force, but our skills improved as the day wore on.

As my lips became stained red with cherry juice, the boys turned back to their discourse. The Tasmanian went off on a rant in support of the church's stance on contraception. I felt my ear perk at this controversial and salacious topic. The Tasmanian was in his late twenties, metropolitan, a world traveler, educated and in possession of a rather wild past, yet he was firmly against contraception. At all. Ever. Even in dedicated monogamous relationships such as marriage. I tried to angle closer as my ears absorbed this information, slightly horrified and fascinated at the same time. I knew he'd lived a promiscuous life as a university student with many girlfriends and a posse of futbol friends, but from what he told Francis, he was now a different man and practically medieval in his stance on birth control. I could tell Francis was intellectually curious but rather taken back at this personal religious sentiment and its encompassing rigidity. Just as quickly as it came up, the topic was dropped and another picked up in its place, but my mind seemed to pause on his words, replaying them. Was the Tasmanian just preaching or did he really believe this? The energy that had passed between us since our meeting was not of a platonic nature, and I could almost taste the physical attraction radiating between us. Right before my eyes, he'd become even more of a riddle. I wasn't sure what to believe, the words from his mouth or the energy flowing off of him in powerful waves. I wanted to believe in the energy and the spark. I wanted to sink deeper into the attraction and get lost there, but what if he believed what he preached? What if he was playing both ends against the middle? What was the real distance between what he wanted and what he claimed to want? The riddle was growing deeper, and I suddenly felt weary of the chase.

At noon, we entered a small city tucked in a river valley at the base of a range of mountains. We bought food and sat on the cold church steps in the main square, basking in the cool shade. The Tasmanian carried a yellow rubber ball with him. As Francis bounced the small object, I confessed I'd never see cricket played and didn't even know how the game worked. With distinct British and British colony pride, they jumped to their feet and started a short-sided mock game in the sidewalk between the steps and the street.

After lunch we made our way out of town and kicked the yellow ball to each other along the roadway. It was futbol with the street as our playing field. We kicked the ball between the three of us with no aim but to advance forward and not lose it or ourselves under an oncoming vehicle. Our trio crossed a large bridge and passed Ava and Iris sitting at the top of the rise. The looked hot and tired, slumped in the shade as if they were avoiding something. We said hello as we passed but didn't slow down to chat.

When I looked back, I understood their nervous energy. Konrad and Tomas were coming down the road towards them. Tomas had set off before dawn to find Konrad and bring him back. We could only assume Konrad had slept in a field the night before, and I was surprisingly glad to see Tomas had found him. I could imagine a confrontation between Konrad and the object of his affection was about to take place. I felt sorry for all involved. The group had become exponentially more complicated when romance had entered the arena, and this was the moment of change; the group would either be whole again or Konrad would be gone for good. I ushered Francis and the Tasmanian onward but knew we would hear every detail of the peace accord later in the day. I could always count on Ava for a thorough recounting of the daily gossip.

Finally the trail and our newly minted playing field brought us to a small cluster of homes on the outskirts of the tiny town of Trabadelo. Outside one of the buildings were the telltale red deck chairs and tables with bright red umbrellas. All across Spain, cafés had this exact same look, making it easy to identify them as more than just private residences. As we got closer, I recognized Zara and Jay in the shade of an umbrella. They'd arrived just before us and stopped to eat a late lunch. We said our hellos then ducked into the cool interior of the albergue. It was a private albergue with only thirty beds in four rooms. Everything was brand new and very clean. It felt like a home as soon as we crossed the threshold. A man came out to greet us and stamp our passports with one of the most beautiful stamps I'd seen so far. It was a hand carved drawing of a traditional pilgrim drinking gourd. The hollowed out gourd, called a calabash, was the medieval equivalent of a water bottle and hung from the pilgrim's walking staff.

I'd become less and less impressed with the stamps in the last few weeks, but here, my delight in their history returned. The stamps were a unique and lasting part of the Camino. They'd been integral in the progress of the medieval pilgrim and had served as proof of his journey when he'd returned home. They were equally necessary for the modern pilgrim. The stamps verified my travels. The credential was a stamp record of my progress and would be looked at in the pilgrim's office in Santiago as the only proof I'd traveled the trail by foot. Even as the Camino transformed, there were elements, like the designs of the stamps, which remained steady and unchanged for hundreds of years.

My credential was only filled with stamps from the albergues, but many other places besides hostels had stamps and were happy to press them into your passport. Churches, cafes and historical sights all had their own stamps. For the pilgrim who wanted to seek out more stamps, it was easy to do. I never wanted to wait around for some institution to stamp my passport, but the Brit boys had filled theirs with stamps from many churches along the way.

I followed Francis and the Tasmanian up the narrow staircase, and we found our room at the end of the hall. The three lower bunks in the room had been taken by a group of Swedish women, and two were napping when we entered. One lay sprawled on her back with her mouth wide open. Long droning snores dragged from her lungs, while the other was bundled so tightly in her bedding I wasn't sure if she was alive or an entombed mummy.

I turned and raised my eyebrows at Francis as he shrugged his shoulders and softly tossed his bag up onto the bed near the door. I took the top bunk on the right wall, and the Tasmanian took the last empty bunk directly across the room from me. Even though he was across from me, the room was small, and it felt as if we were right next to each other. I could feel that charge of energy running through me as I took out my things and started to set up my bed. The three of us had landed, and who knew what the night would hold.

TRABADELO

There was something charged about spending the night in the same room with the Tasmanian. I knew we were both aware of the building energy. It had been so long since I'd felt such a pleasant sort of tension that I found myself flustered and boundlessly optimistic. I immediately loved Trabadelo and delighted in its remote location with no city to distract and only this albergue to house us. Once again our group was in a world unto ourselves, but now the Tasmanian was here with us, falling into step with our flock. After unpacking, Francis suggested we go down to the river and have a swim. They day had been hot, and neither of us could avoid the call of swift moving water.

Having grown up in New England, I took ponds and lakes for granted. Everywhere I turned there was clear water to swim in. Along the Camino route we'd found very few places to swim. Francis and I went off ahead of the Tasmanian to scout a way to the river, and I hoped he would follow us shortly. Yet as we skirted a gated backyard and stumbled upon the edge of the water, I was delighted to have a moment of calm with Francis, a pause to collect myself before the Tasmanian joined us. Francis was delighted by the generous berth of the stream and even managed to spot a small dock jutting out from the bank a few yards down from where we stood.

Though the dock was little more that a few old planks nailed together at the water's edge, it would suffice. I lay down on the rough boards as Francis tested the water. The river was only three feet deep in the center but had a swift current. When I placed my toes in the water, it felt akin to arctic snow melt. Even though the sun was high above us, it wasn't warm enough to completely negate the chill of the water. Francis waded in with a determined look in his eyes, and I followed suit. Both of us stood stock still with our arms raised above our heads and lungs pulled up in gasps of shock unsure if we should go further or retreat. I could see the outline of every one of Francis's ribs and the steady inhale of his lungs. It wasn't wholly unusual for a young guy to be such a gangly collection of bones, but still his waist looked impossibly small.

I couldn't tell how much weight he'd lost since the first morning I'd walked with him, but every line in his body suddenly felt so sharp and clear, I feared I might cut myself if I touched him. Maybe I'd been too close to see the change until now, but his whole frame was looking more haggard than ever, and his closely shorn head didn't help matters. We had both been sick from the well water in Manjarin, but such a mild incident couldn't have played too great a part in his appearance. A niggling of concern had been growing in me each time I looked at Francis in the past few days, but I'd let it pass. I'd been lost in the hum of activity since Astorga and only now did I find myself recalling the way it had felt to hug him in Bercianos. I'd been thoroughly delighted to see him that morning yet startled by the touch of his frail limbs. His body felt brittle in my arms; I worried I could hurt him with little effort, and I was rather slim myself. And now it seemed as if the journey itself had taken him up in its powerful grasp and threatened to break him. He'd always eaten very little, but it was something more than hunger eating away at him. There was the hint of struggle in him as if he was fighting some battle behind the calm front lines of his demeanor. I suddenly wondered if he confided in Elliot and quickly marked my jealousy at the thought of Francis placing his trust in someone other than me.

No matter how willing he was to open up, I ached to take care of him and to find some way to halt the progress of the grey pallor spreading across his face. Some combination of forces was causing the bones in his jaw and wrists to become more prominent before my eyes, and I felt helpless to stop it. I felt myself groping around for the cause, watching him with dogged determination in hopes of gleaning a clue. I just wanted to find a way to shift the current of his journey back towards the vitality and joy we'd known on the Meseta.

I often felt the temptation to hug him again, to pull him back into animation by tussling with him and reminding his limbs how to feel, but I restrained myself. He was no albergue kitten or little kid whom I could comfort with touch, and I didn't want to invade the space he held around himself. He seemed to be drifting away from his body, but all I could do was hope the icy waters would snap him back into physical life and whatever internal fever ailed him would break and dissipate.

I was distracted from my thoughts as Francis suddenly plunged into the river and leapt out just as quickly with a resounding yelp. His vocal cords were clearly as strong as ever, and I even caught him grinning at the joy of being water bound once more. After a few minutes splashing around, I returned to the riverbank and fell asleep. When I awoke, more of the group had arrived. The Tasmanian and Francis were both in the river, absorbed in throwing the yellow ball across the water's surface to each other, while Jack and Ivan stripped down to their matching boxer briefs in preparation for a swim. Jack boasted how he and Ivan had purchased the special fiber boxers with the assurance that these briefs could be washed half as often as normal boxers. They were the lazy man's travel briefs and apparently gave the guys a carte blanche to do way less laundry than they should have. Ivan's tight black briefs only served to highlight his brutal tan lines and accent the affects of the sun on his pale skin. For the first week of the trail he'd worn the same tank top and no sunscreen. When he was shirtless, it looked almost as if he was still clothed in a very, very white tank top. The phenomenon was dubbed the invisible shirt and though amusing, it wasn't a fashion highlight.

As I jumped back into the thigh high water, it traumatized my newly warmed skin and felt even colder than before. The Tasmanian came and stood by me. We taunted each other over who would be the brave one to fully plunge below the surface first. Beyond the obvious flirting, I felt I had something to prove, some test to pass in order to draw him closer. Even as the water brought convulsions to my legs, I flashed him a bold smile and without hesitating dove into the water. The icy current crashed into me as I slid below the surface, and the gravel of the riverbed scraped across my limbs. My clothes pulled away from my body as they flooded and wrestled with the current. Every surface was shocked alive, my lungs bursting. I knew I'd been reckless in the shallow water, but I'd been so many years before.

It had been over ninety degrees every day that week. No air had moved through the mammoth building that housed my college dance studios. Everything had been sticky. The floors had swelled with moisture and my skin had been in a continual lather. Everybody in class had moved at half speed, craving escape. I'd craned my head out the window, hoping to see storm clouds coming to break the heat. When we'd been let out of class, my best friend had dragged me away from the studio to go for a swim.

As we'd walked arm and arm out of the building, Dancer Man had come running after us. As I'd faced the last few days of my senior year, I'd been deeply concerned about how to survive the end of school and the unknown of where my love for him would go. He'd stood with us in the road and had asked if he could come along.

The sky had been clouding over as we'd piled out of the car and run for the shoreline. Throwing clothes off as we'd gotten closer, the three of us had paused at the edge of the chilly water. It had been early May. I'd looked over at him, hair ruffled with sweat and blue eyes plugged into my own with mischievous delight. He'd always been so transparent in those unguarded moments. When his feelings had mixed with his fair features like that I'd often lost my balance, and here again, I'd found myself swaying and suddenly craving action, I'd dived deep into the spring water, laughing back at him as I'd come to the surface with weeds tangled around my ankles and rocks crunching under my toes. Later, I'd sprawled on the wooden raft in the middle of the lake, bleeding water all around me as he'd stood next to me and watched a storm drawing towards us. As he'd practiced back flips off the side of the raft, dark clouds and rumbling filled the sky. I'd watched him move about the raft, feeling his weight rock the surface underneath me. Every movement had been easy and locked seamlessly into the next as if the moment on the edge of the storm, adrift and soaked to the core had been planned, choreographed by some greater force. I'd felt his eyes trace the edges of me as I'd watched the arc of his hair shake water onto my skin. A rumble foretelling the future had reverberated through us, and I'd suddenly believed it would all be OK, and we would find our way forward from this echoing moment. As he'd turned towards me, the skies had opened. Rain had filled the air until there'd been no way to tell where the surface of the lake and the surfaces of us had begun and ended.

And here I was, thousands of miles and many years from that moment, but still caught in the echo. The echo of energy I'd known before in another. As the Tasmanian drew up beside me, I felt the pull towards something great and terrifying, beautiful and wrenching. There was an intense river of energy between us, but I couldn't be certain if it would bloom or break, if I would fall onto solid ground or drop off the edge. How could I be sure it wasn't simply an echo of another love lodged in a new frame. Yet it was everything I craved and all the things I feared. It was nothing I'd expected days from the end of this journey, but it was suddenly something within my grasp.

Konrad arrived at the side of the river with a beer in hand and Ava and Iris in tow. Tomas came around the corner as well, the whole group was eager to be near the cool water if not in it. I felt the Tasmanian's focus drop from me. When he started to chat with Ivan, I knew I'd lost his attention. Francis looked over at me with thinly veiled concern, but I wouldn't meet his eyes. I felt he was seeing it all and brimming with things unsaid. I couldn't handle his judgment at this juncture in time. I knew he meant well and cared for my wellbeing, but I didn't see the harm in pursuing someone who was clearly drawn to me. Yes, the bursts of being ignored didn't sit well in my core, but I needed more than the platonic friendships my posse of boys was offering. Francis might be evaporating before my eyes, but I wanted to be in a body and feel something more than distance. I crawled up onto the side of the dock and walked back to the albergue alone.

After taking a warm shower, I pulled my clothes onto my damp limbs and sat in the cool dark of our room. I wanted to lie with my back on the cold floor and find my center. The slumbering Swedes had vanished for the moment, and the albergue was filled with empty silence. I could feel a pleasant buzz humming through my body even in the stillness. Every nerve was awake and fully invested in my growing attachment to the Tasmanian. I couldn't put the energy down, tuck it away or let it go. Instead it moved through me in an endless loop and as it circled again and again, I recognized there was a familiar thread of anxiety tucked in amongst the pulse.

So the Tasmanian had a habit of setting me aside to connect with others as if he'd lost track of his craving. Was this an insurmountable behavior? Even Francis couldn't deny the Tasmanian's strong attraction to me. Francis might counter that such things were not enough and this I agreed with, but I'd only begun to unravel the Tasmanian. I needed more time to see what lay beneath the surface.

I could sense the Tasmanian's infatuation, but at moments, he became distant. Even though I'd only known him for a short time, the days on the Camino were heightened. Everything took place with great vibrancy. Plus, he wasn't like the rest of us. He had the aura of one who was a bit dazed and shell-shocked to be back in the world. He'd spent the last two years walking alone, never having people traveling the same direction as him and always leaving people behind. For this reason, I felt it might be a self-protection reflex to draw close and pull away in corresponding intervals. Making friends was easy. Following an attraction was more nerve wracking after two years away from the game. He was still a bit feral, and I wondered if he just needed time to ease back into the rhythms of human life.

Yet, I wasn't sure I believed my own logic. I'd so long been without in this area of my life that I feared I might be following the energy without being clear about why. Did I really feel there was genuine potential in my connection with the Tasmanian? Or did I simply like the feeling of being desired by someone I desired in return? Or did I recognize a familiar type of man and feel drawn to echoes of a past some part of me still longed to justify? In the past, my love life had been defined by tension and conflict. I'd constantly thrown myself into relationships defined by immovable objects and unstoppable forces. Did I want to take one more try at pushing an old pattern, or was I coloring the present with the past because I simply didn't know anything else when it came to romance? I didn't feel particularly desperate these days. In the past, I'd admit, I got my highs from attraction. I'd thrived off being drunk on love, drunk on the angst of unrequited love and smashed on the euphoria of sparks and lingering sexual tension, but only because that was all I could take away from such toxic and tumultuous bonds. I'd taken what I could and tried to make a love life out of meager scraps. Now I was asking for more, but I still felt thrilled to finally stumble across a viable romantic target who looked at me with passion. I'd longed to cross paths with a decent man who wanted to be more than my friend and wasn't hairy, creepy or ancient. The feeling of hope and joy was my own and not the property of the men I'd wasted it on; so if it was alive again, I had to see it as a good thing.

The intensity of the vibration between the Tasmanian and me felt like gravity tugging on my insides, but I knew I would wait to dive in deeper. This dance we were spinning around each other was magnetized, but it wasn't love. I knew in the past I'd confused this feeling for love, and it was never anything to do with love. This left me more than a bit gun shy. So how could I be sure what I was getting with the Tasmanian until I knew him better? Our spark reminded me of my affection for that first love, but maybe with the Tasmanian it would have the real love piece that the past hadn't been able to give me. There was time, and I could absorb every moment as it came, make choices and trust my emotions wouldn't get the better of me. I had to trust my ability to pick love, or I would be lost. I wasn't so sure Francis had the same faith in me. Nobody, not my family or friends from home nor my dearest trail confidant could help me now. I was on my own with the puzzle of the Tasmanian at my feet.

But Francis's unspoken yet obvious disapproval rumbled around inside me. Was I being lured in by the familiarity of attraction and ignoring important undertones? I didn't know how to reconcile our growing attraction with the dogmatic beliefs the Tasmanian championed. I was too muddled to see him clearly. Perhaps I'd willed myself into a state of temporary amnesia about the past, so I would give the present a fighting chance. Nonetheless, I wasn't in favor of stepping out of the ring. I knew I had to get into the mess of connection and not withdraw before I could be sure. I wasn't afraid of the chaos, and I wouldn't regret having gotten a bit messy on the Tasmanian's behalf.

As I sat cross-legged perched on the top of my bunk, I tried in vain to calm my scurrying thoughts and get quiet. I knew the same wellspring of guidance that had brought me here to this strange land that I now loved with deep affection, could also support me in finding the way forward with the Tasmanian. But part of me didn't feel ready to pause and listen. Soon it would be dinner. I could hear life stirring in the kitchen. The outside world was calling. The groups were returning from the riverside, flush with sun and looking for supplies for the next meal. I jumped off my bunk and stepped back into the fray without a second thought.

When I left my room and entered the kitchen, I found most of the group had disappeared in search of the only restaurant in the village. Only a few had stayed behind. Ivan and Jack went with me to shop for dinner as the shadows fell. Once back at the albergue, we dropped our loot on the big table in the small kitchen. I sat on the end next to the Tasmanian as he went through the videos in his camera and shared clips from earlier in his journey. He had filmed today, and it was fun to see us playing in the streets and laughing into the camera. He stopped after a few minutes and picked the small video camera up to his eye, pressed the record button and began a lighthearted interrogation of Ivan. For some reason, Ivan fascinated the Tasmanian or at least Ivan's grandiose schemes caught his attention. Ivan had made no secret of his waning opinion of the Tasmanian and had even voiced his concern with me down by the river. He was wary of the Tasmanian's desire to be the center of attention and his overtly religious agenda that excluded everybody not under his banner. Nonetheless Ivan was in a mood to entertain and happy to detail one of his many future dreams: to own a custom made submarine the way pop stars own luxury yachts. Ivan stirred a pot of pasta on the burner and talked into the camera, describing all the reasons a personally outfitted submarine was the ultimate thing to buy if you had a spare eighty million dollars lying around. As Jack, the Tasmanian and I provided the laugh track, Ivan managed to hold a look of serious focus, never faltering as he presented his fantasy to an adoring audience.

I could hear the Iron Six return from dinner and set up camp out on the deck, lounging around and laughing with each other. There we were, cut in half again. Me, the five boys and the Tasmanian were in the kitchen while the Iron Six were outside. I longed to talk with Ava or Iris to find solace and support in female company as I wrestled with the situation at hand, but it was hard to get through the guard dogs to find a moment alone with them. Plus, I wasn't sure they'd even noticed my growing connection with the Tasmanian. I knew I wasn't the most discrete person and often felt unwilling to hide my feelings, but I'd been more poised and restrained in my public moments with the Tasmanian. Despite my most adult-like attempts at being mysterious, I knew Francis was aware of everything. His eyes traveled between us, and his silences hung heavy as if his mind was whirling as quickly as mine. Much of this was the reason I'd been steering clear of him all evening, refusing to catch his eye and avoiding any moments alone with him. If I confessed to my growing entanglement, I didn't want to have to digest the truths I might see reflected back in his knowing eyes. I had a strong feeling he wouldn't hold back his heartfelt opinion if given space to voice it, and I wasn't sure I would be able to disagree with the things he said.

The talk of submarines and wild dreams drifted into the evening. The light faded outside the windows causing me to flick on the soft overhead lamp. The Tasmanian heated a pan of milk and made hot cocoa for the group. I shared the last of my tinned peaches with Francis, knowing they were his favorite and hoping to keep the peace, at least on the surface.

When all the dinner dishes were drying by the side of the sink, Jack asked to borrow my guidebook. I dashed back to the room, leaping across my bunk to pull the book down. He and Ivan sat next to each other at the kitchen table and counted the days ahead. They were the only two members of the larger group who had to hold to a tight schedule. They planned to return to Pamplona for the running of the bulls and needed to be back in Basque country by the opening day of the week-long festival. They had macho dreams of strapping on sneakers to run with the crazy Spaniards, and none of us was about to stop them from following their passion. I wasn't sure if they'd fully digested the danger involved or the likely chance of being gored, but their enthusiasm was infectious. Even John seemed ready to sign up for the blood sprint after Ivan explained its lure. No matter what happened or didn't, their adventures in Pamplona would be the stuff of legends and offer many impressive stories to future generations. I hoped I'd get the chance to hear them someday. But right now, they were focused on their schedule and the number of kilometers that lay between them and the end.

The Iron Six still talked noisily out on the porch. They were planning a short day tomorrow for several reasons. One was Ava's newfound desire to slow down and stop our rush to the end. She had time to spare, loved the communal life and already felt Camino withdrawal. I understood this and shared many of her sentiments, but I was deeply weary. Tomorrow would take us to O'Cebreiro and the beginnings of the wild province of Galicia. This was the last province on the Camino, and it would bring us to the sea. We were drawing close after so many days in between. The trail out of Trabedelo to O' Cebreiro was a steady climb, the biggest single day elevation change since the hike over the Pyrenees, but it would only be eighteen kilometers. Most of our days as a large group had been at least thirty kilometers. This shorter day was a departure from routine. The other major reason the Iron Six wanted to stop in O'Cebreiro was to give proper time and due celebration to Konrad on his twenty first birthday. I felt quite certain Konrad would prefer to celebrate with those he actually liked, and I wouldn't be overly welcome at the festivities. I wondered what the Brit boys and American guys felt about the impending party and our obvious lack of VIP status.

Hunched over the table, Jack and Ivan decided they couldn't afford to walk only eighteen kilometers. They would need to hike an extra ten kilometers beyond O'Cebreiro to keep on pace. All evening I'd been distracted by the Tasmanian's plans, but I was suddenly upset to hear that Jack and Ivan planned to go ahead. I felt my stomach drop when I realized they were serious. They really were prepared to leave me and the Brit boys behind to fend for ourselves amongst the larger pack. I'd finally found my place in a group, begun to feel safe and balanced only to find it suddenly splintering in my hands, and I felt powerless to do anything about the cracks.

Ivan's declaration of intention was nothing compared with the bombshell that followed. Without missing a beat, the Tasmanian volunteered that he also intended to walk on maybe even more than ten extra kilometers. Though he was three days ahead of his schedule, he said he wasn't interested in doing a short day. I felt myself trying to bring us all to the same place the next night, seeking some solution to the shifting dynamics, but the energy in the room was darting in all directions. No one but me seemed worried about the split. Jack and Ivan had already told me they weren't fond of the Iron Six and wouldn't sacrifice their timeline to stay connected to them. Nor could they help it if the Brit boys and I were casualties. Elliot said nothing, and John looked glassy eyed. I knew they were just as upset as I was but unwilling to speak up. Ultimately they still had each other, and that left me as the only person in the room attempting to keep all the divergent players together. I was going to lose the most with this break up. And I was reeling from the Tasmanian's strangely dispassionate declaration and behavior. He was three days ahead of his schedule, yet he wasn't planning to stay with our group? He didn't look in my direction as he spoke about going on and didn't seem flustered in the least. It was chillingly clear this hadn't been a hard choice for him. He knew it would mean never seeing any of us again. He knew this meant not seeing me again. I felt taken aback. Was this a move of indifference? Was he really ready to just walk away? If so, I had bigger problems than the departure of Jack and Ivan.

I went back to the bunkroom and climbed up on my bed. The room was dark. Francis had left dinner long ago and was already asleep in his bunk. His arm dangled off the edge of the bed, but he didn't stir as I moved around. Part of me longed to wake him, open the floodgates and ask him what he thought, but I didn't. He looked too peaceful, and I knew it might make things more complicated rather than less. I felt a squirming agitation in my limbs. I didn't know what to do. Down at the river, Ava and Iris had asked me to walk up to O'Ceberiero with them tomorrow, and in hopes of a little bit of girl time, I'd agreed. I wanted to spend more time with them, but now my plans were wrought with confusion. I was upset about losing touch with Ivan. He'd been a kind friend to me and his sense of humor was invaluable, but the real issue weighing on me was the cavalier nature with which the Tasmanian had announced his decision to go on and leave me behind. There was only one loophole and though he hadn't said it, I'd felt it hanging in the air. He was going no matter what, but I could change my plans. I could leap and go too.

I didn't want to follow after him like a lovesick puppy, yet I wasn't sure his impending departure was a bad thing. It was forcing my hand, and if I played my cards right, this moment could be healthy for me. I just couldn't figure out which cards to play. I was on a razor's edge of change and knew this hand would define the rest of my trip.

If I stayed, I could let him go and perhaps know he was a ghost of old loves past and that falling for him had just been the last taste of a pattern of falling for the wrong men. To let him go might prove I had the wisdom and guts to make a different choice in the face of an old foe.

Yet within me lived another line of thought. I could travel with him until the end, place all my cards on the table and jump. I could trust the pull and block out all the cautioning voices. Maybe my worry was really just springing from the wounded doubting part of me, the part that feared the worse. I loved the rush of energy coursing through me as I let the trail take me towards romance again, but I couldn't shake the deep thread of something dark, something I couldn't explain. But the Tasmanian was still the only person in my current Camino universe who seemed willing to offer me romantic love, and that was a hard piece to let go of without a fight. I wanted this blooming courtship to work. I could almost taste it after so many days on this trail with not a glimmer of such things in sight.

He was the last one to come into the dark room and move towards his bunk. I sat against the far wall and wrote in my journal under the soft beam of my flashlight. He turned to me as he came in and walked over to the side of my bunk. He placed his hand on the edge of the mattress, and I could feel my weight being pulled towards the depression. I couldn't see his face very well in the dim light as he spoke in a low whisper and drew closer to me.

"I am going on tomorrow." he said softly. The words hung in the air for a moment until I responded,

"That upsets me. You have to know that upsets me, right?" my words came out low and tight. I couldn't tell if they sounded cold or saturated with emotion.

He waited, flooding the room with silence. I could tell he was looking at me, but I couldn't see his eyes. The air between us was dark and thickly strung as if we were locked in this configuration, our limbs braced against the energy. I could feel anger rushing off me in waves but didn't know exactly why. Was it anger at his brush off and decision to push on without me? Or at myself for falling for this man who had drawn me in and now wanted to leave me behind? He broke the silence.

"You can walk with me tomorrow if you like. I could wake you when I leave." he said slowly.

Were his words meant to be warm and inviting or simply courteous? I couldn't read him without a view into his eyes and the lines of his limbs. The energy swirled around us, and I couldn't feel anything but its pulse.

I knew he was leaving at four in the morning, and now he'd offered to wake me. I sighed and felt his limbs shift ever so slightly towards me. My anger had evaporated, and he knew it. Yet the air between us was still charged with the undertone that had been there all along. The gravitational pull of attraction tugged at my center, drawing me towards the edge of the bed. Even in the darkness, I knew the space between us had narrowed, very nearly evaporating altogether. I wondered if he would find my warm skin, find the line of my jawbone with the wide surface of his palms and bring me to him, drawing the surfaces of me to him in the dark, seeing without eyes and finding me with the simple words of touch. And then he spoke,

"I will wake you at four and ask you again."

Before the last syllable trailed off, he lifted his hand from my bed, pulled back and retreated. The moment was over. I sat rooted in place, my eyes looking into the blank darkness around me. I could hear him climb into his bunk, and soon the room dropped back into silence. The air hung still and heavy; no one snored. I couldn't even hear the gentle inhale of another human. Falling backwards, I wrapped my arms around my ribs and closed my eyes. I wrestled with the soft lining of my sleeping bag all night in a drugged and groggy sleep, flooded with an indecision that stayed with me into the darkest hours.

I dreamed of snow. The ground was covered in a thin layer of white, and the prints of our feet traced away behind us. It was the end of November. I'd stayed on after graduation to work for my college and still be there for the Dancer Man. He walked beside me as we crossed campus. I was cold, and he was silent. His hands were deep in his pockets and his blonde hair ruffled with sweat from dance class. The years hung between us unsaid. The years of dance, endlessly tangled movements, words unspoken and the torturous way it would neither begin nor end.

It had long ago lost its luster. Now the current was little more than a ragged shell of the intensity and recognition, emotion and infatuation it had once been. We'd moved in the same space, looping around each other, drenched in a familiar desire for years. I didn't remember how it felt to move unaccompanied by the haunted threads of us. I knew his every gesture of desire, and he knew every breach in my armor. As I grew into my limbs, the intensity of the space between us was everyday reborn to what was before and what could be after these moments in limbo. Yet some pieces of our struggle were growing more rooted with time. His grasp on his emotions and the flow of his life was slipping as he refused my help. I was forced to watch him drown in other loveless connections, locked into a cage he himself had engineered. He adored the theatrics of victimhood, and for a time, I agreed to watch, rescue and ground a life that was undercut by his own hand.

His eyes bled with sorrow at what his life had become, and when he went numb, I took on the job of feeling for him. Since I loved him, I wanted to rescue him. Since I knew him, I wanted to believe in the rescue. But he had embraced the surface of life over the substance. And so I learned that a drowning man who refuses help is sure to drown. I began to fear if I couldn't give up the love, he might pull me under with him. As the years dragged on, the love threatened to crush me and sapped the marrow from my bones. Though the rush of desire might never cease and the truth of how we could dance together might never alter, something in me would soon snap. I would only wait so long for him to leap, to break the chain of many lives, follow the pulse of truth and pick me over the cast of illusions.

As winter began, I told him again of my love, arriving at his door with bloodshot eyes and sleep disheveled hair. He turned away from the choice. He would keep the course. He would march to the beat of false gods, pulling fame and praise, pride and soul erosion to his chest. He wanted to flood his life with the movement and buzz of the surface world, turn away from his eternal truths and connection to the light. I knew this course would bring him what he sought, but not what he needed. He assured me he was done with me, yet he wouldn't stop touching me, wouldn't stop seeking my eyes, pleading for energy, for love, for comfort.

On that cloudy November day, there was nothing left in me for him but aching silence. We walked past a small group of young children making snow angels in a fresh layer of white. In that moment, I knew we would never have children together, never get the life I'd imagined. He walked me to my apartment down the small dirt road. At the door he turned and walked away. I entered the warmth of the empty building but couldn't help looking back, knowing this was the end. This was the way love, broken and abused, must end. My bones were brittle under my skin. I'd laid bare my chest and the delicate filament of my heart, and he'd taken it with no hesitation or intention to be kind and value my love.

Maybe if I'd been older and wiser I would have seen the ways I'd been prey, the ways he'd abused his power. He adored the attention too much to do anything but take and was too broken to see the way he broke others. He was lost when I'd stumbled upon him, and he was still as lost many years later. I shuddered and suddenly knew he might be lost his whole life, leaving a wake of destruction in his path, being the cruelest to those who loved him the most. As I stood in the doorway, my muscles reverberated with the November words he'd spat at me, the words that cursed me for my caring heart and belittled the love I'd given him. He'd trashed the treasure and treasured the rubbish in his life, and I couldn't stop him.

As I looked back, the world was flush with the white fields of winter. His small figure stood at the top of the drive. He glanced back and paused. Like a frozen moment from a film, he turned back for one last look at the life he wasn't brave enough to embrace. I closed the large storm door with its chipped paint and turned away. The next day, I packed up my belongings, quit my job and left the existence I'd known for three years, never to see him again. Even as these memories flooded through me in the guise of a dream, I knew a crossroads awaited me in the Spanish dawn.

I awoke with a start as a firm hand touched the side of my curved body. I knew it was the Dancer Man. I couldn't think straight. I had no idea where I was or what he was doing here beside me after all this time, after all had long faded between us. It wasn't until he spoke my name that I was no longer sure it was blue eyes looking down at me in the dark.

The figure was too tall and the voice thick with unusual tones. He said my name again and told me he was leaving. I snapped back into the present. It was the Tasmanian. I was on the trail. He was leaving with or without me. Yet I had thought he was a figment of my past, and with absolute clarity rushing through the dark I knew why. He was shaped from an identical mold. He was the same pattern, the same lost boy in a new incarnation with a different accent. I knew I couldn't follow him. I knew this attraction would never be the good love I needed. I couldn't take another single step in the direction of the old pattern. It was over.

"I am going to let you go." I said in a soft whisper.

His hand lay on my side for a moment, and then the touch evaporated. Darkness rushed upon me. I didn't hear him leave. The last of the night swallowed me into the protection of sleep. The trail had taken away as quickly as it had given, and I knew little about where it would move me next.

O'CEBREIRO

STAGE TWENTY ONE- 27.4-17M
TRABADELO TO ALTO DO POIO

The room was a dark cocoon until I awoke to Francis slipping off his bunk and moving towards the door of the sleep silent room. I wondered if he'd found the note I'd left on his pack. The looping letters were a plea for him to stay in O'Cebreiro tonight with the rest of the group, to hold tight to the fellowship and not abandon me. I didn't call to him as he slipped out of the room but instead glanced at the empty bunk across from me. It looked shockingly tidy and utterly vacant as if the Tasmanian had never been there at all, as if four a.m. had been years ago rather than hours.

I couldn't trust my ability to think clearly that morning and felt caught in a hollow fog. Everything was trapped in the aftershock of the pre-dawn moment that no one knew about except me and a stranger long gone. Later, I hardly noticed as other pilgrims slipped out of their rooms and joined me at the kitchen table.

Jack and Ivan had already left when I arrived in the kitchen. The morning felt even emptier knowing they had parted from the group. Both the Tasmanian and the American guys had chosen to break apart our configuration of travelers, and I wondered if they even cared about the aftershocks of their choices. There was no real need to break the group, yet they had put other factors above that of community. It worried me about the kind of choices others might make in the days to come. I felt acutely aware I'd arrived at the Camino alone and was now in serious danger of departing the same way.

Since I'd promised Ava and Iris I would walk with them on the morning trek to O'Cebreiro, I intended to do so, but it was hard to wait around for them to be ready. All my muscles ached to go, to leave this place behind and go onward in the wake of all who'd already vanished. Iris was always the first up and had to spend at least half an hour coaxing Ava out of bed and out the door. Once we got going, I started to feel better.

I was ready to be distracted and invest my energy in a long overdue gossip session. Since Zara was sleeping in, for this brief moment, I felt there was space for me in the girl posse. It was up to me to put in the effort, entertain and strengthen our bonds. The morning was spent regaling them with the train wreck of my first love affair with the Dancer Man. I could sometimes fall into a mood where the story was funny and entertaining in a black comedy sort of way. That was the version of the story they heard on the trail up to O'Cebreiro. For the girls, it was like reading a juicy gossip magazine, and they hung on every word.

The details I shared with Ava and Iris were only a small taster, but somehow I was able to tell the story with a clarity I'd never had about this particular chapter of my life. I realized the narrative was losing it hold over me, the power of the tale was fading, and soon it would be just a story. It was as if the characters were becoming fictional, and I was now the wise and objective storyteller. Perhaps my mind had gone over the memories so many times it had worn them clean of any feeling. But then, there was nothing like a fresher and more twisted broken relationship to help the old love lose its oomph.

Yet even with the complicated layering of two polar opposite relationships back to back and the eventual ruin of both, I felt as if healing was within reach. So it would take more time to bury the remains of my last relationship with its freshly decomposing dark elements and bitter sting, but it could no longer define me. Nothing of the past could, especially with this trail in my life. The Camino was more than a rebound. She was going to be the relationship that healed me. I could feel it vibrating through every moment. My life had moved on from who I'd been. I'd stepped across the milky white line and become someone new. The Camino had given me new chapters, so I could begin to put the old to rest. Now I would need all her support and the rallying of all her troops in the wake of Trabadelo.

Eventually I tried to coax Iris into talking about what had happened with Konrad. She assured me it had been nothing important. Apparently he'd told her he wanted to be with her, there had been a kiss, and she'd turned him down. So it was true, Iris had spurned Konrad's advances, and yet he'd returned to the group. I assumed Konrad had fled the night in Ponferrada to protect himself or in defense of his pride, but his return had proved he was made of stronger metal. I was curious how he would navigate his homecoming now that he knew he couldn't be with her. I'd watched him keep a distance during the afternoon, sipping his beer by the river, but I noticed he was still focused on her. The emotion was still there, and though he looked at her less, he still looked. I'd rarely, if ever, seen someone remain loving and connected after he or she had been rejected, no matter how kindly the rebuff. Was it possible he cared for her without possessiveness? I just didn't know him well enough to guess, but if so, he would earn a bit more of my respect. It was hard not to judge him entirely on his behavior towards me, but I was trying to give him the benefit of the doubt.

Iris explained she was very private when it came to relationships and just wasn't interested in having one in her life right now. She disliked public displays of affection and had been terribly embarrassed by Konrad's note on the pavement. I felt his attention was truly wasted on the rare girl who didn't like to be doted on. I knew I would have savored any such tokens, but we were very different girls and in very different places in our lives.

As Iris talked, Ava interjected comments every other sentence. At one point, she even began to narrate the story and explain the reasoning behind rejecting Konrad. Ava made it very clear that Iris's first priority on this trip was their friendship. Yes, they had come together, and yes, they had been friends since they were young, but there was a strange intensity to her remarks. Ava talked about the need for the two of them to be there just for each other. In some ways I understood. If I'd come with my best friend then I would have felt she was my first priority, but I hoped I wouldn't have kept her from connecting to others or finding a bit of romance.

I suddenly understood the tension. Ava felt this was a battle for Iris, and she was willing to fight tooth and nail to keep her to herself. She saw Konrad as a major threat and some of the rest of us as minor ones. I had to wonder if she'd been instrumental in keeping the romance from taking flight. I could suddenly identify the energy around the girls that had eluded me for so long. A thread of possessiveness bound them, and Ava was very focused on keeping them together. No wonder I'd felt challenged when trying to connect to the girls separately. I was a rogue element who could come between their duo.

As we started to climb into Galicia, I sought an audience to help me process what had just come to pass. Everything with the Tasmanian had accelerated and evaporated at an alarming rate, yet it was a familiar rut. I wasn't sure Ava and Iris would understand the depth of the pattern I'd just turned from, but I needed them to contain the story. I needed female listeners to understand how I'd just said no to my biggest addiction, turned away from my own personal drug of choice and faced the void in my romantic life once again. I needed two girls to acknowledge how it had taken all my will power to do what was right and not chase after another lost boy. For reasons I couldn't understand, I knew Francis wasn't the right person to talk to about this issue. He was entrenched in the dynamics, too close to the players and too invested in the outcome. I knew his words and feelings on the matter would likely have been more sound and wise, but I wasn't sure I could confess all my feelings on the matter to Francis. Light-hearted Ava and Iris, on the other hand, had been blissfully oblivious but were more than willing to gossip about what had happened last night.

As we chatted and moved slowly up the first part of the ascent, we ran into John sitting on a rock by the side of the trail. He'd been waiting for either Elliot or Francis to come along. Instinctively, we all wanted to stick with other people as we climbed into Galicia. After a brief visit with John, we started out of town. Iris was eager to keep up the salacious girl chat, but first we needed to form a line along the side of the small road so a bright red car could get by us. The car was moving quickly, and it was up to us to get out of the way. As it zipped by, we looked back, and suddenly time slowed.

As the car moved away from us, a dog ran out from a house beside the road and right under the front tires of the car. My body went rigid with shock. Ava uttered a mangled scream as the tan limbs of the dog tangled with the tires of the swift moving car. The moment fell into slow motion and then sped up with frightening clarity. The dog yelped and was spit out behind the car.

The three of us were rooted in place as the animal tumbled into the hedgerow on the far side of the road. A woman came out of her house and ran into the road. We told her the car had hit the dog. She crumpled on the roadway, then squatted with her hands over her face, weeping. As we stood in shock,

Francis arrived with John by his side. The two of them quickly went in search of the dog, and I turned back to Ava and Iris.

Ava stood very still with her poles dangling limp from the straps around her wrists. She was crying large wet tears and telling Iris she couldn't handle the sight. Iris took Ava in her arms. Holding her tight, she rocked Ava's body. All I could hear was a soft murmur coming from Iris. I would never know what had called forward the uncharacteristic flood of emotion in Ava. It seemed we all were on the rebound from some trauma or another. In large and small ways, we all had post-traumatic stress reactions to life and could only hope we would have someone to hold us close and tell us it would pass. But they couldn't hold us and contain the echo of the past if we weren't let into the inner circle of their life, and for this reason, I didn't hug Ava even though I wanted to comfort her. I wondered if I burst into tears if either of these girls would embrace me, or if perhaps Francis was the only person here who knew enough of me to hold me in such a flood of emotion.

Iris glanced at me with anxious eyes, and I helped her get Ava moving away from the scene of the accident. We didn't see John and Francis again before we were up the road and out of sight. Quickly the trail began to climb into forested tunnels of green. We were on the final ascent to O'Cebreiro. After a few minutes, I launched myself forward. With the light chatty atmosphere of the morning thoroughly broken, I needed to clear my head, and I felt the girls also wanted some space. Ava still looked distracted and raw. It felt right to give them this time so they could soothe each other on their own.

I tried to extinguish some of my anxiety in the push up the mountain. I noticed the rush of blood to my muscles and the way my quads took control, making me swift and strong even as the incline increased. My breath started to come deep from the bottom of my lungs. Each small breeze hit my back and cooled the sweat where my bag lay close to my skin. This was the first real mountain we'd climbed for weeks, but I didn't hesitate. I'd been born and bred among hills and mountains. Every trail that led from my family's farm went downhill to circle and loop across several hilltops. To return home was always an uphill journey.

Since Manjarin, I'd felt not only that all of us were fated to walk the trail at the same time, but that the members of our group had known one another in other times and places. This connection wasn't just one layer or simple to untangle. The web was endless, and each fresh moment revealed a new angle or brought forward another bond that had been there all along. It was amazing to know the universe could arrange all the tributaries and bring our group of souls to the trail. Perhaps we'd all marked our cosmic calendars for this moment. The Camino must have always existed in the plan for each of our diversely different lives. This subtle and eternal structure made me doubt myself when I let go of connections. I worried I might be breaking off from the love and community I'd asked the universe to send. How could I know? I wanted to trust the choice to let the Tasmanian go on and keep Francis and the Brit boys in my life.

As I drew towards the summit of the mountain, I could see the rim of clouds falling away along the far slope. I passed through hedges of bright yellow flowers. They clung to every surface and filled the air with their strong musk. When I first smelled the blooms, their fragrance was bold and sweet, but soon the smell turned sour in my nostrils. The flower's cloying perfume filled the air and was inescapable. Their tang attracted and repulsed at the same time. I knew people whom I felt the same way about. All the contrary feelings were tangled around each other, and it was hard to see the person clearly. I wondered what this meant about our group and especially the Iron Six. When all was said and done, I wasn't sure if my bond with some of them would fall into the sickly or the sweet category. And if they were a package deal, how long could I stay connected to those who so openly regarded me with distain and indifference? How long could I push against Konrad's energy for the sake of Tomas and the Brit girls?

Reaching O'Cebreiro, I arrived at the top of the sky, high above a layer of white clouds drifting along the surface of the earth. A small market of local fruit and vegetable vendors clustered in the main square. For the first time in a long while, there were big crowds of tourists piling off buses. I skirted a large group of brightly dressed families and older folks. I felt out of place in this town of expensive tourist shops. The sunlight fell directly from the apex of the sky. I pulled my hat down a bit farther to keep the light from my face. I didn't think anyone else in the group would be here. In my mind's eye, I could see them dotted along the trail curving up the side of the mountain. A fruit stand with sweet cherries glistened like soft red lights. I couldn't resist buying a small bag of the tender fruit from a kind man with weather beaten hands. I pointed and he filled the bag. I paid, and he tossed in another handful with a twinkling smile.

I headed toward the albergue but stopped short when I noticed a cluster of outdoor tables near a café. Konrad and Jay sat at the table. Jay had his hat tipped over his face to shield it from the sun. I couldn't be sure if he was awake or taking a light nap. Konrad sat deep in his chair with his long legs flung out around the table. He looked at ease, and I remembered he and Jay had woken before dawn to climb to the summit. It was Konrad's birthday. They'd headed out very early like explorers seeking adventure in the pre dawn glow, wanting to feel alive before the evening of celebration.

I walked over to the table and pulled out a chair. Neither of them looked up. Tomas came around the corner with a few drinks. Even though he greeted me with a warm smile, I knew I wasn't wanted. My chest started to flutter. I wondered again what I was doing with this group that merely tolerated my presence.

Since childhood, I'd been in a constant tussle with groups; I'd never felt at home in their dynamics. As I sat in the melting sun in O' Cebreiro, I was crushed by the realization that another group had thrown me to the outskirts for no obvious reason, and the people whom I cared for like Tomas and Iris had let it happen. Had I not been friendly, warm and engaged in their lives? What more could they want? Were they simply prepared to stick to the code and keep the doors to their inner sanctum closed because I'd met them too late? It was very worrying to know Jack and Ivan were gone, for they had been shelter from the Iron Six storm. I would sorely miss their easy company. The British boys were also distraught with the departure; somehow the two rather comical boys had acted as a buffer and broken up the unbalanced dynamics.

Tonight promised a strange mix of the Brit boys, the Iron Six and me. I left the table after offering a happy birthday to Konrad. I wasn't sure he even heard me as I scurried away. I walked into the first café and surprise, surprise there were Jack and Ivan at a table piled high with empty dishes. They offered cheerful greetings as I plunked down in a chair. I was thrilled to see them and deeply relieved. The end of the trail lay not far ahead, and I knew these boys would be kind enough to let me walk with them as long as I kept up. I felt a deep childlike fear at the idea of walking to the coast alone. It churned in my stomach and started my mind whirling on a change of plans.

What if I managed to convince the British boys to walk the next ten kilometers too, and we stayed on pace with Jack and Ivan? What if we became our own six? It was a band-aid sized solution for feeling I didn't really fit anywhere in the fragmenting groups. A large group always had buffer space for extras. The Tasmanian became one for a few days. Luc was always in and out. Everything was more fluid. But now with the departure of Jack and Ivan, my position felt painfully secondary and vulnerable. In the eyes of the Iron Six, I was always going to be an outsider. I had to finally accept this.

Jack and Ivan decided to take off down the backside of the mountain but told me where they planned to spend the night. I wandered the town while waiting for the British boys. Francis arrived first with sweat seeping out from under his floppy hat. He seemed pleased to find me in the courtyard. I remembered the note I'd written him and sensed he did too. It was lovely to feel the tension had broken between us like a passing storm. The Tasmanian was gone, and the skies were blissfully clear. Even though I longed to talk at length with him, sit and eat cherries in the shade, I knew it would have to wait. Time was of the essence. As his lean frame settled into an empty chair I told him about my master scheme. I'd sensed for a while that he struggled with the large group and really only cared to spend time with his boys, the American guys and me. He was too polite to show this openly and probably felt he ought to socialize with the rest of the crew even if he didn't enjoy it, but now after many days, I could see the pressure of being part of the social hurricane was wearing on him. Yet he felt torn in half by this moment of splitting, maybe as much as I did. I couldn't be totally sure, but if his desire to stay here was mainly to honor my written request, then I had a solution. We could follow the American guys on their breakaway and retain the bonds we found most precious.

As we sat in the open sun of the courtyard across from each other, I suddenly realized Francis was the only member of the whole group I couldn't, under any circumstances, bear to part with. As he sat quietly, mulling over my scheme and drinking water from his pack, I knew I wouldn't flee O'Cebreiro unless he came too. He was my rock, my dearest confidant and the only person here that I never tired of. I looked over at him and felt I'd always known him. Maybe I'd always known he would meet me here on the Camino, that this was the place where we would find each other again. Seconds later, Elliot and John bounced into town. They'd fallen behind Francis to search for the dog hit by the car and announced with big grins that they'd found the pup in a roadside bush miraculously unharmed.

Within moments, the four of us made the choice to go. As we sat around the plastic table in the bright midday sun, we agreed unanimously. No one resisted or brought forward any arguments to stay with the Iron Six. The choice was turned into physical action almost immediately as I leapt from the table. John and I agreed to be the advanced guard. I stuffed my fruit and supplies into my bag and took off at a half jog. John came bounding after me, determined to prove he too could walk with speed. Francis was sent as the messenger to tell the Iron Six we were pushing on. Only later did I realize how tough an assignment that was and how he took being the bearer of the news with true grace. I am sure I would have made a horrible mess of explaining and done us all a disservice.

I had very few coherent thoughts in my head as I tumbled down the trail next to John. After half an hour, the path spit us out onto a few kilometers of dark tarmac. Somehow leaving in this manner felt like an escape. Everything was rushing at great speed through my system, thoughts and feelings alike. I didn't know if I was running away from something or to something.

I hardly spoke to John as we put more and more distance between us and the Iron Six. I could feel my adrenalin fading. Something else started to set in as we arrived at a small petrol station. The parking lot was coated in dust and the air of abandonment. I wondered what I'd done. With one fell swoop, I'd left people behind again, and as before, it had been all my idea.

LIÑARES

I stood in the shade of the petrol station and felt as if all my roots had been pulled from underneath me. It had been a single choice after weeks of so many, but it still caught in my chest. My heart told me it was the right one, but I felt horrible. The choice was the final acknowledgement I would never be allowed full entrance into the Iron Six, but I'd felt this coming for sometime. It was wise to choose the people who cared for me, but the break up still flooded my bloodstream with sorrow. Suddenly I was tired of being alone. Even when things were good with the large group, I felt as if I was only just piecing together enough moments of intimacy and interaction to sustain me. The hunger for a vibrant and full community was proving extremely hard. Maybe I just couldn't feel fully grounded without a best friend or a boyfriend? And if so, why did I find myself with neither after weeks on the trail? Was this my Camino fate? I craved home like I had that first lonely night in Roncesvalles. I didn't know what else to do but keep walking. Elliot and Francis had caught up to us, and we started off down the trail again, moving further away from O' Cebreiro with every step. Elliot and John went ahead, but Francis stayed by my side. He was quiet and made no judgments about the choices we'd made; he didn't even probe me about what I was feeling. I felt a rush of gratefulness towards him and his continued willingness to hang in with me through the rough seas of my journey. He was an anchor I'd come to rely on, and I suddenly wondered if he would have been able to fill the best friend void if he hadn't had a prioritized allegiance to Elliot and John or if there wasn't a sliver of hesitancy in our bond. Our closeness was already a source of some tension among their camp, and I knew he struggled with the conflict. But on the trail off the mountain, Elliot and John were clearly distracted by chasing down Ivan and Jack and had left us to ourselves.

After several minutes my eyes began to silently overflow, and my voice caught in my throat as I tried to let the wave of sadness pass unnoticed. Under the shade of a tree, Francis begged me to stop and wait for my tears to end. I wasn't sure if they would end or why they had even begun. I wasn't sure I wanted to spill my messy emotional insides all over one of my few allies. What if he pulled away? What would I do if I didn't have the solace of his company? Francis turned to me and handing me his stick, tilted his head questioningly and waited for me to begin. He could see the waves, so maybe he wasn't afraid of getting soaked. Francis listened with unending patience as I sobbed and slurred my words, trying to explain things I myself didn't fully understand. I wondered where the root of the tears lay. It certainly wasn't the loss of the Tasmanian himself but rather the loss of the idea of him and all the hopes I'd pinned onto the dashing stranger. Maybe it was the way he brought to the surface all the many other losses of the past few years and crushed my optimism that I might still find the dream of love at the end of the trail.

I managed to slow my breathing as Francis walked beside me, an empathetic grimace on his face. "You feel things so deeply," he said to me in a soft voice after one of my long exhales.

I did feel deeply, but I wasn't sure what belonged to the present and what was simply left over emotion from the past. I felt myself dipping into the grief and finding it was not for Iris and Ava, nor Tomas and certainly not for Jay and Konrad. It was for the men who shared the same ugly name, the friends who had taken paths that led them from my life and all the other blurred faces of people who had vanished without a rhyme or reason. I felt empty and let Francis's voice soothe me. I let his words comfort me and felt reassured he wouldn't have broken away if he too didn't feel it was the right thing to do. We both agreed it had been looming on the horizon for some time, but I was scared of what was to come as we entered Galicia and the last leg of the voyage. Time was rushing forward, and I felt raw after so many weeks on the move. It was hard to imagine who could possibly arrive in the days to come and how I would feel safe to open up to them.

At the top of the next steep climb, John waited to walk the last kilometer with us. He kicked his boots in the dirt on the side of the trail and was oblivious to Francis's irritation. Both Francis and I wanted to be on our own as I tried to pull myself together. I craved the space to carry on with our conversation without emotional censorship. I wanted to confide in Francis alone. At the same time, I felt Francis wanted the space to openly comfort me, yet there was nothing we could do about John's entrance. It was annoying but not egregious. John was rather endearing, like a muddy dog seeking an embrace at all the wrong moments. I could empathize since I knew I could be the same way myself. I squeezed Francis's arm, gave him a weak smile and tried to let him know that it was OK. What could we do? He nodded his head in agreement. We hardly had to speak any more when it came to communicating, and we both knew there would be time later to pick up the thread where we had left off. The trail was the trail, and on it, privacy was a rare creature. Whatever had flooded over me would hopefully pass. With Francis and the rest of my boys still here, still on the same trail forward, I would recover my zest again.

Not long after, the trail crested the mountain and spit us out on the edge of a road with two large buildings on either side. Jack and Ivan sat in the shade of a run down and virtually deserted hotel. They sprang from their seats as we approached. The hugging and general high spirits distracted me. They were elated we'd chosen to walk onward with them instead of the Iron Six. It was comforting to bask in their genuine glee at our arrival. They were transparently happy to see us and effusive with their welcome. Their high spirits were without pretense and lifted my mood.

As we pulled up chairs, they warned us that the albergue was very strange. In fact it wasn't an albergue at all but a ramshackle hotel with one large bunk room in the attic for stray pilgrims who got stuck here. Apparently, few pilgrims chose to stop here for the night, but some were caught by impending storms or nightfall. It wasn't promising to hear this, yet I figured as a group we could survive one night almost anywhere.

Dinner proved to be as dismal as the accommodations. After the meal, we guzzled glasses of water in attempts to drown our raw and parched taste buds, abused by the saltiest meat and eggs I'd ever tasted. The dinner won first prize as the vilest meal I'd eaten on the entire trip against a stiff crowd of contenders from the early days.

I tried not to wonder about the Iron Six or feel bad we were trapped in this creepy hotel rather than in O'Cebreiro's quaint environs with its circular thatched houses like something out of the shire. The one and only consolation was being with the boys. I felt safe and stable as long as they were with me. That night, we slept in the dusty attic, happy to have the space to ourselves even if the door didn't lock. As I unpacked my bag, Francis and Elliot went off to say their night prayers. John dozed in his bed per usual while Jack went to shower, but Ivan lay on his bunk talking about his childhood fear of spiders.

After an hour or so, the rest of the guys returned. Though our sleeping quarters were dark and dingy, the boys were in high spirits and excited about what awaited us in Galicia. Our small group sang songs, laughed about the strange nature of our night's abode and fought over who would get to read my book before the lights went out. I gave it up to Elliot in the hopes I would be able to fall asleep quickly and leave the day behind me sooner rather than later.

The combination of tired muscles and frayed nerves was making me the most forlorn of the bunch, but I tried to hide it as best I could. We all sat around in the bunks closest to Ivan as he perched on his bed in a reclining position. Elliot lay on his back, dangling his legs off the end of John's bunk as Jack rifled through his pack on the ground. My bed was on the far side of the room, so I came over to Francis's bunk, saw the open space and instinctively curled up next to him. The attic had grown cold in the last hour, and I felt a chill cross my skin and reach for my core. Francis was leaning up against the wall with his long legs in front of him as I tucked my body up along his left side, mimicking the same posture, but slouching lower so I could curl my head into the space above his shoulder. I'd already carved my way into the space beside him before I realized how close we really were. We'd never been an overly affectionate duo. In fact, we'd hardly ever touched. I could recall the handful of moments, and each had been as smooth and stylized as a court dance, a social pleasantry among crowds of onlookers. We had long been close but only emotionally, and I hadn't sought physical comfort from a fellow pilgrim since my arrival in Spain, least of all Francis. It had been a luxury I'd simply gone without. Yet now, I needed his warmth to extend beyond his words and wondered why it felt so strange to ask this of him. Was it because he was naturally reserved and unreceptive to physical displays of affection or was it something else? I felt his limbs clench as I sunk down beside him, but his reaction was hardly visible on the surface. The others were too busy with their fun and games to notice the shift in his energy, and his placid expression gave away nothing. I felt myself hold my breath, unsure if I should retreat and give him space or refill my lungs. I wanted to pause the frame, still the moving characters and ask Francis what he was feeling, ask him if he wanted me to move away and seek comfort elsewhere.

I was unraveling under the stress of the last few days, and I desperately needed human comfort, but Francis's reaction unsettled me. Why had he suddenly become cold and tense as if all his energy was pulling away from me at once? It almost felt as if he was afraid of me or annoyed or both. I'd never felt this tone reverberating through him, especially not directed towards me. Of all the boys in the group and all the many people I'd met along the way, he was the only person who could truly understand this simple plea for connection. He'd seen me cry, make massive social blunders and fall in and out of a messy crush. I wasn't trying to redefine the boundaries of our friendship. I just needed to feel close to him. We were friends in a tiny room with four other guys. Such innocent nestling should have felt harmlessness, but as soon as I touched him I knew it wasn't. Not for me and not for him. As I felt the warmth radiating off his body, I suddenly wondered why we had hugged so little, so often refrained from linking arms or wrestling as most good friends do. Was it his British reserve or some unspoken rule of our male to female friendship? I'd just accepted our quirky bond as I found it, but now I knew there had been a hidden friction for some time. Ever since Manjarin, something had lingered unspoken. The trail had offered plenty of distractions, but suddenly they were gone. Now I could pick out the individual notes of tension and the ever-present vibration radiating between us. I knew at times I'd deflected it as concern over my growing infatuation with the Tasmanian, but with the adventurer gone, I was surprised to find it still lingered. I felt as if I had, with one swift movement, stumbled into a deep pool of energy I'd failed to see at my feet for the past weeks. This realization hummed through me as I looked to Francis, wondering what he was feeling, but his face was turned away from me focused on Ivan's performance. I sought reassurance that I wasn't unwelcome in his space. I wanted to hunt around in the energy and prove he was merely shy and feeling self conscious with me because I was a girl. I wanted it to be general or impersonal, anything other than a subtle comment on his feelings about me. So the Tasmanian had been hot for me but hadn't liked me, and Francis liked me but found my touch disconcerting? It was all deeply confusing. Too many games had been played across the battlefield of touch in my life with men, and even though Francis was simply a friend, I still cared about his actions. I still wanted to be clear about the buzz between us and its physical tone. I wanted it to be as warm as all deep bonds should be, but I felt he feared the power of the heat.

I was weary and knew all my circuits were frayed and overloaded with the double hit of the Tasmanian's exit and our secession from the Iron Six. So as the boys quieted down for the night and found their own bunks, I retreated and decided to let the whole incident drop, chalking it up to lingering Tasmanian backlash or worry about the end. So Francis had been annoyed by my uncouth

American ways or my needy girlish behavior and acted strangely in response. He would calm down and tomorrow all would return to normal. I needed our sturdy friendship in balance to navigate this last province and face the end of the world. Tomorrow, I would have my loyal band of pirates by my side. I would rise above the worry and the rumbling insecurities in my chest and boldly charge forward. I still had things to prove and trail to conquer before this journey was done.

TRIACASTELA

STAGE TWENTY THREE- 37.1K-23M

ALTO DO POIO TO SARRIA

That first night in Galicia I dreamed of birds. This time they were coming out of the layers of fog that clung to the mountains, darting though the curling waves of white clouds that rolled through my skin and evaporated. The wings of the birds were warm and golden in the early morning light. I could hear every noise rushing off the edges of their small bodies.

Maybe the dream was an omen or maybe a prediction for I didn't know it at the time, but I would be lost in a foggy chamber, white and soundlessness, for the next two days. In the pre-dawn hours, the boys and I rose and made our way into the lush green hills of Galicia. I was thrilled to step out into the dark morning. The crisp air washed clean all the unsettled feelings that had haunted me in the night. We watched the sun rise from the roadway then slipped silently down the backside of the mountains. The fog flowed off the mountains like the tumbling waves of an ocean. Two by two, we moved through fields of endless mist, cut open by segments of rich orange morning sun. Everything was either drenched in milky white hues or bold golden rays. The pathways were narrow. Mountain streams flowed to the edges of the trail, and water trickled through moss and tree roots before running out onto the rocky track. We shared the trail with cows as they migrated from one pasture to another. It was clear who had the right of way as the large creamy colored beasts filled the path, forcing us up and off the trail. The sheer size of the cows was intimidating, and I wasn't sure how they felt about humans. After a herd moved by us, a small man in a tweed cap with a rush in hand came up the trail in a pair of worn rubber boots. He said good morning as he passed. If the words hadn't been in Spanish, I would have sworn I was in Ireland. For all I knew, I'd gone to sleep in Spain and awoken on the emerald isle. The smell of the fresh damp land, the trail littered with ripe cowpats and the soft touch of the air was the language of the western shores. It was no mere coincidence this land had a long history connected with Ireland and its Celtic culture.

The group broke into staggered pieces as the morning wore on. Francis disappeared ahead and Elliot slowed to be on his own at the back. The rest of us ambled along, eventually coming upon a rest spot at the side of the trail. Tucked under the shade of two large wizened trees a cluster of tables made of long stones appeared. They were low to the ground with short legs and squat tree stumps as seats. It was a picnic area build for hobbits. Ivan was enchanted, declaring we must stop and take a break in the miniature scene. His faithful followers, Jack and John, agreed. I spent much of the break wrangling with my gear. The mouthpiece to my water pack had broken and now leaked all over me like an unruly tear duct.

When we returned to the trail, we descended further into the belly of the fog, and the green vegetation grew even more lush and dense around the edges of the path. Trees formed a dense canopy overhead, and gnarled roots spread over the surface of the pathway. Stonewalls marked the boundaries of the trail, and small cottages tucked into the side of rambling plots of land were silent and cozy. We passed wild trees that must have been hundreds of years old. Some of the trunks were slim and tough, while others were three to five meters in diameter with speckled uneven skin and long thick branches. It was as beautiful as a fairytale, drenched in the hidden magic of elves and mythical creatures, the perfect backdrop for times when princesses disappeared into dark woods and gallant knights cut through overgrown vines to find them. These were the sights and smells of my childhood spent deep in the pages of a fairytale book. Before long, the shady path wound us into the heart of a village, tucked in the nook of the green valley.

In Triacastela, we waited for two hours on a street curb for a supermercado to open. We knew the likelihood of coming across another food shop before tomorrow morning was slim to none, and so it was worth the wait. The group sat close together to keep out the early morning chill. John leaned against Ivan and Jack while the three pontificated and blew on their cold fingers. I was on the end of the line beside Francis, and without thought I tucked my arm through the crease in his elbow. It was the cold that made me sit close with my knees gently bumping up against his, but once again I felt it was only politeness and a desire not to make a scene or offend me that kept him from shaking off my touch as soon as it landed. What had been startled curiosity last night now bloomed into full-scale irritation; I was officially pissed off. What was his problem? Why was it wrong to link arms for warmth when John was practically sitting on Ivan's lap for the same reason? I wanted to pull my arm away and swing it back at him with force but knew I would only be pursuing the edges of my reaction, for at the core I felt the familiar feeling of rejection. I'd never cared what he thought of my appearance or if he found me desirable, but now I suddenly did. Now I wondered why he was having such a complex reaction to a simple moment. The thin but tough layer of buffering around his frame spoke of what lay between us and maybe even described the blooming complexity. I felt the pool of energy again flooding around us, rising like a quick moving tide. What had happened to our open and unconditional state of friendship? Why were we suddenly so deep in a push and pull dynamic? Who was doing the pushing and who was doing the pulling? Sensing this new conflict between us made me feel raw, distressed and ready to withdraw, back off and move out of the energy. I needed to be moving again, for the cold was now reaching into my chest, and my toes had gone numb. Was I crazy to feel the trail crumbling underneath me while the rest of the group bounced about in cheerful oblivion?

As we waited for the store to open, the group assessed each person's strengths and gave out corresponding superhero personas. Ivan gave himself the oddly poetic role of Indestructa boy and even cheerfully accepted the challenge of being a hero that could never be hurt but easily killed. Ivan relished the magnificent futility of such powers and embraced the catch 22 with a gracious swagger.

Mercifully, the shopkeeper arrived at eleven and pulled up the metal gate to open the shop. We loaded up on supplies and set off with heavy packs. The trail branched at the bottom of town. One route followed the road and ran by a large monastery. The other dove deep into an old forest and curved up through the mountains. We chose to bypass the monks and go by way of the magic forest instead. Elliot had read in a guidebook that this area had a deep connection to fairy lore and the elemental forces of nature. Nonetheless, we didn't move through the woods in reverent silence. Instead the boys created rap lyrics about our journey that made my sides ache with laughter. Francis held down the steady beat as Ivan and Elliot took center stage, free styling with astounding ease. I didn't dare join in, knowing I could never come close to the deft and clever turns of phrase, rhyming and imagination the boys innately possessed. I was happy to merely walk along and listen as the musical interlude broke the mood that had lingered since town.

As the afternoon wore on, the trail emerged out of the deep woods and wound us along a series of open fields. The group sifted out and suddenly I was on my own. Ivan and Jack were lost in a conversation about home, and Elliot had slowed his pace to drop off the back of the group again. Francis and John were up ahead, entrenched in what appeared to be a tense argument. Before leaving England, Elliot and Francis had been given a series of envelopes from a friend with the instructions that they open the packets along the trail when different things occurred. Some were light hearted and bent on inciting a laugh. One such envelope that the boys had been directed to open in the French town of Condom had contained its namesake. Some were simple like the envelope for a cold and rainy day that contained a few tea bags, but others were more complex. And those seemed to be the ones left by the time I met the boys. There was one for when two of them had an argument. Francis and John had opened that envelope this morning before we set off on the trail. I hadn't been 100% sure about the reason behind their argument, but I had an unsettling suspicion it had something to do with John interrupting my tearful conversation with Francis on the backside of O' Cebreiro. I felt bad for my part in their argument, especially since they'd gone for nearly two months without having to open that envelope. The envelope directed the boys to trade packs for the day. I could tell as I scanned ahead that they both felt a conversation was needed to resolve things as well. I gave the boys space but secretly craved a view into their dynamics. Maybe there were clues in Francis's words of amends that would shed light on our current tussle, anything but stoic silence would be helpful.

In the late afternoon, our ragged group landed on the outskirts of Sarria. Though we didn't talk about it, a pervasive feeling of the end filled each of us. With Sarria's streets under our feet, we had officially entered the final stage of our journey. At just over one hundred kilometers from Santiago, Sarria was famous for its position on the trail as the last city a pilgrim could start from and still get "credit" from the Catholic Church. The credit in question was the official Compostela, given to pilgrims who walked at least one hundred kilometers to arrive at Santiago. The Compostela was a document from the Church, much like a diploma, giving the owner iron clad proof of his or her journey in the eyes of the Church. I cared very little about the document but knew it matter greatly to the Brit boys. As long as I added a Santiago stamp to my passport before walking to the coast, I would be happy.

Sarria was unlike any other trail city we'd navigated. There were over a dozen albergues along the main street, and men stood on the corners handing out fliers for different accommodations, seeking pilgrims to patronize their albergues. After so many weeks of a different ethos along the Camino, the scene was startlingly commercial. One whole section of the city was even tailored to accommodate pilgrims. It had a touristy sheen to it that took me by surprise, but the albergues were new, inexpensive and very clean. I was pleased when the group settled on the first albergue we stumbled into as I wasn't in the mood to shop around for the best deal. I was weary and perfectly content to make a choice and stick with it. The building was long and thin with well-lit bathrooms. Everything shone white and clean. The water was warm, and the sinks even had soap. The dormitory was a spacious room painted in soothing shades of yellow with long wispy curtains fluttering along the lengths of the tall windows. There were over twenty bunks in our room, but they all hugged the sides of the walls. The open space in the middle created a sense of privacy. Yet it was the lovely garden with a porch swing and a bit of lawn that was the centerpiece of the albergue's charms. Even though the space was small and cluttered with clotheslines and lawn chairs, it felt inviting and offered a view out over the rest of the city. Ivan and Jack took up residence on the swing for most of the afternoon as I hung washing, and the Brit boys played fierce rounds of Uno in the grass. I felt back in the contented rhythm of trail life again and relished the peace in the wake of all the past drama.

In the evening, Jack and Ivan convinced the group to go out for dinner before heading to a bar to watch a bit of futbol. After the meal, I felt tendrils of worry and agitation creeping back in but tried to keep my mood high as we set off to watch the match. The championship game of the European Futbol Cup had arrived, and there was no way the boys were going to miss being among Spaniards when Spain was the favorite to win. We all wanted to partake in the celebration and subsequent drunken madness of a triumphant nation. The bar we chose was packed to the gills. Scores of people stood, sat and crouched with breathless anticipation. The crowd was almost as entertaining as the game itself. I watched the first half of the match squeezed in among the boys. After the lead striker Torres, in all his golden glory, scored, I called it a night. I'd seen the swell of jubilation from the home crowd, the clinking of beers and the rollicking banter. I'd mingled. I'd witnessed. I'd conquered. Now sleep was filling my thoughts even more than hunky Spanish strikers. The albergue was still and dark when I returned. It was comforting to turn on my small flashlight and write in my journal. I needed time to collect my thoughts, to sort through my own energy in a space free of others. I hoped writing down all I'd felt in the last few days would illuminate what had passed, but in the end, my writing trailed into a flow of anxious ramblings, so I cut myself off and went to sleep.

The past few days had taken the wind out of my sails. I felt fatigue creeping into my body in a new way. My muscles were stronger than ever, my feet could practically walk the last hundred kilometers on their own initiative, but my resolve and my spirit were battered. I'd suffered tough losses of late, and though some were right and necessary, they hurt none-the-less. Change exacted a high toll, and now the alteration in my friendship with Francis was pushing me to the edge of myself. I suddenly wanted to go backwards, repair the fracture and mend our friendship at the very moment it began to splinter. Yet I also felt this was futile. Maybe we were always destined to arrive here, and maybe what lay on the other side of this struggle was nothing to fear. I hoped this was true but didn't know how to cross the gulf that now lay between us. The end was only a few days away. Three or four at most. I knew time was dwindling, and my connection to Francis wasn't the only thing on my mind. I could no longer delude myself that I would find love along this path. The trail was drawing to a close, and I was powerless to stop its momentum. It was pulling me forward to Santiago and the coast and there was nothing I could do about it. There was no way to halt time and wait for the elements of the dream to arrive.

For the second night in a row, I dreamt of birds. The air was alight with colors, wings brushing my face and grazing the surface of my body. The crimson of the cardinal moved around my solo figure in infinite swift loops, circling up into the endless sky and vanishing into two horizons of blue.

Suddenly I was awake. Two fellow pilgrims were standing next to my bunk. One of the strangers was handing me a flashlight and the other offering a small lighter. I'd clearly been talking in my sleep and apparently asking for a light. Maybe even yelling for one. I blushed in the dark. I'd let my guard down, let my concentration slip and this nighttime scene was what I got for it. I knew my sleep talking and walking tendencies came out only when I felt fully comfortable with my surroundings, and I'd found that changing locations every night kept me from these nighttime rants. Until now that is. I'd grown comfortable somehow or vulnerable or too tired to keep control as I slept. Maybe it was being with the guys or maybe it was something else. I couldn't know. Now, I awoke to my crazy behavior and the need to convince a set of pilgrims I was OK, and whatever I'd been yelling about could wait until morning. I hoped they believed me as they moved away to their own bunks. Even more so, I hoped the guys had slept through the theatrics. As I tried to fall back asleep, I realized I'd been speaking in Spanish; I'd been clear and decisive. I was calling for a light. I needed a light. It was true, I couldn't see. I felt blind in every direction. I couldn't see the way forward, and I couldn't see what lay around me. All the birds were auspicious signs, but I felt far from clear about what they were trying to show me.

PORTOMARÍN

STAGE TWENTY THREE- 22.9K-14.2M
SARRIA TO PORTOMARÍN

Our group met in the empty pre-dawn kitchen then fled the streets of Sarria as fast as possible. I walked with Francis in the lead pack, and soon we lost sight of the other boys, but neither of us spoke. Outside the city, the trail turned into a winding corridor of rutted dirt paths blocked in by stonewalls. The morning was damp and chilly. The cold seeped through my layers, and I wondered how long it would be before the sun cut through the blanket of fog that swallowed us. Francis was swift and determined with his long strides, but I sensed he was also battling fatigue. I felt as if the weather had invaded my brain and covered everything it touched.

If I was fogged in, so was Francis. He seemed weighted down by something, and neither of us dared to extricate the other from this mood. All we could do was walk. I suddenly wondered if we would be like this until the end; if the one duo that was known for their boundless ability to talk for hours on end had finally run aground and gone silent. I'd always felt we were the closest of all the freshly formed trail bonds, but maybe this wasn't so. Even the way we walked had now changed. We drifted apart and then back together over the course of an hour, shifting like floating debris on the tide of the trail. Yet he never disappeared completely out of sight, and I never let too much space build between us. He walked with his head down, lost in his own world. I had no idea what lived and breathed in that world today but wondered if I resided there. He was certainly alive in my thoughts, even if I could make little sense of his presence. If anything I wanted to share my current worry and struggles with him, to once more divulge my fears and desires about the end of the world. Even though we walked with a marked space between us, it was as if we were still connected by a very long cord. It seemed to be the only way Francis could handle my company this morning, staying close but at a distance. I held onto the chord and kept going.

The foggy path was quiet at first, but as the sky lightened and the hour grew, things began to change. With jarring swiftness, the pathway became clogged with herds of people unlike anything I'd seen on the Camino before. For the past weeks, the trail had been an experience of familiar community, a shared eight hundred kilometer event. Before Sarria if I didn't recognize fellow walkers, I still assumed they were engaged in the same long pilgrimage. Their clothes and packs told the same tales as my own. We were obviously of the same breed; they moved like seasoned walkers, and I knew they were on the Camino for the long haul. Now on the outskirts of Sarria, I came upon the first of hundreds of walkers who were not of our variety. They swarmed the narrow pathways, filled the air with voluminous noise and were oblivious to the shared nature of the trail. Many were sullen teenagers with book bags, gold sneakers and Coke cans in their hands or adults with daypacks, crisp white clothing and binoculars dangling around their necks. Their every detail alerted the world they were one hundred kilometer pilgrims.

Many were part of large school groups that walked the sixty miles stretch in a week and a half. The herds would walk short distances with their belongings shipped to their next destination. Their bags, shoes, hair and skin were clean, all tell tale signs they were new imports who didn't intend to linger on the Camino for long. It was strange to move past them and feel distanced from the people I was sharing the trail with. I wanted to make a sign and post it on our bags: "We started in France!" I wanted these newcomers to snap out of their self-involved travel, notice the life of the trail and understand where it had come from before they joined its stream. I felt intruded upon, violated on home turf. We all did, and there was nowhere to hide. All we could do was move faster. As Francis passed a horde of kids moving at the speed of molasses, I noticed no one even looked up to see him pass. Completely distracted by flirting with each other, gossiping or munching on candy bars, the kids failed to experience the trail. They failed to see the people, the epic journeys and the stories as they flowed by. They missed it all in the blink of an eye. If I hadn't looked up, said hello and reached out, it would have been easy to miss connecting with the guys, meeting the Iron Six and all the many characters I'd encountered. I could've kept my head down, remained in my own world and missed the Camino itself. Just the realization took the wind out of my lungs and jolted me back to life. Without a moment's thought, I darted through the mass of kids, skirted the oblivious adult leaders and walked as fast as I could until I drew up beside Francis. Suddenly, the distance, this space between us on the trail, was too hard to sustain. Suddenly, I wasn't content to keep my head down and let Francis drift away from me in the final lap.

I walked beside Francis until we came to the infamous one hundred kilometer marker. This was a major landmark, an indicator of how far we'd come and how little was left between us and Santiago. As we cheered in celebration and high fived, the touch of his cold hands left a chilled imprint on my own. I'd known for sometime that Francis had trouble with circulation in his hands, and that before the trail, it had become so bad, he'd been hospitalized. That trip to the hospital and worry over his health had almost kept him from coming on this journey. I wanted to warm his hands, retrieve his gloves from his pack and put them on his delicate fingers, but I restrained myself. I knew he could take care of himself, but I still I felt an intense tenderness for him. I wanted to take care of him even as the air between us still held unresolved conflict. His contradictory nature often struck me in these small moments, sliding sideways into view and reminding me that behind the serious and centered appearance of manhood he was still a boy. I wondered what he would be like when all the last remains of boyhood had vanished, and he stepped fully into who he would become.

Francis decided to stop at the one hundred kilometer marker to wait for Elliot and John. He wanted to cross the threshold with them in a moment of unity. As he leaned against the way marker covered in bright graffiti, I felt the sting of resentment return. This was just the beginning of feeling left out of celebrations, just the start of days when it would be hard to forget that here on the trail, I belonged to no one.

I left Francis as he wished and walked ahead alone. I was comfortable with my own company but afraid I would never get to a place in time that held a community of my own. In no way did I want to revisit the truly solo feeling that haunted me at the start of the trail, but as I strode along ahead of all the guys, I struggled to figure out if being alone in a group was any better than simply being alone. As I walked down the trail and away from the one hundred kilometer marker, the two options felt one and the same.

A few hours later, I stopped in a trailside field and waited for the boys. It was nearly noon, and the sun had burnt away the fog. I propped my bag under my head and rested my body in the long grass. The guys arrived in a rowdy clump, their spirits high, thoroughly prepared to stop and eat a hearty meal. After dropping down into the meadow around me, they proceeded to construct gourmet lunches as trail tradition required. I let my eyes close and pretended to drift in and out of sleep. I was weary but not tired. I knew I was withdrawing emotionally but tried to cover my tracks by pretending to nap. I was astounded at how gathering all of us together often negated, at least for the moment, any brewing conflicts. It was as if everything was put aside while we sat merrily lunching together. The tension between Francis and John had either gone or been put down in a temporary cease-fire. And whatever was happening between Francis and me slipped below the surface away from the eyes of the group. In fact, I felt it had hardly crossed their radar to begin with. If asked, the boys would state that Francis and I were close, but they would never guess at the complexity or intensity of our bond nor its quickly shifting terrain. Even with the larger group of twelve, nobody had seen the undercurrent. Maybe that was due in part to how distracted I'd been while we traveled as a circus group of twelve. I'd let group dynamics and the Camino gossip, or "Camino G" as Ava and Iris called it, overtake the real emotional thread of my trail. Now in this pared down group of boys, there was no way of skirting the extremely intense dynamics with Francis. Maybe my entanglement with the Tasmanian had caused a disturbance in our bond and laid bare pieces of our friendship that had been hidden. My feelings were blurring all the carefully constructed lines I'd created for us, and I knew he felt the same out of control sensation yet was hesitant to admit it. Part of me wanted to talk about it, and the other part was freaked out by his freaked out energy. Our emotional turbulence had become a never ending loop yet managed to fly right over the heads of the five other boys living cheek to jowl with the two of us.

I couldn't tell if the blindly oblivious nature of the group, especially Jack and John, made me feel less tense or just plain crazy. Ivan, however, could always be counted on to gather all of us into silly banter. It was his gift. He could lift the mood of any group, and the more he lightened our spirits, the more he enjoyed his role. And he was in top form during lunch, delighting us as head jester and even prodding me into a few genuine laughs.

One of the things the group couldn't deny was the change in the land. I felt haunted by it. I couldn't pinpoint why until I realized it echoed my days in the west of Ireland down to its very sounds and smells. The stonewalls caging in the trail and the endless rolling hills all caused visceral flashbacks to my Irish summer. I felt cradled by the land again with everything close and comforting. It was a stark contrast to my state of mind. In this soft welcoming track of land I felt cold and isolated, but in the barren Meseta I'd felt warm and cared for. What a strange reversal of fortunes.

I wondered if the land would change as we neared the sea. Would the ocean strip away some of these soft green layers? After so many days of land, part of me craved open water. Though I knew we would one day reach the sea, I was unable to guess what the first view would feel like. We'd been tied to the land, tracing its every contour for so long. Would the sight of the ocean change everything?

As always, my limbs refused to stay inactive for long, and I took off for Portomarín, informing the group I would meet them at the albergue. The land swept down through tiny clustered villages into a valley filled with a large river and reservoir. Portomarín sat on the far side of a narrow bridge with a separate lane for foot traffic. I was glad not to have to walk amongst speeding cars, but a large group of teenage boys clogged the center of the bridge and seemed prepared to stand in the way of pilgrim traffic all day. From the look of them, they were one of the student groups walking the trail. As I drew closer, I heard them speaking German and watched as they shoved each other with brute force towards the drop. Absorbed in throwing stones off the bridge and roughing each other up, they didn't see me as I approached. The space between the guardrail and the side of the bridge was narrow, and I had to move through the mob to get to the other side. The energy of this group got stranger as I passed. One of the boys yelled and reached out as if trying to catch me as I slipped by. I couldn't tell if he was cat calling or flinging profanities, but his eyes were dark and hooded. One of his friends thrust his hips and smiled a dirty grin. I ignored their taunts, picked up speed and cursed how vulnerable I felt without the guys around me.

Once in town, I sat in the park eating peaches out of a tin, trying to sooth my nerves. Portomarín was nothing impressive, but the water at its feet changed the nature of the place. This was the biggest body of water I'd seen in Spain. No mere pond, it was a lake fed from a strong river and looked invitingly cool.

I waited to check into the albergue until the boys arrived and was glad I did. We'd always tried to stay in the less expensive municipal hostels; up until this moment, our strategy had worked well. We'd been able to roll with the less than modern facilities or lack of private bathrooms, but the albergue at Portomarín was a particularly ugly monstrosity. As I lined up to check in with the guys, I saw the nasty German students from the bridge were staying with us in the prison-like building. Thankfully, I was once again entrenched in my posse and could create a safe space free of groping German boys.

The large albergue was unwelcoming and cold. Everything that could be chained down was. We were given a bland government stamp on each of our passports then asked to move along and not block the line. A security guard with a gun stood in the entryway. Later, I would see him flirting with the grumpy young woman who'd checked us in. Once upstairs, we entered a long and narrow room with tiny windows near the ceiling that did little to shift the stagnant air. We moved about in a sweaty daze as a thick cloak of heat clung to every surface.

Settling in, I realized I had a problem. The bunks in the room were packed so tightly that every set was pushed up against another like double beds. I would have to sleep right next to someone, and in no way did I want it to be a one of the German boys or a large frisky Spaniard. I wasn't about to let down my guard in this place, but fortunately I didn't have to. There were five strapping young lads by my side; even John would do as a suitable buffer. I glanced around sure one of them would step forward and offer his assistance. I would settle for Ivan or Jack if they could bear to be separated, but I really wanted Francis to claim the empty bed beside me. Even with all our complications, I would find the most solace in his close proximity.

I held my pack in my arms as the guys looked around at the bunk arrangements. Before they could pick bunks, I spoke up and asked if one of them would be so gallant as to fill the place next to me. The all nodded with relaxed nonchalance, and Jack patted me on the back as if to imply there was no reason to get all worked up. But nobody stepped forward. Didn't they see the large Spaniard with small white underwear and a dark hairy chest lurking just down the row? Didn't they get how few centimeters lay between the narrow bunks? Was I being crazy or was I simply being a rational girl among a group of clueless boys? I wondered how Jack would fare if someone leered at him for minutes on end and made a swing at his butt as he passed by. It might give them all a bit of perspective into the female experience. Then I noticed Elliot turn to look at Francis who lingered in the hallway. Even Ivan seemed to be waiting for some mysterious cue from the doorway. Suddenly, I understood they were waiting for Francis to take the spot. Even though much of my bond with Francis had escaped their notice, our preference for each other hadn't, and they all assumed he was the heir apparent to the bed next to mine. But Francis wasn't stepping forward to take the spot. I waited for something to happen, for Francis to make a move, for anyone to make a move, but nobody would. Finally after a painfully strained pause that seemed to last for days, Francis aggressively threw his stuff on to the bunk next to mine, turned to the door, and without a word, stalked out. As soon as he disappeared, the boys came back to life, talking animatedly as if nothing had happened. I stood still at the end of my bunk, rattled, annoyed and completely baffled at what had just occurred.

Much later, Francis came back to collect his washing. He appeared to have shifted out of his irritated mood and seemed resigned to the situation at hand, but he didn't volunteer any details about his dramatic exit. I gave him his space and hoped we could both let our hackles down. The tension was pushing me towards some sort of meltdown, and I had a feeling such a scene wouldn't be pretty. Plus, I felt hurt by Francis's transparent annoyance at being my bunkmate. It was the same response all over again. It was the same energy he'd flung at me in Triacastela, but I had no clues what it meant. He'd dropped into a silent private mood and put up the do not disturb sign.

As Jack and Ivan had already fallen into a somewhat indestructible napping coma, I wandered the building and found three distressing things to be true. The first was that there were no pots, pans or plates in the kitchen. The second was that the supply of toilet paper was now officially gone on all three floors. There had been scraps here and there when I arrived at midday, but now there wasn't a sheet in the whole building. Third, the showers in the large public bathrooms had no doors, curtains or palm fronds, just wide open air.

The afternoon dragged into night. The only break in the long hot hours was a trip down to the reservoir for a swim. No sooner had we found our way to a section of marshy waterfront than the guys stripped down to their boxers and ran hollering into the water. After a swim, I sat on the shore while they slapped around like a pack of sea otters. Ivan swam out deep, took off his boxers and swung them around his head yelling with glee. When the others followed suit, I watched like a proud mom from the shore, enjoying the silliness of my boys. Once back in their clothes, they posed for a picture on a large fallen tree that sat halfway out of the water. As I took the photo, their behavior reminded me of bathing beauties or pin up girls. In a strange way, I sometimes felt like the only boy among a pack of rambunctious girls.

Evening and the awaited promise of sleep arrived. I wanted to leave this town, and sleep would bring a faster departure. It was disheartening to stay in yet another dismal place. Even at nine, the air was thick with heat, the light dim and the room full of dozing pilgrims. I wore a tank top and shorts but wished I could shed more layers. Everything stuck to my skin. Francis sat next to me writing in his small journal while I wrote in mine. His was a very tiny leather bound notebook about the size of his palm, and he wrote in the small pages with even smaller script. My handwriting was, in comparison, wild scribbles that ate open pages with fierce speed. Yet I liked the way his book could fit in his raincoat pocket or tucked into the narrow folds of his pack. Its size made it magical and had me wondering what thoughts he was pouring onto the delicate squares of paper.

After our trip to the reservoir, the tension from the incident with the bunks faded, and we returned to our truce of not talking about anything of substance. Neither of us seemed willing to discuss what happened, and I, for one, felt nervous about what might be said. It was too hot to fight, and I couldn't withstand another dose of his irritation with me. I could feel his buffer layer wrapped tightly around him again, but I didn't push the edges of it. Not tonight. In some ways, we didn't even have a window for anything to be said, since the thirty other pilgrims in the room negated any sense of privacy. Once again, we were stacked like sardines but relieved to be lying down after a long day. To write in my journal, I propped myself up with my back against the wall and my legs splayed out in front of me. Out of the corner of my eye, I watched Francis write with focus, only lifting his eyes every once in awhile to mull over a phrase. We both faced across the room to another set of occupied bunks along the far wall.

After a while, I noticed I was being watched. Looking up from my journal, I saw two middle aged Spanish men reclining in their bunks, arms crossed over their burly chests, staring straight at me with unflinching interest. They had no books to read or journals to write in. It appeared I was the entertainment of the moment. Once I caught their eyes and they noted my awareness and subsequent disapproval, I assumed their behavior would cease, but it didn't. I looked up a minute later to find them still staring with the same dogged focus. I turned to Francis and asked him for his opinion on the matter at hand. He looked over, his eyes drawing together in consternation and quickly turned back to confirm what I'd felt. There was no doubt about it, they were settled in for the long haul. I grew uncomfortable and sensed Francis was agitated by their attention as well. I wanted to stow my journal and duck under the covers, but just the thought of trapping myself in my insulated sleeping bag made me choke, I would surely perish of heat stroke and suffocation. Apparently space wasn't as foolproof a form of protection as I'd hoped.

For years, I had been aware there was something about the way I looked that attracted attention from lecherous older men, but it never made moments like this any easier to bear. To have these men leering at me brought nothing but discomfort, and I didn't experience it as a compliment. Why would I be glad if they liked my appearance? It wasn't me, not really. It wasn't the me that could hold them. It wasn't the me they could love. It was only the me they could see from afar, possess and covet, put on a shelf or hold at a distance. My looks weren't the substantive parts of who I was, and admiration of the external wasn't proof that someone cared about the person behind the looks. I'd learned the hard way about predatory men. I'd been manipulated by them too many times to find this anything but demoralizing. It was one of the reasons I liked Francis so much. He'd never been caught up in my looks but had been drawn in by who I was, and this was a refreshing change. Even though things were odd between us, I sensed his desire to protect me. He even looked as if he was seriously considering defending my honor, but then darkness dropped a veil of semi-privacy over us, and sleep was possible.

In the night, I rolled close to Francis. I awoke at dawn to find our bodies inches apart. We'd both let our guards down in sleep and unhinged ourselves from self-conscious worry. Unhampered by his well constructed boundaries, I'd gravitated across the divide, instinctively drawing closer to him. As the light spread across us and broke the warmth of sleep, I quickly rolled back to my own side of the bed. I was quite sure he wouldn't have wanted me so close, and I suddenly felt upset that sleep and my unconscious had lured me towards him. I had to respect his wish for space, for distance and clarity, even though I didn't understand it, and he refused to be honest about his reasoning. Part of my confusion over the energy swelling around us lay in his maddeningly contradictory behavior and his mixed energetic tone. I could sense now in every movement, word and look that he was struggling with two divergent feelings. He was wrestling with a jumble of attraction and aversion, and neither seemed to be winning. As we packed up our things in the half light, I couldn't tell how the night had affected him, or if he'd awoken at any point to notice the way I'd strayed across the line. Regardless, it had shaken me more than I cared to admit.

We escaped the cold utilitarian walls of the albergue before the German students awoke. A handsome Italian man passed me in the stairwell, turned around and winked at me. Francis made an annoyed groan and grabbed my arm, slightly exasperated by the sheer volume of overeager males, then led me down and out of the building into the dark morning. In a cluster, the six of us crossed the edge of the reservoir on the way out of town. We walked two by two and talked about politics, the municipal albergue system and dreams of Santiago. We aimed to walk a bit beyond the next big town and cover just over thirty kilometers. Seared by the horrors of the municipal albergue, we decided to pay extra for a place that felt a bit more like home. The unanimous decision wasn't due to a need for more lavish amenities but a desire for a place with a more wholesome atmosphere. We all needed more of a sanctuary than had been offered of late. The most astounding places where I'd spent a night had been run by people who loved the trail and cared about the pilgrims who traversed it; we needed one of those places to greet us again.

Francis was distant during the morning, and I let him be. If he needed to be far away, I would give him space. Once again, it was calming to be surrounded by a blissfully unaware group acting as a buffer between the two of us. In some ways, the days between our meeting and O'Cebriero had been a light social interlude and a distancing confluence of events, filled with scores of people, activity and stimulation. But now that season of the Camino was over, and we might not be able to avoid the vibrancy of our bond in the final throes of the trail. I wasn't ready to shy away from my connection to Francis, but I couldn't tell how much was on the line. What could be won and what could be lost?

SAN XULIÁN

STAGE TWENTY FOUR- 31.1K- 19.3M
PORTOMARÍN TO SAN XULIÁN

Tucked in the sleepy countryside and consisting of little more than half a dozen houses was the town of San Xulián. Walking though a wide shaded grove of trees, we stepped out on to a curving dirt road that cut a swath through a cluster of buildings and brought us to the front door of the albergue. The low slung house was a compact square of thick stone that nestled into the ground. From the outside, it looked extremely tiny and delicate as if it was built for elves rather than humans. The true magic of the place further revealed itself as we stepped through the rounded doorway. The low vaulted ceilings formed a tight warm space that made me feel I'd entered a living room worn by generations of people. The energy held a tone of tender care and proud inhabitance without striving to be anything grander than it was. There was a wide family table, a row of welcoming stools by the bar and a matching set of cushioned chairs all inviting us to sink into the settled air of this small kingdom. It was as if everything had been tailored to fit humans as perfectly as a well cut piece of clothing. There was no excess of space, but I didn't feel cramped or confined. This building had found the golden ratio of proportions that put us all immediately at ease. I could feel the general exhale of relief travel around our group. After the prison style hell of Portomarín, this was a dream come to life.

Miguel Angelo, the man behind the worn wooden bar, completed the picture with his long white beard and cheery features. He'd been born in this very building and lived here still with fierce pride for his lifelong home. His family had owned the four hundred year old building for many generations, opening its doors to pilgrims for as long as they'd resided there. The ancient building, along with the town church built in the 12th century, had been spared during the Spanish Civil War. Galicia and its infrastructure had been relatively unscathed during the war. One local's love for place had saved them. Maybe it was luck or maybe it was fate, but Miguel Angelo owed the preservation of his family home to one of Galicia's most famous natives: Generalissimo Franco.

Miguel had a clear fondness for our traveling kind and confided in me as I rested up against the bar, letting my eyes soak in the thousands of magical details of the place. He had dreams of opening a restaurant in the house across the narrow road. Even with the language barrier, his kindness swelled around me. I was endeared to him and desirous that all his dreams for this sanctuary and a restaurant come true. He'd welcomed us into his home, and now I felt we were part of his tribe. Even though the rough wooden table filling the front hall suggested a history of decades if not centuries of boisterous feasts, this peaceful afternoon the wall had the most tales to tell about who had come before us. Carrying beams were carved into mythic figures while ancient sideboards overflowed with stoneware dishes An ethereal bird cage dangled below a skylight, glowing as if illuminated from within. Faded black and white pictures held court around the back wall of the bar while a small pair of baby shoes hung from a nail next to a set of hand carved wooden tools. It was a place out of time, yet it was cozy and modern with clean sheets, a fireplace and soft surfaces to sink into. The public spaces were open and welcoming while the bedrooms held comforting nooks built into the edges of their stone walls. The window in the small dormitory was a battlement window, a deep square hole in the stone without a pane of glass between the outer world and us. In the night, it would rain enough so that a light spray would reach my cheeks. Elliot, John, Ivan and Jack chose to eat dinner in the main dining hall, but I'd felt ill all afternoon and retreated to the quiet of my bunk instead of joining the cattle call to the table. The narrow room was soothingly dark, and I relished the chance to curl up in a soft corner and be by myself. After a few minutes, I heard the door open and looked up to find Francis standing beside my bunk. He asked me if he could keep me company since he too had no appetite. I said yes and pulled myself up to sitting, wrapping my sleeping bag around me like a cloak.

He sat down and pulled his long limbs onto my bottom bunk. Again stillness fell in the stone room. The faint clatter of silverware and idle chatter could be heard as a far off rustle coming from the dining room. My back rested flat against the wall as my knees drew up to my chest. The cool stone room felt soft and close, removed from the flow of time and deep as a well. Francis sat beside me, his hands folded loosely in his lap, his shoulder blades flush against the wall. I felt empty of words and was glad he didn't speak either. Our truest conversations had always been in silence; words only seemed to bog us down, cause roadblocks and keep us from this stillness. I owed so much to this place of calm and stillness where my guidance could take root. This was where I stopped all external whirling and felt all the way to my core. It was the only sanctuary left to me now when it came to the destiny of this trail and my way forward with Francis. Suddenly I wanted both of us to drift to the bottom of this stillness and find what lay there. I was ready to stop fighting and avoiding each other. I wanted Francis to lay down the push and pull and simply feel. Only a few inches of air hung between the outer edges of my shoulder and the lines of his arm bones, but it was enough. Enough to feel the distance, to be aware of every slight shift and every rocking inhale. It was enough space for the particles to charge. And with little effort, our intensity bloomed and unfolded in the air between us.

Everything had rushed upon us like a flood in the early days of our meeting, but very quickly the diversion of the Iron Six had descended upon us. The days we'd traveled as a band of twelve had been like joining a circus full of dramatic and colorful shows. There had been dancing girls, festive meals, daring acts of entertainment, even bold group theatrics. The social world had erupted in excitement, and I'd been drawn in more than anyone else. I'd longed to escape the shadow of the early days and build a wider trail community, but with our departure from O'Cebreiro, the boys and I had slipped out a side door of the circus tent and into the night. After that it had been just the six of us, and the days had revealed a stripped down trail and the bones of intimacy that had been there all along. There had been no more distractions or flashing lights. The group who'd pulled me into lively commotion and the dashing stranger with ulterior motives and slick skills were gone. Suddenly, I couldn't avoid the truth that had been growing unattended for weeks. I couldn't be still and not feel the pulse of my affection for Francis and see an equally strong pulse flowing through him. We had to face it here. We had to face the truth of us.

I waited for my breath to calm itself as Francis also dropped into a place of deep quiet. When we left the three-ring circus of the Iron Six, Francis and I had nowhere to hide from each other. I couldn't fake neutrality about our friendship, and he couldn't avoid me. For the past three days, we'd both been trying in our own ways to avoid such a moment. He'd seemed torn, and I'd felt gun shy. I wanted to open the floodgates, but I feared what might come out. I was frightened by the tangle of emotions I felt right below the surface and dreaded knowing the reasons he didn't want to touch me. I feared he would retreat from my life, and I feared I would let him go because I was afraid to be hurt. Now, I felt the only way forward was asking him to sit with me in the quiet of San Xulián and listen. I wanted him to listen, not to me or his own muddied thoughts, but to something deeper and more eternal in his core. I wanted to know what his guidance said. I wanted to hear how he really felt below the surface and the struggle. I would trust the truth. On the edge of the soft rosy skin of my sleeping bag, under the eaves of the top bunk, he acquiesced to my request to sit in silence without a word.

And then, I had nothing left to do but wait for my insides to stop their churning fear, bring myself back to steady rhythm of my lungs and listen. Listen to the space beyond worry, beyond avoidance, beyond sorrow, beyond hesitation. If I listened, maybe Francis would listen too. Within a few moments, I could feel light energy threading through my body, pouring across the wide ceiling bone of my skull and into the long and tightly strung muscles of my neck. The golden light rushed down my upper arms and through the gentle twist of my forearms then out my fingers like beams. The light was now liquid cascading into the core of me, soaking all my internal organs, rushing through my pelvis and down my folded legs. The room had fallen away. The ceiling peeled back to reveal a darkening sky, and my skin shed every particle of weighted anxiety. I knew if I kept the light moving through me, everything would be well. If I could keep this flow alive, we could find the path forward no matter where it led. I would be OK, and Francis, dear Francis, would be OK too.

As I sat very still in San Xulián, I could feel this convergence of skin and breath, fluid and muscles, bone, and light. The moment became a key. A bright key that fit perfectly into the keyhole in my chest. It unlocked my life. The light and the guidance, the stillness and the energy was proof there was a plan. The dream at the end of the world and the forces that had brought me here had never left me, and they wouldn't lead me astray here in the final stretch. I could trust this journey wasn't just a practice in futility and fortitude. And if I let go, I would know the way forward. We both would. And I would survive whichever path Francis chose. I would survive if this energy between us wasn't destined to unfold.

I felt this dear friend beside me and wondered at the universe, wondered at a journey that offered up such vibrant and divergent men as the Tasmanian and Francis. I'd longed for it to be right with the Tasmanian, for our attraction to have legs, but now I trusted its end. It hadn't been easy, but it had been right. I knew Francis was pleased with my move, and glad I'd dug through my connection with the Tasmanian until I found the truth. That was all I was trying to do now with Francis, trying to understand what our shared trail was meant to be and how to do our bond justice. After many weeks, I needed to know if Francis felt more than he'd shared.

Maybe all I'd sought was a love who would stay by my side, stay in the building and stay in my life. Along the trail, I'd tried on many different suitors and learned much from the echoes of the past. And now I knew I needed someone who could hold the light with me rather than expect me to supply the missing parts of his life. I felt Francis breathing beside me and knew, at least for now, that he was here with me. But change was afoot, and things between us couldn't stay as they were. All the light surging through me confirmed this. I felt the tide moving. I drew closer and closer to the edge of an answer, the edge of knowing what to do and how to move forward with Francis.

I awoke as if from a dream. Francis was silent beside me. His eyes brimmed with tears as he look forward and away from me. He didn't move or speak, but I could sense the sea of grief that lived in him and how it had come to the surface again in this silent place of protective stone. In this moment, I felt he was as wounded as the day he'd lost his first love. My heart ached for him. I knew I had to tread gently with him and follow the thread of light in every now, for I didn't want whatever was to come to damage him again. I didn't want to inflict that pain and add more sorrow to his weary frame. In his brokenness and tender heart, I saw a reflection of myself.

Finally he turned to me. His walls were down. The last few days of keeping me at a distance had fled like shadows. As he looked at me, he laid down his armor and in one intense surge of energy he seemed to show me the scars and the desires of his heart without speaking a word. I didn't know where his energy field began and mine ended. We were so close, almost touching, and I could feel prickling heat on my skin. Suddenly, the room felt as if it was ours alone, our own vessel moving with a current we couldn't stop. I felt the reels of energy he'd expended to push me away evaporate and the pull of desire sweep over him. I was the most alone I'd been with anyone on the entire trip, and I knew he wanted to draw me into him arms and unhinge our platonic friendship. I turned my face towards him, and he spoke, telling me about the energy he'd experienced and the way the space had filled with something he'd never felt before. The sweet swell of a current I felt he'd been fighting for some time had overtaken him, and he seemed to glow with the surprise of someone who was amazed he hadn't drowned, amazed he felt closer to the light than ever before.

"There was so much energy, I just wanted to kiss you." he spoke softly. He didn't move towards me, but the words hung in the air, vibrating every molecule in the sliver of space between our bodies. We both paused.

Bang. Crash. Clunk. The door swung open and John bounced into the room, knocking into a chair and dropping his book on the hard flagstones. The delicate web of light and intensity, desire and tenderness snapped. The moment was over, stolen from us on its ripe edge. I felt Francis retreat back into himself, and a wave of angst washed over me. I wanted to hold onto his open frame, but it was gone. Then painful memories of the past washed over me, echoes of others who had recoiled just so. John hardly glanced at the two of us as he broke into an enthusiastic description of dinner and its many courses. He hummed to himself as he rummaged through his stuff, pulled out clothing and emptied the entire content of his bag onto the stone floor. I sat very still, shell shocked into a state of immobility. My jarring re-entry into the normal flow of reality was as smooth as a blindside tackle, and I feared it had been worse for Francis. I feared his retreat had been greater than his advance. I suppose we both should have been prepared for John's talent at choosing an entrance, because one thing was for sure; there was no privacy on the Camino. There was no place to be alone even in the light.

Francis crawled off my bunk, and I drew my arms tighter around me as the rest of the guys flooded back into the room with full bellies and happy banter. My skin felt raw, and I needed to hold tight to the edges of my body. My first reaction to John's entrance was severe disappointment but right on its heels was a flood of questions. The pendulum swing had been jarring and caused my chest to surge with worry. I'd finally turned and begun to face my growing feelings for Francis, but he seemed more confused than ever. I'd felt the edge of his desire more intensely than before, but I'd also felt the sting of his withdrawal, the voice of consternation in him that believed his attraction was wrong. I knew he was aware of the current of energy between us now, but I also sensed he was more determined to fight it than ever before. And I hadn't a clue why. Was he shocked that I'd tangled with the Tasmanian in hopes of a little passion and unabashed desire? It was the one piece I always knew Francis was afraid to give me. And I could tell he was afraid still. Even after the silence. Even after the light.

Francis's face was drawn and weary that night as we all got ready to go to bed. I'd gravitated towards Ivan as soon as he'd arrived back from dinner. I was thirsty for a distraction, thirsty for an interaction that was insignificant and unemotional. Yet my energy system was now utterly linked to Francis's. After what had happened, we were magnetized to each other, sealed with the stamp of this ancient place on the edge of the ancient trail. I wondered if we had been here before or known each other in another time and been locked in this same configuration. Was our story layered deeper than we could both know and guiding us toward a connection or convergence that had been a long time coming?

The sky rumbled in the middle of the night. I awoke in the darkest hours as rain drove down upon the impenetrable building. I wondered if it would feel good to stand outside and let every surface of my body be touched by rain. Maybe then I would feel enough to ease myself back to sleep. It had been too long since I'd been held, and tonight I felt it. The soft embrace of my sleeping bag wasn't enough. I needed a warm body curled next to me and the feeling of skin upon skin, the evidence that love was close and solid, not an ephemeral wisp of a dream or a complicated tangle of un-actualized emotions. I suddenly hated Francis for his inaccessibility and hated myself for placing so much of my affection in his chilly and hesitant hands.

If touch were a mineral, I was utterly deficient. It was sorely lacking in the body of my life, weakening the bones and muscles that kept me evolving forward. Now I was suddenly anemic without it, yet the link between the emotions of my heart and such physical love remained disconnected. When would a full love life manifest? I'd survived too many romances where one piece or the other was denied. I shivered, curled closer to the wall and fell back into a well of rain soaked sleep.

ARZÚA

STAGE TWENTY FIVE- 24.4K-15.2M
SAN XUILÁN TO ARZÚA

I walked next to Ivan the following day. As we left the small sleepy cluster of buildings and bid farewell to the albergue walls, I sidled up next to him and stuck like glue. He didn't seem to notice my fierce need to be entertained and distracted or the way a pensive Francis hung near the back of the group. I felt a desperate need to energize the group, re-inject it with the humor that had been the best part of our days with the Iron Six. The edges of our small band were fraying as the end loomed. After all these weeks the mental, emotional and physical toll ate away at everyone in different ways.

But if Ivan felt weary he didn't show it. He seemed as full of zest as ever. He was in his element now that there were only the six of us. His easy humor and confidence had faded slightly during our circus days with the Iron Six but had charged back in full force in the last few days. I knew Ivan's humor was about as helpful to my current struggles as a white-hot lamp bulb was to a moth, but I couldn't resist the glowing promise of a laugh or two. My emotional circuits were overloaded, and Ivan was uncomplicated.

After all the weeks of hobbling, Ivan had finally regained a normal stride. His foot wound was fully healed, and it was much easier to walk beside him now. That morning as we left San Xulián, his current preoccupation was the weather. Ivan's only rain gear was a ragged poncho he'd pinched from a dumpster outside of Pamplona. The sides now flapped open, and water seeped through the seams around his neck, but he remained faithful to the sheet of plastic that had come so far with him. It wasn't warrior like to complain about gear or buy a replacement in the final throws of the journey. As our group moved away from San Xulián, I glanced back at the other boys absorbed in conversation. My friendship with each held a different tone, and even though I felt warm affection for them all, I was most drawn to Ivan and Francis. Since I didn't dare glance back at Francis, let alone seek him out, I was relieved that Ivan accepted me at his side.

We stopped for breakfast in the large village of Melide, a place known for its seafood cuisine. Since it was early in the morning, we didn't partake in their famous octopus dish but found a café down a side street and ate sitting on the curb, soaking in the morning fog. Everything smelled wet and green, and I found myself in wonder at Galicia's vibrancy. There was something tactile and ripe about the land even when interrupted by wide streets or dim storefronts.

As I sat next to Elliot on the damp sidewalk, a young man rounded the corner. I recognized the bulky form coming towards us and felt a jolt of shock. It was the Hungarian Lover boy. Seeing him was like crossing paths with a character from the past and made the early trail seem long, long ago.

Since the sun hadn't broken through yet, the Lover boy wore a checkered black and white scarf around his neck and long sleeves. When he saw us his face lit up, and he strode over to where we sat. I glanced down the trail and saw no sign of company. He was alone. The Actress was nowhere in sight. The slightly frazzled look on his face suggested the Actress had slipped through his fingers yet again. He explained that she'd fled in the night, and he didn't know where she'd gone or when they'd meet again. I felt a shiver of déjà vu but was at a loss as how to help the Lover boy's quest. I hadn't seen the Actress for weeks now, and I couldn't possibly guess where she was, but most of all, I couldn't explain her actions. The Lover boy seemed utterly devoted to her and had always been kind and respectful to everybody. It was her prerogative to avoid him if she chose, but that wasn't the issue at hand. It was the coming and the going that made the whole situation so unbearable. She was playing a pushing and pulling game of her own. I'd heard her speak with excitement about her growing romance with him, so why did she feel it was acceptable to spin him in intervals of intimacy and distance? What did she really want? Why didn't she simply pick and spare the poor boy's feelings? The whole dynamic made me anxious and upset for the Lover boy, since I could tell by the tone of his voice and the carriage of his body that he was emotionally invested. And because of his feelings, this intoxicating girl was dragging him down the trail and wearing him out. The Lover boy only stopped for a moment, looking as if he wasn't willing to waste time on pleasantries. Once he found out that we hadn't seen the Actress, he waved goodbye and pushed on. As he dashed up the block and out of sight I had to give him credit. He was certainly dogged in the face of the Actress's erratic and seemingly thoughtless behavior. I fervently hoped he would be rewarded for his pain.

After a few minutes, Francis rounded the corner of the trail, deep in conversation with a Frenchman. His head was tipped slightly to the side as if he was listening very carefully to gather each word's meaning. The Frenchman stopped for coffee and bid Francis farewell so he rejoined our group, and we all headed out of Melide. The streets in the center of town were lined with flower shops stuffed to the brim with a riot of colors. Closed panaderias also taunted us with chocolate and pastry delights. Nothing but a handful of cafes were open at this hour, so we walked on by. The road became tight then spit us out on the far side of the village. The next cluster of civilization wouldn't be for another fifteen kilometers. With the sun hot on our backs, the enthusiasm that had abounded during the morning hours burned off.

A weariness of heart infected my every step. I walked on my own for a while, drifting ahead of the group. I tried to listen to my music, slip under the lyrics and submerge in the beats. I wanted to hide but found little solace in my old tricks. I tucked my ipod back in my pack and soaked up the sounds of the trees creaking overhead and the crunch of my feet hitting the path. I was startled by the effort it took to lift each leg. Everything required more energy than before, and it made no sense. After all these weeks, I expected to be a walking machine, able to cross vast tracks in my sleep and hardly break a sweat, but instead I struggled and felt more drained than ever before. Maybe I could keep my emotional exertions from taking a physical toll for only so long. Perhaps my feelings had finally caught up with my legs. Or maybe this trail with all the energy it demanded from us was cumulative. Perhaps like childbirth, the last few pushes were the hardest.

Just looking at the outside of the municipal albergue in Arzúa, I could tell it was much better cared for than the albergue in Portomarín. Tucked comfortably into a row of older buildings, it blended with the architecture around it. At eleven in the morning there was already a line of people waiting to sign in. I placed my bag at the end of the line and sat down on the sidewalk. Some of the pilgrims left their bags in line and sat in the café across the road. They drank coffee, had a bite to eat and watched over their bags with sharp eyes.

When the albergue doors opened, people rushed to their packs, and a long line formed. Ivan had offered to sit with the packs while Jack and I went to buy supplies for lunch. When we returned, our packs were almost at the front of the line. The woman checking us in was businesslike but kind as she pointed us up the stairs. We were housed in one of two large dormitories with thirty beds in each. The room had a high ceiling, lots of windows and clean sturdy furniture. I was immediately relieved.

The only similarity this albergue had to its cousin in Portomarín was the double bunk scenario. As soon as I noticed this feature, I took charge, unwilling to face the same tortured scene for a second time. I asked Ivan if he would be my bunkmate. He gladly agreed, and we hoisted our things onto a set of top bunks. It was settled, and I breathed a sign of relief. A large floor to ceiling window opened out into the ally next to my bunk, and a soft breeze pushed in the sounds of the street.

In the afternoon, the noises ceased, and the lull of siesta took hold of Arzúa. The heat acted like a sleep drug, and many of the pilgrims in our room dozed peacefully. On the bunk below me, Elliot read my book with obvious glee while Ivan and I sat next to each other and talked softly about home, his girlfriend and his plans to write a book. His body was easy and relaxed, but he was focused on our conversation, more so than I'd ever seen him. He often surprised me with moments of depth when I least expected it, and somehow he knew I needed a serious ear to listen that afternoon. Maybe it was the subject matter drawing out his roots to home or my descriptions of all the dreams I'd held for the trail that took our conversation somewhere new. Or perhaps it was his subtle sensitivity when I shared my tumultuous sentiments about the end. No matter the cause, I felt less adrift with him beside me, and my fondness for him grew. It made me forget, if only for a moment, the things I had to sort out before the end of the trail. It almost made me forget that Francis dozed in a bunk across the room or that Santiago and the sea awaited me up ahead.

Before dark arrived, I walked to the center of town. I could see a bit of park ahead and sought a patch of green space where I could watch the night fall. As I darted out of the front door of the albergue and started down the street, a voice called me from behind. Francis had been out on his own wanderings and now stood in front of the albergue, looking as dazed and disoriented as I felt. He walked towards me, asking if he could join me. I nodded my head, and we traveled into the inner circle of the city. The park was full of families pushing strollers, old couples sitting close to each other on benches and the steady gurgle of a large fountain. We settled down on a wide stonewall on the outskirts of the park. Neither of us said anything nor looked at each other. I felt my skin soaking up the night, willing my nerves to cease their frazzled surges. This was my dearest friend and trusted ally for much of this journey, so why was I suddenly unnerved to be alone with him?

Here we were in silence again. Not in the hallowed walls of stone but in the living breathing pulse of a city. We were in the light, in the shade, among people and set apart. My insides ached, and I felt unsure. He looked drawn and troubled. I felt we were both preparing our own strategies of self-preservation. I wanted so much to open the floodgates again, pull him back towards the energy of us, but I couldn't read his face. I couldn't tell if he wanted that. Did he need me to say it? Did he need me to voice the flow of fresh desire that moved through our friendship? Or did he feel it and wish it had never been? Was he mounting the courage to express his feelings or mounting a defense against mine? I wanted to believe he was being cautious and shy. I wanted to believe John's graceless entrance caused a momentary blip in on the surface of his feelings but wouldn't change the current of genuine emotion underneath it. But his face showed no clues, and his eyes roamed with inscrutable ease. I felt if I made one false move all could be lost, and he was giving me no clues where the edge lay.

That moment, that split second before John had bounded into the room and broken the ring of stillness, I'd seen farther into Francis's heart than ever before. It had been no miracle of my eyesight just a simple opening of the doors. And what I saw was a heart very much like my own. I could see all the layers of scar tissue, all the ways the Camino had helped to heal parts of him. I could see the marks of his last broken love affair and the way he worried he wasn't enough. I could see how deeply he felt life and how intensely he cared for people. But most of all I could see the core of our friendship reflected back to me. I saw the strong fibers of connection and warmth. I saw the best relationship I'd ever had with a man. And then I felt the wave of desire. And I knew I wasn't the only one. The pieces weren't strung together, but they could be if we wished it so. In that moment I knew we both understood that we'd backed off our relationship for a reason all those days ago. We'd let distractions and complications flood in because we'd reached a level of intimacy where we couldn't avoid the question any longer. We would have to ask ourselves could this be more? I knew I was battered and bruised by relationships of the past, and this had made me gun shy, but I wasn't sure what Francis felt behind his defenses. I needed to know where he stood, for I was suddenly terrifyingly certain of where my feet were planted.

Before San Xulián I'd cared deeply for Francis, but now I knew I loved him.

All the tiny details and all the delicate words had rolled themselves into a living and breathing love. Our connection had been so effortless and intricate yet so sturdy and magnetic that we'd always drifted back towards each other. He had the potential to be the whole balanced romantic partner I'd never known before. I'd survived messy destructive relationships, but one thing they all had in common was their fragmented nature. I'd come to the relationships with my full self, but the men on the other side had always wanted one piece of me and not the others. I'd so often been broken down into pieces, shredded myself in order to please those I loved, and in the bargain, I'd felt utterly devastated with the loss of myself. This trail had helped those pieces of me return, and now I had to know if I could have a whole love with Francis. I felt it could be so, but I was a believer that relationships were not balanced by luck or fortune but by a willingness to be open. Those men of the past could have shown up and given their all to our connection, but they made a choice not to. We all chose how much we gave and how much we sought balance. This path had helped me grieve for the times I'd abandoned myself in destructive relationships and it had given me back all the pieces I'd forfeited. Now I knew I couldn't accept less than wholeness. And I knew there was the potential for this with Francis but only if he also stepped to the line and jumped.

If he'd been able to see into me as we sat in the park, the same way I'd seen into him in San Xulián, he would have found clarity and chaos. I was clear on what I needed know now, clear on the potential and the beauty I saw blooming between us but submerged in the chaos of uncertainty about how he felt and what he wanted. I knew the last few days were littered with proof that he was holding back, censoring himself both emotionally and physically. I could tell when he wanted to touch me but didn't, when he got a wistful look in his eyes but held his tongue. I could still read him like a book when he didn't think I was watching. So many of his movements and his energy reminded me of a wounded animal and to tell him everything that flowed through me would only send him back into retreat. So I paced myself and chose a different tactic.

My voice was smooth and low when it finally emerged. On the surface, I reflected nothing of the chaos. I was the picture of calm, cool and collected. The words flowed out of me easily and fell into the space between us. I offered words of comfort for it was all I felt I could give him. He was at the center of a push and pull, and it wouldn't stop if I got in the middle of it. I wanted to ask him why he was afraid when our connection was so strong. I wanted to talk him through his rational for distance, but I would have been a biased listener, so I gave him space and time instead. I offered another truce of sorts as I felt the gift of more time was all I had to give either of us. We might have had another round of battling and verbal sparing in us, but not tonight.

Francis listened to me speak and seemed to agree to the ceasefire. I drew my legs to my chest, wrapped my arms around them and hugged tight as he leaned ever so slightly forward and looked at me with earnest eyes. When he spoke, his words were flush with relief and other subtle tones I couldn't identify. Perhaps for tonight we were both playing our parts in a guarded dance around the white elephant in the room. What if we were a good match all along? What if the universe and the energy of the trail had arranged for us to meet here? What if this, even with its imperfections and complications, was destiny? And what if it wasn't and we would never be as close again? Yet for me, the biggest question was if Francis wanted to love me; if he would at least give it a try.

If Francis felt the buzz of lingering unknowns, he didn't let on. Instead our eyes turned back to the activity in the park: the kids running around a bench, the group of ladies posing for a picture and the tall street lamps flickering on in the dusky air. We walked back to the albergue and slipped in before they locked the doors. We parted at the edge of the dark room full of sleeping pilgrims.

LAVACOLLA

STAGE TWENTY SIX- 39.8K-24.7M
ARZUA TO MONTE GOZO

I awoke before dawn. The kitchen and garden were locked for the night, so everyone awake in the building was crushed into a small entryway. I ate a couple handfuls of dry cereal then packed away my meager supplies. I hoped we would come across a fresh food market at some point in the day. After breakfast, we followed the arrows out of town. The street lamps cast shadows that trailed us into the dark outskirts of Arzúa. The sky was blanketed by a fog that turned our skin an eerie shade of white. Francis and I didn't speak of the night before but once again took solace in the fabric of the group. There was safety in being part of a crowd, and we clung to the inadequate comfort. Our group of six had quite a distance to walk, and I could feel the anticipation in each of us. By late afternoon, we would be looking out over the city of Santiago. For better or worse, our journey was drawing to a close.

As light started to fill the sky, my night vision faded. I was able to see more of the trail ahead. I'd learned from one of Ivan's lectures on the life and habits of pirates that the eye patch of the common pirate had more to do with light than eye injuries. I'd always imagined an infamous pirate had lost his eye with one bloody swipe and by donning a patch had revolutionized pirate fashion, but I was wrong. The patch rarely held a gored eye socket behind its fold; it wasn't a handicap but instead a sly fighting tool.

When a pirate fought above deck, he would keep the patch on one of his eyes. When the swordplay drove him below deck, he would switch the patch to the other eye and continue fighting. The patch allowed the eye to retain its night vision while above deck in the light of day. The patched eye was always ready to be put to use in the dark galleys below deck. It was a way of seeing clearly in both the light and the dark. I could feel the rods and cones in my eyes flicking back and forth in the morning light outside of Arzúa. I squinted and wondered if it wasn't just my eyes that were having a hard time adjusting to what lay ahead of me. The half light forced me to pay attention to each step, but it couldn't keep my mind in the foggy present, no matter how hard I tried. I looked around and knew I wasn't alone.

I could see all of our minds rapidly flicking forward in time to the end and then quickly back to the present, repeatedly jumping back and forth over and over again. Within my own anxious thoughts about Francis, I wondered if it would be better to be able to patch over the part of my brain that allowed me to sweep forward in time, keeping only the part of my brain that lived in the now, fresh and alive. Was there any way to do such a thing, especially when it pertained to matters of the heart? How could I stay in the present with so many unknowns?

The universe answered my idle question with deft speed. In mid stride, the tendon in the front of my right foot suddenly seized. I said nothing but leaned more and more of my weight onto the pole in my hand. The boys were chatting away beside me, but I was now only alive to the present. I felt all my concentration settling down at the bottom of my leg where the muscles and tendons arced into my foot. We had over forty kilometers to walk that day, and there was very little chance of deviation from that plan. The boys wanted to look upon Santiago that afternoon, and there was virtually nowhere to stay between here and there. I started to slow my pace as the burning tightened its hold on me. I could feel a grimace settle on my face, and then I had to stop.

The group drifted on ahead of me. Everyone was clustered together except for Francis who'd disappeared down the trail long ago to say his morning prayers. The rest of the guys were in a heated debate about something or other. As I slowed, I declared nonchalantly that I was taking it easy on my legs. Since I didn't throw up any major red flags, they kept walking at a normal pace, putting more and more space between us. This was it. Here was the injury I'd feared for so much of the trail. This slim right tendon might just be the instrument of my downfall, the thing that could cause me to be left behind in the last lap.

I told myself I could make it as long as I kept hobbling. I might have to walk much longer into the day, but if I had to, I would drag my body to our destination of Monte Gozo. Then my left supporting leg buckled from the strain. I couldn't take another step. I stood frozen in place. Tears splintered from my eyelids and dripped off the edge of my chin. I felt as raw and vulnerable as the day I'd arrived in St. Jean, and I was just as alone as I was then. I found a large rock on the side of the trail and sat upon its rough surface. There was no one in sight, no strangers, no friends, no love interests, no sound except the wind.

I closed my eyes and waited. I waited for all the noise in my jumbled head to stop, for the images of the Camino to cease whizzing across my mind's eye and for my breathing to slow. I knew it was still dark at home in the states. I imagined my younger siblings asleep on our screened porch with deer grazing just yards away. I pictured the riot of green gardens and vibrant blooms waiting in the morning light to feel the sun again. I saw the dogs asleep at the foot of my parents' bed. I felt the still air of morning just waiting to rise. The farm would always be there for me, but I also knew my childhood was no longer mine. It was a stolen season, a dream I had to part with. I was a grown up now. The trail had shown me this. The trail had been my home. It had taken me in on my way elsewhere. But where would my life take me now? I wasn't even able to get up and walk to our night's destination. How would I ever find my way to my life?

And then a hand reached out and touched my shoulder. I opened my eyes to find Elliot looking down at me.

"I've come back to walk with you," he said in a matter a fact tone.

"I don't know if I can walk." I uttered in a wavering voice.

He smiled kindly as if he already knew that. I could see the patience in his soft eyes. All I could do was be where I was, and he had come back to be there with me. I stood gingerly, and we started to walk with slow steps. He walked beside me with a serene demeanor that conveyed he had no problem going my pace, in fact, he actually enjoyed it. I wouldn't have predicted that of the whole group, he would be the one to come back. This trail was a mysterious creature.

It took us over an hour to meet up with the rest of the group at a small café. The boys dug into large bocadillos filled with fresh omelets and melting cheese while I ordered a coffee. It was good insurance to get my weary body to the end of the day. Francis was nowhere to be seen, but the other boys didn't seem too concerned.

Elliot let the group in on my ankle conundrum, and they generously agreed to ratchet back their pace to keep together. Half an hour later we came across Francis pacing on the side of the trail. The path split two ways up ahead. He'd taken one route but had been nervous he'd chosen a different way than us so he'd retraced his steps. He was agitated and grumpy over the hassle of miscommunication. He didn't noticed the group was walking like a slow herd around me, and I didn't speak up. He was the last person I wanted feeling sorry for me and my gimpy leg.

After a few more kilometers, we took a break in a railroad underpass to eat chocolate biscuits. I rubbed arnica into my lower leg as Francis sat next to me, and Ivan climbed up the high wall of the underpass to practice his balance. In the light of day, I noticed my legs were now quite hairy. This had been a razor free trip, and it was now showing in the fair down on my legs. The tendon in my leg had swelled, and as I rubbed the strong smelling cream into it, Francis lightly touched the surface of my leg, tracing the unbroken line of my shinbone. I felt a shiver cross my whole body. I caught his eyes for the briefest second, before he was distracted by John's attempts at mimicking Ivan's acrobatics. It was the first time he'd reached out to touch me in days, and I felt the move was made even before he realized what he was doing. It was as it he couldn't help himself, as if he forgot for a moment that our connection hung between us in a tenuous state of unknown. I was startled for several reasons, one of which had nothing to do with Francis. Girls across the western world, and especially my sister, would be horrified I had such hairy legs, let alone allowed a boy to touch them.

I felt as if our popular culture had become disconnected from many real experiences of the body. We'd lost touch with the real substance of human life, the basics both internally and externally. It was as if we had veered away from the core of things and busied ourselves with the surface. From what I'd heard from my college age sister that meant waxing, plucking, straightening one's hair and generally beautifying oneself all the time. As I sat rubbing my injured leg, one that had walked over five hundred miles in the last month, such surface activities felt hollow. All the primping and preening wouldn't have saved me from heartbreak or loss in the past, and it wouldn't save me now.

I'd found essential parts of life and myself on the trail and did it all with hair that I washed in cold water with a bar of soap and dried as I tossed in my sleep. I went days without seeing my face in a mirror, let alone the rest of my body. My experience of myself was a felt one. It was the deep breath flowing in and out of me as I charged up hills or the first flush of sweat prickling my skin each morning, waking the surface of me from the inside out.

I thought less and less about how the world saw me and more about how it experienced me. I knew everybody in my world was seeing me as I woke in the morning with my hair tangled and in the evening as my eyes blurred with sleep. They saw me befallen by injury, bleeding and squatting behind trailside bushes to pee. Their experience of me was whole. And I saw my friends with the same holistic view. As I looked down at my dusty battered legs, I realized I would be loved in spite of my humanness or maybe because of it.

Noon arrived with bright heat. We started up a sloping incline that opened out to a series of wire fences and loud noises. At first, the drone confused us, but then a large aircraft tore up through the clouds and out of view. We had reached the outskirts of Lavacolla, the site of the airport that serviced Santiago. As I walked next to its runways I thought how strange it was that some of us might leave Spain on planes from this very spot. The end had always been a blurry far off image, out there somewhere but never in clear view. Now it was coming into focus, and it was unfathomable.

After stocking up at a small shop in Lavacolla, we headed down to the river for a picnic lunch. As was tradition in our group, we sought out a prime soft grassy spot where we could construct a feast, eat and lie in the sun. Because the river Lavacolla was the last body of water before Santiago, it was a major fixture in Camino lore. In the middle ages, pilgrims had used the river as a place to bathe themselves in preparation for arrival at the cathedral. I could only imagine that after months and months on the trail, they'd been sorely in need of a good scrub.

As we moved closer to the river, Elliot and Francis couldn't contain their excitement. They'd told me long ago in Carrión that they wanted to bathe in the river and share in this ancient rite of passage. I wasn't sure if I would strip down to keep with tradition but was willing to be enticed. As we came down to the bottom of the slope, we could see a riverbed twisting across the small valley. The boys practically skipped with joy to its side, but something was not right. As we pushed through the small vines and shrubs that lined the river, we looked down. Disappointment crashed into our troop with a heavy thud.

The river was four feet across and at most, a foot deep. We'd all imagined a mighty beast of a river, tumbling with white froth and flush with life. This was a tepid stream clogged with algae and weeds. Francis bent down, pulling his long delicate hands from the insides of his pockets. He slid them into the water and washed the dusty surface of his skin. After a moment, he pulled out his hands, shook then dry and walked over to a tree along the edge of the field to put down his pack. Even though the boys were disappointed not to be able to frolic in the waters, I knew it wouldn't stop us from having a celebratory lunch beside the river.

We'd bought a few extra pieces of fruit for later in the afternoon, but Ivan had other designs for the under-ripe orange and slightly crushed kiwi. He pulled us into a tight circle with our arms wrapped around each other. Then one of us threw a piece of fruit into the air straight above the group. As soon as the fruit was launched, we all ducked our heads and waited to be struck from above. There wasn't much threat of serious injury from an orange hurling down upon us, but the rush of energy that came from the unknown was wonderful. In those seconds after the fruit was hurled skyward, grips tightened, bodies hunched and each of us flinched, waiting for impact.

It felt childishly silly and made me laugh until I gasped for breath. I threw the kiwi high above us and listened with joy when Jack yelped as the green orb spewed its insides down his back. I'd never played such an idiotic but delightful game. With our bodies intertwined, we were all part of a tight-knit group. I wasn't an outsider. I even felt a flush of pride that I was the only girl and had earned my place among this tribe of boys. After a few rounds, John refused to play and stood beside the circle, wringing his hands. Something about the anticipation of being clonked with a piece of fruit was too much for him. We closed the circle up and went for another round, seeking another high stakes tilt with flying fruit.

Later, as the boys finished eating, I lay on my back with my head resting on my bag. Ivan and Francis jumped up and danced around the open field, breaking out their best modern dance moves. In vaguely matching outfits of tan shorts and white shirts, they turned their serious faces towards the audience, spinning, leaping over each other and artfully twirling their walking sticks in the air. The dancing ended as Ivan misjudged the height of Francis's legs and kicked him in the middle of a graceful leap. The two tumbled over each other into a squirming mass on the ground, and the piece came to an dramatic conclusion. I was honored by their homage to my beloved medium and felt Francis's giddy smile melting the space between us again. I loved it when he freed himself from lockdown, forgot his sense of propriety and became the magical and charming person I knew was in there. I cheered loudly and felt I hadn't had moments of lightness like this in years.

As we left the banks of the mighty Lavacolla, I wondered what it would feel like to look out across the great city of Santiago. We were headed for the albergue at Monte Gozo. The Galician name of this spot is Mon Xoi which literally meant "mountain of joy". This was where we would spend the night before slipping down into Santiago early the next morning. In the middle ages, pilgrims had climbed the small mountain to gaze out across the city. They'd seen the mighty spires of the cathedral rising up, drawing them into the great belly of the city. But over the last fifty years, the Spanish government had planted trees on the mountain, and they were now so tall, it was difficult to get a clear view.

We followed a narrow road up to Monte Gozo until the river was out of sight below us. The trail twisted through a neighborhood of new homes with fresh flowers blooming in the window boxes and ancient granaries in the front lawns. Each step brought us closer to our last ones. The group conversation focused on our impending arrival. John bounded beside me, confiding that the moment at the cathedral was the aim of his whole trip. He seemed to be frothing with anticipation as his prime target drew closer.

My jaw dropped. This was not the way I felt about the Camino. My most precious moment could be any minute of this journey. It might be right around the corner, sweeping over me at any time. The arrival in Santiago was simply another piece of the whole. To me, the attention Santiago received only represented the outside world's need to manufacture times of importance instead of letting them happen of their own accord. Just like graduations and other benchmark ceremonies, it was a way of locking down times of value and change.

John remained firm; his arrival into Santiago would be his high point. I understood his logic, but it didn't seem realistic. I worried for him as he waited for this moment to arrive. The elation, the joy, the sense of accomplishment might not come or might happen in a fleeting second that would slip by him. Would this hurt him? I, on the other hand, had my crosshairs turned towards another kind of cathedral; the all mighty panaderia. I wasn't hoping for the best chocolate croissants of my journey, and I didn't expect this to be an apex of sweets, but I knew Santiago would deliver something delicious nonetheless. I wasn't sure if John would find what he wanted in Santiago, but I felt more confident that with my low expectations, I might actually be satisfied.

Walking stride for stride with Francis and John, I was suddenly overcome by the fact we were tracing the steps of millions of pilgrims taken over the course of a thousand years. We were migrating along a route that millions of feet had known. Walking the trail was one of the few things a modern person could do almost exactly the same way it was done by a person a thousand years before. Human feet have not slowed, become faster or changed in shape and action since the middle ages. So the journey, at its very core, was essentially unchanged. It took breath, muscles and strong legs to bring us to the door of the city. We would arrive in Santiago the very same way as all the pilgrims before us had. The time we lived in and the nature of our gear mattered little, for we arrived with the same spirit filling us, having carried us through sweat and toil all the way to the end. Under the surface appearance, we could be a part of any time, and we weren't removed from the ancient trail by our modernity. We were a part of the flow of the trail that paid little heed to time. We were part of the eternal life of the Camino.

Monte Gozo was situated to the east of the sprawling city of Santiago. A large modern sculpture sat atop the hill, and groups of people swarmed around it. A couple of wagons selling cold sodas and ice cream rested along the edge of the road, and clusters of bikers stood in the shade. The spot felt strangely touristy, and we quickly moved past the scene. Striding down and away from the sculpture, we skirted a track of pine forest in search of a view. To see the cathedral and the city required walking down a long field.

I stood sheltered by trees at the top of the field as the boys leapt down the wide grassy slope, arms high above their heads, walking sticks dangling from their hands and cries of triumph rushing from their lungs. Francis, Elliot and John held each other tight in a hug that formed a closed circle. Ivan jumped around

Jack as they laughed at this moment so long in the making. I stood very still. The world rushed and blurred around me. The end was in sight. If I kept moving down the slope to where they celebrated, I too would see the end. I would see the city we had navigated towards for all these weeks. That place ahead, ever out of sight, was now near. It filled the eyes of my companions as they stood holding one another. They were woven together in this moment, in clusters of two and three. They had a place. They belonged. Even Francis was part of something other than us. He was the most important link here for me, yet Elliot and John had always held that spot for him. It was a sobering to watch them play in the fields of the finale and never look back up to see if I was coming down. After a few moments, I slowly walked down the hill to face the beginning of the end alone. The sweat had dried to my skin, and I was cold again.

That last night before Santiago, we stayed in a large barracks style albergue. Stacked next to each other like dominos, the rectangular buildings held over eight hundred beds. As we moved down the wide walkway that lay between the buildings, I felt as if I had stumbled into a military base of cold grey lines and utilitarian amenities. Inside, the buildings were slightly less harsh, and the energy of other pilgrims cut the sterile spaces. It was hard not to warm to a place when people sang in the bathrooms and the smell food wafted from the kitchens. Chatter, movement and pilgrim gear brought a place to life like nothing else.

We checked in at the main desk and were told we could stay in municipal hostels near Santiago for three nights. Everywhere else on the trail pilgrims were alowed only one night in a hostel, then they had to move on or find alternative accommodations. The only exceptions to this rule were for the injured or the ill, and the validity of those conditions had to be backed up with a doctor's note. This rule was put in place to keep non-pilgrims out of the albergue system. The government didn't want young travelers to take advantage of the albergues as cheap places to stay. And for this reason, albergues had managed not to become youth hostels for the young and aimless.

We were housed in a building near the top of the hill and given a room with eight beds. Since the albergue was nowhere near capacity, it was just the six of us in the space. I wondered if in the high season this place filled every one of its eight hundred beds. I took a bottom bunk by the window, and the boys scattered into other bunks. Francis took the bottom bunk across the narrow room from me. He looked grey and distracted as he unlaced his boots. Ivan dropped his pack on his bed and announced a need for sustenance. Jack did push-ups while he waited for us to go to the food shop, and I rummaged through my pack to see if I could avoid going shopping with the boys. I craved the escape of a nap. I even hoped the nap might bleed into night, and I would sleep on through until morning. For some reason, I suddenly didn't want to be awake, but I had no food left, so I went with Jack and Ivan to the shop. Elliot wanted to get some washing done with John's help, and Francis hardly seemed to be functioning. He was lying very still on his bunk and looked as if he wouldn't be interested in food anytime soon. I wasn't sure when he had gone from giddy to gray, but I knew another draining sickness was the last thing he needed. I wanted to talk with him, find out what was going on before I went shopping, but I hesitated. His eyes were closed, and I didn't want to wake him. I knew Elliot would look after him while we were gone. The Brit guys were kind to each other in that way, tender almost. I suppose over the course of so many weeks, they'd all had their chances to care for one another and be cared for in turn.

When we arrived back, it was clear Francis was sick and in no shape to get up for dinner. He'd spent most of the afternoon asleep or throwing up. I wasn't surprised he was unwell. The end of anything is traumatic, and the unknown of our bond was certainly not helping matters. After making sure Francis had everything he needed, the four boys went off to make dinner in the kitchen, and I lay in my bunk. Staring at the metal beams of the bed above me, I felt numb. Francis lay across the room from me on his back not moving but breathing evenly. I assumed he was asleep, but I'd been wrong about that before.

Unbeknownst to me, he'd been awake during many small yet pivotal moments. He'd been awake in the sleepy afternoon in Ponferrada when I'd flirted with the Tasmanian across the sea of bunk beds, and my infatuation had taken hold. And he'd been awake in Trabadelo when the Tasmanian and I had whispered in the dark. Maybe he'd been awake in all the moments I'd been hopelessly asleep.

Now I felt we were both moving through our days asleep, escaping the shifting trail up ahead. I felt as if we were building towards another round, preparing to strip back another layer of our friendship in search of some kind of knowing. But this albergue with its air of hollow expectation and cold surfaces had pulled apart our whole group and drawn a distance between us. He was only five feet from away. I could have sprung from my bunk and been next to him, curled up beside him and holding him in a split second. But such swift movement felt impossible. The five feet felt like an un-crossable gulf, and I couldn't tell which one of us had created the abyss.

I ate a mushy banana and tried to read my book. I moved about as silently as possible and felt my whole being willing it to be dark. Francis woke after an hour of tossing and turning. He rolled to face me but didn't say anything. I continued to read. Eventually I sat up and asked him if he needed anything. He looked tired as if the very surface of his body was worn thin. It was terribly distressing. He'd never had much reserve padding on his body to begin with. Had he never recovered from the bout of sickness from the well water in Manjarin? I felt a stab of worry. I should have paid closer attention. I should have been making sure we beefed him up, but I'd become so distracted. And now I couldn't claim I hadn't added to his stress and helped draw him to this place. I pressed him harder, asking if there was anything at all I could get him. But he refused my help, saying he needed to wait for his body to calm down. I could sense he both craved and feared that I would come and sit beside him, touch him and cross the line he had held for so long simply because he was too weak to stop me. Suddenly the push and pull in his energy made me as immobilized as him, so I waited and did nothing.

I went off to shower and spent an extra amount of time under the hot flow of water. It was a safe refuge. The women's bathroom could only admit people I didn't know. I thought of Ava, Iris and Zara and wondered where they were.

Would we see them in Santiago? What would it be like to reconnect with the Iron Six? Did it even matter in the whole scheme of things? I was so angst ridden about the dynamics in our own band of six, what could the Iron Six bring to the mix? Distraction, maybe, especially if Ava was in a celebratory spirit. I felt in dire need of some form of distraction.

I hurried out of the bathroom. I wanted to go from the warm water to the tight cocoon of my sleeping bag as quickly as possible. The rest of the boys were back. Each was busy preparing his pack for the next morning, planning his own version of a dramatic entrance into the city. As I crawled into my bunk, I noticed Francis had left a note on my bag. I slipped the note into my journal, pulled my sleeping bag up over my head and curled up into a ball against the wall.

I knew what the note said without having to open its folded wings. Francis had taken pencil to paper to tell me he still wanted to walk with me to the coast. We'd talked about the three day walk beyond Santiago before, and he'd soothed my worries with an iron clad assurance that no matter what happened he would go with me. With deep sincerity in his voice, he'd told me not to fear being at the end alone; he would go with me if nobody else would. At the time, it had been a welcome balm, another layer of devotion between us, but now the waters were muddied, and more was on the line.

The group plan was clear all the way until Santiago. The six of us would stick together until we reached the city, but after tomorrow the fate of our merry band was uncharted. Would we stay together somehow or dissolve at the threshold of the city? If the group were to disperse, I would be the one to feel it the most. I would have to pick a group to cling to and hope they would keep me around. Jack and Ivan would be hurrying to the coast so they could rush back to Pamplona for the running of the bulls while the Brit guys weren't sure how long they would stay in the city or even if they would go to the coast. I couldn't fathom undertaking the trek to Fisterra alone. Yet the closer we drew to the end, the more acutely I felt like the odd girl out. I knew Francis was aware of this and still wanted to be the person I could rely on. I knew his offer was genuine, but I was at a loss as to how to answer.

Everything in the group was shifting, and suddenly I felt a tightening in my chest. I heard Francis turning restlessly in his bunk and wondered if he lay awake like me. I had a choice to make, but there were too many dangling questions in the air between us to see the trail ahead. I had to choose how to go forward, and I felt utterly disorientated. Which move took me forward and which would throw me back? Which would draw me towards my life and which would lead me astray? As night arrived in our noisy barracks above the city, I waited for the lights to go out. Finally, a hushed restlessness fell in our room, and I found sleep.

SANTIAGO

STAGE TWENTY SEVEN- 5K-3.1M
MONTE GOZO TO SANTIAGO

Ivan shook me awake in the dark. Our room was a scene of chaotic packing and giddy action. Elliot and John were practically bouncing off the walls. We all moved at once, hurrying as fast as we could to charge out the door and towards the city. No one else was awake in the building. The stars were still vibrant on the surface of the sky as we ran through the outdoor corridor between the silent barracks. It had rained in the night, and the world was wet and opalescent. Ivan and Jack hummed The Star Spangled Banner to the bright arc of the Milky Way. It was the fourth of July.

The outskirts of Santiago looked the same as all the other cities we'd known, but our steps were fast and direct. Large apartment buildings hung over our heads, forming dark shapes against the sky. The streets were dirty with paper in the gutters. Stunted palm trees along the sidewalk attended the procession of arrows that curled us down into the city. After a brief rousing chorus of patriotic American songs, we grew silent.

John looked pale. I wondered if his mind was racing with built up expectations of the moment so tangibly close. Francis look tired but alert as if he was soaking in every detail, every smell, sight and twist of the street that pulled us deeper into the center of Santiago. Jack and Ivan bounded down the sidewalk as if it was Christmas morning, and they were eight. After an hour, their infectious spirit rubbed off on the Brit boys, and a festive mood prevailed. I was the exception but tried to hide the gulf forming inside me. I felt distant from the moment as if it wasn't my own. These streets and their anticipated aura belonged to the boys. I would tag along and support them as they sought out the cathedral, but I felt numb and detached. After several minutes of walking in a daze, I looked over at Francis, and my chest tightened. I was jolted back into awareness of my lungs and limbs, my feet hitting the solid ground and the growing flutter in my chest. I needed no further proof than the sight of him to show me there was still plenty of feeling and emotion left in this journey.

We crossed a large intersection, mixing with people on their way to work. Then we caught our first glimpse of the old city a few blocks ahead. The sky was a dull shade of grey. It would stay this hue and spit rain on us all day. We wrapped ourselves in layers of gear, but I kept my hood down and let my face feel the rain.

The raw weather was our welcome, and somehow it was fitting. The roads turned to cobbled alleyways built for foot traffic then suddenly the arrows vanished. There were no more way markers. We had crossed mountains and deserts, rivers and empty tracks of land, always following the arrows, always knowing they would be there. But here in the destination city, we faced our first moment without them. We were so close, yet we had nothing more to guide us forward. We could see the massive spires of the church ahead but didn't know which twisting alley would take us to its hallowed halls.

With the aid of a storekeeper and a bit of rough Spanish, we carved our way to the center. Under the arch of a courtyard, the damp ghoulish exterior of the cathedral appeared. The Brit boys cheered, and Ivan and Jack embraced. We had our picture taken by the only other pilgrims standing in the early morning drizzle. The boys took individual group shots, while I waited off to the side. The Brit guys had walked a thousand miles to arrive at this very spot. They had stuck together through injury and illness, disagreements and inner struggles. They had walked together for months, sharing nights and days, albergues and the open road. They had an endless supply of overlapping memories, and they got to return home together and be in each other's lives to reminisce in the days, months and years to come. They would always have this time folded into the root of their friendship, and the same could be said for Jack and Ivan. They didn't have two weeks bouncing around on their own before finding each other. They didn't have lonely gaps in their journey or a fear that the people they'd shared the trek with would vanish from their lives. Theirs was not a patchwork journey as mine was, and I felt they might never understand the visceral difference.

Eventually the rain started to fall in earnest; it was time to seek shelter and sustenance. I was relieved since the only sensation breaking through my numbness was hunger. I suddenly longed for a hot cup of coffee. Francis and Elliot led the way as our posse moved away from the cathedral in search of a café. It was interesting to see the two of them take charge of the group. This moment and this city were important to the both of them. Elliot was especially well prepared to navigate Santiago. Only a few blocks away from the cathedral, we found a small corner café and pushed several tables together before taking off our wet layers.

I sat next to Francis in the buzzing excitement of the group. I couldn't stop myself from drawing close to him. Somehow even amidst all the chaos between us, we still needed each other. In the warm elegant confines of the street café, I could tell that behind Francis's rather withdrawn façade, he was awash with a complex mix of emotions. At the same time, he could see my numbness was a front. So we exchanged very few words but used our aptitude at reading the other to navigate the gathering. Francis's ability to be a rock of support both relieved and unnerved me at the same time. It was an intoxicating blend of comfort and vulnerability when he glanced over the group and caught my eye. I felt I could have curled up at his feet like a devoted animal, assured I was close to one who truly cared for my wellbeing. I'd always felt this from him and knew this piece of our bond was never the element in question.

And the life of the group rolled on, unaware as ever. Elliot described the pilgrim office and what we would have to do there in order to get our Compostelas. Jack moaned in delight over his hot chocolate as he dunked pastries into the thick syrupy drink. I warmed my hands with small cup of coffee. I worried about Francis's hands as he rubbed them together, trying to ease the chill. We'd all become wetter and colder than expected. John looked like a soaked puppy, and Elliot complained he was feeling a bit off. After we paid the bill for our large and expensive breakfast, we slipped back into the street, delighted to find the rain had stopped. The skies remained ominously grey, and everything was slick.

Our post breakfast destination was the pilgrim office. The tall four-story building was the hub of all pilgrim activity and the official place to report our arrival in the city. The office was off a side courtyard of the cathedral. Even though it was only ten in the morning, the building was already buzzing with activity. Climbing three flights of wide stairs, we entered a large room with a long desk at the far end. There were three stations where officials checked credentials, verified each pilgrim's journey and gave out the coveted Compostelas. The room felt like a lively modern office with clean surfaces, walls covered in maps and posters and an efficient sense of order. It was a well-oiled pilgrim processing machine.

I waited in line behind a biker still wearing his tight shorts. In such a hurry to be validated, he'd left his bike shoes on too, and they clicked as he moved up to the desk. The boys waited in lines parallel to mine. We were all headed to the desks for the same reason, to officially confirm our journey and receive our Compostelas. The room was filled with chatter in many languages. When I reached the counter, the woman was pleasant but brisk. She looked over my credential and scanned the dates and locations of my nights. She typed small bits of data into the computer and then asked me to fill out the sheet on the counter under my elbows. It asked about my nationality, gender and, finally, my reason for walking the trail. There were three categories: religious, religious and other and non-religious.

I stopped with the pen poised above the paper. This wasn't a question I'd been prepared to answer in an official capacity. The sheet was a group sheet that held other names and info above mine. Everyone above me had checked religious. And here in the shadow of the cathedral, I paused. The church and its old walls meant very little to me, almost nothing in fact, and it couldn't compare to the beauty of the land I'd traversed for so many days. The gloomy spires didn't hold a candle to the days of fog and rain, the mornings of stars and new light. I'd walked the course of the Milky Way and traversed the lay lines of the earth ever westward. I'd come here to be reborn into my life, to unburden myself and to form deep bonds. I'd come to embrace the land, my fellow travelers and the newly blooming version of myself. I didn't come because of the dogmatic institutions people build around belief, and I didn't come for religion. I came because of the marrow of faith. And I came because I was guided, nudged, corralled, channeled and called to the trail. Something deeper and greater, wiser and kinder than I could fathom knew what I would find here and who I would become on this pathway. My oneness with the trail was my real Compostela. The way I'd become part of her fabric and found that effortless flow of belonging was my document of proof. For like a flow of water, none of the particles could be divided with the naked eye. It was all part of the whole; nothing was greater or lesser, stronger or weaker. No places were more holy or less and no movement more altering than another, for it was all part of the same current. The three choices were too narrow. Too black and white. Too reductive. The third choice was the only true one for me, for it was the only choice that wasn't divisive. It held the right tone of oneness. I believed such beauty was boundless and part of every cell and every second of this pathway.

I checked the non-religious box and handed the woman the sheet. As she scanned the information, her eyebrows lifted slightly. She turned the sheet to me and asked me if I was sure of the box I had checked. I was.

Twenty minutes later, I sat on a large sofa on the far side of the room holding my Compostela document in my hands and staring blankly into space. My name hadn't been written in Latin. The artwork was crude and plain. The design was totally different than the others I saw around me. I didn't get the official Compostela but had been given a lesser version because I hadn't checked the "right" box, because I didn't believe in the power of the box. I stood by my truth, but it was extremely upsetting to see my friends clutching different documents. I suddenly felt separate from them as if we hadn't done the same trail, as if they got something more that slipped through my fingers.

It was a relief to return down the stairs and pass the long line of people waiting to check in. I avoided Ivan and Francis. I wanted to get away from the pilgrim office before I broke down in a flood of tears. I wanted to be able to collect myself and not make a scene. As we spilled out onto the street, the cobbles were drying, but the world was still grey. I could tell the sun was out behind the clouds, but its warm light had no way to reach us. My rain jacket was sticking to me, and I could feel the chill creeping into my clothes.

We moved through the streets in search of the tourist office. Elliot assured us they would be able to help us find a place to stay close to the cathedral in a private but relatively inexpensive lodging. These hostals were for pilgrims and though they worked like small hotels, they were actually guest rooms in locals' apartments. After weeks of spending no more that eight euros on a night's stay, it was a shock to pay for a regular priced hotel room. This was a compromise between the two.

We found the tourist office to be another well-oiled machine run by young attractive multilingual women with manicured nails. With phones tucked behind their silky curtains of hair, they handed us maps and called hostals to see if rooms were available. The office was a mixture of glistening white surfaces and glass displays. Under the glare of bright lights, it felt like a high-end boutique. After a few phone calls, we got a lead and headed off to the hostal.

We arrived at the large door of the hostal, and Elliot rang the bell. He'd become the man in charge. I didn't care where we landed as long as I had a safe place to sleep. An older gentleman answered the buzzer and called us up. He had two rooms available. One was a double, and the other was a quad. Both John and

Elliot wanted to pay more for a space to themselves, and the rest of us didn't mind cramming into the quad. We'd slept in old barns and rooms with scores of people; in comparison, this was a luxury.

As the man took us down the hall, I felt my mind slip backwards. The narrow space with its wallpapered surfaces was just the same. Just the same as the Barcelona apartment that had been my surrogate home during my fifteenth summer. I was suddenly reminded how unbearably unhappy I'd been in that apartment belonging to my exchange hosts. I could trace the beginning of my adulthood to that very summer.

Before that trip to Spain, I'd spent my summers in one-piece bathing suits, playing cards with family, singing cheesy pop songs and building bonfires. I'd felt peacefully invisible and disconnected from the adult world and all its expectations for the fairer sex. I'd still been a kid, tucked in the safe fold of my wonderfully grounded family. But as soon as I'd touched down in Barcelona, everything had shifted. In Spain, I'd been looked upon as an adult. I'd been expected to drink and stay out until three in the morning. In Spain, I'd been categorized as a woman. I'd gathered stares from men on the streets, and my host family had harassed me about finding a Spanish boyfriend. I'd become self-conscious about my childish clothing and tall awkward body. In Spain, I'd been unprotected, unsupervised and neglected. Many would have felt liberated, and grown up. I'd simply felt abandoned.

My family had been my community and source of comfort, and I'd expected to find this with my Spanish hosts. Instead, the immaculate first floor apartment in the ritzy neighborhood had been empty, trapped in endless darkness behind thick curtains. My host sister had spent two happy summers with me in the states, but once back in Barcelona, she'd preferred kissing her boyfriend in public parks to showing me the city. My host family had worked all hours of the day and had stayed out until dawn. They'd refused to speak to me in anything but Spanish, encouraged me to go out partying and treated me like an adult. But I hadn't been an adult, and I'd felt like I was drowning in my new role.

When I'd returned home thin and gaunt, I'd had to cut off my hair. It had knotted so badly I couldn't break the snarls. Yet more distressing than the loss of my hair or weight was the collection of ideas I'd brought back with me. I'd returned with the frightening knowledge that to the world outside of my family, I was now officially a woman. Things were now expected from me by society, I was no longer OK as I was. I'd have to look, act and be a "woman" from then on. The prospect had overwhelmed me.

Spain had been the turning point. In that summer, I'd found out I was a woman and lost my grounding in an authentic sense of my womanhood all at the same time. I would spend the next decade wrestling with the issues born during those sweltering Spanish days.

Now I was back in Spain, and everything was reborn. My view of this land, its culture and my relationship to it was revolutionized. Now I loved Spain with a fierce ache and loved the version of myself I'd found along the Camino. Perhaps I had to return to Spain to reclaim what I'd lost to this land so long ago. I'd returned to take back the grounding, zest and joy that had filled my childhood. Maybe if I could hold tight and take back these missing elements, I would find that wholeness again. This trail had given me so much; I just hoped I could keep it all.

In our Santiago hostal, the room was small and filled with three beds. Two single beds clung to the walls, and a larger double was pushed into the back corner. Jack quickly claimed a single bed on the grounds he was too tall for the double. I'd thought he and Ivan would claim the double. I wasn't opposed to sleeping in a double but was suddenly back in the same old conundrum and anxious about who would claim the space beside me. Thankfully Ivan settled the matter before I could utter a word, volunteering to sleep in the double next to me. I could feel Francis's unease with the decision, but I acted as if I didn't notice and began to unpack. Unfortunately, this obvious and practical arrangement didn't calm the energy in the room, and within the span of a couple of minutes, the vibration became thick and tense with the unspoken. All of a sudden, I wanted nothing more than to get away from the small room and the swirling emotions.

I dropped my things and escaped into the buzz of the old city. It was a change to be over stimulated. I wound my way through cobbled streets, crossed busy intersections and moved through a sea of umbrellas. A medieval fair was taking place in the main square, and vendors were setting out their wares. Under rain tarps, I found stalls overflowing with fragrant spices: baskets of vibrant orange saffron and deep black peppercorns. There were falconers with mews full of birds and miniature ponies dressed in festive cloaks. The scene filled my senses and made my mouth water. There were barrels of olives, perfect ovals in dark green and black flooded with salty liquid, heaving boards filled with an array of cheese wheels and all varieties of roasted meat seeping delicious smells. I bought a bit of chocolate from one of the stalls and sat alone on the large courtyard steps. Men and women dressed in bright medieval garb moved about selling jewelry and cloth. The sky was still dull, but the air had grown warm again.

Jack and Ivan came to find me and explore the medieval fair. We wandered the stalls together, seeking out all the magical mysteries. Unlike the British boys who had receded into a depression moments after we settled into our room, the American guys were amused with the whole arrival experience. Ivan reported that despondency had descended on all three of the Brits in subtle ways. Francis still felt ill while Elliot had hurried off into the city to call home. John had volunteered to stay with Francis and doze away the afternoon. I wondered if they had set the bar too high, if they had too much riding on this arrival moment, and now it felt desolate and anticlimactic. And the strangest side effect of this disappointment with the arrival was how they were missing the experience because of the buildup. It felt cruelly ironic that they came the furthest for this moment yet were missing the spices, ponies, chocolate treats and suckling pig roasting over an open fire. They were absent from the festivities and the laughter. Part of me wanted to go drag them out into the streets to join us, but the other part of me knew to let go and let them be.

At the top of the plaza, Jack and Ivan found a stall selling old weapons. The woman running the booth was delighted to let us play with the hardware, and once given the green light to touch, Ivan wasn't shy. He picked up each sword, assessing its weight and moving it around his body as if he was test-driving it. Jack looked over the small hand carved knives then watched as Ivan posed in battle helmets that came down over his forehead and the bridge of his nose. Jack challenged me to a mock battle, and I eagerly accepted. After picking our weapons, we took our spots and began. Falling into some unconscious, long dormant place in me the sword moved in my hands swift and sure, my feet shifted below me without command. I had Jack on the defensive from the first strike, and it didn't take long for all watching to see that the fight was mine for the taking from the first move. Jack had never stood a chance.

It was an ornate cow horn with a leather holster that captivated Ivan's attention most ardently. Pulling it down from where it dangled on top of a long pole, he practiced sounding the call. At first the noise was wet and pathetic, but the woman in the booth took pity on him and shared a small secret. On his next try, the cow horn performed, and the sound resounded throughout the plaza. The grin of accomplishment didn't leave Ivan's face for nearly an hour. He swore as he parted with the very expensive horn that it was the horn of Gondor, Boromir's horn, and someday he would have one just like it.

We explored the fair and enjoyed the chance to be around other people. Jack was determined we attend the free concerts taking place throughout the city. It was nearly six by the time we set off to the next performance. We hurried through the streets, wound around corners and dodged through crowds to make a mad dash up the steps of the Santiago modern art museum. We slowed our tempo as we walked into the interior courtyard to find seats and listen to a famous Spanish cellist perform. Sitting in a small crowd on the outskirts of the museum's gardens, my ears flooded with finely crafted sound. I found I was desperately thirsty for such a moment, a vignette of sheer beauty, a convergence of skill and passion. It seemed to stir all my dormant creative longing. I wanted nothing more than to move and be moved. I pined for dance and craved a creative life so badly it ached. I was so drawn into the performance energy that I hardly noticed when Elliot slipped in to join us.

When the show was over, Elliot reported that Francis had taken a turn for the worse and couldn't keep anything down. He was quite worried about him, enough so that he felt he should go back to the hostal and look after him instead of staying to watch the next performance. He looked downtrodden by this turn in events, since the next show was a jazz quartet he'd been especially interested in. Before I fully understood what I was saying, I leapt from my seat, volunteering to go in Elliot's place. I wanted him to stay and soak in some of the magic of this day, and I felt drawn to the cause of caring for Francis. I remembered how stressful it was to be sick in a foreign place, and the difference it made to have familiar company by one's side. I also felt my thoughts swirling with images and words I longed to share with Francis. I was wistful for the easy days we'd once had and hoped I could recapture them even if only for a short while. I agreed to send John back into the city so he too could see the show. Elliot gratefully sank into his seat as I took off with the key to the apartment in hand.

I still felt flush from the emotion of watching the cellist play and hardly noticed anything around me as I maneuvered back to the hostal. Earlier in the day, I'd felt overcome with loneliness, and as I skirted the crowds I felt it tug at the edges of me once more. Here in the busy metropolis, our group was dissolving. The trail had been an almighty uniting force, a shared experience of great diversity and change. It had fueled our connection and linked us in a deep web that only grew tighter as the days progressed. The journey along Camino was our shared purpose and now, in this city, that purpose had evaporated. We were no longer pilgrims on the trail but just a group of kids moving aimlessly about the place, unsure how to exist without the backbone of walking and unsure who we were to each other now that we didn't need one another. I wondered where the Iron Six was and if they were hitting the same group roadblocks. I kept scanning the crowds looking for a familiar pilgrim, sure I would turn a corner and come face to face with their posse.

I arrived at the hostal, climbed the three flights of stairs and let myself in. I found John in his room then set him free to go see the concert, informing him I would look after Francis. He took off with a grateful smile, and I made my way down the hall to our room. I opened the door as quietly as possible and slipped in to find Francis half sitting up in his bed with his eyes closed. He looked as if he hadn't moved from that spot in hours, but as soon as the door clicked behind me, his eyes opened. A weary sheepish smile crossed his face, and his eyelids seemed to ache with the effort of opening. I told him I'd come back to watch over him and let Elliot go to the jazz performance. I stood by the door for a moment, unsure of where I belonged in the room. He patted the edge of his bed as if calling me towards him, and I stepped forward then veered off to sprawl on my double bed across from him instead. He seemed unperturbed by my change of course and waited for me to settle. Lying on my back looking up at the ceiling, I confided how bereft I felt now that my connection to our group was fading. He agreed that our shared purpose had evaporated the moment we arrived in the old city, leaving each of us with something akin to emptiness. I wondered for a moment if this was at the core of the Brit boys' sudden implosion. Francis spoke about the drama of the end, and I felt myself settling into his soft slow cadence. We both knew we had hours to talk. We could have claimed that his illness and my weariness kept us bound together in the small room at the end of the hall, but I knew that was far from the truth. We weren't going anywhere, because this was where we both wanted to be the most. I could feel it humming through us. This was the most alive space in our journey, and I couldn't help being drawn back to it and back to him.

After a few minutes, I tilted my head up and looked over at him. He smiled again, and his face seemed brighter, full of energy that hadn't been there half an hour before. Galvanized by the sight, I confided how much I'd missed his company, and how I'd let Elliot stay in my place more out of selfishness than selflessness. He laughed as if I was confessing something rather funny but ultimately endearing. I was telling him he was my favorite, he was my person and I knew he found it funny only because it had been so very obvious for so very long. I rolled over onto my stomach and glanced at him again to find his smile had disappeared, and his eyes were trained on me, seeking my own with a sudden intensity. He didn't break the thread as he told me that I too was his person. I could tell by the way his voice dropped that he was reaching deep down inside himself for the words, seeking to saturate them in as much earnestness as possible. He wanted me to feel their weight and believe them. And it was quite a confession. For me to declare who I cared for the most was of little consequence. I was a solo, but he had others who should have outranked me. It had never occurred to me that he could have believed my connection and energy lay anywhere but in his hands, but now he knew unequivocally.

After a silence, I started to tell him about the concert, the passion of the playing and how it filled me with the overpowering urge to dance. I knew he would understand how the energy of the musician had sent a shockwave through my system and made me crave my own outlet for such things. I was waving my arms in the air as I spoke when suddenly he cut in and asked me to dance. Without a pause I began to move. At first I flitted around in slightly silly twirling circles, narrating the feeling of the music, but then I felt the current take me, and my words dried up on my tongue and rolled down into limbs. And so I fell into the energy and began to dance around the tiny room filled with three beds, four packs, a desk, a nightstand and Francis. Even with all its bulk and pointed edges, the furniture was the least complicated of the elements in the room to maneuver around. The desk's sharp corners didn't scare me half as much as the sharp focus of my audience. I could feel every nerve in my body humming as his eyes trailed my every move. I didn't dare catch his eyes or stop the flow. I felt unsteady on my feet but waded through it to the other side. For only the second time on the entire trail, I danced. I danced for my closest companion in the small third floor room above the Praza Galicia as evening fell in Santiago on the day of our arrival, and I let him see all the way through me.

Many years ago, I was told a story about a magnificent dancer who was out hiking in the Alps with her spiritual teacher when he asked her to dance. It was the first time she'd ever danced for him, and she was on the side of a mountain in a pair of hiking boots after a long steep climb. Even under the least ideal of circumstances she'd danced and made do with the stage that was given to her. The image of this beautiful dancer moving for her beloved teacher despite her surroundings always brought me courage. She'd shown grit and poise, but most of all she'd demonstrated vulnerability. She'd allowed herself to reveal an imperfect beauty to the one she cared the most about, and such acts of bravery mattered. Was this the perfect moment to let Francis become part of my dance and open my heart all the way to him? I couldn't know, but perhaps it was just as it was meant to be, even in all its imperfections. I'd lost much in being open before, but I still believed I would have lost more if I'd stayed closed.

So I danced for him, and it was a truly human moment. And when I was done, I suddenly felt the space was close and intimate in a way it had been in San Xulián, yet now it filled the whole room. My whole body vibrated with the energy. As I danced for Francis, I'd opened the door again. I'd talked to him in the language of my soul. A language even more evocative than the silence we'd known in the stone room.

After a moment he spoke, "I wonder why you don't dance this beauty every moment of every day." His eyes seemed to be full of the movement, replaying the echo of every arc, but his arms wrapped tightly around his core as if he were locking his body in place. The small gesture felt suddenly defensive and detached from the obvious joy surging through his eyes. He'd seen another side of someone he cared deeply for, and I knew it had brought him joy, but I could feel his body was closed off, his physical connection to what had happened was retreating. I wanted him to leap up and come towards me, to enfold me and refuse to let go. I wanted him to move on the momentum of light around us and kiss me. I wanted us to leave the outgrown shell of our friendship behind and wrap ourselves in one another.

But as I waited, swaying in stillness, I suddenly knew he would stay in his corner. He wasn't going to come towards me with the desire I knew he felt. He wasn't going to actualize the attraction. He wasn't going to touch me, even though a part of him craved to. The other part of Francis was striving to keep us as we'd been, keep us from change, and he'd chosen this part of himself even after I danced for him.

All of a sudden, I was drenched in sorrow. I wanted to evaporate or escape the energy that would never thrive. The trail had helped me heal in many ways. It had been a true detox of the past, allowing me to sweat out all the old remnants of previous relationships, but I was still battle weary. Even if I was scrubbed of the past, I still feared a repeat of the same dynamics in the present and was horrified to find myself falling head first into just such a configuration. Here was a man that I knew loved the internal workings of my soul and who had been a friend unlike any other. He had all the elements I'd so often done without in the ones I'd loved. So when I felt the stirrings of desire, I'd wondered if here in Francis was a person with whom I could have it all. Maybe with him I could be loved for my entirety.

But now, I knew that having the raw materials for a whole love connection between us didn't guarantee a romance. We both had to want this. We both had to embrace this. And though I was on board, I suddenly knew Francis was undecided, worried and hesitant. I could see the coils holding him back, the issues that tugged at him and eroded the energy of his longing. He'd imagined this journey as one of solitude and devotion to God, yet he'd stumbled across the likes of me and wasn't sure I was really meant to be in God's plans for him. He wanted to follow the energy and the light around our bond but didn't know if loving me was the right path for his life. The transparent messages filtering through him were crushing, and I felt helpless. I could see he felt the same way as if he couldn't stop gnawing at all the fears about following his desire in the face of his belief system. I wanted to shake him, snap him out of doubt and indecision but knew this wasn't a battle I could win. I wasn't even in the fight. He had to choose which part of his life he wanted to grow. Was it to be the vibrant and messy human world or the life tucked away in the hollow walls of his religious ideals? This conflict was all his, and the outcome would determine our fate. My path forward had so often hung on the whims of men that I knew this place well and simply wished to hibernate until the verdict was read.

So I retreated to my matching corner and pretended to read. After a while he closed his eyes again. I looked over and noticed he was like a tightly wound spring. Even in sleep he was torqued. His body was eating away at itself, and there was something scary about the tension in his frame. I'd noticed this for the past few days, but as he lay in bed that evening, I could see he'd become very, very thin. As I sat on the far side of the room from him, I scrolled though my emotions and realized all I wanted was to be held; to feel physically safe in the wake of that vulnerable moment and its crushing reality check. But clearly he was in no state to offer me such solace. His thinness made him utterly unapproachable when everything else about who he was made me want to cross the room and hold on. I wanted him, but I also wanted warmth and softness, arms and closeness, and he was evaporating into sharp lines before my eyes.

Francis arrived in my life out of left field, and even from the first moment, something in me knew he would be important to my life. It was as if he was a part of me. He'd been there all along, and I just hadn't known it. There'd been a mark of destiny to our meeting on this sacred pathway. Yet now, with the trail at an end, I didn't know if I got to keep him. I didn't know which way Francis would go or when staying on the edge would be too much for the both of us. I kept reading until night fell, until he turned onto his side away from me and fell asleep. I slid into my sleeping bag and faced the opposite wall. We were an evenly matched pair, each turned away from the other as night came.

THE CATHEDRAL

I awoke to bright morning light. The sun was shining on the city for the first time since our arrival. The raucous noise outside our window had remained constant during the night. Voices called out at all hours. I was now convinced Spanish youth never slept. In most cities, there was a lull after two or three, but here there was no break in the activity. Even at five in the morning, the revelers were still out and about.

It was a pilgrim tradition to go to the noon mass at the cathedral on the day of arrival in Santiago, but our group decided to wait and go to mass on our second day. Seeing the sunshine, I was glad we'd delayed. Hopefully everyone would be less morose in accordance with the change in weather. As was tradition, each of our nationalities and entry points on the trail would be read out during pilgrim mass. The boys were thrilled by the prospect of being recognized within the cathedral walls. It would be entertaining to pick each of us out from the long list of pilgrims arriving in the city. I had no idea what the mass would be like, but we'd heard rumors a giant thurible of incense would swing during the show. The thurible in the Santiago cathedral, called the Bota Fumero, was renowned for its size. Apparently it took several priests to make it swing.

I didn't doubt there would be a show of bold theatrics at the mass, but I wasn't inclined to attend. Yet after some group cajoling, I agreed to go. Ivan wouldn't let me miss out on the moment and assured me he too was there purely to witness the curious sight of a foreign culture's pomp and circumstance. I would stray into dark halls of hostile territory in the name of group harmony but only for a brief visit. Actually the anthropologist in me was slightly curious about what lived in the gilded belly of a group I didn't belong to. So much on this trail had been new. I told myself this was no different. The mass started at noon, and we agreed to meet up at the cathedral's side entrance beforehand.

Elliot, Francis and I arrived at one of the side entrances ten minutes before the hour. The courtyard was already thick with people funneling through the wide cathedral doors. We flowed in under the door jam towards the center of the cathedral. The walls were stunningly ornate, almost gaudy. Everything was crusted in golden hues, but because the chambers were so large, the decorations didn't overpower the room. Rows and rows of pews stretched towards the altar. The space was already full of hundreds of people sitting, milling around and talking with one another. The three of us made our way up the aisle to find seats. I didn't care where we sat but hoped for a good view of the proceedings in the central nave.

Walking alongside the pews, I scanned for a spot that would fit all six of us. Suddenly, I saw a double flash of bright blonde hair. There tucked in a pew close to the front were Ava, Iris and Konrad. The girls looked relaxed and clean, while Konrad appeared at ease sandwiched between them. Without a moments thought, I ran over and hollered a joyful hello. I was unexpectedly happy to see their familiar faces. The girls stood up, and we hugged while Konrad stayed seated, looking bored. If Santiago had brought out one thread, it was the preciousness of friends in a strange city. Ava and Iris were even more of a sight for sore eyes after a day of feeling oddly uprooted from Camino life. They were links back to what had been; I'd missed them and the excitement of the circus. We'd shared much of this journey with each other, and their presence allowed me to feel it wasn't all ending. Together we could still be pilgrims, at least for a bit longer. The girls chatted in a polite way for a few minutes but kept scanning the crowds for the arrival of the rest of their group. Even after so many days, some things hadn't changed, and the girl's focus on Iron Six unity was the same as ever.

We parted after we agreed to meet outside following the mass. Elliot, Francis and I found a section near the back as Jack, John and Ivan arrived. Within moments Tomas, Zara and Jay came through the backdoors behind them. There was no room with Ava, Iris and Konrad so they took second best and claimed seats around us. I sat squished between Ivan and John. The pew grew even more crowded when Jay slid himself in at the last moment. I had to press tight up against the boys, holding both my arms out in front of my body. Even after all this time, John appeared flustered to sit so close to me. A giggle rose in my crushed chest as I felt him fluttering beside me. Sometimes he certainly did earn his role as the baby of the group. I found it amusing but sympathized too. Females could be pretty intimidating, and he appeared to be generally terrified of girls. But he was young; it would pass. Ivan, on the other hand, seemed completely at ease, undisturbed that I was practically sitting on his lap. I was glad to have him by my side since we were both on the same page when it came to the ceremony. What he hoped most from the experience was to watch the giant thurible rocket around the space. We would both be disappointed when the Bota Fumero didn't swing. Later we learned it was only swung during pilgrim mass if a large monetary donation was made in advance by a rich visitor or if the mass was attended by an elected official, celebrity or member of the royal family.

Once the mass started, most of the group grew still and focused. Zara, who sat directly behind me, began to weep and continued to do so until the end of the service. I was stunned. In all the days we'd traveled together, I hadn't seen her come close to melting her icy core or shedding a tear. I peered into the row in front of us and noticed Francis looking distant and grim. I was restless. My body itched to be on the move and outside in the warm sun, but I was pinned into the hard pew for the duration.

To my surprise, even after the service began, people kept walking up and down the aisles chatting. The service might as well been out in the crowded streets. There was no hallowed silence here. The much anticipated announcement of our names was so slurred we couldn't even distinguish the words. The priest spoke in a particularly heavy accent and mumbled into the microphone with an evident lack of enthusiasm. It was a horribly anticlimactic moment. The only person we could identify was Zara who was un Austrialiana a Roncesvalles. At the end of the service, we were encouraged to hug the people on either side of us, and it was the only moment in the two hour mass that held any authenticity. The bonds between us all meant more to me than any of the gilded surfaces, adorned holy men or mumbled words coming from the altar.

At two, we emerged into the blinding sun of the main square. The courtyard that yesterday was empty and grey was now awash with people. Where they had all come from I didn't know, but suddenly it felt like an adventure again. People milled around in groups, took pictures and lay on the warm stones of the courtyard. The six of us went off in search of lunch but arranged to meet for celebratory pre-dinner drinks with the Iron Six. They were staying in a series of buildings that looked over the main square. The British boys were envious of their prime realty, but I was pleased with our abode off the Praza Galicia. Ava seemed especially smug with their accommodations, but I was thoroughly unconvinced by her insistence that this enhanced their Santiago experience.

There were so many other factors at work, combining to shape this stretch of the journey. As I stood in crowds of hundreds of people celebrating the end, I knew I wasn't done. The end of my Camino was a three day walk beyond Santiago, and I was ready to go. I missed the trail and longed to dive back into the rhythm of walking. I felt positively aimless without it. I craved to be back in the trail's embrace. This urban life, even in small doses, didn't suit me.

Since our arrival in Santiago, Ivan and Jack had been obsessed with tasting the famous Galician pulpa. After mass, they cajoled the group into joining them at a restaurant to dine on the food in question. The word pulpa sounded like some juicy citrus or sweet dessert, but it was neither. It was the chewy buttery tangled body of an octopus cooked in the local style. I tasted the dish but must admit that for days afterward even the memory of pulpa was enough to make me gag. True to character, Ivan was thrilled with the new taste and happy to finish my pulpa and wipe the plate clean. I laughed with him as he entertained the table, but everybody else was in undisguised ugly moods. Elliot was grumpy, felt ill and left half way through the meal. Francis was silent, boiling with words unspoken. I didn't have to try and guess why he was so pissed off. My harmless banter with Ivan didn't help matters. After lunch, Jack and Ivan went off to see another jazz show. Francis traipsed off in one direction and I in the other. I felt horrible but unable to face his dark mood when I knew I had little chance of fixing it. I wandered the city alone, moving through the fair to distract myself but feeling deeply restless. I finally found a bench on the side of the main cathedral. Sitting in the sun, I watched people flow in and out of the space. It was like viewing a time elapse film, watching things arrive, unfold and drift out of the scene altogether.

Tomas found me an hour later. He wanted to go see the medieval fair before dinner and asked me if I would accompany him. As we wound our way through the stalls, we bought slices of gooey chocolate pie and watched a couple perform a tango in the streets. I walked him back to the hostal where the Iron Six were staying, and we talked about his plans for getting home. He wanted to walk back to Belgium but was open to the universe's directions. Maybe he would take a boat back instead of walking. I envied his ability to choose his homeward course and to keep the journey going. We paused and took a seat around the edge of the central square with the cathedral looming above us. The rest of the Iron Six were nowhere to be seen. Tomas explained they were staying for several more days in Santiago before traipsing off to a beach holiday for just the six of them. I would most likely never see any of them again once I left this port of call, and I had a feeling we might once again part ways without a proper goodbye; but perhaps I'd never had a real hello.

How could I know that months later, Konrad would write me a series of letters. In the blunt tone I'd come to expect from the gruff German, he explained how he'd actively worked to keep Jack, Ivan and most especially me out of the Iron Six. He didn't apologize for his actions but explained his desire to keep their group, whom he called the Golden Six, on their own private Camino. He'd been given the role of the bouncer for the group, setting up boundaries and growling at anyone who sought entrance. I just happened to be the person who'd banged loudest at the gates of their alliance.

He would explain how the six remained tight all the way to the beaches at Fisterra but no further. Konrad would be surprised and disheartened to discover that for the girls, the bond was simply a means to an end. It gave them company for the length of the journey. Sitting in his empty apartment during cold German nights, he would write me with a forlorn air about how his group had moved on, made new friends and forgotten the long summer days in Spain. Ironically, I would be the only one in the whole group who wrote him back. Me, the person he most loathed on the Camino, the person he had continually manhandled out of the inner circle, would become his closest post trail confidant. He'd wanted his Golden Six to be exclusive so they'd form tight bonds, and he'd turned on his blinders to other souls who could have become deeply rooted in his experience. I understood his instinct but could see how it had led him astray. Had he welcomed me in, I was perhaps the one person who would have stayed close and kept the Camino bond alive. Even with our tense history, I would like the Konrad I met through the letters better than the one I'd known in Spain, and we would grow close for a time. I would lament the fact we hadn't been friends when we'd lived side by side, but through our letters, we would give ourselves a second chance.

As our correspondence deepened, I would discover he had a lot of regrets about his exclusive Camino, and I would became his safe harbor to discuss them. I appreciated his honesty after so many days in the company of the Iron Six where the truth was never aired. The letters helped me realize how young the group had been. They were in their late teens, a time when community comes easily and seems never ending. Maybe later they would realize the way life shifts once this period passes. Perhaps if they'd been older, they would have appreciated how precious and rare the trail bonds were. They'd thought life would continue to present them moments such as these summer days. Even sitting by Tomas's side in the courtyard in Santiago, I'd known it wasn't so. I felt the threads of our trail slipping out of my fingers and the community fading. I knew the season of twelve was truly over. Only later would I understand the reign of the Iron Six was waning as well. In Santiago, they might have felt they were golden, but time would reveal their nature to be nothing more than iron.

After a time watching the flowing crowds with Tomas, we fell into companionable silence. It was effortless to be with him again and talk about the chaos of this journey's end. Ever since our day in Rabanal, I'd enjoyed his company. Our calm oasis didn't last long. Not soon after the cathedral clock tolled the hour, Francis strode into the square, eyes scanning the crowds. I knew he wanted to talk, and I felt unable to hold him at bay any longer. I'd craved this moment and feared it, but now I couldn't stop it. Tomas marked the grimace on Francis's face and politely left to go shower before reconvening with the group for drinks. Francis took Tomas's place beside to me.

In the heart of Santiago's old city, we sat side by side as we'd so often done along the winding path. We'd lived our Camino lives parallel to each other for so long that the trail before we'd met felt like a distant memory. The energy between us was so vibrant, even in the midst of our struggle, even when neither of us wanted its pulse. Against all logic and odds we'd found each other, met on neutral territory and moved forward together. It was impossible to walk the forward flow of the trail and not feel things change and accelerate, evolve and shift. This was the growth curve, and I knew my internal life wasn't the only part of me that had leapt into the current. Our connection had bloomed, sometimes even against our will or personality desires. We'd unfurled something precious between us, and now we were hovering on the edge of the end of the physical trail and clutching unknowns. The oneness of the guidance and the road, the choices and movements all combined to bring us here. We were always destined to meet on the trail, to find each other on this path in Spain, but what came next neither of us knew.

The trail had been our glue, our common ground and the comforting roots to our bond, but we both knew it was drawing to an end. I felt my stomach drop as I recognized it was time to know which path he wanted to take next: the one that moved him towards me or the one that led him away.

I loved him and saw deep gifts in his soul. I believed he had the momentum to be part of my life, to jump aboard the fast moving train and hold tight. I knew we could contain a thriving friendship and dive into the growing attraction. There was certainly heart, and there was the promise of heat as well. He had proved he was loving enough to be with me, wise enough and strong enough but only if he took the brakes off his life. Only if he left the confines of dogma and compartmentalization. Only if he broke down his sense of right and wrong and trusted the flow of his life. Maybe we could work if he began to see the expansive nature of God and the universe and let go of his embattled view of what should be. His whole body seemed to wedge itself into the smallest box, into a place where he failed to imagine his life could be for God as he hoped and also full of vibrant passion for another. He was unwilling to trust he could have it all. I wondered if this trail had been able to impart its cardinal rules on him: nothing can be planned, nothing is out of bounds and we can't miss our destiny if we follow the energy. Even though souls had been walking this trail for a thousand years, the trail was a wild improvisation not a rigid and lifeless repertoire. I believed following the path of life was the same way; we were on a track that was somewhat known, but what happened along the way was a mystery.

I wanted him to feel how his rules about his life and about us were eating him alive, literally. He wanted to blame the suffering on his weakness or my role as his Jezebel, but he was the jail keeper here not me. If only he could trust his heart and trust me. If only he would give us a chance, I knew he would feel the shift in his whole being. I could sense I'd become a fearsome creature in his life, a dangerous minx even when I wasn't trying. I was the temptress pulling him outside of his rules about what his life and his faith should look like, and I felt unfairly cast. Francis had walked this trail for God, but I felt he was unwilling to ask, to truly know if what God wanted was for him to embrace our relationship, embrace the love that had taken root between us, to have passion and family and to embrace all the physical gifts of life. I could feel he was drawing each layer of fear close to him, wearing his ideas of right and wrong as a shield and pulling the emergency break on the signals of his body and heart. He would let his body waste away before he let it follow its desire, and I didn't know how to turn the tides.

I was overwhelmed by the cosmos of conflict and emotion swirling around him and knew all I could do was ground to the center of myself. I had to find the core of trust and silence I'd known so viscerally in San Xulián, go to the place where I knew it was all going to be OK, no matter what. The internal re-sourcing was nearly impossible for me at this point in the struggle, but I knew it was the only way to survive this inevitable moment. All my habits and personality instincts wanted to rush into his energy field and force him to fight for us, force him to take off the brakes and trust his life, trust his feelings and his desire. I'd attempted such acts of coercion with others, but with Francis I ached to persuade him more so than ever before. I wanted to roll up my sleeves and get to work, pledge my dedication to the cause and start pumping energy into the project, but I felt myself hesitate. I knew the base of love that we had for each other, his spiritual momentum and love of God, were exponentially greater than the toxic men of my past. If anything he was the one case where I should have fought tooth and nail to make this love happen, but I knew even with such stakes, it would all be in vain. He had to make the choice. I had to respect his free will. If he was unwilling to pick the path towards me even though he loved me, there was nothing I could do to stop him. Free will was the one escape clause in destiny, and he had the right to step away from us. If he was going to walk by my side to the coast but refuse to be with me all the way, then I couldn't go to the end of the world with him as much as I wanted to. We couldn't go as friends, for in many ways our friendship was over. We would either draw together or fall apart.

We couldn't go backwards on this trail.

Everything hung on this moment, on the words and the energy from his lean frame and weary eyes.

I told him I wanted to walk to the coast with him because I loved him but was afraid of the trail beyond this land. He was silent, but I felt a charged energy building in his body as if all the forces were fighting inside him, waging war on my words and his conflicted emotions of duty and desire, piety and purpose.

Finally he turned to me and told me I had it all wrong. He told me he didn't feel that way for me. He told me he didn't love me that way and never would. I could feel the energy hemorrhaging out of his downcast eyes, yet I could also feel a foreign object, a cold metal plate of steely reserve clutching tight to his center. There was a tortured and contorted stillness to his limbs. Just the sight of him hit me like a strong gust of icy wind diving through all my veins and sending shivers out across my skin. I wanted to gut his words, rip their vowels apart until I could find the emotion I knew lay there, until I could hold the energy up and force him to see what he really felt. I wanted to tackle him, pin his battling insides to the ground and force them into a ceasefire under the breathing weight of my body. I wanted to break his lies before they could rain down upon me and pierce my skin, but I had no such defenses. So I let his words fall and slice all the way down to my core. Others on this trail had been given my affection, but he had been given my heart. I loved the best in him but recoiled at this part that had come to the surface, this part that had made such a crushing choice about us. I had no strength left to battle and no belief in the fight against his free will. It was his free will to say no, and I had to prove I'd grown and would no longer seek to change the choices others made even when my heart hung in the balance.

I felt a rushing warmth around my body as if some current was picking me up and holding my aching body close. The energy had me on my feet and suddenly I was leaving, walking away once again. I left Francis with his head bowed into his hands in the shadow of the cathedral, weighed by his own words and the markers of his fate. I slipped out the far side of the square. My body moved under the steam of some deep and benevolent force I felt too weary to disobey. I was moving onwards under guidance my mind had yet to digest. I'd never thought it would come to this with Francis. I never thought I would lose him in a fight for his love. As I walked away, I knew the trail was calling me back to finish what I'd started so many weeks before. It was time to face the end.

I fell asleep in our empty room before the light left the sky. Thankfully no one had been about when I curled into my cocoon. I'd called my parents and wept silently into the receiver before returning to the apartment. I was at the end of my rope, feeling the dangling ends of this trip. I was so tired that the glimmer of home on the distant horizon seemed the only source of comfort. Nonetheless, I was determined to go to the coast. I'd asked Jack and Ivan if I could tag along with them. They'd agreed and said they would wake me in the morning. I wanted to slip into the night stream of the trail and put space between me and this city. But most of all I needed to part with Francis and go forward without him.

Santiago had called us for so long. It had drawn us forward, yet such ends as this place were empty. The real destinations were the moments tucked into the trail behind us, dropped along the wayside, in the albergues and in each other. This group of souls had been my destination all along. The walls of Santiago were just walls. I would wake and move beyond them, move beyond the echo of this end.

NEGREIRA

STAGE TWENTY EIGHT- 34.4K-21.4M
SANTIAGO TO VILARSERÍO

At the time, going to the coast with Jack and Ivan felt purely circumstantial. I had to leave Francis, and I had a strong suspicion the American guys wouldn't pry into my fragile emotional state. I also felt I needed a bit of protection and was willing to trade being the obvious third wheel for safe passage.

The last factor was timing. Jack and Ivan were leaving the city before the Brit boys, and I wanted to exit Santiago as quickly as possible. We decided to wake early and leave the city before dawn. We said goodbye to a dark room of sleeping bodies, and I felt as if I'd ripped a piece of my chest out and left it behind, but I didn't wake Francis. I didn't force him to open his eyes and watch me go. Our lives were interwoven and just as quickly they were wrenched apart. I was suddenly sad there was no turning back, no reverse, no undoing what had been done.

It was before sunrise when we slipped out of the building. I jumped as the heavy thud of the door pushed us out onto the trail again. Lamps guided us down the streets toward the center of the city. The trail out of Santiago was down a small lane next to the cathedral's main square. We assumed if we kept the towering spires of the church in sight, we would arrive at its feet. This was a harder task than anticipated, and there was little hope we would meet any sober people to guide us. Eventually we came upon the chillingly empty space in front of the cathedral and hurried across the void as quickly as possible.

The trail to the coast was roughly one hundred kilometers, and our trio would attempt to do it in three days. More level headed pilgrims split the distance into four or five days, but the boys and I were disinclined to play it safe. Ivan led the way, looking for a Camino marker low to the ground. After half an hour, we stumbled upon the arrow and cheered with relief. I hadn't anticipated the city would be so hard to shake, but what did I expect after the poorly marked welcome it had provided us. With three full and grueling days of walking ahead of us, getting lost or turned around before even leaving the walls of the city would surely have brought me to tears. I was teetering on the edge of emotional collapse, and I prayed this trek would be smooth and swift.

We found our way to the outskirts of the urban center and very quickly the land started to roll into hills. Trees crept in, and the pavement trailed off. Looking back as we crested a hill, we could see the sun rising behind the three spires of the cathedral. Ivan stopped in the middle of a story, the breath caught in his throat. The sky was a warm purple as it flushed up from the earth and lit the towering cathedral from behind. It was the start of a new day. The light felt holy and fresh. It was the most beautiful moment I'd experienced in the city, and ironically it arrived as I was fleeing its walls.

Jack led the way, and Ivan took the spot in the middle of our small processional. Ivan spoke of men and myths in a low voice, telling us the story of Achilles and Hector. His stick clicked with every step, and I let my mind sink into the diversion of listening to a voice outside my own head. I was glad the American guys didn't make a habit of talking about emotions or the shifting energy of the journey. I was in no state to unearth or share anything other than simple monosyllabic responses to straightforward questions. The dirt path wound up through a young forest of eucalyptus trees; their stripped and shredded trunks were tightly packed together with a canopy of leaves whispering above us. Ivan's tale continued as the pathway spit us out into a recently built housing development. Each cookie cutter home sported tall walls and wrought iron gates, drawn blinds and darkened windows. At this hour, nothing stirred. After our ascent out of the city, my limbs were warm with newly pumped blood. As Ivan came to the part in the story where Achilles slays Hector in grief and rage, his body became tense. The still and empty world around us fell away to the power of the story.

Suddenly noise and fury exploded around us. At first, I could make no sense of the attack. As I walked the narrow sidewalk, I'd seen no movement, but now I felt saliva and hot breath breaking over me amidst a deluge of noise. A large muscled body flew at the gate again and again, shaking the metal with brute force. The dog wasn't chained, and I could sense how his mouth sought my soft throat with raw focus. I dove off the sidewalk and skidded into the road. Part of me waited for impact, sure the only way to defend myself against the teeth and muscle of the beast was to run.

I was a hundred yards ahead, sprinting down the road with my pack banging against me before I realized I wasn't being chased. I turned back and saw that the dog was still raging against the fence but going nowhere. I was safe for the moment, but by the way the boys scurried after me, they also felt it was only a matter of time before the old fence failed, and things got ugly. Panting hard, we agreed it was best to be on or way.

Ivan looked pale, and Jack muttered invectives as we slowed back to a walk. There were many stories about dogs on the trail, but until that moment, I'd met only shy strays and harmless lap dogs. Today would be different. Little did we know, but we would spend the rest of the day with every dog we passed leaping out from its front stoops to test the strength of its restraints. After several attacks, I walked in the middle of the empty road to avoid being repeatedly startled by another aggressive lunge. We lived in a heightened state of anxiety, fleeing from hidden foes with twenty pounds of gear on our back. None of us voiced the fear, but I knew we all wondered what would happen when we stumbled upon a house where the gate wasn't strong enough or where there was no gate at all.

It wasn't until we turned a bend in the trail that the road fell away before us, and the first town outside of Santiago gave hope of a hot cup of coffee and a bit of food. The light shifted from dawn into the first golden tones of day. We had already lived a long morning, yet the sun was only just coming into full view. I walked a few paces ahead of the guys and returned to the narrow strip of sidewalk. Jack, who was chatting softly with Ivan behind me, abruptly fell silent.

I looked up. A young woman walked up the road towards us with her dark hair in wild clumps around her face and a slight hiccup in her gait. She wore a tight short dress and a glittering jacket. This was the first person we'd seen since leaving the center of the city. She came up the hill towards us with her head down. One hand fell to her side and from her fingers dangled a broken shoe. Closer and closer we came towards each other with us clamoring down the hill as she gingerly made her way up it. As we drew near, the guys and I jumped off the sidewalk to let her pass. The girl didn't speak to us or even look up. A flash of bright red trailed along the side of her hand. It flickered before my eyes then fell into shadow. Turning back as she passed, I looked at the back of her lower leg and foot. They were streaked with thick trails of blood. She was cut and bleeding. The color and coppery tang cracked the stillness of the new day. I shuddered. Ivan turned his worried face to me and asked if he should go back and offer her help. I wasn't sure what to do, but when we turned back the girl had disappeared down a side street, and we were alone again.

No buildings were open as we passed through this first village outside Santiago. I could feel the push behind my knees, drawing me forward just a slight bit faster than they had before. Something felt off and unsettling about the trail. I couldn't tell if it was the aftermath of Santiago, the rhythm lost by our rest days or simply this place. Or maybe it was the way the trail no longer comforted me in the face of what awaited me in the empty life I'd left behind.

Moving through a long strip of houses on a wide road, we didn't see a single person or car. The land rose up around a small bit of dull green forest and past the sturdy stone gate of a large estate. I wasn't sure if we were leaving the town or on the outskirts of a new one. I knew the trail from Santiago only went through a few towns and no cities. It was one of the more desolate stretches of the trail. The lack of accommodations pressed pilgrims into logging long days. The town we would enter in the next hour was one of the places pilgrims often stopped, but we hoped to go another two hours beyond it. We turned uphill as trees crowded the sides of the road. All through the morning, the only noises were those of dogs and a few small birds far above our heads.

My breath came thicker and deeper as my quads vaulted me up a steep incline. Suddenly the sky reverberated with a deafening roar. The large boom of a big gun or a plane hitting the sound barrier flooded our ears. Again the noise rained down on us. And then again, causing me to cover my ears. Over and over, it came loud and close, massive in scale. And it didn't sound harmless. With the trees shielding us from all evidence of modern life, it felt like we'd slipped through time and were in the middle of a war. In response, we moved faster. I wondered how our morning could become any more stressful.

The trail followed a side street of derelict houses down into the center of Negreira. We passed row houses where bedraggled women hung wet clothes on long sections of line while children with dirty hands and feet scurried around them. A man with dark slick hair came out from one of the rundown buildings and climbed into his car but not before he turned to stare at us as we drew close. I knew he was looking at me, watching me like a creature in the zoo. I could feel his eyes trailing my every step. Once I passed on the far side of the road, he drove off but continued to stare until his car disappeared out of sight. I released a nervous sigh of relief, and let the boys catch up with me before we moved quickly onward.

The trail had always felt safe, but here it felt shockingly different; the supportive net had evaporated. I was utterly grateful I'd followed my intuition and insisted on walking with the American guys. I had a deep feeling of unease and knew it wouldn't have been safe for me or any woman to walk this section of the trail alone. Even in the turmoil of Santiago, I'd felt clear about my guidance that this section of the trail required backup. I might have been emotionally alone, adrift without my most trusted confidant, but I wasn't physically alone, and when it came to dodging the advances of creepy Spanish men, Jack and Ivan were proving themselves to be essential.

We stopped in a small café, and the boys ordered cocoa. They were convinced the hot drink would help them ease down their breakfast of dry bread. On our last day in Santiago, Jack had decided he and Ivan should eat only bread on the three-day trek to the coast. Jack had purchased twenty pounds from a street vendor at the medieval fair, and it was game on. This notion was another of their schemes of greatness, and they'd informed me it would help in their warrior training and also insure the feast at the end of the trail would be a moment to remember. Alas, after only a day, the dense brown bread had become the enemy, and warrior training had lost its luster.

The guys pushed the bread into their mouths with force, but their throats refused to accept the material. At first, the commitment to the nut and fruit laden loaves had been a great novelty. It had been their very own lembas bread from The Lord of the Rings. Now, it just made them cranky, focused on exactly how they'd worded their pact with Poseidon, because Poseidon was a big player in the scheme. According to Ivan, they couldn't make a plan like this without invoking the gods. He'd felt it was fitting that the contract to eat only bread should be struck with none other than the god of the sea himself. This way, the deal paid homage to heroes of the past as well as the mighty Atlantic coast. But right now, their stomachs had another, more mortal agenda. They were hungry and pining for anything other than the food of the gods. As I sat across from the boys, they cycled through all the many questions that arose from the fine print of their agreement. Were all other foods off limits or was it simply solid food? Could they eat around the nuts and pick out the dried fruit? And was the official end sunset on the third day or sunrise?

The night before our departure from the city, the archetypal pilgrim fuel seemed an excellent choice of trail food. Now as the debate over hot chocolate drinks raged on, most of their breakfast bread lay untouched. I munched on handfuls of cereal but hardly tasted the food. The boys wouldn't have to worry about me ordering gooey bocadillos or chocolate pastries and taunting them with delicious sights and smells. I was through with sugar. I'd even given up tinned peaches. My favorite trail vice had come to an end. My bag had hardly any food in it, and I didn't worry about where the next supply would come from. It felt like an unimportant issue. Everything in my body was hollow except my stomach which was tight and solid as a rock, unwilling to admit much of anything. I was facing my own self-induced plight right alongside the guys. I already felt the echo of Santiago eating away at me, even without a diet of lembas bread.

At first, I didn't expect my lack of fuel to keep me from tackling the long days of nearly forty kilometers. I'd previously walked under similar constraints, but somehow each step sapped more energy than ever before. I'd hoped that with nearly thirty days of walking behind me, I would have an edge, but the departure from Francis and the chaos of Santiago had taken it out of me. Jack was picking the raisins out of his bread, creating a small pile on the table in front of him as Ivan went to the bar to buy a cup of coffee. I changed out of my leggings and felt the warming air coming in from the open door. It was so much easier to have the full mobility that shorts gave, but I worried now about attracting more attention. I felt fragile. In this last leg, I didn't want to be observed by strangers or even by those with whom I was close. That was why Jack and Ivan had been an excellent choice of bodyguards. On the whole, they hardly bothered to observe me at all. At times, it felt like I was walking in the company of my parents' eager golden retrievers. They could spot danger, point the way and keep me company at night, but they weren't going to pry into my psyche.

Even though it was Sunday, Negreira was filled with people, and many of the stores were open. Jack and Ivan darted into a large supermercado with a collective yelp of joy. The boys could buy a few new drinks with which to wash down their daily bread. I bought a small bag of peaches, a few granola bars and some yogurt. This appeared to be the moment to buy whatever supplies we would need for the next few days.

This stretch of the Camino was a land unto itself. It felt strange and off balance. The greater distance between clusters of civilization made me edgy. The only guide we had for these three days was the worn and frayed piece of paper from the pilgrim office in St. Jean. It had lived in my guidebook for many weeks, surviving long enough to act as our only source of information about the trail from Santiago to Fisterra. The sheet had been wrong before and wasn't proving to be much help. In Santiago, we'd been advised to seek out an old school building in a very small town where we could stay for free. A friendly pilgrim who'd just returned from the coast explained that staying there would help break up the stages into three more even parts.

Though most of the pilgrims stayed in the busy town of Negreira, we pressed on to the schoolhouse ten kilometers beyond. It made no sense to stay in Negreira, for as we left the supermercado in the center of town, it was only eleven in the morning. Many more hours of daylight stretched before us. We all knew the social part of our trip had ended in Santiago. There was no point getting to an albergue early so we could have an afternoon off. There was nothing to do with that time now, except wait and hope for nightfall. I was glad I still had a good portion of my book left to read. With a book, I could escape my reality inside and out. Jack and Ivan hadn't brought any books, and I wondered if they longed for something to fill the empty time. In fact, the guys had left their larger packs and most of their belongings with the proprietor of our former abode in Santiago. Our cheerfully efficient hostess at the hostal in Santiago had agreed to store the boy's packs while they traveled to the coast. Jack felt it was important to walk to the ocean as unburdened as possible, hence the logic that one food supply would streamline their lives.

Before leaving town, Ivan and Jack headed down the road to an outdoor market in search of cheap sneakers to wear while running with the bulls in Pamplona. They were on a mission for shoes that would help them burn bright and fast as they ran for their lives. Whether the shoes lived to tell another tale wasn't as important. The sneakers' lives were destined for that sprint and that sprint alone. I followed behind them and watched a local marching band trail through the street to celebrate the town's saint's day.

As I sat down on the edge of the market, Ivan ran back to me. Clutching my arm, he began to shake with laughter. Apparently he and Jack had also been watching the band and noticed a young tuba player who'd been a bit distracted by my presence in the crowd. As the tuba player craned to keep an eye on me he'd stumbled and bumped into the person in front of him, knocking that person forward in a chain reaction that momentarily derailed the whole procession. Ivan found the mishap delightfully entertaining, even as he feared the poor guy would drop his tuba in embarrassment.

As we found our way out of the city, I bought a bag of fresh cherries from a farm stand while Jack gleefully clutched his new pair of shiny white shoes. The day was long and hot. There was vegetation along the trail, but it was brittle and dry, offering no shade and giving the land an unwelcoming feeling. As I walked a few paces ahead of Jack and Ivan, I felt unsettled by the barren and pilgrimless trail. Late in the afternoon, we arrived in a one bar village on a desolate roadway. There wasn't a soul in sight. Dark curtains hung across the windows of the few homes we passed. There were no noises, voices, car engines, dogs barking, nothing. Further down the empty lane, we were thrust onto a wide road with fresh tarmac and glaring yellow lines reaching away into the distance. Built for heavy traffic, it was a road that had nothing to do with this village. It was merely the shortest route from one more important place to another.

We walked down the center of the deserted road, trying to figure out which of the ramshackle buildings was the albergue. I wasn't thrilled to be here for the night, but it was our only option. The next albergue was another twenty kilometers down the trail, and it was now late afternoon. We were stuck here for better or for worse.

I tried to convince myself the albergue would be warm, filled with other pilgrims, a place of refuge from all the strange sights and sounds of the day. As we navigated one last rise in the road, the sun shone in my eyes and was hot on my skin. Suddenly, I felt a small chill run down my arms. A lone building sat on the side of the road with its face turned away from us. The carcass of a rusted swing set stood beside its grey walls. The front yard was no more than packed dirt and sparse tufts of sharp grass charred brown by the relentless sun. The building was two stories with a single row of windows at the top of the first floor. Half the windows were fractured with large cracks running down the length of each pane. A broken sign dangled above the entrance. Though faded, it read albergue. This was the building we were looking for. This was our home for the night.

The abandoned schoolhouse was free of charge. I had a sinking feeling the monetary savings would be the only silver lining, and our night's accommodation would be worth exactly what we paid for it. I followed Jack and Ivan through the entrance into a large room stripped of everything and anything valuable or useful. Thin dingy mattresses stacked in the far corner were the only objects in the hollow room. Later would we discover the mattresses were not only dirty but damp as well. There was no sign-in sheet, no evidence of other pilgrims and no longer a set of stairs to the second story. The stairs were now a heap of broken beams crumbled in the tight stairwell. Flies buzzed against the windowpanes as we placed our things on the floor. Even though there was no one to check us in, we needed to get our passports stamped if we wanted to get our Fisterra Compostelas. The guys suggested we head back into town and find someone who might be able to help us. I wasn't hopeful, but I needed to escape this desolate space. There was still plenty of daylight left in the sky, but the albergue had already fallen into shadow.

The three of us agreed we had time to kill before going to sleep. Up the road we might find something to distract ourselves until dark, or at the very least, someone to stamp our passports. We just needed to get through, survive this night and wake up tomorrow to move on. With a bit of trepidation, we left our packs in the albergue and headed back towards the bar. The first house we passed was clean and freshly painted in a warm shade of blue. Compared with the rest of the village homes, it was grand. Compared to the albergue, it was the Ritz. Soft white curtains fluttered in the windows, and a set of bikes leaned against the sidewall. Even the small gardens out front looked well loved and carefully tended. The place was an anomaly, a mirage that called to weary pilgrims and drew us up its front steps. I knocked and a woman with strands of grey running through her hair, a bright apron around her waist and a pair of muddy boots answered the door. She smiled down at us, and I was flooded with relief to see a kind face in this strange place. She happened to be the very person we were looking for. As soon as I held up my passport, she ran into her kitchen and came back with a stamp and a dark blue inkpad. Her Spanish was thick with a Galician accent, but she smiled between every word. The sleeves of her shirt were rolled up to her elbows, exposing forearms browned and worn from the sun. I could see every line, cut like deep grooves in her palms as she carefully stamped my document. I understood most of what she said, but at one point I felt she was telling me something about the schoolhouse. She leaned in towards me, her eyes turned a darker shade and her voice came out in a low tone. I didn't catch the exact translation of her words, but I got the gist of it. She'd already cheerfully resumed stamping our passports before I could ask her to repeat what she'd said. I felt the creeping chill across the surface of my bare arms again. Her words felt like a warning or perhaps I was imagining things.

In an effort to distract ourselves until nightfall, we walked back to the bar in town. Rafael Nadal was playing Roger Federer in the finals at Wimbledon. Once again we found ourselves amongst Spaniards as they cheered on a national champion. Nadal won the tournament as darkness descended. Back at the schoolhouse, a single florescent bulb hung outside the entrance and flooded the front yard with sickly yellow light. The room was dark, but the floor was now littered with other pilgrims. We stepped over their sleeping forms and crawled into our sleeping bags. I knew the shapes scattered around the room were others just like us, but in the night, they looked like strange corpses. I willed myself not to think about the building or my growing feeling that something haunted this space. I was safe inside my own cocoon. I had to be. My sleeping bag was my first and only line of defense against my childhood fear of the dark and the unknowns of the world. With night fully upon us, the room creaked in a high wind. Gusts battered the frame of the building and whistled through the cracked windows. Currents of air pushed the building in one direction then pulled it back again. The trees along the backside scratched against the rough surface of the walls. The world outside was thick with darkness, rumbling as if possessed while the wind off the ocean blew harsh and antagonistic circles around us.

I lay awake for a long time among the slumbering forms in a space charged with an old and sinister air. Even the natural world outside banged around us in hostility. If I could get there, sleep was the only escape. I curled my arms around my rib cage and buried my head in the folds of my sleeping bag. Eventually sleep came, but when I awoke, the world was still dark. It wasn't yet dawn, but it was time to leave. The guys were awake and as eager to flee this place as I was. I flicked on my flashlight, but everything outside of the beam remained trapped in darkness.

CEE

STAGE TWENTY NINE- 39.1K- 24.3M
VILARSERIO TO CEE

We packed our things in the dark and stepped out into the open air. I sat on the front steps in a daze, looking out beyond the florescent light into the empty morning. Mercifully the wind had calmed in the last few hours, but the rusty swing set still creaked in a slight breeze. I choked down a few bites of food while Ivan and Jack washed down their lembas bread with a bit of water. It wasn't unusual to start walking before the sun rose, but today the forty kilometers weighed heavily upon us. The tone was set, and the day hadn't even begun.

I stepped onto the dark roadway and turned west towards the sea. A hearty slice of the waning moon was out, and once our eyes adjusted, we didn't need flashlights to guide us. Trees cut black shadows on the roadway and whispered into the air. We didn't worry about cars because their noise and lights would alert us long before they came upon us. I walked ahead of the guys on the centerline, tracing its slightly florescent glow with my feet. The stars lay across the sky in blooming clusters. Some stood bright and solitary. The Milky Way hung on the arcing panorama above our heads.

I breathed in rhythm with my footfall but couldn't shake the feeling I was being stalked. Though I was glad to have Jack and Ivan near, it was what lay beyond our circle that worried me. What lay in the shadows. What lay in the unknown. I chewed anxiously at the strap of my backpack and felt my hands growing stiff and cold in the exposed air. A shooting star lit the sky in front of me and fell away towards the western horizon.

We followed the main road for an hour and arrived at a four-way intersection. The only way to find the arrows in the dark was with my flashlight. We tried to guess where we might find the next marker, noting how long it had been since we'd seen the last one. The arrows on the trail from Santiago to Fisterra were proving less consistent than on rest of the trail. I wondered if we'd bitten off more than we could chew by starting in the dark. At the crossroads without an arrow in sight, I felt my heart sink. There were no clues, no hints, nothing. I swung my flashlight to the left and right but felt no closer to an answer about the way forward. All we had was Ivan's compass to guide us west. After several minutes, we choose the road bearing left, hoping it would keep curving westward. The road was wide but empty. Its painted lines stretched off into the distance. There were no houses, no signs and no lights.

I hunted in the dark for any clue we'd picked the right path. It felt utterly demoralizing to be lost. I scanned the scrub on the side of the road for a stone way marker and traced the beam of my flashlight over the surface of the road. Jack and Ivan trailed behind me.

Then in an instant the quiet was shattered and the dark broken as a set of blinding lights rushed up over the crest of the road. Two glaring yellow beams attached to a giant metal beast were coming directly at me, about to crush me. I threw myself into a ditch on the side of the road and felt the earth shake as several tons of metal screamed past me at lightning speed. Once the ground steadied, I gathered my shaking limbs and stood up. With my adrenaline pumping, I ran back towards the boys, panicked they might not have seen the truck in time. It only took a few seconds to close the distance between us, and I knew from the easy tone of their voices cutting through the stillness that they were fine. More so than myself. They'd stopped by the side of the road to rest and hadn't been anywhere near the thundering machine. As my breathing calmed, we agreed this road was wrong. It had been too long without corroborative arrows, and now it was taking us east not west. With weary steps, we turned back towards the intersection and arrived at the crossing disheartened. Though the sky was growing lighter, we still couldn't find any clues about the way forward. I didn't want to spend more time following threads in the wrong direction, but that's all we could do, for as always, going back was simply not an option.

On our second guess, we chose straight ahead along a smaller dirt road that also had a westward bent. I was encouraged by its direction but only for about twenty minutes. There were still no yellow arrows even when the road came to another T. We'd taken the wrong road once again. Ivan suggested we stop searching for the trail but go west towards the cluster of homes we could see in the distance. From there, we could gather directions and reconnect with the trail. Between us and the cluster of houses lay a series of smaller roads bisecting endless fields. They were little more than narrow lanes used for farm equipment arranged like a spider web looping around us. We couldn't know what would lead us through to the houses in the distance and what would terminate in the lost land in between. As was my habit, I walked ahead of the boys, always eager to resolve the unknowns as quickly as possible.

I followed a rutted farm lane, climbed over a barbed wire fence and glanced back to make sure Ivan and Jack were still in sight. They were there, slowly ambling along unworried by our current state of affairs. I had a suddenly flash of envy at how relaxed they were no matter what came at us. Up ahead, I could see a mass blocking the trail. At first, I thought it was a large grove of trees, but as I drew closer, I realized it was a hedgerow arcing over the path to form a tunnel. I moved in and under the edge of the tree canopy. As I went deeper the new light in the sky vanished. Under the wings of the trees, it was still the darkest night. I expected it to be a tunnel with an entrance and an exit, but once in the middle, the space branched out in several directions. It was a living, breathing maze in the middle of ordinary farmland. Each pathway led away from the center with equal width and authority. Caught up in the enchantment of the space, I spun around several times before I realized what I'd done. I'd lost the bead on where I'd come from. I had no idea which way was forward and which way was back. Rooted to the ground, I reached for my flashlight, but the bulb flickered and went out. After weeks of inconsequential use, the batteries had died. The dark clustered around me, and I knew this was the bottom. I was lost.

I'd worked so hard to protect myself from this very moment and yet here I was. In this dark lost place, everything revealed itself as still broken. All I wanted to do was curl up in a ball and be lifted homeward. My shattered hopes, so long strapped down below the surface of my skin, rose into the space around me. In this place, I had nothing of the dream that had brought me to Spain and carried me across the length of this trail.

What was worse than being lost in the endless maze of fields in an unknown land? Knowing I'd lost so much along the way. Some of the loss had been cleansing, a washing away of the past, but other pieces had been harder to part with. Other people had been harder to let go. Breaking free of the men of my past was profound, but necessary, liberating even. But letting go of Francis and my trail community was devastating, and I suddenly felt as if I'd nothing to show for my journey. I was empty handed. Part of me feared I'd abandoned my own cause of finding love and connection, but most of me knew Francis was never going to be mine to have. When I'd signed on for this trip, scrawled my name on the cosmic consent form, I'd feared this place the most, the darkness and the emptiness of being alone.

I worried I'd lost my way and lost my dream of this trail. Even though the trail had given me gifts without measure and set me free, I could no longer feel the pulse of my dream at the end of the world. Everybody wants to be cured of past broken hearts, released of guilt and shame, doubt and sorrow, but no one wants the story to end with just a healing. I didn't want my tale to simply end with me having recovered from the wasting sickness of past romances and tortured love affairs; I wanted it to end with the new. I wanted it to end with love. But I was alone in the dark. I felt my reserve of blind hope about the Camino slipping away and draining into the earth. What was recovery and the repairing of the past, if it didn't guide me into the joy and expansion of the next chapter? Had the universe and God drawn me to this growth accelerator and detoxifying pathway with a baited hook? What had become of the end of the world and where did Francis fit in the puzzle? I felt he was still with me at times, and then like awaking from a dream, I would remember our parting. I would remember we'd broken apart, that he had told me he didn't love me and let me walk away. I wanted to see, and yet there was no light, no answers or arrows pointing the way forward. Everything was still. I waited. All I could do was wait and listen. Wait and listen; they were my old friends now, hard won and battle tested allies in this journey, and they would get me out of here. I hoped.

The emptiness crashed around me like waves. Time passed. It might have been a few minutes or a few hours, but all of a sudden, out of the silence, I heard a voice. And the voice was calling my name. The voice drew closer and closer, then Ivan appeared at the mouth of the tunnel, calling me out of the dark. I felt my legs move towards him, out of the shadows and into the light.

Bearing west, we walked the pathways for another hour. In the daylight, a rainbow arced through the sky as we crested a hill. The farm trails ended, and a road lay beside the field. A town sat to our left, unmarked by arrows. Maybe we could bang on doors to find out where we were. We flagged down a sleepy eyed man on his way to work and asked him where the Camino was. He told us it was just a few minutes up the road and clearly marked. It turned out we were never as lost as we'd believed. We'd been running parallel to the trail the whole morning, cutting our own way. I wanted to believe this was true of my own life. Maybe I was running parallel to the answers and the fresh starts. All I had to do was step over into their flow.

In the afternoon as we approached the sea, black scrub filled the terrain around the trail. Finally, I stood at the crest of dry land, opened my eyes wide against the glare of the day and looked out over our first view of water. The sky broke into two layers of blue. The top blue was deep and free of clouds and the bottom was the sea. It could have been a trick of the eyes or the sky, but it wasn't. It was the rough seas of the Atlantic breaking against the Costa Muerte. It was our first sight of the Coast of death and a glimmering preview of the very body of water that would terminate our Camino in little over a day. In all my time on the trail with land pirates and warriors in training, I'd felt the sea calling us forward, yet to finally look upon it meant the end. For so many weeks, I'd been unprepared for this moment, unsure if I wanted the stolen season of Camino life to close, but now I was itching to end the physical march for my journey as a pilgrim seemed to have already vanished.

As I looked over land to the sea, the weeks I'd lived on another west coast came rushing back to me. During the summer before my senior year in college, I'd gone to Ireland to live in the wilds of the west coast among cousins. I'd spent my days walking to the edges of land and sea. I'd sat on wide beaches covered in worn stones and had waited for the rain to stop or to start or to do both over and over again in endless loops.

One of my elderly Irish cousins had told me he'd once saved a boy's life on a Connemara beach. He'd plucked the boy from the water as his mother watched from shore because neither mother nor child could swim. My cousin had explained they were following in a long line of sea people who didn't learn how to fight the pull of the water even though they lived on an island. To the modern mind it was inconceivable, but sailors and pirates had long been wary of learning to swim. The reasoning behind this choice had more common sense than a lack of it. Historically these men didn't learn to swim, because more often than not, if they went overboard the ship wouldn't come round for them. No rescue was possible. Knowing how to swim only delayed the death that was now their fate. If one's fate was set once one plummeted into the icy waters, was learning to resist just prolonging the struggle of what was destined to come?

Had we all been pushed around by the mighty winds of the trail and tossed over the edge or was it just me? Was I the only one fighting to stay afloat and connected to a dream at the end of the world? I didn't know if I had any struggle left in me.

I looked across the bay to the white smudge in the distance that was the lighthouse marking the end at Fisterra. I wondered what would happen if I stopped wrestling with my fear of this moment? What would the end feel like if I let its current take me and faced the stillness of the choices that had guided me here? What if I could know that each choice to draw close or break away was the right one? Was the chaos and darkness in this stretch of trail an aftershock of a poor choice? Was this like Sahagún only on a much bigger scale? Or was this shadowy leg of the journey some sort of threshold guardian I had to push through in order to finish the quest I'd begun so many weeks ago? If I kept my eyes on the sea, would I find my course again and reach the real ending in the wake of the false ends of Santiago?

We arrived in Cee near the end of siesta. It was the last night we would spend on the trail. We were all weary and covered in a chalky layer of dirt that clung to our skin. I almost lost the guys in the streets of Cee as we hunted down a place to sleep. Their company was my last element of comfort. I wasn't sure if I could have held it together if we'd lost track of each other. If I was destined to face the end on my own, I still wanted to stick close to these guys until the last kilometer. Maybe then it would be an easier moment to bear.

The albergue was really no albergue at all. It was the basement locker room of the local high school. Two flights down, the space was strewn with hard black gym mats. The room smelled strongly of cleaning supplies and had only three tiny windows to the sky. It was another free night's stay, but after sleeping in the haunted albergue, I would have shelled out a few euro for better accommodations. Unfortunately, Cee didn't have any other pilgrim albergues, and the guys seemed excited to have another economically beneficial night's lodging. I was too tired to argue.

There were several other pilgrims who also unwittingly wandered into the school in search of a place to stay including a group of three South Africans and two German guys. Both groups seemed equally unsure of the albergue but were just as tired as the rest of us. At this point in the journey, it was easy to see why we'd all resigned ourselves to what the fates offered up. The trail from Santiago to the coast was notorious for emotional complexity and grueling days. She was certainly living up to her billing.

Technically, we weren't in our final day of walking, but as night fell, Jack and Ivan abandoned the last rock hard chunk of lembas bread by flinging it into the sea as a gift for Poseidon. They told me this was in honor of the last night on the trail and assured me they had lived up to their pact with the gods. After the ritual, they treated themselves to a restaurant feast that included a pile of lamb kebabs and multiple ice cream cones in a variety of flavors.

We sat in a daze outside the restaurant. My brain was foggy due to weariness and disbelief about what tomorrow meant. Jack and Ivan's semi-coma was likely attributed to the enormous dinner and its sedative effect. I hadn't seen them so happy in days. Finally we returned to the basement to sleep on the hard mats among strangers. Since Santiago, the other pilgrims had come to feel like strangers. No one spoke to people outside their group, and everyone was closed off in their own world. I tried to be friendly, but nobody rose to the bait. All sense of community had vanished as we hovered at the edge of the end.

After a night underground, we rose in the early light of day and walked through Cee. We moved up and away until we crested a mountain into the next bay where our hazy destination sat in the distance. Fisterra was only eleven kilometers from where my feet stood. The morning turned hot, and Ivan walked shirtless. My legs were sore and each step weighted. The ground seemed to suck me backwards. It took all my concentration to keep plodding onward. We all suffered from the energetic quicksand that made every movement towards our destination more and more of an effort. We were in the home stretch of a very long race, and it caught each of us like weights around our legs and lungs.

Even though this day was a very short one, it felt longer than my fifty-kilometer day to Burgos. The emotional toll of dragging myself to the end far outweighed any other factors. My pack was heavier than ever before. I walked a few paces ahead of the boys, and there was little talking. We passed a fisherman gutting his morning's catch while a swarm of cats hovered around the scraps, and an old women in a kerchief beat a rug on her front stoop. We'd been walking for two hours and hadn't seen a single pilgrim. The smell of the sea grew stronger, and the wind took on a salty bite. The breeze hit my face in gusts as it rolled off the open water from the south. The sea was steely blue and glinted with the promise of cold depths.

I'd seen this ending for many years in my imagination. Long before I'd even heard about the trail, I dreamt of the end of the world and followed her scent through a series of radical changes in my early adulthood. The image of this ever shifting place was my most powerful ally, but I'd never met her in waking life like this. We'd never arranged such a dramatic rendezvous, and I didn't know what would come of meeting a dream I'd cherished for so many years. Was I prepared or had I lost something or someone precious along the way that would reveal an emptiness when I arrived? This moment under my feet was one of uncharted waters, and so like an insecure lover, I both feared and longed for reunion.

We turned off the main road and went up through a forested stretch of land. The trees had been burnt to their roots, and everything was covered in dark soot. The landscape was stark and unforgiving. The sea had shaped it into a hard form, and it was nothing like the interior wilds of Galicia. This felt like land unfit for human life. Nothing soft and nurturing, just the consistent push of wind and water fighting us, battling our physical limits at every turn. And this was where I would arrive at the end of the land, the end of the trail and the end of the world.

FISTERRA

STAGE THIRTY- 15.7K- 9.8M
CEE TO FISTERRA

After we left the burnt forests, the trail became very straight. It appeared to lead us into the sky then suddenly the path crested and before us lay a curved bay with white beaches and a tightly packed village. The lighthouse at Fisterra rested on a spit of mountainous land high above the town. We would have to go down to sea level then climb up again to the last way marker. The beaches into Fisterra were long empty strips of pale sand. Not a single person could be seen in the perfect white arcs, and nobody swam in the rough waters. Concrete breakers divided the beach, and boats bobbed on their moorings. With the boys still a few paces behind me, I climbed up into the guts of the village, my eyes always on the lighthouse in the distance.

Fisterra was like many of the other large towns we'd passed through. The only marked difference was its proximity to the water. Cutting across it, we made a direct line for the lighthouse, three kilometers beyond the town. The lighthouse was only accessible by a busy roadway that twisted up the mountainside. As we navigated the steep incline, we shared the space with speeding cars and bulky camper vehicles. It was disheartening to know they would all be with us when we arrived. Cresting the incline, the lighthouse beckoned us in.

The building was large and angular with smooth white walls and a glass tower housing the light itself. The three of us left the road, crossed the parking lot and pushed our way through the raucous midday crowd at the base of the lighthouse. We didn't speak but moved with purpose to the way marker that stood ahead. I arrived at the bleached stone pillar first and bent down to confirm what my eyes could hardly believe. I'd seen hundreds of these stone markers along the way. Everything was familiar, except the numbers. They read 0.0 kilometers. This was the end.

There wasn't a cloud in the wide blue sky. The ocean rumbled against the cliff below the lighthouse. All the noise around me merged into a cacophony of nothingness. After glancing at the way marker, Ivan and Jack left me and went down to the water. It was time to cast their walking sticks into the ocean and share their moment of triumphant glory with each other. I watched them disappear down the side of the ragged cliff, and then I was alone.

People flooded around me. Chatting, laughing, chasing after their children, posing for photos and moving to and fro aimlessly. I stumbled back against the low wall around the lighthouse and lay my bag next to me. I drew my legs to my chest, let my head tuck into the space between my knees and closed out the sunlight. I was hemorrhaging numbness. I wanted to feel connected to the breadth and depth of the journey, to be filled with a rush of energy and understanding, but I only felt empty and alone. I could feel the trail fading within me. She was the last constant to abandon me and take the dream with her. I was powerless to stop this arrival, powerless to hold onto those I'd loved along the way and unable to locate the heartbeat of my dream at the end of the world. I'd been nurturing and fostering the promise of love and community for the length of this mighty trail, but now I worried I'd miscarried in the final steps. The end of the world was under me, above me in arching light and rumbling in liquid motion against the land. Suddenly I felt terribly sick as if everything was contracting. My body was in revolt. And just like that, stars blanketed the back of my eyes. Then all was still and dark.

Once during my early days as a dancer, I'd passed out in class. During the seconds I left consciousness, I'd dreamed I'd stayed in bed and hadn't gone to class. I'd taken solace in the illusion until I'd awoken a minute later to find my classmates huddled over me, welcoming me back to reality. I'd never disappeared like that before.

I didn't dream in the unconsciousness that crashed upon me as I leaned against the lighthouse at the end of the trail. I simply fell into the light. It embraced every cell and flooded through the memory of every step. It washed clean every muscle, restored every breath and tended to every question. It was the same light that had visited me in the dream for the past few years and the very same light that had flooded through me in San Xulián. Suddenly I knew it was this light that had brought me here.

I'd followed the dream to this very moment and was now swept up and above it all, drawn into the embrace of an aerial truth. All that had appeared disjointed and fragmented suddenly had flow and rhythm, purpose and direction. I could feel my heart absorb the truth of the plan without question. I suddenly trusted everything that had been and all that would come. I was overwhelmed with the destiny of all events on this trail, understanding that both the good and bad were essential to the journey. No false step had been wrong, and no wrenching parting had been a failure of heart. The light had drawn me onward along the trail, leaving not a single cell untouched. I was meant to feel the wholeness of the trail, her cruelty and her benevolence, her loneliness and her community. Each piece had helped to free me from the past and guide me forward. The trail was an indivisible thread of the universe, a small-scale version of our bigger lives, and I knew I'd done her justice even in all my humanness.

It had been wrenching and painful to stumble around in loneliness, fall prey to injury and eventually have to leave the love I felt for Francis, but such trials were not in vain. As I'd parted ways with Francis in Santiago, I'd been acting from a deeper instinct, a power cultivated over the length of the trail, an insistence on an essential truth that in the past, I'd denied myself. I'd walked away from a beautiful but fragmented love because it promised to erode my wholeness.

I'd protected myself in the most profound way, and buoyed on the current of this trail, I'd found the strength to trust my move. I'd stumbled to this final way marker carrying shame and blame about being alone like weighted stones around my chest, but I was wrong. To have stayed with Francis and walked here in our divided relationship would have been the weaker choice, the scared and broken choice. A choice I'd made many times before.

Yes, I feared being alone, but now I feared it less. What I really feared was the compromise, the parts of me I would have to sacrifice to be in community and be loved by those who didn't embrace all of me. The Camino had given me back my totality, challenging me for it at every turn. Told me I would have love but had to be intact to find it, know it and absorb it. She'd rekindled my sense of myself as whole and placed me in situations that would threaten to shatter it. She'd given me the gift of myself back after so many wounded years, and in the same instant, she called me to defend the integrity of my heart. How could I know all this training wasn't leading me toward love and family? How could I know that it wasn't the soul boot camp I needed in order to be ready for whomever was coming towards me? How could I know I wasn't on the right path; the path that had always been leading me forward?

I felt the current of light rush through me again and again and knew I wasn't at the end alone. That was the gift of the light; it filled everything inside me, spilling out of my skin, soaking into the ground, air and breath. There was too much energy, too strong a sense of belonging and oneness with this moment for loneliness to win. If I let the surface dictate my emotions and my view of my life, then I might always miss what was really flowing through it. In the microcosm of this place and my life, I was far from alone. I felt myself shedding all the layers of belief that divided me from the land, the weather, the people and the energy around me. I even felt the light cross the edges of time and blur the present into something deeper, more expansive, something that included a view of love. It made time disappear all together, and I could feel beautiful things yet to come pressed around me and fill my body.

I just had to trust. This was the coast of death, and it had brought me to the death of many things, but things were born as well. I knew now that I'd walked all the way to the end of the world because it had been the way forward on my trek as a soul. It hadn't been a painless comfortable road or a road of guarantees, but it had been the road my guidance and link to the divine had called me to take. I hadn't come for outer rewards or because it had been easy. I'd survived the trail and not just because I'd signed on, but because I'd fought for it. I'd thrown my body into the instructions, embraced the sweat and the tears. I hadn't taken on this challenge half-heartedly for I'd needed my whole heart to make it to this very spot. When it came down to it, I'd been willing to place all my trust in the universe even when I hadn't known what would become of me. I'd surrendered to the divine current of my destiny. I'd lived it imperfectly and with my fair share of mistakes, but I'd shown up.

Now the trail was turning, shifting like the wind, redirecting my course to another end of the world. Perhaps the dream was less a spot in my life that I was moving towards and more of a string of moments along an unending thread. Maybe I wasn't leaving the Camino behind, maybe I didn't have to part with my beloved companion and dearest of mentors just because our physical tryst was through. Maybe I'd become this waking dream, and no matter what lay forward, she would be part of me.

I awoke with a start. I didn't know how much time had elapsed or where I'd gone. No one had noticed my dip into unconsciousness, and I felt sleepy and warm. I'd been still all the way to my core and come to a truce with this moment, this end of the world. Suddenly I knew it was time to go. This part of the journey was done.

Standing on wobbling legs. I turned from the lighthouse and walked down the mountain without looking back. Now my compass pointed me homeward. The hand didn't waver.

THE RETURN

I spent my last night on the trail in a municipal albergue in Fisterra. When I arrived, the Hungarian Actress and her Lover boy were cooking pasta in the kitchen together. He smiled as he told me they were going on to Barcelona tomorrow. Together. Finally together. Their journey was only changing venues, becoming deeper and intertwining in a way the Lover boy had always longed for.

The next morning as Jack, Ivan and I sat on a bench in the center of Fisterra, a bright red sports car pulled up to the curb. A young very attractive woman in a short skirt climbed out of the passenger seat. And in one swift movement, the Cowboy himself emerged out the driver's side door. With a wide grin on his face, he noticed me and came over to say hello. I asked him where his horse was, and his face dropped.

"I had to shoot him." he said sadly, his eyes dark and his bushy eyebrows drawn. My breath caught, and I stood in horrified silence. I felt like I was going to throw up.

The Cowboy turned away from me, waited a half a second, then turned back to declare it was a joke, and the horse was fine. He'd left Fernan back in the stables outside of Santiago. As the Cowboy took off with his arm around his new companion, I realized he was moving on too. Changing gears, meeting hot young things and trading the sturdy feet of his horse for a sexier mode of transport. At this point, nothing surprised me.

I called my parents and arranged my flights back to the states. I would take a bus back to Santiago, spend the evening there and travel home the following day. It was Tuesday. I would arrive at my parent's farm by Thursday night. So much distance to be covered, but this was my path forward now. I resettled myself on the bench and resumed my wait for the bus, a bus that would make us all seasick after more than a month on foot. It would deliver us back along the path we'd traversed. I would be drawn backwards at warp speed, first with Jack and Ivan then on my own.

The guys and I said our goodbyes in Santiago. It was the last and the gentlest in a long string of farewells. They were off to catch a series of trains to Pamplona. Ivan hugged me with genuine warmth, and Jack looked restless as if he were already thinking about their next adventure with the bulls. They set off side by side and left me on my own. I waved to them until they were lost in the crowds streaming through the narrow streets.

I sat beside a fellow American pilgrim on the flight out of Santiago to the

UK. Also in her twenties, she was a mid-westerner living in London who relished the chance to talk shop about the trail. She'd traveled in a raucous group of thirty something men who club hopped their way down the trail, camping in tents. Hers had been a vastly different Camino than my own, but we did share one common thread; an adoration, delight and slight unhealthy addiction to the dream of Camino love.

Despite our divergent trails, the American gave me a gift as we parted at Stanstead. In keeping with the generous spirit of the Camino, she helped me navigate the airport and find the connecting bus to Heathrow. As I hugged my new trail acquaintance goodbye, ever so grateful for her helping hand, I wished her luck. She turned to walk away then stopped. Coming back, she gave me her name and email so we could be in touch.

"Don't worry," she said, "Hey, your journey isn't over, maybe your Camino Love is still out there just up ahead."

Even though she was a stranger, a passing traveler on my path, I felt her words rush through me and gift me with something akin to hope

Hours later, I thanked the security officer as he stamped my passport in Boston and welcomed me back home. My parents rushed towards me outside the gate and wrapped their arms around me, pack and all. I slept that night out under a familiar sky but rose early and looked east, waiting for the light from Spain to reach me. Finally the sun appeared from the direction of the land that was now behind me. I was back. Back to a world unchanged but with a body and heart so altered.

I found myself still on the Camino. The memory of my Camino loves and my love of the Camino clung to me as if it were woven into my skin. Even after the end of our physical romance, I still believed in the tenacity of the love born on those hot summer days. It had proved itself to be resilient and powerful like an inexhaustible current, fueling my feet and my thoughts well into the winter months, long after I'd returned to the normal rhythm of everyday life. In stillness, I began to write. To write of the trail, sift through each moment and draw forward all the deep threads of connection. I wrote into the night until my eyes blurred with sleep. I woke before dawn, scribbling notes to myself in the half light. My dreams filled with images and characters from the Camino. With every word, I drew closer to understanding where my path had come from. I even started to gather fresh clues as to where it might lead. The stories of the trail unraveled from within me and I found Francis there too along with the memories and the last remains of our story.

ONE YEAR LATER

DEAR CAMINO ONE

A GOODBYE LETTER

Did you know I was coming back? It was late spring before I dared to dream of a reunion. I hoped it would be OK to just show up at your door as I'd done a year before. To see you again was the recovery of a dream long dormant, buried beneath layers of well thumbed memories and winter tides. I wanted nothing more than to come back to you dear Camino, after our year apart.

I hoped you would be just as I remembered you, but I also hoped you would meet me full of new promise. I hoped even after a year's absence, you would have the same familiar tone to your voice and that easy way of making me feel at home. I hoped you would still have sway over me, cover my skin in shivers, drench my muscles in sweet exhaustion and encircle my every surface with endless hours of golden touch. But I am shy, and you are vast. Maybe I should have known you would be changed, maybe even I would be changed. Perhaps I should have understood that I would find us both inexplicably altered and that I could never really return to you.

I must confide that among all the change, I did find echoes of our history. I found that community again. I bumped into the six of them in the streets of Sarria. Their backs were turned inward around a large table under the wide wings of an umbrella. The blond one at the head of the table wore a silvery scarf around the crown of her head and rested her elbows on the edges of her chair as if it were a throne. The group swiveled in their seats to catch every laugh that fell from her wide lips while the unshaven German ordered another round of beers. The group was done walking for the day. No packs lay nearby, and the only sign they were pilgrims was the thin guidebook a tall girl with dark hair held between her slender hands while she addressed the group in a voice that drew all eyes to her. I could see from several paces away that she was the one in control.

None of them looked up as I passed like an unseen spectator, slipping down the street and away from their pilgrimage. I'd heard Camino gossip about them several days before. I'd learned they were young and exciting, international and uber cool, but one glance was all it took to see it was them again.

Maybe now they were older, no longer satisfied with salads in the park and eighty-nine cent Rioja reds. Maybe this year they were ruled by a set of blond Norwegians instead of lively Brits, and the scruffy lovelorn and utterly enraptured boys had come from Brazil and Switzerland rather than by foot from northern Europe, but I remembered them all the same. It was the six of them as tight and thick as iron. I knew I could stop, introduce myself and try to belong. I could try once more to prove something or force entrance into their circle, but after a moment's hesitation and with the heat of siesta hours descending, I suddenly knew my days as a locksmith were done, so I walked on.

And the rogue was there too, striding into town in the last stages of the trail, his impossibly long legs eating the distance with magnificent ease. His face was tipped down as he walked up to where I sat in a gaggle of pilgrims. Like that night in Astorga, he lifted his eyes and scanned the group, tilting his head slightly and flipping back his dark brown locks for maximum effect. He was in search of someone to listen, on the hunt for someone to adore him.

I remembered him in soft faded shirts and thick-soled boots, but today he was wearing all white. The linen shirt and pants formed one seamless line, adding to an aura that suggested he was something holy, something purely pilgrim. When he draped himself on the wall across from me, one knee bent while reclining like a swimsuit model, he spoke with a smooth confidence. He hadn't been on the road for two years and didn't have a pack full of papal documents, but it was him all the same. The long narratives, the endless tributaries of his own story and all the dreams of future greatness; they were still there. Now home wasn't down under but down over in South America, and the dream was a Camino of his very own on his native soil. But once again, any heart to fall for him would have to board his dreams and hold on for the ride. The sun grew hotter, and his liquid eyes sought anything to grab on to. They wanted affection, and they craved adoration even if only for a moment.

But I remembered the end of us just a year before, and the pull was gone. My rampant desire to cross the road and slide onto the wall next to him, to listen and believe in his dreams had evaporated. Suddenly he was harmless. Even his handsome face was inconsequential. The beauty that echoed a dancer from my past was swept aside. I no longer chased him or his kind, no longer felt drawn to his ever-forward pace, even when the alternative was to wait alone and let him stride out of town. I was too attached to the parts of me he would have demanded I leave behind to move to Peru or Australia, to make a trail from his faith or live on a cattle ranch on the far side of the world. Loving him would entail the death of too much: the dreams of my life, the marrow of my faith and the roots of everything essential in me.

And the lost boys. They were there too, pacing around in circles with fifty pounds on their backs, being hunted by what lay beneath their boredom and consuming experiences like trading cards. Always collecting but never knowing. They were there spinning non-truths and letting sweet girls be led on about love. But this time the sweet girl wasn't me, and I stood out of the way as they prowled wildly up and down the length of the trail, moving like ones possessed. I wasn't drawn in by their boyish good looks or how such facades allowed them to hide from themselves.

When they finally took off, kicking dust as they fled, I was relieved to see them go, relieved to know they no longer had any place in my life. Their toxic circles cut grooves into anyone who cared for them but had no effect on me now. I was finally free, so free I no longer worried I would try and love a lost boy ever again. By meeting with them once more, I knew the pattern was dead. Everything that ever drew me to their trauma clusters was long extinguished and in its place was a clear view, a lightness and strength. I knew as they ran away from our group on the side of the mountains that I would never again get caught in the cross fire of their retreat from the truth.

And my lost love, he was there too. Even though Francis said he wouldn't come back with me for round two, he was there. He'd written me letters in the winter months and sent sprigs of lavender in the spring. He'd told me once again that he loved me but couldn't be with me. He loved me but couldn't be in love with me. I'd beseeched him to return to the trail with me, and he'd refused.

Yet he was with me all the same. And one morning, days into my return journey, I knew it was time to write him one last letter. I left the sleep drenched albergue in the early darkness and stepped onto a straight and empty trail. My words were less clear. I still wore the same blue pack on my shoulders and worn banana around my throat. He'd known me in those colors, desired me in those colors. He'd seen them in every shade of light. I'd ached for him in those colors. We'd been here before under skies stitched to the edges of land. We'd collided and diverted along this road. We'd sought intimacy and distance in the moments of wayfaring. We'd been alone in vast lands of endless sky and in nooks of grass and stone where nothing existed beyond the span of our touch. But now, moving alone on the trail we'd both known, I wrote to him out loud in a voice I hoped would carry across the space between us.

I wrote him every word unsaid. I told him of crossing the land we'd walked together. Of how I'd traced back through the lush trailside nooks of fresh grass, hoping they would be just as we'd left them. I told him I'd found those places on the edges of the trail bright and harsh, clogged with dust and forgotten by all who passed. Our fingerprints were no longer there, and no ring of grass swirled out from the center bent under the circle we formed together. The seeds of the tart apples we'd eaten hadn't lived on, and the tree that had given such remembered shade was frail and near death.

I wrote to ask him why he'd acknowledged the love between us but had withdrawn at its growing pulse. As I passed the way markers of us, no one noticed my eyes were thick with the past. I was the only keeper of the memory of us, and I wanted to leave it there, release the memories to the Camino like a stone I was unable to carry anymore. But I couldn't. It was too sad a burial place for a thing of such beauty. So I'd tucked it away in my pack and had gone on.

Dear beguiling Camino, it was only as I walked you again that I knew I'd be the one he'll always regret. There was light in what you gave us, love to be nurtured and a life to be made. This second time, I could see my love had never been the flawed element. The flaw was in the person I'd loved and his inability to trust what you gave him along your pathway.

In the months before I returned to you, his letters had trailed off, and finally he'd delivered one last missive, shaped like a blade. Its purpose had been to cut all ties of love between us, step off the Camino and away from me for good. Unlike all the words that had passed between us before, these had engendered no compassion or kindness in me, for they hadn't been made of such things. He'd meant this blade to cut us apart in one fell swoop. And it had done the job. We would never be. We would never be friends or lovers even though we'd had the ingredients in us for both. I'd mourned the death again on my side of the ocean as the sting of his words had crackled across the wide sea. He'd called me crazy for following the pulse of our bond; now I knew I would be crazy to ever again give him the precious resources of my heart.

On the empty morning trail I exhausted what remained of the ache, saying everything I might never get a chance to say, waiting until the words dried up and ceased to flow. I paused for silence to slip down into my lungs and nestle against my heart. Writing him an honest letter from afar, dropping it into empty air and knowing he might never hold the energy of its delicate scrawl was an imperfect way forward, but it was the only choice he'd given me. To write to him along the road cluttered with the memory of us was the best way to speak my peace to a vanishing bond. It was the only way to say goodbye when he refused to walk with me again. It was the only way to say goodbye to a love abandoned into my charge. It was now mine to mourn, mine to resolve and mine to finally bury in Spanish soil and walk away from.

With the light awaking the edges of my skin and the sky ripening behind me, I sealed the letter. I sealed all the untidy moments of loss, failed attempts at bestowing him with love and the cold ends he'd brought to us with a few silent breaths. And then I mailed it with no return address.

As for the girl who went on a quest empty handed, got lost, grew up and eventually found her way forward, she was there too. I saw her striding past me in the early morning, tuning out all the sound around her while pushing each and every muscle to its last fiber. Her sneakers were encrusted in layers of dusty mud; varying shades marked how each day had nearly swallowed her whole. I saw her eating on the run, and when she looked me in the eye, I saw the hungry way she was searching for something.

I saw her in the park desperately trying to scoot herself into the inner circle of a group, and I saw her sitting with a young man on a crumbling stoop in a deserted town. I saw her try to ignore the way he'd let her close but never let her in. I watched her hunt for the scent of love along the edges of the trail out of town. Now this second time round, I turned back into the oasis of green lawns and flowers in bloom. I sipped my tea, settled deeper into my new pilgrim skin and watched her run off and away.

No one else in my group noticed the young girl on overdrive. Maybe I was the only one who saw her. Maybe I was the only one who knew that she ate while walking and gave herself stomachaches from chocolate when she finally allowed herself a bit of sustenance. I even saw her wandering through the streets of Mansilla with a forlorn look in her eyes, wondering how she could have found herself on the outside of yet another group. I saw her bent over distance charts each night, counting the number of kilometers with obsessive drive, calculating and recalculating the time and space to be crossed, trying to pull the end closer while also holding it at bay.

And I saw the profound hunger. The aching hollow below her ribs that drove her to find love and pushed her aching body to cross fifty kilometer stretches in one arc of daylight. I saw her running in the dark hours before sunrise. I saw her dash through herds of fellow pilgrims and even felt her brush by me. Once she looked back at me and straight into my eyes. My face softened, and I craved to drawn her close, pull her into a deep embrace. To kiss her forehead and hold her. I longed to hold her for I knew that was all she wanted: to be held. Held without restraint or judgment, pity or possessiveness, just be held by arms that loved her.

But she fled, slipped away into the past, and I did not join her. I knew her and understood her every move, but I wouldn't go back. The year had been too long, too deep a scouring for me to ever go back. So I let her run on by and fade until she was nothing more than a ghost only I could see. I knew she had lived here once, crossed open plains, sat on dusty benches and curled up tight in lofted bunks, but I was no longer her. And this trail had welcomed me back anew, as if it could hardly recall the way I'd once been. As if I was a new pilgrim to her shores.

DEAR CAMINO TWO
A LOVE LETTER

I didn't recognize you at first. I watched from a distance and tried to see if we belonged together. I knew you had potential when a hundred vultures circled over my head on the very first day and that night I found myself taking refuge on the side of a mountain in a village of tents. But like all things most precious, you were coy in revealing your true self, and I had to wait before I could get close to you.

Once again, you reminded me that along your pathways people find each other with the aid of some deeper form of gravity. Once again, the very cells of my journey were drawn towards the unseen orbits of those I was meant to meet. You even reminded me of how souls always seem to find each other when the time is right, against all impediments and all odds.

My favorite divine appointment brought me weary and worn to stay with a trio of singing nuns who smiled with such infectious joy that I caught their symptoms. And there with the nuns, you delivered me to a meeting with a shy girl on the halfway line. This very familiar stranger was a doe eyed Canadian who I would discover wasn't shy at all. In those middle lands of heat, I found she was much more than that; she was open, curious and fearless with her questions about the world around us. She wanted to know the unfiltered truth and routinely asked for it without a shred of hesitation. She braided my hair with tenacious patience, joined my endless warbles about love and above all, made space for me in her journey unlike any before her. Hers was an open heart. She would cross the longest stretch of nothingness by my side, and stay with me until the very end, even traveling through the bowels of Madrid to hug me one last time among rushing trains before she launched me into flight back across the Atlantic.

Oh, Camino two, I can even say I loved you when we fought. As I faced dull lifeless slogs on roads deep in the body of the Spain, the curses I flung at you were only half hearted. You knew I could barely muster a fight as I faced the impossible soul sucking climbs along busy highways once again. And yet you served me up another unfiltered trial, a brutal measuring stick by which to test the sheer fibers of my resolve and the guts of my faith. In your own way, you were seeing if I could survive you again.

I suppose I loved those fights because they brought us closer, but at the time, they also made me hate you and wish never to see your endless pathways again.

I swore I wouldn't miss your clustered circles of civilization and open tracks of echoing loneliness.

But as I lay in my bunk one afternoon, limbs soaking up the pure release of stillness, you rested on the edge of my bed with that look of wistful regret. I knew you were sorry you'd brought us to this tired impasse again. The flicker of compromise in your eyes held me, and I knew there was too much life in us to quarrel so. We could change. I'd already changed in the long absence from your touch. I proved it the next day by remaining calm as my small rag tag band walked only a handful of kilometers. And you proved your contrition by giving us solace at a hidden gem in a ghost town, a place where the kitchen was stocked with tea and milk and the bright colored sheets in the bunkroom smelled of fresh laundry. It only took a day to remind me you were still you. Still full of unending twists and turns, heartbreakingly beautiful views and impossibly warm human life. You were still light and God. You were still part of me.

And before my eyes you bloomed into places I'd once hastily passed by, rambling buildings where I'd never slept inhabited by a new cast of unfalteringly colorful hospitaleros who welcomed us into their homes. You filled my senses with pastry shops where I'd once failed to linger and cafes with steaming cups of warm milk. You shared the pure bliss of a bit of shade and a kilo of local cherries, and you reminded me how beauty is ever reinventing itself.

And as before, I sought tales of Camino love. Of love both fleeting and cinematic, sturdy and stormy. I still craved the stories, pined for new accounts and collected tales like stamps in a passport marking the course of love down this ancient road. The words and looks, gestures and names were unique elements of the one kind of journey I could feel and see but had yet to walk. I curled in my bunk at night among the details of those who had found what still eluded me and rolled the vibration of their pathway into my dreams. I followed the stories like way markers down the length of the road and sought to find my own place among their folds.

Nothing about you, Camino two, was love at first sight, but over time, you took root and made me feel safe. You didn't offer security; you hardly offered the guarantee of a bit of food and an open bunk. You didn't give me a built in companion or an immediate posse. You made me work for what I found, and you even kept your deepest self from me for many days and hundreds of kilometers. You kept me waiting to understand what we would be to each other and what you would let me take forward from this time along your current. Perhaps you keep me waiting still.

Then in your silences. Oh, those silences. The ones coupled with rain that fell like tears and winds that pushed with unnecessary force, during days of open heat and times when my fingers burned with early morning cold. Only then did I know what you had to say. Only then did I know you were telling me in the only language you spoke, how you were the proof that my time as solo journeyman was drawing to a close. All my past maneuvers were abandoned. The days, months and years of dragging broken relationships along behind me, befriending circles with no warmth to share and placing love in all the wrong hands were over. Loving you, Camino two, was like playing tag with acceptance and realizing after darting around, evading your touch that I would rather be caught and held by the present than try and live in the past.

And then you whispered to me on the banks of the Lavacolla of all the promises of the next chapter, a cluster of light inside of me and of the great turn toward a life of Camino love and a family of my own.

You navigated me through the current of the trail again to show me I'd evolved. The fading outline of memories was all that remained of the past. Even your land had forgotten, let go of all my old chaos, absorbed it back into dirt and grass, sky and rain. You, Camino two, taught me how to do the same. There was no use fighting your flow; only beauty in finding someway to let go. And for that I will always love you.

Love,
Elizabeth